ONE

ON

ONE

ONE

ON

ONE

TABITHA KING

A DUTTON BOOK

DUTTON
Published by the Penguin Group
Penguin Books USA Inc., 375 Hudson Street,
New York, New York 10014, U.S.A.
Penguin Books Ltd, 27 Wrights Lane,
London W8 5TZ, England
Penguin Books Australia Ltd, Ringwood,
Victoria, Australia
Penguin Books Canada Ltd, 10 Alcorn Avenue,
Toronto, Ontario, Canada M4V 3B2
Penguin Books (N.Z.) Ltd, 182–190 Wairau Road,
Auckland 10, New Zealand

Penguin Books Ltd, Registered Offices:
Harmondsworth, Middlesex, England

First published by Dutton, an imprint of New American Library, a
division of Penguin Books USA Inc.
Distributed in Canada by McClelland & Stewart Inc.

First Printing, March, 1993
10 9 8 7 6 5 4 3

Acknowledgments

"Victory Dance," words and music by John Cafferty. Copyright © 1987 John Cafferty
Music.

"Let's Stick Together" written by Wilbert Harrison. Copyright © 1962 by Longitude
Music Co. Copyright renewed 1990. All rights reserved. Reprinted by permission of Longitude Music Co.

"Life During Wartime" (David Byrne, Jerry Harrison, Chris Frantz, Tina Weymouth).
© 1979 WB MUSIC CORP. All rights administered by WB MUSIC CORP. All rights reserved. Used by permission.

"Be True to Your School," words and music by Brian Wilson. Copyright © 1963 Irving
Music, Inc. (BMI). All rights reserved. International copyright secured.

"Boys Will Be Boys" copyright © 1988 Steve's Pizza Music (BMI). Lyrics by M. Zellar.

Courtesy of ROIR Cassettes, the Dickies' "We Aren't the World" (ROIR-A140). Written
by Phillips/HUFSTETER.

"Pumpkinhead," by Dharma Bums. Written by Jeremy Wilson. Copyright © Mother
Found Out Music (BMI).

REGISTERED TRADEMARK—MARCA REGISTRADA

LIBRARY OF CONGRESS CATALOGING IN PUBLICATION DATA:
King, Tabitha.
  One on one / Tabitha King.
    p. cm.
  ISBN 0-525-93590-8
  I. Title.
PS3561.I4835O54   1993
813'.54—dc20   92-30421
                                                                        CIP

Printed in the United States of America
Set in Sabon
Designed by Leonard Telesca

This is for my home team
who coached me and ran the plays with me
and
for
my sister
Marcella Spruce.

Several people made huge contributions to the published form of this novel. They include my agent, Chuck Verrill, and my editor, Audrey LaFehr. I had terrific copyediting from Barbara Perris. My first readers, Stephen, Naomi, Joe Hill, and Owen, did more than offer editorial advice; their commentary in the margins of the original manuscript constitute a conversation I cherish. My sister Marcella shared observations and memories of her experiences as a teacher. And the prank on the roof really did happen on Penneseewasee Lake in Norway, Maine, some years ago, but since I do not know the identities of the mischief-makers, I can only gratefully acknowledge their inspiration.

What'sa matter, buddy, ain't you hearda my school?
It's number one in the state . . .

"Be True to Your School"
Brian Wilson

I wanna shoot one in from downtown
to end the double overtime . . .
I wanna do the Victory Dance . . .

"Victory Dance"
John Cafferty

Prologue

■ ■ ■

An Iridescent Confetti of Snow tarnished by
sodium arc light sifts from the void over the glowing horizontal
bulk of Greenspark Academy. It is 1:40 A.M. of a Sunday morning
in early March. On the school's front lawn, the letterboard spells
out *1990 WESTERN MAINE STATE CLASS A CHAMPS 1990*.
Underneath, smaller type declares *Winter Carnival Week*.

A garden of ice sculpture enlivens the school grounds. One is a
rendition of the bust of the warrior chief on the Indianhead penny,
wearing Walkman headphones. There is a rampant bear, a Big
Bird, a Bart Simpson. Monumental sports gear—a football helmet
big enough for a small child to hide inside, a hockey mask acces-
sorized with a chain saw, and a baseball and Louisville Slugger—is
strewn about as if some giant high school jock has emptied his
closet. In their midst stands a ten-foot-tall hoops trophy—a basketball on a plinth—inscribed *Western Maine Champions '90*. The
smooth surfaces of the various sculptures are frosted by the precipitation. It filigrees the diamonds of the hurricane fence enclosing the basketball courts near the gym and the bare rims of the
hoops.

Despite the day and hour, Greenspark Academy is burning every
light and the parking lot is full. The gymnasium currently holds

more people than actually live within the limits of the small town of Greenspark. A live-TV van with an enormous thick pole antenna erect on its roof idles between the parking lot and the double doors of the gym.

The noise of the mob inside the gym resembles a distant rumorous surf. With a rain of sighs, the needle snow isolates the thud of a basketball on one of the outdoor courts. The shuddering beat of the cold ball on snow-streaked pavement is driven by the rubbery creak of a pair of high-tops, the snap of a loose lace and the open-mouthed breathing of slightly congested lungs. Snow glistens wetly in eyelash, in the arc of eyebrow and a cockscomb of spiked hair. It gleams on the taut skin of a narrow, raised face and silvers the curve of gold in the lobe of the nose.

Momentum claws back the flapping skirts of an unbuttoned man's overcoat on the scarecrow figure. From the tips of chapped fingers the ball flies in a long, sweet hook. The whicker of its fall through the rim is lost in the whisper of wind-driven precipitate. Catching the ball as it bounces up, the shooter stops to knuckle a wet upper lip and snorkle back mucus.

With an exhuberant whoop and burble, police sirens implode the silvery hush and red and blue lights pulse on the main road. The gym doors are thrown open explosively and a cheering crowd spills into the net of the blinding TV lights. Manic and colorful as a troop of Shriner clowns, Greenspark's five police cruisers sweep up the school's curving drive, leading two yellow school buses and behind them, a parade of honking vehicles.

■ ■ ■

The kids on the buses begin to hoot and bellow from every window at the first sight of the school. Some of them jam head and shoulders through the opened windows and are held back from falling out by others clutching them at hip and waist.

"Check it out," one of the celebrants of the first bus calls out. "Look who's getting the edge on next season."

The ripple of laughter at the lone shooter on the snow-riven court is immediately drowned by crowd-roar greeting the buses.

A gauntlet of students forms to welcome the Greenspark Academy Indians, for almost five hours now the Class A Schoolboy Basketball Champions of the State of Maine—and for the third consecutive year. First to emerge from the bus into camera flash and TV spotlight is Coach, with a looted net around his neck. He is followed by the two assistant coaches and the team managers. They trot the short parade line to the open doors of the gym, to be taken up by welcoming dignitaries. The second bus empties simultaneously and its passengers—cheerleaders and band members—are absorbed into the crowd.

As Coach disappears into the gym, there is a sudden blossom of bottles and cans from under jackets and out of pockets into the hands of the impromptu honor guard. The team members descend from the bus into a popping fusillade of tabs and caps and duck through sprays of beer and sparkling cider. Each of the boys who exits the bus receives a rousing welcome but the last boy off, the biggest one, is greeted longest and loudest. Someone thrusts a bottle of beer into his hand. Sam Styles upends it, aiming it at his mouth, and manages to get most of it down in one swallow—an act that raises another cheer.

■ ■ ■

Sam blinks sticky cider from his lashes and shakes his head. His ponytail whips from left to right, scattering droplets that halo in the saturated air. At the edge of his vision he glimpses the solitary shooter on the basketball court. For an instant, their eyes meet. The noise of celebration is, for that moment, as insubstantial as the light precipitation. Silently, the shooter on the court raises both middle fingers in sardonic salute.

One of the other boys, looking back, sees what Sam sees and laughs. "Check it out," he says and those team members who hear him turn and look. And laugh.

"Come on, Sambo," another boy urges, yanking at Sam's sleeve.

The shooter on the court picks up the ball and backs casually toward the hoop. Effortlessly the ball leaves her fingertips, rises and falls behind her, through the basket.

Sam whoops and cocks a spatulate thumb high in approbation.

The mohawked girl on the court pivots away to catch the ball.

■ ■ ■

Inside, the hastily reassembled and owl-eyed Greenspark Academy Band greets the championship team with a nearly recognizable version of "We Are the Champions." This year the band is a little drum-heavy, with ten kids on sticks.

Despite the hour, the gym is packed with parents and grandparents and siblings and schoolmates, with teachers and administrators and town officials, and with hundreds of citizens of the school administrative district which Greenspark Academy serves, sharing the team's victory. The players are engulfed by the folks who already mobbed them on the floor of the Portland Civic Center in the delirium after the buzzer. Gradually the boys grope their way to the center of the gymnasium. Again they hold aloft the trophy gold ball, in a fireworks of camera flashes from dozens of snapshot cameras recording the event for family albums. The powers-that-be voice the clichés that on this occasion are perhaps more true than usual.

Scattered among the students are the members of the girls' basketball team, also called the Indians, whose season ended in the Western semifinals. They had a chance at a state title too until their point guard, Gauthier, got her skinny ass kicked out of the game against Breckenfield for diving into the bleachers to punch out an abusive fan. They couldn't quite do it without her, which didn't make her any more popular with anybody.

The co-captains of the victorious boys' team, junior center-forward Sam Styles and a senior guard named Scott Cosgrove, are called out. Scottie makes brief appropriate remarks and then it is Sam's turn.

Sam easily picks his father out of the crowd. Reuben's breadth and height make room for the woman in front of him, Sam's heavily pregnant stepmother. She leans into Reuben to ease her back and smiles at Sam, a slow and tired two-in-the-morning smile.

From the mass of faces, another suddenly emerges; the shooter has come in from the cold. She stands against the doors, watching.

Sam blinks and gropes at the microphone Scottie has stuck in his hand and manages to make it shriek. While everyone laughs, he touches the trophy briefly and applause erupts.

"Next year," he says, and the applause swells as the crowd assumes he is about to promise next year's title. But he goes them one better. "Next year," he repeats, "the girls are going to bring one home too."

The response from the crowd is deafening. The astonished principal shakes Sam's hand and the girls' coach does the same. The members of the girls' team are pushed forward to join the boys at the center of the gym. Except for the mohawked Gauthier. The doors whisper she was there.

■ ■ ■

A couple of hours later, Greenspark Academy is dark against the curdled sky. The snow has stopped and the wind come up a little more so it is miserably raw. The parking lot is empty except for the rows of yellow buses stitching its northern edge. Though one is tracked with frozen sneaker prints, the basketball courts are now abandoned.

A ten-year-old Ford van riding heavy in the back slews from the main road onto the drive. Bouncing around to the rear of the school, it comes to a skidding stop. The five boys inside fortify themselves from a bottle of rum.

The parents of four of them believe—maybe—that their sons are at a chaperoned party at the home of the fifth, Scott Cosgrove. Scottie's parents subscribe to the theory that the kids are going to booze anyway so the smart thing to do is provide the liquor in the safe environment of their home. Having invited the entire team and their female attachments, if any, to celebrate in their basement rec room, the Cosgroves have gone to bed after consuming quite a lot more California champagne than was wise.

Scott is driving—having promised to stay sober enough to take the wheel. He isn't but he's not quite as loaded as the others. Last out of the van, Sam Styles wraps a paw over the roof and hauls himself out of the backseat. The van rises on its springs. He gets a lungful of raw wet air. Unsurprisingly, it makes him dizzy. He's not used to drinking and it hits him hard. He blinks into the cutting wind. The others—Scottie, another senior guard named Josh Caron, and Todd Gramolini and Rick Woods, both juniors like Sam—have stumbled to the rear of the van to open its doors.

"Come on, Samson," Woods shouts.

In the back of the van, cradled on a nest of rope and tackle, is a cylindrical bundle about eight feet in length. Its circumference is difficult to judge in its canvas shroud but looks to be something under two feet. Sam gets a grip on one end. They all lend their strength to extract the massive thing and lower it to the ground. The others stand around and watch Sam lay out ropes and tackle on the ground and then they all roll the thing onto the ropes and he finishes rigging it.

Sam tosses another line with a grapple on it to the school's roof. Gramolini scrambles up the line and secures it for heavier freight. Sam and Scottie use it to go hand over hand after Gramolini. It takes considerable snickering and obscenities and an occasional burst of uncontrollable merriment to get them up there. Once on the roof, they hoist the thing, guided from the ground by Woods and Caron. When the thing thumps onto the roof, the ground crew comes up the rope, bringing additional tools inside their jackets.

Sheltering behind a ventilation shaft, they pause for another round from the bottle. The darkness is beginning to thin along the eastern horizon. Todd squats to undo Sam's rigging and then unwrap it. He works with the concentration of an old-fashioned obstetrician gently bringing a breech baby to a more favorable presentation. The others keep an eye on the main road. They fall silent and then conversation breaks out again—the game, the season, the bus ride home, the party, how hammered they are and how bad their hangovers are going to be.

The last flap of canvas thumps against the roof and Todd releases a huge relieved sigh. The others gather round solemnly. It is, they agree owlishly, awesome, and entirely undamaged in its transit from hiding in the fishing shack on the lake to the school. A work of art. They compliment Todd, the executor of the design for this particular ice sculpture, from an inspiration by Sam Styles, in conspiracy with the rest of them the previous Saturday after practice. The five of them roll it to the front edge of the roof.

Below them are the double glass doors of the school's main entrance. With much effort they raise the sculpture into position, jutting out from the flat roof. They adjust the angle to forty-five degrees and sweep up most of the snow on the roof to wedge it more securely. Then they pass the bottle again. It comes last to Sam. He empties it, then winds up and hurtles it toward the main road. It explodes on the centerline.

■ ■ ■

Lonnie Woods wakes up for the second time in the kitchen, standing at the counter with the coffee scoop in his hand. He remembers he was filling the basket of the coffee machine but has lost track of the number of scoops. Dumping the grounds back into the can, he starts again. He took Saturday night off to go to Portland to watch Rick play in the championship game and had to take a Sunday shift in exchange. At least it would be quiet. Filling the pot at the sink, he nearly drops it.

"Shit," he mutters.

His wife is still sleeping and he doesn't want to wake her. But as he opens a cupboard, looking for a mug, he hears the shuffle of her slippers in the hallway upstairs and then the bathroom door closing behind her.

Keyed up as they were from the big game, it's a wonder either of them slept a minute. Worse is having Rick out all night. They had only agreed to the blowout at Cosgrove's on Rick's promise he wouldn't get into an automobile to go anywhere for anything. If he wanted to come home, he was supposed to call for a ride. But he hasn't called and they have spent hours staring at the ceiling, wondering if they did the right thing.

Wishing he had a cigarette, Lonnie shaves in the downstairs bathroom. By the time he's finished, the coffee is ready and Fern is sitting at the table, warming her hands around her cup. She raises a blank face for a kiss and exchanges a mumbled *'morning* with him. She has taken the chair that will give her a view of the back door. He reaches to squeeze her hand. As she glances over his shoulder, her eyes widen and she jumps up.

Rick is coming up the path with Sam Styles in tow. Looking very young and half-grown with their beard stubble and red eyes, both boys move as if their bodies were clothing bought several sizes too large.

Lonnie opens the door for them.

"What a sight for sore eyes," Fern exclaims.

Rick sweeps his mother up and whirls her around the kitchen.

Laughing with undisguised relief, she scolds him. "You bad boy, you're trying to jolly me."

"Right," Rick admits cheerfully.

"You boys had enough celebrating?" Lonnie asks Sam.

Hangdog and bleary, Sam blinks and shuffles his feet and nods shyly.

The phone rings. They all fall silent as Lonnie picks it up. Fern tenses with long experience of early-morning weekend calls, thinking of all those kids out partying last night. The two boys sneak glances at each other.

Lonnie hangs up and buttons his shirt collar. He reaches for his uniform tie, dangling from the back of his chair.

"Somebody," he says, raising an eyebrow at the two boys, as he knots the tie, "pulled some numb stunt at the high school. Dispatcher thought the first call was a prank but now she's gotten two more say the same thing."

He checks himself in the mirror by the door—straightens his *SGT WOODS* nametag—and Fern hands him his jacket and hat.

"You two heroes, if this is for real, you'll want to have a look at it. Come on."

Sam and Rick look at each other. Rick shrugs.

"Come on," Lonnie repeats a little impatiently. "You got all day to sleep it off.

■ ■ ■

When the high school comes into sight, Lonnie breaks up. Like the figurehead on the prow of a ship, eight feet of tumescent penis sculpted in ice thrusts out from the building's roof over the main entrance doors. Someone has troubled to detail it with meticulous accuracy.

"Damn." The cop grins. "Talk about morning stiffies."

In the backseat of his cruiser, Rick and Sam struggle briefly to keep their composure and then lose it. They laugh until they are weeping and they clutch their aching stomachs and squirm like a couple of little kids.

Along the main road, passing traffic has slowed to look and some vehicles have pulled over and parked. A few people have gotten out to stand by the side of the road with their hands on their hips, the better to gawk. Phones are ringing all over a hundred-mile radius of Greenspark Academy.

■ ■ ■

Dawn has cleared the skies and the air is crystalline and mild. For a while there is some standing around talking with the janitor and the principal and the chief of police and various other self-appointed experts. First off, the principal wants the janitor to go up and cover the sculpture with a tarp.

"Go ahead," says the janitor, George Moody. "You do it, Bill. My back ain't up to it. Anybody asks me, I say the first thing is get the damn thing off'n the roof."

Bill Laliberte, the principal, suffers the janitor addressing him by his first name with a pained grin. Moody has been known to leave a dead rat clogging Laliberte's private can as a protest against work he doesn't want to do.

Sitting on the hood of Lonnie's cruiser, Sam Styles and Rick Woods dare not look at each other directly.

The fire department shows up. All of it. There isn't much to do in Greenspark on a Sunday morning, and it isn't every day there's an eight-foot ice sculpture of a stiff prick on the high school roof.

Eventually the hook-and-ladder is backed into position and the firemen clamber to the roof. Quite a few other people get up there too—the chief of police and the head selectman and the principal—until somebody notices the number of camera lenses pointed their way and it occurs to the dignitaries, more or less simultaneously, that being photographed with a giant ice dildo could be embarrassing.

It is almost eleven o'clock by the time the fireboys have the sculpture rigged for removal. By then most of the student body, some of it severely hung over, is part of the audience. Lonnie Woods is too involved in traffic control to keep track of Rick and Sam. They continue to use the hood of the cruiser as a beach blanket, where they lounge in weary splendor. Gradually, the rest of the basketball team assembles around them to watch.

At last, the ice dick rises from the roof to cheering and applause. The fireman at the wheel of the hook-and-ladder throws the truck into gear and it begins to roll away from the building.

Sam sits up. "Oh, oh," he says.

The ice dick sways dramatically in its cradle of rope. Suddenly something lets go. Sensing the shift, the driver brakes the truck and the abrupt stop propels the sculpture backward. To the gasps and screams of the spectators, the thing slips its cradle and goes hurtling through the glass doors. It shatters on impact with the lobby floor. Fragments of ice and glass commingle like white confetti.

Sam slides off the hood of the cruiser onto the pavement of the drive, so convulsed the only sounds he makes could be taken for inconsolable grief. Around him, his teammates bay and shriek.

■ ■ ■

Forty minutes later, the two boys trudge up the stairs. Rick flops onto his bed and rolls over to undo the laces of his high-tops.

"On the floor," Rick says. "I ain't sharing my bed with nobody with a dick."

The blankets and pillows Mrs. Woods has left to spread out on the carpet are just fine by Sam, who is beat enough to sleep on nails.

For a little while there is silence and then Rick groans. "Don't know if I can sleep, Slammer." He pounds his pillow. "Fuck! We won the fucking state!"

Rick squirms to the edge of the bed and hangs his head over to see if Sam is appreciating it all.

But Sam is silent, his eyes closed. Rick knows his friend is far from fragile—without Sam's drayhorse strength they never could have gotten that thing to the roof without a power winch—but he hasn't slept in over twenty-four hours. Had himself a game. And partied with the rest of them. In his own weird way. Could have had any girl he wanted last night but spent most of the party with headphones on, sucking up beer and playing DJ for them with Scottie's music.

Sam's sudden lapse into unconsciousness is sleep as crashing, a sudden precipitous loss of elevation. In his exhaustion, Sam's dreams are as intense and violent as the physical exertion and emotions of the past day might be expected to provoke. Of his dreams, on waking, Sam Styles recalls only the image of the solitary shooter out in the cold, an image with the eerie quality of an instant Polaroid. The figure is flat and grainy, the sole color and clearest focus the ghostly but still warmly dirty-orange basketball grasped by fingers so perfectly formed they seem sculpted of ice. There is no way to tell if the picture is fading or still developing. Weirdly the memory evokes the chemical smell and taste of the rubber ball, like nothing so much as dirty tears.

1

■ ■ ■

The Back of the Room—his natural haven—has no space for his legs so Sam Styles folds himself like a Hide-A-Bed into the tube-frame angles of the desk at the outside corner of the first row. Gradually he relaxes until his size-sixteen Converse All-Stars are in the no-man's-land where the English teacher, Mr. Romney, paces.

"People," Romney says, in a tone that suggests he wishes he had a cattle prod handy. "You *have* all read the material, haven't you? Why am I asking?"

Sam struggles to focus on the teacher. The heel of his palm rests against his crotch underneath an open notebook, hiding the semi that has popped up from nowhere. Frigging thing has a life of its own. He is, he has long since concluded, merely a life-support system for a dick.

Romney strides to a window and opens it. The rush of cold air at least makes them all stir about a little.

Sam tugs his unbuttoned red flannel shirt forward over his T-shirt, which bears the legend *Dope Is The Opiate Of The People,* and hunches against the sudden chill. He gives Romney an apologetic look.

The teacher cocks an eyebrow at him but Sam continues to

slump there taking up space. Too vividly, Romney recalls his first class with Sam, three years earlier, when the boy's posture made it clear he was doing his best to be invisible. He supposes it's a kind of progress when Sam is confident enough to be just another thud.

"Mr. Styles, will you tell us, please, what Huck Finn means by 'you can't pray a lie.' "

Sam draws in his feet and straightens up, starting to sweat, slipping back to that agonizing moment when Paul Romney had called upon him to read aloud in that first freshman lit class. He scrubs his face with his huge hands and for a moment it is a blank as he searches for a response.

"You can't bullsh—con—God."

Romney mops at his brow mockingly.

"Thank you, Sam. Succinct as always."

As the teacher moves on, searching his class for signs of brain activity above the flatline, Sam takes a deep breath. His armpits are greasy with the stress and his stomach churns but he has survived another challenge. He glances around at his classmates, all kids with whom he has been in school since seventh grade. One or two grin at him.

Paul Romney ignores the interplay. That first day three years ago, as Sam stuttered and then fell catatonically silent, the other kids were hot-eyed with fury at the teacher. One of them, Todd Gramolini, lingered after class to tell Romney bluntly to quit picking on Sam.

"He can't help the stutter," Todd insisted. "Everybody leaves him alone."

Paul Romney went directly to Sam's records and found what he'd suspected. Since coming from the Nodd's Ridge grammar school into the Greenspark system at the junior high level, the boy had taken only low-track courses that required little more than a warm body to answer the roll call to pass. With the exception of straight A's in shop classes, his grades were suspiciously at the exact minimal level required for athletic eligibility. This kid evidently got the flu every time somebody handed him a test folder and a #2 pencil, for his state assessment tests were all marked incomplete. No makeup tests had been recorded. Speech therapy for the stutter supposedly completed in the fourth grade. No discipline problems, a good school citizen—but one teacher more honest than the rest had noted: *Rarely have I seen so much effort expended to so little result.*

The educational mill had simply passed the kid on, year after year, filling in the minimum marks to keep him playing ball and get him to the next grade level. Hardly unique, Romney knew, but it had infuriated him anyway. He yanked Sam from a study hall, sat him down in his office and tested him informally. The boy wasn't able to flog his way through a confiscated X-Men comic book. When Romney let him try the Harley-Davidson owner's manual from the teacher's own bike, it was clear Sam was faking it, using practical knowledge to cover the fact he couldn't read anything more than a handful of words strongly associated with specific objects—stop, yield, Texaco, gas, McDonald's—and a smattering of obscenities that only added to his confusion with the variant spellings to be found on restroom walls.

Further testing confirmed Romney's guess that Sam was dyslexic. Romney became Sam's tutor and over the intervening years, the boy achieved grade level. It was Sam who chose summer school with Romney over invitations to basketball camps. Thinking of how far Sam has come—he almost never stutters anymore when he is called on in class—Romney experiences a brief flicker of satisfaction. Then he humbles himself, recalling how many failures he can count against this one particular success—Sam's older sister Karen among them. Karen—primarily a disciplinary problem rather than an academic one—Karen had defeated Romney.

Romney worked as hard as he did with Sam as much to compensate for Karen as for the points he would make with the administration for keeping the school's basketball star unchallengeably eligible. Of course Sam was relieved to have his secret exposed and eager to make up the deficiency. It had been a pleasure to watch the boy discover he could bring the same concentration to bear in his studies that served him so well in his sports.

The teacher stops to squeeze the bridge of his nose. He is amused to realize he is having as much trouble concentrating today as his students are. *Something in the air. A virus you contract from the lags who run the system, or the kids themselves,* he thinks tiredly. *Who gives a shit. Nobody.*

"I want you all to consider the contrast between Huck Finn's and Tom Sawyer's ideas of right and wrong, particularly as regards the issue of slavery. Be thinking in terms of Friday's exam, which will be, I remind you, a choice of essay questions."

■ ■ ■

Another day of Sam Styles's senior year gurgles away.

Changing for practice, Sam is grateful for the few moments in the locker room. Lately, it seems like he can't turn around without tripping over some babe—or into a whole gaggle of them—a giggle of girls, he amends, because that is what they do, in sulfurous soprano geysers, just as he realizes that once again he has just committed some oafish act—elbowed some babe's boobs or trod upon her toes. It seems as if he spends most of his time backing red-faced away from females laughing at him.

During practice, of course, the girls' team and the cheerleaders and assorted other loiterers will be in the bleachers but that's different. Once he's playing ball, he's focused. The wenches could be wallpaper then. Almost.

Slamming into the locker room, Kevin Bither calls out, "Hoss!"

Sam resists the urge to strangle Bither on the spot. Any hint how much he loathes being called Hoss and Bither will never let up. It is bad enough to be known as Samson and Slammer in the sports columns of the school newspaper and the local rag. If Hoss and Bigger and some of the other stuff they call him in the locker room ever gets out—someone will have to die, that's all. He gathers his hair at the nape of his neck and twists an elastic around it.

"Hey Hoss," Bither continues, "I think Romney's hot for you."

"Spare me your homoerotic fantasies, Mouth," Sam retorts.

The others break out laughing. Bither puts his hands on his hips like an angry girl and tosses his head and makes a gross wet smooch at Sam.

Stupid, Sam chides himself. Once started, Mouth never stops. He'll find a way to be a pest in practice. Kev can be a major friggin' weasel.

Running patterns to start, Sam loses himself in the rhythms. After hours of inactivity in classes, his body is eager to be exercised, sweated, used for something besides a brainrack. Not that the brains, such as they are, mind; this is work they like—running, handing off, stealing, hooking, pivoting, jumping.

The team splits to scrimmage. With Pete Fosse, the team's backup center, Bither double-teams Sam. The two of them crowd him relentlessly, Mouth talking trash, fast and gross, every time they are out of earshot of Coach. The object is not insult—the insults are too convoluted and extravagant to be taken seriously—but to make Sam laugh.

When Sam makes a sudden feint, Fosse follows it and Sam pivots to drive between Fosse and Bither. Surprised, Bither trips over his own feet. As Mouth flails for balance, Sam attempts to rise over him. The two boys tangle and plunge over the empty bench and into the girls' team, waiting for their own practice in the first two rows of the bleachers. The shorter Bither is caught on the first bleachers as he and Sam descend into the shrieking girls, who scramble with limited success to get out of the way.

Sam tumbles into female bodies in nylon jerseys and shorts, into a perfumed chaos of legs and arms and breasts, bottoms and braids and bangs, velvet hairbands and delicate winking little earstuds. He comes to rest between bleachers, on top of the slippery nylon of a practice uniform filled with girl.

Long muscular legs splay on either side of him. A hard-breathing tummy heaves under him. He stuggles to get off her but they are walled in, his shoulders wider than the space between the bleachers. He will have to turn and lift himself out at an angle, the way he came down. Desperately he gropes for purchase, finds he has hipbone in one hand and a clutch of small, springy breast in the other. In a roar that is greater inside his head than the noise of his teammates convulsed at his expense and this unfortunate girl's, Sam heaves himself up and looks into the ironic bitter-chocolate eyes of the Mutant.

■ ■ ■

Deanie Gauthier, a/k/a the Mutant.

Once a scrawny anonymous townie, the nobody child of a long-gone daddy and a biker mama, Deanie Gauthier has transformed herself, by this her sophomore year, into the Mutant.

The mohawk fashion history, she now shaves her head to a stubble of black hair. Her eyes are kohled in thick eyeliner, her mouth a slick of unnaturally colored lipstick. By contrast her skin is the fragile, easily bruised white of a narcissus petal. To play hoops, she is compelled to remove most of her normal jewelry but off court, the ring in the lobe of her left nostril is the terminus of five chains from five separate rings in her left ear. A single chain scallops through five rings in her right ear before falling to a collar of cruder, thicker links around her neck. While she is unchained for practice, the tracks of her facial chains are marked in siftings from her mascara across her left cheek.

In her practice uniform, her tattoos are fully visible: a winged death's head holds a rosebud in its teeth on her nicely formed right bicep and on her more powerful left, the man in the moon weeps from one eye. A very small broken rose spills its petals like teardrops of blood above her bony knee. One leg she shaves; the other sports a natural growth of fine black hair, as do both armpits.

Even as a freshman point guard, she was good for twenty points a game. The Mutant plays as if she is possessed, intimidating the hell out of other teams. Five feet seven inches and a hundred and nine pounds of skinny, self-balded scare queen, she has wrested for herself the peculiar status of Greenspark's Bad Girl. But everyone knows she is in fact merely Deanie Gauthier, weirdly shaved, tattooed and wrapped up in chains and rags, a scrawny little townie gone Mutant.

■ ■ ■

"You okay?" asks Sam.

From her sprawl between the bleachers she shrugs ungraciously. He reaches down. She hesitates. Accepts his hand and lets him set her on her feet. Her sulky underlip is like a sullen squeak of hunger.

Sam remembers the cage of her ribs against him, her rapid heartbeat inside it.

"I'm sorry," he says.

"Asshole," she spits, and drops back onto the bleacher, crossing her arms and staring up at him scornfully.

Jesus. Sam retreats.

The Coach dusts off Bither, who has bitten his tongue and scraped his chin on the edge of a bleacher.

Rick Woods digs an elbow into Sam.

"Smooth move, Sambo. Copping the entire girls' team at one time. I was gonna do that, I'd try to land on the Jandreau twins. The Mutant, that's too close to necrophilia for me."

Sam's head feels as if he has gone Mutant himself; left his locks on the floor around the barber's chair, had black lines and the word *Spalding* tattooed over his shorn skull. He thinks of a Dharma Bums lyric, a wailing lament:

I'm gonna crawl, I'm gonna fall, gonna be a punkinhead.

■ ■ ■

The Mutant watches him stumble, wretched with blown cool, to center court. Whispering and sniggering, her scattered teammates settle around her again like birds on a wire.

Melissa Jandreau crouches behind her. "Did you feel it? How big is it?"

The Mutant rolls her eyes up and drops her head back abruptly as if her neck were suddenly broken.

"Fuck off," she says.

Melissa leans toward her twin, Melanie, to whisper audibly: *Bitch.*

■ ■ ■

Sam knots himself into a fury. The incident will be a school joke for weeks. Possibly forever. A Legend. He makes himself take slow, deep breaths, groping for his concentration. She is a black cat in his path, a ladder he has walked under, a crow swooping straight into his eyes. Seven times seven years of bad luck. He plays badly.

■ ■ ■

The Mutant watches, taking a sardonic pleasure in his undoing. Mr. Sam Styles, a/k/a *Double-Zero,* after the number on his jersey, also rumored cattily to be his IQ. *Slammer. Shammer. Sambot. Sambo. Samson. Preacher. Saint Sam. Godzilla. Samgod. Mr. God-To-You.* He has more names than God, for sure. She hears in the locker room they call him Bigger, for Bigger Than God. Numb as a pounded thumb but they love his ass in this frigging hole. Bet they blame her for the way he's fucking up. She should give a shit.

What does Samgod do at parties? Reps, maybe. Chows on the Doritos. Looks under the hoods parked in the driveway. Clicks around the cable, pausing for a few seconds to check out Club Meat on MTV. Settles on something involving men chasing a ball. Goes home early to rewire his speakers. Is almost asleep before he remembers he was going to choke the cobra. Decides he's been doing it too often—might be affecting his game—and rolls over, to dream of a new four-wheel-drive with a plow attachment. The Mutant grins.

■ ■ ■

Toweling her sweaty face, she streaks the cloth with grime. She grabs the water bottle. Some of the boys have emerged from their locker room to watch the girls from the sidelines. Samgod is among them, no doubt itching to escape home to Center Cowshit. The vision of a long-haired blond giant dribbling through a herd of black-and-white Belted Galloways transports the Mutant. She adds the thinnest flurry of snowflakes to the scene: a cow's long tongue unrolls to catch the wet flecks of cold. The gamboling mooseboy blinks against the spit of snow, and laughing, imitates the cow, tasting winter.

She hopes he has seen her play. Nobody can touch her; she is quicksilver. Coach is yanking her to yammer bullshit about pacing herself, meaning the frigging twinkies can't keep up with her. She could keep up with Samgod Himself. Anyway she'd like to try. She wipes her nose on the back of her arm and gets a whiff of her armpit. She likes it. Sourly, Coach signals the Mutant back to the scrimmage.

■ ■ ■

Watching the girls on the court, Sam drifts into his own fantasy: Round and pumpkin-colored, he spins from fingertip to fingertip, bouncing rhythmically under the damp palm of the blonde forward as if he were being petted. Shooting into a sudden underhand pass, then driven around, among, between long bare legs. Aware of rapid breathing, swish of shorts, sweet tang of girlflesh, vibration of the floor, the squeak of sneakers like hungry little birds. And rising, rising in a long elegant arc to apogee, an instant's weightlessness, spinning in perfect balance with the planet—and then the grab of gravity through the hoop, a belly-jumping rush into eager reaching hands.

Abruptly he is himself again. Sweating piggishly, though he is just out of the showers. He tries to concentrate on the girls' moves. At last and inevitably, his eye is on the Mutant, drawn first by the fluidity with which she moves and then her obscenely naked skull and desperate little face. She is as quick as a frog's tongue, slick as wet leaves over drowned sand, nasty as a needleburst of freezing rain. Everything moves like she has first-class suspension. She has fresh bruises and scrapes on her legs he realizes guiltily are the result of his falling on her between the bleachers. And there is that hair in her armpits. It looks kind of soft and silky, like the fur in his old bear's armpit, the one that is currently being drooled all over by his baby sister India. Which reminds him—home and supper are on the other side of Greenspark and the Narrows.

■ ■ ■

Tony is having his wake-up beer at the kitchen dinette.

Without speaking, the Mutant passes him and goes into her room, a narrow space under the stairs scarcely big enough for her cot. Judy and Tony sleep upstairs in a low-ceilinged room that was once a storage loft. The Mutant closes the door between her and Tony. A hook and eye hangs together on the back of the door and the frame is splintered.

The room is windowless, every surface painted black. Mounted on the black ground is an alligator skin of reflective glass composed of cheap handmirrors and tarnished framed mirrors from junkshops and yard sales. Here and there an oval looking glass with a handle punctuates the mirror mosaic like an exclamation mark. When the Mutant is stoned, the black ground becomes a web trapping bright nodes of reality.

Spilling books and notebooks from her backpack, she flips open her biology text. In the gap where the human reproduction segment has been sliced out is a roach. She reaches across the cot to flick on her clock-radio. Sitting cross-legged, she lights the weed with a paper match and listens to Axl Rose singing about finding a safe place.

Tony opens the door. He leans over her to snap off the radio. "Gimme a hit."

She hands it to him. He would take it by force if she didn't.

"I need this," he says. "I gotta look at a freak like you, I oughta be stoned."

She doesn't respond and he goes away, taking the roach with him.

She turns the radio back on and cranks the volume to hear Axl still wailing. The hell with the roach. She needs to get her homework done, keep her grades up to stay eligible to play. Just a toke or two was all she wanted but Tony has to be a pig and take it away from her. She doesn't dare to be grateful he didn't stay. He might come back.

And he does. He comes back and turns off the radio again and lets her have the last couple hits while he fools around with her. She does what he wants so he will go away and let her do her homework.

Once upon a time, she had needed to close her eyes but now she never does. She sees herself and him in the mirrors, broken and multiplied, minimized and magnified, a jigsaw of bodies and faces. *Picasso,* the Mutant thinks, remembering the colored plates from

a folio in the high school library. *Maybe he was into mirrors too. Did they have blotter back then?*

She hears Judy arrive home. The cupboard opens, the heavy bottle clunks on the counter. Jack Daniel's gurgles into a coffee cup.

"Tony," Judy calls.

He doesn't answer.

"I'm home," Judy says.

The couch creaks under Judy; the TV blares on. It's *Family Feud.* Judy laughs with pleasure. She never misses it.

Huffing dirty words, Tony does the funky chicken and collapses on the Mutant. His weight crushes her for a moment while he catches his breath and then he rolls off her. His pants are tangled around his ankles. He pulls them up, buttons his shirt, tucks it in.

She studies the reflection of her left shoulder in a wedge of mirror. When she can save the money, it would be a good place for a tattoo, except sometimes she gets a zit there. Tony turns around, gives her bottom a hard slap that makes her body jump on the mattress.

"That's a good girl," he mutters.

He is still zipping up when he opens the door.

The Mutant looks back over her bare shoulder. Briefly Judy glances away from the TV screen. In the blue flicker, her eyes are moist with terror. The Mutant meets her mother's eyes calmly. Hastily, Judy returns her gaze to the TV. A fraction of a second later, Judy starts to laugh. She laughs hard and for a long time, but by then Tony has closed the door on the Mutant's room and joined Judy on the couch. *Family Feud* is one of his faves, too.

The Mutant puts on her clothes again and picks up the papers and books Pig Tony has shoved on the floor. She turns on the radio again. Sitting cross-legged on her rumpled cot, she does her homework.

■ ■ ■

Sitting at the kitchen table, Sam holds his baby sister and massages her sore gums. She chews furiously, wetly, on his finger, while clutching at the headphones riding his collarbone.

The kitchen radio is putting out Axl Rose.

W. Axl Rose. Waxl. Possessed by Janis Joplin, Sam thinks, and he's even wearing her old clothes.

Reuben washes the pots while Pearl puts away the leftovers.

Sam's stepmother embraces his father from behind and bumps him gently against the sink counter. Reuben laughs. Sinuously she slides around in front of him and he pins her against the counter. She locks her arms around his neck and he lifts her up to kiss her and pushes her back toward the sinkful of soapy water. She shrieks and struggles. He tickles her. They are getting foamy water all over themselves and the kitchen and having a fine old time. From his angle of view, Sam cannot help noticing that his father is getting a hard-on.

Slinging Indy over his shoulder, Sam ducks into the living room. He flops onto the carpet, lets Indy down to crawl, and pulls his headphones up over his ears. He gropes for the play button of the Walkman hooked to his belt. When he glances toward the kitchen he sees his father and stepmother swaying in each other's arms to something on the radio he can't hear over the dub of hardcore grunge in his Walkman.

The baby clutches at his thigh. In the gold iris of her left eye is the same piewedge of brass as in her mother's grey eyes; it is a familial stain that comes down in the female line. Pearl's light eyes against her gloriously mahogany skin are certainly arresting. Rick Woods has told Sam that his grandmother calls such light eyes in a person of color devil eyes. Sam guesses his little sister qualifies as a person of color too, but hers is amber, her thick ringlets not black as Pearl's but tawny. Indy is rapidly losing her infant frogshape. She crawls along Sam's prone body to tug at his lower lip. She breaks wind and her alien golden eyes widen in surprise.

All at once Reuben is stooping over Sam to pick up the baby. He says something and Sam nods, though he doesn't hear it over the Bastards' confessional "Shit for Brains." Sam rolls to his feet and bounds upstairs. In his bedroom, he goes to his knees on his bed, startling Pearl's Siamese cat from her nap on his pillow. Tearing his headphones and Walkman off with one hand, he thumbs the power buttons on the sound system on the wall at the head of his bed. The cat scampers from the room.

From outside, below his bedroom window, comes the sound of Reuben's truck's ignition. His father is taking Pearl and the baby to the farmhouse. They are rebuilding the original Styles homestead, fire-gutted shortly after Reuben married Pearl. For now, they crowd this smaller house she inherited. Evenings and weekends, if he doesn't have work at the garage or caretaking to do,

Reuben works at the farmhouse. Pearl and the baby often accompany him.

With basketball, homework and the few hours he can put in at the garage himself, Sam has little time left to help with the farmhouse—a few hours of a Sunday afternoon at best. And it feels weird to be there. It was hard enough to see it in ruins from the fire but now it is becoming something else—Reuben is not rebuilding it exactly but altering it in various ways.

With money and time so short, the rebuilding has gone slowly and now it looks as if it won't be finished before Sam graduates high school. He wonders if he will really ever live in the farmhouse again—or should. Maybe he should bail out in June, find his own place and let his father's new family make the farmhouse its own.

He jacks in the system headphones and scans the airwaves, not sure what he's listening for, but trusting he will hear it. It will reach out of the static and the garble and grab him by the earlobes and lift him out of his socks. It's out there. He just has to be patient.

2

■ ■ ■

Winter Has Crept In like a cat to suck his breath when Sam wakes. Frost scratched on the windows, the bedroom is brittle with cold and as gloomy inside as it is outside. The clock-radio is only three minutes from going off. Coughing, he rolls over and hits the off button on the alarm.

When he peeks into the nursery, Indy is sitting in her crib, wide awake, drooling around a pacifier she has managed to plug into her mouth. She squawks at him. He holds out his fingers and she curls her tiny digits around them and tries to tug herself to her feet. Loosing her grip, she sits down abruptly with a squishing sound. She reeks of baby pee.

In a pair of sagging pajama bottoms, Reuben comes in behind Sam. It is always first thing in the morning that it strikes Sam how much white there is now in his father's beard and chest hair.

"How's my little Miss Take?" Reuben asks.

Sam laughs and so does Indy.

Reuben picks her up. Lower limbs pumping, she shoves the binkie purposefully into the corner of Reuben's mouth.

"Oh yummy."

With the baby under his arm, Reuben disappears into the bathroom and a second later, the shower erupts.

Sam and Pearl nearly collide at the door of the bedroom she and Reuben share.

"Oops," she says. "Need a traffic light this time of day."

As she hustles past him to the bathroom, he catches a glimpse of her red bikini underpants under the shirt of Reuben's pajamas.

"Use those drawers for a stoplight," he teases.

"Sam!" she says, but her outrage is all show.

There are two bathrooms but only water enough for one shower at a time. With all of them up and going to work or school at once, they can't afford an excess of privacy. Sam does his showering before bed and shaves in the downstairs bathroom in the morning to free the upstairs conveniences for the rest of the family.

■ ■ ■

Overnight the hard freeze they have been awaiting has turned the ground to iron, the air to rust in Sam's lungs. His truck—a 1978 International Harvester four-wheel-drive that despite its unimpressive appearance has a lot more under the hood than when it came off the assembly line—starts reluctantly. From now on, he needs to remember to plug in the engine-block heater before he goes to bed.

Though it is too cold for hanging around outside the school, the Mutant is alone on one of the outdoor courts, shooting hoops through a netless rim. The pavement is greasy with frost and fallen leaf. Her hands and nose are scarlet in the frigid atmosphere. She wears a man's overcoat, unbuttoned so the skirts will not hamper her, the too-long sleeves cuffed back to uncover her hands. Her exposed skull makes Sam think of a baby abandoned in a garbage can.

Inside the school, it is almost too warm. He crouches over the lost-and-found carton outside the Office and scavenges a home-knit marigold-yellow scarf, a pair of gloves with a couple of fingertips popped and a shapeless pilly watch cap. He stuffs the items in his jacket and leaves the building again and lopes to the court.

The Mutant comes to a standstill, holding the ball on the flat of her left palm. Silently, he drops the scarf over her thin shoulders and winds it loosely around her neck. She is as passive as a little kid being dressed. When he tugs the watch cap down over her skull and ears, her skin is cold to the touch. Her nostrils glisten and a snail's trail of clear mucus begins to slide toward her upper lip. Sam finds a handkerchief in his jacket, performs the practiced to-and-fro swipe under the Mutant's nose he has learned on Indy. He takes her right hand, puts a glove on it, transfers the basketball from her left to under his own arm, and gloves her left hand.

With her head covered, he sees how she would look with hair. Her narrow face with her dark doe's eyes under really fine eyebrows is like an eighteenth-century portrait—the frontispiece of some mildewed old book, matted in an oval frame with a little veil of tissue to protect it.

Stepping back, he tips the ball to her. She just stands there, rigid, holding it. Feeling as if the frost has gotten to his brains, Sam falls back. When he looks over his shoulder from the entrance of the school, he sees cap, scarf and gloves in a tangle on the ground. The Mutant pivots in a red-handed, bald-headed, snot-nosed turnaround jump shot. The ball twangs angrily on the iron rim.

■ ■ ■

The warmth inside is suffocating now. Sam lets himself into the gym and helps himself to a ball from the rack in the equipment closet. He flicks on the sound system, drops a cassette into the tape slot. It is just a few minutes past six. When Sam first started at Greenspark, there was no morning gym. He lobbied it into existence and now he has the keys because he's always there first. Though it isn't compulsory, most of the team turns up before school, even in buck season. As eight o'clock creeps up, students and teachers and administrators are apt to stop and watch awhile. Coach usually wanders through too, but he thinks it's important that his boys continue to regard the game as fun so he's usually content to let Sam set the pace and tone.

Sam is unable to forget the Mutant, outside courting frostbite. For the first time it sinks in that the girls don't use the gym before classes. The boys own it. It's not fair. Something will have to be done about it. Some kind of rotation to give the girls time. Immediately he founders in the consequences. Will it affect his game if he gives up some of his morning time? Maybe they could start a lunchtime session. It makes his stomach growl to even think of such a sacrifice.

■ ■ ■

Second period: Sam is in the weight room. It is a jocks' P.E. option, filled up with senior lettermen, plus some competitive pumpers and wide boys for whom muscle is a major preoccupation.

One of the non-lettermen is J.C., who answers the roll call as Jason Chapin. Though he has built himself a physique even the bikers respect, J.C. streaks his asymmetrically cut blond hair with an electrical rainbow of color and hangs with the burns, among them the Mutant. He must pump out of vanity, as he's not into team sports and it's apparently not a health thing—his fingertips are yellowed with nicotine. Doubtless just looking tough is a business asset. J.C. deals. That's axiomatic; everyone does who uses. It's the economics of dope. But J.C. is bigger than mere economics; he is The Man at Greenspark Academy, or at least he thinks of himself that way. He is a happy camper, a popular dude who smiles a lot and gives no grief to the administration. Chapin and Sam Styles keep a careful distance between them.

Sam finishes early enough to corner Coach in his office.

"Sam, Sam," Coach exclaims. "Did you crack your coconut on the edge of a bleacher when you fell all over those girls? I hope you haven't been talking this around. The girls'll get the idea they're entitled."

"But they are."

"Oh Jesus Jumping Christ."

Sam grins. "I'm going to the Office with it."

"You're going to your next class is where you're going. Those morning loosenin' up sessions just might be our edge. Why do you want to mess with a winning situation?"

"The girls almost took their division last year. Maybe with a little bit more court time, they can go all the way."

With a moan, Coach throws up his hands. "You're the only guy on this team has any interest in any of those girls going all the way outside the backseat of a car. One of those twitches put this numb idea in your thick skull?"

Sam glances at the clock.

"Just trying to be fair," he says, and splits.

■ ■ ■

By lunch hour when Sam catches up with the principal, Coach has already weighed in with his opinion.

"This is all your idea," Laliberte says, with the practiced reasonableness of an authority who has already made up his mind. "Why don't you let them fight their own battles?"

"What's fair is fair. Why should they have to ask for what's their due?"

"What brought this on, Sam? You've been using the gym in the mornings for three years without sweating the girls' access to it. All of a sudden you're on a crusade."

From the principal's office windows Sam can see the empty outdoor courts. The multicolored tangle of lost-and-found rags appears to be frozen to the ground amid the clutter of dead dull-bronze leaves.

"Deanie Gauthier was out there this morning, shooting hoops in the below zero."

Laliberte snorts. "So she hasn't got sense enough to come in out of the cold. Gauthier's just one member of the girls' team. They seem to be content with the current situation. She wants to go out there and freeze her buns off, that's not your lookout." The principal shifts restlessly in his chair. "Sam. Think. You want your team distracted and upset about something like this when they should be winning another state title?" Leaning forward confidingly, Laliberte speaks in the earnest tone Sam recognizes as the principal's bullshit voice. "You're a good kid, Sam, and we're proud of you. You carry a lot of weight with your peers. Don't misuse your influence and start something that could divide the school into camps."

You're just a kid, Laliberte means, *and the only thing you know beans about is how to get a rubber ball through an iron hoop, so shut up and get back in line.*

Sam thanks the principal for his time and heads for the cafeteria.

■ ■ ■

It is team policy to lunch together if possible. They shove together a couple of tables and horse around a little and it makes everybody feel a little bit more connected. Some of the guys, like Rick Woods, who is going with Sarah Kendall, have their girls sitting with them too. The girls who get to sit at the team table strut and toss their heads a lot to make sure everyone sees where they are.

Sam scarcely hears the dirty joke of the day being repeated as he empties his lunch pail into his gut as quickly as possible. The tension in the pit of his stomach doesn't make him less hungry but it does diminish his ability to savor fully his stepmother's chicken stew and biscuits.

The Mutant is nowhere in the cafeteria. The people she hangs with don't do lunch. They have more pressing engagements in the smoking area.

Selected for maximum discomfort and inconvenience, the designated student smoking area is outside, on a blind back corner of the gym. It is often wet underfoot, exhaust from the metal shop in the basement vents nastily nearby, and there is a draft that feels like it originates in the Antarctic. Hunched over their butts, the smokers huddle like sheep in a blizzard. Generous to a fault in their pariah fellowship, they often share their smokes. Somebody always has a boombox, so there is music or at least a perceptible beat. There are enough smokers to break down into smaller groups: bikers, burns, hipsters and scrubbers, townies and shit-kickers—all with jackets wide open, if worn at all, no gloves or mittens, bareheaded, jeans strategically rent for maximum exposure of chapped skin—a literal interpretation of cool and its current intensifier, chill.

Sam does not bother to close his denim jacket either, and with his fingers trying to find refuge in his pockets, he too hunches and shivers.

The Mutant loiters with the burns, nothing in her hands by way of smoking material that could get her bounced from hoops, but doubtless she is getting a whiff of the communal haze. On the outdoor court before school, she had been wearing thready Levis. Apparently in concession to the game-day dress rules—skirts or dresses for the girls, jackets and ties for the boys—she has simply removed her Levis, retaining the ragged tights underneath. Her "dress" is a long shapeless extra-large man's T-shirt that clears her bottom by three inches, and over it, a man's sweater vest, with the edges unraveled and the buttons removed. The T-shirt is sweat-stained and torn, the grey vest pilled and disreputable. The two pieces look like she raided some fat old man's ragbag. She gets away with mocking the code because the administration is nervous about enforcing gender-specific rules.

At the Mutant's side is Shasta Grey, a junior who used to live in Nodd's Ridge. Grey nods at Sam. Remembering her in the second grade, a pallid little worm of a girl, her mouth ringed with cold sores, Sam nods back. She is a chainsmoker now, her butts burnt down to lipstick-stained filters.

J.C. has a pumped-up arm around Gauthier's waist. She leans her bony hip into him.

"Talk to you?" Sam asks her.

The Mutant's eyes are scornfully amused. "Fuck off."

Grey and J.C. both laugh.

"Later," Sam says. "First I need to talk to you."

"You heard her, Samson," J.C. says, genially flicking a lighted cigarette at him. "Fuck off, man."

Sam's hand snakes out and catches the tumbling butt before J.C. finishes speaking. Unsmiling, he hands it back to him. J.C. looks at it with raised eyebrows and then plugs it back into his mouth with a laugh.

"Didn't know I had to check with your appointments secretary, Deanie," Sam says, and turns away, too cold to put up with the bullshit.

The Mutant hasn't heard her given name in so long, it takes a second to realize he has used it. It has the shock of a broken taboo. She presses J.C.'s arm and bounds after Sam.

"Wait a minute."

Sam stops.

J.C. watches a moment, then turns away with a shrug to take another drag. Grey leans close to whisper in his ear.

Sam is irritable, sick of the Mutant's attitude, of *Attitude,* period. Inside his sneakers, he curls his toes against the cold. The wind cuts like a rain of razors through the layers of his longjohns and fleece sweatpants.

"You want to win the state this year?"

Her eyes narrow. "You need to ask?"

"You can't do it with frostbitten fingers."

She sets her mouth in a sarcastic scar. "Oh fuck you very much."

He returns the sarcasm. "You're welcome."

She starts to turn back to her burn buddies.

"It's too cold outside," Sam says. "You should be able to use the gym. Get your team to ask your coach and the principal for equal morning access with the boys. Hit them with it on the bus tonight after the game, when they're pumped. I'll work it from my end. We ought to be able to work something out where we alternate three mornings one week, two the next."

She stared at him. "No shit. Why are you doing this? It'll cut into your time."

" 'Cause it's fair."

He walks away before she can say anything more. He's not doing it for her. She may be the drive wheel but she's not the only talent. The Jandreau twins, Billie Figueroa, Nat Linscott, Debbie Michaud, they all deserve another jab at the state title. Just a few words with her are enough to confirm she's a burn, a scrubber, a foul-mouthed butthead.

The Mutant is his sister all over again, only worse. Karen doesn't shave her head—yet. Somehow she missed that numb stunt, but it must be the only one. One of these days, the Mutant will drop out of school, just like Karen, and he'll see her on some street corner with a bellyful of another nobody's child. It was some kind of union rule with girls like them.

■ ■ ■

J.C. ignores the Mutant's return for a moment and then, in a bored tone, asks, "What was that about?"

Hands in her pockets, the Mutant swivels away from the others. J.C. moves with her, leaning close.

"Just b-ball shit."

J.C. hauls out a handkerchief and wipes his nose.

"What's this shit about Samson falling all over you and the rest of the babes yesterday? First I hear about it is just now from Grey."

The Mutant shrugs. "You want to know every frigging thing I do, hire a camera crew. Go to the videotape."

J.C. clears his throat and spits but then he grins.

Teeth chattering, the Mutant hugs herself and stamps her feet. After disbelief, her first reaction to Samgod's curious initiative is she wants it, for herself, for her team. She is angry that she didn't think of it herself and even more furious that it's any kind of question. Why should the gym just automatically belong to the boys in the morning?

■ ■ ■

In the girls' room nearest the cafeteria, someone is barking up lunch in the stalls. The Mutant gags loudly, setting off an imitative chorus among the girls doing hair and makeup in front of the mirror.

In response comes an angry choked cry: "Fuck you, you fat bitches!"

The Mutant recognizes Cady Flemming's voice. "Come on, Flem," she shouts, "chuck it *up,* baby!"

A roll of toilet paper comes sailing over the stall door, spinning out a comet tail as it flies.

"Eat it, Mutant," Cady screams. "Choke on it!"

The Mutant grins into the mirror.

Cady's been doing Puke Watchers all semester. The Mutant admires the cheerleader's dedication. The Gag Squad bitches can all go puke in their fuck-me hairdos as far as she's concerned. She watches them as they bounce through their little rah-rah routines and can't believe they have the nerve to call shaking their tits and asses while chanting moronic doggerel a *sport*. If that's a sport, then jerking off should be in the Olympics.

Though the Mutant is eligible for free hot breakfast and lunch, she has trashed the application since she was in fifth grade. All that bullshit about confidentiality and everybody still knows who gets the charity chow.

The Mutant has coffee for breakfast and scavenges a muffin or a Danish from the teachers' lounge or the cafeteria trash. When she's really starved, she boosts somebody's lunch between morning classes. The school is full of food if you're not picky and your fingers are quick. Sometimes she's hungry but a drag takes off the hurting edge and anyway, she's used to it. Maybe if old Flem had to work harder to get something to eat, she wouldn't be so quick to stick her finger down her throat.

Cady Flemming exits the stall. She yanks a huge green bottle of Scope out of an enormous handbag and gargles, spitting a geyser of the mouthwash into the basin next to the Mutant. Cady looks up into the mirror. Her eyes are puffy.

"Feel better?" the Mutant inquires.

"Someday I'm gonna stuff my fist down your throat," Cady says. "See if you can gag it back up."

The Mutant make a kissy face at her in the mirror.

"Gauthier's gagged a lot more than a little puke," Melissa Jandreau puts in from across the room.

Almost everyone except the Mutant laughs.

"That's disgusting," an outraged, high-pitched voice squeaks.

Everyone looks at little Kerry Hatch, suddenly blushing furiously.

"So's that john you used, Flemming," the Mutant says.

"Just like your face, freak!" Cady spits back.

"Eat me," the Mutant counters, flipping Cady a double bird. "Your boyfriend's got your lunch in his zipper."

As Flemming shrieks and pitches her hairbrush, the Mutant ducks out the door.

■ ■ ■

By three, they are headed to the first game of the regular season, away at Castle Rock and a big deal because the two schools are neighborly rivals. The boys' bus is less crowded than the girls' because the cheerleaders travel with the girls' team, but it is easily as noisy.

Sam Styles seals his ears with his headphones, closes his eyes. Tuned to the beat throbbing through the bones of his skull and the soothing vibration of the wheels of the bus over the lonesome rural roads, he goes to sleep. Still growing, he sometimes corks off as unexpectedly as his baby sister. On the trips to away games, he deliberately exploits his susceptibility to the soporific effect of the road and unplugs himself.

Next to him, Rick Woods, who is his regular seatmate, listens to his own Walkman and translates a French assignment. A glance at his friend makes him shake his head. How can Sam just crash like that before a game, when his own gut is churning, his right foot twitching uncontrollably?

The combination of Sam's capabilities and a total lack of ambition beyond this year's states are a frustration to Rick, whose own dreams of a professional athletic career have faded during his high school years with an almost literal painfulness. Talent Rick knows he has but his long rangy body exhibits an odd fragility. He is plagued with sprains, splints, torn ligaments, bone spurs and every other athlete's curse. With a nervous stomach, he has trouble maintaining a reasonable weight and his stamina is unreliable. The community saddles Rick with the expectation that his skin color is proof he is a natural athlete—meaning it all comes easy. Coach and a good many local fans think he is temperamental and spleeny, if not an out-and-out hypochondriac.

In contrast, in the guise of a slow-witted, overgrown, shitkicking grease monkey, Sam Styles can do no wrong. It's a perverse joke, a con job that lets Sam avoid dealing with his own potential. Sam could be a prince in the world and chooses to be a pauper. Every straight wench in school damp for him, the doofus is still cherry. Ever since his idiot sister Karen went off the rails, Sam's gotten steadily more tight-assed and not just about sex. Never mind getting loaded—to the best of Rick's knowledge, Sam hasn't cracked a solitary beer since the prank with the ice dick. For all Sam's mockery of religion, there's a streak of genuine Holy Roller in him. It's no secret Sam carries a paperback Bible in his duffel bag and sometimes reads it, right in front of everybody. Rick used to think it was just Sam's way of countering the rumor that he can't read, but it wouldn't shock him at all if Sam suddenly announced he'd accepted Jesus as his personal savior and coach.

Rick checks on Sam again. Sleeping like Smaug the dragon on the gold of his own life. The big boy draws the deep even breath of the innocent. Well, maybe not innocent. Sprawled in his seat, Sam's developed a noticeable rise in his Levis. Considerately, Rick blankets Sam with his own duster.

3

■ ■ ■

Between Greenspark and Castle Rock, Sam
dreams. He is on the floor of the Bangor Civic Center. Above him
the cavernous roof is studded with television spots like miniature
suns that turn the polished floor into a glassy field of light. The
shining court is vast, with just him on it. As the bleachers fill, he
banks shots, gleefully making the backboard thrum and rattle. It
feels good to be here again, this one last time before his childhood
ends for good and all. Suddenly he knows it is the state tourney he
is about to play. And it's game time. He looks around: where is his
team?

The crowd roars as the opposition team bursts onto the floor.
He sees he is playing the girls' team. He looks around again, expecting to see Rick and Todd and Kev and Billy and all the others
on the bench, grinning at him, enjoying this peculiar prank at his
expense. But his bench is empty.

He looks at the board and it clearly reads *Sam vs. the Babes.* At
center court, the ref is waiting, ball in one hand and whistle between his teeth. The Mutant steps from the cluster of five girls
who will start and positions herself for the tip. Sam feels unbeliev-
ably stupid. He has at least a foot of height on her, a hundred
pounds of weight. She rockets up next to him, close enough for

him to feel her body heat, and of course the ball is his, an easy tap away from her, the only problem being he has no team. Rick isn't there to receive the tip. Nat Linscott hooks it clean from midair. Before Sam's feet are fully on the floor again, the babes flow around him, down court toward their hoop.

Shee-it.

How is he supposed to play an entire team by himself? He shakes his head and lopes after the girls, who chorus something at him. It takes him a moment to realize they are shouting *Pussy* at him. *Puss-zee-puss-zee-puss-hey-Sam.*

His ears are chili-pepper hot.

Suddenly pissed off, he crowds Melanie Jandreau, who has the ball. Melanie sticks her tongue out at him as she passes the ball to Melissa. His hand follows the ball but it's not there, Melissa has it and *her* tongue is out at him, and the girls are chorusing *na Na na Na na Na na* while Melissa dances triumphantly from one foot to another, dribbling the ball. Every time he goes for it, his hand seems to pass through a ghost.

The Mutant slips between him and Melissa, taking the ball, driving it toward the hoop. He tries to move between the girls and they are all over him. *Jesus, where's the ref?* Doesn't the idiot see them fouling him left and right, it's *Night of the Living Dead* time out here.

He blocks the Mutant from the hoop. She feints but he's with her and she can't get the ball past him and he can't get it away from her and they are locked in a weird dance. Why doesn't she pass the ball back out to Nat and let her shoot it over him from outside? He can't seem to get his hand on the ball when she dribbles it but goddamn it, she's had possession too long. *Where's the fucking ref?*

All at once, he realizes he's stark naked, except for his high-tops. And he's getting a boner.

The Mutant is just as suddenly bare-ass. Her creamy tits tremble and sway with every movement and her bush appears in brief glimpses between the rise and fall of the ball. The detail of the ball fades; he wants the damn thing down, so he can see her bush. Frantically he struggles for his concentration—and *oh shit,* all the babes are in their birthday suits. They move around him and the Mutant in a witch's coven, Deb's breasts larger than he would have guessed, Nat's bush blazing red and her areolae as big as gold pieces, and there's gold dust freckled all over her. The M & M's are mirror images of each other, four perfect, perfectly identical breasts, twin elegant little navels, twin dairy-dream swirls of golden pubic hair. Their beautiful mouths making mocking kisses at him. His crotch feels as heavy as if he were dragging a ball and chain with his works.

The ref drifts into his peripheral vision, bucky too, except for his whistle and his black shoes.

Half-blind with the sweat running into his eyes, Sam lurches toward the ball. His heart leaps as his fingers succeed in closing on it. At the same instant the Mutant's fingers coil around his arcing penis—the sensation a jolt of burning electrical cold, as if she has a handful of dry ice. With an angry shout, he shoots off instantly, his semen falling in a slow-motion silvery spatter over the ball between them. With the closed fist of her free hand, the Mutant casually bops the ball out of his grip from underneath and his spill rides it over her head, into the basket.

As the ball drops through the hoop and the crowd roars, he realizes all his family and friends are in the bleachers, and now his team is on the bench, and all of them are cheering the Mutant's score.

■ ■ ■

Sam moans in his sleep. No one hears over the racket of the boys on the bus, growing ever louder as they approach Castle Rock.

Rick nudges him. "Wake up, man. We're here."

Tongue thick in his mouth, Sam's face feels as if it melted while he slept. His headphones are askew. He hooks them down around his neck. He's sweating heavily. Rick's coat is over his lap. He pushes it off and sits up.

Rick leans close. "Thought I'd better cover you up, guy. You were getting embarrassing, you know?"

Blood hot in his face, Sam is suddenly aware of a puddle of stickiness drooling through his body hair. Then he begins to remember his dream and his embarrassment thickens.

"Shit," he mutters.

Rick pushes his glasses up his nose. "Anyone I know?"

Sam ducks it. "You ever have one that was a nightmare?"

Rick laughs. "No. Sounds like the kind of thing happens to a guy who's been cherry too long."

Sam yawns. "Big friggin' help, Doc."

■ ■ ■

The girls have the court first. In the bleachers, with Rick and Sarah next to him, Sam swats away the immediate recall of his wet dream their appearance evokes. He groans inwardly at the stupidity of it. Why is it in dreams, no matter what weirdness is happening, you-in-the-dream just go along with it, like the dopey teenagers in the slasher flicks who are always falling asleep in class when Freddy Krueger is sitting right behind them, as if a person could fall asleep with a homicidal maniac fanning fingernails like gutting knives and grinning at you? Staring at the Mutant, he feels a little ill to remember what happened when she touched him in the dream. Or else he's getting excited again. There's something really sick about getting turned on by a freak like her, even in a dream. Next thing, he'll be getting hard for Freddy Krueger.

To his relief, the game finally gets under way. The Mutant isn't having a banner night. A minor fumble gets her angry at herself and she tenses up and starts making mistakes. Her coach sends in Billie Figueroa to replace her before she blows up. Fortunately, Figueroa turns out to be hot.

Reuben touches Sam's shoulder and Sam glances up at him. Indy rides the crook of his father's arm and Pearl is at his side.

"Good luck," Reuben says, and Sam reaches up to grasp his father's hand.

Reuben shakes Rick's hand too and Rick grins at him, at Pearl, and tickles the arch of Indy's foot in her soft leather-soled booties.

Sam watches them moving to the upper bleachers. They stop to greet Rick's mom and dad.

There can't be more than twenty blacks in the whole county. While everyone knows the Woodses—as a cop, Lonnie is everywhere day in and out, and Fern runs childbirth classes at the hospital as well as working a regular shift in the maternity ward—after five years' residence, they remain somewhat isolated. Sam sees Pearl straightening her spine and putting on her most dazzling smile for Fern Woods, who jumps up to kiss the air next to Pearl's face. Fern never seems to realize the way her mouth tightens at the sight of Reuben and Pearl together but Sam's sure Pearl has noticed. It didn't keep Pearl out of Fern's LaMaze class and Fern was there for Indy's arrival but still—the two women remain at arm's length.

Indy bounces on Reuben's arm, recognizing Fern, who goes all gooshy over her. The baby dives for her, Fern catches her with delight and Pearl laughs with them. Maybe Indy would yet make the two women friends.

■ ■ ■

In the locker room, Bither is flying up his own ass from nerves. He roams around, yammering, in nothing but his jock.

Rick looks up from taping his left ankle. "Somebody give Mouth a 'lude. He don't shut up soon, I'm gonna need one myself."

Bither hops onto the bench next to Rick and makes an armpit fart.

Sam applauds. "That's talent, Mouth."

Bither beams. "Hey, Sambot, you get a good feel of the Mutant? Is it true her puss is as bald as her head?"

Woods groans loudly amid an outbreak of jeering and prurient laughter.

Todd Gramolini hoots and raises his voice to announce the question to the whole locker room. "Mouth wants to know if the Mutant shaves her muff."

"Mohawked," Pete Fosse shouts.

"You must have been drunker than me," Tim Kasten puts in. "Her twat's as bald as Michael Jordan's skull."

"No it isn't." Matt Michaud is dramatically puzzled. "She's got bush from her belly button halfway to her knees."

"And a tattoo on her ass," someone else calls.

"Yeah," Fosse elaborates. "It says *This End Up,* with arrows pointing both ways."

Sam hauls up the tongue of his left sneaker and holds it firmly while he laces the shoe. This kind of crude bullshit starts to get tacky for him when girls get named. It makes him uncomfortable if only because they could be talking about his sister—probably do when he's not around. He tries not to be paranoid but is resigned to the likelihood the old scandal about his mother is also sometimes a subject for lewd derision, and even more likely, his father's marriage to Pearl and the baby eight months later. It makes him dislike the Mutant even more.

■ ■ ■

The boys line up to give the girls congratulatory high fives for their 49–43 win as they leave the floor. Grinning, Sam extends his hand to the Mutant. She pauses, rolls her left hand over ritually and gives him a finger. He looks at it and shakes his head.

"Good game," he says.

She thrusts out her chin. "Fuck you very much, Your Holiness."

Her coach is suddenly behind her. "Gauthier, I heard that."

The Mutant looks back over her shoulder as she skips away toward the locker room.

"Break a dick, guys," she says.

Her coach slams past the boys, screeching, "Gauthier!"

The boys break up, displeasing their own coach. But they go out loose and stay that way.

■ ■ ■

Though the Rock's center grins up at Sam from just six feet tall, he is a solidly built kid, a junior who knows his job well. He wears rec specs and a mouthguard and has two fingers, dislocated in practice, taped together on his right hand. His name is Lucas Priest and he is related to half of Greenspark as well as most of Castle Rock.

Like Sam, Lucas is a junior volunteer firefighter and emergency medical technician. In previous summers, they have worked an occasional multiple-alarm house fire, major automobile accident or search-and-rescue together. They like to rank each other about their tastes in music—Lucas listens to country. Between junior and senior high, Lucas even made a serious attempt to convince his parents to let him live with an aunt in Greenspark so he could be on Sam's team. The two boys give each other double fives so exuberantly the crowd laughs.

By the third quarter, the Indians have a substantial lead. Sam goes out of the game to allow Fosse, the backup center, to get a good workout. It's fun to watch Lucas break out and rally his discouraged guards. Pete is momentarily flummoxed. Woods, Gramolini, Bither and Kasten pull together to compensate but Pete is trembling like a winded horse at the end of the quarter. Coach calms him down. Billy Rank goes in for Rick, who has simply run out of gas. There is a momentary wobble in the defense and Lucas drives past Pete to lay in a clean shot. Like a gymnast, Lucas tumbles over Billy trying to claim the rebound. Todd Gramolini gets a hand on the loose ball and pivots off balance, only to find the Rock's Lennie Clutterbuck waiting to steal it and lob it back in for three. Coach calls out Pete and sends Sam back in. Trusting him, Billy steadies and relaxes again and The Big Machine kicks into overdrive, taking down Castle Rock 70–58.

■ ■ ■

Outside it's colder than the gulag but the windows on the girls' bus start rattling down and the boys are showered with candy bars, notes, tape cassettes and blown kisses. With his hands in his jacket pockets as far as they will fit, Sam walks up to the side of the bus, right to the Mutant's window, and blinks up at her. She stares down at him for a fraction of a second, then gobs at him. Seeing her pucker, he jumps back and she misses.

Suddenly Sam reaches up and grabs the edge of the window and climbs the side of the bus. It rocks under his assault. Inside the girls shriek. All at once the entire boys' team is climbing the sides of the bus with him. He shoves his head through the window. The Mutant holds her ground, kneeling on her seat within his reach. Sam looks around the girls' bus, which is in hysteria. He grins.

"Thanks," he says. "You loosened us up."

The Mutant regards him coolly.

"Asshole," she mutters.

Up and down the bus, boys have their heads and sometimes shoulders through the open windows. Some of them are getting kissed—the M & M's are being particularly generous. Other guys are being shoved back out.

"Take'm," the Mutant suddenly shouts. "Go for their pants."

Screaming girls hurtle themselves off the bus as the guys wriggle back through the windows. The ones closest to the bus door are in immediate trouble as girls haul at their jeans or sweats before they can escape.

Since his shoulders prevent him from getting more than his head in the window, Sam drops easily to his feet. Rick Woods, Billy Rank, Tim Kasten and Bither are not so lucky; their pants are variously somewhere between their hips and their ankles.

The girls' coach bellows through a megaphone she has found somewhere on the bus, "Any student not on the bus and in their seat at the count of ten is suspended!"

As girls scramble to their seats, the boys are either frantically hauling up their pants or diving for their own bus, just ahead of their coach and the bus drivers, who move among them like game-beaters in a grouse shoot.

Retreating toward his bus, Sam glances back and waves at the Mutant. She still kneels in her seat—the only girl to stay put during the melee. The girls' coach can be heard raving at them. The windows on their bus slam closed in a toneless crescendo.

The Mutant's window alone is still open when the girls' bus

jerks into motion. Turning away as her bus passes the boys' stationary bus, she calmly hikes her oversized shirts and drops the tights underneath to flash her bare bottom at them. No tattoos.

Roaring with approval, the boys lunge to Sam's side of the bus to catch the view. Coach goes nuclear and the poor bus driver hunches forward over the wheel and covers her eyes. On the girls' bus, their coach plunges down the aisle toward the Mutant. Before she can get there, the Mutant has her tights back up and is sitting down.

Rick Woods writhes in his seat, his laughter becomes a loony, breathless hooting.

Coach's bugged eyes are suddenly in Sam's face, causing him to start violently. "Jesus Jumping Christ! You two are supposed to captain this team!"

Eyebrows raised, Sam spreads his hands in mystification, as if he has been listening to his Walkman all along and missed the whole thing.

■ ■ ■

It takes a while for the girls' bus to settle down. At the front, their coach flops wearily and closes her eyes. Quietly the Mutant begins to move around the bus, speaking softly. *Meeting*. She indicates the back of the bus, beyond Coach's hearing thanks to the chatter of the cheerleaders. Some of the girls are reluctant but curiosity gets the better of them, especially since it involves something the Mutant wishes to keep secret from Coach. As much as they loathe the Mutant, her mooning the guys has given her a momentary authority.

"We're the captains," Melissa Jandreau protests. Melanie adds, "We should call the meetings."

"Anybody can call one," the Mutant points out. "You'll wish you had when you hear this."

She tells them about Sam's initiative.

"All right, all right," Melanie admits. "I never thought about it before but if anybody'd ever offered me the option, I'd have been there."

"Is it worth it?" Melissa says. "It's gonna take some hassle to get permission. We can't even be sure it will make any difference."

"It all comes to one thing," the Mutant says. "You want another try at that state this year?"

The girls look at each other.

The answer comes out of Melissa in a throaty growl. "Jesus, yes."

The Mutant grins. "Then here's how we do it."

■ ■ ■

His teammates are shouting objections before Sam finishes. Even Rick shakes his head in disbelief. Arms crossed, Coach glowers at Sam. Everywhere he looks, Sam sees negative body language.

"You take this up with them?" Todd Gramolini demands.

Sam nods.

"You oughta lay off the cheap drugs, Sambot," Pete Fosse says. "They need more time, let'm take it in the evening."

"When? After both teams have played games? After they've taken two hours' practice and waited another two hours for us to take ours?" Sam counters.

Rick Woods hugs his elbows and studies the floor.

Unsurprised when the vote goes against him, Sam slumps into his seat and stares out the bus window. He sees the reflection of his own face, like the ghost of a moon traveling over the hulked, spiky black fractals of woods, the bumpy geometries of walled and fenced fields. A heavy ceiling of snow cloud blinds the sky. The Mutant's moon, already set, is the only solid one to rise to-night—an upside-down heart, not moon-shaped at all. She has beautiful dimples at the narrow base of her spine. Hanging it out the window on a night this cold—that took some iron.

"*I will forget my complaint, I will leave off my heaviness,*" Sam murmurs to his reflection.

"Do that," Rick says.

Sam glances at him, raising an eyebrow. "*Are the consolations of God small with thee?*"

"Shut up, preacher, and read your Bible," Rick says, "or you'll be consoling with God bigtime."

"*Shall vain words have an end?*" Sam demands.

"Amen, brother Styles," Todd Gramolini says, catching the pul-pit rhythm if not the words of Sam's speech.

Rick Woods gives up and joins in the chorus of *amen, brother*s and *give-us-The-Word*s from the rest of the bus.

Sam waits for it to die down to expectant silence. He stands and looks up and down the aisle with great solemnity.

"E-e-eat me," he says in an eloquent stutter, and the boys on the bus explode in laughter, cheers and applause.

■ ■ ■

At Greenspark Academy the girls' bus is emptying when the boys' parks next to it. As Sam unlocks his truck, he sees the tails of the Mutant's coat whipping around the corner of the building, headed for the path that climbs the wooded hill behind the school. It will take her east to Kansas Street, exactly in the opposite direction of her home on Depot, in the village. At the main road, he turns east himself, takes the left onto Kansas and spots her a block ahead.

He beeps; she stops and cocks her head at him.

"Ride home?" he asks.

Hopping the curb, she skids around the truck and hauls ass into the cab in the intake of a frozen breath. She hunches on the seat, shivering.

"Jesus," she whimpers, "it's so fucking cold."

Sam spreads a hand in front of a vent; the truck won't be putting out heat for a couple more minutes.

"You want my jacket?"

She gives him a sour look. "Fuck no. Just drop me at Scotia."

Chapin lives on Scotia. Sam nods.

"Between hanging that moon and the way you dress, you should have frostbite of the fanny," Sam ventures. "You talk to the girls about the gym?"

The Mutant stares out the window. "Yeah."

"The guys didn't go for it."

She is unperturbed. "Who needs'm? Drop me here."

Out of the truck as quickly as she was into it, she flies up the Chapins' walk with her coat skirts billowing open.

"Deanie!"

She glances back over her shoulder.

"You're welcome," he calls.

She flips him a double bird and bounds up the Chapins' front steps. He watches her smack the front door with the flat of her palm. Dropping her backpack and gym bag, she hops from foot to foot. When J.C. opens the door to let her in, Sam drives away.

4

■ ■ ■

As the Closing Door Shuts out the cold the Mutant snugs up tight against J.C. for the warmth. He lifts her up and puts her down again with her feet on top of his and walks her through the foyer into the living room, where the fireplace is throwing feverish heat. Tipping her right off her feet, he picks her up and drops her onto the couch and hands her the Walkman he has just abandoned to answer the door. When she settles the 'phones over her ears, she hears Dylan insisting everybody must get stoned.

J.C. disappears toward the kitchen and returns with a mug of hot black coffee and a sugar pot. It's not granular sugar but cubes, in which she takes a childish delight. She dumps four into the coffee. J.C. unhooks the 'phones and takes back his tape player, dropping it and himself onto the couch next to her. He puts his sneakered feet on the glass coffee table. In pirate drag, he wears a black silk scarf around his head, a muscle shirt and baggy pants like pajamas in the colors and images of regurgitated pizza.

His parents are not at home. In all the times she has been inside the Chapin house, the Mutant has never actually seen the Chapins and suspects they may have forgotten how to get there.

"Win?"

She nods. It isn't important to him but she appreciates the effort he makes. J.C. has a salesman's ability to interest himself in his customers long enough to convince them he is their close friend. The smoothness of his con amuses her.

Producing a joint, he waves it under her nose. "Wanna get wrecked?"

"Yeah. I earned it."

He raises an eyebrow. "Oh oh. What'd you do, D.?"

"Mooned the guys' bus."

J.C. curls up, sniggering. "Oh, shit, I miss all the good stuff."

The Mutant shrugs. "You don't miss much, J."

Grinning, he takes a drag on the number and passes it to her. "Samson must have appreciated it, he chauffeured you over here."

"He wanted to give me a tract, tell me about how Jesus changed his life," she lies, to be witty. "It's a short ride and it's so frigging cold out, I figured I could stand it that long."

"Right. Must have been the cold making your titty-bumps stand up when you came through the door."

The Mutant brings her coffee mug to her face to feel the warmth.

Slowly, J.C. stretches his legs, shifts his hips and relaxes against the back of the couch. He sucks in a lungful of smoke, closing his eyes while he holds it.

"C'mere," he says after a while, his voice smoky with dope and seduction.

Putting down the mug, she moves within his reach. She takes another toke and leaves the jay burning in the ashtray.

J.C. undoes the scarf around his head and she wraps it around hers, tying it at the back to make a kind of wimple. He likes costumes.

"Sister Mary Doobage," he laughs into his fist.

She straddles him and he slides his hands under her shirts and inside her tights, squeezing her buttocks, grinding his crotch against hers as she works her tongue around his tongue. She lets him nudge her head down to his crotch. She's tired and would like to have this over quickly, as it usually is when she blows him, but after only a moment, he stops her and tugs her tights down. Kneeling between her legs, he lifts her bottom and shoves his spit-wet cock into her with deliberate crudity.

She closes her eyes and inhales the musk of his healthy sweat, the complex scent of his expensive aftershave. This is business but it's nothing like the way Tony goes at her. J.C. never hits her, he shares his dope, and his body is young and feels good to her. Warm. For a moment she forgets the ludicrous writhing and grinding. Gently, she strokes the back of his neck as he labors. She is far from her body as he rides it. Suddenly he searches frantically for her mouth and bites her lower lip. Reflexively jerking away from him, she cries out in surprise and pain and he slams himself down on top of her, shaking and groaning.

■ ■ ■

"All right," he says, lifting himself away from her after a moment's breathless collapse. "All right."

He pulls up his pants and goes upstairs.

Silently, she yanks off the scarf and swabs her bleeding lip with it. The blood is just a dampness on the black silk. She curls up close to the fire. It's a trip to watch, and so warm. It makes her sleepy. The Chapins' house is the nicest she has ever been inside. She would probably let J.C. screw her just to spend a little time in it once in a while.

J.C. comes down again with a small paper bag he tucks into her gym bag. It contains weed—most of which she will stash away from home to keep Tony or Judy from appropriating it—and her b.c. pills.

J.C.'s dad is a pharmaceuticals salesman—like father, like son, J.C. likes to joke. The Chapins want J.C. to go to med school. He fully intends to oblige. He can't wait to get his hands on his own prescription pads and samples. In the meantime, he is too smart to steal from his old man, except for mere trifles, among them birth-control pills for the Mutant. It's easy to make a single month's supply disappear; the old man just assumes he miscounted or somebody at the factory fucked up.

He presents her with a piece of ice in a wet facecloth for her lip before he flops down next to her again.

"Sorry. I lost it."

She shrugs. But for the soreness between her legs and her tender lip, already it seems as if the sex never happened.

"Boys win tonight?"

"Sure."

"I've been thinking about Samson," J.C. says, reaching for the cold number.

The Mutant's lashes drop suddenly.

"Slammer's an android," she says. "He has the brains of a video game. His circuits just sit there, blinking, waiting for somebody to insert either a shop cartridge or one for round ball. Yank the cart and the meat machine goes on walking, talking and whacking off but there's nothing going on upstairs but radio static."

J.C. chortles and extends the fired-up joint. She takes it, drags on it and holds the smoke in her lungs.

"If you could get him interested in some product," J.C. finally says, "I'll give you some samples to lay on him. Maybe he's looking for boosters. You let him know I can get him anything he wants—powder, uppers, steroids—anything on the jock aisle. He buys anything, I'll give you a little something on commission."

She's willing to risk suspension from the team—there's a certain boot in flirting with it and she never wants to look in the mirror and see another ass-kissing conformist jock—but only suspension. She never carries more than a single easily disposed-of joint or a couple pills at a time. And she adamantly refuses to deal for J.C.

"Come on, he's so straight I could use him for a T-square in drafting class. I told you before, I won't hold shit for you. If—and this is right up there with the likelihood I'm in the running for Miss America—if Samson should happen to get a Post-It note from Jesus to get in touch on the 800-blotter line, I'll set it up but that's all."

J.C. pauses, the jay an inch from his lips, and smiles. "Whatever. Your trip, babe."

■ ■ ■

With a plaintive yowl, the Siamese spooks from the shadows and twines around Sam's ankles as he climbs the steps to the back porch. Hunger pangs triggered by the woodsmoke in the air deepen almost to cramps as the first warm whiff of supper leaks out the door his father opens for him. Reuben gives him a high five for the good game. Pearl, with Indy climbing distractingly on her, pecks his cheek.

Headachy with hunger, Sam has his spoon in his supper before Reuben lets go of the soup plate. Pearl has knocked herself out; her paella is spicy and thick and filling. While he tucks it away, he shuffles the little pile of mail next to his plate—college recruiters and other unwelcome reminders the future is bearing down on him.

He's got a file full of shit from recruiters, from summer basketball camps. Though he's played exhibition games, he's never accepted any invitations to sneaker camps or to tour colleges. When Coach tries to talk to him about His Future, Sam remembers compelling business elsewhere.

His spring SATs were a disaster. He froze. It was like he'd never taken the practice ones with Romney, or the state assessment exam that was so similar. Everybody in school knows he handed in his book forty minutes into the exam and went directly to the lavatory to puke his guts out. Romney has tried to persuade him to sit for them again and he says he will but he keeps losing the application form. With substandard scores, he'd have to take the Prop 48 back door to play college hoops—maybe even do a year or two at some junior college that specializes in academic rehab. *Not smart enough to compete academically with your peers? We'll do you a favor because you won a genetic crapshoot that made you big and strong and athletic.* It's humiliating, a reminder of those forty minutes trying to keep his sweaty grip on the pencil and his guts. Somehow it sours his genuine accomplishments, on and off court.

There's a postcard, the usual brief cheerful scrawl from his brother Frankie, in the Persian Gulf where it's been heating up to a shooting war since August. Sam doesn't know how he could live with himself if he was collecting free sneakers and faking his way through bullshit courses in some juco, angling for a college berth, while his brother puts his life on the line for whatever the Holy Cause is this time—oil, the hordes of the infidel, it doesn't matter—it's always some weenie-measuring contest between one old man and another.

He takes dessert—chocolate-coconut-cream pie, his favorite—upstairs where he can eat it while jacked into the FM.

■ ■ ■

The baby, crying, wakes him. It is very cold and still dark out. The clock says 3:50. The house is way too quiet. Shit. The furnace.

He hauls on several layers of clothes and goes downstairs. Bundled up in blankets, his stepmother is settling into her rocking chair next to the woodstove in the kitchen. Inside the turn-of-the-century firebox, the fire is roaring, stoked up by Reuben on his way to the cellar. Indy is somewhere inside Pearl's quilts, to go by the muffled little cries escaping. Pearl shifts and suddenly Indy is making frantic snuffling noises, something she does when she knows the nipple is right there. It's her version of scraping a spoon over the cell bars. She keeps the mess hall riot going, slobbering and snorting for a few seconds even after she finds it. Pearl winces as the baby chomps down. She smiles sleepily at Sam.

Sam shrugs on his jacket and heads for the cellar. Reuben is on his back on the dirt floor, shining a flashlight into the guts of the dead furnace.

"Know what's wrong?" Sam asks.

"Mostly this frigging little burner was never meant to heat this whole house all the time. Joe put it in as a backup to keep his pipes from freezing when he wasn't here to stoke the fires. Old fart never in his life heated more than the room he was squatting in."

"I do anything?"

"Make some tea for me," Reuben grunts. "Check the wood-stove."

Sam trudges upstairs and puts the kettle on. He adds another chunk of wood to the fire. It is putting out good warmth now. From the cellar, he hears Reuben curse. Not a good sign. His father rarely uses bad language. Sam goes back down and passes tools to Reuben until the furnace grumbles on again.

Before breakfast, Sam tries his truck and it does a fine imitation of the furnace earlier. He has forgotten to plug in the engine-block heater. He'll have to write it down on one of his reminder lists. He jumps it from Reuben's truck and leaves the battery charging. In the kitchen he makes himself a cup of instant cocoa.

"I want to sell a piece of the woodlot and use the money for a new furnace," Pearl is telling Reuben.

Reuben shakes his head. He's still wearing the jacket he put on to go down cellar to work on the furnace. Indy is sitting in his lap while he spoons applesauce into her mouth.

"No. It's yours. Indy's. We've spent enough of your money. Besides, the real estate market is flat. Right now you couldn't give away a condo at the Right Hand of God, even with free cable and a clock-radio thrown in."

Pearl flips a pancake impatiently and slaps it with the spatch. "Sell the timber on it, then. We've got to have a new furnace. The baby's going to be sick all winter if we have to live in this cold."

"Jesus Christ," Reuben explodes, "tell me something I don't know."

Startled by his raised voice, Indy starts to blubber.

"I'll tell you something," Pearl says. "There's no good reason for us to get up at three-thirty in the morning because it's too cold to sleep, except your goddamn Yankee pride."

Reuben rocks the baby to calm her but his mouth is tight and angry. "All right. Give me a chance to ask around and find out if I can work a barter deal with someone."

Pearl sets a plate of pancakes down hard in front of him.

"The next time I wake up to a dead furnace, I'm going out and buying one myself."

Coming abruptly to his feet, Reuben hands her the baby. He sweeps up the plate and slings it against the wall. The baby shrieks at the explosion of the china and Pearl ducks. Grabbing his jacket, Reuben slams out the door in tight-lipped rage.

"You pigheaded asshole!" Pearl comes up onto her toes to scream after him.

Indy's wails of terror jump another decibel and Pearl jounces her, instantly passing from shrew to earth mother. With her hand on the back of the baby's neck, she shushes and strokes and pats until Indy hiccups and whimpers.

Wordlessly, Sam picks up the pieces of the plate and the fragments of pancake and wipes down the wall with a rag.

In the yard, Reuben stomps around for a few moments before he shuffles back into the house with downcast eyes.

"I'm sorry," he says. "Pigheaded asshole?"

As she wipes Indy's nose, Pearl's mouth quirks into a smile.

Sam conciliates. "We're all up too early."

The three of them look at each other and Pearl laughs.

"I guess so," she says.

Reuben tugs her and the baby into his arms. "I'll do something about the furnace today."

Later, as they are all leaving the house, Reuben stops Sam on the back porch.

"Sorry about the blowup," he says.

Sam glances back toward the kitchen, where Pearl is bundling Indy to go to work.

"Let's take her to dinner tonight," Sam says. "I'm up for some Chinese."

Reuben grins. "Why not? On a day I'm blowing off the price of a new furnace, one more MasterCard charge'll feel like a pack of gum."

■ ■ ■

The courts outside the school are empty of everything but dead leaves and some hardly distinguishable frozen rags. Rick Woods hops and skids across the parking lot to meet Sam and they enter the school together.

Most of the girls' team loiters expectantly in the corridor outside the gym. Poker-faced as hoods on a street corner waiting for a challenge from a rival gang, several of the guys cluster at the very doors. The Mutant poses, hip shot to one side, observing what she has wrought.

Giving all a pleasant nod, Sam unlocks the doors. They follow him into the gym, the girls with murmurs and giggles, the boys silent and tense. When he opens the equipment closet, the Mutant appears at his elbow and pops the basketball he hooks from the rack from his hand into hers.

"We're taking the gym," she announces.

Sam watches her lope to center court. The girls are already on the floor. At the sidelines, the boys stand together, giving angry, disgusted looks to both Sam and the girls. Sam crosses his arms and leans against the door of the closet.

"Fuck this," Pete Fosse says, striding across the floor toward the Mutant. "Gimme the ball, bitch."

Stonily, she passes it to Billie Figueroa and flips Fosse a bird.

Tim Kasten closes on Figueroa. When she attempts to pass the ball to Nat Linscott, Tim snatches it away. Laughing, he bounds away from the girls. In an outburst of angry cries, the girls start after Tim and suddenly the rest of the boys are there, forming a wall like some enormous law firm marshaling against a class-action suit. The girls falter and come to a stop.

"Get the fuck off the court," Fosse says, jerking his thumb toward the sidelines.

The Mutant walks up to him. "No way. This court is ours today."

Sam approaches and curls a finger at Fosse, to whom Kasten has handed the ball. Sam holds out his palm. Pete hesitates. Woods, Sam's co-captain, is suddenly at Sam's side. Pete releases the ball into Sam's hand and is rewarded with a smile.

"Five on five," says Sam.

Amid an outbreak of cursing and protest from the boys, the Mutant whoops triumphantly. Fosse grabs for the ball but Sam holds it high over his head.

"Now, now, Peteybird," Sam reproves gently. "Gram, Woods, Michaud, Fosse and me for the guys."

"Black, Carver, the M & M's and me," the Mutant calls.

All the girls but the ones she names drift to the sidelines. The boys hold their ground, arguing among themselves. Finally they also go to the sidelines, leaving only Rick Woods and Billy Rank to represent the boys.

"Volunteers?" asks Sam.

Joey Skouros, everyone's nominee for Nerd of the Universe, shuffles back onto the court, wincing at the curses and insults heaped on his badly barbered head by his teammates. Acting as ref, Sam places Skouros to tap for the boys' team. Shaking, Skouros manages to lift his six-foot three-inch gantry of a body high enough to knock the ball into Woods's hands.

The scrimmage, such as it is, commences. Sam leaves the court long enough to plug a cassette into the sound system. When he turns around, the Mutant has stolen the ball from Woods and is taking it to the girls' hoop. Rick looks extremely pissed. The boys on the sidelines jeer at Woods, at Skouros and Rank, who falter and come to a standstill. Skouros abruptly walks off court. Hands on his hips, Rick Woods glances toward Sam and then also abandons the court. Billy Rank gives Sam a beseeching look and follows Woods.

The Mutant smoothly hooks the ball into her hoop. It comes down into Melissa Jandreau's hands. Melissa dribbles it, looking toward Sam to see what happens next.

He shrugs and lopes down court as the sound system finishes feeding the leader of his dub past the tapehead. There is an easy jingly island-sounding pump and then the vibrant guttural voice of Wilbert Harrison urges,

> Together we will stand
> divided we fall
> come on people,
> Let's get on the ball
> and work together.
> Come on come on
> let's work together.
> Now now people
> say now together we will stand
> every boy girl woman and man.

His choice of music has the Mutant grinning. Almost dancing to it, he fakes, Melissa buys it, and he plucks the ball away from her, pivots, and heads toward his hoop, the Mutant on his heels, her team racing to get there ahead of him.

" 'Aw yeah,' " he shouts with Wilbert Harrison. " 'Aw look a here, look a here,' " as he rockets straight up from just short of the key and sinks a three-pointer over the heads of the defending girls.

He descends into applause and cheers, finds the floor solid under his feet and the atmosphere suddenly rowdy and gleeful. Shaking his head, Rick Woods trots back onto the floor and high-fives him. The Mutant takes the ball and moves down court again.

"Defense!" Todd Gramolini shouts, bounding onto the court.

Grinning, Joey Skouros stumbles behind Gram and Billy Rank follows.

On the sidelines, the members of the two teams dance one on one, girls with girls and girls with boys and one boy—Kevin Bither—with two girls. Anyone looking into the gym would wonder is there a dance going on or a basketball practice. The only holdout is Fosse, who stalks away.

Sam bears down on the Mutant again. The matchup is ridiculous; she's so much smaller and lighter than he is but Jesus is she into it. If he's dancing, she's kick-boxing. She has less power than he but a magnitude of fierceness he doesn't expect from a girl. He has seen her on court enough to be familiar with the intensity of her play, but this morning she is tuning herself up to try to meet his overwelming height and weight advantage and it's so quixotic, he is tickled.

As Sam advances on the Mutant, he is aware that between them they have created the circumstances of his dream on the bus. It is reassuring to know this time he is not wearing his uniform but a union suit and sweats, most unlikely to suddenly dissolve. And she wears cutoff Levis over one of those whole-body tights things, only the legs stop at mid-calf. Totally thready, of course, so when she lifts her arms, a slight pale bulge of breast is visible in a ripped seam under one arm, and the rusty black tights show through the rents and unravelings in the skintight bleached-out cutoffs.

But the music lifts him and it all feels right in a way the dream had not. He is glad of his choice of hard-driving ZZTop for the second cut on the dub.

"Shut'm down," he shouts.

His boys grin at each other. In moments, the girls are giving each other frantic looks. The glee vanishes. The nonplayers stop dancing to watch and exchange low-voiced commentary. The Mutant calls for Deb Michaud to replace Megan Black and Meggie looks relieved.

Sam takes the ball from Nat Linscott—again—and passes it to Skouros. The Mutant is on Joey in a flash, darting around him, trying to cut him off.

"Prick," she remarks to Sam as she runs past him.

"Eat me," he answers with a grin.

"You wish," floats back to him.

At his elbow, Rick Woods sniggers.

It is part of the ongoing revelation: treat the Mutant like another guy. She reads it as respect.

When the warning bell for classes rings, the Mutant bends, panting, to grasp her knees.

Cradling the ball, Sam stoops over her. "Okay?"

"You son of a bitch," she gasps. "I feel like a minge trying to fuck an elephant."

"You want the state or not?"

She glances up at him irritably. "Oh fuck you, 'god.'"

Sam fights to keep a straight face. "You wish."

Still short-winded, she laughs and it turns into a coughing fit.

■ ■ ■

Rick Woods crosses his arms and tips back his chair at the lunch table. His girlfriend, Sarah, is next to him, a proprietary hand on his knee.

"So we beat the shit out of a bunch of pussies."

Sarah slaps his thigh hard and he starts. His face knits in a frown. "I don't like that word," she says.

"Tough shit," Rick snaps.

Sarah jumps up and stalks away. The guys all watch her leave.

"Another thing to thank you for," Rick mutters to Sam. "As I was saying, it was fun, but what's it got to do with the real world?"

Sam extracts a mussel shell from the leftover paella in his Thermos cup. "It's got to do with them taking the state. They can beat us, they can beat anybody."

Pete Fosse claps his empty corn chip wrapper between his palms in a kind of Bronx cheer. "Who gives a shit if they take the state? Fuck'm."

Sam leans forward and speaks intently. "What's gonna beat us is some team from nowhere that shouldn't, on account of they really want it and we're not used to being up against somebody wants it so bad they think they can take us. You can't beat this buncha girls for intensity. Gauthier plays like she's got veins in her teeth. So we play them just the way we did this morning. Run'm into the floor. Don't give'm a friggin' break." He pauses, trying to remember if he's missed anything. "Just don't foul any more than you have to, so nobody claims any of us copped a feel."

"Shit on that!" Kevin Bither explodes. "If you're gonna make us play girls, then we're entitled to a grope if we can get it. You got to cop'm all, Sambot. We got our needs too."

A round of crude commentary as to the perverse nature of Bither's needs erupts.

Rick Woods is quiet.

"I think you've lost it, Sam," he says finally. "That shit you listen to has finally shorted out your brain cells."

Sam rocks the empty shell in his cup with the tip of his finger. "When it's warm we play volleyball with them, we play softball. Chill out, Rick. If it doesn't work, we'll go to alternate days."

Rick shakes his head doubtfully.

Sam pokes him in the ribs and Rick glances over his shoulder. On the other side of the cafeteria, Sarah and the Jandreau twins are demonstrating dance moves they must have picked up from MTV to a circle of girls. Sarah looks Rick's way and undulates her hips.

"Oh my God," Rick says. "She's gonna make me eat shit to make up, you know."

Raising his eyebrows, Sam nudges a packet of Saltines toward Rick and asks, "Wanna cracker?"

5

■ ■ ■

Bepimpled Boogerhookers Clot the corridor
outside the Office. The freshman lockers are located nearby and at
the end of the day the place is a rat maze of glandular wretches
desperate for the exit. Sam's forward passage is halted by two
freshmen suddenly throwing punches at each other.

One of the combatants he recognizes as Kevin Bither's younger
brother Bobby, the shortest male in the freshman class, and the
other is a slobby fat kid with thick glasses and a Bart Simpson spike.
It is not a heroic or edifying engagement, just a lot of grunting and
ineffective pummeling. Sam doesn't care who started it or what the
issue is. The boogers are in his way. He yanks Bobby off Fats Four-
eyes and shoves him ungently against a locker, while Four-eyes, a little crazed, keeps popping the air as Bobby is lifted out of his reach.

"Take it outside," Sam says. "You're blocking traffic."

Laliberte gestures from behind his desk, summoning Sam past
the secretary into his inner office. The two coaches are already ensconced there, sucking up bad office coffee from Styrofoam cups.
Like the Siamese twisting between his ankles at home, the Mutant
materializes disconcertingly and slithers in behind Sam. She drops
into one of the two chairs in front of the principal's desk and
swings her sneakers up to park them on the polished mahogany.

Her coach barks, "Gauthier! Feet on the floor! And get rid of that gum!"

The Mutant promptly drops her feet to the floor and sticks her finger in her mouth to retrieve a wad of gum. She examines it closely, looks around and finally sticks it between her eyebrows.

"Gauthier!" her coach growls.

The Mutant crinkles her forehead and the gumwad drops into her palm. Leaning to one side, she pots it into the trash can next to the principal's desk.

"Bingo," she says.

Sam slouches in the other hot seat, aware of his coach glaring at him.

Frowning, Laliberte leans forward and taps the tips of his fingers together. He clears his throat and smiles his I'm-a-reasonable-kinda-guy smile.

"The use of the gym before classes is a privilege, not a right. This morning the two of you took it on yourself to reinterpret that privilege without approval of the proper authorities or even consultation with your peers. What do you have to say for yourself?"

The Mutant's body slips into a bored sprawl in her chair and she tips her head back to stare at the ceiling.

"Mr. Styles," Laliberte says, with some impatience.

Sam gestures toward the Student Handbook among the reference manuals on Laliberte's desk. "Handbook says the gym is open for hack hoops. It doesn't say anything about boys or girls. We did consult with our team members and got a fifty-fifty break. I figured on negotiating alternate days but this morning the girls were there and ready to go. I wasn't gonna take it on myself to throw them off the court. It seemed like a reasonable experiment to use the gym together. The important thing is it worked."

Sam is perspiring heavily. Pleadingly he looks to the Mutant for support but she is otherwise engaged. Mouth Almighty except when you need her. Then she's got more urgent business mapping flyspeck on the overhead fixtures.

Abruptly, she comes to life, bouncing to her feet to lean across Laliberte's desk and shove her face into his. "It's our gym too."

The principal frowns as if he is considering a complicated thesis.

The Mutant pivots to address the coaches. "When we went in there, we just wanted our time on the floor. Now we're all agreed if we could play the guys regularly, it would toughen us up to where nobody could beat us. We've never played so hard as we did this morning."

Arms crossed, her coach listens intently and then addresses the principal. "I saw some of it. I was surprised at the way the girls fought back. I'm inclined to go along with it."

Sam's coach snorts incredulously. He pokes his chest with his thumb. "Well and good for the girls but what's it gonna do to my team? They'll get used to walking over the girls and lose their edge. Besides, this is a contact sport. There's a size differential. Somebody could get hurt. This galoot here falls on one of those girls, he's liable to do a serious injury."

The principal and the coaches laugh and Sam smiles self-consciously. The Mutant is occupied with picking a loose thread from her T-shirt.

"Besides," Coach continues, his face reddening, "I don't like boys and girls playing together. Next thing you know, they'll be—grab-assing—"

"Oh please," the Mutant's coach interrupts in an offended tone.

The Mutant jumps in. "It's just hacking, mostly running and shooting."

Sam looks hastily at the floor. She's lying and her coach knows it too. They weren't hacking this morning; they were scrimmaging.

Laliberte sighs loudly, a signal he is toying with ordering the baby bisected if somebody doesn't offer him another solution.

Sam clears his throat and they all look at him. "The guys'll learn by teaching. As the girls get tougher, the guys'll have to adjust all the time. I told them the most dangerous opponents we'll have this year will be the ones we're not expecting, the ones who are supposed to be walkovers who turn out to have fire in their bellies. The girls are very gutty, very unpredictable. I think," he takes a huge breath, "it's worth a trial."

Laliberte looks to the coaches inquiringly.

"Me too," says the Mutant's coach.

Sam's coach makes a disgusted noise. "There'll be trouble, mark my words."

Laliberte nods solemnly. "So noted. I wonder if I could have a word with Miss Gauthier alone. Mr. Styles, I'll see you after her."

■ ■ ■

Sam slumps in a chair in the outer Office, trying to find a place to put his feet where no one will trip over them. He catches the high points of the principal's interview with the Mutant; the word *attitude* is repeated several times with considerable emphasis by Laliberte. The Mutant's responses are brief and inaudible. The door opens and she struts out and past him as if his chair were empty.

"Mr. Styles," Laliberte trills.

Sam has to wait for the principal to leave off paper-shuffling. He is being reminded, he knows, that he has made trouble and is taking up Laliberte's valuable time.

"Sam. I feel a little bullied. This has been very precipitous. How much is your doing and how much Gauthier's, I'm not sure. I sincerely hope she is not going to be a partner of yours in further upheavals."

Sam listens attentively. All issues suddenly coalesce for him into the image of the Mutant.

"The only thing in this school Gauthier's ever given a sh—a damn about, is hoops. If it makes her a winner, maybe she'll realize she can be a winner at other things."

Laliberte smiles indulgently.

Hearing the naivete in his words, Sam blushes.

"Very commendable of you. Have you ever heard the saying about the rotten apple?"

Throat tightening, Sam looks away. "You're writing her off, the way my sister got wrote—written off."

Laliberte straightens up like somebody just stuck a poker up his ass. "I'm not in the business of writing anybody off. Let me remind you that I was not principal here when your sister dropped out, but I'm sure no one ever wrote her off."

Sam mumbles an apology.

"Accepted." Laliberte turns conciliatory. "I had no idea you had any resentment about how your sister was treated here. What is she doing now?"

Sam stares at his feet. They don't look as if he could get them into his mouth but somehow he manages to do it.

"I dunno," he mutters, "I never see her." He picks at a callus on his palm. "It doesn't matter."

Laliberte is silent for a few seconds.

"All right, Sam. No more surprise rewrites of the rules, please. Keep this gym thing in order or shut it down promptly."

■ ■ ■

A sunbeam casts its spell over Sam as he tries to read an assignment for Romney's class at one of the big tables in the school library. The light falls over his heavy head and broad shoulders in a warm thick toffee caul, somehow stretching out time like a pull of homemade candy so the baby's cry in the bone-chill of the house seems to have wakened him on an entirely different day. A moment, he promises himself, just a moment, and lets his heavy lids fall.

Almost immediately, someone's shaking his shoulder. Lifting his head, he realizes at some point he has slumped forward over the book.

"Sambo," Rick whispers, "quiet time's over. Time to run and play and clear the old cobwebs out of our headie-weddies. And wipe that drool off that book. It's gross."

Brushing his sleeve over his mouth, Sam blinks and thrusts his neck out of his shoulders like a turtle. The face of the library clock comes into focus and he bolts to his feet with a screech of chair legs. Rounding the table, he slams a hipbone into the corner and yelps. The librarian frowns at him and Rick laughs out loud.

Down the corridor and on the stairs, Rick keeps ragging Sam. "Flaking out in the library, that's one of the seven deadly signals of excessive weenie-wringing, Sambo."

"You're the expert," Sam responds, "you tell me."

Jerking a fist suggestively, Rick chortles.

Coach is at the locker room door. Raising his wrist, he points at his watch, and spreads the fingers of one hand to indicate they are already five minutes late. Every minute costs a lap around the gym.

Muttering *shit,* Rick slams to his locker.

"Styles," Coach says, "I want to see you."

However late Coach makes him, Sam will still have to do the laps. It's Coach's favorite technique for minimizing backtalk.

"I get calls from scouts," Coach begins. "Asking about you, about Woods. I tell ya, Sam, I can't wait to tell'm my boys are playing the girls' team. Monday, I had a winning team and now I'm asking myself how long I'm gonna have a team at all. I dunno what happened. On Monday, you fell into the girls' bench and on Tuesday you're playing monkey bars on the girls' bus and that bald witch with the tattoos is hanging her bare hiney out the winda and this morning the two a ya got my boys taking practice with the girls. Sam, goddamn it, are you on the girls' team or the boys'? I mean, I'm starting to smell Vietnam here. Has it crossed what passes for your mind that you might be destroying your team to save the girls?"

With one eye on the clock and a mounting debt of laps, Sam follows the argument as far as Vietnam and then glazes over in confusion.

Coach snaps his fingers in front of Sam's face. "Pay attention to me, Sammy. I don't give a crap whether the girls win the state lottery or the Publishers Clearing House Sweepstakes or a state hand-job championship. I'm warning you, if this bullshit has even the smallest negative effect on my team, *your* team, the one with the dicks, I'm gonna make your life so miserable, you'll wish you didn't have one."

A life or a dick? Sam wonders but with fifteen laps waiting, he only has one thing to say. "Yessir."

"Just so we got it straight."

Rick has already completed his laps and is warming up with the rest of the team. Jogging the perimeter of the court on his lonesome, Sam has ample opportunity to observe his teammates. He sees no sign that team spirit has been affected by thrashing the girls. If anything, the mood is cocky.

Having had the early practice slot, some of them are threading back into the gym from their locker room to settle in the bleachers. The Mutant saunters to the corner of the bleachers. She has scarved her head like a gypsy in a tie-dyed rag with a fringe that looks like it might once have been a doily in some old tabby's musty parlor. She postures hipshot, legs spread, in the arrogant stance of a movie streetwalker.

Passing her, he offers a high five.

Without hesitation, she slaps his palms with a shout of "Come on, people."

The girls in the bleachers come to their feet to applaud and echo the call. The boys on the floor respond in kind.

Sam's euphoria is short-lived. Coach proceeds to find fault with everything he does. The rest of the team falls into a wary silence. Coach holds them all in the locker room for a pep talk about the next day's home game. He bears down heavily, with repeated digs about playing what he calls, with spit-spraying contempt, *a buncha pussies.*

■ ■ ■

It's as dark outside as it was when Sam woke, reminding him wearily it is still the same day. It's as if the elastic of time, stretched in the library sunbeam, just got snapped back to its normal form. The rollercoaster track of the day is on a dead flat. He finds himself at a rare, disconcerting loose end, with too little time to bother returning to the Ridge but not enough to do anything constructive beyond a minor errand at the pharmacy before meeting the folks at the Chinese restaurant.

Filling Pearl's list, he moves slowly down the aisles. At the makeup counter, Billie Figueroa and the M & M's spritz each other from sample bottles of stinkum, and giggle, with a sound like a string of birds suddenly exploding from their perch on a wire. A little cloud of cloying scent drifts his way and he suppresses a sneeze. Tim Kasten and Pete Fosse are studying the covers of the shrink-wrapped slick stroke books from the top rank of the magazine rack. The bell over the door jangles and Sam catches a glimpse of the Mutant's headscarf before it disappears between the aisles.

When he arrives at the cash register, the fussy little cashier with her glasses on a tether frowns over a bottle of baby lotion that has two conflicting price stickers on it. She draws an exasperated breath and turns away to fumble at her intercom mike. Behind her, packs of cigarettes are ranked within easy reach. As the cashier asks tremulously for a price check, someone jostles Sam from behind. Reflexively he flattens a hand on the counter and manages to tumble the little heap of his goods onto it. As he tries to stop them scattering, he knocks a box of breast pads toward the opposite side, where it teeters on the edge.

With an exclamation, the cashier grabs for it, too late, and it falls past her to the floor. As the woman stoops to retrieve it, the Mutant, in sudden fluid motion past Sam, is up on her toes and snatching a pack of butts from the rack. She is gone down the nearest aisle before the cashier straightens up with the box of breast pads in triumphant custody. As if he has just come in from a long time in extreme cold, dull heat kindles in Sam's face and ears. His own fingers feel suddenly thick and guilty.

There's no sign of the miscreant by the time he's outside. Behind the wheel of the truck, he considers his options. He could claim a table at the restaurant and drink Chinese tea and read the book he dozed off over in the library. He could check out the Corner downtown, still open and at this hour full of kids snacking on pizza and fries, feeding the video games, hustling each other, hanging out. Still undecided, he catches a pinpoint wink of red, hanging impossibly in the dark void beyond the wooden railing fencing the small shopping center from the gorge of Mill Brook.

Two-armed standards lift arc lights over the parking lot, spilling a fringe of light down the side of the gorge. A handrailed wooden stairway stutters down the steep slope to Mill Brook, from a break in the weathered-grey post-and-rail fence. The waterway snakes through Greenspark like a tapeworm. Downtown, where Mill Brook is a placid stream that stays between level banks most of the year, some of its spring floodplain is a pleasant strip of park. Along the stream at the perimeter of the few blocks of downtown, the park grows wilder as the banks rise, until the brook and its overgrown, jungly margins lie below the paved streets of the small town. The shopping center—laundromat, supermarket, pharmacy and feedstore—is built above the very place where the tame stretch of the park, with an elaborate, newly constructed Creative Playground, sinks away under the overpass of Grant Street into the gorge of the widening, rising banks toward the ruins of the old red-brick and grey-stone Mill. The lights of the Playground are not yet operative and so it is closed at night.

Vaulting the fence rail, Sam crunches through the frozen crosshatch of tall grasses and weeds to the stairs. Below him, off the stairway now and moving in the direction of the crenelated, towered Playground, the dot of red blinks at him. He catches a whiff of cigarette smoke rising up the chimney of the stairs. The overpass rumbles with traffic. Shrugging his jacket higher against the back of his neck, Sam follows the turning stairway down to Mill Brook. As he descends and the artificial light and susurrations of the overpass fade, his vision adjusts. At the bottom of the stairs an enormous bank of wild rosebushes overhangs the steps with a flagellant grab of thorny branches.

The miniature red star glows from the unlighted Playground. He makes no attempt to quiet his steps on the gravel path. It is a moment before the single red eye opens again. By then, his night vision is sharp. He sees the Mutant's outline, the fringe of the scarf swaying as she tosses her head and then the red wink of the cigarette reflected and twinned in her eyes, the faint rust it paints on her nose ring and the nearest links of facial chain. The leather of her swing creaks gently as she rocks in it.

"Samson!" she drawls in mocking surprise.

Calmly he cocks his chin to her in greeting. "Gimme a butt."

Raising her eyebrows, she reaches automatically into the breast pocket of her reefer coat.

As quickly as she snatched the pack from behind the cashier's back, Sam plucks both pack and lighted cigarette from her fingers. He pitches the butt toward the Mill Brook. The red tumbles and disintegrates into multiple points of fire.

The Mutant jumps to her feet, trying to grab back the pack he holds beyond her reach. "You fuck!"

Sam launches the packet toward the brook. From the darkness comes a soft chilly plash. Sheer luck—it's found the blind bucket of open water between the ice crusting from the banks.

The Mutant pounds both fists into Sam's gut. "Son of a bitch motherfucker!"

He steps backward, making her follow him to land her blows. As she lunges forward, he feints to one side, catches her by the wrist and twists it behind her to put her into a neat armlock. Still swearing, she kicks back at him. As the force of her kick unbalances her, Sam lets go. The Mutant sprawls face down on the fine sand of the Playground.

Panting, she rolls over and glares up at him. "You Nazi bastard," she spits.

Sam shivers and works his fingers into his jacket pockets.

"I put my ass on the line for you," he tells her, "you go straight out and boost yourself some butts. Never mind the frigging things are bad for your wind and you signed a contract you wouldn't use them in training. You get busted shoplifting, you won't just be suspended for a couple weeks. You'll be off the team with no chance of reinstatement, ever."

She vibrates with undiluted rage. "Fuck you, asshole! It's my goddamn business! I didn't ask you to put *dick* on the line for me. I don't need any fucking favors from you!"

"Your goddamn business!" Sam is incredulous. "You thieving wench, you used me to pull that ripoff! If you'd gotten busted, it could have looked like I was in on it. You could have got me busted too and cost me my eligibility. Looks to me like you made it *my* goddamn business."

Sitting up, she hugs herself. Realizing the ground must be fiercely cold, he reaches down to give her a hand up. The Mutant gobs at him. Bingo.

"Cute." He wipes his hand on his pants. "Look, I don't give a shit if you play hoops or if you don't. Make you a promise, though. I ever happen to see you kite so much as a pack of Big Red again, I'll shop you. It's the least I can do, seeing as how you were willing to put my ass on the line for a pack of Camels."

Turning on his heel, Sam takes only a couple of strides toward the stairway when she launches herself from behind him and is on his back, driving her knees into his kidneys as she gets him by the windpipe. He staggers back, choking. He can't breathe, let alone shake the bitch-monkey. Panicking, he throws himself into a forward roll, so she is underneath him and his weight knocks the breath out of her. He comes up on all fours and she is flat on her back, gasping for air. When he touches one of her outflung hands, their coldness shocks him. Crouching next to her, he gets his hands under her shoulders. Her wiry muscle can't disguise how close to the surface her bones are. As he boosts her to her feet and holds her upright, she is too busy shaking and shivering to offer resistance.

"Are you okay?"

She jerks away from him.

"Come on," he pleads. "I'll take you home. What are you doing down here, anyway? There must be warmer places to have a smoke."

Using the trailing end of her headscarf to wipe her running nose, she mutters, "Shortcut." She gestures upstream. "Go by the Mill and through the woods and come out on Depot."

"In the pitch dark?"

Her voice is weighted with sullen scorn. "I know my way."

A glance around locates her gear next to the swing and he picks it up. Wordlessly, they trudge up the steps. He slings her backpack and gym bag into the cab of his truck. When he tries to give her a hand up, she swats away his hand. Inside, she curls up against the closed door to sulk.

Sam hunches over the wheel. His basketball on the floor of the cab rocks and rolls with the forward motion of the truck. The shivering Mutant hugs herself in her corner.

"You want something hot to drink? Some cocoa?"

She kicks at the glovebox. "I want a fucking drag!"

Looking away in disgust, Sam sticks the truck into gear.

The Mutant boots the glovebox again and then in a fury, delivers a fusillade of kicks that pop the box open. Papers, maps and assorted junk come vomiting out.

Sam pulls over to the nearest curb, yanks the stick into park and lunges across the seat toward her. All he means to do is to put her out of the truck. The flare of terror in her eyes as she cringes, warding him off with her palms, tucking up her body to protect herself, stuns him. He withdraws hastily to his side of the cab. She peeks warily at him and then straightens up, pretending she hadn't been visibly intimidated.

"I wasn't going to pop you one," he says. "Just put you out on the sidewalk."

"What difference does it make? You're a fucking fascist bully!"

Shifting gears again, he snorts. "With a busted glovebox. That was mature, Deanie, very mature. As always."

"Yeah, well, fuck you, 'god."

"You wish."

She can't suppress a giggle.

On Main Street, he pulls over to the curb and pops out of the truck with a promise to be right back.

Buying her a pack of butts, the Mutant hopes, as Samgod foots it to the Corner, where the plate-glass windows throw glowing cold light into the street. She shivers at the instant's alchemy as he moves from shadow into the gilding light. He leans over the counter to speak to the girl, in a proletarian tableau vivant Hopper might have painted. Samgod wouldn't know about Hopper, of course; Art is just short for Arthur to guys like him.

Swiftly she searches the junk from the glovebox, the contents of his gym bag—shit, a Bible! the idiot drags one around with him! all marked up too with highlighter like he actually reads it—looks under the bench seat and runs her fingers into the cracks of the bench and seatback. Nothing. She doesn't expect a bag of weed or a vial of powder but everybody has something, if only change fallen between the seats. Except Samgod, the bozo. Not even a frigging returnable empty kicking around on the floor.

■ ■ ■

Opening the driver's side door, he finds her going through the pharmacy sack. Unabashed, she keeps rummaging in it without so much as an upward glance. His own hands are fully occupied with two cardboard cups of cocoa.

"Anything you can use?"

"What the hell are breast pads? I never heard of them."

"Yeah, well some people got nothing to brag on but their ignorance. My stepmother's nursing the baby. Sometimes her milk leaks."

"Yuk," the Mutant says.

This from somebody who regularly gobs on other people. Jesus. Fishing a paper bag from his jacket pocket, he extends it to her.

The Mutant snatches the bag, letting the pharmacy stuff fall to the floor. Her fingers crab at the little bag but it contains only a couple of jelly donuts. Disgusted, she slams herself back against the seat and stuffs most of one donut into her mouth. Jelly squirts red onto her fingers. She slurps and swallows noisily. Eats with all the finesse of Indy gumming up mashed bananas. Sam watches her licking her fingers, working her tongue around her lips to get the dribbles of jelly and the powdered sugar. She looks inside the bag, hooks out the second donut and stuffs it too, without asking if he wants it. He is reminded of Pearl's Siamese, with her face in the dish before he has finished emptying the can into it.

The illumination from the cafe highlights a pattern in the glossy weave of her headscarf. After a blank second it comes to him: brocade, linen brocade. Nice sound, nice way with light.

"Boosting smokes. Why take the chance? Maybe Camels are a little steep but couldn't you smoke Mistys or something? Buck ten, something like that, aren't they?"

"Ain't got a buck ten," she says through a mouthful of donut.

"So get a job."

She sticks her tongue out at him. It's stained with the jelly. There's a dot of it on the tip of her nose too.

"Up yours. I got one. Clean house for a couple old bags on Saturday. That's all I can swing and play basketball and go to school. Nobody's hiring skinheads to flip burgers."

"That's your choice, how you look. If you don't make enough money to burn, that's another good reason not to smoke."

She crumples the bag and tosses it at him. He catches it and drops it to the seat.

"How 'bout I'm hooked on the frigging things? I'm also hooked on eating, at least a couple times a day. What d'ya think, I should cut the designer rags and my masseuse outa my budget?"

The Mutant's mother is a clerk in a convenience store, which can't pay much, but she shacks with a factory worker, so there's another income. The Mutant can't really be feeding herself. She did go at the donuts like a junkyard dog at a bag of garbage but she must burn a lot of energy playing ball. How much could she smoke in one day, if she maybe snuck a couple at school and she could really only do it at home? Even at minimum wage, she has to earn more than the price of a carton of butts a week. He doesn't buy it; it's self-serving bullshit.

"Maybe you ought to cut the doobage outa your budget."

"You don't know shit, do you? I never paid cash money for rope in my life."

Sam tightens like a slipknot. Crushing his empty cup, he lets it fall to the floor. "Right. What I admire is your ambition, Gauthier. You're not going to let anyone stop you from petty thievery or doping or sleazing. That's the kind of class you showed in the semifinals, getting your ass kicked out—"

The Mutant throws the last of her cocoa at him. "Who the fuck gave you a license to preach? Just take me home, asshole."

"My pleasure," he mutters, biting back *you bitch*. He won't lower himself to her level. He won't make himself a dog—that's what Pearl says calling a woman that word makes a man. It's one of the few words on which his stepmother holds strong views.

Wiping his face with the sleeve of his jacket, he throws the truck angrily into gear. Depot Street is only a few minutes away. She stops him a good two blocks from the end of the street where she lives.

"This is far enough."

"I'll take you to the door."

"No!"

"It's no big deal."

"No!" She is growing frantic. "My mother's boyfriend gives me crap when a guy brings me home. I don't need it tonight."

Wrestling clumsily with her gear, she's out the door.

"You're welcome," Sam calls sarcastically after her as he stretches to close the door she has left open.

She flips him a bird and stumbles down the broken sidewalk toward home.

6

■ ■ ■

In a Sweet Haze of Cigarette Smoke,

Tony's watching tube. Judy isn't home yet.

The Mutant pauses by the couch. Takes a deep breath that makes the craving worse. "Bum a smoke?"

He doesn't take his eyes off the screen. "What'll you gimme for it?"

She flings away from him, furious. No way will she fuck Tony for a drag. Dumping her junk in her room, she slips upstairs in hopes of kiting a pack from the carton Judy leaves on the top of her dresser but wouldn't-ya-know the shitting thing is empty.

Tony cranes back over his shoulder as she slouches down the stairs. She stares at him. He grins at her.

Bolting into her room, she throws her books around and slams herself onto her cot. She could puke, she is so angry at Samgod. There's no hope of Judy letting her have any of hers when she gets home. Once Judy's taken the edge off her day with a mug of J.D., though, maybe she can lift some from her bag. Goddamn Samgod. For about three seconds, she actually considers blowing Tony for a pack of butts. Attempts to bargain with him always bring more grief than profit. She could never trust him not to go back on it.

■ ■ ■

To celebrate her departure, Sam palms a dub into the truck's tape player. The first cut is Shinehead's reggae cover of "One Meat Ball." He cranks the volume. It's offbeat enough to restore his sense of humor a little. What a bitch she is. There are at least two guys on his own team he loathes but he makes himself leave that personal shit behind when they're on the court. He can do it with her too. The girls had better not count on her, though. Next practice, he'll take a closer look at their backup quarterback, Billie Figueroa. If he can help Billie, he will, and the Mutant be damned.

Reuben's restored '63 Eldorado hulks like a sleek, beautiful beached whale outside the Chinese restaurant. Sam's suddenly hungry enough to eat the Eldorado. It ticks at him in passing. He walks his fingertips affectionately over the still-warm hood. It only gets out for special. There's no reason to baby it; it's a tank with a monster mill under the hood. On a few occasions he has driven it himself, each time with rediscovered wonder that his father doesn't drive it every day. He would, if it were his. He would drive it all day, do nothing but drive it. Possibly that was why his father used it sparingly, so he could have time to make a living, rebuild the farmhouse, shit like that.

■ ■ ■

Next morning as the radio weatherman warns of snow, Sam checks the contents of his duffel. He fingers the caps of his high-tops where the rubber has begun to shingle and split. Already more Shoe Goo than canvas and rubber, the shoes are beginning to hurt. Should have been replaced two weeks ago. The cheapest high-tops won't take the punishment of four or five hours a day on the court. It's almost impossible to avoid a hundred-dollar hole in his bank account. During basketball season nearly every bit of cash that comes into his hands goes into the truck for gas and parts and for walking-around expenses. Almost nothing goes back into the account because he has so few hours for work.

He could accept free ones, of course, along with T-shirts and shorts and gym bags and every other damn thing from one of the sneaker companies or some college coach or a shoe store. But he refuses to let himself become beholden—seduced by seemingly harmless favors into vague obligations toward this coach or this school or this pricey brand of shoes. It is bred in his dense and outsized bones, as his father's son, and reinforced both by the experiences of his short life and his Bible-reading: there is no free lunch, so you better know who's picking up the check and why.

■ ■ ■

Come the revolution, a mood of postcoital tristesse promptly follows, Sam discovers. His troops in the gym are fewer, some sullenly mutinous. Not only has Coach had his influence, the very fact of the world turned upside down, as it always does, undermines Sam's authority as effectively as it has the old regime. Counterrevolution is in the air and along with fewer bodies, it makes the gym seem vaster and somehow colder. Sam has, of course, no authority to command their presence or discipline their absence. A few more AWOLs and he will be playing the babes by himself again.

The girls are out in force but are uneasy, struggling between theory and blood. Overnight has brought the first arguments with their boyfriends. The girls have been shocked to discover that what seemed a minor reinterpretation of their rights is perceived by many as a radical and extremist departure.

Sam deposits a couple of gallons of apple cider on a bleacher and opens two boxes of muffins he has promoted from his stepmother. The Mutant appears instantly at his side and helps herself. She's in a new getup today. Over her spandex unitard and cutoff Levis, she has hung a series of interconnected chains around her waist and hips. One passes through her legs from back to front. She doesn't speak to him.

"You're welcome," he teases.

She ignores him. Not even a thank-you finger.

The muffins and cider succeed in breaking a little ice among the others. In a few moments, the atmosphere is much looser. The holdout is the Mutant, hastily unchained, who grabs a ball while her mouth is still full and takes it to the floor to do ballhandling drills by herself.

Later, loosened up and feeling good, Sam takes himself to the sidelines to watch. He is not alone. Both coaches are there along with the assistant coaches. What he sees pleases him; the girls have left their doubts off court and are working their hearts out. He is reminded again these girls nearly won a state championship last season and it wasn't all the Mutant's doing. No fault to her today, though. Even as the boys repeatedly deny her the bucket and overreach her to score at their own, she never falters. Her doggedness infects the others. In the most recalcitrant of the boys, disbelief gives way to a grudging respect.

■ ■ ■

The Mutant rotates out to allow Billie Figueroa to take her place. In a kneeling crouch, she watches the unequal struggle. Outrun, outreached, outgunned, the girls score only when the boys make an error. The only strategy they have is to play smart, exploiting every mistake and accident and making opportunities for more.

One of the M & M's—Melanie—falls out and collapses next to her. "This is insane," Melanie gasps.

"Right. Basketball-fu, candypants."

Melanie gives her a look of total disbelief. "You been smoking booberry already this morning?"

The Mutant starts to wipe her nose on the back of her hand and winces. She has forgotten the Band-Aid over the burn there.

"We even come close to shutting the door on these jackoffs, we can beat anybody," the Mutant tells Melanie.

"You keep saying that," Melanie complains.

The Mutant barely hears. She begins to hook herself into her chains, blessing the beauty and elegance of the pelican clasp, which makes life a lot easier in roundball season. When she stops playing ball, she's going to make several of her chains permanent.

Her coach hustles over for a word. "Good workout, Gauthier. What's wrong with the hand?"

"Cat scratch."

Frowning, Coach warns her not to let it get infected.

Not a chance, the Mutant reflects, Judy fucking cauterized every hapless germ under her lit cigarette.

■ ■ ■

Toward the end of the second period in the weight room, Sam is spotting Rick when Chapin approaches. J.C. is pumped from his workout. His shirt issues a universal invitation: *Sit On A Happy Face.*

"Samson!" He grins. "That was real thoughtful of you, giving the Mutant a ride to my house the other night. You could make a business of it, delivering take-out pussy. I feel like I owe you a tip."

At the word *pussy,* conversation around them quiets and ears prick up. On the bench, Rick exhales as he lowers the bar.

Sam reacts with an agreeable but slow and confused smile. "Come again, Chapin?"

"Once was enough," Chapin quips.

The other guys laugh and Rick makes a strange noise in his throat.

Sam only seems more confused. A beat after Rick's strangled snort, he manages a chuckle as if he has finally gotten the joke. Then he frowns in fierce concentration.

"Mutant—did you say Mutant?" Snaps his fingers. "Oh. You mean Gauthier? Right! I did give her a lift the other night. That was your house?"

Chapin laughs. "Yeah."

Sam nods as if relieved to have a significant mystery cleared up. For an instant, he is pleased with himself but then his brow wrinkles again.

"Maybe you could tell me, Chapin, I always wondered—what does that mean—Mutant? Does she have one of those inherited diseases that makes her bald? I notice she's wicked skinny and pale so I wondered, maybe she was sick and had to have, like chemo or radiation or some shit like that?"

Chapin confides genially, "Samson, she shaves her head."

"Sure."

"She does," he insists.

Slow puzzlement dawns across Sam's face. "Why?"

Nobody is this shit-numb, J.C. tells himself. This is a put-on. But he has to say something. "She's a freak. Get it?"

Contemplatively, Sam nods. "Wicked sweet hook shot, though."

Chapin forces a polite chuckle. "That's only one of her talents. You ought to have a bald chick go down on you."

Blinking in momentary confusion, Sam is amazed. "Go down? You mean, like—?" He looks down at his crotch as if he cannot quite visualize the act.

J.C. cups his hands in front of himself and pops his hips at them and winks. "Talk about giving head."

Suddenly J.C. is aware of Rick Woods staring up at him from the bench with an expression of disbelief. Belatedly he hears the locker room braggart in his own words. It stings to realize Rick Woods finds him uncool. J.C. is no great fan of the local jocks but

Woods is by definition cool. There is nothing more cool than a black jock.

"Oh." Sam studies the floor for a moment, lashes fluttering with the unaccustomed effort of heavy thought. At last he shakes his head. "Don't get it," he confesses solemnly. "Maybe you could blow me, Chapin, show me how it's done."

Around them, the other guys break up and Rick is making strangled noises again.

J.C. makes a huge effort, smiling to cover his fury at having been had.

"You're cute but not that cute, asshole," he says.

Smiling innocently, Sam shrugs off his disappointment.

Chapin backs away, smile fading with him, to make a hearty pretense of socializing with the other guys.

Rick heaves the bar into its cradle and sits up. "Goddamn. You were awesome, Sambo. I was getting hot, all that talk about oral sex."

"I'm sort of relieved he didn't take me up on it," Sam tells him. "He's such a romantic guy, he'd probably think it meant we were going steady."

Rick coughs violently and Sam pounds his back helpfully.

They change places, Rick spotting Sam while he lifts.

"Tell you what, I could not get it up for that freaky bald chick." Rick shudders eloquently. "No shit, Sambo."

Sam exhales.

"I was wondering how she can stand making it with a douchebag like Chapin."

"Hey, dude, you know it ain't romance. It's capitalism. She's closing her eyes and pretending his tiny white worm's the doobie she's earning. I don't know what he's pretending and I don't want to think about it either, or it'll make me a sexual cripple. Like you."

"What do you mean? Sarah seems to like my corncob collection—"

"Shut up, Sambo," Rick interrupts.

"Yessir," Sam says humbly.

■ ■ ■

On his way to lunch, Sam spots the Mutant going upstream against the flood and heads after her. The Mutant's hand is on the pushbar of the exit, on her way to the smoking area, when he calls to her to wait up.

Leaning against a locker, her hand tucked behind her, she stares up at him. "Make it fast."

"Be nice if somebody else brought some music in the morning. I thought maybe you'd like to bring in a mix."

"Hey, genius, if I could dub from a yardsale clock-radio to a Walkman, I could break into the Pentagon's mainframe with a pencil and start World War Three."

She has the pleasure of seeing the face of 'god nonplussed.

"Oh." He blinks. "I didn't know. Maybe one of the other girls could do one."

With her head back against the locker, she grants him a disdainful smile.

"I'll ask. Don't blame me if it's some shitkicking country twang and I have to puke on the court. Now if you don't mind, I need to get out there and suck in some passive smoke before I die."

"You mean so you will," he twits.

Sardonically she shows him a double bird as she backs toward the door.

"You do that better than anyone I know," he mocks her. "It's the kinda skill a person can really use in life, too. What happened to your hand?"

"Your fault, asshole." She rips the Band-Aid off it and thrusts it in his face. "I was kiting a butt from my mother and she put out the one she was smoking on me. All right? You happy now? If you'd minded your own fucking business, I'd have been smoking my own."

Sam flinches. He reaches for her wrist and she allows him, briefly, to turn the hand to look at the wound before jerking it away and stuffing it into the sleeve of her coat. She flings herself against the pushbar and stumbles out of doors.

■ ■ ■

For some reason the lights glow a little more strongly, not so much as if there has been a surge on the line but more as if Sam himself has faded, from a loose plug, a bad connection. His stomach cramps. Without haste, he turns down the hall toward the cafeteria and enters the lavatory near it. It's crowded, lines at the urinals, all the stall doors closed. For a fraction of a second he stands still, as if he doesn't remember just why he came in here.

The wound on the back of her hand had looked like a nail hole. The pale skin had been red where she tore off the Band-Aid.

"Shit," he mutters.

For a fraction of a second he wavers, his head nodding weakly as if he were fighting nausea. Then his whole oversized body seems to contract like a spring. All the tension releases at once as he goes straight up to drive his fist through a ceiling panel. It descends in a rain of fibrous shards. Spinning on his heel, he kicks up into the mirror over the nearest handbasin, twisting away from the explosion of glass and staggering against the adjoining wall.

At the urinals, cursing boys hunch to protect themselves from flying glass. There is an immediate general exodus.

Breathing hard, Sam slides into a crouch against the wall, with his head bowed. For some moments, the only sounds are his breathing as it settles, and the sigh of the door. It creaks suddenly.

"Jesus," Rick says, peeking in. "Rock n roll, Sammy. I hear you're taking the place apart. They weren't kidding. You okay?"

Disgusted with himself, Sam shrugs. "Stupid."

Rick shuffles his feet through glass and broken ceiling panel. "You got that right. What the fuck happened?"

"Nothing."

Rick snorts. "Looks to me like a classic case of hopeless sexual frustration. You get your rocks off—"

The door slaps back and the vice-principal, Mr. Liggott, is standing there.

Rick hastens to offer a hand up to Sam, who gestures it away and hauls sheepishly to his feet. Rick smiles glassily.

"I just lost it, Mr. Liggott," Sam says quickly. "I'll clean it up."

"I guess you will," the VP responds. "See me in my office as soon as you finish. Woods, you can keep everybody out until Sam gets this cleaned up."

■ ■ ■

Liggott isn't alone in his office when Sam gets there. Laliberte and Coach are there too. In similar stances, arms crossed and chins gravely tucked, the three men circle the VP's desk. Their faces are stamped identically with the cast of a hanging jury.

Liggott clears his throat. Discipline is supposed to be his particular jurisdiction, so he goes first. "What's this about, Sam?"

Realizing he will have to look his father in the eye later, Sam decides he had better get some practice and lifts his gaze to meet theirs. He knows he's looking at an immediate suspension—meaning out of the game tomorrow. And Romney's exam this afternoon. He won't be allowed to make up an exam missed while suspended and if he misses this one, he'll blow his hard-won B.

"I—I lost my temper. I'm sorry. It was stupid."

The three men exchange glances.

"Why'd you lose your temper?" Laliberte asks.

"Somebody make some kind of remark to you?" Liggott prods. "Something offensive?"

Sam drops his gaze to the splits in the toecaps of his high-tops. His hand aches. Probably not as much as her hand hurts, though. The words are lodged in his throat: *Deanie Gauthier's mother put a cigarette out on her hand.*

If he tells them, they will have to report it to the child welfare people. Almost certainly, nothing much would happen except Gauthier would be in deeper shit with her mother and her mother's boyfriend for telling. Sam knows how these things work. When it comes to child endangerment, the system is pious but limp-dick.

Sam shakes his head. "No sir."

The VP sighs in exasperation. "You'll be d.c.'d Monday afternoon. You know, if you were anybody else, you'd have been suspended already and on your way home. Think about it. Don't expect the Disciplinary Committee to do you any favors on Monday if you won't be candid with us."

The principal uncrosses his arms and leans on the VP's desk. "Whatever the cause, whatever the outcome on Monday, you'd better make sure it doesn't happen again." He smiles faintly. "The plant can't take it."

"You need to work off temper," Coach interjects, "there's a bag in the weight room. Just remember to use gloves. How's the hand? You get that looked at right away."

"That cover it?" Laliberte asks Liggott.

The VP nods. "That's all, Sam," he says, dismissing him.

■ ■ ■

Rick is already in shop. He has enough credits in his college prep courses to take motor shop for fun.

"How's your hand?"

"Bruised it a little, tore some skin off it. Nothing, really."

Rick shakes his head. "What bit your ass, man?"

Sam grins. "It was just an attack of raging adolescent hormones."

The two of them snicker.

"You gents like to share the joke?" the shop teacher inquires genially.

"It's not that funny," Rick admits.

"Too bad you're wasting your time with it then. You two gonna do anything today besides whisper pee pee and poo poo to each other and giggle? You got a—what is it?—Bulgarian limo you're supposed to be putting back on the road, you can find the cow pats to run it on. I trust you on that one, Styles."

"God, I love this class," Rick murmurs. "This town."

"What's that supposed to mean? You shitting on us rubes, slick?" Sam asks, tugging at the hood of the little subcompact import.

The whole vehicle lifts slightly but the catch is sticky or jammed and the little car settles again, unopened. Sam gives the Yugo's hood an impatient yank. There is a screech of shearing metal and the hood dangles from his hand. Around him, the class convulses hysterically.

7

■ ■ ■

Sparks of Snow Fall Out of the Darkness
into the headlights of the truck. So far the accumulation is minor—
frosting the road surface, smudging the edges, blurring the darkness—but it means slow going. Sam feeds himself one-handed from
the lunch bucket next to him. Along the roadside a quarter mile
from the high school, the Mutant trudges like a tinker with her
burden of backpack and duffel. Giving a lick to his fingers, wiping
them on his pants leg, Sam pulls over reluctantly.

Against the farther door, she curls up, shaking, inside her coat.

He'd just as soon not have any conversation at all with her but
out of politeness, turns down the volume of his Gear Daddies tape.

The Mutant snuffles, nose running as usual.

Groping for a hankie, he hands it to her. "You need a ride, just
ask. I have to go through town to go home anyway. It's no big
deal."

She clears her nose wetly. The blower erupts with her, blasting
heat into the cab. With a moan of "Oh god," she spreads her fingers over the vent.

Sam swings back onto the road. "Deanie." He hesitates, then
plunges into it. "I'm really am sorry about your hand."

She makes no immediate response beyond snuffling and shivering. When he glances back at her, silent tears gloss her waxy cheeks, running channels of mascara to her chains.

"Hey," he says, reaching out impulsively to pull her up against him and in the process, knocking his lunch bucket to the floor.

Her chain belt and the ones between her legs click faintly in her brief passage across the seat. Her face is buried against his jacketed shoulder; her shoulders shake but she makes no sound. He can feel the chains on her face through his jacket. Hand on the back of her neck, he is intensely aware of its odd, scratchy fragility. His fingers follow the channel of the indented stalk of her neck up over the bulge of her skull, in an instinctive soothing gesture. The skin is cold and pallid, prickly with stubble the color of black pepper. Blue veins pulse visibly in a schemata that reminds him of his baby sister's skull when she was a newborn. But then as suddenly as she has dissolved in tears, the Mutant scoots back across the seat, where she blots her face and blows her nose again. She clears her throat and stares out the window with embarrassment.

"You okay? Want me to stop for some cocoa again?"

She shakes her head negatively and then gestures toward his overturned lunch bucket on the floor. "Hey, 'god, you done with that?"

"Go ahead. I missed lunch today. I was just spoiling my supper when I saw you. You know, you really ought to bulk up some. It would help with your stamina. And lay off the butts. You play ten minutes straight, you're winded."

She dips into the bucket, hooking out the remaining half of his second sandwich. Mouth filled, she settles back with a sigh. "Did you really kick the shit out of the boys' room? Put your foot through the ceiling?"

He flexes his hand in her direction. "Hand. Put my foot into a mirror. Minute I did it I felt like a major asshole."

Laughing, the Mutant kicks the glovebox reflexively and it pops open, spilling its contents again. That makes her laugh harder.

Sam leans over and rips the door off the glovebox one-handed. "Fuck it." He flips it to her. "Put a couple crimps in it and use it for an ashtray."

The Mutant punctuates the offer with a few more kicks to the dash before she settles down. She helps herself to the banana in the lunchbox. "I told you you were an asshole, 'god."

The odor of banana makes Sam's mouth water. He waggles his

fingers at her, begging for some of it. Getting up on her knees, she leans across the cab to feed it to him.

"What's this God shit?" he asks. "You keep calling me that."

Sitting back on her heels, she twirls the banana skin. "Short for Godzilla. Then I heard the guys call you Bigger Than God. And that's the way you act and you get treated, isn't it? Like you can do no wrong. Bet the d.c. gives you a fucking medal for renovating that shithouse. Probably name it after you, put up a plaque."

Sam grins. "This is the first time I've ever had to go before the d.c.," he admits.

"Shit. It's about fucking time you found out how us scum live."

"I could have waited." Sam rolls his shoulders uneasily. "Anyway, it's not the d.c. I'm sweating. It's my old man."

The Mutant drops the banana peel and wipes her fingers on her coat before she shrugs him off. "What's the worst he can do? Bruise you up a little? You're as big as he is, almost, and younger—you can give as good as you can take." She grins. "If he wasn't bigger than God too, I'd figure you were doing steroids. They come to all your games, don't they?" Her tone is wistful, then turns resentful. "The only way my mother would come to a game is if they gave away free beers and shots."

Sam peers into the beams of the headlights. The snow is beginning to blow. There'll be work tonight.

"My mother's never seen me play either," he admits. "She gave me some bullshit once about how she wanted to but my father might be there. I ask her what she thinks is going to happen, she runs into him at a game. She says, it might be unpleasant." He is surprised by a sudden dryness in his throat. "Well, shit. You know. Unpleasant."

The Mutant is staring at him, her eyes curious and bright and unreadable. He feels like some kind of specimen.

"Sorry," he mutters. "Family shit sucks."

"No shit. All the same, your old man's there for you. It must be something to have somebody proud of you."

Everything she says is disconcerting, like the faint shuffle of those chains she wears. He can't think what to say in the face of the shame that overtakes him at his ingratitude.

"Bitch if you want," she says, "nothing to me." Her voice cheers as she changes the subject. "Those mixes you make. You like moldies? I'd have figured you for a headbanger."

"Grew up on moldies." He jumps at the chance to move on to

something less painful. "I'm not too discriminating. I like noise. Grunge, industrial shit, hardcore, rockabilly, it's all fine by me. Any kind of fusion—you ever heard any punk-reggae or zydeco-reggae? What does it for you?"

She gropes in her gym bag for her Walkman and pops the tape into it.

He takes a hasty glance. "Sisters of Mercy!"

"I lifted it in Lewiston a couple weeks ago."

Sam flips the cassette back to her in disgust. "Jesus, Gauthier, you know what a terrific advertisement for brain damage from drugs you are?"

"And what'd you do to get so fucking stupid? Jerk off?" she retorts.

Pissed at her, he forgets he is supposed to stop at the corner and starts to turn onto Depot Street.

"Shit!" she yelps. "Stop! Right here!"

He reaches past her to yank the door handle for her. "You're gonna catch your death, tramping around half-dressed in this shit."

"Fuck you, Mom," she yells up at him.

He extends a middle finger. "You're welcome."

■ ■ ■

Great. Now she's got him speaking her language. Next time he gives her a lift anywhere, he's gonna tape her mouth shut.

He turns for home. There's nothing on the radio but stomach-turning saber-rattling. He plugs in another tape but can't concentrate on it.

Something I did, he rehearses, *something I did got this girl hurt. I mean, not seriously—I bet it scars. I bet it hurts like a mad bastard. Goddamn it, I didn't hurt her. It's not my fault. Her freaking old lady did it. What kind of person puts a butt out on another human being, on her own kid? What am I supposed to do about it?*

No way can he tell the old man this shit. His father would be on the phone to Laliberte before Sam finished stuttering *butt*.

He got off lucky himself, when he was in state custody during his folks' breakup. His foster mother, Ma Lunt, was the best but it had still been a nightmare. Suddenly he had no mother, no father, no home but a caseworker and a judge ordering him from place to place in a state police cruiser. His grandfather Frank had been a Smokie and his Uncle Terry still was, so he hadn't been afraid of the cops the way some kids might be. Somehow he didn't think the Mutant would find the backseat of a cop car reassuring.

Maybe nothing would happen except he'd make himself extremely unpopular with the Mutant's old lady and her shack-up—not that he gives a shit how that pair of losers feels about him. Weird as Gauthier is, though, her mother could probably get away with saying the Mutant did it to herself. The thought brings him to a full mental stop. She couldn't have. She's not that screwed up, is she? It's a jump from tattoos to self-inflicted cigarette burns. All the same, she's wicked bitched up, the Mutant is.

Screw it. The worst the old man will do is make him feel like he's let him down. He's sweating this shit all out of proportion, starting with punching in that frigging ceiling.

All at once, he's okay. Maybe it's crossing the line and being back on the familiar roads of Nodd's Ridge but he definitely feels more like himself. It's another universe than the one the Mutant lives in. Another dimension.

■ ■ ■

The wrecker is on the apron, ready to roll, at the Texaco. His father is visible in the office window.

As Sam enters, Reuben flicks his reading glasses from the end of his nose to the papers spread over the desk. He sits back in his chair and rubs the back of his neck.

"Bill Laliberte called. You want to tell me about it?" He smiles reassuringly at Sam's chagrin. "Spit it out, kid."

Fingers digging into his hip pockets, Sam shuffles and stares at the floor as the silence lengthens.

Reuben's smile fades. He pushes back in the chair. "You hungry?"

Sam shakes his head.

Reuben shrugs toward the truck in the near bay of the garage. "Help me put the snows on this rig, then."

Sam hangs his jacket on a hook and for half an hour, father and son work wordlessly and efficiently, changing the tires. Finished, they stack the off-season shoes on the truck's flatbed.

Reuben shakes the kettle on the hot plate and makes himself a fresh cup of tea. Unasked, he makes one for Sam, loading it with honey and fresh-squeezed lemon. The familiar childhood nostrum eases Sam's throat, making him realize how tense it had gotten.

His father slumps into his chair again. "Soon as Bill told me you'd busted up a lavatory, I thought of myself smashing that plate at breakfast the other day. I felt small when I did it, Sammy. Now I feel even smaller. I feel like I gave you permission to throw a tantrum."

"It didn't have anything to do with you."

Picking up his bifocals, Reuben waggles them thoughtfully. "So what was it about?"

Mousetrapped. Shit.

"Nothing."

Reuben folds the glasses carefully and slides them into their leather sheath. "Sammy. That's bullshit of the purest ray serene."

Sam grabs his jacket and takes a stride toward the door.

"Sammy." In his father's voice there is as much reluctance to pursue him as Sam feels to answer his question. "I know it's tough for you to talk but pretending it was nothing won't erase what you did or why."

Hand on the doorknob, Sam is horrified to find himself on the verge of tears. He grips it tighter but he doesn't turn it. Slowly he leans against it, closing his eyes. The cold glass chills his forehead.

"Are you worried about Pearl and me?" Reuben prods.

"No!" Sam lets go of the door, straightens up and turns to meet his father's anxious eyes. "Whatever happens, you'll both still be my friends."

"What?" Reuben laughs painfully. "Jesus Christ, Sammy." He rubs his chest as if it hurts. "It was just a tiff. I'm not leaving her and she's not leaving me. I'm putting the new furnace in this weekend."

The last, almost irrelevant assertion provokes a weak laugh from both of them.

"It wasn't about you and Pearl," Sam repeats.

Sufficiently distracted by the glimpse into his son's grim view of the state of his marriage, Reuben lets it go.

"I'm going home to eat," Sam tells him. "Be back in half an hour. You want me to bring you something? Looks like it'll be a long night."

"Pearl left supper here for me on her way home from the diner."

They look out on twisting sheets of wet snow.

"There's been plenty of warning on this one," Reuben observes. "Most folks should be off the road by now."

Sam grins. "If not now, we'll have to yank them back onto it."

■ ■ ■

After school the next day, the girls get the first home go at Hamlin. In the bleachers with his teammates, Sam notes coldly that the Mutant is winded by the end of the first quarter. She snorkles mucus so noisily it is audible over the thudding of feet and cries of the players in the reverberant gym. The Band-Aid on the back of her left hand makes him queasy every time he looks at her. Billie Figueroa comes in to spell her. In the third quarter, the Mutant's on the floor again and playing well, until she tangles with the Lady Pipers' off guard under the net. Flailing, she strikes the back of her hand against the post.

"Shit!" she shrieks.

People laugh.

Though she is visibly fighting the discomfort of using the hand, she throws herself back into the action. She begins to guard it and rely on her right. Her coach takes her out. The Mutant sulks on the bench, cradling her hand and chewing her lip. By the last quarter, when Sam and his teammates adjourn to the locker room to change for their game, the outcome is in doubt despite a rugged effort by Billie and the other girls.

When the girls are defeated, Sam leads the line of boys in offering each of the Greenspark girls a handshake and a consoling pat. The girls have their chins up and are dry-eyed. Sometimes girls cry when they lose but not this team. Rumor has it any girl who even clouds up suffers the Mutant's apparently terrifying scorn.

The Mutant glares at his hand and stalks by him. He wants to laugh. She is so ridiculously fierce. It's like one of Indy's all-body freakouts when the baby's chubby fingers lose their grip on her water bottle or plastic keys and she goes rigid with fury. Somebody should give Deanie Gauthier a good tickling and make her laugh until she hiccups. But it's hardly the moment to assure her it's just another game.

■ ■ ■

On court, Sam slips the cat's cradle of his life. Tugs the string and the knots disappear as if they never had been. Here is the place where for all his many names, he is most himself.

During a time-out, he glances up from the huddle around Coach and catches a glimpse of the Mutant, returned to the gym with the rest of her teammates after showering and changing. She is next to Nat Linscott—some pair they make, Nat with her flaming red hair and Gauthier with her cueball skull and her face chained up like it was something dangerous that might escape.

A while later, toeing the free-throw line, Sam wipes his face with his shirt. There is some discussion going on between the two refs. Everyone else is still sorting out their position. Again he glances toward the Greenspark bleachers and sees the Mutant turning in her seat to say something to Nat. The ivory curve of her throat and jaw remind him forcefully of her hands before the cigarette burn.

He returns his focus to the ref now poised under the post with the ball in his hand. Then it's in his hands and he tries to empty out everything except the easy arc that drops the ball into the peach basket. As he releases the ball, the sudden image of the fiery orange coal sinking into the back of a pale, slender hand wrenches him. He knows the shot is a brick even before it wobbles around the rim and then tiredly slips the channel. He is in motion with the surge into the paint.

■ ■ ■

The old bagmobile humps and stutters to a lame halt in front of the supermarket and Miss Reggie Rodrigues unfolds her rigidly corseted six-foot, two-hundred-pound frame from under the steering wheel. With her big high rump and stiff gait, she looks like an exotic flightless bird of some long-extinct species.

Saturday mornings begin with the old biddy piloting her late father's 1954 Buick Century Special to the market, where she and the Mutant do the weekly shopping. After the groceries are stored in the Buick's capacious trunk, they go to the pharmacy. There may be a stop at the dry cleaner's or at the self-service pumps down the street to put a few dollars into the Buick's bottomless tank. Filling up is the Mutant's job as Miss Reggie's knobbled fingers are no longer able to exert the initial pressure on the gas nozzle to set the trigger guard. Last stop is the bakery, for the afternoon tea-break goodies, one of which the Mutant is allowed to choose for herself. With the whole glass case of pastries at her command, she always winds up choosing a slice of lemon-coconut cake.

With seven elderly and incontinent cats, the Rodrigues sisters live in the late Dr. and Mrs. Rodrigues's home at the eastern edge of Greenspark village proper, a mile from Greenspark Academy on the Main Road—Route 302. Set among aged evergreens that block the light, the narrow wood-frame farmhouse is high-ceilinged within and clad without in fading yellow-painted clapboards. The furniture-crowded rooms smell of cat piss and lavender, of lemon polish and musty old upholstery and disintegrating horsehair plaster under mildewed wallpaper. The kitchen features a slate sink and a handpump, a wood-fired cast-iron range supplemented by a small enameled gas one, and a Kelvinator with a compressor on top.

Miss Katherine is waiting at the kitchen door. She is the older of the sisters. As stout and heavy-framed as Reggie, she is much more crippled by arthritis, depending upon a walker for anything more than a step or two.

The Mutant scours the kitchen top to bottom. The linoleum is so old it has long since been rubbed raw. Every bucket of dirty floor water she pours down the toilet carries off a quantity of the crumby tarry substance of the eroded lino, like topsoil into the Mississippi. She picks a comber of cat hair from the edge of the disintegrating floor sponge. It takes most of the forenoon to scrub the kitchen, where the old women and the cats spend most of their time, particularly in the cold months when it is the warmest room in the house.

The afternoon is consumed with changing the sisters' beds, cleaning the two bathrooms, vacuuming, dusting and polishing the herd of heavy-limbed Victorian furniture. On her hands and knees, scrubbing bathroom fixtures with baking soda and an old toothbrush, her Walkman blasting decibels into her ears, the Mutant is as content as she is anywhere out of reach of a net.

While the Mutant makes the tea, late in the afternoon, and sets the places at the table, she reflects this is her real work in this house—entertainment for the bored old women. Someone to talk to, to make them feel they are still connected to the world. The sisters are nicer to her than anyone else. They feed her. They allow her to smoke on the back porch and in the little room that was their late father's study, saying the smell of cigarette smoke reminds them of him.

The presence of their dead parents is still in the house, from the formal photographic portraits in nearly every room, to the inherited furnishings still sitting where Mama arranged them in nineteen-ought-fuck-all. The airless continuity of this anachronistic, nearly extinct family is comforting. Just to have a sister with whom to grow old, to share cherished memories, let alone to have beloved parents to mourn, seems as wildly luxurious as the lemon-coconut cake that is all hers at tea.

8

■　■　■

Pale Melting Windows of a thin, heatless light fall
over the honey-colored floor of the meeting-house hall. The cavernous room distorts the sound of the Cramps eloquently demanding some new kind of kick—nitrous oxide is one suggestion—from
Sam's boombox on the floor and the bop of the basketball as he
takes it through a series of drills. The thermostat is set at fifty-five.
He compensates with layers of sweats, a handkerchief headband
and gloves with the fingertips scissored off.

Within a quarter hour, Rick Woods arrives along with several
other teammates—as many as could tear themselves away from
hunting or work. Joey Skouros comes all the way from Dickens-
field, Andy Alquist from Lafayette. They come in their own wheels
if they have, hitch rides with others if they don't, or borrow family
vehicles. The mutinous players turn up, to underline the way it
should be: no pussies. Even more than usual, there is a feeling of
conspiracy as the boys gather for this session. Without any discussion, no one has any intention of letting the girls ever know about
it, let alone let them in on it.

It happens the Nodd's Ridge meeting-house hall has a beautiful
floor, a court installed by Reuben Styles a decade earlier. Not co-
incidentally, Sam and his father maintain that floor for the town

of Nodd's Ridge, which gives Sam access to a set of keys to the meeting house. This serendipitous arrangement puts some or all of the boys on court another three or four hours a week, depending on whether any other events are scheduled for the hall.

With a grimace of disdain, Rick ejects the Cramps from the boombox and slots in a Shinehead cassette. The hall reverberates hollowly with the herd thunder and cacophony of the boys, the thump of the ball in and out of sync with the rap, and then reggae, of the music. It sounds a very different song than that of the Greenspark Academy gym. Sam hears it as a kind of whale song reporting auditorily the trampoline topography of the floorboards. It is a familiar lullaby.

■ ■ ■

Very early Monday morning, the day Sam has to face the Disciplinary Committee, the temperature plummets far below freezing. The new furnace has a nervous breakdown and farts oily smoke into the cellar, setting off the smoke alarms. Cocooned in blankets again, Pearl and the baby huddle in the seat of Reuben's truck and wait for the heater to kick on while Sam and Reuben open all the windows and doors to vent the smoke.

When Pearl sees them covered with greasy soot she falls back onto the seat, shrieking and hooting and kicking her legs. On the nozzle for comfort after the shock of being wakened suddenly by the nerve-wrecking alarms, the dopey baby squeaks with surprise.

"It's the Knights of Columbus minstrel show!" Pearl gasps.

Somehow they get the furnace started again. Neither one is exactly sure what they did but that's how it is sometimes.

Sam needs a shower desperately and so does Reuben. Pearl volunteers for a cold one but is dissuaded by Reuben on the grounds it might slow her milk. She and the baby shower together first; then Sam takes his while his father dresses Indy. Reuben comes into the bathroom as Sam is drying off.

"How's the water?" he asks.

"Okay so far."

Wearing a towel around his waist, Sam loiters, slowly combing through the no-rinse conditioner that keeps his hair from being staticky.

When the icy cold water hits Reuben, he shouts in surprise. Sam laughs. An old trick but still enjoyable.

"Very funny," Reuben grouses and then dives from the shower

past Sam to grab a can of shaving cream and squirt it over Sam's bare chest.

Sam defends himself with a tube of toothpaste and shortly they are both smeared and pasted. He winds up having to take his shower all over again, shivering in the same dead cold water as his father.

Leaving the cold house early seems providential so they go to the diner for breakfast. The truck dies in the diner lot. By the time it has taken a charge from Reuben's Silverado, Sam is running late.

■ ■ ■

Chapin's yellow Sunbird is in the high school lot, engine running. The Mutant hops out as Sam locks his truck. She's inside the building before he is—no wonder considering the temperature— and at the gym doors when he arrives. Nat Linscott is next to her with a cassette in her hand. As they enter the gym, Nat passes it underhand to the Mutant, who pivots and shoots it at Sam. He plucks it from the air, pitches the Mutant the keys to the equipment closet, and slots the tape while she sheds her coat onto the floor and snags a ball from the rack. With some relief, Sam hears the outer-space Musak burble prelude to Van Halen's "Jump."

At center court, the Mutant flips him. Sam's fingers close around the keys and he passes behind her, stripping her of the ball with pickpocket finesse.

The Mutant screams in outrage but when she lunges after him, he points an accusing finger at her chains and she falls back to remove them and her jeans. Over her tights, the same ones she wears every day she doesn't wear her unitard—Sam's got all the holes memorized—she pulls up a pair of cutoff Levis, with what's left of the legs rolled into cuffs right up to her crotch.

Today there are defections among the girls. The Mutant would be there if the gym were held by a joint Libyan-Iraqi terrorist squad but if the morning session is going to make it, they can't afford to lose Nat or the M & M's or Billie. At least the boys have all turned out.

Sam and Todd Gramolini are teasing Nat Linscott with the ball when the Mutant explodes onto the floor between them. Todd passes the ball to Sam and he spins it on one fingertip high overhead while the two girls leap futilely after it. He keeps it there until smatterings of applause break out from the other players and spectators trickling into the gym.

"Hot dog!" the Mutant hisses in his face.

Laughing at her, he dances down court, tantalizing her with the ball. She stays right with him. All at once he is aware she is suppressing the shakes. Her ribs and hipbones protrude hungrily. He hasn't felt the cold in the gym but then he's dressed for it.

Backhanding the ball to Rick Woods, Sam fades to the sidelines, where he watches the Mutant relieve Rick of the ball. The boys can't get it back. She hooks one neatly in the bucket and Todd snags it on the rebound.

Sam pulls his well-aged shapeless orange sweatshirt over his head and catches up with her in the backcourt, wordlessly extending the shirt. She spares only a fraction of a second of attention, hesitates, then grabs the shirt and disappears inside it. It reaches past her bottom. The sleeves hang well below her hands. She rolls the sleeves back into great thick fuzzy cuffs and races to join the traffic at the boys' post. The shirt bounces and billows and swirls around her.

Sam covers his grin.

■ ■ ■

On Tuesday afternoon, the buses depart for Ravenswood Academy in Prosper with Sam on board and still eligible to play. The Disciplinary Committee has let him off with a written contract to repair the damage, a written apology and a warning, all entered into his record.

The rivalry with Ravenswood is much nastier than the one between Greenspark and Castle Rock, for it is founded in class. As several boarding schools in Maine do, Ravenswood also acts as the local public high school but regards itself as a prep school and has a headmaster to prove it. The sight of all those smooth-skinned beautiful inheritors of the earth with their perfect teeth provokes Greenspark to displays of blue-collar crudity. Ravenswood always reacts with well-bred surprise before bringing to bear a ruthless capitalist blood-thirst.

As usual, the girls meet first. The girl facing the Mutant for the tip cannot suppress a derisive giggle, triggering an explosion of muffled amusement in her teammates. Sneering, the Mutant wipes her nose on her arm. Ravenswood controls the tip but the Mutant drops sharply onto the terribly amused Wren's left toe.

With that, her amusement value for Ravenswood fades rapidly. She uses the floor as if it were a water slide, diving into otter-sinuous slides that take her over yards of the court and into the middle of everything. Already scabbed and lurid with bruises, her bare legs and arms acquire fresh abrasions and contusions.

The crowd gasps and groans as she hurtles herself through the game with the abandon of a hockey player. The row of Wrens perched on the bench flutter, covering their mouths in trepidation. The Greenspark girls grin, give each other thumbs-ups, high fives, pats on the ass. Before the half, the Mutant succeeds in putting the Wren who giggled at her in danger of fouling out. In the fourth quarter, she fouls out herself with two minutes on the clock. A three-pointer by Nat Linscott gives Greenspark a 50–47 decision.

The Ravenswood bleachers are feeling resentful when the boys come onto the floor. At first sight of the ponytailed blond giant in the green-and-silver of Greenspark's travel colors, there is a flutter in the home bleachers. Like the Mutant, Sam is well remembered from previous seasons' encounters.

"Steroids! Steroids!" cry a trio of slim, beige-cashmere-to-their-bones daddies' darlings. They burst into giggles at their temerity, fingers fluttering to their throats to the ghosts of pearls that await them in family safe-deposit boxes.

In response, Sam hunches forward to drag his knuckles on the floor and gibber. He curls his lip and scratches an armpit, sending the bleachers into waves of laughter and even producing a faint smile from an official.

From the upper bleachers, Reuben's roar of laughter breaks over Sam.

A wave of exceptionally good humor lifts him. He takes Ravenswood to school, driving his teammates before him until they are nearly as exhausted keeping up with him as the Ravens are. It is one of the occasions when he outplays both his own team and the opposition. He doesn't usually let that happen— sometimes exuberance gets the better of him, or even more rarely, he gets a little ripped at the opposition. Even this time, he doesn't really unleash himself. He tries never to forget that the rest of the team has to believe in themselves or there won't be a team anymore.

■ ■ ■

Leaving the building, the Greenspark teams discover Ravenswood is taking its losses with ill grace. The buses have been spray-painted with much edifying advice: *EAT SHIT GREENS-*

PARK and *THE BIG MACHINE SUCKS* and *MASSACRE THE INJINS* and *STEROID SAM SUCKS* and *BURN THE BALD WITCH* and *RAZORHEAD FREAKAZOID BITCH* and *SHIT-KICKERS GO HOME*. It only makes the Greenspark players more raucous in their victories. The last sight the Ravenswood campus has of the Greenspark buses is massed rigid middle fingers arrayed against the windows as they pass the Ravenswood dorms.

■ ■ ■

At the edge of the Greenspark Academy parking lot Sam slows to a stop next to the Mutant. He stretches across the seat to open the door and she heaves her gear in and hops in without hesitation. She gives him a high five, throws herself back against the seat and props her feet on the dash. She is wearing her tie-dyed headrag again.

"Hey, 'god! Great fucking game!"

Sam nudges his lunch bucket in her direction. With a quick grin, she dives into it. He's packed extra but she doesn't need to know it.

"You got a hoop at home?" he asks.

"Had one. Just an old rim I took off an old abandoned house. It was a bitch getting it up onto the side of the house by myself, too. Tony tore it down one night when he was shitfaced. Sometimes I go to the court in the park or the one at the grammar school. They're closer than the high school."

And out of doors, Sam adds to himself. He ticks his head toward the glovebox. "Made you a mix. All punks. It's in the glovebox."

She yanks off the piece of cardboard he has gaffer-taped over the doorless glovebox and rummages for the cassette with his carefully printed listing of cuts on the jacket card.

"Mostly it's classic stuff you probably know already—Ramones, Dickies, Buzzcocks—"

She tucks the tape into her gym bag.

"Couple years ago," he says, "my mother was hassling my old man, trying to get custody, so I cut out to visit my aunt who lives in Oregon—anyway, while I was there, my cousin got me into some clubs in Portland and Seattle." Remembering excites him and he founders, struggling to convey the experience. "It was amazing," he blurts, and blushes at the lameness of the phrase.

The Mutant tucks her knees under her and stares at him. "No shit? You got a fake ID?"

"Most of the places we went weren't fussy if you had the cover charge in your hand. Lot of times there'd be about seven people listening—well sometimes they were listening—and the band. One of the best I heard, it was like that. But sometimes it was packed and totally out of control. It was great."

Her eyes are wide.

There's a funny warm feeling in the pit of his stomach—he's impressing her. He starts to sweat. "I heard about a job in the school cafeteria. It's just the lunch hour, serving the line, busing. You'd get paid and you could eat for free, not just lunch either. Be easy to pick up breakfast and snacks and stuff. Help you bulk up some."

The Mutant flops against the door. "I gotta wear a hair net?"

"To keep your hair from falling in the food?" Sam can't help a snicker.

Swinging a leg across the seat, she boots him in the thigh.

"Hey! That hurts."

"Would you wear one of those stupid things?"

"No! I wouldn't shave my head or stick a ring in my nose either. Come on, Deanie. You gotta put some weight on and get your stamina up. The bigger players are gonna blow you away."

She grabs his lunch bucket. "Right, right. 'god's always fucking right."

"Anyway, they want something on your head in the cafeteria, maybe you could wear that tie-dye thing. I kind of like that."

She glances up. "You do?"

He rolls his head as if his neck were stiff. "Well, yeah."

When he lets her out at the corner, he yells after her. "Turn those witches of yours out tomorrow! Burn some ass!"

"My pleasure!" floats back to him.

"You're welcome," he calls.

■ ■ ■

Guys Our Secret Weapon, under the fold, headlines the brief interview with Greenspark Indian sophomore star Deanie Gauthier in the morning Portland paper. It's all a matter of mutual support, the controversial point guard has told the reporter who covered the Ravenswood-Greenspark contests, in which first the Greenspark Indian boys exhibited a notable enthusiasm while the girls were on the floor and in turn were cheered on by the distaff Indians. A photograph of a struggle for possession between the Mutant and a Ravenswood player accompanies the piece, along with one of the guys, on his feet in the bleachers, cheering the girls' action.

Asked for comment, the Ravenswood girls' coach remarks her girls had a bad night, that's all, and it is amazing that Greenspark tolerates Gauthier's disruptive appearance. As to reports the Greenspark buses were vandalized with obscenities and personal attacks against players, both Ravenswood coaches agree Greenspark's got an attitude and the whole incident was overblown.

Sam rolls the newspaper and taps out the processional opening beat of Queen's "Under Pressure" on the edge of the kitchen table before he tosses the paper to his father. Everybody'll be at practice this morning. Stroke of genius. Thank you, Gauthier. And thank you, Ravenswood, for being piss-poor losers.

■ ■ ■

At lunchtime, the Mutant is behind a stainless-steel steamtable, with a ladle in her hand. It feels zooey. She's one of the feeders and the animals are on the other side, dragging their trays down the gutter, studying the contents of the steamtables like scavengers turning up their noses at insufficiently fragrant carcasses.

Everything—food, utensils, kitchen workers and kids—smells overcooked, like canned tomato soup on a back burner until it has a wrinkled skin on the top and a pebbly layer of black gunk on the bottom. The animals mutter and whisper and giggle and chatter. Her pits are wet, she's nauseated with the overwhelming smell of it all and she wants a drag in the worst way. The poisonous suspicion has come upon her that this is all a plot by a certain overgrown grease monkey to keep her from the smoking area at lunchtime.

Only he's too stupid to be that devious. She remains convinced that most of the time there's nothing going on in 'god's cranium but mental basketball, played to a tape loop of Coach's clean-living bullshit punctuated with little-boy varooms and automobile crash noises. Like one of those video games that plays with itself when nobody's punching in quarters.

And still the animals shuffle along, whining and carping and jostling each other. When they get to her they all have to say or do some witty shit. Mime barfing. Cover each other's eyes. Clutch themselves, screaming they've been poisoned.

Kevin Bither, Mouth Almighty, stands in front of her, staring at the goop in the steamtable.

"Hey, Mutie, you didn't like hawk into this crap or nothin', did ya?"

He looks around him at his friends for approval of his wit. Then he tucks his chin and wrinkles his piggy little nose in distaste. He is the same color as the food—worm pale, tinged tomato soup red.

The Mutant scrapes up a Mount Saint Helens of American chop suey—limp macaroni, canned tomatoes and scabs of fried hamburger, blandly flavored with bits of slick tick-like onion and boogery chopped celery—and plops it onto his tray.

"Jeez-us," Bither moans, "do I have to eat this shit?"

The Mutant plunges her fist into the macaroni, reaches across the gutter with her other hand to grab Bither by the front of his shirt and jerk him close enough to wash his face with the goop.

"Eat me," she tells him calmly and then shoves him backward.

Sputtering and blowing, the spud staggers against the guy behind him.

"Food fight!" someone screams.

The cafeteria erupts.

A meaty hand falls on the Mutant's shoulder.

"Gauthier," says the supervisor, "we have to talk."

■ ■ ■

Sam ducks a flying brownie. Grabbing his Thermos and his lunch bucket, he safeguards his grub. No way is it going for ammunition. He zigzags through the battle toward the cafeteria line where it erupted. The double doors are flung open by the vice-principal and several teachers rushing in. They start shouting for order. Sam catches a glimpse of Liggott taking a square-on face hit of something that looks like a fistful of pale pink maggots. Bither straddles the steamtables abandoned by the cafeteria workers.

Coming up behind him, Sam wraps gorilla arms around Bither and hauls him down as the yelping Mouth rubs a fistful of cooked peas into Sam's hair. The outcome is inevitable; Bither falls under Sam's superior assault force.

■ ■ ■

This time, he promises himself as she climbs into the truck cab after practice, he's not going to say one damn thing to her she can read as a put-down. She reaches for his lunch bucket without asking and holds it in her lap with her back against her door and legs stretched out straight on the seat between them.

"You lucked out," he says. "I thought they'd boot you."

She grins. "Me too."

Like she's done something clever. Irritation gets the better of him. "First day on the job, you get your ass fired. And on probation, too."

"Hey," she snaps, "fuck you. I didn't ask you—"

"To do dick," he finishes. "I know, I know. You're welcome, Deanie."

She kicks out at him, connecting solidly with his thigh.

"Ouch. Shit, cut that out!"

She keeps on doing it and he grabs her ankle and shoves her leg back toward her. Her knee buckles with the force, which drives her back against the door.

"Shithead!" She heaves the open lunch bucket at him.

He deflects it with one hand. Braking, he spins the wheel right and fishtails into the breakdown lane. He throws the truck into park, jumps out and strides around to jerk open her door. Grabbing her by the waist, he yanks her out and dumps her on the ground. He hauls out her gear and drops it next to her.

He holds up his palms. "You win, Gauthier. I'm done doing dick for you."

"Fuck you very much!" she screams at him as he turns on his heel and stalks around to the driver's side.

When he looks back in the rearview, she is still sitting there, her legs Y'ed straight out, and her middle fingers straight up. Her small face chained and icy.

9

A Twenty-Watt Bulb of Sun Lurks behind the dirty sheet of cloud ceiling. The cold has tightened its grip overnight and there is no relief in the forecast. Out of doors, everyone walks in a heat-conserving hunch.

Most of the players turn out for the morning session. As the Mutant drives the girls and herself furiously, the boys begin to respond to the relentless pressure with a certain admiration. On Friday, the last holdouts—Fosse and Dupre—wander in, jauntily pretending they were never boycotting the session. And that day, both teams record another win in after-school games at home, pasting Dyer's Mills—the Weavers, the Weaverbirds—as expected.

"You going to make it to the dance tomorrow?" Rick Woods asks Sam in the locker room. "Be some women there. You make a little effort, you could take care of that problem of yours."

Pumped from the win, Sam feels the pull of the suggestion. It's just easier to go to work than have to deal with some of his teammates—possibly including Rick—sneaking beers and blowing weed in the parking lot and the invitations to him to do the same. As an underclassman, he had gone along, uneasily, to get along, to the extent of cracking an occasional beer. His choices come down to participating in the wink of conspiracy at the violation of their athletic contracts to stay substance-free during training or trying—gag—to play team cop. Or team rat. He reverts to a holding pattern: he can still keep his face out of it when the rest of them are into it.

"Working," he tells Rick.

Stuffing his uniform into his gym bag, Rick snorts. "No wonder you work so goddamn hard to win the state. It's gotten to be the only time you ever let yourself party. It's frigging unhealthy, Sambo. You ever heard of moderation? You don't have to get puking drunk, you don't have to burn any bud if you don't want. Couple beers, get some loving in the backseat of your daddy's Eldorado, you'll feel like a whole new man."

"I got Bible verses to read. And," Sam repeats, slinging his duffel over his shoulder, "I'm working. I need the money for new sneaks, Woodsie."

Rick's grin fades and he grabs his gear and follows Sam. Lengthening his stride to keep up with him, Rick speaks with some urgency, in a tone meant for just the two of them to hear. "No you don't. Ask and you shall receive and you fucking well know it. One thing, Sambo. You ever think about how this holier-than-shit goes down with the rest of us? You want to win, you have to put the team first."

"Right," Sam says, "that's why I signed that contract that says I won't booze—"

"It's bullshit!" Rick explodes.

Sam shrugs. "See you tomorrow. Good game, Rick. You were on top the whole time."

■ ■ ■

Outside in the below zero, the Mutant is crabbing along the side of the Main Road. She looks half-dead from the cold. Sam toes down on the gas. Before he passes her, though, he closes his fist and thumps the steering wheel in frustration. He sighs in unison with his brakes as he pulls over.

She throws all the cold she must be feeling into a freezingly scornful glance and keeps on trucking.

Under her coat, she is wearing a couple of layers of those oversized shirts that are supposed to pass for a dress, over tights, with her ragged Levis pulled on after the game. At least she has her head covered with her piece of brocade. It strikes Sam as funny, how he is getting used to her looks. The headrag no longer seems to cover nakedness. During the girls' game tonight, it suddenly struck him that the other girls all seemed to have an awful lot of hair on their heads.

Creeping along next to her, he calls, "Don't be stupid. I won't put you out on the road again."

She trudges a few more steps before she comes to a sudden halt.

He stops, throws the truck into park and jumps out to help her in—and she needs it. Her whole body is so tensed against the cold, she's almost incapable of flexing her joints adequately to climb into the truck, or even to let go of her gym bag to let him take it.

"You had a good game," he says, as soon as she's on board.

Huddling in the corner, she makes no response. Maybe she can't—her teeth are chattering. They'll be in the village before the truck's heater kicks in.

He shivers himself. "Want some cocoa?"

She nods.

He plugs in an old tape and they listen to the Droogs without conversation until he stops at the Corner.

One of the first books Romney had gotten him to read was *A Clockwork Orange*. The teacher had noticed a Droogs cassette sticking out of Sam's unzipped duffel and asked him immediately if he knew the name had been taken from the Burgess novel. Sam hadn't. As it turned out, for Sam it had been no more difficult to translate the invented slang in the novel than it was to decode standard American English in print. It had been a major revelation that a writer could actually make up words to tell a story more effectively, the way musicians sometimes invented sounds to make a song.

Leaving the truck running, he ducks into the Corner to buy them cocoa and a couple of jelly donuts. Settling behind the wheel again, he pops out the Droogs and inserts a blues dub. He drinks his cocoa and concentrates on Earl King's "Time for the Sun to Rise." At the bridge, he is almost swept away with it—almost forgets he is not alone and he is embarrassed to open his eyes and realize he has been crooning along with it.

"Wow." The Mutant shudders in admiration as the cut ends. "Good shit." She wipes her fingertips over her lips. "I was hungry." She seems surprised. She is looking at him curiously, as if she hadn't particularly noticed him before.

He reaches for the gearshift. "I'd better take you home."

"Tell you what, take me over the Mill. It's spooky." Suddenly cheery, her eyes sparkling as the sugar energizes her, she shivers and hugs herself. "You ever been inside? I'll give you a tour."

He hesitates. "Maybe some day it isn't so frigging cold?"

"Those walls are a couple feet thick. It's not bad inside at all. It's really an amazing place. I can't believe you've never been inside."

He doesn't have to meet a schedule nor ever work on a game night. It's up to him whether he wants the hours and the wages in his pocket. Friday is the night his father's only other employee, Jonesy, takes off, but keeping the place open only requires one man. How long could it take to shine a flashlight around the abandoned Mill and make Gauthier feel like he's impressed with how spooky it is? She's trying, in her ignorant way, to say thank you. She needs to feel like she's doing something in return. And he wants to make up for putting her out on the road.

■ ■ ■

She has him park the truck in the lot at the newly lighted Playground, which strikes him as spooky enough on its own— nevermind the Mill. With the flashlight he keeps under the seat and the one from his toolbox in the flatbed, they each have something to light their way through the tangle of icy underbrush along Mill Brook's edge to the hulking darkness of the abandoned structure. Sam follows the Mutant, hoping she knows what she is doing. The arc lights from the Playground help them find the path. Against the cold black sky the outline of the building is like a cut-out, a long rectangular mass with a square tower on one end.

He can smell the decay and abandonment of the Mill before its mass looms over them and blocks the cutting wind from the frozen brook. It stinks of birdshit and worse, as if the Mill itself were still spilling human waste from its nineteenth-century sewage system into the water. The Mutant shows him a small wooden door in the narrow end of the building, a service access of some kind, he guesses. It is padlocked but she has a key.

"Broke the old one off and installed this one myself," she says, with an unabashed grin.

As they step into a void, Sam has a fraction of a second of vertigo when he feels as if he might be falling down a rabbit hole. But the gritty floor underneath his feet is solid. The place smells like a wet-brained bum with DTs. Swinging the beam of the flashlight above him, he locates rafters a good thirty feet overhead and then realizes they are not rafters but the remains of floor joists—there is another three stories of building above the floorbeams. The floorboards of the upper stories are entirely gone. The beams are massive, beshitted things carved from whole tree trunks. There are structures he doesn't comprehend up there, and ropes and pulleys and hoists, some of them dangling actually within reach, hanging past those enormous beams with a gallows gloom in the shadows. High up, the wind soughs distantly through broken windows as if far down a tunnel. A particularly strong gust makes something rattle and disturbs some of the lines. Their lights catch one thick rope swaying, as if something had just skittered up it. Its shadow shivers on the wall.

"In the summer," the Mutant tells him, "this is a great place to party. Get a bunch of people wrecked, crank up a boombox, it's a blast. Nobody ever fucking comes down here. Except the winos. We chased 'em out a couple years ago. Sometimes some of 'em come back but we just run them off again."

The thick walls do cut the wind—probably keep the summer heat out too. She leads him across the floor into shadows that hide another, unlocked door. It is knobless, a hole where the original fixture protruded. Passing down corridors and up and down stairs and through partitioned spaces that might have been offices, in the gloom Sam loses any sense of where they are in the Mill. He loses his grip on time itself, not just the passing moment, but his connection with the late twentieth century. What fills his lungs is nineteenth-century air, the stale dungeon exhalation of the Industrial Revolution, grim and dim and oily.

Entering a narrower space, definitely not a corridor but exactly what he doesn't know, it becomes markedly colder. Suddenly, weird old machinery is all around them, rising through the floor from some space underneath, running ahead of them as far as the light goes, climbing above them. At first sight, it could be the rusted iron bones of some enormous newly discovered dinosaur. In a moment it resolves itself and his stomach tightens with a nearly sexual excitement. It is a huge power train of some kind and looks substantial enough to operate yet. A terrible cold soughs up from underneath them and he realizes they are over the frozen Brook, over the millrace itself.

"Isn't it freaky?" she asks. "It looks like you could use it to torture a giant if you only knew how."

He laughs delightedly. But he doesn't think it's strange, just an amazing relic of a past era. All at once the Mill isn't the least spooky to him. He wants to see it in daylight to explore the old gears and shafts.

She stoops to play her light over a metal plate.

Tarnished brass, bolted to iron. Beside her, Sam bends close and is stunned by the calligraphed inscription: *SAM'L R. STYLES, 1849.*

"D'you believe it?" she whispers, voice congested with awe. "I 'bout shit when I saw it the first time. Must have been your great-great-granddad or something, huh?"

With shaking fingertips, Sam traces the letters. No one has ever told him his family ever had any connection to the Mill. Yet here is his own name, as it is repeated for generations in the family Bible Aunt Ilene keeps. Which Sam Styles is this one? What else could the plate mean but that this enormous device was the work of Sam's own ancestor?

"Come on," she urges.

He tramps after her, distracted by the discovery and ready now to get the rest of this tour out of the way and go home. He doubts there can be anything else of more consuming interest than the relic power train with his forebearer's nameplate.

Behind another padlocked door to which the Mutant has a key is a kind of night watchman's cubby, outfitted with a stained mattress on a cot and a kitchenette counter in which a cutout rectangle marks the former location of a sink. The former locations of a refrigerator and stove are easy to make out because someone has helpfully cartooned substitutes for the missing appliances inside the outlines on the linoleum and the walls. Empties, food wrappers, butts and crushed cigarette packets litter the floor. The webbed, encrusted panes of glass in the single small window are like black mirrors in the night.

Surveying the room, he asks, "Party town?"

She sticks her tongue out at him.

He hardly notices, as he is distracted by what his light shows of the wall above the cot. A hallucinatory hand has graffitied the faded-to-wash-blue painted plaster with caricatures and fragments of lyrics, in greasy colored chalks. The drawings are all melted together, like somebody took a fork and swirled it through the images before their outlines could solidify. At first impression he thinks it would take hours of staring at it to sort it out but all at once he can see some of it's pornographic. Hastily he flicks the beam away.

"One weekend in September I got fucked up on blotter," she says. "Couldn't stop drawing. I'd like to do all the walls in this place. Take me a lifetime and a shitload of acid, though."

"I didn't know you—could draw. It's—interesting."

"It's not like hoops. I'm no fucking good at it."

He can't tell. It ain't the Sistine Chapel, that's for sure.

"It's not a bad hideout when the weather's decent. I'd live here if I had some heat," she continues.

Christ, it's her *lair*. A place to go to ground. It creeps him out completely, raising the hair on the back of his neck and goosebumps all over.

In his childhood, he and Frankie had made a clubhouse in the hayloft of the barn—a place to play hearts or poker, to shuffle through their baseball cards, to sneak peeks at the pictures in his brother's raggedy *Playboy*s that Frankie obtained along with cigarettes through the older brothers of various pals. The hayloft had been a warm and dusty place, smelling of horses and the wet stench of doused cigarette ends in Frankie's ashtray—an old tuna-fish can half full of water. This dank, dark hole is the exact opposite of the hayloft. Hiding out here must be like being buried alive.

She jumps on the cot, trampolines on the mattress. All her chains click and whisper and chatter. They rise and fall in fluid waves in the light. Her face is alight with glee. She wants him to like this wretched, abandoned place.

"Great," he says and she sticks out her tongue at his obviously false heartiness. He grins and she laughs.

There's more to see. She takes him back to the first vast space and leads him to another door and around corners and up and down until they are at the bottom of a stairwell. Sam knows where they are then—in the tower at the north end of the Mill. The plaster has flaked from the walls but the steps seem sturdy enough and she is absolutely confident, bounding ahead of him, taking them two at a time, excited about something ahead of them. The stairs march at right angles around a square core. They emerge in a square dark gallery, smaller than the previous floors and with a pitched roof. Pigeon shit is thick on the floor and the windows are blocked with deteriorating shutters.

"Was this a clock tower?"

"Uh-huh," she says. "There used to be a clockface on the village side. It's been gone since nineteen-ought-fuck-me-if-I-give-a-shit. But I think the tower was really some kind of freight elevator. Check out the view."

He peers past her through a broken shutter at most of downtown Greenspark. Below them, the silvery ribbon of the frozen Brook snarls through the eerily lit village. Sam has never seen Greenspark from such a vantage. All at once the history of it is palpable. It is a whole organism on the banks of the Brook, its every brick an insistent reminder that once there was no settlement here. People came here and built it, every painstaking stick and brick and stone of it, with their own callused hands. As they built this tower in which he and this girl stand.

"It's really something," he says.

"Yup."

Suddenly she slips away and clatters down the stairs. He lingers briefly to take a last look and promises himself he will come back to look at it in daylight.

■ ■ ■

Approaching the bottom of the stairwell, he realizes uneasily she is not waiting there for him. Distracted as he takes the next step, he is not prepared for the crack of the tread and the stomach-dropping sensation of wood giving way. He shifts his weight instinctively forward to the foot already dropping to the next step. Thrown off balance, he descends the last few steps heavily, like a horse, a beast too large and too habituated to moving on four feet to be able to negotiate stairs—uncertain where to put his feet down, and when. For a fraction of a second, he thinks he is going to go ass over teakettle. His hand flails hard against the wall and his flashlight flies free. The beam of light bounces crazily and abruptly blinks out. Sam listens in total darkness to the rest of the flashlight's brief tumble to the bottom of the steps.

Blind and breathing hard, he shuffles down the last few steps. As he gropes gingerly about the floor for the lost flashlight, he fights a nauseated panic. He could *die* in this shithole—could have fallen right through the fucking stairwell and broken his idiot neck. The whole ramshackle vastness is an evil maw, waiting to chew up some brainless asshole kid. He probably deserves to die an agonizing, grotesque death impaled on a broken timber for being so incredibly stupid as to wander around in it, after dark, with a malicious bitch who probably thought it was just a *scream*, leaving the big moron to find his way out on his own. She's probably somewhere in the dark, snickering at him, waiting to jump out behind him and make him pee himself. Biting his lip to stop himself shouting her name and giving her the satisfaction of knowing she's got him scared, he forces himself to breathe deeply and evenly.

The flashlight evades him. Surely, he despairs, he's felt up every inch of this disgusting floor by now. Then his fingertips encounter cool smooth metal and he snatches up the flashlight. Depressing the nipple of the on-off button does zip—which means the bulb is either broken or out of contact with the batteries. Carefully, he tightens the lens to force the contact and suddenly—light. It shows Sam the door—disappointingly ordinary, shabby, filthy, knobless and unlocked, and wonderfully, it creaks open at his touch. He steps through it and into the great empty space they first entered.

■ ■ ■

From the darkness overhead there is a giggle and a flicker like a cinder.

He swings his light upward and spots her on high, balanced on a beam, a spliff in her fingers. Smoke dances in the light around her.

"Get your idiot ass down here," he yells. "I'm leaving."

"Suit yourself. If you weren't such a tight-ass, you could find your way up here and have a toke with me. It's good shit."

She shifts, puts one foot in front of the other like a high-wire walker. Sam stops breathing as she wobbles and then steadies herself. He's too scared to yell at her. She waggles the doobie at him in invitation and laughs.

Sam's light feverishly sweeps the walls and beams for her way up. Shadow pleats the plaster-scabbed brick so he can't read what's solid and what might be a doorway or a stairwell. His breath stands in the chilly air like her dope smoke. *Frozen sighs,* he thinks, *I read that somewhere.* Stumbling upon an intersection of the written word and reality is still a frisson strong enough to distract him, like a cobweb on his face, from what is happening. Then all he can smell is her dope and his fear.

She hums tonelessly above him, breaking into an occasional hoarse laugh.

He works backward from her to either end of the beam and finds it, the thick rope that is nearly invisible in the shadows. The light cannot find the upper end at all. Loping to it, he gives a tug and it holds. It took her weight, he tells himself. Securing the flash in his jacket, he yanks harder and still it holds. Hand over hand he goes up, tentatively at first until he trusts the rope and then with a powerful quickness.

Watching, she shrieks with witchy laughter and urges him on. Halfway up, something plummets in his peripheral vision and he freezes. Not her, falling—something lighter that lands with a little thump. Something else flutters by. If it's a bat they've somehow disturbed, it's too woozy to fly for shit. He wants to use his light to make sure she's okay but he needs both hands to stay on the rope.

"Deanie!" he shouts.

She snickers. Her light clicks on and he sees her standing on the beam. She's holding the flash in one hand like it was Lady Liberty's torch and she's taken off her coat and shirts. It was clothing that fell past him.

"Shit," he mutters, closing his eyes.

He sees her still, her partial nudity as blinding as a burst of light in his eyes, the afterimage painful on his retinas. The rope creaks with his weight as he hangs there. It hurts his hands. He has to go up or down; he can't stay where he is.

"Deanie, what'd you do that for?"

She doesn't answer.

He opens his eyes and she's crouched on the beam, eyes shut tight, toking deep, oblivious to the fact she's balancing on a shit-greasy beam thirty feet above the ground. With her gypsy headrag, her rings and chains, her bare torso is somehow natural. She looks as if she might have flown up there, maybe on the back of some fallen angel, for some demonic purpose—lay the devil's eggs up there maybe.

"If I go back down, will you come down on your own?"

She shakes her head. "You come up, take a hit of this shit, then I'll come down. Go first, if you want."

"Why don't I just go call the cops and let them bring you down?"

She giggles. "Oh Samgod, you don't want to do that."

"What's that supposed to mean?"

She comes to her feet and then to her toes. "Guess." She raises her arms and the trail of her flashlight beam is like a strobe, showing him briefly the lift of her breasts, the tufts in her armpits. "I wish I could fly."

Sam moves then, climbing the rope as if he were being timed by a nasty drill sergeant. He passes the beam and then lets himself down onto it. As soon as he steps on it, the Mutant retreats a few paces.

"Don't move," he says. "Please."

The beam seems solid but he stands still a moment, waiting for the sound of cracking. Below him it's totally dark. Taking out his flashlight, he turns it an oblique angle to her so as not to suddenly blind her. Or see her bare breasts too directly. It's just as disturbing when the light finds her from the side. He doesn't point it downward. He doesn't want to see how far up he is.

"I'm not chasing you. Come to me."

She saunters toward him, holding her arms out a little from her sides. Her nipples are rigid little bumps. Hastily he raises his eyes to her face. His cock is thickening—as much a weird reaction to the adrenaline rush of his terror of heights as it is from the sight of her trembling little peaks. Her eyes are as dark and depthless as the void below them. Just beyond his reach, she stops and takes a long hit from the roach. The tang of the smoke makes his nose itch and he is afraid he's going to sneeze.

"Hurry up," Sam urges her, "it's frigging cold and I'm scared shitless up here. Gimme the goddamn roach and let's get off this goddamn thing."

"Don't grab me," she warns.

He nods. He has no intention of unbalancing them with stupid heroics.

"Put your arm around me," she instructs, "slow."

He encircles her waist so they are side by side, hip to hip.

She raises the roach to his lips. "Come on, now, it'll feel good."

For a fraction of a second, the damp paper touches his lip and then he spits it off forcefully. It disappears into darkness. Crying out, she leans after it but he has her firmly by the waist. They sway on the beam. She clings to him tightly in terror and he holds on for them both. After the echo of her cry, he hears his own violent heartbeat in the silence. Her face crushed against his ribs, she hears it too. She sniggers.

It takes him a couple of tries to be able to speak. "Come on, you're scared too."

She moves his hand up to her breast. "Wanna check?"

He snatches his hand away. "Cut it out."

She slides by him to the rope, giggling at the feel of his hard-on against her hipbone. He listens to every inch of her descent. When her high-tops thump the floor, he closes his eyes in relief. Then he takes his guts in his hands and starts down after her.

10

■ ■ ■

Every Creak of the Rope is discrete in his ears, as he strains for the sound of strands snapping. By the time he drops off it onto solid ground, he is praying under his breath—automatically, without conviction, just begging any god that might be out there to keep his ass from falling and dying.

The Mutant has found her shirts and is pulling them on. In the backwash of adrenaline, he's almost grateful for the distraction of another glimpse of her tits. It's all so perfectly Mutantly weird—go into the Mill with her and risk death. But you do get to see her actual bare tits. When she sees he's sneaking a peek, she laughs at him. He finds her coat, throws it at her.

"Ooooh," she teases. "Somebody's cross."

Outside, while she closes the clasp on the padlock, Sam stumbles away into some brambles.

"Where you going?"

"Take a leak."

He's got to piss so bad he can't get it started, he's numb, and then it hurts when it does. It takes forever, while he pisses like he was getting rid of a couple day's backup.

"It's so frigging cold," he mutters to himself, "frigging cold," but the mantra doesn't make him less so. It'll be a miracle if he doesn't wind up with a cold in his bladder.

Crashing out of the brush, he finds her huddled by the door, humming again. He wonders if she's so stoned, she'd sit there all night waiting for him and never notice she had frozen to death. He hustles her toward the truck.

She jerks away from him and skips ahead, calling back, "Still mad at me, 'god?"

He's too cold and ripped at her to answer.

Dancing away toward the Playground instead of the truck, she grabs the ropes of the swing and jumps up onto its seat.

"Fuck it, Deanie!" he shouts at her, "it's too frigging cold for this shit! I've had enough of your crap! You want a ride home, get in the truck right now or I'm leaving without you and you can get your own ass home!"

She stands on the seat, her arms looped around the ropes, swaying and twisting dreamily. Hands shoved into his Levis, he stamps his feet on the gravel to get his blood going. She drops out of the swing onto her feet and shucks her coat.

"Shit!" He breaks into a lope.

She pulls her double layer of T-shirts over her head as if they were one piece. Sam grabs them from midair, snatches up her coat and wraps one arm around her. She is too consumed with the giggles to resist. When they reach the truck and he has to let go of her to unlock it, he shoves the clothing into her arms.

"Put your goddamn shirt on before you catch pneumonia," he pleads.

She lets go of the clothes and they fall to her feet. Sam fumbles the coat from the ground and flings it into the truck. He tries to yank the two shirts, still together one over the other, over her head. She goes ragdoll slack so he is forced to hold her up with one arm while he struggles to get the doubled neck of the shirts to pass over her headrag. Then she jerks away from him. He tightens his grip on her and she struggles and he can't do it, his hands are full of writhing half-naked woman and it feels too much like something bad. The hell with the shirts. Picking her up in a fireman's carry, he heaves her into the cab.

She slides right back out and he catches her halfway and tries to shove her back and she's sliding down the front of him, bare tits in his face and then his hands. Her legs wrap around his waist and he can feel the hard ledge of her pubic bone, the softness of her sex against his navel. She grabs his face and wipes her mouth over his frantically until he jerks his head back. The coldness of her skin and the chains across her cheek startle him, raising goosebumps all over him. The shiver knots his scrotum, becomes a jolt to the root of his cock. He tears her off him and bundles her back into the cab. Scooping the T-shirts from the ground again, he tosses them into the cab and scrambles, breathless and trembling, behind the wheel.

He slams his door and shoves the key into the ignition. In a cold sweat of sexual excitement that's all mixed up with being furious at her, he refuses to look at her. Still he's intensely aware of her, crouching against the opposite door with her hands between her knees, bare breasts shivering with spasms of giggles. Suddenly she jerks down on the door handle. He lunges after her, grabbing her by the hips as she twists toward the opening door. She manages to flip the shirts through the crack before he yanks the door closed and punches the lock button.

He's on top of her and her left hand is on his cock. He reaches to shove it away but when his hand covers hers, he can't, he finds himself pressing both their hands against him and he moves instinctively against the pressure. Now it is Sam who seeks her willing mouth. She tastes of marijuana smoke and cocoa and jelly donut underneath and her tongue is a slippery urgent muscle. Her chains are part of her skin, a cold silky scar, a mysterious new mechanical organ, rolling over his cheek and mouth. The metallic taste makes him moan, is absorbed by his brain and rushes through his nervous system like a drug to turn his penis iron. The chains at her waist and crotch are hard against his leg, his stomach, his penis. The hand that isn't on the ridge of his cock presses at the small of his back and strokes down over his ass, urging him against her. He lifts himself into a crouch over her, abandoning her mouth for her breasts. Grinding against his leg, she finds his hand and tugs it to her pubis. He nuzzles her armpits, smelling her, tasting her. As his tongue explores the tuft in her armpit, his fingers rub the crotch chain into the warm soft notch between her legs. He pushes the chain to one side and his fingertips slip over the silky threads of her pubic hair, palpable through the frayed denim and her tights. Thumb stroking down, hand closing, knuckles rolling over the yielding heat of her sex, encountering the hard curves of the links of the chain. Her thighs tremble and she clenches them to trap his hand. She unhooks something at her waist and the rig between her legs lets go and falls away. Her fingers are at his fly buttons, then grope below to cup his scrotum and back up to squeeze his hard-on. As he fumbles at her buttons, one flies free and rattles against the dash. Suddenly the vent exhales and a rush of heat washes over their struggling bodies.

Even as he tugs at her buttons, he covers her hand on his crotch to stop her. "No," he gasps. "Deanie, no. I don't have a—any," and she shushes him. "It's all right. I'm on the Pill."

Though his hand relaxes, letting her continue to unbutton him, he falters. Her hand is inside his shorts, and he closes his eyes at her direct touch, her fingertips on the head on his cock. She hovers over him, her face in his. When she gives him her mouth, he drives his tongue into it. Her Levis are undone, and he drags at them, at the tights underneath, and she's so close, heat under his fingers, the yielding heat.

A burble of colored light sweeps over the truck from behind and the burp of the police cruiser's siren makes a mocking raspberry.

■ ■ ■

The beam of Lonnie Woods's flashlight catches Sam with his fingers working frantically at his own fly buttons, and the Mutant against the far door. Slow to grasp what is happening, she is still bare-tit, her Levis and tights halfway down her hips and the edge of her pubic hair exposed. Sam flops his jacket over her. She giggles. An idiot can tell she's wrecked.

"Hi, Sam," Rick's father says. "Saw your truck down here, thought it might be stuck or dead or something. You want to shut off the engine? Deanie, honey, where's your top?"

She can do nothing but snicker.

"On the ground on the other side of the truck," Sam answers for her.

The policeman gestures with his light. Sam opens the door and gets out to retrieve the shirts. Sergeant Woods coaxes the Mutant from the far door; surprisingly, she cooperates. While she sits on the edge of the seat, Sam tugs her tights and Levis up around her waist, puts her arms into her shirts and pulls them over her head.

Lonnie looks Sam over casually. "Been drinking too, Sam, or just smoking?"

"I wasn't smoking. She was."

"No kidding. You got any more dope in the truck?"

Sam shakes his head. "Maybe there's some in her gear."

"Deanie, you got any more dope?" Woods asks her.

"Ooops," she snickers. "Sorry, have to get your own."

The cop laughs. "You want me to trust you about that, honey?"

She smiles. "Check my stuff. There's no more shit."

While the cop is tossing her gear, Sam presses his crotch and winces and then looks up to realize Woods has seen him do it. Woods grins wolfishly. Sam looks quickly away. It takes only a moment more for the cop to toss Sam's gear too and have them empty their pockets.

"Okay," he finally sighs. "It's goddamn cold for this shit, kids. What I want you to do, Sam, is take this girl and then yourself straight home—no stopping to finish what you started either. This is gonna stay between me and you. You better not let me catch you down here again. It's a public park, not a motel."

Sam chokes out a thank you.

The policeman studies him a moment as if he were considering saying something else. Then the two of them bundle the Mutant back into the truck and Woods closes the door and leads Sam a few steps away.

"Sam, I'm surprised at you. You can find yourself better company to keep. I'm sure you weren't thinking about anything but getting laid. But that girl's legally intoxicated and I don't need a test to know it and neither do you. It don't matter she's easy and willing, if she's impaired enough, she can't give consent, legally. Maybe it's not likely this one would ever claim it was rape but she's not going to be the last girl you're ever around who's impaired. You could find yourself with a lot more serious worries than keeping your eligibility to play basketball. Don't get yourself in this situation again, son. It's not worth it."

Sam can't meet his eyes. "Yessir," he mutters.

"Go on, now."

The cop walks away as Sam restarts the truck.

■ ■ ■

"Whooo," breathes the Mutant. "Thank you, 'god, for making me lose that roach. Any amount's enough to get me booted off the team." And she laughs and claps her hands.

"I'm glad you think it's funny."

He swings the truck around and climbs the access road to Mill Street.

The Mutant finishes rigging up her chains again and slides across the seat to drop a hand onto his thigh.

He lifts it off. All he can think of is he's never gonna let the druggie bitch into his truck again. "Don't touch me again."

"Come on, I'll give you a handjob, make you feel better."

"Get away from me, just go back on the other side." His voice rises with fury. "I never wanted to do it in the first place, I didn't want to, Deanie, so get away from me! Get the fuck away from me!"

Only then does he realize he's frightened her again. Cowering on the floor of the cab with her coat yanked high over up the back of her head to protect herself, ribbons of streetlight spilling over her huddled form, she's like a porcupine on a back-road stretch of midnight. Abruptly, Sam's eyes brim and his throat locks. He reaches down and tentatively touches the crown of her head. The brocade under his fingertips is both silky and pebbly. She shrinks away from his hand.

"I'm sorry," he murmurs. "I'm sorry."

Depot Street is a very short distance. He stops at the corner as she has always insisted. Putting the gear into park, he gets out and helps her out. She holds herself away from him. Behind them, the police cruiser idles.

"Do you want me to carry your things the rest of the way for you?"

Wordlessly, she tugs the straps out of his hands. She wipes her nose on her wrist, smearing a glaze of snot over her chapped skin. Her kohl-ringed eyes are opaque, shining like black mirrors in the streetlight. Grubbing a tissue out of his pocket, he takes her hand and wipes the smear away. She gives him a shy, tired, childish giggle.

"Go on home now. It's cold."

She shivers obediently and shoulders her duffel. Sam closes her door. She's still standing there so he gives her elbow a nudge and she stumbles toward home.

He makes himself move, get back behind the wheel and drive away. Suddenly he's shaking again, as if he were coming down with the flu. His crotch feels like he's taken a line drive in the nuts. His fingers close around the wheel and for an instant he wants to tear it from the column and pitch it through the windshield. She shakes her tits at him and turns him into a total hard-on. It isn't her fault, any more than it's the basketball's fault it's round and orange and slippery. She's just ignorant and bitched up.

At the town line, the police cruiser's lights fall away behind the truck.

On either side of the Narrows, the neck of the long narrow lake that hooks southeast to separate Greenspark from Nodd's Ridge, the water is solidifying in the darkness, shrinking away from the causeway. Sam can't see it but he can smell it and feel it—the contraction of the water, a long slow tightening, squeezing, hardening up, faster at the edges like a callus. His eyes are scratchy with what feels like crystals forming in his fluids, a microscopic accretion in the clouds of his cells, impurities building infinitely unique and differentiated structures. It is as if some fundamental misalignment is trying to right itself; this sense of shuddering on the edge of coming apart, of being on the verge of blowing a circuit, a rod, an axle, something vital, is what makes him more than aware, makes him feel the complications of his own machinery.

■ ■ ■

'god lies. Never wanted to. Who's he shitting? A stiff prick may have no conscience but it doesn't lie about what it wants.

That blues song had taken Samgod like a shower of gold, evoking the same intensity he brought to bear at hoops. Being on court focused him, as if somebody was adjusting the picture, sharpening it up, erasing the dim, clumsy ghost of his off-court self. All at once, she had known it was time to show him the Mill, with his own name signed to it like the autograph of some Elder God.

When she found it two summers ago, the loops and curves and swooshes and hollows like a rollercoaster as she traced them ignited in an aurora borealis of colors at her fingertip. At first she thought it was all a blotter vision but the signed plate was still there when she beamed down again. It had been such a great secret to have, of meaning only to her and to him, a deity who hardly knew she existed. The longer she kept it, the more powerful it had grown, so that even in the disclosing, it had worked for her. She could see he was impressed—Samgod! only the most monstrous star in the state—and she wanted to get to him even more.

First it was just a tease, to see if she could get him worked up, but the shit was too good. It made her feel like she could do anything. She just wanted to yank 'god around, fuck with his head. Turn him on and loosen up his tight ass a little. For once, she'd gotten turned on herself, more than she ever had with anyone else. She's still all knotted up inside with excitement. He's so big and powerful, he scares her, like a rollercoaster ride. Like teasing a tiger in a cage. To have him hard for her, totally concentrated on her, in her power—what a rush that was. It would be worth having him treat her like any amount of shit to have that power over him, even once.

As if under the influence of some unfolding spell, the Mutant's footsteps grow heavy and slower as she approaches home. Tony grabs her as she passes the couch. Judy doesn't even look up from the tube.

"Hey, hey," Tony wheezes, "what's this? Somebody a little wrecked already? How 'bout that? Bringing the party home to Tony, cookie?"

He doesn't hesitate to shove his hands under her T-shirts and squeeze her tits right in front of Judy—that wrecked himself already.

The Mutant pulls away from him, stomach churning at the thought J.C. might already have gone out partying, and goes to the phone to call him. When he answers, she can hardly do anything but giggle in relief but she gets it across to him she has to get out. He doesn't ask questions. She dumps her shit into her room and bolts right back out, flipping Tony the bird as she goes out the door.

"Hey, fuck you, you wasted little cunt," he bellows after her and laughs at his own incisive wit.

The Mutant floats to the corner to wait for J.C.'s Sunbird. She's not going to tell J.C., she decides. Her teeth are chattering and her nose is running and she can't jump up and down fast enough to get warm. *Jesus, he's taking his frigging time.*

■ ■ ■

Jonesy's pulling Friday night at the Texaco.

"Your dad asked me to cover for him. I don't mind. Me and Patty weren't doing nothin' but renting a movie anyway," he assures Sam.

There's not enough work to keep the two of them there.

At home, supper's waiting to be reheated and there's a note on the table saying Reuben and Pearl and the baby are at the farmhouse.

Sam bounds upstairs, drops his junk on the floor. His basketball bounces gently and rolls into a corner. Picking it up, he automatically bops it down again. He's not supposed to dribble it on the second floor of the house—shakes plaster dust from the old ceilings. He flops down on his back and rests the ball on his stomach.

He doesn't even like her. She's a druggie burn and she's ugly— well, she's made herself ugly. Have to scrunch up one eye and look at her very closely to see what she could be. She's a thief. A scrubber. A witch. And he'd been two buttons away from fucking her. Two buttons away from being one of those dinks in the locker room talking about screwing the Mutant. Being a sleaze like Chapin. He hadn't even been drunk. If Rick's dad hadn't turned up when he did—

Eyes closed, Sam rocks the ball over his groin. She is . . . a cage of bones, a trap. A drowning place.

Touching him. The way she touched him. Jesus. Rolling her fingertips over the head of his cock. Educated fingers; she knew what she was doing. It filled his guts with queasiness to think of it. How many guys? If a tenth of what he hears in the locker room is true—

He sniffs his own fingertips. Her chemicals, salt, copper, something else, he doesn't know the name but it drives him crazy to remember. The musky tufts in her armpits. Her skin fine-grained as the water of the lake and shockingly cold against his, but her mouth, hot and wet, hard edges of teeth like the ridges of her chains against his face. He can taste the chains still. Smooth and cool as scars, they are also intricately textured and flexible, organs of some strange and wonderful mechanical function. Sweet meringue tits against his face, hard little button nipples rolling under his thumb. Funny little silky pebbly things. She reacts like they're wired straight to her furnace. Tight little bottom flexing in his hands. Thighs open to him, legs around him. The fleshy heat of her sex against his hard cock, the bump of her clitoris palpable. How two bodies flow and change and rise to meet each other, harder here, softer there, opening up and enclosing, tightening and releasing. So close. So close. Almost there. Oh Fuck Almighty. He squeezes the ball so hard it squirts from his fingers and bounces on the floor.

■ ■ ■

He wakes up Saturday with a thickheaded cold. Six A.M. in the meeting-house hall, working on free shots, he is feverish, eyes watery, lips cracking. His head is so clogged he can't concentrate, can't think. When the guys show, he can't get enough oxygen to play for shit and his lungs burn as if he were underwater. Pushing himself too hard, he has a coughing fit and pukes up bile and phlegm in the men's room. With no appetite, he skips the knife-and-fork workout at the diner and goes straight to work, where he sucks up honeyed and lemoned tea by the quart.

The Attack of the Rhinoviruses does not, unfortunately, distract his congested libido. Weirdly, it makes it worse.

A dark-haired dark-eyed college girl in a little black Mercury coupe—Bowdoin sticker on the rear window—pulls up to the pumps.

"Fill it, please," she says sweetly.

Watching the swing of miniskirted hip, scissor of mesh-stockinged legs on the way to the restroom, Sam assaults the Merc's fuel intake with the leaded-gasoline nozzle. That's why the port's designed to prevent the entry of the wrong-grade nozzle, he tells himself in disgust as he holsters the wrong gun, yanks out the unleaded one and shoves it into the neck of the gas tank. They know about guys like you.

While he makes out her credit slip, the babe from Bowdoin stands right next to him. She smiles at him and he frigs up the numbers, which he never does, and has to write a new slip, with his face flaming and his mouth open to breathe. And the whole time he's so grateful for coveralls he could weep.

A logger tips a load of softwood into a ditch halfway down Partridge Hill. Sam and Reuben go out together to help the predictably hung-over Sonny Lunt put the log truck back on the road. Crawling over the turtled flatbed to kick a sapling out from under an axle, Sam finds himself staring at the chains on the truck's tires, on the verge of caressing the goddamn things.

Back at the garage, he ducks into the restroom. Again. Frantically he shifts through the stack of magazines in the restroom for one that doesn't have any naked women in it—anything will do, he wants *Popular Mechanics, Reader's Digest, The Watchtower*—but first he has to get past the girly glossies—*Population Mechanics, Whacker's Digest, The Snatchtower*. Someone has abandoned a *People*—but it turns out to feature a piece about sexual activity among adolescents which makes it clear nearly everybody except him is getting laid, or claiming to anyway. The article informs him the male sex drive reaches its peak between nineteen and twenty-six. It gets worse? Throwing the magazine at the wall, he locates the *Playboy* with the tall chesty redhead in it whose every freckle he has already committed to memory.

"You okay?" Reuben asks him when he reappears. "I'm thinking 'bout charging you roomrent on that can."

"Tea's going right through me," he mutters.

"That's good," his father says. "Flush out your system."

"Right," Sam agrees.

Late in the afternoon when he takes two hours to run to North Conway to pick up the new high-tops he ordered three weeks ago, he scores some over-the-counter decongestants too.

■ ■ ■

Waking up is hard to do. All she wants to do is sleep and J.C. won't leave her alone, he keeps at her, murmuring, making her get up. It takes a little while to sort out she's still in Jimmy Bouchard's older brother Dickie's apartment. J.C. lights her a butt and makes her instant coffee. He holds her head when everything comes back up. He decides there's no point in giving her a booster if she's just going to barf it back up.

So long as she says she's with J.C., Tony doesn't give a shit if she stays out all night. He thinks J.C. is queer, on account of his dyed hair and his twice-pierced ear. Of course J.C. is too smart not to play to the delusion around Tony. Besides, J.C. has the most endearing quality Tony could imagine—he's a reliable source of good shit.

J.C. makes sure she gets to the supermarket to meet Miss Reggie. Buys her another cup of coffee. She gets teary. Sometimes he's so sweet to her, she doesn't know how to react. She can't figure out what he wants.

The Mutant manages to get through the grocery shopping but when she's putting the stuff away, she starts coughing and nearly strangles on the phlegm. Miss Reggie has already noticed her hot eyes and bloodless skin and how bad she's wheezing. But the Mutant insists it's just a cold—she can't very well tell them it's too much toot and way too much Popov vodka.

At teatime, the Mutant gropes her way rustily down the stairs. She apologizes for her uselessness. The old women fuss stoutly. They feed her. In the middle of listlessly stirring her tea, she begins to cough again.

"Well, I know rales when I hear them," Miss Katherine de-clares. "You're going straight to the doctor's, young lady."

The pain in her chest when she coughs scares her. Miss Reggie drives her, very carefully, not to the doctor's office, because of course that's closed on a Saturday night, but to the Emergency Room. Pneumonia it is and the Mutant is too sick to argue about it when Miss Reggie drives her straight home.

It's just bad luck Tony and Judy are in the middle of a fight.

"Tell somebody gives a flying fuck," Tony tells Miss Reggie when the old woman tries to explain about the pneumonia.

From the depths of hot-eyed fever, the Mutant is furious with him and humiliated too, as she creeps to her room. She pulls her blankets around her, slides off her cot with her pillow clutched in one hand and crabs her way under the cot. Her chest feels like it is full of broken glass but she tries not to cough so as not to draw Tony's attention.

11

■ ■ ■

Like a Guilty Smoker sneaking a drag, Sam sits in the truck on Monday morning, working up courage to go into the school. What's he supposed to say to her? How's he supposed to act? What will she say to him and how will she act? Maybe she's already told all her burn buddies how she had him going, or that she sent him home with his nuts in a knot, or maybe that they really did it. What if he gets excited just seeing her?

The inside of his nose itches. Drying up from eating decongestants like M & M's since Saturday afternoon and *why did he have to go thinking that?* He'll be on his knees at center court with his face in the crotch of Melissa—or Melanie, it doesn't matter—Jandreau's shorts. He has to get a grip on himself—there's an equally unfortunate thought. He doesn't want to think about how often he had his hands on himself over the weekend. Jeez-us, Jeez-us, his head is blocked, like there's a big bubble of air under pressure between and behind his eyes that wants to explode. He gives his raw nose a swipe and grabs his gear.

It all goes to prove what a distraction women are. All he did was make out with a girl he can hardly stand and it's ruined his concentration all weekend, to say nothing of having given him a frigging head cold. Even the Sunday pickup game with his dad that was usually so much fun had sucked.

Just imagine if he were going out with someone. He isn't so dim as to believe having a girlfriend would solve the problem, not right away. First you sweat do you like each other or not, and you make out a little and get all worked up, and then you make out more and you're out of your mind with horniness and if you don't break up, you start doing it and *then,* to go by the way Rick and Sarah and his father and Pearl and other couples he has observed, you're more obsessed with it than you were when you were just hot for each other. And that's just the sex. Nevermind you have to make friends with each other, go out, spend time on the telephone, get involved in each other's lives, all of it distracting and time-consuming. And expensive. And if anything goes wrong—you say the wrong thing or she sees you talking to her best friend or you see her flirting with somebody, one of those idiot things that happen to his friends—you're fighting and maybe breaking up and your head's fucked up with that kind of shit when you should be thinking about basketball. So far, nothing that's happened to him, nothing he's observed has contradicted his own assessment you have to be smarter than he is to make it all work at the same time.

Everybody's waiting for him except the Mutant. For a moment, he can almost breathe. Once on court, though, he feels like he is moving in another medium. Underwater. Or in cold molasses. Or on another planet. He doesn't know why he isn't leaving gummy fingerprints on the ball, trailing gooey slime wherever he steps.

When the practice breaks and there's still no sign of the Mutant, he asks Nat if she knows where Gauthier is. Nat shakes her head, says she'll find out.

Just outside the gym, he runs into Coach, who moans at the sight of him.

"Jesus, Sam, look at you. Raccoon eyes, white as a sheet, and you're breathing through your mouth. You look like you spent the whole damn weekend whacking off."

"Just a cold," Sam protests, feeling the heat flood his face. "I'm okay to play." He has a sudden inspiration. "Lot a colds around."

"Yeah, yeah," Coach glooms. "You'll give this one to the rest of the team. Try not to French any of 'em, okay?"

■ ■ ■

Catching a glimpse of Shasta Grey while changing classes, Sam shoulders his way through the hordes and corners her. "Gauthier missed practice. The office never got a call from her mother. Is she sick?"

Shas snaps her gum and grins. "I bet. Friday night, she was doing some severe partying. Probably still hung over."

After what she pulled at the Mill and the park, the wench *went out* partying? Whatever made him think she was ever serious about a state title?

"You got a number for her? I should call. She could lose her eligibility if nobody calls her in sick."

Shasta fumbles a pen. "Oh, yeah, I forgot. You jocks, it's like you're in kindergarten. Gotta sign up to pee practically."

Abruptly she gives up the search and pats his chest as familiarly as Aunt Ilene, full of bonhomie and sherry on Christmas afternoon. "Better let me call her, Samson. That creep lives with her mother is a real shit to her when she gets calls from guys. I mean, we're talking *major* asshole, you know?"

At lunchtime, Shas finds him to tell him the Mutant's home sick with pneumonia.

"Tony—Mr. Buttcheese—answered the phone. Said one of those old bags she cleans for brought her home Saturday. She's got pneumonia. The asshole says she's keeping him awake, hacking. Do you believe it?"

Pneumonia. No trouble at all believing that. He wishes he'd never gone into the Mill with her. It had all started there.

The school secretary agrees to call and check. This is not a favor for the wretched Mutant, of course; this is strictly for Sam.

Then he hurries to lobby the cafeteria boss, Mrs. Hobart, to hold the job open. He makes a powerful argument: everyone knows how valuable the Mutant is to the girls' team. She really needs the job. The fattening up. If she needed to eat before, coming back from pneumonia, it could be crucial.

Mrs. Hobart's a soft touch for a sob story, especially if it comes from a growing boy. They're all puppies to her, hanging around the kitchen wagging their tails for crumbs and handouts. Teasing him about his ponytail, she tucks a couple of brownies into Sam's shirt pocket.

"Take care of that cold yourself," she admonishes him. "You kids."

■ ■ ■

Everything short of redemption, promises the label on the liquid cold medicine Sam slips out to the pharmacy to pick up after school. What matters is it won't make him drowsy. The dosage chart doesn't cover his size so he doubles the high end. Tastes—yuck—like it should turn him into a frog. Though he feels weirdly light-headed, the potion gets him through the two hours of drills, patterns and scrimmage in real time instead of slow motion.

All of the distaff Indians except, of course, the absent Mutant, are hanging out after their practice to watch the boys. Not cheering, not flirting anymore. Scouting. It makes him grin inside.

While the truck warms up, he gulps another double shot of old Froggie's glug. The nasty taste makes him decide he's definitely mutating into a frog. A two-hundred-thirty-five-pound (thereabouts) six-foot-ten-inch (start of the season) frog, with his mouth and throat all glassy with this fermented-fly-flavored muck. Skin cold and damp, he sure feels green inside and out.

He runs his tongue out and flicks it around at an imaginary insect. *Froggie went a courtin', he did go, Unh Huh, unh huh.* Time to hop down the road to Center Slime, back to the old Pond, the old lily pad. Hope he doesn't get squished by an eighteen-wheeler. Already he feels very flat, oozing and leaking onto the pavement, an attractive treadmark ironed down his leathery back. The right tape comes easily to hand; the Buzzcocks croak and thump from his speakers.

The road seems strangely empty without the Mutant. He feels like he's forgetting something, not picking her up. Abruptly it strikes him he doesn't know how she gets to school in the mornings. Four miles between Depot Street and the high school at the edge of town. The buses don't roll early enough for her to make the early session in the gym, of course. Sometimes she gets out of Chapin's Sunbird, sometimes out of Shasta's rolling wreck of a Chevelle, but the morning she was outdoors on the court so early, she was all by herself and he doesn't recall either of those vehicles being in the lot. She must walk, at least some of the time.

He should go see her. Make sure she's all right, or as all right as she can be, with pneumonia. Bring her a box of dead flies. There are things he really has to say to her. But let it go today. Let her rest and get better. Go home and take care of his own cold. He'll go see her tomorrow. The hell with her mother's boyfriend.

The way Sam feels, the thought of thumping some asshole's head into a wall has considerable appeal.

■ ■ ■

Next day brings a home with Chamberlain.

The Chamberlain girls—the Lady Colonels—blitz Greenspark in the first quarter. Without the Mutant, the girls seem unfocused. At the half, the Indians are trailing significantly. When Melissa Jandreau takes a tumble, her sister, coach and assistant coach bend over her anxiously.

Sam wedges himself in behind the girls' bench and leans on Nat and Billie.

"You're letting them get to you," he tells the two girls. "Gauthier's gonna be out awhile. You gonna have to do it without her. Get your shit together. Billie, get your head up. Where was your concentration when Mellissa made that pass? You acted like you never saw a ball before and you got stripped, didn't you? Why aren't you setting screens? Now calm down, tighten up, and tell the babes you lose this game and tomorrow morning I'm gonna shave your heads and put rings in your noses."

Nat and Billie laugh and they give him high fives and take his threat to the team huddle.

Among his own team, Sam thumps up some bleacher support. It helps that the guys are feeling restless and frustrated at the way the game is going for the girls. It's child's play to kick-start the kind of rowdy obstreperous mood they had the night of the Ravenswood wins.

When the girls go to the floor again on a wave of manic enthusiasm from the boys, the girls' coach crooks a finger at Sam.

"Who made you assistant coach?" she growls but she's got a twinkle in her eye.

It gets brighter as Greenspark rallies.

Frogged out on cold medicine, Sam croaks and stamps in the bleachers.

From the locker room as the boys change for their game, they hear the uproar as the clock counts down the final few seconds on the end of the girls' contest: someone has pulled Greenspark ahead at last. Then the cheers of triumph falter and flutter away. The team manager slams into the locker room and kicks a locker in frustration.

"I don't friggin' believe it!" he screams. "Chamberlain scored

on a wild throw from the side with five seconds to go! One goddamn point!"

Sam is as stunned at the reaction of his own team as he is at the
heartbreaker. They go berserk, as if it were their loss. What has he
wrought? The explosion of anger is phenomenal. Even more startling is its object.

"That fucking Mutant!" Pete Fosse curses. "You *know* what the
bitch did this weekend! Partied her whorin' ass off!"

Rick Woods drop-kicks a sneaker over the rank of lockers.
"Freakin' little burn. They should kick her off for letting her team
down."

"Wait a minute, wait a minute," Sam objects. "She's sick. She's
got pneumonia. I checked on it myself."

Kevin Bither crouches like a gargoyle on the bench.

"Bullshit," he snarls. "What world you livin' in, Sambot? You
think she's gonna admit she was at Dickie Bouchard's with Chapin? Everybody knows she was, everybody knows she got so
wasted, she fucking passed out."

"Everybody knows shit," Sam answers. "Anybody else here go
to Bouchard's, actually witness any of this famous partying?"

In the subsequent silence, Gramolini tosses Rick his high-flying
sneaker.

Hauling it on, Rick leans close to Sam. "Saturday night at the
dance, Slammer. You weren't there on account of you had that Bible reading to do? Chapin was bragging on how bad they got
fragged Friday night."

"Chapin likes to talk. Everybody likes to talk. It's a frigging
shame the girls lost tonight. Maybe they would have anyway."

His team is distressingly sullen. Their faces, their shoulders, all
say they think otherwise.

"An average game, she's a twenty-point shooter, Sambot,"
Bither says. "Get fucking real. That's twenty points the girls didn't
have tonight. It could have been a nineteen-point win."

"Hey, bud, all right," Sam soothes. "That game's over. We gotta
play our own now."

■ ■ ■

In the bleachers, Reuben glances at Pearl. Indy is quiet in her
lap, concentrating on her fob of plastic keys. Pearl looks up at him
with an encouraging smile.

He'd be a liar to pretend that how the girls do means as much to him, though Gauthier makes their games interesting. They don't seem to have be able to do it without her—though to be fair, they all look tougher than they did last season. He could swear they have picked up some moves from the boys.

With their faces tight, the Greenspark boys take the floor. All tensed up, except for Sammy. As always, Reuben is struck with the change in his son that occurs when the kid steps onto a basketball court. His very frame seems to enlarge and he moves differently. His face changes. Though it is more masculine, more adult in its planes and shadows, there is an eerie transparency to it that evokes the six-year-old Sammy, with an angelic tranquility to his features.

Right from the tip, though, Sammy seems a little off. A tick slow, and widening his eyes and blinking every once in a while. Probably his damned head cold getting to him. Rick Woods comes on strong. Gramolini's hot, able to take the ball whenever Rick and Sam can get it to him, to do the necessary. A minute and a half into it, Kasten twists an ankle and Coach replaces him with that goofy kid, Skouros. He looks like some particularly stupid moose mistook his mother for a cow, but shows instinct and guts in the big guard position. Bither at small forward flubs a couple of free throws after being fouled.

While the Colonels double-team Sammy, the other four Greenspark starters outplay their trio of Chamberlain defenders. Sammy amuses himself playing to his guards, faking them out with an exhibition of tripping on his own feet. They are under the Greenspark post, players weaving among each other, when Gramolini dishes off to Rick, Rick rises from the floor to bop the ball in midair toward Sammy, and Sammy's there, one enormous hand thrust casually overhead as he pistons upward, his guards falling away like rocket boosters. Their faces are caricatures of surprise. Gently he taps the ball and it drops through the hole.

The tally is not two but four. A Chamberlain guard has fouled Sammy in trying to block him. The ref calls two free shots and Sammy makes them. Chagrined and desperate, Chamberlain goes to triple-teaming Sammy and he settles down to making sure they foul him repeatedly. He makes most of his next quarter's points at the free-throw line. While the Chamberlain guards rack up fouls, the only real gain for them is exchanging an occasional three-pointer for Sam for two at the line.

Toward the end of the quarter, Rick goes out for a rest. Coming in for him, Billy Rank makes two turnovers out of sheer nerves. Gramolini goes nuts on the second one, hotly dressing down Billy right there. A hastily called time-out to cool out Gramolini and steady Billy down gives Chamberlain a chance to regroup too.

After halftime, Sammy comes out of the locker room with a loopy grin on his face. He just squirts from between his guards whenever he wants. With every pass and shot, his tongue seems to flicker after the ball. Making a baseline jump, when his feet touch the floor again, he takes a couple of hops. The last huck he takes is at the post, and his thighs piston, driving him up and up and up, until he reaches out and drops the ball into the hopper. When he comes down, he grabs the rim with both hands and hangs there, a goofy ecstasy spreading over his features. A wild speculation lights his eyes and he rolls his eyes back in his head as if he is trying to see the backboard—contemplating swinging up and over to kick off it and into a backflip to land neatly on all fours at center court. Instead he chins himself a couple of times and drops to the floor.

Amid the crowd roar, Reuben's own laughter fades and he glances at Pearl. She cocks her head at him, squinches up her features quizzically.

On the bench, Sammy buries his face in a towel while a Chamberlain player shoots the technical Sammy has earned for hanging on when it wasn't necessary to avoid injury. It has no effect on the outcome of the game. At the buzzer, Chamberlain is down seventeen points. And Sammy seems to reel through the ritual courtesies to Chamberlain before bolting for the locker room.

■ ■ ■

Hugging his cramping guts, Sam vomits horror-movie green bile violently into a john. There is a weird tickle in his nose and when he sneezes, projectiles of vile mucous gout simultaneously from mouth and nose and the pressure behind his eyes is instantly gone.

Staggering to his feet, he finds Coach and the AC and his teammates standing there, staring at him. Hot-eyed, but otherwise cold and clammy to his bones, he grins.

"It isn't easy being green," he croaks.

Coach pats his shoulder and nudges him toward the showers.

"Better stay with him," Coach tells Rick. "Don't let him faint in there."

While Rick strips hastily, Sam wanders fully dressed into the showers. Rick yanks him out and makes him take his high-tops off. Uniform covered in lurid glory and still in his socks, Sam drifts under the nozzle again. He raises his face and opens his mouth to the sweet water that sluices away the coat of slimy nastiness that seems to go all the way down his throat and all the way up into his nasal passages. Ten minutes later, Rick pushes him gently out from under the showerhead.

Sam confides in Rick. *"Froggie went a courtin', unh huh."*

Rick flings a towel over Sam's head. "Get a grip on it, Sambo. You'll be pissing in a bottle, you don't calm down."

"Just a horny toad," Sam mumbles.

His friend shakes his head. "Man, oh man. Come on, you don't need a chill on top of that cold."

By the time he's dressed, Sam can assure Coach he is fine. He is. He feels much better, gut empty, clearheaded. A little tired. He's purged the poison. He just needs to go home and sleep about ten hours.

■ ■ ■

Outside, Nat Linscott's little Honda is next to the truck. She rolls down the window. "Are you really gonna shave heads tomorrow?"

"No. Not over one wild shot."

She giggles with relief, waves, and whips up the window.

Rick nudges him. "I think she's warm for you, dude. What's this shit, shaving heads?"

Rick's teasing but Sam nevertheless experiences a certain slimy shiver at the thought of Nat being warm for him. Distracted, he admits the threat.

"You're a very sick man," Rick says. "You developing a fetish for bald chicks? We got one too many around here, you ask me. I never thought I'd hear you defending some druggie burn. Not you. She let her team down, Sambo."

"She's sick."

"Yeah, yeah. Made herself sick—if she really is."

Leaning against the side of the truck, Sam closes his eyes in weariness. It feels so weird, knowing for sure it's no con because he was with her when she was prancing around half-naked in the cold. Be a miracle if she hadn't gotten pneumonia right then, nevermind whatever partying she did later. He isn't up to debating with Rick. It isn't just a matter of protecting himself from embarrassment or declining anything that sounded like braggadocio. What had happened was between them; she owned it as much as he did.

"Hey, get your ass on home," Rick advises, as he heads for his car, where Sarah is checking her lipstick in the rearview mirror. "Take care of yourself."

"Yeah."

■ ■ ■

He recognizes the bleary-eyed woman at the door as the chainsmoking clerk from the convenience store. Before she can organize herself to ask his business, a man shoulders her aside.

Tony. Shas had called him Tony. Mr. Buttcheese. Sam lets his mind drift, the way Romney taught him to do when he finds himself unable to remember something. Unplugging himself adds to the perception he is slow and of course at this moment his mouth is open so he can breathe, but the method works. He pulls the rest of Tony's name from nowhere. Tony Lord.

"What d'y want?"

Lord is beefy, muscle going to fat but plenty of power left in his veined forearm. The man is freshly shaven and his work pants are clean, suggesting he is on a night shift. Headed to work or not, his breath is beery; he has a can in his right hand.

On the verge of extending his hand and introducing himself, Sam realizes civility is a futile effort. "Stopped to check on Deanie."

Lord thrusts his square, dented chin out at him. "You're a big bastid. Styles' boy, aren't you? No doubt about it, I'd say. Went to school with your old man. He's a big bastid too."

"Right," Sam agrees.

He has been hearing much the same commentary since he can remember. Even as a little boy, he had been the biggest little boy in the county.

"How's Deanie?"

"She's sick. I had a dog sounded like her, I'd put a slug in its head."

Lord turns toward the woman, who has drifted back to the couch and stares at the tube. "Turn that fucking box down, Jude! How'm I s'posed to be able to think with that faggot screeching?"

The woman quickly points a clicker at the television and shoots down the volume.

"Where was I? You wanna beer?" The offer is automatic, distracted.

"No thanks." Still standing in the doorway, Sam peers past the man into the small house. It's poorly lit and there's little to see. Woman in front of the tube, a dinette and kitchen appliances on the other side of the room, a rickety stairway, a couple of doors, to a bathroom, to the cellar, to a shed maybe. The place smells like a party the morning after, stale cigarettes and booze—the man's beer, the hard stuff the woman's knocking back, and the odor of stale empties from a trash bag slumped on the kitchen floor like an alcoholic Santa's forgotten sack. There's another smell, the one underneath all the others, far worse than any of the fetid odors in the dark corners of the Mill. He can't put a name to it but he's smelled it before and it makes his already queasy stomach reel.

"I'm on my way home. Just stopped for a minute."

The man empties the can in his grip and crushes it. He looks at it thoughtfully. "Yeah, well. Waste a your time, buck."

The creak of a hinge draws Sam's eye to the wall under the stairway. The Mutant huddles in the crack of the door, her hand tight on the knob as if the door were a shield. She's smaller and thinner, in a pair of boy's flannel pajamas printed with cowboys and Indians on a faded red ground. She hasn't shaved her head in several days and her skull's covered with a dark fuzz, like a newborn's. Eyes huge with fever, she is chainless and barefoot.

Any worry of an embarrassing surge of lust for her is ludicrous. It seems impossible he ever felt an instant's horniness for this sick waif, let alone ever touched her intimately.

She snuffles. "Whatcha want?"

A beer, Sam thinks. A case of it. A tall hot redhead. A smile. Jesus, anything but to be here.

"How are you?"

Shuffling her feet, she shrugs. "How'd it go?"

Sam hesitates. "Girls lost by one point."

Her pale face tightens. "Oh."

"Guys won."

"The goddamn door's open," Lord says. "We're heating the fucking outadoors here, buck."

Sam steps inside and closes the door.

Anger contorts Lord's face and he starts to turn toward the Mutant. She flinches. Only then does Sam realize he's missed his cue. Lord had been telling him to go.

The Mutant opens her door a little more but still holds it between her and Lord. She says quickly, "Sorry I wasn't there."

For an instant, Sam can see into her room. It makes no sense at first, before he understands the ghostly multiple Sams and fragments of Sam are reflections, as are the pinpoint flames rippling like Pentecostal fires from lighted candles in her room, a room full of mirrors like a funhouse.

"I'm better," she is saying. "Be back at school Friday."

Sam fumbles for the door behind him. "Thought you'd want to know. Hope you feel better."

For an instant only, she looks right at him. Her face is like her mirrored room, a melting montage of anger and shame and terror. He even sees himself reflected there, a distorted batrachian monster. Like a feral animal retreating into its earth, she shrinks away behind her bedroom door.

Sam backs into the winter night.

12

■ ■ ■

The Candleflame Quivers at the end of her cigarette as she lights it with shaking fingers.

Tony kicks open the door and she drops the butt and the candle and he punches her in the stomach. She falls to the bed, retching and coughing and clutching herself.

"What's Hotshot comin' 'round for? Take your fuckin' temperature?"

Anxious not to provoke him with a defensive gesture, she uses wiping her nose with her forearm to protect her face, if only for a fraction of a second. Even that ephemeral reassurance helps steady her nerves.

"I dunno. He's a big stupid retard. Numb as one of those Irish setters. Catch a Frisbee like a frog zapping a fly but after he's got it he don't know what to do with it."

To the Mutant's relief, Tony laughs.

"Yeah, I can see him humpin' your leg." The vision so amuses Tony that he elaborates on it. "Christ, him and you, almost be worth seeing. Saint Bernard jumpin' one of them bald ratty little beaner mutts—what d'y call 'em?"

"Chihuahuas," she mutters.

Tony wraps a hand around her wrist. "You with Hotshot last weekend, you didn't come home?"

"With J.C., I was with J.C. Friday night. I just got wasted, Tony. Passed out. That's all."

"That faggot Chapin. He didn't peddle good shit, I'd break his faggot ass for him. He like to watch? Is that it? You pull a train and he gets to watch? You think I'm stupid or something? I know what you get up to. That's how you pay me back for everything I've done for you. I put a roof over your head, I feed you, I take care a you, I love you better than your mother. And you whore around. Just like she does."

The Mutant throws her arms around Tony's thighs. "No, Tony, no I don't."

Tony presses her face into his crotch. "You think anybody else would ever be so good to you? You're just as ugly inside as you always been outside. Hotshot comes 'round here again, I'll break your fuckin' face."

Frantically, the Mutant rubs her face against his erection. "He won't be around again, Tony. I promise."

Burning paint fumes tar the air.

Tony pushes her away. "That fuckin' candle's burning the floor."

Hastily the Mutant recovers the candle and the butt. The floor paint is alligatored with black blisters.

"Gimme that candle."

She fails to respond quickly enough and he wrenches it from her hand, grabs her by the back of the neck and forces her face to the blistered paint. It is still hot.

"Eat that," he says.

■ ■ ■

Sam notes in passing that the town office is burning lights and his father's truck, along with others, is in the parking lot. At home, he lets himself into the kitchen. His supper is on the table. Upstairs, it sounds like bath time for Indy—plashing and chortling and Pearl singing

> She drank up all the water,
> She ate up all the soap,
> She tried to eat the bathtub
> But it wouldn't go down her throat.

Slipping past the bathroom to his room, he flops wearily onto his bed. There is an unpleasant gluey cobweb behind his eyelids and in his throat that is either hangover from the cold medicine or a fit of weeping waiting to happen.

Some time later he is vaguely aware of Reuben's hand brushing back his hair to check his damp brow and the solidity of his father sitting on the edge of the bed next to him. Drifting, he weaves his fingers through his father's on the bed. He is a big strong boy who sleeps as easily and suddenly as an infant. When his father tucks the covers over him, the boy in his oversized man's body takes a long shuddering breath and snuggles into their warmth.

■ ■ ■

Hobbled hand and foot, he struggles frantically to free himself of the tangle of sheets trying to drag him back down into nightmare. In this abrupt wakening the dark sits on his diaphragm like a malevolent succubus. He is wet, snared in soaking linen. Sweat—just sweat. His stomach muscles tremble with relief that he hasn't pissed the bed. His headphones are askew, poking into his neck. A glance at the clock: it's only just past midnight; he hasn't been sleeping all that long.

Then he hears her, in throaty ecstasy. His father finds voice for some urgency and then she cries out again. Slipping off his 'phones, he rolls over and yanks the pillow over his head. Down the hall, his father and his father's wife whisper to each other.

■ ■ ■

By Thursday morning, Sam's cold is on the run. As he works out in the weight room, he feels as if he is sweating yet more poison out. It's like he's been compressed and now he's expanding again into his normal shape and size.

Spotting Rick, Sam overhears Chapin holding forth to an audience around the Soloflex machine he is using. One eye on the assistant coach prowling the room, Chapin keeps his voice low enough so the details fade in and out but the tone is clear. The Mutant. Lexie Michaud. Deb's little sister. Jesus, Lexie's a freshman.

The girls were back in the gym first thing Wednesday, back to work, putting the loss behind them. The Mutant's pneumonia and what it cost the girls means nothing to Chapin, the way the Mutant means nothing to him but lumber to build his own bad legend. The Mutant isn't the only one the noisy little prick is damaging.

As Chapin gladhands his way out, his gaze passes over Sam and stops.

Sam jerks his head toward the corridor. "Word with you."

"I don't feel like fucking around, Samson."

Sam's reassuringly earnest. Air of a man looking for a deal. "Not," he says.

The empty corridor is only a few steps away.

"What's up?" J.C. asks once they are there. He pats himself for a cigarette before he remembers he's in sweats.

"You and Gauthier, you're buddies, right?" Sam asks haltingly. "Hang out, party, whatever."

Curiosity wars with caution in a sudden restless shifting of Chapin's stance. He's not buying the village idiot act again. The last time he had a conversation with Samson about the Mutant, the bastard put him down hard. Buying time while he figures out what script they're playing, what role he's going to create for himself, J.C. delivers up a little amiable corridor chitchat. "Myself, I haven't talked to her but Grey did last night. Said she was better. But upset the girls dropped it."

"Heartbreaker," Sam agrees.

Still mentally gossiping over the fence, J.C. shakes his head sympathetically.

Sam leans back against the wall, studies the laces in his new tops. "Some people blame her for the loss, being out sick when her team needed her. Say she parties herself sick."

J.C. laughs.

Loitering in the corridor, shoulder to shoulder with Sam, he is suddenly conscious of the sheer physical presence of the fucker, the space the gorilla takes up. He breaks into a sweat and babbles. "Yeah, well, Friday night was a maximum blast, no argument. She was stoned when I picked her up. That was for starters. Never woulda guessed she was getting sick."

Sam stares at Chapin's all-American happy face. Good teeth, good skin, well nourished, muscled and handsome, a child of indulgence and prosperity. The ripple of rainbow hair like a flag of exuberance. The urge to send J.C.'s boy president's face a Sluggergram is almost irresistible.

Instead Sam is confidential. "It gets back to the Office Gauthier was partying with you Friday night, they could drop a drug screen on her. You're a friend of hers, you'll want her to be clean so she can keep on doing what she likes. Playing ball."

J.C. shakes his head. Get real. It's the Mutant's lookout whether she can pass a drug screen. She can always just say no. This numb shitkicker doesn't seem to understand she likes being loaded as much as she likes playing ball. And considerably more than she likes balling.

"And so nobody ever asks where the fuck she gets the shit you supply her," Sam continues.

Chapin's smily face freezes. "What is this shit?" he protests. "You're talking like Sister D.'s some kind of junkie and I'm the mean old pusher hanging around the schoolyard. She parties a little—what's the big fucking deal?"

Sam speaks softly. "The big fucking deal is real simple. Shut your friggin' trap, Chapin, so I don't have to open mine."

"Fuck you, jack. Maybe you'll open your gym bag someday and have an ounce of blow fall out."

In a blur of movement, Sam slams Chapin against the wall with one hand and knocks the breath out of him. He leans into his face.

"And maybe you'll eat a baseball bat, motherfucker," he says. "Try me. I never wanted to fuck anybody up so much in my life." Keeping Chapin jammed against the wall, Sam lifts him off the floor to speak directly into J.C.'s ear. "Keep her clean or you'll be smoking your own dick, shithead."

The AC hustles out of the weight room. "The hell is going on here?"

Sam drops Chapin to the floor.

Sullenly, J.C. mutters, "Nothin'."

Sam smiles and pats the top of Chapin's head. "Chapin said he wanted to get high. I was helpin' him."

"Spare me the cute bullshit," growls the AC. "Styles, lemme remind you, you got a warning flag up. You looking for a vacation?"

■ ■ ■

Next morning is as raw as a clam slip-sliding down a gull's gullet. The Mutant's walking; she's walked the whole four miles from Depot Street. She and Sam arrive at the juncture of the Main Road and Greenspark Academy's curving driveway simultaneously. Muttering in inarticulate disbelief, Sam pulls up next to her. He stretches across the seat to pop the door. She ignores him.

"Come on," he says. "You've walked far enough."

"Another few yards won't kill me."

"Wanna bet?"

Haughtily, she accepts a hand up and settles back against the seat. Breathes like it hurts.

"Couldn't get a ride?"

"Sure," she drawls, staring out the window, "had eight or nine offers. It was such a nice fucking day and I need the exercise. I get sick of the limo all the time, you know. People could start thinking I'm impressed with myself."

His gaze skitters over her. She still looks sick. Maybe that's why he isn't afflicted with an embarrassing surge of lust, just a surge of plain old incredulity that anything had ever happened between them at all. Maybe it was something like the way electricity discharges when it can between two points of conduction. His accumulated frustration had just had to go somewhere—try to go somewhere—and she *was* female, even if she did everything in her power to negate it.

"You okay?"

He thinks that's about right. He's stopped himself from telling her she shouldn't be there; she should be home in bed.

She shrugs.

"The job's still open," he goes on. "See Mrs. H. about it. Maybe you could start again next week, you feel up to it."

When he peeks at her, her head's down and he can't even tell if she's listening. Fringe on her headrag shivers a little as she stares out the window. She's out of the truck as soon as it stops.

"You're welcome," he calls after her.

She pauses long enough to show him two world-weary rigid middle fingers.

Rick catches up with Sam at the edge of the parking lot. "Did I see an ugly bald wench get outta the truck and flip you off or am I having a drug flashback?"

"The Mutant's back." Sam grins. "And meaner than ever."

Rick points a finger at his temple. "Go ahead, make my day."

■ ■ ■

Bopping the basketball comfortingly with his left hand, he closes the equipment closet and risks—purely as a scientific experiment—looking at her again. She is unhooking the chains from between her legs. Observing this as a mechanical operation, he notes with increasing cheer that it has no effect on him. With the chains between her fingers, the Mutant raises her eyes and looks at him. Her narrow features are impassive. There is no flirtation, no coyness in expression or body language. She merely catches him looking and her eyes glitter with irony.

But in a few moments she is crouched on the sidelines, rocking on her heels, her body racked with coughing. She hides her face in her arms. Sam brings her his old sweatshirt again and she submits wordlessly to his tugging it down over her head. At the end of practice, she's gone and the shirt's gone with her. Oh well. He'll get it back from her later. What can she do with it—blow her nose on it? Use it to work some voodoo on him?

■ ■ ■

At the gym doors, Sam catches up with Nat.

"You know, Gauthier walked all the way this morning," he says. "She shouldn't be taking any four-mile strolls this time of the year, not after having pneumonia. You need her healthy, Nat. Maybe you girls could fix her up with rides?"

Before he's finished asking, Nat's got her arms crossed and she's already shaking her head. "Not me, guy. My mother is convinced the Mutant's a Satanist. She finds out I'm giving rides to her, she'll have me into church for an exorcism and probably never let me out of the house again. Why doesn't Mutie ride with her burn buddies?"

"None of 'm get up before the first bell. Besides, the less time she spends with that bunch of thuds, the more likely she is to stay healthy enough to play. And stay eligible."

Nat shrugs. "You have to come right through town. Why don't you pick her up?"

Sam had been hoping she wouldn't think of that question. He can't help blushing.

Nat grins at his discomfort. "Gimme a break, Sam. You're bigger than her. You can fight her off. Hey, how come you haven't asked me out since last summer? Didn't you believe I really had another date?"

He can't bring himself to meet Nat's eyes; his vision fills with his own restless, enormous feet.

"Maybe when the season's over," he mutters. "You know how it is. No time."

"Sure," she says. "It's a bitch, isn't it?"

He thinks he hears her say it's *the* bitch. Backing away, he bumps against a bleacher.

"I gotta talk to someone," he says.

He bolts to the water fountain and wets down his throat, does some deep breathing, wipes his sweaty face and then the bell warns classes are imminent.

Between first and second period, he stops the Jandreau twins.

"No way," they chorus and burst into derisive sniggers. "You're shitting me," Melissa gasps. "Excuse me while I puke," Melanie adds.

Deb Michaud's right behind them.

"Ask Deb," Melissa says, "she lives near the Mutant."

With the malevolent twins watching, poking each other in the ribs and covering each other's mouths, Sam makes an approach to Deb Michaud.

She gives him an incredulous look. "Give that c-u-n-t a ride? I see her on the road, I'll step on the gas and run her over."

Rick pushes through the mob of students changing classes as the trio of girls moves away with their heads together. They glance back at Sam with expressions of mingled amusement and disdain.

"What'd you do, Sambo?" he asks. "Invite Deb and the M & M's to perform a black Mass with you?"

Sam ignores him. There must be somebody on the girls' team who doesn't absolutely hate the Mutant's guts but he's making a fool of himself finding her a ride. Discouraged, he submerges himself in his workout, hoping some answer will come to him from the blessed nowhere.

■ ■ ■

The Mutant goes along to Helsinki, suits up and sits on the bench, though in isolation from her teammates. The girls do more than play well without her—they crush the Raiders. For each other they have hugs and squeals when they win but not for the Mutant. They show the same enthusiasm for the guys when they win, which confirms for Sam again that the best thing coming out of the morning practice sessions together is mutual support. Which makes it that much more important not to leave the Mutant standing alone. When he approaches her with an encouraging smile, bringing his hands up to offer high fives, she whirls around and strides away.

They emerge into the first blowing snow. By the time the buses reach Greenspark Academy, the going is sluggish. The lot has not yet been plowed and the tracks of buses and other vehicles cut a good three inches of heavy wet stuff into deep relief. It seeps through the fabric of his new high-tops—his boots are in the cab of the truck where they'll do the least good. But he sticks his tongue out contentedly to taste the snow. What a stroke of luck it is, this minor storm. His bank account is a hurting unit. With school out, he can work all night if need be.

On the roadside, the Mutant slogs against the rough slop underfoot and a headwind. Visibility is compromised by the snow blowing into her face as well as the shit blown up at her by passing traffic.

With a sigh, Sam pulls over for her.

He has to wait for a UPS van and Rick in his Skylark to pass him before he can swing back onto the road. Rick waves at him and gives him a shiteating grin.

"How you feeling?" he asks her as she tucks herself up on the seat, waiting for some heat from the vents.

"Like shit." She shrugs it off. "You sound snotty yourself."

"Caught your cold," he admits.

"But you played."

He gropes among his tapes and shoves in the first thing that comes to hand—The Dharma Bums. "Pumpkinhead."

"The day I fell on you in the bleachers I felt like this one," he confesses.

She cocks her head the better to listen.

In the rearview, he gets a glimpse of Nat's Honda. Shit. He might as well paint *Mutantmobile* on the side of the truck. He is doing exactly what he doesn't want to do but he can't leave her on the road again, still half-sick. Why didn't she just stay the hell at home?

"Maybe you shouldn't try to make practice during the break," he says.

"I'll be there."

Right. With him to haul her druggie ass back and forth.

"I tried to find a ride for you today so you wouldn't be walking in the cold. You know not one of your teammates was willing to do it?" He doesn't want to sound angry but it comes out that way and he realizes he is furious. It makes him even angrier not to be able to control his emotions. "You're their star, for Christ's sake.

And you can't count on one of 'em for a lift in the frigging cold. Can't get one from your burn buddies, either, can you?"

The Mutant's mouth tightens. "I got friends! J.C.'s my friend, Grey's my friend—they're just not numb jocks like you. You think you're better than they are, you fucking bonehead hard-on!"

"Some friends. I hardly ever see Grey at your games. Chapin gets you wasted. He doesn't even care if you get busted off the team for it, that's how good a friend he is."

She grabs the basketball off the floor of the cab and thumps it against the dash. "You're jealous of him."

"Jealous!" Sam points at himself. "Jealous! Of what? Of you?"

Kneeling on the bench, she turns toward him and opens her coat, clawing the skirts behind her.

"Yeah, me. Why else are you doing me a bunch of favors I don't want?" she taunts.

He shakes his head in disbelief.

Slowly she opens her thighs to the circumference of the ball until her crotch rests against it. She begins to rock on it.

With one hand, Sam yanks the ball from underneath her and bats it to the floor. "Cut it out, Deanie."

She knee-walks across the bench until she's right next to him, her chained crotch up against his forearm.

Jerking his arm away, he locks his eyes on the road. "You can't shake your tits at a guy and not get a reaction. It's not fair. I don't want to have that kind of thing with you. What's the matter with you? Don't you know how to be friends with a guy without screwing him?"

She grins. "Guys don't know how to be friends to girls without screwing them, you dope. Prime example's sitting behind the wheel of this truck right now. Get real, dub."

Her hand drops to his thigh and he pushes it away.

"Stop it. I'm taking you home. It's the only ride you're getting from me."

Sitting back on her heels, she's still too close.

"You think I'm ugly?"

"No! Jesus, no."

And he realizes he means it. He takes his eyes from the road long enough to look at her. Not ugly. Even her head isn't ugly to him anymore. The ravaged scalp is as delicate as the shell of a bird's egg, the studs and chains like rickrack outlining the curves and convolutions of her ears, the ring violating her nostril, a mysterious contradiction. Tonight the chains keep the narrow porcelain of her child's face from shattering. With his fingertips he traces her arm to the curve of her neck and cups the side of her skull to draw her head to his shoulder. He can hear the rattle in her lungs when she breathes. The place in his chest where the anger was empties out. Taking a deep breath, he spreads his hand over her face, touching her chains, her skin.

"You're beautiful, Deanie. I don't why, but you are."

"Then what's the big deal?"

"I never did it before," he blurts.

With a little laugh in her throat, she licks the palm of his hand like a kitten.

Reluctantly he returns his hand to the wheel. She's doing it to him again. She's not beautiful, he tells himself. She's a freak. Some of her is beautiful, he amends, her skin and her hands and her eyes, her eyebrows, her mouth, her tits, her body—right. Jackoff.

"You need it," she tells him with the confidence of a mom urging spinach on a reluctant three-year-old. "No wonder you're so tight-assed."

At least she doesn't laugh.

Sick to his stomach with arousal, he speaks to himself as much as to her. "It ain't gonna happen. Go sit on the other side right now."

"Why not?"

The willful bratty cry ignites his anger again. "Maybe I don't want to be another guy in the locker room blowing off about getting wasted and screwing you. Like that sleazy fuck Chapin, making jokes about you giving him head."

As if the sharp intake of her breath actually hurts her, her hands cross over her breastbone and she shrinks away from him.

It's the truth, Sam wants to say, but his throat constricts a moment too late. When he forces something out, it's a mutter. He doubts she can hear him saying he's sorry.

Suddenly she snatches the basketball from the floor and drives it into the side of his head.

For an instant there is only the burst of pain in his ear that makes him jerk the wheel inadvertently. The truck starts to slide. Blinking back the pricking tears of pain, he manages to reassert control. He makes a careful turn onto Depot with a headache knotting behind his eyes.

She cries silently, shoulders heaving, back of her hand wiping at her face. Great. Got her crying again. He's found his special talent in life. Streetlight washes over her with the weird penetration of an X ray, rendering her more than exposed, more than naked, almost transparent. When he reaches out to touch her arm, she knocks away his hand. All at once, she grabs her gear and dives for the passenger door.

"Wait a minute, wait, what are you doing?"

Yanking the door handle, she heaves her gear ahead of her and tumbles out of the truck. He hurls himself across the seat after her. As his feet hit the ground, they gain no purchase, just keep on sliding. Sam grabs at the open door and for an instant it's in his grip. Then his weight, still moving as his feet skate through the slushy snow, pulls the door forward on its hinges. He skates in the slick. His feet leave the ground. Body twisting as he clutches at the door, he goes down flailing, streetlights spinning in his eyes like oncoming headlights.

13

. . .

In a Storm of White Flecks the world comes all
apart. It's as if the color and shape and substance of reality were
flaking away like brittle wallpaper, the black universe showing
through behind it. Streetlight spatters into myriad feeble points
like candleflames wavering in mirrors. Then Sam knows he's on
his back in wet cold snow, blinking flakes out his eyes and tasting
them in his mouth as he gasps for the breath he's knocked out of
himself. Taste of blood in his mouth—bit his tongue somehow.
He's wrenched his shoulder and the back of his scalp feels like
somebody bludgeoned him. He stares up into the snowspill from
the sky. Slowly, he rolls and hauls himself to his feet. On touching
the back of his head, his fingertips come away wet and red. A second feel is reassuring; he's cut his scalp but it's minor, maybe an
inch long.

She's gone, disappeared into the snow. Probably home by now.
Shit, he forgot to ask her to give him back his sweatshirt. It's his
favorite; it used to be his father's. Frankie gave it to Reuben one
Christmas and Sam grabbed it out of the dryer one day a couple
years later when he was desperate for some clean duds. For a
while the two of them teased each other, kiting it from each other's
dresser or the laundry, but then it was his, like his father knew

how it made Sam feel tight with him to wear it. And after a while it was just another sweatshirt. Only he hates the thought maybe he's lost it for good.

■ ■ ■

His eyes still seek her as the world begins to spin out from under him and 'god falls in a stuttering descent. His body tumbles and twists, the back of his head bounces on the edge of the door, as he pours bonelessly to the white ground. When the fan of descending images closes, there is silence. Her vision is grainy with the snow, colors diluted, edges blurred. And the snow under his head leaks a pool of darkness.

The Mutant struggles to a sitting position in her bed. She hacks into a clutch of tissue. There is still a twinge in her chest, like her ribs are made of glass.

He got up. She saw as she backed around the corner. He got up and drove away. Fuck him.

If she could stop seeing him fall, maybe she could sleep. A little smoke would do the trick too but what little she's got is stashed at the Mill where Tony can't get at it. She curls up and pulls the blanket over her head.

After a while her head spins and it feels like falling. She can see herself becoming the first fold of a kaleidoscopic separation of descending Mutants. As the shutter slices her into fractions of motion, she closes her eyes against the vertigo, against actually seeing the blade descend like the blink of a glass eyelid. Slowly, slowly, she comes to rest, folded into herself again in a chaste snow. It is all cold edges, microscopic crystalline feathers, flakes of glass, weeping from the corner of the moon's blind eye.

■ ■ ■

Though he works late, Sam's at the meeting house first thing Saturday morning. The small cut on his scalp is a little tender and his shoulder has stiffened up some, though not as much as it might have if he hadn't used it as much as he could manage during his evening shift at the garage. He tests his shoulder, works the ball. Walks it, runs it, trots and paces it. Explores its every inch, circumnavigates it, orbits it, kicks it into warpspeed, sails solar winds on its humpback and beams back. By the time the other guys turn up, he's warmed up and loose. He feels the shoulder but it's going to be okay.

"You coming to the dance?" Rick wants to know.

It's the Christmas dance, a significant occasion. He should turn up for at least a while, be one of the guys.

"I was going to but Dad's sick. He's got my fucking head cold. I'll have to work until at least ten."

Rick looks skeptical. "Suit yourself. I can't do the diner this morning. Gotta work myself."

Sam feels the same judgment from the other guys, most of them cutting the usually high-spirited breakfast at the diner, refusing to look him in the eye. A harsh laugh drifts back from Fosse as he leaves, his head bent to make some remark to Dupre. Maybe it's not about him, Sam thinks, and then Pete glances back, and he knows it was.

What makes it so unfair is for once he really wants to go to a frigging dance. Nat had been pretty direct. Maybe she would be there on her own—last he heard she wasn't going with anybody just then—and they could—dance, or something. Talk about basketball and get comfortable with each other and maybe he'd ask her about a movie or something during the break.

■ ■ ■

The snow has sweetened the air and it's mild out, as it often is after a storm. It doesn't look as if the few inches that fell are going to stick either. The roads are already mostly clear, shining black with melt, and there are puddles on the pavement around the garage.

"Isn't there a dance tonight?" Reuben wants to know. Sick or not, he's at work, eating aspirin and drinking juice and tea.

"I should work. I need the bucks."

Coughing into a fistful of handkerchief, Reuben waves the off hand dismissively. "It'll be quiet tonight. Jonesy can handle it."

"I need the bucks too," Jonesy chimes in.

"Why don't you quit at eight, eight-thirty and go anyway? Thing doesn't even start until eight, does it?"

Sam shrugs. "You should be home in bed."

"You sound like Pearl. I can be sick just as well here as I can at home. You're just trying to change the subject. It's your senior year, Sammy. You ought to have some fun."

Sam zips his coveralls decisively. "I am having fun. I'm saving up to get a Harley tattoo. I figure it's the closest I'm ever gonna get to a bike. With the right tattoo, at least I'll meet some cute bikers."

Jonesy chortles.

Reuben shakes his head. "It must be that stuff you listen to. Look what the stuff we listened to did to my generation. Yours—I dunno. Probably be cannibals."

"Dad?"

Reuben looks up from his workbench.

"There's a card on the board at the diner. Alf Parks has got a litter of beagles."

"We already talked about this, Sammy. I miss having a dog too. It's just a terrible time for a puppy, with the baby on the floor all the time and putting everything in her mouth, and the house crowded too. Imagine that kitchen with a dog underfoot at suppertime. Next year'll have to do."

"Right," Sam says. "Nevermind."

Frowning, Reuben looks down at the workbench with an air of trying to remember where he left off.

"The hell with it," he says abruptly. "I'm going home." Shrugging into his jacket, he pauses at the door. "Why don't you go to that dance, Sammy?"

Sam looks up and nods. "If I do, I'll be home early."

■ ■ ■

The weirdness of melt overwhelms him from the time he leaves the garage—not at eight-thirty but at ten-thirty, when he makes the decision impulsively as he closes up the garage. Twenty-four hours earlier he was pushing snow around and now it's *balmy,* though with that little rusty tinge of cold on every deep breath.

There is as much going on in the parking lot as in the gym—people standing around cars and trucks, bullshitting and sneaking beers or passing smoke around. Some of them have come from partying in houses where the parents are conveniently absent or willing to look the other way. The cops will pass through the lot at irregular intervals through the evening but it's impossible to sneak into the place unnoticed and so there's plenty of warning to dispose of the evidence.

In the morning, the parking lot will be littered with empties, a few baggies with a residue of seed and stem, heaps of ash and cigarette ends from dumped ashtrays, a used condom or two. The pavement will be spattered with vomit and at least one pair of bikini underpants will decorate one of the juniper bushes around the school. Some few of the partyers will manage to get their asses busted behind the wheel or if the cops move on a particular make-out site but there is a world of homes empty of parents out partying themselves, and back roads, gravel pits and camps within reach of anyone with a ride.

In the cluster of bikes at one end, Sam spots Romney's Harley. Romney must be one of the chaperones. If he's got the parking lot duty, he's wandering around with an eye out for potential fights, and discouraging with his presence any standing on the roofs of other people's vehicles, guzzling openly, throwing bottles, public pissing or other mayhem.

Inside, the amplifiers are cranked to nosebleed levels and the gym reverberates to Skinny Puppy's kettledrum synthesizer assault, a deafening apocalyptic chant just right for Hell's waiting room. In deference to the holiday, the decoration committee has gelled the lights in red and green, producing a bilious bad-trip atmosphere. The writhing dancers over which the peculiar light spills could easily be the tormented denizens of the Bad Place itself. A life-size Santa Claus has been lynched from one of the raised basketball backboards. The late Merry Old Elf sports Freddy Krueger's razor fingerblades, strung with tinsel made poisonous and bloody by the red and green gels. It looks as if the Mutant had a hand in the decor.

Todd Gramolini comes up to hang an arm over Sam's shoulder and deliberately huff beery breath into his face. "Slammer!"

"Seen Woods?" Sam asks.

"Token was here with Sarah but"—Todd pumps his eyebrows lasciviously—"they left."

Deliberately, Sam works the room. He ignores a lot more beer breath from his teammates. Making a joke of it, with his hand to his ear, he pretends to be deaf to invitations to sample Christmas cheer in the parking lot.

When the season is over, he assures himself, he will treat himself to a major blowout. In the meantime there is a kick in the noise and exuberance and the girls strutting their stuff on the dance floor. The clashing lights highlight and kaleidoscope their forms into moving parts, a jazzy cubist vision of the infinite variety of the female body. He's suddenly hellishly horny.

Drifting to the refreshments, he is buying himself a Coke when

Nat sidles up. Blinking, she pops out a contact and deftly reinserts it.

"Oh shit," she giggles, and then grins at him. "Wanna dance?"

She's a little bit toasty, he realizes, and bending closer, he picks up the hot scent of booze on her breath. Not the yeast of beer but a creamy coffee smell—coffee brandy is popular with the girls because it's sweet.

The music's frenetic, so it won't be a slow dance and there won't be any contact between them. Then her hand is in his and she's looking up at him, a warmth in her eyes that makes him feel a lot warmer himself in every way. It's a little bit surprising she's not with someone and it occurs to him, with a little jolt, that maybe that was on purpose—maybe she was hanging out, looking for him. All at once, he wants the music to change, he wants something slow so he can hold her against him. Nat's one of the most popular girls in school. He's suddenly sure she's had a hard-on pressed against her at least a few times. Maybe she's not even a virgin. Probably not. Most unlikely. He wants to hold her real close and see what happens, see if maybe she presses back.

Something flutters down from overhead and he reaches out automatically to catch it. It's his sweatshirt. Letting go of each other's hand, both he and Nat take a step back to look upward.

"Check it out," Nat giggles.

The Mutant straddles a lighting catwalk in the shadows of the roof above them. Face impassive, she waves desultorily. Around the eye on the unchained side of her face, she's blackened a distorted joker's diamond with an elongated, downward point. Though her skull is naked, her headwrap knotted at one hip, she's at least not bare-tit; for the occasion she wears a red lace bra with her ragged jeans and chains. She's not even the only girl with her bra visible—sheer or semi-sheer blouses are on every other girl tonight.

Sam's face heats at the immediate evocation of the night they were on the verge of making it. His hand clutching the shirt is sweaty and he doesn't know what to do with it.

"Yo, Nat baby," the Mutant calls down. "Come on up. The view's awesome. Bring Bigger with you. It's the only way to get him high."

Around them, everyone is turning to look at them. Suddenly Romney shoulders his way through the crowd.

"Come on down from there, Gauthier," he advises her with a grin.

She sticks her tongue out to jeers, cheers and pleas to take it off, but she comes down. Romney heads off to intercept her as she reaches the floor.

Sam realizes Nat is looking at him curiously.

"Bigger?" she asks and giggles again.

She really is a bit tight. She's hectic and her makeup's a little smeary. He takes her parking, it could change their whole lives— and not necessarily for the better if she's not on the Pill and he isn't able to score a rubber off Rick or somebody else who won't retail him looking for one all over school.

He remembers the shirt in his hand. " 'Scuse me, I should take this over to Gauthier."

Nat blinks. "Sure."

But in the mob, he can't locate Romney, let alone the Mutant. Maybe Romney hauled her off to the Office or her locker to find her something to put on. Nor does he see Rick. Until he does, he'd rather avoid Nat and the pull to take a stupid chance. At least he's got his shirt back.

■ ■ ■

Going outside, he tosses his shirt into the truck. Beer is in the air, smelling too frigging tempting for words. On impulse, he grabs his basketball. He dribbles it slowly across the lot toward the outdoor court.

"Give it a fucking rest, Bigger," Bither bellows from the flatbed of someone's pickup truck.

The net's gone, of course, but the mild temperature has left the pavement exposed. He intends no serious exertion, just wants to kill some time before going home. Keep his hands filled so they won't wind up wrapped around a beer bottle or groping some girl. He spiders the dribble, shifts it to his knees, lets it rise and converts to walking figure eights. He forgets the parking lot and the noise from the gym and the uneven light.

Sardonic applause startles him and he spins around to find the Mutant grasping the hurricane fencing around the court. She rattles it furiously.

"Shirt!" she hisses.

Loping to the truck, he retrieves his sweatshirt and reenters the court. Rather than go around the outside, he keeps the fence between them and stuffs the shirt through one of the diamond-shaped holes. She drops her coat. She is wearing a black Harley T-shirt that must have come out of Paul Romney's tool kit. It's greasy and full of holes—fits right into her look. Her tits in the lace bra stick out the tears in the shirt; the tips are like candied cherries before they disappear under the sweatshirt. She's tied her headrag at the side with a hint of twenties flapper. The details lock themselves into Sam's brain at first glance; he can't help it. And the horniness in the gym is back in spades. She resumes her coat hastily.

"You shouldn't be out here," he says. "You ought to be home getting well, not prancing around showing off your tits."

"Up yours," she says.

He thinks about it a minute. "You wish?" he tries.

"Ha!" She slaps her hand against the fence, vibrating it.

Curling the fingers of his left hand through the wire, he stops the vibration. "You going to be able to make the practices during break?"

"Of course. I'm okay."

On opposite sides of the fence, they have unconsciously adopted mirror poses with one hand on the fence. The chain links cast shadows all over her, cutting her into Mutant diamonds.

"Didn't like the music?" she asks.

Sam gestures toward the gym. " 'This ain't no disco, this ain't no party, this ain't no foolin' around,' " he quotes.

She bursts out laughing. "What is it then? You can't leave it alone."

"Trying to leave the other stuff alone," he admits. "Booze to the left of me, babes to the right. Thought I'd be safe out here."

She grins. She gives the fence an emphatic shake. "Everybody else partying their heads off and I'm as straight as you are. Thought I'd at least have a smoke. Came outside looking to bum one. But I don't really want to. I mean, I don't want to but I do. You know? I don't want to get sick again. Miss any more games."

"Yeah."

Their gazes meet in a moment of silence. Her dark eyes are level with determination; she wants him to know how serious she is about playing. About winning. The tightness of her mouth, her fingers around the wires, the tension of her leg muscles telegraph the same message. He nods, smiling approval and encouragement.

She strolls around the corner of the fence and onto the court. With a shrug, he drops the ball into her hand.

She dribbles it thoughtfully. "I thought maybe J.C.'d be in a good mood tonight and I could make up with him, but he's more interested in Lexie now. I'm still cheesed at him anyway."

Stay cheesed at him, Sam thinks. *I'll keep him in a bad mood.*

She pauses. "You fell kind of hard yesterday."

Sam gently taps the ball loose from her hands.

"I'm okay. One on one?"

She grins at him. The chains on her face ripple in the light from the parking lot.

"Hey," she assures him. " 'This ain't no foolin' around.' "

■ ■ ■

Coat skirts swirling dervishly, the Mutant pirouettes beneath the hoop and rockets to dunk the ball. It drops through the hoop into Sam's extended palm.

The fence caroms, this time under the flat of Rick's hand, with a noise like dragging chains.

"Sick, obsessive behavior," he calls.

The Mutant answers with a double bird.

"She can't help it," Rick explains to Sarah. "Drug damage."

Snickering, Sarah ducks her face against Rick's chest. A little drug-damaged herself. Rick too.

The Mutant gives Sarah a disinterested once-over. "Got a butt? Better yet, a jay?"

Sarah whips out her cigarettes. The Mutant hesitates.

"They're French," Sarah says.

"Gauthier's in training," Sam objects. "And just getting over pneumonia."

"Yeah, yeah, yeah." The Mutant kicks at his foot. "Mind your own business, Preacher."

But she waves off Sarah's pack. Sarah shrugs and lights one for herself.

The parking lot's noisier and busier.

"They're shutting this place down," Rick says. He has his arm inside Sarah's coat, around her waist. One hand under her sweater.

"Right. I'm outta here. You need a ride?" Sam asks the Mutant.

"See my limo? Chauffeur's fucking off again," she says.

Rick and Sarah are playing grab-ass, chasing each other around the court.

As Sam gives the Mutant a hand up, she looks past him and hoots at somebody. When he turns to look, he sees it is Nat, just leaving the gym with Deb Michaud and Kerry Hatch. Eyes narrow, Nat smiles acidly.

Shit and double shit. Shit to the tenth power.

He ducks behind the wheel. Hugely pleased with herself, the Mutant leans back as if she really were in her limo. He grabs a tape and slots it angrily, punching up the volume to eliminate conversation.

"All right!" The Mutant twitches on the seat. Very shortly, however, she thumbs down the volume without a by-your-leave and points out a yellow farmhouse set back from the road, less than a mile from the school. "That's where my old bats live. The ones I clean for."

He doesn't care. He doesn't want to know anything more about her than he already does. Which is too much.

"They took me to the Emergency Room when I got sick and paid for my medicine. It's gonna take me half the winter to pay them off."

She still looks peaked to him, and she was out on the frigging court with him in the raw night air. He flips up the volume again and steps on the gas. She knocks it down again.

"Put me out on the Main Road once we get to town, okay? Unless you want to go parking?"

"No," he says, reaching for the volume button again. "And don't bring it up again. And don't touch this button again either."

She sticks her tongue out at him. He ignores her.

■ ■ ■

She trips down the hill, cutting steadily down through backyards to cross Depot and skirt her own block, into the fringe of swamp and trash woods along the banks of Mill Brook, over the abandoned tracks and to the Mill. She gropes the candle and matches cached just inside the door and lights her way to the cubby. Fixing the candle in the neck of an old bottle and wrapping her coat around her, she curls up on the dirty old mattress on the cot. She could find a party and be warmer—get high too, of course—and not have to go home. Anything beats going home. But the very mildness of the night seems to recommend this choice, just as finding Samgod on the outdoor court and reclaiming his sweatshirt struck her as an omen, a cosmic whisper assuring her he's hers. Hadn't she cut off Nat's move like a chain saw through butter?

His sweatshirt still smells of him. When she is wearing it, she feels as if she has crawled inside his skin. She knows things about him. How scared he is. Of her. It's a trip having power over him. Knowing he's cherry. He's going to be a pushover. Then she'll have all his magic, all his strength.

The damp chill holds her in a trough of shallow sleep, dreaming a dream she cannot recall when she wakes in a frigid, silvery pre-dawn, her upper lip wet with mucus, a curious tension in her groin. Like a cramp.

14

■ ■ ■

Sick as a Yellow Dog on Christmas Eve, Reuben gives up and lets Sam take him to the ER.

"What happened to the glovebox?" he asks, on seeing cardboard taped over the doorless compartment.

"Oh." Sam grimaces. "It fell off."

Reuben closes his eyes. Given the kid's proclivity for misjudging his own strength, it's a safe bet Sammy's managed to rip it off. Too embarrassed to mention doing it—no doubt he was going to quietly repair it without a word.

The doctor scolds Reuben and sends him home after sinking a spikeful of high-octane antibiotic into his hip. Twenty-one days of a cephalosporin-class bug-killer turns out to be a ninety-buck pop. Reuben gropes his way into the pharmacy to use his bankcard to cover it. He dozes off on the ride home. And sleeps through the rest of the day and the evening.

Sam and Pearl put the tree up and decorate it—a considerable project involving stringing cranberries and popcorn and other obeisances toward tradition. When the holiday is over, the tree with its natural garland intact will go outside to feed the birds, who won't care that the popcorn has gone stale and the cranberries gooshy and bitter. While they are hanging the ornaments and putting presents under the tree, Indy grabs at all the shiny going by. It's a year or two too soon for her to have even the vaguest understanding of the festivities but she enjoys it at the most primitive level and without reservation, self-consciousness or expectation.

Observing her, Sam envies his baby sister's purity of experience. He cannot help missing Reuben's participation. He misses Frankie, he misses the Christmases of his early childhood—he even misses the latter Christmases after his parents broke up. There had always been the small and reassuring traditions like the popcorn-and-cranberry garland even as the family itself fractured, diminished and most recently, grew again. His stepmother's gaze meets his and he understands she is feeling the same shadow of Christmas Past.

"My mother always said it never really felt like Christmas to her in Florida," Pearl says, pausing to dig a raw cranberry Indy has pried from the garland out of the protesting baby's mouth. "Wish she could be here now."

"Want to look at the old albums?" he asks.

Her whole face lights up. "Let's. I'll make some cocoa."

■ ■ ■

Christmas is unwrapped in slashing sleety snow. At four-thirty in the morning, Sam is on the phone, sleepily switching the service to Maxie Sweetser in Greenspark. Maxie doesn't mind; he loves bad weather. It keeps his three wreckers paying for themselves and keeps Maxie out of the house when his in-laws are infesting the place. Jonesy turns up at five, offering to work, and Sam tells him Maxie is already covering them. They have a cup of cocoa together, wish each other Merry Christmas and Jonesy departs to spend the rest of the day with his girlfriend.

The bad weather intensifies the warmth and closeness of the indoors but it is not suffocating, only a reminder to be grateful for shelter. Sam grabs the excuse to call his mother, who now lives fifty miles away, to tell her he can't make it over to see her because of the weather. She seems to be as relieved as he is.

Deliberately he says nothing about Reuben's illness. It isn't her business anymore. She has to get her gossip about his father's life now from Karen, on the rare occasions mother and daughter see each other. The last time Sam answered—or rather didn't answer—a question from his mother about Reuben was when she asked if it was true his father was seeing a colored woman.

"Colored?" Sam had responded incredulously. "Hold on, I'll look." And had walked away, leaving the phone off the hook. An hour or so later, he picked it up again and the line was dead, so he guessed she had found something more useful to do with her life.

Since Indy isn't old enough to care, Sam and Pearl decide to put off opening gifts until the afternoon, in the hope that Reuben will be better. There are phone calls to make and take, making the holiday connection to far-flung relations and friends, to break up the day.

Once Reuben comes around, in the late afternoon, it takes him a while to understand it is Christmas. He is distressed to discover they are still waiting the holiday on him and insists on coming downstairs and having their tree.

For Indy, the unwrapping is a kittenish festival of ripping bright-colored paper and snatching after ribbons. The contents of the packages are less interesting than the outsides. Everything goes directly to her mouth to be gummed and gnawed and drooled upon. Eventually she drops whatever it is to the floor and forgets it. Her chin is discolored with dye from various papers and ribbons. Sam has decorated her as well with three self-sticking bows from his own packages and they bob loosely upon her curls.

Reuben unwraps a pair of pajama bottoms from Sam and Pearl unwraps the top, a mild joke that amuses them enough to have been worth the effort. Sam also gives his father assorted oldies, including a few forty-fives—Reuben likes old wax, old vinyl, not just old rock—scavenged from cut-out racks and has-bins. Their gifts to Sam are utilitarian—socks and shorts and so on—but there is a new basketball.

When everything is dispensed, Reuben looks around as if he is confused and frowns.

"Isn't there one more thing, sugarbabe?" he asks Pearl.

She frowns too and then her face relaxes.

"I must have left it upstairs. I'll go get it."

When she won't let Sam do it for her, he suspects the byplay with Reuben was just theater. He takes the baby for her but Indy is restless and he puts her on the floor among the discarded wrapping. She slaps and grabs relentlessly.

Sam waits expectantly, wondering if Pearl could somehow have smuggled a puppy upstairs during the day. But she returns with a good-sized box. As he unwraps it, he can't suppress a little disappointment. He didn't really expect a pup, any more than he expected to get a Harley, though he had cut out and pasted a picture of one next to the stick-figure dog on his Christmas list. He smells the leather before he folds back the layers of tissue.

The dog is instantly forgotten. As he shrugs on the bike jacket, he registers the zippers, the buckles, the fact that it fits, which means it was made to order—serious buckage. He knows his eyes are shining when he thanks them. It's reflected in the delight they take in the success of their gift. Reuben and Pearl reach out blindly to squeeze each other's hand and the mutual confidence in the gesture hits Sam harder than the gift itself. To cover the depth of his emotion, he models the jacket with brio, sweeping back his hair dramatically and snapping his fingers.

■ ■ ■

Their applause is interrupted by a petulant drumming at the back door. Pearl rises but Sam gestures her to stay where she is—he is already up and moving. He recognizes his sister's fist.

Though the sleet has stopped, it's still raw and cold. On the back porch, Karen clings to a mildly intoxicated and fuzzy young man. She has none of the Styleses' height and is as slight as her mother but in the face she is the spit of the photograph on the mantelpiece of Reuben's mother in youth. From that lady too Karen has inherited a disproportionate abundance of bosom. With her red eyes and nose, her hair and makeup looking like an unmade bed—like she just rolled out of one, anyway—it's a safe guess she's spent the weekend partying. Flinging her arms around Sam, she kisses him smearily. Her breath is as boozey as a cordial-centered chocolate and she moves sloppily. She notices his jacket and rubs the chest of it.

"Oooo, Sammy! Sex-ee!" she squeals.

Her carrying voice draws Pearl with the baby on her hip and Reuben close behind her from the living room.

For a moment the kitchen is a confusion of embraces, Karen at once teary and laughing. Sam and Reuben and Pearl exchange quick worried glances as Karen makes over Indy. Fueled by whatever she's done up on, her emotions are too highly colored and rapid. She is in a state like a cheap Christmas-tree ball, little more than a brittle shell of brilliant color.

Sam introduces himself to her companion, who seems to be a good-tempered shit. The guy's name is Bobby Somebody and he calls Karen "Kare." Bobby gives her very warm, pleased looks, which suggests to Sam ol' Bobby hasn't known Karen very long. Probably picked her up Friday night and is still under the impression he's found himself a good-time-loving girl. She hasn't emptied his wallet while he sleeps yet, or stolen his credit cards, if he has any, or wrecked his car, or any of the other tricks she pulls sooner or later with every guy who's still around when she wakes up.

Indy panics at Karen's too-enthusiastic jouncing and the shrill strange face in hers. Reaching small frantic hands for Pearl, she bursts into tears. Karen nearly loses her grip on the baby and clutches her too tightly, triggering a shriek of pain. At that, she all but throws Indy into Pearl's anxious arms.

Shushing the baby, Pearl retreats to the rocking chair, where she offers Indy the most reliable comforter. Though it is a discreet act, the baby's head disappearing under Pearl's loose shirt and the shawl she tugs down from the back of the chair, Karen's Bobby turns red in the face. Karen giggles inanely.

"Sweetheart," Reuben tells Karen, "there's something under the tree for you."

It's a decent exit from the kitchen. Sam trails his father and Karen and Bobby to the doorway and loiters there, as if to shield Pearl nursing Indy by the woodstove from any further contact with Karen.

In the living room, Karen unwraps her gift while chattering at Bobby. "I told you they'd have popcorn and cranberries on the tree, didn't I? Daddy always says it's traditional but really"—she addresses Reuben—"you're just too cheap, Mommy always said you were just like your old man, only"—now she turns to Bobby—"my grandpop decorated his last Christmas tree with his brains."

She runs down just as Sam is about to strangle her. It is a vintage Karen performance. She's too loaded to understand what she is doing to her father, who has sunk back onto the couch, grey in the face and looking as if he wants to throw up.

Karen shakes out the handmade sweater—Ma Lunt's work, made to order in the same blue as Karen's eyes, with enough room in the front for all of her endowment. Dumping the box on the floor, she jumps up and yanks her T-shirt over her head. She's not wearing a bra and for a moment she is naked from the waist up, her oversized breasts rising and falling in all their breathless centerfold extravagance. She is oblivious to the stunned embarrassment of the three men. Then she pulls on the new sweater and shakes her tits at Bobby.

"Like it?" she teases, glittery-eyed, running her palms over her breasts.

But it is only a reflex, and she leaves Bobby standing there grinning uncertainly.

"Daddy," she demands from the kitchen where she has opened the refrigerator, " 'd'ja drink all the booze already? There's not a single fucking brew in here."

Coming up behind her, Sam lifts her hand from the fridge door and closes it firmly. "There's no booze in the house. No coke either. No pot. No pills—"

"Sammy," his father says, following them into the kitchen, "maybe Karen and her friend would like to stay to supper."

Karen looks at him blankly, then turns on Sam.

"Fuck you," she says. She grabs the corner of the bike jacket he is still wearing and yanks down on it. "You may be bigger than me but you pissed the bed until you were eleven, you moron, so don't you try to pull that shit on me." She struts toward Bobby, who is holding her discarded shirt and clearly wishing he were somewhere else. She points at Sam. "Dimbulb, over there, he couldn't fucking read until he was fif"—

"Karen," Reuben interrupts, taking her by the elbow, "that's enough. You're loaded, honey. Why don't you sit down in the living room with your friend for a while and settle down and then we'll have a meal together? You two stay overnight. Stay out of this rough weather."

She shakes off his arm violently. "Just leave me the fuck alone! I don't know why I bothered to come here. I thought on Christmas maybe I'd get treated like a human being. No fucking way in this house. It's the same old shit from my prick brother and you— 'there's no booze in the house,' " she mocks. "You're the one who doesn't dare have it around, you're the one with the problem, and every fucking time I come through the fucking door, you lay it off on me. Karen's fucking loaded again." Her face is wet and blurry. "Bad old Karen."

Reuben tries to embrace her but she jerks away from him, raising her hands in a warding-off gesture.

"Enough," he says, backing away. "I love you, Karen. It hurts us all when you're like this. I'd like you to go now. Come see us when you're sober."

In the silence, Pearl makes a choking noise, and Sam realizes behind the hand covering her face, his stepmother is crying. She hates to cry almost as much as she hates scenes. Reuben moves toward her, putting his hand on her shoulder.

"I'm outta this shithole," Karen says.

With an automaton clumsiness, Sam lurches after her. She slams the door of her friend's rusty Maxima between them.

Bobby shuffles up, mild brown eyes cloudy. "Sorry, man. I didn't know what the situation was." He hesitates and scratches his head. "I just met Kare last night."

Sam raps on the window and Karen rolls it down angrily.

When he stoops to speak to her, he's startled to see how exhausted and pale she is. She's looking very hard-used for just nineteen. It softens his heart toward her.

"Dad's sick as a dog. Why don't you sleep it off and come by and see him tomorrow? Tell him you didn't mean all that garbage."

"Go fuck yourself," she snarls. She struggles with the sweater and he looks away as it comes flying out of the car and lands on the ground.

Sam picks it up. "And Merry Christmas to you too, Kare," he mutters.

■ ■ ■

The leather of the jacket is stiff in the cold and he has to fumble at the pockets to get his fingers a ways into them. A rigid edge of paper stops his fingertips in the left-hand pocket. It's thick like oaktag. Then a fingertip slides over a satin surface and without seeing he recognizes it as a Polaroid snapshot. He pulls it out as he trudges up the back steps and the porchlight shows him a picture of the horsebarn at the farm. He flips it over and on the back is printed: *Look Inside.*

The puppy. He can see it in his mind's eye, a bright-eyed little beagle huddled in a box with a blanket and a chew toy, and nearby, to keep it warm, one of the electric space heaters his father's been using to heat the farmhouse while he works.

The kitchen is empty. He hears the television in the living room. He props himself against the frame of the archway, two fingers behind him clipping the snapshot out of sight. Reuben and Pearl and the baby are on the couch together under a quilt, in the dreamy blue passivity of television light. Not paying any attention to the tube—it's just a sound machine, like waves at the beach—all three have closed their eyes. Reuben opens one eye at Sam.

The only sound is the dialogue from the television: some version of Dickens's *Christmas Carol*. *These are the chains I forged in life,* Jacob Marley explains to Scrooge in a ghastly croak.

"You okay?" Reuben asks.

Sam nods.

Pearl's eyes pop open. She moves to sit up and Reuben pulls her down.

"Pretty gruesome, huh?" Sam says.

His father strokes Pearl's temple and she makes a sound low in her throat. Indy is belly down on Reuben's chest. Pearl rests a hand on the baby's back, rising and falling smoothly in sleep.

"Let's not let it ruin the rest of the evening, okay?" Reuben asks. "What's left of it."

Sam produces the Polaroid and holds it out questioningly.

His father grins and shrugs. Not telling. Sam looks to Pearl and her mouth curves faintly in a little Mona Lisa smile.

"It's nasty out. I guess I can wait until tomorrow."

Reuben raises an eyebrow. "Up to you."

The puppy will be lonely and scared. It's not a long trek and his truck has four-wheel drive.

He hears the soft murmur of their laughter behind him as he goes out the back door.

■ ■ ■

The old farmhouse stands on the height of the Ridge, its roofbeam a blind leviathan spine against the sky. With Reuben sick and Sam tied up with basketball, no work has been done on the house recently and the sense of abandonment is as cutting as the wind on the ridge. Leaving the truck, Sam walks past the farmhouse up the yard toward the horsebarn, which stands far enough apart to have saved it from the fire. He's always had more of an affection for the barn than his father does, who had lived in it for a time while in high school. In fact, it is precisely the evidence that still remains of the time his father made a home of the tack room—raw shelving, nail hooks in the wall, gaps in the wood caulked to keep the wind out, the handmade wooden seat in the earth closet—that endears the place to Sam.

Despite the faint frozen odor of manure, the horses have been gone since his mother left and there's no point in locking the doors. Sam steps through the opening into a sudden cessation of the bitter wind.

"Hey, Cujo," he says.

He rolls the swath of his flashlight over the lightless interior. The beam splinters the bits and pieces of things salvaged from the farmhouse fire and still stinking of it—leaded glass from the front door and the parlor, a box of ceramic doorknobs, brass or copper fixtures, a claw-foot bathtub—and shocks a gleam of black sleek curves he recognizes instantly. Numb, he reaches automatically for the light switch by the door, finds it blind and flicks it. The inside of the barn leaps into detail as if he had tumbled into it from a dark hole. In the middle of the floor, a flathead Harley Electra Glide sits in splendid potency, keys in the ignition, brain-bucket glinting like a black mechanical skull on the tail.

Cujo forgotten, Sam strokes the cold silken steel of the bike's muscular curves.

Clipped to the keys is an envelope—ownership papers, registration, the thing is already licensed. Stuck to the papers is a note: *She's eleven years old, been through three owners, and every one of them dicked with her so she's no virgin. Jonesy found her. He fixed the immediate previous owner's balls-up of the transmission. She still needs some work but nothing major. Ahem. Goes fast. You don't have a bike license yet. Also you have to pay for your own insurance which is going to be outrageous so I figure you'll have her on the road in about five years. PLEASE DO NOT KILL YOURSELF ON THIS THING.*

As he reads his father's printing, he swings a leg over and mounts it without thinking about it. Like the jacket, the bike fits. When it comes to life, he thinks he should have put on the helmet first to keep his brains from exploding out his ears with the rush. It brings to mind a Duke Tomato song that demands "More Love, More Money." Who needs money, Sam counters, who needs love, with a machine like this between your legs? It *is* love and money and the proof is there in his father's words: *Goes fast.*

While he hasn't qualified for a bike license, as a matter of course he has wheeled other people's bikes around the garage or the parking lot or shop at school. In any case he is a natural and instinctive operator, adapting smoothly to the shift from four wheels to two. He rolls out of the barn without a second thought. Testing brakes and gears automatically, he leans his weight joyously into the curve around the door. It's a big heavy ride. The rollercoaster thrill of planing on icy mud pumps his adrenaline a little higher. He feels perfectly in control at the edge of control. The wind bites at him and he slows, idling at the bottom of the yard to zip his jacket to the throat and don the helmet and his gloves.

He knows the road conditions are moderately greasy with occasional plaques of black ice. New riders almost always dump their bikes at least once, usually within a few miles of their first ride. And he's unlicensed. But it's nearly eleven on Christmas night and the cops are all at home with their families—everybody's at home with their families. Nodd's Ridge is a map of empty roads, byways Sam has driven constantly since he was fifteen. Working with his father on the tow truck and the plow, he knows every bad patch on them. Anyway, he notes for when his father asks, he's wearing the brain-bucket.

As the bike's weight and his own combine to tip dangerously on one particularly sharp corner and he compensates, the twinge of protest in his right shoulder reminds Sam of the damage he might do if he goes down with the bike on that side—nevermind the season or the state basketball title, he could wind up jerking off with his left hand for the rest of his life. Immediately he slows and becomes more cautious.

From the crest of Partridge Hill he sees the void of the frozen lake and the Narrows and swoops down on it, shooting across the Causeway and over the town line into Greenspark. His first impulse is to roust out Rick and give him a ride, but the quietness of the town reminds Sam it is getting late. The conjunction of his lack of a license and Rick's dad being a cop gives him further pause. His own father is waiting at home. Worrying about him. He wheels the bike around and heads back.

■ ■ ■

Reuben is reading the paper and drinking tea at the kitchen table.

"I took the bike out," Sam says.

His father looks over his reading glasses. "Looks like you're still in one piece."

"It's beautiful," Sam blurts fervently. "Thank you."

Reuben laughs. "It is, isn't it?"

Pushing back his chair, he glances at the clock on the wall. "My mother used to say tomorrow comes early. My experience has been it's usually already here."

Sam pegs his jacket and rattles the doorknob to confirm he's locked it. "I shouldn't ask this, Dad, but it must have cost—"

"Then don't." Reuben cuts him off. "It's used, Sammy. We found a way. I wish I could have swung the insurance too but I couldn't. It's not a free and clear gift. You can't ride it again until you've got the insurance, you know. Except at the farm. Big deal, right. So basically you got yourself a fancy paperweight. I suppose you'll have some fun working on it, anyway."

"I shouldn't have asked for something that expensive," Sam says. On the way back from the farmhouse, he recalled the blowup over the new furnace. How much of the tension between Reuben and Pearl over that had proceeded from already having committed a major chunk of change to the bike for Sam?

For a moment, his father looks at him. "Don't apologize for wanting what anybody might want. I made a choice to try to give you what you wanted."

Sam nods.

"Finish locking up, will you?" Reuben says. "I've got just about enough beans left in me to make it up the stairs one more time tonight."

15

■ ■ ■

Mother and Child Make a Picture framed by
the bedroom door as Sam stops, intent on saying thank you again
to his stepmother for his Christmas. The baby is suckling inside
her mother's pajama top while Pearl reads a novel. From the bathroom beyond comes the sound of Reuben brushing his teeth. Sam
goes in and kisses his stepmother, who puts aside her book with a
sigh.

"Thanks for the bike."

"Sure, baby."

Wanting to say goodnight and thank you again to his father as
well, Sam loiters.

On the dresser, Pearl's jewelry box is wide open as usual, pieces
strewn on the fringed silk scarf that protects the old oak. Often
she sits Indy next to the box while she picks out her earrings or
whatever she's going to wear and lets the baby rummage among
the sparklies. It's all costume stuff. Once she had some fancier real
stuff but when she left her first husband, she found he had emptied the safe-deposit box not only of the pieces he had given her
but of several things that had been hers alone, earrings and rings
inherited from her mother and a ring given her by a man she had
loved and lost in youth. Telling Sam this story, she said with a rue-

ful laugh that it had been a lesson in the futility of storing up trea-
sure in this world.

Sam stirs the baubles with his thumb, churning up the stuff at
the bottom. He thinks about the Johnny who gave her that fancy
jewelry and took it back. She hasn't cut him out of her photograph
albums, the way his mother has his father from the photographs
she kept. Sam likes Johnny's face in the first pictures, the ones
around the time she married him. Then Johnny's face grows closed
and the two of them, Pearl and Johnny, are literally farther and
farther apart in the group photographs of family gatherings as the
years of their marriage pass.

The dogtags seem to come to his fingers without him really
looking for them. Tangled with them is a gold rope chain with a
small Celtic cross on it. The cross is engraved with the name on
the dogtags. Looking down at his fingers, draped with the chains
of the tags and cross, Sam thinks of his brother, wearing tags of
his own now. He recognizes the tags and cross—there is a snapshot in one of Pearl's oldest albums of a young man, with Pearl,
on a boat in nineteen-sixty-something. In the picture, that bare-
chested young man—her lost first love—had been wearing the tags
and cross.

Her voice startles him. "Would you like to have those things?
The tags and the cross?"

It's so unexpected at first he thinks he has misheard her.

"The cross was like a civilian dogtag. All the shrimpers and sail-
ors wore something like them for identification. He used to say a
face doesn't last long in the water but gold lasts forever." Very
gently she slides Indy from underneath her pajama top. "Those
things went all the way to Vietnam and came back. He died after
the war. I used to wear them to remember him until I married
Johnny."

Blinking, Sam touches the chains again, lifts them out. "Really?"

"Unh-huh," she says. Her hands are quick and practiced under
the quilt and her pajama top, discreetly slipping a breast pad into
her nursing bra and closing it. "I hope they'll be the only dogtags
you ever wear, Sam."

Reuben emerges from the bathroom. "What's this?"

"Pearl says I can have these. Gonna ward off the draft board."

Reuben shudders. "God, I hope so."

Sam says his goodnights and thank yous and Merry Christmases one last time. As he bends over Pearl to kiss her forehead, she closes her hand over his, the one with the chains in it, very briefly—almost a caress.

■ ■ ■

Talking Heads lullabies tongue in cheek from his stereo as he puts on a pair of old sweatpants—all he ever wears for pajamas when he wears anything to sleep. Rolling his arm in its socket, he feels no more than slight discomfort, though he still has some bruises healing in their lurid way from the inside out. When he gingerly touches the place where he cut his scalp, it gives a little. If he presses it, it makes him sick to his stomach. He guesses there is some fluid there, a bruise, still healing too.

As he raises the gold chain to close it around his throat, his gaze is arrested by the reflection in the mirror on the wall. Slowly he lifts it to his cheek, drapes it against his face, first studying its track between his nares and the lobe of his ear and then closing his eyes to feel its slightly cool, silky braid. He turns toward it, letting it pass over his mouth, trail over the tip of his tongue. With quickening breath and nervous fingers, he fastens it around his neck. It falls against his collarbone, the edges of the cross catching in the curls of his chest hair. The steel tags on their chain click against the cross.

Clicking off the overhead, he rips back the quilts. A gleam in the mirror catches his eye. By the single light of the reading lamp clamped to the headboard of his bed, he is a shadowy hulk in the looking glass. The chains at the base of his neck could be the crude seam of stitches holding his head to his shoulders. Unfocusing his eyes, he lurches experimentally.

He knows—having read the book under Romney's tutelage—that the movie monster is erroneously known as Frankenstein, who was in fact the scientist who patched him together out of corpses. The monster had no name. Victor Frankenstein's big goof, after reanimating the grab bag of dead meat, was to neglect the poor monster's education. The monster, it seems, had just enough brains to want more but ultimately had no soul.

No soul, Sam thinks as he squints into the darkened glass, no brains worth educating, and serious motor control problems. Sam doesn't remember the movie monster speaking—had it roared inarticulately from time to time, or giggled just before it oopsydaisied the little girl?—but he wouldn't be surprised if it had stuttered.

Crashing stiff-limbed to his bed, Sam chokes and gibbers what he hopes are appropriately inarticulate expressions of desire for a soul, a brain, a monstrous piece of ass. Then he lies still, savoring the pleasant pressure of his own weight on his engorged penis. It feels so good. The memories of making out with Deanie are unavoidable. Groping each other, the taste and textures of her armpits, chains, mouth, breasts. Candied cherry nipples in her red bra. Turning on his back again with a groan, he uses his right hand. The chains quiver with light like a Christmas garland.

■ ■ ■

Like a signpost or a traffic signal, the Mutant's on his way. He stops. What else can he do? Jumping up into the truck, she thrusts her hands into the heat from the vents.

"Nice jacket," she says.

"Thanks. How'd Santa treat you?"

She shrugs. "Same old shit."

The offhand way she says it warns him off the subject. Probably she was glad if they *didn't* give her anything—a black eye, some new cigarette burns. Christmas at the Mutant's house—it gives him the creeps to even try to imagine it. Wordlessly, he pushes a paper bag with a tinfoil package of Pearl's Christmas pastries and the Christmas-wrapped tape mixes he has made toward her.

She sits up straight. "Oh, jeez." She doesn't unwrap the cassettes, just holds them on her palm a moment. "Lemme guess. Could it be tapes?" Then she slips them into her backpack unopened and digs into the pastries. "Oh my God," she moans.

■ ■ ■

Sam executes a long pass to Bither. The Mutant descends on Mouth with burglary in her eyes. A thoroughly spooked Bither underhands the ball to Rick.

The Mutant glances Sam's way with a quick lift of one eyebrow. She breaks eye contact with him immediately. Dances like a Hindu goddess with a multiplicity of braceleted ivory arms into Rick Woods's face. She's wearing her sprung spandex tights that stop at midcalf, and those cutoff denim shorts, with a cutoff sweatshirt— not his, she better not cut it off—over a man's ribbed sleeveless undershirt. She has visible bruises on her arms and her legs where the skin shows but that could be from the fact she plays basketball like it was hockey.

All he really knows is her mother has mistaken her at least once for an ashtray and she's scared of that guy Tony. Shit-scared of him. The memory of her cringing from Lord suddenly infuriates Sam. If he ever is sure that fucker is punching her around, he won't stop to phone the child-abuse hotline. He'll just strain the fucker face first through a piece of hurricane fencing.

■ ■ ■

The following two days are a pair of old maids, Thursday frigid, Friday gloomy with snow coming on. Picking up the Mutant on the road on the way to practice, Sam waits for her to say thank you for the tapes but she says nothing.

After practice he slides a bag of sandwiches he has made for her across the seat. She licks her lips and grabs them like she thinks maybe he's going to change his mind. About halfway through goffling them, she stops and takes a deep relieved breath, and then plunges in again. She is dusting crumbs from her hands when they reach Depot Street.

"Oh," she says, shoving a tube of paper at him, "I ripped this off for you. Merry Christmas and all that happy horseshit."

She's out of the truck before he can react.

It is a page razored from an art folio, a picture of a man in an oddly old-fashioned and ill-fitting black suit, like something a nineteenth-century circuit rider might have worn. Too-short sleeves expose the man's wrists and large hands. Weirdly, the man's head is covered with a jack-o'-lantern. *Pumpkinhead Self Portrait 1972 James Wyeth*, it is captioned. It gives him a strange punched feeling in his solar plexus. Or maybe he is just hungry, he decides. Ripped it off. He laughs, too bemused to be angry.

■ ■ ■

Work fills the hours of Christmas break when he is not at practice at the high school or the meeting-house hall. At various times, Rick drops by the garage to visit with him, as do others of his teammates—the bike, brought down from the barn, is a draw, much envied and admired. He lets a dozen proposed plans for New Year's Eve flow over his broad shoulders with the remark he needs to work.

The snow finally hits on Friday, heavier in the foothills than the lowland, and keeps them busy all afternoon and into the evening. Reuben fades suddenly in the early evening and takes himself home, leaving his desk cluttered with the books he has been working on between calls.

Later, Sam sits down at the desk with a cup of tea to take a break. The books are right there in front of him. He's been reading the ledgers since he was a kid—numbers have never been the mystery letters were. What the books say about the state of the business is no surprise; Sam sees the work orders and distributors' bills and the totals on the cash register regularly enough even during basketball season to map the financial seismography. Winter's always harsh, he tells himself, pushing the garage accounts aside. Always. Harsh.

Underneath is another ledger, an old and dog-eared one he's never read though he's seen it in the cabinet. Curious, he tips it open. It enumerates the whole history of his father's ownership of the garage and the total family financial situation—farm rents, property taxes, caretaking income and so on. Flipping toward the current year, he ascertains Pearl's assets—the diner, liquid assets, house and land inherited from old Joe Nevers and Joe's sister, her grandmother, Gussie—are not recorded, which is what he expects. Considering both his father and Pearl got nuked in their respective divorces, it's not surprising they were extremely reluctant to mingle their finances. Pearl gave up the two vehicles she owned at the time of the marriage as lightly as dusting flour from her hands, with the remark they were a needless expense, and it was she who announced her willingness to sell her property to buy a furnace, so he guesses it is his father's pride that continues to keep the accounts separated. Ignoring the farm, which given the current real estate market could only be sold at a serious loss, if at all, and without Pearl's assets, Reuben teeters on the edge of bankruptcy. Historically, nothing new—he's never really recovered financially from the divorce.

Sam closes the ledger and pushes it away. A scrap of paper drifts toward the floor and he catches and smoothes it against the satiny oak of the old desk. It is his father's running summary, the bottom line slashed so boldly it's almost ripped through the paper. The quarterly tax demand, the distributors' take, the mortgage payment comes to a sum that makes Sam queasy. He doesn't see how they can make it. He grabs both ledgers back and picks through them again, looking for the way his father's going to get through the next quarter.

Suddenly Sam is struck by the realization there is no accounting for the bike. Which means it must be in Pearl's books. It must have come out of her money, costing his father only another blow to his pride. Or else Reuben borrowed the money from her and keeps, somewhere, a secret accounting of how much he owes her.

He can't stop thinking about it. He's been colossally immature and self-centered, nothing but basketball and his dick on his mind. Sweating a new pair of high-tops and the cost of Christmas presents while his father's been worrying about losing his life's work unless he can bend to accept his wife's help. He well knows how his father's mind works; it isn't just the humiliation of being financially dependent on a woman and after having been out on his own since he was Sam's age but the suspicion her hard-earned money would be following bad, ruining her too. No wonder Reuben was upset about her wanting to sell some of her land to buy a new furnace; he must have heard the click of the first domino falling. Reuben believes with a feudal fervor that land is capital—once sold, almost impossible to recover, and the too-liquid money goes, and then you've no land and no cash either.

On Saturday, Sam finds an excuse to go to the farmhouse to reassure himself it hasn't got a for-sale sign on it yet. Wandering through the yard with his fingertips in his pockets, face burning with the wind that embitters this point on the Ridge most of the winter, he finds his old hoop, the one they'd taken down after the fire and never got back up again. In the barn something else catches his eye: a bundle of electrical cable. The power company had used the fire as an excuse to run new line into the farmhouse, replacing the cable that had been there for four decades. Naturally he and Reuben had picked up the discard; never know when something like that could be used, if only to secure a bumper or a door temporarily.

Seized with a sudden vision, Sam welcomes the distraction. He takes both hoop and cable. A rusty little space heater from the farmhouse—if his father misses it, he will admit to tripping over it and then throwing the damaged thing out in embarrassment. He stops at the hardware store and charges some other items to Reuben's account. And blushing furiously, with a tap on Reuben's shoulder to get his attention, lies to his father.

"Suh-Suh-Sunday," he stutters, "gotta guh-guh-go fix that ceiling panel at the school. George's gonna let me in. I bought some stuff at the hardware store to do it. I'll puh-puh-pay you back."

"Good." Reuben turns back to the oil pump he is rebuilding. "You want New Year's Eve off?"

"Rather work."

Reuben pauses. "There'll be many New Year's Eves in your life you may have to work, Sammy."

Sam shrugs and turns away.

■ ■ ■

At six on Sunday morning, with the pickup game scheduled for nine at the meeting house, Sam parks his truck in the Playground parking lot. Counting on the scant traffic of the early hour, the poor light of winter dawn and the isolated location to protect him from prying eyes, he shimmies a pole to tap the power line that feeds the new playground lights. As he works, he considers how he could possibly explain what he's doing to the cops: his best bet would be to mew piteously and hope they will think a very large mean dog chased him up the pole. But shortly he's down without incident. Up a tree overhanging the Brook to hook the cable there and now it's overhead, just another piece of utility line invisible among all the others crosshatching the sky. Then onto the Mill, using trees and brush to camouflage the line.

The padlock's easy: squeeze one hard and they almost always pop right open. From inside, he draws the cable through a hole drilled in the frame of the window in the watchman's cubby and to the fusebox on the wall. It looks like something Fred and Barney put together out of dinosaur vertebrae and jungle vines. Boom boom boom: the Mill's electrified again. He does a triumphant little Irish jig. Has visions of juicing the power train. Maybe he can use the Mill as his Science Fair project in physics, spring semester: The Greenspark Mill Reanimated—he likes the sound of it.

There is still an ancient lightbulb dangling from the ceiling and the cubby actually has a couple of outlets. Into one he plugs the small space heater salvaged from the farmhouse. No reason to work in utter misery and he can leave it here for her. She's been here—left candle stubs on the floor. No cigarette butts, though. No roaches or empties but then returnables are worth a nickel or a dime and roaches not eaten are saved for another go.

From the other outlet he runs extension cord to the cavern of the main floor and in darkness climbs the rope and clips a floodlight to the beshitted beam. By this light he installs permanent floods on pulleys to make the bulbs easy to change. Once he has light, the last bit is easy. Bring in the ladder and the rest of the gear from the truck, mark the wall, drill the holes in the brick. Set the backboard and hoop.

He squares to it, lays up a shot, watches his new ball shiver through the nylon. Even with the new net, the rusty hoop looks shabby. He ought to have derusted and painted it. With the floods spilling ruthless light everywhere, every grim defect of this place is revealed so it looks as bad as it smells. What's he done? You can't make hell cozy or a whorehouse innocent. Let down, Sam picks up his ball, gathers his tools and heads for home.

■ ■ ■

A very thin turnout at the meeting house increases his sense of discouragement. He hoped more of the guys would care enough to put in the extra time to make up for taking Christmas Eve and Christmas off, but the partying started Friday night and continued on Saturday and the guys who do turn up are showing it. Sam and Rick linger behind to do the floor—winter weather brings in a lot of grit.

"Cheer up," Rick urges, in reaction to Sam's moroseness. "It's not all bad. I'm getting laid."

"Right," Sam agrees. "I can sleep without my chastity belt now."

Rick grins. "I got an idea. Why don't you get a date?"

Sam gives the broom a push. "Rather not. I'm working."

"What else is new?"

Knowing how Rick is going to react, he almost doesn't say anything. "I'm thinking about quitting."

Rick thumps a mop to the floor. "Jerking off? Too late. You're already brain-damaged."

Sam laughs. "Basketball."

Rick stares at him. "You're shitting me."

Sam shrugs. "It's just a game. I'm not going anywhere with it. It's over in a couple months anyway. You guys can take the state without me."

"I do not fucking believe you, man. What do you want to quit for? Don't tell me you got something better to do?"

"If I had the hours to put in, Dad could take on a lot more work."

"Your dad wants you to quit?"

"No! Of course not."

Rick shoves his mop into Sam's hands. "Here, try this on for size. It's another couple months and then you got the rest of your life to be a blue-collar thud."

"Nevermind. I was just thinking about it. I got a bike to support, you know."

"You can't even ride your goddamn bike for another three months." Rick flings his mop aside and picks up a loose basketball. He backs to center court. "You're a sick mother, Samurai." He pivots. "You don't need to quit basketball. You need to get your head out of your ass and wake the fuck up." He whangs the ball into the backboard.

"It's not that easy—" Sam says, shaking his head.

"Yes it is," Rick interrupts. "Yes it is." He points a finger accusingly at Sam. "You're chickenshit."

And stalks out, leaving Sam to finish the floor.

■ ■ ■

Steamed with a pearly glow, the windows at the Corner beckon warmly. From the sidewalk the Mutant spots J.C. in his favorite booth. Once inside, she leans over the back of his booth and tickles his earrings and he leans back and smiles at her.

"Stranger," she says.

"Stranger and stranger," he responds. "How ya doin'?"

Climbing over the back, she drops down next to him. He slips an arm around her waist automatically as she snugs up against him like a cat. Under the table, his hand strokes her just above the knee. She slips a hand up the inside of his thigh and cups his scrotum.

J.C. exhales, a grin breaking out. "You just glad to see me or is this a hernia check?"

Her boldness turns J.C. on as much as the slight pleasurable pressure. *Fuck Samson.* When she wants something, it opens up all kinds of possibilities. He bends to her ear to ask if she wants to go to the house in a little while. She listens closely, her hand tightening steadily around his balls and it begins to hurt, a discomfort that immediately increases as the rush to tumescence goes into painful reversal.

She licks her lips. "Looking for action?"

Fumbling for her wrist, J.C. gasps, "You're hurting me!"

"I should rip'm off, you shit."

He thinks he's going to faint from the pain. "Leggo. Please."

She lets go. If it weren't a public place, J.C. thinks, he would—he pushes the thought away. Payback later. He closes his eyes, takes a deep, steadying breath, and finds a thin smile for her.

"Jesus, D., chill out. What's your problem?"

"How come some guys are so nice until you put out for them, then presto, you turn into a slut? Can't wait to tell their homo buddies who they banged, what little sleaze went down on them? You know anybody like that?"

The light glimmers for J.C. and he relaxes.

"You been talking to Samson?"

"Sure. And you, you prick, you been talking to anybody who'll stand still for it."

J.C. frowns. "Really, baby, you gotta chill out. How 'bout a 'lude?" He begins to grope a pocket for a little med. "You know, you shouldn't let other people's hangups get to you. It's no big deal." He presses the cap in her hand.

Funny how *shiny* they feel. It's not a real 'lude—those are about impossible to get anymore—just some rip-off junk, margarine for butter. That scared little tremor in her tummy is still there. This will make it go away. She helps herself to his Pepsi to wash it down.

"Lemme get you one," he says, jumping up to go to the counter. When he comes back, he pats her leg. "Better?"

"Better."

Relieved to be back in charge, he grins. "Lookin' for something?"

"You never forget."

"Ah, baby." His finger smoothes her eyebrow. "Grey says you're not partying."

"Not till hoop season's over. I can't afford to miss any more games. Just need my b.c., is all."

"I might want something special," he says.

Sure he will. He'll need to get back for her giving him a hard time. The best she can do is get everything she can for it.

She moves his hand up her thigh and speaks in a light mocking tone. "Pig."

He laughs. "Hey, I was just talking you up. Cross my heart, baby, it's just between the two of us from now on."

She lets him squeeze her breast before he slides out of the booth. He does it hard too, on purpose.

"Is tomorrow night still hoop season? I'm going to Lewiston, do a little partying. This high school scene is getting old, you know? You want to go with me?"

She shakes her head no. "Not this time. How 'bout Wednesday? After practice?"

"Too bad," he says. "All right, I should be recovered by then. You're skinning it though. I gotta split or I'm gonna be late. See ya around."

She doesn't bother to watch him leave—he has to work the room as he goes, leaning into people's faces, flashing the smile, gladhanding jerking them off too cool for school blah blah she could tell them a few things about Mr. Smooth. If she's skinning it, it's his doing. He could give it to her early if he wanted. It's just more payback for getting hard on him. He's holding out on her to make her nervous, squeeze her tit a little harder. No big deal. Mr. No Big Deal. Right. Every fucking breath is a big deal to him. He makes deals with his own dick when he has to pee.

16

■ ■ ■

Through the Stutter of Black Light, the
Mutant skywalks over the surf boom of the music and the choreic
crosscurrent of dancers. When the black light blinks over her, it lu-
minesces the white of her T-shirt, slit in the front to reveal the
cones of her red brassiere and the white spandex capri-length
tights underneath her raveled jeans and jumps along her chains
and the dancing miniature plastic skeleton in her ear. The lacy
cups and the cross-threads of the jeans, the leather laces from her
high-tops to her thighs and the mime's malevolent pinched diamond drawn around her right eye flash black. The effect is a weird
striptease, the lighter clothing become a more naked skin, lace tit-
ties and jungle stripes modeling the shape of her body, the crotch
of her jeans a black delta in the confluence of the silver flowing
chains.

Shivering over the turbulence, the tight wire of the lighting catwalk vibrates with the music. It feels trippy to spy unnoticed, at
least so far, above the crowd. She has a god's-eye view of a dozen
interactions, approaches, rejections, tiffs, making-ups. Who's making time, who's getting panicky, bored, wrecked. Pete Fosse snarl-
ing at Cady Flemming, Cady shoving his class ring halfway up his
nose in fury before stalking off. Sarah Kendall with her tongue in

Rick Woods's ear, Rick squeezing the amazing Kendall ass with both hands. The Jandreau twins targeting Todd Gramolini as victim of the night—Melanie gives him the come-on and Melissa moves in as soon as Todd loses his grip on his skepticism that this is happening to him. After fifteen minutes of hot-eyed attention from the twins, he has a stupid grin on his face and an obvious boner. And he's unaware of Deb Michaud observing the circus with growing fury. Bither herds Kerry Hatch onto the floor and proceeds to make a spectacle of himself doing his Vanilla Ice act, until poor Kerry is cringing and peeking at him through her fingers.

The chaperones look as sappy and chagrined as ever, anxiously guarding the punchbowl but not closely enough. While the Mutant covers her mouth so she won't laugh aloud, under cover of the closed bleachers, Jimmy Bouchard pisses in an empty soda can. Sidling up to the punchbowl while a confederate distracts the chaperones, Jimmy spikes it with vitamin pee. Wherever the chaperones aren't looking, kids spill soft drinks from cans and bottles into sinks and fountains, onto the parking lot or into the bushes around the building, and top the remaining soda with popskull vodka or rum. From her perch, the Mutant can smell the alcohol.

Grey hangs on Jimmy and the bikers. She had wanted to go to Lewiston with J.C. but he had ignored first her hints and then an outright request, and finally told her to fuck off, he was sick of her whining. Just the thing to make her bite her lip and stick her chin out. Out to the parking lot repeatedly, she's gotten shrill and ragged.

Lexie too has been turned down. J.C. can get into bars with his fake ID but she's just too obviously underage to pass. But she isn't Grey. She's going to prove herself to him. So the younger girl works the crowd, flirting, taking a sip of a spiked soda here and there, making connections for J.C. All the soda she's drinking seems to take her to the girls' room repeatedly. Guys loiter outside the lavatories, seemingly waiting for girlfriends. Within a tight radius of the lavs, Lexie lightens her handbag and fattens J.C.'s wallet.

■ ■ ■

As midnight approaches, there are departures to parties in various homes or parking spots where the New Year can be greeted with California fizz out of sight of authorities. People come in from the parking lot with juiced sodas in their hands and bottles of sparkling cider to blow off when the year changes. From above, the Mutant watches the foaming geysers erupt from shaken bottles at the appointed instant of celebration.

A few minutes later, she tromps down the snow on the outdoor court. The parking lot is emptying steadily but there are still quite a few kids hanging on, and canned music erupts spasmodically as the people exit the gym.

Grey and Lexie peer through the fence. Grey lights a cigarette, drops it, picks it up, muttering to herself.

Lexie rattles the fence. "Mutant, you evil bitch, come on. Let's go find a party before they're all fucking over!"

The Mutant slams her ball against the backboard. The ball squishes into the snow and lies dead. The Mutant picks it up, places it carefully and then kicks it over the fence. It sails in a high, graceful curve, thunks down on the roof of an unoccupied truck and then bounces onto the hood of a Chevy Blazer.

Pete Fosse erupts from the Blazer, followed by Todd Gramolini, Tim Kasten, Bither and Billy Rank.

Billy scoops up the ball. His eyes are as opaque and rubbery as the ball he holds up over his head with a sloppy grin.

Loping across the lot, the Mutant jumps for the ball but Pete lunges forward to pluck it away.

Rank laughs foolishly.

"No way." Pete tips her ball into his Blazer. "I'm keeping it."

The Mutant shrugs and raises one finger.

The guys hoot mockingly.

"She told you, Pee-ter," Bither observes.

Grey and Lexie pick their way, stumbling and giggling, from the outdoor court.

"Party time," Pete murmurs to Todd.

Pete inserts himself between Lexie and Grey, an arm around the waist of each girl.

Todd flings a convivial arm around the Mutant's shoulders. "Ladies, it's cold out here. We do anything to warm you up?"

The Mutant snorts derisively and ducks out from under Gramolini's arm.

Lexie squints at Pete. "If you got the bucks and some matches, I got something to build a fire with."

She opens her bag and he peeks in. "No shit. How much?"

Lexie hangs on his neck to whisper in his ear.

"Pass the plate," he tells Todd.

"Not here," Todd objects. "Someplace private."

"Count me out," Tim Kasten says. "See ya around, guys."

They watch Tim lope across the parking lot and catch up with other friends of his.

Pete squeezes Lexie. "How's a little trip to camp sound?"

Bither and Billy Rank clamber into the Blazer. Pete picks up Lexie and passes her, wriggling and squealing, back to them and Grey climbs in behind her. Leaning into the open front seat, the Mutant makes a grab for her ball. Behind her, Gramolini grasps her by the waist and boosts her to the front seat. He jumps in behind her and drops an arm over her shoulders again, giving her an ironic little smile. Pete takes the wheel.

The Mutant kicks back, heels to the dashboard. Fosses' camp. Bound to be warmer than the Mill. She doesn't have to do anything but be friendly until they get there, then she can tell them all to fuck off and find a corner to crash in. They won't stop partying just to drag her back to Greenspark.

Todd slips a hand under her T-shirt. "Want a beer?"

Scornfully, she removes his hand and he laughs.

Pete straightens up behind the wheel. "Play it smart, guys. Beer on the floor, no horseshit. I mean it."

The Mutant glances behind her at Lexie. Bither's whispering in little Lexie's ear. Eyes wet and blurry, Grey is smoking a butt. Billy has the glassy stupid look of a mutt thrilled to be getting a ride in the family car.

"Pete," the Mutant says.

"Yeah?"

"Lexie's thirteen."

He winks. "I won't tell if you won't."

Lexie kicks the seat behind the Mutant. "Mind your own business, bitch."

The guys laugh the way guys do.

Pete squeezes the Mutant's knee. "Relax, Gauthier. This is going to be a good time. I got a couple bottles of champagne."

Geez. If Flem hadn't picked New Year's Eve to have a bustup with Pete, Cady could have gotten blasted on Pete's champagne and had a legitimate reason to puke. It is a thought to make the Mutant smile.

■ ■ ■

Fosses' camp is nicer than the house on Depot Street—two bedrooms and a loft, a living room, a kitchen, two full bathrooms. A television set and stereo components sitting there unused most of the winter. Knotty pine and chintz and a fireplace. From the first, Pete is nervous about being there, threatening murder if any one of them leaves any sign someone's been in the place. Won't let them build a fire on the stone hearth. He wouldn't hesitate at a nice romantic fire, the Mutant suspects, if it were just him and Cady. The party is an impulse, a way to fill his suddenly empty night.

He does allow the Mutant to turn on the tuner in the stereo rack and find a year's-end countdown. He pops the corks on the champagne and they pass it around, drinking directly from the bottles. The air is sweetened with its cidery scent. At the coffee table, he rolls the weed he bought from Lexie into joints. When he lights one up, the Mutant slips away into the kitchen. The smell of it is too enticing. All she needs is a contact high to make sharing it seem harmless. A restless rummage through the cupboards turns up a glass jar of popcorn and a little oil. Air popper in another cupboard. So she makes popcorn.

Todd wanders in. Leans against a counter and sips a beer. He offers it to her and when she shakes her head, smiles and raises it to her.

"Saint Sam'd be proud of you," he mocks.

The Mutant shrugs. "Nothing to do with him. Just staying healthy, that's all."

He smiles knowingly. "Whatever. I don't mean anything about Sam. So he's got a few hangups. So don't we all. I've known him to tip a brew now and again but since his sister sort of went over the edge, he's a little tight-assed about it. His mom's a religious nut too. He probably caught a little of that. Who gives a shit as long as he can sink a three-pointer when we need it?"

Lexie shrieks happily from the living room—somebody's squeezed her tit or goosed her or something. Todd shifts nervously from foot to foot. Runs a meditative fingertip around the channel in the lid of his Bud can.

"Tell you the truth, I still like Deb. She got kind of possessive and I wasn't ready for that shit, you know? But we still like each other all the same and I'd feel seriously weird having anything to do with her little sister. I mean, I remember when Lexie had a mouthful of braces and no tits."

The popcorn begins to fire from the throat of the air popper.

She nudges the bowl closer to it and picks up a stray blossom of popcorn from the counter.

Todd's hands fall lightly on her hips from behind and one hand slides down over her chains to her crotch.

"Mmmm," he murmurs, hot yeasty breath in her ear, "not much to you but it's all put together right. When you gave up getting high, 'd you give up going down?"

She pistons her elbow rudely back into his solar plexus and he gasps and backs off.

"You get a cramp in your brain thinking that up?" she mocks him.

He rubs his diaphragm thoughtfully and then grins. With a laugh, he reaches past her to scoop up a handful of the fresh popcorn.

She tips out a smaller bowl for herself and hands him the rest to deliver to the living room. Nibbling the slightly tough puffs—kernels stale from sitting in that glass jar for months—the Mutant pokes around some more and finds a can of coffee grounds in the freezer. Reads the directions on the can carefully and starts a pot in the Mr. Coffee machine on the counter. Never made anything but instant before at home. Pete's dad is a lawyer of course and they're all rich, which is why the Fosses have a houseful of appliances keeping cold for the summer. The heady smell of the coffee mingles with the drift of marijuana from the living room.

Pete sticks his head in the kitchen. "Coffee? When did you go all domestic?"

With another charge of popcorn spitting from the machine, she ignores him.

He waggles a roach at her invitingly. "Good shit."

The Mutant waves it away.

"What is it?" he asks. "You in a bad mood or you got your period or what?"

"Fuck off," she answers.

He shrugs and goes away.

When she brings the second batch of popcorn to the living room, Billy is muttering to himself and moodily shaking open beer cans, looking for a forgotten mouthful. The others have disappeared into the nearest bedroom and taken the dope with them. There's nothing left on the coffee table but a roach and some crumbs. Billy picks up the roach and offers it to her. When she shakes her head, he looks at it and then sticks it in his mouth and swallows it.

"I'm fucked up," he explains seriously.

She pats him on the shoulder and flops onto the couch. He slides down onto the floor next to her and rests his head against the outside of her knee. The tang of the weed standing in the air smells good; she breathes deep. Billy laughs and reaches for the popcorn bowl.

Pete comes out of the bedroom. Climbs onto the back of the couch and opens his legs to pull her back between them. She leans back, slips her hands under his knees and tips him backward. He goes down cursing and flailing, comes up laughing.

"Cold, cold." He shivers, hugging himself. "You didn't used to be so cold. Is it true you've got a ring in your cunt now?"

Face flaming suddenly red, Billy Rank makes a strangling noise.

Sardonically, the Mutant flips Pete a double eagle.

He shrugs. "Ah hell, you're a lousy lay anyway. Good thing I unloaded my gun already. Guess you'll have to see what Rank's up to." His derisive tone suggests Billy isn't up to much.

Billy hides his face in his hands. "I couldn't help it. I'm too baked, Pete."

Pete leans over the couch to tug the trailing tags of her headrag. "It's gotten very freaky in there. Grey's a circus all by herself. Come on in and watch a little while—maybe it'll warm you a little."

"You're an asshole, Pete," the Mutant says. "You touch me again, I'll tear your dick off."

Pete laughs and wanders back toward the bedroom.

The Mutant finds her coat and tucks herself into a curl under it on the couch, and closes her eyes. In a moment, Billy nudges her, shivering.

"I'm cold," he complains.

She lets him snuggle next to her and share her coat like a blanket; it's nice to have his body warmth, even if he smells a little sour. The noises from the bedroom rise above the countdown of this year's hits from the radio. She closes her eyes a little tighter but she can still hear too much. At one point, Billy moans and she opens her eyes and his eyes are open too, wide and fearful. He blinks and wipes at them. "Oh, jeez," he murmurs and he clutches her tight and buries his face between her breasts. Wrecked as Billy is, he only understands he is scared; the why is beyond him. Reluctantly, she lets one hand come to rest over his ear, in a gesture that is as close to comforting him as she can bring herself. She hates guys, she thinks, she really hates them. They are all pricks, nothing but pricks.

The first one out of the bedroom is Todd, who heads for the bathroom. She hears him throwing up. Bither staggers out, and keeps on going, right outdoors. In a little while, Todd emerges from the bathroom and Bither comes in from the cold and the two of them slump into chairs, heads back, eyes closed, looking sick.

Pete appears and starts nipping at everyone's heels, harrying them to tidy the place up and get a move on so he can haul ass for home. The Mutant looks in at the bedroom door. In the light of a single low-wattage bedside lamp, Grey sits in a wicker chair, smoking a butt. Her knees are tight together in her tight jeans, one hand rests palm up on the opposite thigh, and she is reapplying her lipstick. Her mouth looks bruised. A crumpled paper towel is stained with the makeup she has removed. Pausing, she uses her free hand to grope for a lighted cigarette resting in the ashtray. She has an embarrassed little smile on her face.

"Okay?" the Mutant asks.

Grey's smile broadens, wavers, and then steadies. She sniffs.

The bed is unmade—stripped of linen for the winter and encased in a a zippered plastic envelope and there is no disorder but Lexie is wiping the plastic with a wad of paper toweling. She is meticulous, precise, almost polishing it. Stoned. Lexie stands back to look at the mattress and it passes inspection. Then she peers at herself in the mirror over the dresser. She traces the edges of her mouth—like Grey's, rather swollen-looking—wiping away a trace of lipstick that has overrun the margins of her lips.

"Christ," she says, "some party. Beeg fucking jocks. Buncha limpdicks. I thought my jaw was going to lock." Glancing at the Mutant, Lexie grins, and pulls a wad of bills from her jeans pocket. "J.C.'s gonna shit," she brags, "look what I took off those assholes. I told'm Grey and me weren't giving it away. Shit, they got a bargain." Lexie giggles. "Hey, the idea of paying for it got Pete harder than anything either one of us did."

Todd comes in and empties the ashtray on the bedstand into a plastic garage bag; he scoops first some empty beer cans and then gingerly picks up a champagne bottle from the floor. Lexie suddenly grabs his forearm and he flinches but she only wants to drop her wad of paper towels into his trash bag.

Grey starts to stand up and her feet go out from under her. Todd and the Mutant between them catch her as she collapses.

"Baked," Lexie snickers.

■ ■ ■

In the back of the Blazer, the Mutant snugs up against Billy Rank and closes her suddenly heavy eyes. Gotten just enough of free-floating smoke to make her sleepy. Practice tomorrow oh 'god. Lexie and Todd are into the front with Pete. The guys have shoveled Grey into the back too. Bither is on her other side from the Mutant.

"She pukes on me," he threatens, "I'll puke too."

He quiets when he locates a forgotten six-pack and breaks it open.

"Gimme one a those," Pete demands.

Bither takes one, holds it up to Billy, who moans and wards it off with his palms. Sniggering, Bither passes the rest forward. Pete pops one; Todd puts the remainder on the floor.

Before they reach the main road, the Blazer slips suddenly into a slow-motion slew. Pete, swearing, spins the wheel into the skid, overdoes it and all at once the Chevy is off the road, jolting into the low banks of snow that fill the ditches. Once into the snow, Pete proceeds to dig the Blazer in up to its hubcaps. They all pile out again so the guys can have a try at pushing it out.

"Great driving," the Mutant mutters to Pete and he backhands her so suddenly she is in the snow with her face hurting before she can react.

"You got a big fucking mouth and I'm tired of it!" he shouts at the girl sprawling at his feet.

Reactions dulled by intoxication, the others are slow to even realize what is happening. Pete steps forward threateningly. Todd moves then to try to restrain him. For an instant, she thinks it will work, before Pete throws off the lighter Todd and lunges toward her.

She scrambles away and he tackles her and knocks the wind out of her. He uses his weight deliberately to keep her down. The struggle excites him. He grows angry in frustration as he is hampered by her clothing and rams his zipper-armored hard-on into her crotch to hurt her.

"Fuck her!" Lexie shrieks. "Go ahead, fuck her!"

Suddenly she can breathe again as Todd and Billy yank Pete off her. Billy grabs her. Panting and staggering, the two of them hold each other up while Pete and Todd shove each other around enough to get tired out. They are too loaded to land effective blows. Finally Pete leans against the side of the Blazer. Sullenly, Todd finds a tree to lean against while he catches his breath and takes a leak.

"Somebody better go call for a tow," he says as he clumsily buttons up. "Where's the closest public phone? The Narrows?"

Instinctively, Pete covers his ass. "We should call Sweetser's or it'll be Bigger or his old man who turns up."

The Mutant volunteers.

"I'll go too," Billy offers but he can barely stand up.

She squeezes his hand and assures him she can take care of it. He'll only slow her down.

"Let's go back to the camp," Todd says. "Stay warm."

"No way." Pete's agitated again. "It's all cleaned up. It's half a mile back and nobody's wearing anything on their feet but sneakers. We can run the engine to stay warm."

No one wants to argue about it with him.

The Mutant bolts down the road, suddenly aware she is soaked with sweat, shaking with adrenaline. Lexie was right. Some party.

17

■ ■ ■

A Blue Moon in the Frozen Black Sky
bleaches the furniture into ghostly ectoplasm. It scintillates on the
Christmas tree like a blacklight dream but it's real—what Sam sees
when his eyelids snap up like cartoon windowshades at the blat of
the telephone. Half asleep, he rolls over on the living room couch,
right hand dropping over the instrument. Squinting at the radio-
alarm clock, he sees it is three forty-eight. It's still next year. He's
been home and in bed since he and his father finished jump-
starting the dead batteries of half a dozen vehicles of late revelers
in the parking lot at the Hair of the Dog when the roadhouse
closed at two.

The liquid rumble of Maxie Sweetser clearing his throat follows
Sam's sleepy hello. Maxie expectorates noisily. "Hiya, Sammy,"
Maxie wheezes. "Wake you up?"

Sam washes his face with the dry palm of his hand. "Just dozing, Mr. Sweetser."

"Lookie, kiddo, I gotta call from some dumbunny got a four-
wheel-drive dug in on your side a the line. Fire Road Twenny.
Doan know why she didn't call you to start." Maxie blows his
nose enthusiastically. "Doan see no good season for me to come
all the hell and gone over there when you're ri' chair. I got all three

a my rigs out now hauling idjits outta ditches over ta here. You want this 'un?"

"Sure. Thanks, Maxie."

"Think nothin' of it. Regards to your dad and tell him that slant-six is chugging right along, so he got that one right. An' Happy New Year too."

"Yessir. Happy New Year to you."

Clutching his jacket, Sam scrawls a note. He half expects Reuben to come downstairs, summoned by the phone, but the household still sleeps when he lets himself out. Fine as it would be to have his father's company, they have worked together all evening, a tough night, and Reuben is still recuperating. Which is why Sam is on the couch covering the calls instead of his father.

Fire Road 20. South end of the lake, half a mile from the Narrows, where some locals still hold on to a narrow band of old camps in the face of the seductive rise in the value of their waterfront property. The land is low and swampy, the roads minimally maintained. This time of year, whether frozen or mucky, the dirt road is impassable to anything but four-wheel drive. Once you've gotten a four-wheel-drive stuck, though, you're really in the shit.

The frozen night is clean and pure, shadows sharp-edged in the second witchy moonlight of the month, terrain creamy and luscious with snow. Sam's very awake in a way that feels good. There's a secret pleasure in having the world to himself.

At first sight he recognizes Fosse's Blazer, up to its hubcaps in a snow-filled ditch. Great. Just the asshole he'd been hoping to spend some quality time with instead of sleeping. Pete's folks have a camp down this road, he suddenly recalls. Somehow he doubts the Fosses were having a cookout there tonight.

The Blazer's engine idles to warm the passengers, windows steamed, familiar music from its radio sounding smothered and fragmented. He pulls up behind it and hops out. When he raps on the driver's window, Pete is tipping back a beer. Startled, Pete drops it. His lips form the word *shit*. Sam opens the door and Pete nearly falls out, tumbling down the driving climax of Zep's "Stairway to Heaven" that spills from the radio.

"Oh fuck." Pete's can of Bud tumbles to the road. The air is immediately tangy with marijuana. "Sambo! Jesus!"

Sam grabs Pete by the back of the neck, yanks him from behind the wheel and throws him up against the side of the Blazer to the accompaniment of Sam's absolutely least favorite Zep lyric.

"Shit!" Pete gasps. "What's your fucking problem?"

"You are, asshole."

The others scramble from the Blazer. Todd Gramolini, Bither, Billy Rank, the little Michaud girl. Last out is the Mutant, with a crooked smile on her painted and chained face. Sam covers the shock of her being among them by leaning past her to check out the interior. Shasta Grey slumps in the back seat. Passed out. The rest of them are all wasted to one degree or another. The inside of the vehicle is smoggy with smoke and littered with empties.

"Gauthier, you numb cunt," Pete complains, "I told you to call Sweetser."

A large hand takes Pete by the throat.

"Shut up." Sam growls through gritted teeth. "Just shut the fuck up."

When Sam lets go, Pete stumbles away from the vehicle into Todd Gramolini, who catches him by the armpits. They stagger in a grotesque dance, both of them trying to stay upright. Bither backs toward the safety of the woods. The Mutant puts her toe out and Bither trips over it, flat on his back. Billy Rank sways in confusion.

Sam kicks the Blazer's rear wheel. It rocks with the force of the blow.

"Take it easy, Sambo," Todd pleads. "We were just partying."

Sam's fist swings up under Todd's nose. "You stupid dink. I should leave you out here. Fuck you all. I'm going to."

Striding to the wrecker, he hauls into it and throws it into reverse. A few yards back, he stops and sits in fuming silence. He pounds the wheel with his fist.

They stand there in his lights hugging themselves and stamping their sneakered feet against the cold. The Mutant in her chains, looking like a clown in Satan's own circus. At Christmastime she gives him a line about staying straight to stay healthy and here she is, a whole nine days later, partying her skinny ass off with his own teammates. Maybe she thinks he's so dazzled by her tits in that red bra he'll believe any amount of shit.

They stare at him with all the acuity of a riff of stoned Zepheads at a laser show. Dazed and confused. You thuds want a light show, climb this fucking stairway to heaven. He flicks his brights up in their eyes. Flinching, they throw up their hands in the familiar horror-flick gesture of defense, as if he had crossed his fingers against them.

The Mutant emerges from the glaring lights. She opens the other door and climbs into the wrecker. She sits on her knees, head cocked like a curious puppy, the tag ends of her headrag on one side like a big floppy ear. "What are you gonna do?"

"Quit. Quit! You people don't give a shit about anything except partying. So go party. I got a life, I don't need this shit. You got no right to ask me to cover up for you when you blow off the rules. How old's Michaud anyway? I don't even want to know if one of those bozos screwed her. Probably they all did. You got weed in that truck, you got booze, you're all fucked up. Grey's fucking passed out. You know what kind of box I'm in now? Now I got knowledge those stupid dinks were out here blowing dope, they had some underage kid out here, got her loaded and probably gangbanged her. Why'd you have to come pull this shit in my town?"

"You gonna leave us here or not?"

"Why the hell not? You put me up Shit Creek without it bothering you too much. You march back and tell your asshole buddies they can walk their wasted asses right down to the Narrows again and call Maxie or the cops or their mummies and daddies or W. Axl Rose and the United States Marines, I give a shit."

The Mutant sinks back and rests her cheek against the seat.

He refuses to look at her anymore. "Get out of my truck. I've had it up to here with you too."

"No. I didn't do anything."

"You're here. You didn't mistake Pete's Blazer for the last bus to Depot Street, did you?"

"There wasn't anyplace else to go. I didn't drink anything. I couldn't help breathing the smoke. I kept my pants on, not that it's any of your business."

"Oh, then, I guess you get a gold star," Sam gibes. "Now get out of my rig."

The Mutant crawls across the seat. "What was I supposed to do?" She rests her head on his thigh like a repentant puppy. "She was willing, for fuck's sake. I just wanted a warm place to hang out so I didn't have to go home."

He closes his eyes. The knot of her headrag digs into his thigh. The tips of his fingers pass down her jawline to tickle the chains between her nose and ear. Any more time out here in the cold, she'll get sick again. Not that she doesn't deserve to get sick, the lying druggie slut.

In silence he chains the Blazer and extracts it from the ditch. When he's finished, he motions Lexie back of the Blazer.

"I'm taking the girls home. You guys help Grey into my truck."

Pete and Todd look at each other, shrug and do as they're told.

Lexie grins. "Ta ta." As she sashays past Sam, he grabs her handbag. She yelps in protest but he searches it anyway, takes out several baggies of weed and pitches them into the woods.

"Shithead," she shrieks.

Before she can get in next to Lexie, he tosses the Mutant's bag too, turning up nothing for his trouble but a smug smile when he hands it back to her. Probably ditched whatever she was carrying—if only cigarettes boosted from the supermarket. Amazingly, she has her basketball with her. Great. They can all go to the high school and play HORSE on the outdoor court. He can't wait.

He crooks a finger at Pete. "That'll be thirty-five bucks, asshole."

With an exasperated moan, Pete strips his wallet, bums the rest from the others. Billy Rank smiles dazedly as Pete shoves his hands into Billy's jeans to pick his pockets.

Sam folds the money into his jacket pocket.

"You fuckups better haul your idiot asses back to Fosses' camp and crash there so you won't be picked up OUI and get kicked off the team. And if you put it in the ditch again, don't bother to call. You can freeze your dicks off. Oh, and fuck you all."

Pete's pale face flushes with anger. "Fuck you too, Samson."

"Shut up, Pete," Todd mutters. "Shut the fuck up."

"Whose idea was this anyway?" Bither complains.

"I don't feel good," Billy Rank says in a clear plaintive voice. Covering his mouth to cough politely, he clutches Bither for support and vomits all over him.

■ ■ ■

Like a faraway star, the porchlight at the Greys' farmhouse gleams weakly. Grey slung over his shoulder, Sam pounds on it. Her grandfather, a bent old man with white stubble on his chin, comes to the door.

"She's loaded," Sam says.

The old man backs up, gesturing toward a rump-sprung couch. A light comes on upstairs and a middle-aged woman appears in her bathrobe and slippers at the top of the stairs.

"Damn girl's drunk as a sailor," the old man rasps.

"Is that Sam Styles I hear?" the woman demands.

"She was with some people I pulled out of a ditch," Sam says. "Guys weren't fit to drive. I thought I'd better bring the girls with them home."

"Boy's driving a wrecker," the old man says. "Couple other girls out there."

"All right," the woman says. "Thank you, Sam Styles. Dad, you put a quilt over Shasta, will you? I've had about enough of this crap from her. She comes to tomorrow, she's gonna hear some home truths. Goddamn it, I got the early shift."

In Greenspark, Lexie slides out down the block from the Michauds' ranch house and Sam watches her trip down the sidewalk. Before she can get her key in the front door, her old man jerks the door open from inside and grabs her by the back of the neck. She yelps and disappears behind the slamming door.

The Mutant relaxes on the seat.

"I don't want to go home," she tells him. "Let's go someplace. The Mill. Or maybe you know someplace. I don't care, just so long as it's warm. We can make out and I'll put you in a better mood."

"I don't want to go someplace and make out with you. You think I want those guys' seconds?"

"Oh fuck you!" she exclaims. "I told you I didn't do anything with them."

"That must be a new experience. Jesus, Deanie. You hang out with wastes like Chapin, you pull crap like this. And those guys, they're no better. So maybe they didn't do anything so terrible, getting loaded, making a couple of willing girls. You can argue that if you want. Somewhere along the way I got the idea fucking a wasted kid who's probably jailbait is dirty pool. Sleazy. A shitty thing to do. Am I getting this into language you understand? And weed's illegal, and so is booze for anybody our age. What if you'd gotten busted?"

"Nobody got busted," she reassures him. "Chill out. Nobody gives a shit."

"Bottom line, huh? Is that good enough for you? It's not good enough for me."

"So far as I can see," she snaps, "almost nothing is fucking good enough for you." Curiosity darkens her eyes. "You're not serious about quitting?"

"Never more."

With a sigh, she slips across the seat to pillow her head on him again. He wants to push her away but he can't. Reluctantly he cups one big hand over the side of her face, fingers the skeleton dangling from her ear. He can feel the chains that cross her left cheek and the rings in her ear where they terminate against his thigh. When he glances at her, her eyes are closed. The starving diamond that stars her right eye is an explosion of darkness like a terrible wound.

He feels it in his stomach, a black rip of pain and confusion. She says all she wanted was not to go home, just someplace warm. If she'd gone to the Mill, she'd have found the space heater he left in the cubby and she could have stayed there. How long were they all at Fosses' camp? Time enough. What's he going to have to listen to in the locker room?

From the corner, though the snow in the yard is much trafficked and littered with empties, the house on Depot Street is quiet. Party over or moved somewhere else.

Clutching her basketball, she slips from the wrecker before he can go around to open the door for her. He watches her go, does not call *you're welcome* after her, and she throws him no mocking birds, just disappears into the huddle of that grim little house.

Fuck her. He should go to the Mill and tear that fucking hoop down. Fuck them all. He throws the truck into reverse. They don't want it bad enough. Fuck them all.

■ ■ ■

In deference to the holiday, practice on New Year's is at mid-morning. The Mutant is at the Corner when Sam wheels through downtown, and she bears a peace offering of sorts—cocoa. Pulling over, he accepts the cups she hands him and she slings her duffel in and climbs up after it. The cab fills with the sweet comforting scent of cocoa.

"Thanks," he says shortly.

She shrugs. "Still pissed?"

Not deigning to answer, he turns up the radio. Just the sight of her is enough to make him sick to his stomach again.

Coach's wagon is in the lot. Pete's Blazer too.

Rick hauls in behind them and Sam warms his hands in his pockets and waits for him at the edge of the parking lot while the Mutant hastens in out of the cold.

"How was last night?"

Rick grins. "Started the night at Kendalls' with Sarah trying to soften up a wheel of Brie in the microwave. Frigging thing blew all over the inside like a big cheese bomb."

Sam laughs.

"Thought I was gonna herniate myself trying not to laugh too hard." Rick glances at Sam curiously. "Went fine after that. How 'bout you? You look like you were up all night."

"Yeah."

Punching the door bar, Sam opens it for Rick and they step out of the cold into the cleaning-fluid smell of the school on break.

"You do some smoke last night, Rick?"

The quiet casual question brings Rick to a halt.

"Don't ask me that, Sambo."

"Is that a yes?"

Rick's gaze is steady. "Fuck you, Sambo. I told you not to ask."

"You signed a contract—"

"Which you know I've violated before, so what's the big deal? It's a stupid piece of paper they make us sign so we can play. Means shit. You think a little smoke's gonna affect my game? That's bullshit. Bullshit. So mind your own fucking business."

Sam nods as if Rick has just given him good advice on a play.

It only makes Rick angrier and he stalks away.

The janitor has opened the gym and most of the players are already there, exchanging tales of New Year's Eve. Todd and Pete sit on the bleachers, in subdued conversation with each other. They glance up at Sam, look down hastily. Kevin Bither pretends not to see him at all. Billy Rank squats on the floor, eyes glazed with a paralytic hangover. The entire squad is here, along with most of the girls and a fair number of ambitious jay vee players of both sexes.

Sam walks through the gym to the locker room, past Coach's office—no Coach inside, for which he's thankful—and sweeps the contents of his gym locker into his duffel. Going past Coach's office again, he slips under the door the laconic resignation he printed out in his awkward hand when he gave up trying to sleep.

A silence falls behind him as he crosses the gym again, still wearing his jacket, duffel slung on his shoulder.

"Sam!" Rick calls, in sudden alarm, as the doors swing closed between them.

They slam open as Rick races after him, catching him at the

outside doors. The Mutant's only a few steps behind Woods, having paused to grab her coat and duffel.

"Where are you going? What about practice?"

"I quit," Sam confides and steps out, smiling slightly, into the cold.

■ ■ ■

In the doorway, Rick stares after him. The Mutant slips under Rick's extended arm, which holds the door open, to scoot after Sam.

"Hey," she calls. "You're my ride. You can't leave yet."

"Oh? See me throwing my gear in the cab? See me getting in? See this key? Makes this heap go varrooom."

She whips around the truck and clambers in breathlessly as he throws the truck into gear and skids across the lot toward the exit road.

"Jesus!" she yelps. "Slow down!"

Sam tromps the accelerator, deliberately spinning them into a donut while she shrieks and throws out her arms in an infantile reflex. He swings them casually onto the access road and she starts to laugh.

"Hot shit!"

"You wanted a ride," he says. All at once, he feels fine. Lighter. Needed a little relief from gravity.

Sobering, she tucks up onto the seat. "You're nuts. You can't quit."

"Sure I can. I just did."

"You're too good."

He laughs. "Thought you were going to tell me the team needs me."

"That was the next thing I was going to say. Hey, if I can quit smoking and partying for the sake of my team, then maybe you put your team ahead of whatever hair you got across your ass."

"Quit smoking and partying? Right. What was that last night?"

"No big deal if you don't make it one."

Sam shakes his head. "I'm not gonna argue with you, Deanie. You twist everything around to suit yourself."

She grins and toes his thigh. "That's how you win arguments."

"Not with me. Where you going? Home? Or you want me to take you back to practice?"

"I'm not going back to practice until you do. In fact, I'm not getting out of this truck until you agree you're not quitting."

"You'll get out when I put you out," Sam says. "Anyway, I was looking for a reason to quit. I'm sick of basketball running my life."

"Liar, liar, pants on fire."

She should know.

His hands slacken on the wheel and he drums at it restlessly. He's free. He feels unjammed—unchained. His life is his own again. It feels so good, he doesn't know why he didn't do it sooner. Hours and hours suddenly his again. Hours he can turn into buckage. Another set of hands, they can take in more business at the garage. He can help his father at the same time he's earning the insurance on the bike. He'll have time to put into the farmhouse. It seems so obvious now, like pulling a loose thread.

A few blocks ahead is the turn that could take them to the Mill. While he was hauling her ass home after midnight, she didn't mention finding the hoop so he guesses she hasn't. His anger at her was so great, if she'd brought it up, he'd have swallowed his tongue rather than own up to having done diddly for her. But now his mood is as balmy as the air of the melt after a storm. He's a free man, and heady with it.

"Been to the Mill since Sunday?"

The change of subject focuses her intently. "Why?"

"I left you a surprise there. Sort of a belated Christmas present."

She sits up straight. "Take me there then."

They park the truck in the playground lot. The turrets, castellations and slides are gingerbread, sugarfrosted with the recent snow. The air crackles and there is a blue cast to everything that makes him think of last night's New Year's moon. Sam pauses to collect his basketball from the floor of the cab. The Mutant trips down the path toward the Mill. Catching up with her as she pops the padlock, he reaches a long arm past her for the light switch.

18

■ ■ ■

A Blue Spark Explodes the switch. The shock trav-
els from the tip of his finger to deep in his armpit, causing him to
drop the ball. The crackle and the burst of light startle the Mutant
as well as himself and she jumps back and comes down on his
toes. Failing any traction on his sneakers, her feet start to go out
from under her. She begins to twist toward him, flailing for her
balance. As he scrabbles to catch her, he takes a sharp Mutant elbow in the balls. His loss of interest in rescuing her is immediate
and severe. Clutching himself, he opens his mouth and a pathetic
croak falls out.

Managing to save herself, she moans in distress. "Oh 'god!"

He waves her off. Crouching against the wall, Sam grits his
teeth and waits. And cups his sack. The only known treatment,
chiefly beneficial on a psychological level, he recalls his father saying after a summer baseball game in which Reuben, on the
mound, caught a line drive the hard way.

After the outrage in his testicles eases, he considers the numb-
ness in his right arm. Flexes it gingerly and feels only a shadowy
ache. The shock hadn't been strong enough to make him piss himself. Flexes his toes in his high-tops. Draws a deep breath, ignores
the protest as his sack shifts. Aside from aches and twinges, he

feels like somebody just jumped his batteries. Totally recharged. Buzzed.

In the meantime, the Mutant backs off. And registers the changes. Eyes widening, she wanders into the cavern of the Mill's main floor and stares at the basketball hoop on the wall. In the harsh glare of the floods, the shadow of the hoop on the wall is a hangman's loop waiting for the stickman's parts to be drawn.

She clasps her hands and whoops in delight. "You did this?"

Sam nods. He essays standing up and makes it.

The Mutant scoops up the ball and dribbles it slowly over the crumbles and cracks of the cement floor. Positioning herself almost reverently at an imaginary free-throw line, she bounces ritually on her knees and lofts it up and in with a soft, smooth motion.

He applauds.

The Mutant throws herself into a cartwheel and comes out of it into a jump, prancing about with her hands on her hips like a cheerleader. She snatches up the ball. "Come on. Even 'god can't skip practice."

The place is so grubby in the light. There's no one else to enjoy her secret court with her. A few shots wouldn't kill him. His first few shots as a free man, for whom basketball is just an occasional recreation. Then he's out of there. Ignoring the ache in his testes, he shambles toward the hoop.

With a little use his arm comes back. And now it's just a game again, he remembers why he loves it, the way it takes him out of himself. Sam the Sham becomes Sam the Slam. And scrawny Deanie Gauthier becomes the Mutant, superpowers flashing from the tips of her fingers. Once they are warmed up, they discard their jackets and she unwraps her headrag. She wears her chains heedlessly, though they snap and whip against her jeans and against the thin flesh of her cheekbone. At one point he stops her and tickles them questioningly. She shakes her head.

With a pretense of slapstick clumsiness, Sam mysteriously gets the ball into the bucket and then scratches his head in buffoonish puzzlement at his success. The Mutant becomes a dervish thug, mugging him for the ball, climbing his back to knock it from his hands, squirting between his legs and rolling away across the floor like a cartoon hedgehog, arms hugging it tight. He picks her up by the ankles and she yelps and lets it go.

"Too bad we didn't have a boombox," he says, "music to hack by."

"Yeah." She's on one foot, then the other, arms crossed. Almost shyly, she says, "You got chains."

■ ■ ■

Reminding himself by touch, he fingers the chains, the thin hard edge of braided metal warmed by his body. They are already so much a part of him he hardly ever thinks about them except when he takes them off and then puts them on again to practice. It must be the way her chains feel to her.

"All you need is an earring and a stud in your nose and some tattoos," she says.

He can't help grinning at the new and improved Sam she imagines. "S'pose I should shave my head too?"

She reacts with genuine alarm. "Don't you dare!"

He doesn't know what to say and a sudden awkwardness widens up between them. Slowly, stealing glances at her, Sam picks up his ball. "I should be going."

The Mutant shuffles her feet. "Don't quit the team."

He studies the ball. "I'll think about it."

There is a sudden flutter of relief through her thin body and then she presses herself against him and slings her arms around his neck. The quickness and enthusiasm of her embrace startle and move him. Laughing in surprise, he drops the ball to hug her back. She rises on tiptoe and quickly kisses him, startling him again. Before he can react, she pistons upward, legs scissoring around his waist like a monkey up a pole. Her mouth is hard and wet on his. He grasps her waist instinctively to keep his balance and then to hold her there against him. The taste of her is irresistible. He takes his time, savoring the slick heat of her mouth and the silky hardness of her chains against his face, his mouth when he traces them with his tongue. His hands move to her bottom and telegraph the way it tightens straight to the root of his balls.

She wriggles against him and their mouths are together again. When he lets her down and their faces lose contact, she presses against him. Butts her head into his chest, rolls her pelvis against his thigh and moves his hand underneath her shirt to her breast. It is a powerful argument, reinforced by repeated sexual fantasies about her. All the words and reasons against it have gone out of his head, leaving only a numb thick protest jammed in his throat. In a dry-mouthed daze and ferociously tumescent, he lets her lead him to the watchman's cubby.

When she sees the space heater, she raises an eyebrow mockingly. "You planned this!"

All he can do is shake his head as he scooches to turn it on. The little room is an icebox, holding the cold as if it were precious.

When he boosts her to the old countertop, she wraps her legs around him again. He kisses the tattooed death's head on her right arm and the tearful man on the moon on her left before he lifts her shirt to taste the raspberry bumps rising to little points. When she pulls the shirt over her head, her breasts rise and fall in his hands. He buries his nose in her armpits, tasting the fresh metallic salts of her sweat. Undoing his fly buttons, she cops his boner, squeezing him and stroking him.

"You're buh-buh-beautiful," he says.

"Jesus," she says, rolling her eyes and pushing him away.

A second's confusion resolves itself; she wants to unlace the rawhide ties that wrap her legs up to her thighs. It seems to take forever but he's grateful for a breather, respite from intense excitement. She does it teasingly and then laughs at the expression on his face when he realizes she has still to remove chains, jeans and the spandex tights underneath. Her fingers unhooking the chains rivet him. Watching her peel out of the jeans and tights, he scrabbles blindly at the laces of his high-tops and fumbles with his own clothes.

Once naked in the spreading glow of warmth from the little space heater, she cocks her hips and stares at him not seductively but with defiance. She seems smaller, softer, with her clothes off. She has scabs on her knees, like a little tomboy—in fact, she has a lot of bruises, all over. She's such a physical player. He has bruises himself all the time, scrapes, nicks and scratches.

At the last moment, when it comes to taking off his jeans, he shies. He begins to look around desperately for his sneakers but they seem to have walked off on some mysterious errand of their own. Buying time, he stutters the first thing in his head. "Wear your chuh-chuh-chains."

Surprised, she laughs and backs off to comply.

Her fingers have gone rusty on her so he helps her clasp the one around her waist and passes the others between her legs from back to front, his fingers brushing through the floss of her pubic hair, the heat of her vulva against his palm.

Wishing he didn't blush so easily, he tells himself this must be the most difficult thing, taking off your pants. Having that stupid thing sticking out announcing the state you're in. What if she laughs at him? What if it's all just a big come-on to her, a chance to make a fool of him? He sees instead that she is unnerved herself as she realizes that with his clothes off, he is as big as he looks, and bigger. She steels herself visibly, intensifying his distress. Peeking at her from under his lashes, he swallows with a painfully constricted throat and squeezes his cock nervously before he realizes his hand is even on it.

Again she makes the first move, pressing her body against his, chains cool against his skin, a hard edge against the crest of his hipbones shadowing the rigidity of his penis against her. She sucks his right nipple, producing such an intense sensation the hair on his arms stiffens. Suddenly she sinks to her knees, taking his cock in her fist and tonguing the head. His throat closes in panic.

"No, please, don't," he whispers.

Seeming to take no offense, she does stop. She draws him down to the cot. It shudders under their combined weight. She's so narrow, so much smaller than he is.

He tries to remember the mechanics as he understands them. Lubrication. The lush crinkle of hair on her pubis seems to part naturally as he rolls his fingertips through it but when he touches the small protuberance of her button directly, she jerks violently. Hastily he lifts his thumb.

She settles down against him again. His thick fingertips probe crevices, separate damp folded wings, silky inside. He closes his eyes to help visualize the structures his fingers inform. Finger finds an aperture, a slick tight channel. Oh it's hot and slippery. With the intrusion of another finger, the envelope of muscle seems to grow wider and slicker.

To his fondling and groping, she is astonishingly submissive, almost disinterested, as if she has something more important on her mind. She tangles his hair around her fingers, plays with his chains, tongues them briefly, but with seemingly no more curiosity than his baby sister examining an unwanted cracker.

He takes a deep breath. Coupling. Hose to coupler, executed at the proper angle. A simple principle. Parts her legs with his knees. She lifts her pelvis.

Lips close to her ear, he blurts, "Help me."

Her fingers close around his cock and he holds his breath as she guides him between her thighs and there he is, there she is. From the first contact with her flesh, he meets resistance and she crabs against him. He freezes in a sweating panic.

"You're not ready. I'm hurting you."

"No, no," she murmurs and shifts again and when he pushes, she opens a little.

And he can't stop anymore. He sinks into the sensation of opening her. The grip of her body on his is a magnitude of difference from pleasuring himself. He feels held, possessed by the heat, the silkiness, the distinct muscularity of her cunt. He tips her face to taste her chains and she rolls her head and they are tongue to tongue. When he moves, the breaking wave of silken friction feels so fine he can't stop. Instinctively making the necessary mechanical adjustment, he presses the small of her back with one hand, lifts her and himself simultaneously. Fills a little deeper and backs a little. Her hips roll under his easy guidance, her cunt clips his cock and he almost faints with the sudden clutch.

And when he looks at her, her eyes are wide. They grow wider yet as he sinks again and then rides the undulation of her hips. She gasps with him, seemingly as amazed at this movement as he is.

"Oh," she breathes. "Oh 'god."

Her hand finds the small of his back, follows the swell of his gluteal muscles tightening and relaxing as he rocks against her, inside her, with her. And she begins to roll with him, around him, against him. The cot moves with them, creaking and groaning. Around his cock the wet seems to flood, as if the friction were melting a viscous lubricant. The cot's metal frame shrieks suddenly and all at once the world drops out from underneath them. In the briefest fraction of a second of freefall, as he rides her body down, he cannot stop the sudden sensation of letting go. Of a great power train turning abruptly over, gears meshing, wheels turning, the violent ejaculation of fluid from a spillway.

"Fuck!" she gasps in his ear.

He does not hear the grinding of gears in his own throat, the rending crash of his own cry.

Then they are on the floor, on the mattress still, with the wreckage of the cot's frame around them.

■ ■ ■

For a long moment they pant heavily in the quiet of the abandoned Mill. Her fingers twist anxiously in his hair. It hurts.

"Jesus," she gasps.

He tips her chin to look in her eyes. Her face is damp, pupils wide and depthless. Dark eyes cores to the center of the earth. Mouth swollen. The loop of her chains across her cheek is damp to his touch.

"You okay?"

She blinks. Clears her throat. "I feel like I fell off the edge of the fucking earth."

There is a visible pulse in her carotid artery. He licks salty damp from the hollow of her throat.

"Thank you," he says. "Thank you."

She laughs, still a little breathlessly. It is an unexpected thrill, feeling her laughter from the inside. He is still half-hard and the slick of heat rippling around him is a new excitement.

"You didn't get hurt by the cot collapsing?"

"Not the cot," she says, "you landing on me. Knocked the wind out of me. That was the weirdest thing that ever happened to me having sex."

"I'm sorry if I hurt you. And about not being able to hold back too. You didn't make it, did you?"

A slight roll of her head confirms his guess.

He wets his lower lip. "Something I can do to help you?"

This time her laugh is disbelieving.

He sucks the lobe of her ear, enjoying the shiver of her body against him.

"No big deal," she says and draws his mouth to hers. A small kiss, like one taken at the kitchen door on the way to work. She wriggles under him, eases him out of her. "I'd kill for a butt."

He watches her twitching through her clothes, poking around the cubby, finding nothing. In the pallid light of the unshaded lightbulb hanging above her, her skin is mottled with bruise and scab and tattoo. The startling sculptural hairlessness of her skull makes her ears seem naked despite her earrings. The nipples of her small breasts are contracted with the cold. Her pubic hair and the black tufts of her armpit hair so conspicuous against her ivory skin, her eyebrows, her dark eyes emphasized with heavy dark eyeliner, her small face so fiercely chained—*a comely cannibal,* he thinks, remembering a phrase he has read.

She knows he is looking but she ignores hm. His cock lies semitumescent and wet on his leg.

"Were you close?"

"I never come." Defensively, dismissively, "Lots of girls don't."

"Never? Not even on your own?"

She's scandalized. "You mean play with myself? I don't need to do that. That's for people who can't get laid."

Sam hoists an eyebrow. "Jesus," he mutters. He's supposed to be the one doesn't know jackshit.

"I told you it's no big deal."

■ ■ ■

Like a soap bubble bursting, the momentary euphoria is gone. It's just a claustrophobic dirty little room in a desolate place. The fractured cot frame staggers at the corners like a busted orange crate. He can feel the cold coming up through the thin layers of the mattress from the floor. The only reason the mattress isn't crawling with crabs or some other bug is it's too cold for vermin this time of year. Except maybe for rats. There are rat turds in corners here and there.

He finds his shorts, his jeans, and legs clumsily into them. "If this isn't a big deal, Deanie, what is?"

"Very goddamn little. Winning a state title, that's a big deal. Doing up a little beer and weed, that's no big deal. Training contract, no fucking big deal."

Sam closes his eyes. She's smarter than he is but about this she's screwed up. Why play the game if you're not going to do it by the rules? What does winning mean if you've cheated?

The decayed smell of the Mill is suddenly strong in his nose. In this chickenshit new world, a rule is a curiosity like this Mill. Obsolete. Relic. Let the sweet old machines seize up and rust; they take too much energy. They're too powerful, too scary. Make the world cheaper with microchips and nonunion labor somewhere in Asia or South America. So what if it falls apart, if it doesn't work. So what if it's cheesy. That's what dumps are for. This place has his name signed to it in brass; he wonders if he might as well have sprayed it on the wall.

"What about Lexie?"

"What? Jesus, are you still ragging about that?"

"It was wrong. She was loaded, she's just a kid. How could they do it? I can't close my eyes and pretend it never happened. That would make me one of them."

Her face tightens into a mask. "Oh grow up."

She finishes buttoning her jeans and kneels next to him. Barebreasted. He can feel her body heat, smell her chemicals, hold her tits in his hands—she's that close to him. A few minutes before, their bodies were locked together. At this instant, their very proximity, their partial nudity, is a mockery. It only seems to emphasize what strangers they really are to each other.

Everything has gone sour. The way it always does with her. Stricken into silence, he gropes for his sneakers. She hugs her knees, watching him. With the heater putting out warmth, her nipples have relaxed and she seems unself-conscious about sitting there half-dressed. He sits down again, necks of his high-tops pinched between the fingers of his right hand. Dropping them, he reaches for her, drawing her close to him again. She resists for a little bit and then sags against him.

"I thought"—he struggles with the words and she interrupts him.

"Big mistake."

He slogs on. "I thought you wanted us to make luh—luh—" Her fingers fly to the trembling of his lips.

"I did. It was nice, what you did. Putting up the hoop."

He doesn't know what to say. He hadn't expected more than a thank-you and the pleasure of her surprise and delight over the conversion of the Mill to a place where she could shoot a few buckets out of the weather. Certainly hadn't expected her to *fuck* him—not for a little electrical work, some floods, a space heater and a rusty old hoop. Some wet kissing and he'd have still owed her small change. Just because she'd made it clear more than once she was willing, it had not occurred to him there might be some kind of exchange involved beyond the pleasure.

A dull sour certainty clots in his chest that she is angry at him, whether she understands it or not, for failing to satisfy her. Surely girls must experience some physical form of frustration like blue balls. No wonder she's such a wench so much of the time; all the screwing around she does and she's never had an orgasm even once. If she was expecting more from him, she must be even more pissed off.

"I'm sorry I was so bad at it."

She flicks her head impatiently. "Oh give it a frigging break. You were okay. You got it in the goddamn bucket. You scored. You're not cherry anymore. Maybe we'll even make it again sometime."

All at once, he is aware of having worked most of the night. Numb and flat enough to mail. Lowering his head, he waits for her to lick an enormous stamp and slap it on his crotch, then pound it down with a closed hard fist, before she dumps him into the *LOCAL* slot.

She pushes out of his arms and reaches for her shirt. "Don't get all bent out of shape. We have to work together. There'll be sore losers bellyaching about favoritism if we start playing kissy-face in the parking lot."

He follows her out of the cubby.

She plucks her headrag from the heap of their outer clothing on the floor. "I'm staying here awhile. See you at practice tomorrow."

"If I'm there."

"You'll be there."

She looks different now, he thinks. Her body moves with newly meaningful suppleness.

"What makes you so sure?"

Mocking dark eyes flick up to his and little frown lines knit between the fine slashes of her dark brows. "I need the ride."

The innuendo makes him laugh. A tired laugh but still a laugh. Tugging her closer, he bumps hipbones with her. "I have to go to work."

She steps away from him.

For an instant he hesitates. Shouldn't there be something more?

Ends snapping and flapping at him, the cloth twists smoothly through her hands as she whips it around her skull and turns away from him.

■ ■ ■

The Mutant carries her coat into the cubby, shrugs into it and flops down onto the mattress. Can't go home yet, not with Tony just waking up from last night with a New Year's Eve hangover. Tucking her knees, she curls herself into a fetal shape. She had wanted 'god to go away but now the Mill is huge and cold and empty around her. She doesn't even have a basketball.

She tucks her hands into the warmth between her thighs and closes her eyes. Tender, swollen there. Nobody ever asked her to do anything before besides spread her legs. But it worked too well, felt too right, the way he made her move with him; she is too much of a jock not to recognize improved mechanics. He hadn't lasted any longer than any of them but he was the only one who seemed concerned about it.

Tentatively she tucks her hips a little in that rolling movement.

Something almost happened to her and then it went away, like a dead short. But something was happening. Maybe it even happened. How would she know? Maybe that deadness is what they mean. For girls anyway. So far as she knows what girls get out of fucking is a little mildly pleasant tension. And either babies or a lot of sweat to avoid getting one. And bad reps, of course, provided by guys who seem to resent you for putting out for them in direct proportion to how much they insisted they wanted it before you spread for them. Maybe getting off isn't what they expect it to be either, except they act like it when it's happening. It seems like fucking is really just a way to make it clear they could do what they want to you, the nastier the better.

But when they were moving together, Bigger and her, it didn't seem so much like fucking. It was more like trying to execute a play on the court, being in sync with someone else's physical reactions, only belly to belly. Smooth and rhythmic and going somewhere. Just because she doesn't want to think about it, she can't get it out of her head.

There was also his concern for her. She isn't sure she likes it. It feels intrusive. Suffocating. And humiliating, too, having him, cherry 'god, teaching her moves. In her weariness, she feels empty and flat and defeated when she should be savoring a triumph. 'god falls to the Mutant, not some blue-eyed blonde cheerleader with ten pounds of hair and an IQ to match her bra size. It's a nice sweet secret to hold tight to herself.

But she doesn't feel triumphant. She feels ravaged and irradiated, changed at her most invisible, microcosmic levels. Mutated. Dread and exhaustion pour out of her. That's the only reason she's crying so hard. She's so whacked out and there's this sense of being in over her head no matter how hard she tries. No big deal, no big deal.

19

■ ■ ■

The Cold Brings Stinging Tears to his eyes as he coaxes the truck to life in the parking lot. Sam wipes hastily at his eyes. Frigging cold. Feels like a vacuum, trying to suck him inside out. He turns on the radio and a blast of "Ninety-six Tears" nearly blows out his eardrums. Hastily he punches down the volume, then cranks it up again a little. That pumping keyboard's irresistible.

It's not supposed to be like this. Rick and Sarah are playful and affectionate with each other. Same for his dad and Pearl. But between him and the Mutant, there's a cold fucking cosmos. It's like they were in a transmatter machine when they were doing it and the machine shit the bed and blew their molecules all over several light-years. Frigging cold light-years.

At the stoplight, he glimpses Sergeant Woods in his cruiser in the supermarket parking lot. Rick's dad waves casually at him. The light changes and Sam has to drive on, wondering if the policeman noticed the truck in the Playground lot again.

The question fades immediately as he heads for home.

The way it felt. Even if he wasn't very good at it, it was still—compelling. Somehow it was both less and more than what he had imagined. Of course it was a shitty place—that mattress had a feel and a smell to it, too, he'd be happy to forget. Maybe it was being with her. Maybe it would be totally wonderful with a girl he loved and who loved him. It was all mixed up, the incredible sensations and the sick feeling in the pit of his stomach at what he was doing and the person he was doing it with. To. Knowing too late she didn't like it. Not much, anyway. And finding out there was something inside him that didn't care how it was for her as long as that tight slippery heat was massaging his hard-on. Which made it even more of a cheat that he'd left her hung up.

He knows things about her now. What she looks like naked and what she feels like, inside and out. Her body is seamless, and despite its bruises and scabs, perfect in her way. Her clitoris was easy to find, contrary to what he had been led to expect, but she doesn't like it touched. Though she is so much smaller than he is, they fit all right. It makes him hot inside and out, recalling details. Her hot wet mouth engulfing the head of his cock, the sensation of her sucking it.

He pushes a button to scan the radio for a harder-rocking station and then presses down on his crotch. Another surprising thing is he's more, not less, horny. He has to resist the sudden impulse to turn around, go back to the Mill, and ask her to try again. It must be something to feel a woman's orgasm with her. Maybe if he could make it work for her, it would fix everything else between them. Probably not, though.

She is probably right—in the run of things, no big deal. No reason to be disappointed. The thing stood on its own, like a badly executed play that worked, barely. It was over. It wasn't like he had been planning on dying cherry. It was going to happen with someone, sometime. She wasn't even the first girl who ever made him the offer but somehow he'd always been able to keep his head before. It was past time—and that was why he wound up with her. It suregod wasn't true love. And while he's being straight with himself, how about admitting she turns him on not in spite of her freakiness but because of it. What's that make him? Just another hard-on, really.

The irony strikes him that on quitting the team, he has gone straight out to join the rest of the dicks. But what possible difference could one more guy make to the Mutant? He's just a drop in her ocean.

What she said—it seemed like she meant to keep it between them but she's contrary and unpredictable. So what if she struts it around the girls' room? He doesn't have to answer the question, if it ever comes up. Just keep his cool, shrug and keep on going. What's between him and her, that's their business and nobody else's.

■ ■ ■

Deep in the guts of an old beater, Reuben doesn't look up until Sam's shadow darkens his view. He smiles at the sight of the boy.

"Letter from Frankie on the desk."

With the flimsy sheets of his brother's letter in one hand, Sam shuffles the mail for a Department of Motor Vehicles invitation to be tested for his motorcycle license, though he knows it's much too soon to expect anything. Satisfied the DMV isn't nearly as excited at the thought of putting him on his ride as he is, he works his way through Frankie's thanks for various Christmas remembrances and big-brother advice to him on the care and feeding of the bike.

His father wipes greasy fingers through a rag and asks how practice went.

Trying to work out a way to tell him he has quit the team, Sam faces Reuben but before he can do it, his father's gaze moves past him, out the window to the pumps. Customers. Only when Sam glances around, it's Coach's Connie pulling in. With Rick Woods riding shotgun. Coach didn't come all the way from Greenspark to buy gas. In fact, from the expression on Coach's face, it looks like a shitstorm delivery to Sam.

Might as well jump.

"I qu-quit the team," Sam says.

Reuben's face remains impassive for a second as he continues to work the rag around his fingers. He attacks the grime without irony. The process is ceaseless and futile, for despite the use of protective solvents, particles of oil and grease are embedded in the upper layers of his epidermis and driven deep under his nails and into the quick so that even when he all but flays his hands with harsh soaps and brushes, even when there is no visible dirt, they still smell of petrochemicals. The act of rag-cleaning his hands is a placeholder, Reuben's equivalent of a cigarette.

"Pardon?"

Sam raises his voice. "Quit. I quit the frigging team."

The anger he hears in his voice surprises him as much as it does his father.

Coach fumbles at the door and bursts into the office, with Rick Woods behind him.

"What kinda bullshit is this?" Coach holds the note in his palm, slaps it with the fingers of the opposite hand. "What the hell *personal* bullshit kinda reasons do you have for leaving your team in the lurch, you overgrown clown?"

Dropping a heavy hand on the coach's shoulder, Reuben turns up his palm in a gesture of inquiry. Trembling with fury, Coach all but throws the note at him.

Staring at the floor, face burning, Sam hunches his shoulders in dull resentment against the buffet of the coach's rage. He isn't a fucking jarhead. Coach can't talk to him like that. Why can't they just let him go?

"I don't understand." Reuben raises his eyes to Sam. "Why?"

"Tired of it," Sam answers. "Tired of giving up my time for guys who don't give a shit."

"What d'you mean?" Coach demands. "We've had full turnouts every practice during break. Everybody was there today but you and Gauthier. Woods says you told him you were gonna quit to get more hours working."

Tracking the coach intently, Reuben shakes his head in disbelief.

Sam glances at Rick, who glares back at him.

Reuben drops the rag into the rag barrel. "I haven't had lunch yet. Neither has Sam, if I'm not mistaken. Coach, maybe you and Rick would go down to the diner and ask my wife to pack enough for the four of us and Sam and I could talk while you're gone."

Coach glances from father to stone-faced son and goes with his best shot.

"Tell her we'll eat what she wants to give us," Reuben advises as the coach and Rick start for the diner.

Reuben hooks his chair away from his desk and slumps into it. "Tell me about it, Sammy."

■ ■ ■

Wondering why he never foresees the consequences when he pitches a handful into the fan, Sam suspects they must all be right about him; he's not smart enough to be let out without a keeper. How he could have gotten himself into this without considering how he was going to explain it to his father? He *can't*—not the stuff about New Year's Eve.

"I know how tight things are. I want to help. I don't want you to have to sell the farm."

Astonishment lights Reuben's eyes. "Oh, Sammy. I couldn't sell the farm if I wanted to, the way things are. Fortunately I had the good sense to marry a woman with some means of her own who's willing to support me. She's convinced me it's an insult to her not to accept her help. You don't have to give up your season."

Sam retreats into himself. There's no way he can shop Pete and those other three idiots, not without eventually having to admit he knows of other teammates' violations. Rick's, for one. To say nothing of tearing the team apart. Maybe that's what Deanie meant by her injunction to grow up. Maybe growing up is when you accept that some things are insoluble, unfixable. It's done, can't be undone, what Pete and the others did, like something fundamental was altered, something way down in the tissue of things. Now it's just part of the whole wrong world. Nevermind the training contracts—the *laws* they broke are scarcely enforced anyway. The wrong is still there but there's no righting it, no justice or retribution. Nobody gives a shit except one thickwitted greasemonkey jock who's no kind of saint himself. Maybe they all understand something he's missing.

The brief silence between father and son shatters with an explosive whirr like an exhalation as an overhead heater kicks on.

"Yeah," Sam says, with a nod.

Reuben shoves back the chair and rises to his feet. "Good. Here comes lunch."

■ ■ ■

Coach reads the resolution in their attitudes and closes his eyes to mutter something, possibly a brief prayer, though he's not a praying man. Maybe just an admonition to himself not to get worked up, to remember these are kids he coaches. He departs half an hour later, comfortably full of an unexpectedly gratis lunch and self-congratulation at his handling of an unexpected crisis.

Too close to Sarah to miss the opportunity to see her, Rick calls her and asks her to pick him up and transport him to his three-to-eleven shift at the supermarket.

When Reuben drifts back to his work again, Rick shrugs toward the door and the boys step outside.

"You're an asshole," Rick says. "I'd like to stomp on your stupid face. You know how long it's gonna take to get everybody settled down again? You walked out this morning and left me with Coach shitting the bed and the team all dazed and confused. Trying to get a practice out of those guys was a major assache."

Sam listens stonily, angry responses tangled in a hot lump below his breastbone.

"But we had one, if you want to call what we did a practice. While you were out there turning wheelies with your little bitch buddy."

Sam's fingers trip down his fly buttons, checking if they are all closed, and drift onward to tug at his crotch.

"Don't call her a buh-buh-bitch! Shuh-shuh-she was trying to talk me out of quitting," he chokes out, though it almost strangles him.

"Call her worse than that," Rick snarls. "You're right about one thing. Gauthier is just like your sister. You're so hung up on Karen, it's fucking up your head. Karen's a burned-out druggie slut and Gauthier's going the same way. I don't care how good her fucking hook is. Scrape'm both off your boots, Sambo; they're stinking up your life."

"Fuck you," Sam advises quietly, without a trace of stammer.

It's the trigger Rick's primed for—his fist flies almost on its own volition, catching the already moving Sam with a glancing blow to the left cheekbone. Then Sam's hands cuff Rick's wrists and he is propelled back against the plate glass of the office window with a glass-rattling thump. Inside, Reuben looks up curiously.

"Karen's my sister, you dickhead. She's a mess and maybe she's a lost cause but she's not shit. Neither is Deanie. So shuh-shuh-shut up, Rick. And check your own boots, slick; you been in the shit yourself."

The office door slams open and Reuben stalks out.

As his father approaches, Sam releases Rick. Rick throws himself on Sam again and Reuben shoulders his way between them, making it impossible for either of them to land a blow. Peeling them apart, he holds Sam back. Sam's resistance to Reuben is all show.

"What's the matter with you?" Reuben demands of Sam.

The boy lapses into sullen silence.

"Rick?" Reuben asks.

Rick shakes his head. "Shit for brains, that's the matter with him," he offers sarcastically.

Sarah's Honda appears in the distance.

"Go on in," Reuben tells Sam.

Relieved to get away from Rick, Sam doesn't need a second invitation.

The mechanic shoves his hands in his overalls pockets and cocks his head thoughtfully at Rick. "This keeps up, you guys won't have a team."

Rick finds himself blinking back tears.

"I don't give a shit," he blurts.

"Sure you do," Reuben counters gently.

■ ■ ■

Inside again, Reuben makes himself a cup of tea. He twiddles the teabag in his mug, as if enjoying the amber swirl of the tea bleeding into the hot water. Sam watches his father dip the hot teabag out and squeeze it between two thick fingers—no doubt adding a little oil to the flavor of the tea—then flick the limp remains into the trash, an operation as ritualistic as the working of the cleaning rag through his fingers. The tannic smell of the tea is clean and pleasing.

"Sammy, come listen to this pig and tell me if you hear a whistle around the head gasket."

To Sam, the air leakage is immediately audible. When he confirms it, Reuben nods. "What I thought," he says, with an edge of irritation that brings Sam's eyes back to his father's face in concern. But there's nothing there but the familiar composure.

■ ■ ■

At bedtime, Sam prowls, checking the doors, the lights, the oven to make sure it's off, though his father's already done it. Checks the baby, who's sleeping—like a baby. Leaning over the rail of her crib, he trails the tip of a finger over her open palm and the slack fingers curl instinctively around his. From the corner of her mouth, she bubbles a pearl of spit as flawless as she is.

He tries a book and can't concentrate. Clamps on his earphones and dodges up and down the airwaves until he locks on a college station from Burlington that's putting out wrecking-ball techno-rock. Punches dub to roll tape. This stuff is so toxic it could be used to wash blood cells in one of those experimental cancer treatments. Terrible stuff to listen to this late, really.

Gives up. Gives in. Again already, he wants Deanie fiercely. Her, not just any female. Nevermind the awkward bits, the letdown after—the experience was so overwhelming, he can't fend it off anymore. Has to wallow in it, the sensations, the revelation. Her chains rolling between them as he fucked her. When he comes, it hurts enough to make him choke and cough.

Better call the game, bush, it's after midnight. Any more of this and he'll be coming blood. Still he lies awake, sticky and sweating, bemused at his own insatiable horniness. Since the time in the parking lot, he has been troubled with this guilty lust. The guilt is not in the lust but in being one of the many; he loathes himself for joining the longtime gangbang of Deanie Gauthier. Can't take it back now, gone and done it. And he's guiltier still, for lusting for her even more. Like tigers around a tree, his thoughts chase themselves until they melt, orange and black, spinning behind his eyelids.

■ ■ ■

Next morning she's at the Corner, hugging herself against the chill. The familiar headrag, the bobbing glint of her earrings, bring an immediate stab of desire. Just what he needs. His pecker stirring around like a sleepy hound. She grins at the sight of the truck, climbs in and settles back contentedly, feet on the dashboard like she owns it. She notices the small bag on the seat between them and grabs it. She coos over the huge blueberry muffin inside it, and the carton of orange juice. While she devours the muffin, she surveys Greenspark with a proprietary air as they pass through it.

"How are you?" he asks.

"Sore," she says through a mouthful of muffin. "I think you bruised my fucking ribs, landing on me."

"Sorry," he mutters.

"Don't sweat it, I can play."

After practice, he thinks, maybe she will ask if he wants to go to the Mill. Have to work, he'll say. No he won't. If she doesn't ask, he'll ask her. She'll probably say no, just to be a wench. Maybe she won't. But he doesn't say anything before they reach the school. Neither does she.

In the gym, he keeps his eyes off her while she is unchaining herself. He's all business on the outside. So's she. Inside, he's miserable and confused. Both of them acting like it never happened. He wishes it hadn't and he wants it to happen again.

He has other troubles. Nobody is a happy camper. The girls are uneasy, infected by the dissension among the guys. The boys act like they are attending a wake. Nobody looks anybody else in the eye and they all talk in asides. The upbeat tape mix Sam has prepared sounds ironic as they go through the session, all of them moving as if they were hobbled, physically and emotionally.

"What'd I tell you?" Rick mutters to Sam at the end.

"I dunno," Sam says. "I wasn't listening."

Rick pauses. "All right. I'll save my breath."

"Do that."

■ ■ ■

Second period, Sam is first into the weight room. He slots the snythesizer onslaught taped from the college station and cranks the volume on the boombox. Feeling as feverish as he did after his bout with the Mutant cold germ, he wants to sweat out the congestion of emotion and a restless night. As the others drift into the class, no one ejects the cassette. The music is a hard-wired, heartless robo-dick anthem, an intensifier of the sweaty jockstrap weight room milieu. Everyone concentrates a little harder and there is minimal joking. Quite a few of them are still sweating out holiday excesses, of course, and no one really wants to talk to anyone else, particularly Sam.

Rick greets Sam aggressively. "What is this shit?"

"Front 242, *Back Catalogue.*"

"Makes me want a lead-lined jock. Only good thing about listening to it is it's probably sterilizing you. You need a spotter?"

Sam nods.

And that's the end of the conversation.

Finished first, Sam wants a shower. The locker room rackets with guys changing when he emerges. His duffel's under the bench where he threw it when he entered. He hasn't cracked his locker since walking out the previous day. He drops his sponge bag on top of the gym bag and reaches for the handle of his locker.

"Samson!" Chapin jumps up on the bench and struts down its center lane between the rank of lockers. "How was your New Year's Eve? Big night in your racket, isn't it? You jump anything besides batteries?"

Around them, the other guys quiet. It occurs to Sam they know something he doesn't.

Chapin's happy face has never been more blankly, murderously ecstatic, grin spread from ear to ear, eyes round with clownish glee. "Thought a you, actually. On account of I ran into your sister at a party."

The only noise in the locker room now is the rattle of lockers, scratch of zippers, thunk of high-tops on benches, breathing.

"That Karen," Chapin enthuses, "she's a real party animal." He buddies an arm over Sam's shoulder and leans close to confide in a voice audible through the room. "Yup, you might say Karen *was* the party. First she got done up on every kind of shit we had and then she did everybody there. I myself—"

Sam lifts Chapin's arm from his shoulder distastefully and turns him gently in a mocking ballet movement, locking Chapin's arm behind him.

"—awwk." Chapin's smile vanishes in a croak.

"Must be proud of yourself," Sam mocks. "Bet you were the high point of her night." Releasing him, he shoves Chapin away from him. "Next time I see her, I'll ask her if she remembers the chickendick."

There is an explosion of jeering laughter.

The assistant coach pops his head into the room.

Chapin doesn't notice. "Hey, shit-for-brains," he snarls.

"You talking to me, jerkoff?" the AC inquires genially.

Moving away, Chapin mutters to Sam, "This isn't finished."

"Shaking in my boots," Sam returns flatly without bothering to look at the creep.

He cracks his locker door. On the shelf lies a half-gallon plastic bag. He tugs it out far enough to determine it's a dead rat, starting to bloat. Pinches the edge of the bag, sees it's sealed, and draws it all the way. Silently, he balances it on his palm.

Rick jumps at the sight of it. "Fuck!"

A murmur passes through the locker room. Sam notes guys looking at each other and then looking away. The nearest trash can is the big plastic-lined barrel at the other end of the rank of lockers, twelve feet away.

"Eat this," Sam says.

He pitches the bag of rat underhand. It describes a low parabola, below which guys duck and shout angrily, and drops into the trash barrel, where it explodes on impact. The smell is instantaneous and horrific.

The locker room clears with amazing rapidity amid outraged cursing. Sam dresses deliberately, though the stench is making him sick to his stomach. Long as they all got a whiff, he's satisfied.

20

■ ■ ■

The Bald Medusa on the Lunchline and on his mind, Sam carefully averts his eyes as he enters the cafeteria. At the team tables, his usual place is an island, even Rick moving away from him. He regrets the rat in the locker room. It might have been more fun to serve it up here. From the girls' team table, Nat gives him a little wave. He tries to smile back.

He empties most of his pail into his quivering gut, fighting the urge to goffle as fast he can and get the fuck out. With a mouthful of ham sandwich, he raises his eyes and allows himself to peek at the Mutant. As if she can sense his gaze upon her, she raises her eyes from her work but looks right at him with bemused contempt.

His sandwich sits in his gut in a dry hard lump. Shoving the paper into his bucket, dusting crumbs from his hands, he turns his attention to his teammates, staring at the table, meeting each and every pair of eyes for as long as the owner will look at him. Some of them immediately find their lunches or some conversation riveting. Others look back with stony impassiveness.

This is all horseshit, he decides. He should never have recanted his quitting.

■ ■ ■

The girls have the early practice after classes. Settling behind their bench, Sam notes the multiplicity of moves they have picked up from the boys. Not just moves, either. Not one of them runs like a girl anymore. They play more aggressively, less self-consciously. They play like boys.

Most of his team loiters in the vicinity of the gym—in the corridor around the vending machines or in the weight room—and some drift into the bleachers, to flirt with the cheerleaders and some of the female band members, just finished with their own practices. Occasionally, the action compels all eyes and there are shouts of encouragement, applause and whistles.

Each time this happens, Sam feels a little better, uplifted by the support one team is giving the other. He begins to turn over strategies to try to pull his team back together during their practice.

On court, the Mutant breaks fast and the scrimmage boils after her.

Rick Woods drops down next to him and wordlessly offers him a stick of gum. Fixed on the Mutant, Sam waves it aside but Rick stays there.

"Hey man."

Sam glances at him.

"I got this extra breath," Rick says. "Need to waste it on you."

Reluctantly, Sam tears himself away from the unpredictable fluidity of the Mutant's game.

"You piss me off," Rick continues, "but I hate this shit. Don't you?"

Sam nods. Rick offers him the gum again and Sam takes it and sticks it in a pocket. "Thanks."

Rick thumps Sam's shoulder. "Come on, we gotta change up."

The locker room is quiet—almost resigned. It's like the fourth quarter of a dud game, Sam thinks, when guys are beginning to lose their belief they can win.

As he returns to the floor, the girls are heading for their locker room. Fingers on her hips, the Mutant drifts along with her teammates without even glancing his way. The flaring edges of her hipbones are visible in her spandex capris and practice shorts. The jersey of the shorts folds from the iliac crests toward the vee of her crotch like the crossed tips of wings over her sex. He feels a rush of heat to his face, his groin. Soon she'll be in the bleachers, watching, and soon they'll be in the truck and he'll be asking and maybe soon they'll be back in the Mill. In the cubby.

"Styles!" Coach screams in disbelieving pain. "What are you doing?"

Fucking up. Red-faced. Two left feet and his head up his ass. His concentration's shot. Never mind pulling the team together, he can't pull himself together.

And outside, after the torture is over and Coach has nuked his ass and everybody else has left without speaking to him, outside in the frigging cold dark winter night, she's not waiting. He doesn't see her on the road. Two hours gone, she could be anywhere. At her old ladies', or home, even. With time for a stop to fuck her good buddy Chapin for a little weed. No big deal.

Cranking up the volume of a Godflesh tape until he can't think around it, Sam heads for home with a headful of hardcore noise. It is something like the sound-effects tape Rick once gave him that was nothing but cars crashing, only better. More like Godzilla stomping the shit out of Detroit. He wants to help.

■ ■ ■

Tipping a miniature berm of herb along the rectangle of paper with practiced concentration as he crouches at the low table next to his waterbed, J.C. sings the occasional phrase along with "Hotel California" on his stereo.

"Hurt my feelings, D., you giving me a line of shit about being in training so you couldn't party with me New Year's Eve. Then Lexie tells me you partied with the whole frigging hoop team."

Cross-legged on the bed, the Mutant winds a bandanna around her skull. She has taken off her laces and high-tops.

"I wasn't partying with them. It was just some place to be so I didn't have to go home. And it was nothing like the *whole* team. Anyway, there's two varsity, two junior varsity and two freshman teams, boys and girls, you chauvinist pig."

J.C. pinches the ends and sets the cigarette aside while he builds another one. He grins at her. "One of the worst. You know what I meant. Anyway, at least I heard from Lexie. More than I can say for you."

"What do you care? You never gave a shit before."

J.C. reaches out to pat her knee. "Chill out. Whatever you did, you did. Whatever I did, I did. You belong to yourself. I belong to myself. No big deal. You would have had a good time with me, that's all."

Satisfied with his work, he lights one of the doobies and takes a hit. When he offers it to her, she flips her fingertips at it in a dismissive gesture.

"Sure?"

She rolls over on her stomach, though the undulations of the bed make her feel a little queasy. He tokes again and climbs onto the bed next to her.

"So Fosse put his Blazer in a snowbank or some shit and you all caught the wrath of Samson. And the high-handed prick pitches my goddamn booberry into the fucking woods. Cost me money, D. Somebody owes me."

She ignores his hand settling on her bottom. He strokes the muscular rise and slides his hand between her legs, easing aside the chains. Silently, she cants her bottom a little to make her crotch more accessible to his fingers and he moves closer, losing interest in the whole question of Samson.

"Been a while," he murmurs and tugs her tighter against him, hardening his cock against her bottom. "Jesus, D., you got a primo ass." The waterbed rocks in motion with him. Face away from him, she takes a deep breath of the smoke in the air. He rolls away from her, reaching for the joint, bringing it directly to her lips, approving as she takes a hit. She lies back against him, and he pushes up her T-shirt.

"Off with the hardware."

Slowly, she removes the chains from her waist and he gestures for her to continue. She takes off her shirt and he pulls her down next to him again. He takes a hit from the joint and blows it into her mouth. It comes to her it's been a long time since she was this relaxed. Maybe it's the smoke but she can't get him to focus, he's familiar to her but also strange. Not-Sam. Weird.

J.C. pushes her head down to his crotch.

"Sister D.," he whispers, "Sister Do Me."

Slowed by the dope, she is confused when he begins to be rough with her, suddenly thrusting harder, choking her and hurting her mouth. Before she can react, he pulls out and begins to yank down her jeans and the spandex capris underneath. She tries to help and he knocks away her hands. A little frightened, she becomes passive. To her surprise, he produces a rubber and dons it. He hasn't done that since she started taking the Pill.

As he moves in her, she is surprised by the gradual response of her own body. In a moment, she is moving with him, and he becomes very excited and much rougher, until he's slamming at her and the response in her dries up and she just lies there until he's finished.

Flopping onto his back next to her, he removes the rubber, swaps it for the half-smoked doobie in the ashtray and brings his concentration to bear on relighting.

"Christ, D., I've been waiting three years for you to move your ass. Why'd you stop?"

She takes a toke before she answers. "You were rough. I didn't like it."

"You've never liked it, D.," he reminds her. "So who's been giving you lessons? Not Tony. You never learned anything from him except not to like it. I can't claim to have taught you anything but how to suck and you only learned that to get out of balling as often as you can." He laughs. "Spill it, D."

The Mutant fumbles for her clothing. "I've got homework still to do. You gonna give me a ride home?"

Resting his head on his arm, J.C. watches her dressing. "Sure. D., what's the big deal? Not Samson?"

Yanking up her jeans, she smiles at him. Stung by his put-downs and made incautious by the smoke, she strikes back. "You're so hot for me to screw him, I'm beginning to wonder if you're queer for him."

J.C. laughs derisively but there is real anger in the rigidity of his reptilian grin. He swings his feet to the floor. He tosses her a brown-paper bag, with her b.c. and a baggie of dope in it.

"What a wench you are. I just don't like that sanctimonious musclehead. He needs taking down. Nothing would make me happier than for the Almighty Samson to take my seconds."

The smoke makes magical frost on the window of her brain but through the opaque swirl is a prickly glitter like the razor-edged light of a bright deep-frozen January day. The shitheel. The prick. Her chains in her suddenly clumsy fingers seem to burn and stick to her skin as if with cold.

Casually, J.C. hooks his fingers around the chain at her waist and tugs at it. He grabs her crotch and digs his fingers into her through her clothes. "Be too bad if instead of a dead rat some bad shit turned up in Samson's locker. Or yours." He makes a flushing toilet rumble. "Goodbye states, hello county slammer."

It costs her hugely to look him in the eye but she does and she laughs crazily. Concluding she is too kited to waste any more effort at intimidation, J.C. releases her. He puts the roach between her fingers and she finishes it while he dresses. It helps a lot to calm her.

"It's good shit." He chucks her under the chin and kisses her lightly. "You know I'll always take care of you, D."

■ ■ ■

His right foot has a mind of its own, moving to the brake, gently weighing it down. The wheel slips to the right through his fingers and Sam stretches across the bench seat to yank down on the door handle and push it open. He refuses to look at her, though. She is wearing her brocade headrag and her face is pinched with the cold. She doesn't look at him either as she flings herself and her burdens into the cab. She stares straight ahead and he doesn't say anything until they are halfway to the high school.

"Where'd you go to last night?"

She could say *home* or *to the old bags,* or even *I got a ride with Grey* but instead she thrusts out her small chin and says, "None of your fucking business—"

"Yes it is," he interrupts her, furious at himself for becoming angry when he was going to play it cool. "Yes it is."

Her fists curl and she shouts at him. "I didn't do anything!"

He takes his eyes from the road again to stare at her defiant face. Her eyes are a little red, as if from bawling. Or a good dose of smoke. He can almost smell it on her. And smell Chapin too. Not that he needs to. Wearily, he turns his attention back to driving.

"Liar."

"You don't own me."

It's as good as a confession.

He nods, turning the truck from the access road into the parking lot. "Right. I don't want to own you either. I don't want anything to do with you. I give up. I'll pick you up and take you home until you find yourself another ride but that's it."

Ripped, she scrabbles for the straps of her gear.

"I don't understand why you want to get stupid with that prick. The way he talks about you. Don't you have any self-respect?"

"Oh bullshit." Her voice is clotted. "You don't give a shit about my self-respect. You can stop putting yourself out. I can take care of myself."

She is out of the truck as soon as he stops it.

He rolls down the window.

"You're welcome," he yells sarcastically.

She drops her bags, extends her middle digits in a double eagle without bothering to turn around to face him, and then snatches up her gear and hustles into the school, passing Rick on the pathway.

" 'Good morning to you,' " Rick falsettoes. " 'Good morning to you. We're all in our places with sunshiny faces.' "

"Shine your face," Sam mutters.

"Shine my ass," Rick counters. "Why don't you just run over the wench? I'll testify it was self-defense. You'll get off."

"Just shut up."

"Oh sure. What'd you suppose she's like when she's on the rag? Probably never is. I don't think she's actually female, you know. I bet she got something like a garbage disposal up there, only the blades are like Freddy's fingernails—"

"Rick, shut up, I mean it."

Rick makes a whirring noise. "Ooops, sor-ree," he squeals, "was that your dick?" He laughs maniacally.

"You're sick," Sam observes, reaching past Rick to push the doorbar.

"You're sicker." Rick's suddenly serious again. "I mean it, man."

Sam drops a heavy arm over his shoulders.

"No," he assures him. "I'm cured."

"Right," Rick agrees. "And I'm Larry Bird."

■ ■ ■

The gym is already open. Coach gestures Sam into his office and closes the door. The floor is visible through the glass that forms most of the wall between the gym and the office. Indicating the chair facing his desk, Coach puts Sam's back to the door.

"We got a problem here," Coach says.

Sam slumps in the chair, waiting for the roof to come down on his head.

"You boys," Coach continues with a mournful shake of his head. He gives up a huge sigh. "Jeez. I dunno. Sometimes. What to do with you." He places his hands on his desk blotter in an attitude nearly of prayer and looks at Sam expectantly. "What are we going to do, Sam? What are we going to do?"

Numbly, Sam tries to summon up some formula, some phrase, to explain his silence, his complicity.

Coach breathes heavily through his nose.

"We got this game to play tonight and it really really feels like you guys are gonna go out there and drop it."

Sam closes his eyes and dares a shallow breath. This isn't about New Year's Eve. Just about tonight.

Suddenly Coach slaps his palms upon the desk explosively and Sam jumps, eyes immediately wide, taking in Coach's glare. Coach points a shaking forefinger at Sam.

"You!"

Coach rants a long long time. Sam glazes over, only to have Coach slap the desk or shove a finger halfway up his nose or half-lunge at him over the desk, jerking him back to reality. Huge circles darken the armpits of Coach's shirt, his tie acquires a strangled look from being yanked vehemently several times and his freckled pate is dewy with perspiration. Eventually he runs down and collapses into his chair.

Sam glances at the clock.

Following his line of sight, Coach sits up again abruptly.

"You're here as long as I want you, bud," he snarls.

Hastily Sam drops his gaze to his feet.

"Now we got this game tonight," Coach says. "And we've got to play it whether you bunch a prima donnas feel like getting off your sweet asses and risking your nail polish and your earrings and your hairdos or not. Gimme that folder over there, you over-grown greasemonkey, and if you can spare another few moments of your valuable time—I realize you got so many other things to do, Styles, what with trying to pass shoelace tying and getting your buttons done up in order and blasting out your brains with that noise and don't gimme that old-fogey look, I happen to think the Beach Boys did some classic music which was at least healthy, and I'm not the only person who thinks that stuff you listen to not only makes you deaf, it makes you stupid"—Coach pauses to scatter the contents of the folder over his desk—"if in your case that's possible, here it is, the player roster for Dyer's Mills. If!"—he glares at Sam—"you could give it your precious attention, maybe we could discuss some vague game plan for tonight?"

■ ■ ■

The ringing bell finally frees him.

Glimpsing Billy Rank ahead of him in the corridor, Sam catches up with him.

"How'd it go, Billy?"

Billy squints. "What?"

"The hack session."

Billy slouches and looks nervously about. "The shits. It was the pits and the shits. Everybody's gotten very fucking weird. We could hear Coach ripping your ass too. You gonna quit again?"

Sam rests a reassuring hand on Billy's shoulder. "Think I should, Bilbo?"

"Jeez, no!" Billy blinks rapidly. "I mean, holy shit. What would we do without you?"

"I bet you'd be fine." Sam grins. "Hey, Billy, you guys will be playing without me next year. And Rick too. You'll probably be starting."

Billy grins too but with a distinct uneasiness. He's clearly not at all sure that's such a wonderful idea.

"What do you think about the game?"

Sam slaps his back encouragingly. "I'll play it as soon as I hear the buzzer, Billy."

■ ■ ■

When he takes his seat next to Rick on the bus, there is awkward silence between them. Both boys seal their ears with headphones. Rick cracks a textbook. Sam closes his eyes, though he is too tense to sleep. They're going to lose this game, he thinks. Can't win without a team. As the bus pulls out onto the road, Sam opens his eyes. Sitting up, he tugs down his 'phones and nudges Rick, who glances at him and then stares out the window. Then Rick sighs, closes his book and knocks back his headphones.

"We got a problem," Sam begins.

Rick slumps down lower in his seat, so his long legs knee the back of the seat in front of him.

"Right," he says in a low voice. "You're the problem. Been hot shit so long you forget you're part of a team. You owe the team your first loyalty, man. Where the fuck is it?"

Sam touches the dark bruise on his cheekbone where Rick hit him. His mouth opens but nothing comes out.

Rick leans closer to continue his harsh on Sam.

"I finally hear from everybody but you about you yanking Fosse and those yo-yos out of a snowbank. Might have known Gauthier would be in the middle of it. So how's it feel, blowing off the team 'cause some idiots got loaded with three little sluts and played trains with 'em? Wish you'd tell me how you wrecking the team is gonna stop anybody from getting stupid if they want. You're being a self-righteous prick and over Gauthier. I should have expected you to get hard for a hopeless waste like her. Why didn't you just get in line and fuck her like those other fools and get it out of your system? Might have found out what it's like to be a human being."

Clamping his headphones over his ears, Rick turns to the window.

Beside him, Sam shivers in a cold sweat, his jaws clenched achingly. He flips up his own headphones, punches the play button on his Walkman and closes his eyes. *If that's all it takes, I qualify. A suregod human being. I fucking hate it.*

■ ■ ■

The Mutant curls her lip and struts to the boos of the Dyer's Mills fans. From among his sullen teammates in the bleachers, Sam breaks out laughing at her showmanship.

Three rows below, Fran Pettit applauds, stamps her feet and whistles through her fingers. Sitting next to Fran, Paul Romney swivels around to wave up at Sam.

"I wanna be her manager when she goes into pro wrestling," he calls to Sam.

Always quick to be boisterous, the Greenspark contingent responds to the Mutant's attitude.

The Mutant herself breaks an infectious grin in their direction. For a second, she meets Sam's eyes. He thinks he sees some softening around her mouth but perhaps it is only an illusion. Or a delusion.

He makes himself concentrate on the game. His struggle is more intense than the game itself, for the Greenspark girls take a walk all over the Weaverbirds. Over and over, his attention drifts to the rise and fall of the Mutant's breasts as she lifts her arms to shoot at the free-throw line, or he's riveted by the grace of her long legs, the muscular curve of her ass. It's a relief to leave the bleachers to change.

21

■ ■ ■

The Rowdy Drained Out of Them in the locker room, the boys mill through warming up. Their sullen isolation from each reminds Reuben of news clips of prisoners chained together in the vending-machine courtrooms of the big cities. When they take the floor to play their game, the lack of byplay between the boys is another bad sign.

The Weavers come out strong and tear through the Indian defense all the way to Sammy at the post. The rest of Greenspark's defense line is riddled with holes created by the inexplicable inattention and misplacement of Woods, Gramolini, Kasten and Bither. It seems as if they are more concerned with cutting Sammy out than they are with what the Weavers are doing. Recognizing that the Indians' perimeter defense is disorganized, the Weavers simply go to their outside shooters and batten on an initial run of scoring.

At the offensive end of the court, the other starters play passaround with the ball, refusing to complete the plays that would bring it inside to Sammy. The only consistency is their willingness to turn over the ball to Dyer's Mills rather than feed it to him.

Intrigued, Reuben leans forward. How will Sammy handle his

team falling apart? He sees the tensing of his son's jaw, the narrowing of Sammy's eyes, and then Sammy breaks out, stripping an intimidated Weaver guard of the ball to pump in a twelve-footer. As it drops through the net, he is on the move again, to the relieved outcry of the Greenspark fans. The Weavers' big forward has possession for a fraction of a second before Sam relieves him of it again. Kiss the floor, pivot, hook it in and then he's in the middle of traffic, most of it Weavers. The other Indian starters lollygag their way toward the Dyer's Mills goal.

Coach calls the first time-out. Though he is bent to the circled players, Reuben can hear the rise and fall of his fury, and read in his vehement gestures the riot act he is delivering to hanging heads and sulky faces. He sits down the four laggards and sends Sammy back in with Rank, Michaud, Skouros and an inexperienced sophomore guard, Shane McCleary.

Billy Rank promptly founders in flop-sweat and cramps. Coach replaces him with Woods, who seems to have undergone a bench conversion to the ways of righteousness. Rick resumes his longtime partnership with Sammy and the Indians open a second-quarter comeback in which Sammy shoots three consecutive three-pointers.

The Greenspark fans come alive with the team. In Reuben's lap, Indy is so stimulated by the rising decibels that she pumps her way to her feet and begins to bounce on his thighs. To protect himself from her enthusiasm—she has exhibited a talent for kicking her father in the worst place—Reuben lifts her to his shoulders. Her heels drum on his chest and she squeals with delight at the improved view. When the cheerleaders take the floor at the half, she quiets and Reuben slides her back into his lap. Pearl returns from the concession stand and swaps him a paper cup of Coca-Cola for the baby.

Whatever ass-torching Coach gave the boys in the locker room, it is immediately apparent when play resumes that it has only gotten the boys' backs up. It begins to look like a replay of the first quarter. Sammy gives a signal that he wants to come out and Coach assents and sends in Fosse. The team begins to cohere, setting a screen against Dyer's Mills that denies a score. Then Woods steals the ball. But the Weavers block out Fosse under the post and keep Greenspark from scoring in return. The Greenspark rally stalls.

Coach calls another time and replaces all five men with the end-of-the-second-quarter lineup. The signs of rout excite the Weavers. Though Dyer's Mills cannot control him and Sammy scores steadily, the bench players are hampered by effective blocking and their own erratic shooting. Sammy and the Skouros kid succeed in controlling the Weavers at the post but the Weavers' forward shoots consistently from the edge of the paint over the Greenspark defense, racking three-pointers to maintain the margin gained in the first.

Again Coach calls time and when play resumes, Sammy moves from the post to screen the Weavers' long shooter. The change is effective; tall as he is, the Dyer's Mills forward cannot get over or around him or even pass it consistently to other Weavers. This long-shooting Weaver is tiring, clearly just trying to hang on until the end and there is no one to replace him of comparable talent on his bench. With a minute on the clock, the Indians have stopped the Weavers with the score at 64–58, in the Weavers' favor.

The seconds tick away while Skouros struggles for possession with a heavyset opponent, lays it up and then stands open-mouthed underneath the bucket, watching his nervous shot wobble agonizingly around the rim and then stagger off. Sammy blocks the Weavers trying for the rebound to let Skouros take it back himself, only to see the gangly sophomore fumble it and squirt it directly into the eager hands of the Weavers' center. Somehow Skouros trips—over his own feet, apparently—and Sammy instinctively rises over him, leaving a shaken Skouros on the floor behind him.

It's too late, Reuben knows, with a glance at the clock. There's no way to close the gap.

The driving Weaver center reaches the paint at the other end of the court, dips to pump into his shot. Suddenly, with only four seconds remaining, Sammy is rising with him, his hands closing around the ball in the shooter's hand. Heart in his throat, Reuben is on his feet without conscious volition. The stunned Weaver is suddenly empty-handed. Swiveling as he descends, Sammy hurls the ball toward the other end of the court. It cannot change the outcome of the game but he makes the shot anyway.

Reuben sees in Sammy's face the knowledge that the shot is true. For an instant it sounds as if it is shrieking, and then Reuben realizes it is a girl—Gauthier, the razorhead—pealing with Amazon glee. Her voice blends into the buzzer and the heart-in-its-mouth roar of the crowd. The game is over at 64–61, and the

Dyer's Mills fans are on their feet, laughing and applauding *Sammy*. For them it has been the sweetest of victories, the defeat of a much more powerful team in the face of the extraordinary performance of the best of the opponents.

On the floor, Sammy stands alone, eyes searching the bleachers. Smiling, Reuben thrusts a clenched fist and Sammy tips his chin slightly in acknowledgment. Then Skouros lopes up to shake Sammy's hand and pound his back, and after him, the other three who were on the floor. Coach comes from the bench to pat his jaw affectionately. Rick rises from the bench, hangdog and silent, along with the other miscreants.

"What happened?" Pearl asks Reuben. "I've never seen them play like that."

"I'm not sure." He takes the baby from her. "There's been some squabbling. Sometimes winning spoils a team. Maybe this will wake them up and get them working together again."

She is already fixed on Indy, cooing to her, snapping her into her snowsuit.

These things happen, Reuben assures himself. They're all just kids. At least Sammy did his best. He'll still be bummed about it; he won't be able to help it. A sudden fierce welling of his love for his son surprises him. That shot! And those dinks—Rick, for heaven's sake, who's supposed to be Sammy's best friend!—let Sammy down after all he's done for them. And there's nothing he can do but hope that his son is now strong enough to withstand the betrayal.

■ ■ ■

Windows blind with freezing condensate, the bus is running when Sam, the last player out of the showers and Dyer's Mills High School, lopes through the cold night and pounds on the closed door for entry. The doors fold inward and Sam dives on board.

Coach rises to his feet.

"Think about it, boys," he says, catching the back of the nearest seat as the bus lurches into motion, "think about it good and hard and make up your mind how bad you want to wear this uniform."

Like his subdued teammates, Sam retreats to his headphones to consider the question. For once, it's an easy one. Though he is consciously preparing himself to give it up in a few weeks, he still wants to wear the Greenspark uniform. The more fundamental question for him is, if he continues to wear it, will the final weeks be more of tonight?

How long will it be before Coach winkles out what the real source of trouble is between the team and him? What happens if—maybe *when* is the right word—someone in authority gets even a hint of the New Year's Eve's follies? If Rick's heard, then doubtless there are rumors all over school—exaggerating Deanie Gauthier's participation, unless she's lying to him about it, which is more than likely. The thought nauseates him. The whole business is like a vulture circling overhead, sniffing for rancid meat. He has ominous feelings—aside from what suspicion and resentment and anger about it are doing to his team—but maybe it's just a conversion of his own guilt about her.

Rubbing a little frost from the bus window, he tries to see the girls' bus just ahead of them. The glow of the one taillight he can see is a red coal in the dark. Like a distant cigarette. Little spark.

■ ■ ■

The Mutant is waiting, crouched, shivering, beside his truck in the parking lot after the buses unload. The truck's cab seems chillier than the out-of-doors, as if sitting in the parking lot all day it had stored up cold like an electrical charge. Drawing up the collar around her ears, she hunches inside her coat until only her eyes and the little cross-stitch of frown between the delicate arches of her eyebrows are visible underneath her headrag. Her teeth are gritted against the cold.

"That was an awesome shot. I know you're not speaking to me but I have to say something about it, you know?"

Starting the truck, Sam does his own jaw-clenching against the cold. Once the engine turns over, he idles down and gropes for the windshield scraper under the seat. It takes a couple of minutes to debride the windows of the thin skin of ice that has formed. Respiration fogs the interior, blotting the Mutant into a vague deformed human shape within.

Behind the wheel again, Sam wipes his nose and hunches forward. The vents trip open and the fog on the windshield begins to shrink magically away. He helps the process along, rubbing himself a larger viewing port with the hem of his jacket sleeve.

"It won't help anything. They're more pissed at me than ever," he says, picking up where she left off.

"What were you supposed to do? You played the best game you could. If they looked bad, it was their own frigging fault."

He changes the subject. "You blew those babes away, you girls. You were great."

"I heard somebody put a rat in your gym locker."

"Yeah."

"Heard it stank something wicked."

He wrinkles his nose. "Did."

"What's gonna happen? With you and the team?"

"Dunno. I guess they don't want to win quite so bad as they want to screw up."

"Must cheese you off."

"Hell yes," he admits. "Nevermind. It's just a game. I'm all done with it in another six weeks anyway. I still want you girls to get your title but I'm starting to give shit one whether we take another one. It might be better if I did quit."

"Right, genius. That's so dumb you had to have thunk it up yourself."

"You know it's around school about New Year's Eve?" he asks.

"So? You think any of the suits who run the show will do anything? It's a dead rat in a baggie to them. They don't want the stink."

She makes cartoons in the condensate on the window; he keeps his eyes on the road.

They are closing on the village before he speaks again, huskily. "Let's go to the Mill."

He glances away from the road at her. She pokes playfully at the basketball on the floor with her toe. Then worms herself into a straighter posture, her eyes gone darker, and sly as the night sky.

"Okay."

The constriction in his chest lets go and he breathes again, and the air is warm and Mutant-smelling.

■ ■ ■

Instead of the parking lot at the Playground, he approaches the Mill from the opposite direction and finds an access road to the park near the end of Mill Street, where a strip of woods backs the abandoned structure. Outside the reach of streetlight, once he kills the truck's lights, it blends into the darkness. Of course she knows the quickest way through the woods to the Mill. At the door, he takes the key from her.

"Stay behind me," he tells her with a grin and she laughs.

As he opens it, she stays his reach for the light switch.

"Don't. Somebody might see the lights leaking from those broken windows way up. Candles are safer."

She stoops just inside the door to dig a stone from the wall. Behind it is a battered tin cookie box presently housing candle stubs, a box of kitchen matches and some E-Z Wider rolling papers.

"My old ladies never throw shit out. They had a shoebox full of candle stubs out in their shed, been there since nineteen-ought-who-gives-a-fuck. I kifed it. They'll never miss'm." As she lights one, she smiles with pleasure. The uncertain flicker over her face is unearthly and melting, as if she herself is an illusion of the flame. "I like the way they smell. Real beeswax. Sometimes I boost one of those fancy scented candles but these are the ones I mostly use."

Handing him the burning stub, she closes the box and rises. For a moment, they look at each other and then she turns toward the cubby. Hesitantly, he follows the flicker of the candle into the vast darkness of the Mill.

■ ■ ■

Her eyes mirror the flame as she applies a match to the first stub, as if there were, deep inside her, a pair of tiny fires. Impassive as her face is, the effect is to make her less human than ever. If her eyes suddenly glowed fluorescent green, she could not look more unearthly to him.

While the coils of the space heater redden, she lights the candles and sets them around the closet-sized room. She unlaces and yanks off her high-tops. He goes so far himself and then they furl themselves on the mattress, waiting for the cubby to warm up. The smell of the melting beeswax is clean and churchy, with a tinge of burning wick. The tremulous candleflame gilds her skin and ripples on her chains like the setting sun on the wrinkled skin of the lake in summer. It throws tiger stripes of liquid honey and shadows dancing onto the walls.

"Good it's cold," he murmurs as much to himself as to her.

Waiting for the heater to bring the chill to something bearable, they have to go slow. He wants to go real slow, make it last. She hides her face in his jacket, her hands slipping under his layers of shirts, fingertips whispering over his nipples. They drift into a flurry of clumsy kisses. He forgets about going slow and makes a sudden assault, his tongue feeling enormous to him ramming past hers, making her gasp. Undoing the buttons of her coat, he cups her breasts inside her T-shirt and rocks against her thigh. For too many long moments, they are tangled in their clothing. By the time his jeans are around his ankles and she is wearing only chains, they are sweating with exertion. Her strong fingers close around his cock and draw him down between her legs again. He pushes the head of it against her and meets a maddening resistant heat. A second shove makes her cry out and yank his hair.

Impatiently she rolls up and goes down on him, mouthing his cock. She doesn't suck him, just wets him thoroughly and flops back again. He grasps, with embarrassment, that she is still dry and this will take care of it. When she lies back, he uses his fingers first to make sure of his route. There is still resistance but it is less and he can't stop anyway, is on the verge of emission, and the hard edge of her chains between them is exquisite. This is worth any amount of awkwardness and blushing. *What a sweet machine, sweet machine* is all he can think as he spurts what feels like his brains into her. And then her fingers are burrowed in his hair, lightly stroking the base of his skull. "It's all right. No big deal."

The words that irritated him before bring him an unexpected relief. Suckered to her with sweat, he shivers. He doesn't need to ask if she made it, not after that performance. When he tries to apologize, she stops his mouth with quick fingertips.

"I'll get better," he promises. "We'll get better."

She pays no attention. "You know how long it's been since I had a cigarette?"

From the sweet taste of her mouth, not this day, but of course it's a rhetorical question.

"I miss it most after sex. In fact, it's the best thing about it."

His rueful laugh brings her eyes to his face.

"Oh Jesus, here we go again," she says.

He clamps a hand over her mouth. "Please, don't let's start bitching on each other."

She peels his hand off her mouth. "I'll say what I want."

For a quiet moment he just looks at her. Then he walks his fingers from her flank up over her hipbone to her stomach and begins to tickle her. Shrieking, she tries to wriggle away but he is still inside her. He pins her casually with his body and fills her mouth with his tongue to still her whooping. Her gasping into his mouth is as stimulating as her squirming body. When he stops tickling her, she continues to laugh, swept along with his foolishness, getting a kick of out his being turned on again by a childish bout of wrestling. The giggling fades except for an occasional shudder as they begin to move together again.

When he looks in her eyes, the widening pool of her pupils pleases him. The candleflames are gone; her eyes reflect him. He tugs at her headrag until her stubbled skull is cupped in his hands and he lays his cheek against it, listening to the shortening rhythm of her breathing, feeling the royal-blue pulse at her naked temple under his thumb. She surrenders suddenly with a strangled sound and begins to shudder. Burying himself deeply, he lets the churning rush take him.

■ ■ ■

"Did you?"

"I don't think so."

"What's that supposed to mean?"

"I guess I was close. It went away."

"That's good, then," he encourages her. "Next time, maybe. Soon anyway."

She might as well be wearing an ivory mask for all the reaction her face shows. He doesn't want to let go of her. Her body feels rounder and sleeker to him, more female. He dips the tip of his tongue into the cleavage between her breasts. Go all night, he thinks. Working this sweet machine. By morning they'd be a puddle of sweat and come. Melted tigers. Bottle it up and sell it as an aphrodisiac.

"Meet me here tomorrow night? I'll be out of work by ten."

She shrugs. "Okay."

■ ■ ■

As they tromp through the woods to the truck, she pelts him with a snowball, a challenge he cannot resist. She jumps him from behind, puts a handful of the cold wet stuff down the back of his neck and they tumble into the snow. She straddles him while they scrub each other's faces with it. He begins to lick the trickle of melt down her face and they are in the midst of another make-out session.

"Oooo, Samgod, 'it's too frigging cold for this shit.' " She shivers violently against him.

" 'Come on, it feels good,' " he teases.

He helps her to her feet, then sweeps her off them and carries her, kicking and giggling, to the truck.

"I'll walk from here," she insists. "It's only a little ways."

All at once she's gone, trekking off on her own with a peck on the lips for a goodbye. She's so abrupt, so ephemeral, the way she changes and takes herself away at the very instant when things start to feel real between them.

The sky seems roofless to the whole frigid frozen universe. It feels like his lungs are being tugged inside out by a black vacuum. His skin is damp with cold sweat. The interior membranes of his nose tighten and crackle and his eyes sting as if they are trying to flash-freeze. It's so beautiful and so heartless, this cold universe. No way to comprehend it, no matter how many planetary gears you map. Maybe that's the point of it, to humble you. Just now, he feels his limits right down to the beads of water freezing at the tips of his eyelashes.

■ ■ ■

His father is on the couch in the living room, pillows under his head and covered with a quilt as if he is spending the night there. Clicking off the late news, Reuben flips back the quilt and sits up. He's still dressed, except for his shoes. Hooking them out from under the couch, he peers at Sam.

"You're late."

It isn't a reproach, just a comment inviting an explanation. Sam shrugs.

Unease crinkles the corners of Reuben's eyes. "Relax, Sammy, I'm not sleeping on this couch. I just stayed up to catch the news."

Sam's cheekbones grow warm. Was he so obvious, scanning the floor for dead soldiers?

"What's wrong, Sam?" Reuben asks suddenly.

Sam makes himself look at his father directly. "Nothing."

Reuben's ironic smile acknowledges they both know Sam is evading.

"You did good, even if it was a loss," he says shortly, and stops to kiss Sam's forehead before he climbs the stairs to the second floor.

■ ■ ■

WEAVERS JAM GREENSPARK'S BIG MACHINE, banners the fold of the morning paper. The photograph that dominates the page is of Sam, at full extension and midair in that thirty-foot rainbow jump shot, captioned *Shooting Star*. A smaller one features the Weavers' forward driving past Bither and Gramolini in the third quarter.

The sidebar speculates about the poor Greenspark performance. For this team to come apart so completely and so quickly, the sportswriter asserts, there is likely to be dissension in the locker room—a point illustrated by the anarchic game the Indians played. Indeed, only one of the Indians actually played a game and what a game it was—but it may be unfair to the rest of the team to cast Sam Styles as the unquestioned hero. After having been a star for his entire high school career, should there be any surprise if Styles's head has started to swell? Or that the rest of the team may have accumulated some resentments?

The coverage on the overshadowed girls' game is less fulsome. Deanie's stats come after the usual cocked-eyebrow description of her appearance and style.

Why should it be such a big deal? So she's not cut out of a paper-doll chain. If Sam shaved his head and put a ring through his nose and tattooed every square inch of his skin, he'd be merely another Bad Boy with an amusingly aggressive attitude. But nobody wants to give the Mutant that kind of slack.

22

■ ■ ■

Saturday Night Raw Reuben calls it—the lucrative but frequently tiresome business of wrecker calls to bar parking lots. It means dealing with drunk owners, drunk passengers and drunk onlookers. Sometimes they are abusive, sometimes incoherent, sometimes sick and worse. At ten that evening, Sam is catching one of those, jump-starting a Subaru Justy at the Hair of the Dog.

"I can't fucking believe you dinks got wiped by Dyer's Fucking Mills!" the Justy's owner berates him. "What the fuck happened? You all too worn out from screwing cheerleaders and getting blasted every weekend or what? Somebody slip you pricks some green to take a dive?"

"All three," Sam answers.

"Huh?" The guy is too far gone into his own rant to register Sam wising off. "I lost fifty fucking bucks on that fucking game!"

It is 10:15 on the clock over the cash register as Sam punches up the sale. Reuben comes in from the pumps and Sam steps back to let him ring in a gasoline sale.

"Okay if I split?" he asks, jamming fingers into his pockets to keep them from twitching, but unable to keep his feet in one place.

Reuben looks at him. "Something up?"

"Thought I'd take a run to Rick's and watch a video with him and Sarah."

His father closes the cash register. "Go on," he says. "I'll close up."

■ ■ ■

The Mill is a void, a black hole into which Sam steps with the sensation there will be no floor, just a long blind floating fall. But grit rolls on the cold headstone of the floor under the soles of his high-tops. He sniffs the air; it is dead with the cold and there is no scent of Mutant, not her cigarette or a whiff of burning bud. He peeks into the cubby but sees no sign she has been there since the previous night. It is eleven, an hour after he said he would be here.

He backs out of the cubby. Putting down his boombox, he finds her candle stash, and one by one, lights and arranges every stub in the box in a semicircle to illuminate the hoop. The multiple flames make a cave of dancing light. He slots in a Pigface tape. The hollow space reverberates the executioner's beat, the hoarse agonized vocalization, the jangling guitar of music that is already half-echo. The first bop of the ball startles with its hollow beat, punctuating the musical grunge. An inhalation, a second beat and then on the exhalation the rhythm begins, like something being born into a chorus of grief. The second cut on the tape picks up tempo, drums running steady, driving, vocal now urgent.

His throat feels sandpapered. A few beers would help it. A lot of beer would cure it completely. He wishes he was puking passing-out drunk, as he has only been once in his life, but the only available oblivion is the rubber pumpkin in his hands. It has a beat he can dance to. Nor does he dance alone. The baker's dozen of candle stubs paint the shadows of a whole team across the floor and up the wall under the hoop, rising and falling, stretching and shrinking, folding and twisting and burning up in tiny wisps of shadowed smoke. The phantoms dancing with Sam wipe phantom sweat from their eyes and feel a shadow of the pounding of phantom hearts. They have no existence apart from him as he draws his being down to this ghost dance with himself and the ball.

Rising like a sudden spurt of flame, he slams the ball through the hoop. His hands close over the rim and he drops, into the violent embrace of gravity, as if the trap is falling out from under him. He hangs from the bucket as it jerks against his palms. His twisting shadow, the stick man hanging from the gallows, catches his eye, a nursery rhyme filling his head: *I have a little shadow who goes in and out with me and what can be the use of him is more than I can see.*

The tape runs out with a whisper. He lets go. The stone floor rises to meet him and he keeps on falling, his legs gone rubber, until he is on his knees, crawling after the ball on all fours like his baby sister and then curled up around it on the floor. The floor is boneyard cold and he is overheated. Shivering, he makes himself roll up onto his feet. Inside, he's as sour and empty as the Mill. Shanked. She shanked him but good. He might as well go home now. Hunched over the ball, he licks forefinger and thumb and begins to pinch off the flames, one by one.

"You think I'm weird," she says.

■ ■ ■

He starts so violently, he loses his balance and falls on his ass. "Fuck! You scared the shit out of me!"

Stepping from the shadows near the door, she laughs at his slapstick reaction. Her brocade scarf falls loosely around her head so it is almost a hood and he cannot see her face. The light of the last candle flickers briefly, raising a flare in one obscured dark eye, like a very distant cold star, and a liquid shiver along the chains from her nose to her ear.

"I came in when you dunked. You were totally into it."

He rises to his feet, shoving his fingers into his pockets, leaving the ball on the floor at his feet. "I've been here a good hour." Then, angrily, "Where the hell were you?"

She drifts erratically along the wall toward the cubby.

"You wrecked?" he asks more softly. "Been partying?"

"Fuck you," she whispers. Her ankle rolls on grit and she catches herself against the wall. "Fuck you," she calls in high childish mock. Then the small dark figure disappears into the cubby.

Sam picks up his basketball. He can hear her in the cubby, moving around. Her chains click like knitting needles. Slowly he finds his way to the doorway of the cubby.

She is molting, shedding pieces of her clothing, becoming a smoothly female figure. Serene, rapt—she reminds him of his stepmother rubbing baby lotion into his little sister's skin or anointing her own skin or hair with some fragrant oil. The cubby is cold, since he has not turned on the heater, and her nipples protrude. Naked, she moves fluidly through the darkness; she stoops to gather her fallen chains and resume them. Sinking to the mattress on the floor, she hugs her knees.

He places his ball carefully on the counter. After flicking on the heater, he takes off his sneakers. The cold comes right up from the floor through his socks. He unbuttons his fly and lets the cold mortify his flesh.

Wordlessly, he joins her on the mattress. Her skin is cold. The touch of his warmth makes her shiver as if she hadn't realized how cold she really was and she snugs up against him hastily. The taste of her mouth is distinctively smoky, nearly the same as it was the night in the parking lot. She winces at the pressure of his lips. Her fingertips go to her upper lip and he takes them off it and lightly feels the bruised area himself.

"What's this?"

She turns her face. "Nothing. Walked into a branch in the dark, coming through the woods."

His forefinger against her chin forces her face in line with his again and she meets his gaze calmly. Though he's sure she's lying, he doesn't know why. Maybe she doesn't want him giving her a hard time about being so stoned she can't get out of the way of a tree.

She cups her hands at the back of his neck and draws his head to her breast. Wondrous bare flesh. The puckered edge of areola, the curve of the bottom of her breast. Hesitantly, he touches her between her legs. The threads are silky as ever, the soft wet welcome thrilling. He closes his eyes in relief. She isn't swollen or sticky from someone else.

Her fingers squeeze and stroke his penis while he works a finger into her. She is unhurried, almost teasing, and he tries to match her pace. One finger, two fingers, probing and opening, sliding, slipping. She makes a small throaty noise; she is ready, he's sure of it. He holds back a little longer, in the hope that drawing it out will help her, but when he tries to substitute his cock for his fingers, she is suddenly dry and resistant and it is too late, he is surprised by a sudden orgasm. There is no way to resist; it just happens, in a mindless hot spill.

At first she reacts slowly but as he apologizes, she registers what has happened. "Shit! You got it all over me. What is this, payback?"

"Payback?"

"You know what I mean!"

He rubs his chest, which hurts with a sudden constriction. His stomach is all knotted up too and he has a headache drilling between his eyes.

"You're still pissed at me!" she explains, as if he can't talk for himself.

The flat statement makes his stomach flutter. Jesus. His stomach clenches with the expectation they are about to commence round bazillion in this cosmic mismatch. He wonders how many times he can take this shit before it becomes aversion therapy and he's cured.

"Why shuh-shouldn't I be ripped? How do you think it made me feel, you and Chapin?"

She looks up at him. "You don't understand."

"No, I suregod don't. How could you do it? Why, for Christ's sake?"

"Fuck you, you self-righteous prick!"

Pushing her off him, he rolls to his feet and yanks the chain on the bare bulb overhead.

She flinches and raises her arm to shade her eyes.

"Don't bother," he says, "you already told me. It's nothing to do with you and me. You lay Chapin, he lays dope on you. No big deal, just a little one you've been working for years. This is my own goddamn fault for letting my dick think for me. Rick's right. You're just another shit-for-brains drug whore like my sister."

Lowering her arm, she stares up, empty-eyed as Little Orphan Annie. He recognizes her stony piss-off from all the times he ever tried to get through to Karen. Now her lip is exposed to the light, he sees the dark swelling of bruise on it. It spreads around the corner of her mouth. Her skin is startling white and fragile in contrast.

"Oh, you're all the same," she cries.

He knows just what she means. They are, he is—no fucking argument. It makes him angrier. "I guess you'd know." He grabs the coat and clothing that she has flung over the counter and begins to shake out the pockets. "Where is it?"

"What?"

"The shit. Whatever kind of shit you got for tricking with that creep. Did you smoke it all up tonight?"

Various pockets yield a meager scattering onto the floor next to the mattress. He scooches over the mess to toss it—some small change, a crumple of currency, raggedy tissues, a flat plastic box, a wooden tube, an eye pencil, a mascara, a lipstick, a plastic comb with the teeth broken out. No dope, not so much as a linty Midol.

"Shithead!"

She plucks out the flat plastic box and throws it at him, a straight shot to the bridge of his nose.

"Ow!" Sitting down abruptly, he claps a hand to his nose and blinks away the involuntary rush of stinging tears. His hand is wet and when he looks at it, there is a trace of blood.

"It's just a cut," she says dismissively, thrusting a crumpled tissue into his hand.

While he blots it, she begins to gather up the strewings into a little heap on the mattress.

Picking up the box she hit him with, he opens it. It is a packet of oral contraceptives.

"J.C. gets them for me. If it weren't for him, I'd be out of school and working a shitty job to support a brat by now."

Stunned, he examines the box again. No prescription sticker— but he can't believe it. She's putting him on or else she thinks he's flatline stupid. It's a legal drug and a cheap one too. She can't really be fucking Chapin just for this. Closing it, he hands it back to her.

"Deanie, they only run about twenty bucks a month. Less than your cigarettes. Which you shouldn't be smoking anyway if you're taking the Pill. No shit—I picked up Karen's prescription once for her. Why don't you just get them from a doctor?"

She sticks her tongue out when he tells her she shouldn't be smoking but he doesn't miss the first shock in her face. She really didn't know how cheap they were. How could she be so ignorant?

"It's thirty-five, forty-five dollars to see a doctor just once and they want you to come back."

"There's good reasons to go back. There's side effects. Sometimes women have strokes from them. Women who smoke," he emphasizes.

"Oh, and when did you go to medical school?"

"Same time Chapin did."

It's a relief to hear her laugh, even a short resentful one. Among her little pile of belongings, he notices the comb again and idly picks it up. It is the kind with thick fangs, except this one has most of its teeth broken off. A pick—that's the name—for extremely curly hair. This girl has no hair at all on her head.

"What's this?"

"A key. Unlocks those plastic frames the stores put cassettes in to keep people from stealing them. Made it myself. It works."

"Jesus, Deanie!"

"Jeez-us yourself! Tapes cost a lot of money."

Sam snaps the homemade key in two.

"You prick!" she says.

"You gotta stop that stealing shit."

"No! You gotta stop trying to run my life, you asshole."

"We've been through all this shit already," he says, "about ten thousand times. You start it up as soon as we finish screwing. I think you're scared to death you're gonna make it one of these times."

Ignoring him, she crouches over the heap of her clothing and extracts a sock. He reaches for his own garments.

"Tomorrow afternoon, want to do some hacking?" he asks, trying not to sound as desperate to make up as he suddenly is.

Her face lights up and for an instant she's so beautiful it hurts. When she pleases so easily, it's like a branch whipping him in the face, reminding him of the scrawny bones of her life. Then she looks away.

"I better not. I got a paper to write." She curls back up on the mattress under her coat. "I'm staying."

Trying not to feel rejected, he checks the heater before he goes. She should be all right. He stumbles on the way out, and out of frustration, curses with disproportionate vehemence.

■ ■ ■

The door crunches over icy grit as he closes it behind him. Then she is alone. The sound of the wind wheezing asthmatically through the trees outside makes her shiver, despite the proximity of the heater. Close call—almost lost him tonight. For once it was worth Tony backhanding her when he hadn't been able to get it up. He'd left no evidence for Samgod's suspicious fingers. Once Tony quit bothering her, she'd needed a number, even though she knew 'god would be angry with her if she turned up stoned. But so far His Holiness is still forgiving her when he gets hard.

Bitterly she thinks of the con J.C. has been pulling on her. Fuck him. She'll find another way to get her Pills. Get Samgod to take her to a clinic somewhere out of town. Give a false name and lie about her age if there's any stupidity about contacting her parents for permission. 'god wants it bad enough; he'll pay for them.

■ ■ ■

On Monday morning, the shadow of bruise that spreads around the corner of her mouth could easily be a stain from her purplish lipstick. She wears a different headrag, a red bandanna, with a small wispy blue-jay feather hooked to one of the rings in her left ear. The way she eats the muffins from the paper bag on the seat, it's like it's the first food she's seen all weekend.

"Get your paper finished?"

In the quick glance he takes at her, he catches the flash of confusion; she has forgotten her own lie.

Swallowing, licking her fingers, she covers it with disdainful indifference. "Oh yeah."

Though they are first at the gym, girls start arriving before they have gotten the rack of basketballs out of the closet. Sam plugs in the mix that starts with "Let's Work Together," by way of setting the tone. Guys trickle in and stand on the sidelines, in groups of threes and fours, watching the girls warming up but making no move to join them.

Dribbling to center court, Sam halts there, keeping the beat of the music with the ball. He looks directly at each of his teammates, one after the other. Polling the jury. Only some of them meet his eyes and Rick's not one of them. Behind the sidelined boys, the coaches of both teams appear in the open doors but none of the players notice them.

He palms the ball hard into the floor and then lets it bobble away from him across the floor toward his teammates.

Coach's question on the bus was the wrong one. Of course they all want to wear Greenspark's colors. The real question is whether they want Sam to go on wearing them.

Silently, Sam strips off his sweatshirt. Under it he wears his practice jersey. When he drops his sweatpants to reveal the rest of his practice uniform, the Jandreau twins burst out giggling and the Mutant wolf-whistles.

The only response from his teammates is a few grins at the girls' reaction to his strip.

"Well?" he asks.

The answer is a wall of glares from the bolder ones, head-hanging by the fencesitters.

Suddenly he yanks the jersey over his head.

"Take it all off!" the Mutant calls and the other girls whoop and applaud.

Fixing on Rick, Sam approaches him first, offering him the jersey, but Rick throws up his palms and backs away, shaking his head. Joey Skouros, to whom Sam offers it next, won't take it either. Sam searches out Billy Rank, who's desperately trying to be invisible. Billy pushes the shirt back to him. Sam turns to Pete, who curls his lip contemptuously. There is no way he can accept the jersey after three others have refused it. He looks away.

Sam pulls his jersey back over his head. "Let's play some hoop."

Though he succeeds in sounding calm, he feels like he has swallowed a stone. When he turns his back on them, he doesn't know if they will follow him again. He looks to the Mutant; she nods reassuringly and bounces a ball his way. As he catches it, he sneaks a glance behind him. Rick is shrugging off his jacket and so are the others, except for the enraged Fosse, who still dithers. Sam breathes again. Looking past the players to the coaches, he winks, and they shake their heads in laughing admiration.

He finds himself double-teamed against Nat Linscott and the Mutant.

"Awesome," the Mutant says.

"I'll say so," Nat giggles.

Sam laughs.

"What you blushing for, Bigger?" the Mutant teases. "Talk dirty to him, Nat, he's losing his concentration."

Nat's face flames under her freckles.

So does Sam's.

■ ■ ■

At lunchtime, Sam has the gym to himself. He wants the personal time with the ball but it is also a political choice, a way to give a breather to his teammates. Without him at the table, they are free to talk about the situation, come to terms with it.

Rick enters the gym and squats on the sidelines, watching him. Bopping the ball over, Sam crouches down next to him. Rick reaches for the ball and Sam lets him take it.

"You yanked my yang," Rick says. And laughs. "Picked me first 'cause you knew I wouldn't take your goddamn jersey. Picked Skouros and Rank, couple of lambs to the slaughter. Backed Peteybird right into the fucking corner and stripped him. Hell of a show, Sambo."

Sam's hands hang slack between his knees. "See if it works tomorrow."

"That was a beautiful rainbow last night. Pure hotdog but oh man, it was something to see."

Sam shrugs, glances at his watch and rises. "Gotta eat."

Rick bounces to his feet. "I forget what you can do when you take a break from being stupid. Look, Sambo, things got out of hand. Some things got said shouldn't have been said."

Unwrapping a sandwich, Sam lets the apology pass with a quick smile. "It's all right, Rick."

"Maybe. If we pull it together again. If it's not too late."

■ ■ ■

Rick's trepidation appears to be unfounded. Practice goes well enough to make Coach cheerful. If there is a distinct chill between Pete Fosse and Sam, it is easy to shrug off. They have never more than tolerated each other but—except for last night's game—it hasn't stopped them working together when necessary. Pete knows he has to serve his apprenticeship if he wants Sam's job next year. Sam bears down hard on Pete—tough on the others too—so much that Fosse has to fight his temper. Coach advises Sam quietly to let up. And Sam does and then takes the trouble to pause and compliment every one of them individually, including Pete, on their play as they leave the floor.

"Fuck you very much," Pete responds, though Coach is only a couple of yards away.

Turning around and walking backward, Sam blows Pete a kiss.

"That's a ten-lap fine, Fosse," the coach says flatly.

With a hitch of his upper lip, Pete pivots and jogs back to the court.

Coach draws Sam aside. "I thought the bullshit was over."

Sam shrugs. "With Pete, it's never over."

The coach fights a smile of recognition; he's shoveled his share from Pete. "What's your point?"

"I want him to understand I'm not going to tolerate any more dogging. I earned my place on this team. I don't need to kiss his ass to stay on it. The only way I put up with him is if he plays to win. If he's got another agenda, he'll pursue it with my foot up his ass."

Coach rocks on his heels. He grins. "Whew! You getting tough on me, Sam?"

Sam smiles. "You want me to stand down?"

Coach throws up his palms. "Hell no. He gets the bit in his teeth, he won't be worth diddly next year. I just want you guys working together again, not against each other."

23

■ ■ ■

The Ball Shimmies and Falls Out as the Mutant misses another free throw. Her shooting has gotten weird. She's favoring the inside of her right foot, Sam concludes. Those shitty tops of hers, she's probably developed blisters or strained a little muscle in her instep from lack of support. She's frustrated with herself but actually she's doing very well away from the line, getting the ball where it should be, marshaling her players.

After the practice ends, he goes out to warm up the truck for her. He finds an old Dickies cassette and slots it. While "The Sounds of Silence" and "Nights in White Satin" are savaged by the punk parodists, the parking lot empties out almost completely around him.

She skitters across the icy pavement like a bug on the surface of the water.

"Coach was gabby," she gasps, throwing herself into the cab and yanking the door closed behind her.

"If Stewart could talk, what would he say to me?" the Dickies' lead singer asks, launching into a song about his penis.

"Oh, great," she says, arranging her gear on the floor of the cab. "Stewart. I love it. You got a name for yours?"

"No," Sam says. "*Stewart*'s a bust but guys who name their

dicks make me nervous." He's sitting in his truck talking about dicks with a girl, he realizes suddenly. A girl he's fucked. Talking dirty. It makes him feel a lit bit heady and a lot horny. "Do girls do that? Give their pussies names?"

Offended, the Mutant's ringed nose lifts snootily. "Only guys are that weird."

It's amazing how prudish she is sometimes, for a girl with her reputation. This is the same girl who shook her tits at him in the Mill and the Playground, who put the moves on him from the git-go.

"My stepmother told me someone with lot of pet names is well loved," he says.

"That certainly explains why some guys name their dicks."

Suddenly she snakes across the seat, sinking as she goes until she is prone on the bench with her face below his belt. Her fingers move swiftly to his belt buckle and buttons.

"Are you out of your mind?" he asks weakly, hands hovering above her head as he surveys the parking lot anxiously. Shit. Both coaches' vehicles are still there. The janitor's old van too. Romney's rust-eaten Olds.

He closes his eyes and rests his head against the top of the seat. He isn't sure he likes it any more than he did the other times she used her mouth on him. He fights the urge to move, to thrust, which would be awkward to do while seated and besides, he is afraid if he does he will choke her or hurt her bruised lip. Occasionally he feels her teeth, which also makes him nervous. What she does to him is too obviously a learned skill—it even has a certain rote quality to it. Remembering Chapin bragging, he projects what a major legend it will instantaneously become if he gets caught getting blown by the Mutant in the parking lot. Despite intense excitement, there are so many inhibiting factors, he is almost unable to come.

Immediately after he does, he opens his eyes and the first thing he sees is Coach, slip-sliding his way toward the truck. "Oh shit. Coach!"

As he sits up abruptly, his sudden movement unbalances her. She coughs and sputters his ejaculate back onto him.

While he tucks his wet, softening cock back into his jeans, she slithers floorward and flattens herself into the shadows of the footwell. He gets half his buttons done and his buckle closed and

Coach is there, looming at the window, his long face scrunched up against the cold.

Rolling down the window, Sam leans forward to hug the wheel and incidentally block Coach's view into the cab.

"Hi," he says.

Coach squints at him. "Problem with your truck?"

Sam shakes his head. "Just warming it up, Coach. Listening to some music."

Coach grimaces. "That ain't music. It's a soundtrack for degeneracy."

Sam nods agreeably.

Coach gives him a funny look and then mutters, "Well, goodnight," and wanders off.

Cranking up the window, Sam rolls his eyes.

The Mutant pounds the floor with her fists and sobs a muffled laughter.

"Great, I bet he smelled it, he thinks I was sitting here jerking off," he says. "Stay on the floor till we're out of the parking lot, okay?"

She hiccups.

"You okay?" he asks.

With several spastic gesticulations, she indicates she is. When they are on the main road, she creeps up into the seat and rests her head against his thigh. He touches her chains.

"Deanie," he says and stops.

She waits, attentive to the sound of her name.

"What's wrong with your foot?"

She sits up and tucks herself against the far side of the cab. Staring out the window, she speaks without tone. "Wracked it on a corner of my bed."

"Oh. You know you're favoring it? That's what's throwing off your shot."

"No shit." She's sarcastically bored.

He glances at her. At her mouth. Back to the road and then at her again. Under her headrag, under the chains, her narrow face is set resentfully but the fixity of her facial muscles does not disguise how young she is. Sixteen, supposed to be sweet.

They are nearly at Depot Street before she speaks again, as the Dickies tape spins into silence.

"You didn't like it, did you?" she asks with a tinselly lightness.

Carefully he makes the turn. "I don't know." He tries to soften it. "I mean, with Coach bopping out to pass the time of day, you know."

"Right." Her voice goes flat. "There's no pleasing some people, I guess."

He reaches out toward her but she's out of the truck and gone. He watches her march angrily down the street. Such a ridiculous girl. If she could see herself, with her backpack and gym bag and the way the tag ends of her headrag bounce and her long coat jerks with her stride. She doesn't look back but he knows what her face looks like angry, a glitter of tears in her dark eyes and her mouth set and those chains bouncing light and her hurt little face white underneath them, her skin so transparent. Close up, a veinous blue like an inadvertent mark of blue ink, faded but not entirely washed away, is visible in certain places—near the corners of her eyes, one place near her jawline.

He sees her clearly now. She's not a Mutant. She's Deanie Gauthier. She lies and she thieves and she knows how to do things a sixteen-year-old girl shouldn't know. And she has too many bruises.

He glances at himself in his rearview mirror.

"And you're fucking her, Preacher," he jeers at himself.

■ ■ ■

Next morning, they are back in the gym. A sharp whistle from Rick punctuates the ripple of amusement from the gathering players at Sam's choice of a dance mix of "She Drives Me Crazy" as the first cut on the new dub he plugs into the sound system. The Mutant—Deanie, he amends—Deanie laughs loudest. Though he intends a self-deprecating joke, Sam's ears glow. At least it kicks off the session playfully.

Stopped by Coach in the corridor after his first-period physics class—Coach wants to know what the hell is wrong with Billy Rank, who is playing as if he left his basketball brains on the bus somewhere—Sam is a few minutes late for lifting. Chapin's already into it, working the machines. Sam makes himself ignore the prick. The music on the boombox is Zep.

"Fucking Zep," Rick bitches. "We had to listen to old fuck Zep last time. Gimme a fucking break."

The few objections are too weak to be taken seriously and several guys shout out what they have for cassettes.

"I got new stuff," Sam says.

The revelation provokes groaning and rhetorical vomiting.

"No punks," Rick announces, "and I don't want to hear any of that headbanger crap."

"Hey," Todd Gramolini says, "what's this shit? I happen to like metal."

Nearly everyone in the room backs the sentiment with obscene affection.

"Remember Dread Zep?" Sam asks.

Rick groans. "Too well. None of that shit, either, Samurai."

"Not them. They're not new anymore. This tape I got in my duffel, it's called 2 Live Zep."

Everyone laughs and waits expectantly for the punchline.

"First cut's called 'Suck My Black Dog,' " Sam says.

Rick's shriek of laughter rises above the outburst of the others. Sam blushes; he can't help it.

"Hey hey mama," he sings, mimicking Robert Plant's blues-hoarse tenor, "say you suck my dick, say you suck my dick 'til it makes you sick."

"Make me sick all right," Rick gasps.

The rest of the session, everyone spends revising various classic Zep lyrics to 2 Live Zep versions of equally unredeeming social merit. It is, Sam thinks, a successful shuck. The foolishness relaxes them all and unlike the locker-room sexual boasting, no one is maligned by it. And they are reassured that he is still one of them, still the reliably blasphemous Preacher who was one of the instigators of the most legendary of school pranks.

■ ■ ■

Sam is in the shower when Chapin steps under the spray next to him. Chapin lets his head drop back and the water flushes over his face and down his body. He shakes himself all over like a wet dog and moves closer to Sam.

"Just the man I wanted to see."

Sam turns his back on him.

"You owe me, Samson," Chapin continues. "From New Year's Eve."

On the other side of Sam, Rick shuts off his shower and lets his ears flap while he towels off.

Chapin shrugs. "Hey, man, I'm not going to press it. I'm a reasonable guy. I can make allowances for a misunderstanding.

What's the profit in us being at odds, for either of us? Shake on it, Samson?"

Sam glances at the hand Chapin offers.

"Come on," Chapin urges. "We got no reason to be enemies. Not over Sister D." He looks to Rick and back to Sam for consensus. "We go back, D. and me, you know that, but anybody can do anything they want."

Sam turns to Rick. "What an asshole," he says softly.

Rick laughs.

"Oh fuck you then," Chapin says, still smiling, "that's the way you want it."

Sam buries his face in the water, hosing the rage roaring in his head.

■ ■ ■

The singular beat of the ball on the polished court reverberates in the empty gym as he drives it. Again he is avoiding the cafeteria to meditate alone with ball and hoop. He needs desperately to get his head straight about Deanie Gauthier and it's impossible to do when she's right there in front of him. As he works the ball, he unplugs his brains and lets what his body knows take over. As if he were dreaming, his mind runs its programs randomly, processing basketball, Deanie and sex, overlapping, intersecting, like the shapes of colored glass filtering light in a kaleidoscope.

Billy Rank slips into the gym and squats on the sidelines. Sam drifts his way and hunkers down next to him.

"What's up, Bilbo?"

"Gotta talk to somebody, Sam."

Looking at the tic pulsing under Billy's eye, Sam doesn't doubt it, though he groans inwardly at being Billy's chosen confessor.

"What is it, my son?" Sam murmurs in a grave ministerial voice.

Billy laughs shakily and then takes a deep breath. His pleading eyes lock on Sam's. "I didn't have anything to do with that rat in your locker."

Sam shrugs.

Billy's gaze drops suddenly and his face blotches with embarrassment. "I didn't do anything to that girl, Sam." He shakes his head. "I couldn't. I was too drunk." A nervous hand goes to his forehead, rakes his hair. "Never been so shitfaced, Sam, honest. I was just gonna have a few beers but I got wasted so fast. When we picked up the girls, I heard the Mutant telling Pete Lexie's only thirteen but I couldn't believe anything serious would happen. And then it did and I didn't even want to try but Pete called me a limpdick faggot. I never believed I could be involved in something like that. It just seemed to have its own momentum, you know?"

Sam reaches out to squeeze Billy's forearm. "Take it easy, Billy."

Looking up with anguished eyes, Billy asks, "I can't stop thinking about it. It's all mixed up in my head. I'm not sure of what I'm remembering anymore. What do I do, Sam?"

It's the last question Sam wants to hear.

"You're not sure what happened?"

Billy shakes his head. "Not exactly. Some of it. I mean, you know what happened. We were all wrecked except Gauthier and she stayed away from what was going on with the other girls."

Sam clears his throat.

"Billy, do you want to talk to someone? Coach or Wild Bill or Rick's dad maybe?"

"Shit no!"

Sam relaxes a little.

"I'm talking to you," Billy points out.

"Okay. But maybe you should get some help with this."

"I just want to know if Lexie is okay. That's the important thing. I'd like to apologize to her but what if she laughs at me?"

"You have to do what you think is right."

Billy groans. "I don't know what's right!"

"Well, you can't undo what's done. Try to let it go for now. Maybe what you should do will come clear if you can get a little distance on it. If it makes you feel better to see if she's okay, do it. I haven't heard she isn't—okay, I mean. She was loaded too, right? So maybe she doesn't remember a whole lot more than you do."

Billy nods eagerly. "Yeah, maybe she doesn't. Thanks, Sam."

This is great, another load of shit to put him in the right frame of mind to play. Billy too; if Billy manages any kind of game tonight, it'll be a frigging miracle. Something else to credit to Pete Fosse and Chapin.

They exit the gym together and have the ill luck to meet Rick and Pete and Todd coming out of the cafeteria. Billy blanches and hustles in the opposite direction and Pete stares after him.

Rick falls in next to Sam and they head downstairs to motor shop.

"I'd ask you what that was about but from the way Pete just

looked at Billy, I don't have to. Billy the Kid puking his guts to you?"

Sam grins at him. "What are you asking for if you don't have to?"

"So I can tell you not to be an idiot," Rick answers, grinning himself.

Sam doesn't believe Rick's grin any more than Rick believes his.

■ ■ ■

After school, Sam heads for the library to do homework in the time before the game. The room is full of Greenspark players with the same idea. There is an empty chair next to Nat Linscott, who gives him a warm, welcoming smile. Blushing, he dumps his books next to Rick instead. Going to the card file for the reference he needs, he wanders into the stacks. The free-standing shelving goes eight feet high, making shadowy corridors. Hearing a page turn thickly, he peeks around a corner.

Deanie sits cross-legged on the floor, leafing through an art folio. When his shadow cuts the meager light, she glances up. A bloom of color burns suddenly on her pallid cheekbones.

Holding a silencing finger to his lips, he sinks to the floor next to her. She turns the book to show him the plate.

It is a picture Sam has seen before, in a history textbook once, and several times in magazines. A famous one. *Nude Descending a Staircase*. The figure, presumably a woman, stutters down the curve of the stairs like a multiple exposure. In a monotone of tattered tarnished golds, her motion is mysteriously hobbled and somehow mechanical. Sam pauses, staring harder at the figure. She appears to have no hair.

Deanie touches the plate reverently with her long beautiful fingers. The cigarette burn on the back of her hand is a small dark shadow now.

"I always feel calmer when I look at this. I don't know why. It's so mysterious," she says in a low voice.

They look up from the folio at each other. Sam reaches out and touches her mouth with the tip of his finger. Her lips are warm and full and the tip of his finger rolls over their curve and slides along the slick moist inside. Her eyes fixed on his, she moves her head with his finger, following its pressure. The light wavers and she tips her head away from his finger and stares past him. He turns to see Rick standing there, one hand falling casually to the stack.

"Excuse me," Rick says and moves away.

Deanie takes back her folio and Sam rises. Stooping again to Deanie, he kisses her quickly, and then again and takes his time. She reaches up to grab the chain that dangles from his open shirt collar.

Feeling a little dizzy, he straightens up and backs away, bumping into the nearest stack. The whole thing shudders and he puts out a steadying hand. Blindly he fumbles along it, looking for his reference.

At the table, Rick asks, "You get any?"

Sam folds himself into the chair next to Rick.

"Any what?"

"Any thing. Tongue, tit, crabs, whatever."

"It didn't mean anything," Sam murmurs, dropping a heavy hand on Rick's thigh. "You're the only one I care about."

Slapping Sam's hand away, Rick jumps as if someone has just spilled hot coffee in his lap.

"I'm being molested," he complains loudly.

The librarian looks over her glasses with a pained expression.

"He asked for it," Sam says. "He came on to me."

Everyone is laughing behind their hands.

"Quiet, please," the librarian says, "or I'll have to eject you both."

Sam pouts at Rick.

"Bitch," he murmurs.

Sweeping his books down the table, Rick gets up and puts a chair between them.

Sam makes kissy-faces after him.

■ ■ ■

Twice-twinned in the glass, wearing their hair in spouts, one to the left side of her crown, the other to her right, the Jandreau sisters solemnly adopt mirror-image poses, rising to their toes, lifting their arms to push imaginary basketballs into imaginary arches through an imaginary hoop. Then they burst out giggling. This pantomime is ritual with them before games.

The Mutant nudges Nat. "You think *I'm* weird."

Nat grins. "Go look in the mirror, Gauthier."

The Mutant leaps to center bench and struts down it. Except for her earrings and chains, she is stark naked. The other girls laugh at her; even the twins are distracted from their posturing. At the end of the bench, the Mutant stares into the horizontal mirror above the makeup counter. She narrows her eyes in mock seductiveness and caresses her bare breasts. She runs the tip of her tongue over her lips.

"I can't help it," she pants. "None of us can. As soon as we take our clothes off, we have to"—she whimpers—"touch ourselves."

The other girls shriek and applaud.

Tying her laces while the Mutant skins hastily into her uniform, Nat stops giggling and grows serious. "You're really banged up. What happened to your instep? It's all purple."

"Caught it in a car door," the Mutant says dismissively. "It looks worse than it is."

On the other side of Nat, Deb Michaud sniggers. "Come on, Gauthier, we all know you're into S & M."

"Whip me, beat me," the Mutant begs, "make me sit on the bench."

"Is that a hickey on your tit?" Deb asks.

The Mutant glances down.

"No, but that *is* a hickey on my ass."

Up and down the lockers the girls groan.

"That's gross," someone murmurs.

"No, the one that's gross is on my—"

Coach slaps open the door. "Ladies," she says, "two minutes to blast-off."

"Ladies? Blast-off?" Nat asks the Mutant and they both snicker.

Once uniformed, the Mutant goes to the mirror. Nat is already there, examining a small bump on her chin. She tsks with disgust at it.

"What's going on with you and Sam?" Nat asks. There is a giveaway nervousness in her voice and her cheekbones redden.

The other girls in front of the mirror are suddenly very quiet; there is a lot of interest in this question.

The Mutant's chains puddle neatly in her palm and her face is naked. Again she narrows her eyes in a simulation of arousal.

"We fuck like beasts," she announces, touching one breast and shivering. "Every chance we get. When he takes me"—she crosses her arms over her breasts—"we know nothing but our incendiary passion."

There is an outburst of laughter even Nat can't help joining.

24

■ ■ ■

The Mutant Is Getting Hacked but good. Double- and sometimes triple-teamed by the girls from Helsinki in this rematch with the Raiders, she is drawing a disproportionate and occasionally savage offensive effort.

"I'm blind, I'm deaf, I wanna be a ref!" Sam chants derisively at the officials and instigates wholesale editorializing from the bleachers.

Eventually a foul is called and the Mutant goes to the line and can't get it in the hopper. Her foul-shooting is still off. From the floor she shoots on the move effectively. She compensates for her poor foul-line work with a flurry of rebounding and assists—it is the most generous game he has ever seen from her. After a particularly tricky play, she shoots him a look of triumph.

When he offers her his palm as the girls, leaving the court, pass the boys coming onto it, she doesn't hesitate. High-fiving him, she calls out, "Come on, people!" and both boys and girls roar their response.

■ ■ ■

The Helsinki boys come out aware that Dyer's Mills has shoved a nasty stick into the cogs of the Big Machine. Foremost in all their minds is the question of whether the Indians can pull it together again outside of practice. In the first few minutes, Greenspark is shaky from nerves. Kasten twists an ankle and Coach sends in Joey Skouros. As if Skouros is the vital piece in the puzzle—not the last one, but the one that pulls the jigsawed picture together—Greenspark is suddenly whole and working together.

For Sam, sheer relief releases him into the slipstream of the game. He soars on the warm thermals of smoothly executed plays, everything concentrated in the instant. He comes to earth again toward the end of the third quarter and, as Bither goes to the foul line, signals Coach that he wants relief.

Pete Fosse crouches briefly at the scorers' table and then stops Sam as he approaches the bench.

"Who's your man?" Pete asks.

Sam stares at him in disbelief. "Where's your head?" He shoves his face into Pete's. "You should fucking well know who!"

One of the officials is approaching.

"Styles," Coach calls.

Wide-eyed and sweating, Pete stares at Sam. He is too stunned by Sam's fury to dare to breathe.

"Why don't you see if you can figger it out?" Sam snarls and strides past him.

"What—?" Coach begins.

"Fosse doesn't know who he's guarding," Sam says. "He hasn't got his head in the game. He shouldn't be in there."

Coach's mouth tightens as he glances toward Fosse, gone red and sullen. "I'll coach this game, if you don't mind. Siddown."

Sam slumps into his chair and reaches for a water bottle.

Fosse founders in traffic, trying to figure out who he is supposed to be guarding. Seeing Pete's confusion, Gramolini signals impatiently toward Number 35.

Next to Sam, Coach snorts and crosses his arms. "You keep your head in this game, Sunny Jim. You're going back in about ninety seconds. Be prepared to stay in too. Mr. Fosse is gonna take some serious lessons in bench-sitting from me."

Soon Pete is surprised by Coach's hook, and as Sam passes him to reenter the game, Sam tells him clearly, "You're on three-five, asshole."

Pete reddens again. Coach points him into the seat next to him and drops a heavy hand on the back of Pete's chair.

■ ■ ■

Outside the lockers the Mutant in her fringed headrag and full chains struts the corridor, to the amusement of her teammates, as well as exiting Raiders and cheerleaders from both schools. They go out into a winter night gone suddenly mild and sweet, and the roof is off the sky. From the Helsinki buses and a parking lot full of vehicles, opened windows emit a cacophony of clashing music and raucous young voices.

"Need a ride?" Sam asks, in the midst of the others.

The Mutant slings her gear at him.

"The question is, do you?" she drawls.

Sam reddens and the others laugh.

Ignoring him, she strolls toward the truck.

He tugs his forelock, adjusts his burdens and shuffles after her in the guise of her faithful chauffeur.

"I have to work," he tells her as he keys the ignition. "I really do," he insists and realizes he is telling this lie to himself. "How's your foot?"

She shrugs.

"You hung in there almost the whole game," he goes on. "Your stamina's really improved." The compliments bring only silence. "You mad at me?" he finally ventures.

"No." She twists her body toward him, kneeling on the seat. "Nat asked me if you and I had something going on." Adopting the smoldering narrow-eyed poise of the locker room, she tells him what she said.

Vintage Mutant; he loves it. Sam wipes tears of laughter from his eyes. "Jesus. Fuck like beasts?"

"They didn't believe me," she says, sinking back against the seat. "I knew they wouldn't."

Glancing at her, Sam hardly believes it himself. He feels like two people, the one he used to be and the one who goes to the Mill with Deanie Gauthier.

He clears his throat. "I could be a little late."

■ ■ ■

He stares at the swirling cartoons on the wall over the mattress. Now he sees the influence of that painting she showed him. Not that her cartooning is that much like it but it has some of the same stuttering expression of movement and a mechanization of the figures too. She draws herself in different sizes, sometimes smaller than the figures with whom she interacts, sometimes larger. Sometimes it's only parts of her that change in size, in proportion to the rest of her or the other figures. In a segment that details a scene from a basketball game, her headless body is in proportion to her teammates, all immediately recognizable, but her hands are huge and it is her head that is in use as the ball. In another area of the cartoon, the figures are shattered into pieces in a way he doesn't understand. There are no faces but he recognizes the way she draws herself. Her fragmented body is among the stew of parts. He doesn't want to look at it too closely because this is the most violent and pornographic section of the wall but it draws his eyes. The more he studies them the more troubled he is by the sense it is a kind of code he should be able to read. He closes his eyes to block it out, thinking tiredly of the lie he will have to tell to his father about being so late getting home and not even calling to say where he was.

Holding her is the best part of it so far—having her warmth, the smoothness of her body against him. But he's beginning to worry the rest of it is never going to work. Every failure to satisfy her chips away at his confidence. It isn't enough to get off himself; he can do that with his own hand any time. Until the pleasure is mutual, he is just using her as a wet spot. Millions do this every day, he tells himself. Is everybody lying like a mad motherfucker, claiming it is such an ecstatic experience while suffering similar agonies of embarrassing clumsiness and frustration? Or is he just a total fuckup at this too? If it's going to be like learning to read, he'll be getting the hang of it around the time he turns forty.

Screw it. The two of them don't like each other well enough to be successful at making love. There's just too much underlying hostility. It's just like he can play with either Rick or Billy, and Rick will help him and he'll help Billy, but if he had to work with Pete Fosse as his point man, it would be a disaster.

He manages to get out from under her and is sitting on the counter, hauling on his boots, when she stirs.

"I gotta go. You want me to take you home?"

"No," she murmurs and rolls over, with her arm over her head. He tucks her coat around her. The cubby's warmed up since they arrived and turned the heater on.

"Goodnight," he says, with a quick kiss on the crown of her headrag.

" 'Night," she mutters.

Looking down at her, he hesitates but in the end he just leaves.

■ ■ ■

Friday's away is against the Mount Grace Red Demons and Lady Demons. The boys' bus is unusually quiet. Though the team truce seems to be in place and things appear to be back to normal, there is a sense of unfinished business simmering. Sam pulls his headphones down over his ears as if he were yanking down a windowshade. He slips into an uneasy doze and dream comes upon him as a shadow, winged and ominous.

A church piano reverently and sedately plunks a childhood hymn, the one they always sang at Easter Service in the Universalist-Congo church on the Ridge, but it is accompanied by the disembodied and mournful working-class British nasality of Billy Bragg singing

> And was Jerusalem builded here,
> among those dark satanic mills?

Then he is in the cubby, reaching for the support of the cartooned wall. His splayed fingers upon the plaster sink into it and as the darkness begins to press upon him like a great hand, he is flattened into the wall. He cannot breathe and it is hugely painful and then he feels himself bursting in poisonous colors like some great pustule lanced. He flows for some time and then he is much thinner, hardly there at all, no more than an attenuated web of lines upon the wall.

It is like being in prison, only it is space itself that jails him. Around him the other cartoon figures struggle frantically to free themselves. He hears them but can only see outward, in the direction in which the points of his pupils are fixed. Their struggle is entirely internal. He hears not their hands pounding upon the flat plane of their prison but their hearts, their lungs, the workings of their bodies down to their cells, in a desperate cacophony of anger and fear and yearning. He hears their thoughts like lyrics and they are astonishing, all woven together, polished bright here and rusty there, chains of words looping in a childishly simple pattern that gradually becomes clear to him, in a mocking voice he knows well.

> She linked up all the iron hoops,
> She smoked up all the rope,
> She tried to eat the basketball
> But it wouldn't go down her throat.

He sits up abruptly, wide awake. The bus is warm with bodies but the window next to him is a plane of chilly damp. He shivers.

"It wouldn't go down her throat," he mutters groggily.

"I bet," Rick says. "Be a brave wench to even try."

Sam stretches and rolls his head and then slumps against the window again, fingertips to the cold condensate beading there.

"The basketball," he says. "The basketball."

"Well"—Rick grins—"if we're talking about the Mutant, you had the right idea."

■ ■ ■

Under the lights her bald head gleams disconcertingly among the frizzies and curls and satiny bouncy heads of hair of the other girls. She looks like a baby buzzard, with her thin neck and the bulbous curve of her skull and her dark fierce eyes. Her mascara and eyeliner run as she sweats, in dirty tears and streaks. She uses the bottom of her tunic to wipe her face and smears the dirt around until it is a faded warpaint. At the foul line, she sinks a little, then rises from flexed knees to take the shot and even as he notes her form, his knowledge of her body disturbs Sam in the most distracting way.

"Relax," Rick murmurs, nudging him. "The babes'll pull it out."

The foul shot bounces off the glass and falls away. She spins away, going for the rebound, and shoots another air ball. It is a relief to have the action reverse toward Mount Grace's goal.

"Come on, Bigger," Rick urges, "time to change."

In the locker room, they hear the buzzer and the outburst from the Greenspark fans. Sam grins and Rick describes triumphant circles with a closed fist.

As the girls pass the boys on the way to their locker room, Sam offers Deanie a high five. She looks right through him. They have barely spoken since Tuesday night. Though he's continued to chauffeur her, he keeps the volume up on the music and conversation is no more than the barest exchange of necessary information. Loping onto the floor with his teammates, it hits him with a jolt that what's going on between him and Deanie is eerily like the tight-lipped tension he recalls between his parents back when they were married.

■ ■ ■

Their baggy red uniforms flapping around their skinny white legs, the Demons look woefully boyish. This team is very young and green. Sam sits out much of the game, watching Greenspark's juniors and sophomores try out what they have been learning. Joey Skouros, at big forward, looks better and better to him. On the bus ride home, he will suggest to Coach that Joey has the makings of a center. Though Pete Fosse is supposed to replace Sam at that position when Sam graduates, it wouldn't hurt to have Joey ready to back up and eventually replace Pete. Among the sophomores, there are two other candidates for big forward so the bench would be deep at all positions.

On the bus, after successfully bending Coach's ear, he takes his seat next to Rick.

Rick stretches comfortably. "Sarah rented a couple vids, Sambo. Why don't you come over and watch them with us? My dad's got the late shift and Mom'll go to bed by eleven so we don't have to cover our eyes during the gushy kissing scenes and we can OD on popcorn."

"Sure you and Sarah wouldn't rather be alone?"

"Of course we would. You're the next best thing, doofus. For some weird reason, my mother is under the impression Sarah and me won't do anything to offend your boyish modesty."

"So if it looks like Sarah's going to try to jump you, I should throw myself bodily between the two of you?"

"Nothing that heroic, bud. Just keep your eyes on the tube and if we're a long time in the kitchen, just assume we're popping a shitload of corn."

Sam frowns. "You know how many people die choking on popcorn every year?"

Rick wraps his hands around Sam's throat and pretends to throttle him while Sam shows the whites of his eyes and sticks out his tongue.

"Maybe," Sam finally accedes.

■ ■ ■

As the bus backs into the parking slot behind Greenspark Academy, Sarah calls and waves from the window of Rick's car.

"Ain't that nice," Rick smirks. "Baby's got it all warmed up for me."

The girls' bus pulls in behind them. Sam lopes to his truck to start it, get the heater going. As he shivers behind the wheel, the

Mutant cuts past his truck, headed for the main road. How could she miss him? The truck hasn't moved since she got out of it in the morning. He toots the horn at her and she fails to respond, so he does it again, more urgently, but she doesn't even look his way. All at once he is certain she is shanking him so she can meet Chapin somewhere and go partying.

He pulls up next to her and rolls down the truck's window. "Come on, Deanie."

She answers him with a rigid middle digit.

Spinning the truck into a swooping turn in front of her, he leaps out in her path as she swerves to go around it.

"Get in the truck!" He tries to sound amused but it comes out faked and edgy.

Gritting her teeth, she zigzags. He makes a wall of himself. She loses her grip on her gear as she struggles to evade him and immediately they are a tangle of feet and canvas, grappling at each other to stay upright.

"Get in the goddamn truck!" he commands.

Laughter and catcalls reverberate around them from exuberant students in the process of departure. Sarah and Rick are distracted from their necking in the front seat of his car to watch.

The knowledge that they have a large avid audience does nothing for Sam's equanimity. Seizing her gear, he heaves it into the cab of the truck. When she spins to stalk away, he catches her by the arm and waist and yanks her into her own momentum, so she falls back against him.

"Slug her one, Sambot!" one of the Jandreau twins yells and raises a supporting chorus, Nat among them.

Her eyes go blank and she stiffens in his arms. He is stricken for her, furious with whichever bitch-twin set it off and the others too for participating and enraged with himself for not just leaving her be. He boosts her bodily into the truck. Jumping in behind her, he slams his own door and stretches over her to lock the right-hand door. She crawls away from him, slipping to the floor of the cab.

"Stop it! I'm not going to hit you. I'd never hit you." Tightening his grip on the wheel convulsively, he stares over it and mutters, "Might kill you, though." He glances at her. "I don't mean that, it's a joke."

She wipes her nose with the back of her hand. Crawling onto the seat, she puddles there like a discarded rag.

"What is this shit? You'll get sick again. I don't mind taking you home."

"Don't put yourself out," she spits at him. "Just leave me the fuck alone."

Tight-lipped, Sam puts the truck in gear and turns it for the road.

Her body rigid with fury, she screams at him, "How would you like to be yelled at and pushed around and have those assholes screaming at somebody to beat you up?"

"I didn't mean for any of that to happen. I'm sorry. They didn't mean it either. They're blowing off, that's all. I just want you to be sensible and let me take you home so you won't get sick again. Jesus, Deanie, you got nothing on your feet but those shitty sneakers and there's three, four inches of wet slush on the sides of the road."

She answers with a sullen thump of her sneakers to his dashboard. After a long silence, she shivers and reaches for his lunch bucket. "Right. I forgot you're a frigging saint."

For a moment she concentrates on stuffing half a sandwich. She slurps some tea that must be at best lukewarm from his Thermos, and then starts peeling a banana. She sniffs. "Think they'll use any game footage on the news tonight?"

The smell of banana brings saliva to Sam's dry mouth and he gestures to her to share.

"Maybe. You did good." He stops himself from bringing up the errors he noticed. She is already sore at him and she takes criticism unpredictably. Better hold it until practice.

Walking on her knees, she crosses the seat to put a lump of banana into his mouth. His stomach lurches at the touch of her fingers on his mouth. She stays there, feeding herself, then him, fingertips gooey and sweet, pushing the chunks of fruit between his lips. Her chains ripple under streetlight against her cheek and the lower ones sway with the slight movement of her body as she balances against the motion of the truck. The slick glob of banana clogs his throat and he nearly strangles getting it down. Her hand falls to his thigh and she leans against him, breast against his jacketed arm.

The wet black road is streaked watery red from taillights ahead of him. He feels blinkered, unable to see anywhere but straight ahead. The road just goes on and on, a meaningless slick ribbon through the night. Her touch, her proximity confuses him, panicking him with the knowledge of his susceptibility. The turn comes quickly and he takes the truck to the secluded parking spot he has used on previous trysts.

She offers the last piece of banana and he opens his mouth for it and she pushes it between his lips, rolling her fingers against his mouth and into it and he sucks at the gummy sweetness and she takes them out and her mouth is on his, her tongue and his mashing the soft sweet lump of fruit. It breaks up into a cloying stickiness and he tears his face away from her and pushes her off him.

She shrugs. "I'm going to the Mill anyway. Tony worked the day shift this week so they'll be wasted by now. I don't want to go home until they're under the table."

While it's a relief to hear her say she wasn't going out partying, the matter-of-factness of her plan chills him. He feels stupid for seeing their use of the Mill as a kind of vandalism when the place is her refuge. With the jeering in the school parking lot hardly faded from his ears, he finds the thought of her spending the rest of the night alone in the ruined Mill by herself horrible. But if he goes with her, they will have sex again, or try to, yes they will. He comes to an abrupt decision. They can go to Rick's house later.

Dragging her gear behind her, she slips out of the cab without another word and picks her way through the brush to the path through the dark woods. He closes his eyes for a second and when he opens them, she's gone. Hastily, he kills the ignition and yanks a flashlight from the glovebox.

Blundering through punky snow into the trunks of trees and tangles of brush, he feels as if he is fighting his way through a wall of thorns. A frozen stick cracks loudly under his foot and he realizes he's sweating as violently as if he were in a losing overtime.

As before, she has chosen her candles over the electric light and there is a glow from the watchman's cubby. When he fills up the doorway, she looks up, unsurprised, from unlacing her ties. He clicks off the flashlight and sets it on the counter. When he turns to her, she holds out her hands. He moves toward her, drawing her close. He gasps at the pressure of her chains rolling over him.

■ ■ ■

For once, her urgency is as great as his.

"Do it," he begs her and she gasps and claws at him.

Momentarily he's lost in the shellburst of his own orgasm. She still struggles in its lee and he tries to help, continuing to move in her, but soon they concede to the recession, the ebbing of arousal. Her head rests against his chest as his heart slows again to a mundane rhythm. If he could take her there—he doesn't know what would happen but surely something would change, something fundamental.

"I have to work a double shift tomorrow. You want to try to meet here Sunday afternoon? Work on your foul shot? I'll buy us a take-out lunch and we'll picnic."

Her eyes shine. He likes that. If it weren't so late, he'd take her to Rick's. Next time he gets the chance. No big deal. Just Deanie's with him—sometimes. A friend of his, whatever else happens between them, and so he expects any other friend to treat her decently. Those assholes in the parking lot will just have to eat it and smile to his face.

■ ■ ■

At the edge of the supermarket parking lot, Sergeant Woods smokes a no-count cigarette in his cruiser. He waggles a flipper at Sam as the truck passes—maybe he's only encouraging smoke out the open window.

■ ■ ■

The baby's crying leaks down the back stairs to the kitchen as Sam lets himself into the house. His stepmother's bare feet pad the polished hardwood floor of the upstairs hall and then the baby gurgles and hiccups to her shushing.

He urinates in the downstairs bathroom and is surprised by a hot stinging. Wincing, he glances at his cock resting on his forefinger. Red and chafed. The stinging's hard use, he assures himself. Just like when he first began masturbating to orgasm, he did it so often he had some water trouble too. Scared himself silly, thinking he'd broken something.

But she tricks with Chapin, Chapin takes it where he can get it, from Karen among others—or so the creep claims and it's at least possible—which brings up the grotesque potential of a daisy chain of infection connecting brother and sister. How could he be so stupid? I'm on the Pill, she tells him, and that's all he pays any mind to, as if knocking her up is the only thing to fret.

Suddenly he wants to shower, as if it would make any difference if she's given him the clap or something. In any case, the baby's just settling down and the racket of the water in the tin shower stall might disturb her. He draws warm water into the basin and gives himself a GI bath, wincing at the burn of soap lather in minute abrasions on his skin. No problem, no big deal, nothing but fucking his brains out. Please.

When he comes out of the bathroom, he is surprised by his father, standing in his pajama pants in the middle of the living room with the TV clicker in his hand, evidently on a mission to catch the late news. Still buttoning his jeans, Sam is taken with a violent guilty blush that worsens with the sudden quirk in his father's smile.

"You had a good game."

"Yeah." He grabs the newel post and pivots around it.

"Sammy," Reuben says.

He stops, not looking back. Can't show his face to his father's X-ray vision again.

Reuben sighs. "Nevermind. Goodnight."

Muttering a goodnight he is certain his father does not hear, Sam takes himself upstairs.

25

■ ■ ■

Gathered at the Meeting House in the early morning, there is the continuing sense of reservation, of waiting on something, even though they pulled together for the previous night's game. Rick arrives a little late, with Billy Rank. Fosse, Gramolini and Bither turn penetrating disdainful glares on Billy and he falters. Rick's hand, casual and reassuring, cups his substitute's elbow.

"Hey Bigger," Pete says, "I see you slugging the Mutant around the parking lot, I wondered maybe she put that scratch on your nose last week?"

"Come on, Peteybird," Gramolini chides, "she never fought it in her life."

Pete squints at Sam. "Yeah—but you forget they're into S & M. Looks like a bite mark to me. She must a tried to bite off his nose when they were working each other up sometime."

"How is she?" Bither demands. "Tell us about it, Sambot."

Sam flat-palms the ball into Bither's chest. "Hear you talking, all you studs, I got the idea you wrote the book on her."

They laugh but it has a nervous edge. "Hey," Rick says, "I gotta be at work by eleven. Can we get started?"

Relieved, they fall to the work at hand.

■ ■ ■

When they all repair to the diner to fuel up, Rick and Sam find stools next to each other, at the corner of the counter. This breakfast is the first food Sam has had since sharing the banana with Deanie after the game and missing his supper to take her to the Mill. Like the first snowflakes in November, the first mouthfuls increase the sense of emptiness with the realization of how much it will take to fill the void. He concentrates on chowing down.

Swallowing the last of his toast, Rick asks if Sam has gotten a date from the DMV for his bike license test. With a mournful shake of his head, Sam allows the DMV is still being coy.

"Frigging shame," Rick commiserates. "Gorgeous machine like that just sitting idle."

"Weather sucks for bike-riding anyway," Sam points out.

Rick lowers his voice. "Thought you were coming to my house last night."

Contemplatively Sam wipes toast through egg yolk. "Didn't think you and Sarah needed me."

"We didn't." Rick toys with a fork, stabs suddenly into Sam's sausage links and boots one. "So what happened with you and Gauthier after the knock-down drag-out in the parking lot? You take her somewhere and kill her, or dick her, or what?"

Sam lifts an eyebrow. "That's some choice."

"Come on." Rick belches gently. "See a couple who fight as much as you and Gauthier do and they keep on hanging around each other, it's gotta be a turn-on."

Wiping his mouth, Sam folds his napkin neatly next to his clean plate. "Slick, get a life of your own, will ya?"

■ ■ ■

Bringing in the mail, Reuben frisbees the envelope with the DMV return address across the garage to Sam, who drops a wrench on the floor to catch it.

When Sam rips it open, he groans. "Look at the date!"

Glancing at it, Reuben laughs. "Tournament week. Have to reschedule."

Nothing to get shook about, considering there are long cold nasty weeks to hump through to spring, itself basically more long cold nastiness with mud instead of snow and ice. Before May, won't be more than one or two good bike days like found coins on a wet sidewalk. It doesn't stop Sam sitting right down to make out the form for a new date, though it won't go out in the mail until Monday.

Just before closing, Sam steps into the lavatory, props himself one-armed against the wall over the bowl and makes a pass at voiding. With his eyes closed prayerfully, he produces a painless stream and breaks into a weak grin.

■ ■ ■

Now she has a new woman working for her who appears to be competent, Pearl has decided to take Sunday mornings off through the winter. She wants exercise, she says, and joins the pickup game at the meeting hall. Reuben makes his first appearance since being sick. It is a good workout, not least because only a few of Sam's teammates are there—Rick and Todd and Joey Skouros and Billy Rank—and it's just for fun.

At home, Reuben decides he's going to cook to give Pearl more of a day off. Sam has never minded Sunday breakfast at the diner. This new experience of having it to themselves at home reminds him of what Sundays were like when he was small. It was the day his father most often made breakfast. He supposes it had something to do with the women—his mother and his grandmother—going to church, and his father usually staying home.

While he eats, Sam works his way through the sports section of the Sunday paper and swaps it with his father for the front section. War is barreling down on the Middle East like a fleet of semis and the world is hunkered on the yellow line like a stunned bunny. A fourteen-year-old-girl has been shot by a sniper on her bus on her way to play a high school basketball game on Cape Cod—killed instantly, murderer and motivation unknown. Throwing down the paper disconsolately, Sam stares at a translucent sliver of fried potato in a red puddle of ketchup on his plate. His nose is full of the sugar and vinegar sharpness of the ketchup.

Pearl and Reuben exchange glances and Reuben clears his throat and shifts his chair a little to face Sam.

"What are you doing with the rest of the day?"

"Drugs," Sam answers distantly. "A shitload of drugs. Then I thought I'd go on a tear and stick up three or four convenience stores, maybe blow away a state cop or two."

"Right." Reuben folds the sports section carefully. "I asked you a simple question, Sammy. What are you giving me shit for?"

"Oh God," Pearl mutters.

Rising from the table, she unbuckles India from her high chair and wipes the baby's sticky face with the edge of her apron.

Ignoring his father, Sam clears his plate into the sink and heads for the door.

"Sammy," Reuben says, "sit down."

Turning his back, Sam reaches for his jacket. He hears the warning scrape of Reuben's chair and then his father's hands clamp down on his shoulders and Sam turns rigidly to face him.

"What did I do?" Reuben asks.

"You tell me," Sam answers.

With the baby on her hip, Pearl murmurs, "Please, guys—"

"You stay out of this!" Sam lashes out.

The hurt on her face distracts him and he is unprepared for his father's hands thumping flat into the middle of his chest, propelling him backward against the door hard enough to make him gasp.

"You don't talk to her like that!"

And then Reuben's fingers in Sam's shirt slacken and he steps back, stricken at the use of hard hands on his son.

The baby whimpers, squinting at each of them, her breath beginning to hitch toward shrieking. Pearl scoops her to her hip to comfort her.

Sam swallows hard. "I'm sorry, Pearl."

She glances up, still hurt, a suspicious brightness in her eyes, but manages a wavering smile.

Eyes downcast, Sam picks up his jacket, jerks open the door and stumbles out.

His father, jacketless, follows him out. "Sammy, please, wait a minute."

Poised at the edge of the steps, Sam reaches out to grapple the porch pilasters, stopping himself like a fighter jet catching the hook on an aircraft carrier runway.

"I'm sorry I shoved you, Sammy. Now talk to me. Please."

Where the grief comes from Sam doesn't know but suddenly he is fighting tears, his nose is running, and he feels like Indy, squinting and hitching at the whole loud frightening world, as he rocks on the edge of the steps between the pilasters. "Where's Karen? What's happening to her? She could be dead. You act like she doesn't exist. You threw her out on the street."

Blindsided, Reuben seems to condense, planting his feet, lowering his head, moving heavily as a bull gathering his responses to a provocation. "I think about her all the time. What do you want me to do? Forcing her into rehab didn't work, you know it didn't. She signed herself out. I can't make her stop. For Christ's sake, Sammy, you remember how miserable she made us all."

"Pearl," Sam interjects.

"All of us," Reuben insists. "She was destroying us, along with herself."

"Why didn't you kill that son of a bitch Bri right at the start? She was underage and you let that shithead mess with her. Where were you when he started her boozing and drugging, where were you when he started fucking her?"

Reuben might say he did the best he could without the foresight to see where it was all headed or being able to be with the girl every minute of every day. It isn't a matter of refusing to admit errors but the contrary; he declines to defend or forgive himself.

"Why didn't you just shoot her!" Sam chokes. "It would have been kinder than what's happening to her now."

"Sammy," his father says, moving to embrace him, but Sam lets go of the pilasters to ward Reuben off with a show of palms.

Sam reels down the steps, trips across the yard, literally falling toward his vehicle.

■ ■ ■

Reuben reaches for the support of the same pilasters as he watches his son flee. He shivers. His ears ache. He retreats to the kitchen, where his wife rises from the table, leaving behind the front page and her cup of coffee to meet him with comforting arms.

"Do you think he's all right?" he asks her.

Pearl rubs her cheek against the rough wool of his shirt. "Read the front page?"

"Sure. I managed not to have a nervous breakdown over it, though."

She steps out of his embrace to pluck the paper from the table and show it to him. "The world's going nuts—he's scared for Frankie, and look, some madman's shot at a school bus, killing a young girl. A basketball player."

Reuben raps thick knuckles against the paper. "Out of the blue, he starts talking about Karen. On the porch."

"He must feel helpless," Pearl suggests.

Reuben picks up her coffee mug and sips at it.

"He was fine this morning. We had a good time. Then he goes all to pieces. Been up and down like a rollercoaster lately. Hormones, I guess, but maybe that's too easy," he speculates. "I've had the strongest feeling for a while now there's something going on he's closing me—us—out of."

"Lot of pressure this year," Pearl observes and Reuben grins at her affectionate mimicry of his usually laconic speech.

Pulling her down into his lap in the rocking chair next to the stove, he cups her breast.

It's easy to forget in the business of the day that Sammy's growing up. He's always backed Sammy's decision to keep the recruiters at bay, though he is a little disconcerted to have it go on so long—he had really thought one of these days, Sammy would quietly make some choice, on his own terms. But here it is January, the date fast approaching for signing a letter of commitment to one school or another, and Sammy has done no more than send off the same terse carefully printed postcard in response to all expressions of interest. He hasn't toured a single school. Perhaps he should push Sammy a little about his future. Maybe the kid is confused and feels like he isn't getting any guidance. He resolves to take it up with Sammy as soon as the kid comes home.

"Cut that out right now, you'll get me leaking."

"I like it when you leak. It tastes good," he answers. "Let's spend the afternoon in bed."

■ ■ ■

The road is glassy under his wheels and Sam deliberately slews the truck onto the main road. As his body shifts with the truck, he feels weirdly boneless. It makes him think of a childhood toy, a rubbery mannikin that could be stretched and contorted like Plastic Man in the comic books, only its name was Stretch Armstrong. Body heat made Stretch pliable—and if he wasn't handled enough or if he was just plain cold, manipulating him resulted in the rupture of his unnaturally pink skin and the leakage of the gooshy green substance inside him that was the secret of his plasticity.

"He feels funny," Sam remembers confiding to Frankie. "Like pulling on my dink."

Frankie clapped a hand over his little brother's mouth.

"Don't say that," he advised, his face working the way it did when he got a fit of the giggles in church. "Mom'll have a kitty."

"It's true," Sam insisted.

"Yeah, yeah. Just nobody wants to hear about you playing with yourself."

Thereafter Frankie took to asking him, in front of unknowing grownups, if he wasn't afraid ol' Stretch might rupture, getting yanked around so much. Along with all but a few of the childhood toys stored in the attic, ol' Stretch had been a victim of the farmhouse fire.

Forces beyond him seem to be pulling him this way and that, distorting him into a comic-book figure like Stretch. Just now, he feels as if his skin is so thin at certain points that it is ready to tear and let all that gooshy green shit come dribbling out.

Crossing into Greenspark, he has an impulse to keep on going. He wants—he wants to see his mother. Not just to see her. He wants her back—the same old childish plea for the impossible. If he had her back, he'd hate her worse than he does now; she'd be driving him crazy with her religion and her rules and her hypocrisy. It's her fault Karen's on the street and Frankie's waiting his turn to be road pizza on the other side of the world and he's an uninvited guest in his own home.

Grow up, he tells himself. So the world's fucked up. It's not being run to your specs. Tough shit on you. You're walking on your own hind legs, you get enough to eat and nobody puts cigarettes out on you. Which reminds him—Deanie's waiting. He hopes. Thinking of her overnights at the Mill, he has slipped an old sleeping bag behind the seat of the cab. When he goes home, he'll apologize to his father and Pearl for being a dink. Maybe he'll tell them about Deanie. In fact, he should bring her home for supper. And as soon as he gets a chance, he should get off his blaming ass and go find Karen. If he can bring Deanie home for supper, he ought to be able to bring his idiot sister home too.

■ ■ ■

All its Sunday papers sold, the Greenspark Pharmacy has few customers. The bored druggist is working the register himself. He glances at the packet of condoms and money Sam drops on the counter and reaches for the bill. The instant the druggist claims the money, Sam palms the condoms directly into his jacket pocket. The druggist counts the change back into his hand and then smiles beatifically.

"Have a nice day, Sam," he says, and winks.

Sam smiles back, gathers his dignity and manages to get out of the door without knocking anything off the shelves or tripping over his own feet.

He breathes a long sigh of relief. That wasn't so bad.

■ ■ ■

From outside, as he shifts his burdens to open the door, he can hear the thunk of the ball on the floor, the scratch of the grit under rubber soles. For a moment he watches her work the ball through a figure eight and back again under the floodlights. She gives him a quick grin.

In the shadowy cavern of the Mill, she is a candleflame, her face and body alike alive with her own consuming light. Bareheaded as only she can be, she wears his faded orange sweatshirt, its cuffs and edges excised by pinking sheers—she has cut it and he doesn't mind after all. The fleece balloons as she moves inside it. Her face is clean of makeup and she looks really young to him, more like a kid than a girl of sixteen, her stubbled scalp and rings and chains a childishly extreme costume.

When he turns on the boombox, the emptiness of the Mill rackets the Surf Punks back at them. She jumps with delight and he laughs. Though the Mill stands isolated by the wooded park and banks of the Brook, he adjusts the sound level so if it reaches the Playground it will be no more than a faint beat on the wind that might be heard as wash from a car radio on the overpass or in the supermarket parking lot above.

They horse around, hotdogging with each other, working up a sweat. They play at their public roles as they have before but the buffoonery gradually thins and disappears until they are testing each other seriously, one on one. He wears her down though she never concedes, only eventually making the time-out T with her hands. She sinks, panting, to her haunches.

"Lesson time," he advises.

She groans and comes to the line he toes onto the grungy floor. Standing close behind her, hands on her hips, he straightens her stance, nudges the hollows of her knees into a slight bend, draws her elbows down parallel to her body and steps back. She cups the ball in her hands. Placing his hands over hers, he rolls the ball to the needle point where it is inflated.

"Put your finger on the ball's belly button."

"Belly button?" she giggles.

"That's what I call it. You call it anything you want. Needle head, sweet spot, whatever. Now look for the point on the floor where the key is centered in line with the hoop. Now head up."

She sinks a little, bounces the ball once, spins it a couple of times looking for the ball's navel, all the while never taking her eyes from the hoop. One arm pistons the ball at the net. The shot sprongs on the rim and falls off.

He hooks the ball as it rebounds off the floor and passes it to her.

"Hold the ball close. Do it."

As instructed, she begins with the ball at breast level, elbows in line with her knees, and then she heaves it one-handed again, and the shot misses.

From behind her, he puts the ball in her hands and tucks her elbows again and then his hands cover hers.

"Stop slinging it. Shoot it with both hands, Deanie. Guide and push. All you have to do is sink it. Little spring in your knees, little spring in your wrists."

He takes his hands away and steps back.

And this time it works. She makes it again. And again, and gives him a cocky look.

"Eat me," she taunts.

He sweeps her, squealing, from her feet. "Okay."

■ ■ ■

When he drops her onto the counter in the cubby, she gives him a shove on the chest. Her eyes are narrowed, her mouth wobbly with alarm. Hands on the insides of her knees, he wishbones them against the counter and sinks between her legs, head into her crotch. The worn soft fabric of her jeans, the silk of spandex underneath, the rigid rickrack of her chains, are damp with exertion. They smell of her. He bumps his face into the soft infolding of her pudendum beneath the ledge of pubic bone against his nose. Her thighs quiver and tense under his fingers. He sniffs deeply; the scent's a jolt to his nervous system. The tightening in his groin becomes a whiplash and his cock stands up, swelling against his buttons. For a moment he buffs his face against the crotch of her jeans, before he reaches for the clasp of the chains at her waist and the buttons of her fly and reluctantly raises his head.

She's flushed and accusing. "Jesus, you're weird. Like some big dog."

Settling his chin on her pubis, he growls throbbingly in his throat and she laughs.

While she undoes her traps, he sheds his own, and the sight of his cock, bobbing and swaying as he kicks off his jeans, strikes him as funny. Her nakedness is still riveting, though, the tremble of her bare breasts, the seamless whiteness of her skin against the black pointer of pubic hair and the shy pink underneath. While she refastens her chains, he makes bold to ruffle her muff with his fingers, and drifting over the cleft to cup the whole sex as she passes the chains between her legs.

She tenses again when he spreads her on the cot and looks down on her, the crotch chains slack against the hollows of her thighs. He's seen her sex before, in brief glimpses, and he's seen others, in stroke books, but it's still startling and strange. It's small, for one. And complicated. The blue-tinged pinks blend into one another. In the middle, it is undeniably wound-like and raw. That hooded little bit like the tip of a very small tongue at the juncture of the outer lips is her clitoris, not difficult to find at all.

It strikes him suddenly he has only the vaguest idea how this is done.

She lifts her head from the forearm she is resting it on. "Ugly, isn't it?"

Startled, he shakes his head. "No! It's just I don't know what I'm doing," he confesses. "Bear with me."

"Great," she mutters.

The tongueless mouth of her sex gives him no coaching. He kisses the rosebud tattoo above her knee. Lowering his head, he breathes in the musky odor, not the fishy smell of dirty jokes at all but more reminiscent of her armpits, only intensified and complicated. It makes him think of the dry astringency of unripe banana.

He closes his eyes and presses his face into it, a fringed fleshy sea thing, one of those exotic faceless submarine delicacies, half-plant, half-animal, floating and swaying like a transparent shadow. She flinches away and he grasps her hips to draw her back down. He tries to really kiss her there, rolling his lips against the swelling rim of her labia, letting his tongue slip over them, tasting them, sliding it into the cleft, tip touching the slick curled bud of the closed aperture, exploring the small confusing petals. The taste is of a foreign spice, a dusty mouth-drying ritual flavor. He wonders if it will make his eyeballs turn blue and produce visions like the mystical spice in *Dune*. For sure, it's summoning a giant worm.

He doesn't hear her moaning but he feels the tension in her thighs slackening. He licks upward on the natural channel of the groove toward her clitoris. The tip of his tongue barely reads the edge of the hood before it rasps the bump and she screams, she bucks and twists and the whiplash collision of the chains flail his nose and mouth.

■ ■ ■

He jackknifes onto the floor, hand clapped to his face. Chains clicking and chattering, the Mutant scrambles after him and crouches over him anxiously.

He opens an eye and stares up into her snatch and the vengeful chains dangling on either side and clamps the lid down again. With tentative tongue, he locates the taste of blood in his mouth; he's bitten the inside of his lower lip. The distracted worm is in retreat. "Why me?" he croaks.

Listing on one elbow, he squints at her. His lips are bruised and beginning to swell but the skin isn't broken. Touching the ridge of his nose, he determines he's lost a little bit of skin there. Inside it's feeling pinched but there's no more than a smear of blood from the abrasions and just a little puffiness.

From the mattress where she has gone to ground, she won't look at him. Her cheekbones are a dull red.

"What happened? What'd I do?"

"I hated it!" she blurts. "It was gross! Then it felt like you stuck my finger in a live socket, only it wasn't my finger."

He apologizes. "Guess I'm trying too hard."

She hides her face in her hands. Huddled under the old blanket, she looks cold. He finds her sweatshirt for her, turns up the space heater and fetches the sleeping bag from where he has left it near the door. Tucking the blanket around her, he zips her into the bag like a papoose and she giggles.

"I want some ice," he tells her, reaching for his clothes, "and I'm hungry. I'm going to get some take-out."

26

■ ■ ■

In the Middle of His Bare Face, his nose looks like a cat went skiing down it. He leans into the mirror in the men's room of the Chinese restaurant and touches his swelling upper lip. By tomorrow, he thinks, his mouth won't be particularly noticeable but there's nothing he can do about his nose.

When he returns to the Mill, she's moved the boombox into the cubby and is scanning the radio. Anticipating that the Surf Punks on an endless loop would wear out even the Mutant, Sam has stuffed his jacket pockets with cassettes from the truck; he spills them onto the cot. While she shuffles through them, he unbags the white cartons of Chinese. He's been salivating for it since he walked into the smell in the restaurant foyer and now his stomach growls audibly.

"I don't like Chinese food," she says. "And I can't eat with fucking chopsticks."

"So eat with your fingers. Fill up on rice. And the fortune cookies. Guy gave me extras. I'll eat the rest of the stuff."

But the first bite of the Szechwan chicken zings his wounded mouth and he winces. He's too hungry to let that stop him. Sitting on the mattress while he sits on the floor, she sulks awhile before she pokes around in the cartons with her chopsticks and takes tentative licks on them. She hesitates and then digs in with her fingers.

"Hot," she grunts once.

"No shit," he gasps.

No tea to wash the hot away but he's foreseen the problem and bought a couple of cans of Coke from a vending machine outside the pharmacy. As he watches her dive into the cartons, he suspects she has never in fact eaten Chinese food in her life. No wonder she doesn't know what to do with her chopsticks.

Filling the endless pit improves his mood drastically. He yanks a dub of the Meatmen and plugs Fishbone's epic "Bonin' in the Boneyard" into the loop. She's never heard it before and its unrelenting horniness breaks her up. Abandoning the take-out cartons, he crawls onto the cot and her.

"Recovered?" she asks with eyebrow cocked.

Tracing the sharp elegant angle of the mocking brow with his fingertips, he grins. "Can't win if you don't play."

"Can't lose, either."

He frowns. "Yes you can."

And she blinks, startled by the proposition. "Maybe it's just not my game," she ventures.

Contact with her body and the sensual drive of the music arouses Sam past answering. Moving her hand to his groin, he brushes his bruised lips over hers and even the discomfort is exciting. The ginger and hot pepper undertones of the Chinese food they have eaten add another tingle. He dives under the sweatshirt.

"Oh no, not again," she cries.

He makes a mouthfart—hurts like hell to do it too but it's fun—on her navel while she shrieks and pummels him. He retreats, pulls down her shirt. Cupping her sex with his left hand, he palms the curve of her pubis, pressing it gently. She shivers but she doesn't jump. Intrigued, he begins to rock his hand. She begins to perspire at her temples and between her breasts.

"All right," he murmurs.

Skinnying out of his jeans again, he kneels between her legs, lifting her ass for an easier angle. Then he remembers the rubbers in his jacket pocket.

"What are you doing?" she demands when he sits back and hooks the jacket off the floor.

"You gotta be free. I gotta be safe."

He braces himself for her to be angry but she merely rolls her eyes and looks away. And he's shocked by his own disappointment. He wants her to be offended, hurt, the way he was over her and Chapin. Is still. Only now he also feels cheesy and mean. The thing on his prick is weird and constricting. Looks stupid too. Safe. It won't keep him safe from being a jerk. He deserves it if it spoils the pleasure.

Trying to make up for sinking to hers and Chapin's level, he summons up an increased tenderness toward her. It is clearer with every encounter that despite her greater sexual experience, she is more fucked up than fulfilled. At first she did little more than make herself available but her increasing participation is in itself a revelation of what sex has been for her to date.

Kissing hurts and he gasps, unable to disguise it, and she goes deliberately for his mouth, surprising him and then exciting him fearfully. It makes him a little sick to his stomach, or else it is the blood in his mouth, and not enough time to digest the take-out but the perversity of it, the sense of flirting with something bad feeds their excitement. The spit they swap is threaded with blood from his mouth.

"Ooo," she moans and then she makes a choked gagging noise as she batters herself against him.

He barely hears her. It comes to him like the cry of an unseen bird on a foggy day on the coast. Zero visibility, crash of wave on the rocks, the fecund smell of tidal flats, the goosebump cold of the coast, and he's turning inside out, drowning, in her.

■ ■ ■

"I think I did it," she says.

It takes Sam a few seconds to work it out. Wiping a bubble from the corner of his mouth, he blinks at her. "Think?"

"I was real, like, tense and then it let go. Like going over a speedbump in a parking lot. For the work, it wasn't much."

Sam closes his eyes. Trust her, when she finally makes it, to have an anti-climax. "Sorry. I don't know why you didn't split while I was getting the take-out."

Reaching down to grasp the ring of the condom, he can't find it. Withdrawing, he stares in puzzlement at his unsheathed penis.

"Where is it?" he asks stupidly.

"Oh 'god," she mutters, "you must have lost it."

"Oh shit."

The engorgement of her sex makes him nervous; he's afraid of hurting her. He locates the rubber by cautious finger and eases it out. He comes up with a greasy deflated rag of a balloon, ruptured at the closed end and leaking semen.

She bursts out laughing, distracting him from his chagrin with the shake of her tits and the quiver of her stomach. The spasm brings on a chill; her nipples stand up and she's covered with goosebumps. She disappears into the sweatshirt again before flopping down against him.

■ ■ ■

His drowse is broken by the sudden cessation of her warmth when she leaves the cot to eject the tape. His mouth and nose ache and there is headache knotted between his eyes. He can't think; his head feels as if some prankster has filled his skull with quick-setting cement. There is whirr of the lead being taken up and then Zep's "Fool in the Rain," practically a lullaby after Fishbone, and she's back in the bag with him. Bare legs and all. They do it again—no rubber, the hell with going through that humiliation again and anyway, it's too late for it to do any good.

"You come back fast," she says.

"Live right." He grins.

The collar of his T-shirt rubs his sore nose as he drags it over his head. The twinge reminds him he's going to have to explain it. Lie about it. Not the night, it strikes him, to bring Deanie home for supper. Soon as he opens his mouth to fib about how he got his lips bruised and his nose scratched up, his lie-detector skin will give him away. Just having her in the same room—he won't even have to look at her—will make him blush. He can see them both breaking down in spasms of strangled laughter. And then there was the shitstorm this morning—he should put that right before he brings home a surprise guest.

■ ■ ■

The light's yellow and Sam slows. Sergeant Woods steps out of the pharmacy, tucking a new pack of butts into a pocket, headed for the parked cruiser. In his rearview, Sam sees Rick's old man squinting after him as he stops for the red. He raises a hand and the cop returns the salute.

■ ■ ■

The old truck scoots through the intersection on the green, headed for the Ridge. Sergeant Woods unlocks the cruiser and slips his pack of Winstons under the seat. Smoked two or three a night, they get stale. He gives the half-packs of old ones to drunks when he tanks them—telling himself it's almost necessary to have some butts handy to calm folks down. As he chucks a couple of matchbooks into his glovebox, it strikes him Sam's truck came up from Mill Street. Again. Not the access road to the Playground but the next street over.

With nothing better to do than indulge his curiosity, the cop takes the cruiser down Mill Street. Kids taking shortcuts to the Playground have trampled the snow through the woods skirting the Mill into a snarl of paths. Pulling the cruiser onto the shoulder under the trees, Sergeant Woods gets out and notes the treadmarks in the snow—Sam's truck if he's not mistaken—not a great feat of detection as he's seen the tread plenty of times in his own drive-way. The proximity to the Playground where he broke up Sam's make-out session with the Gauthier girl interests the cop. Having overheard Rick on the phone to Sarah on the subject, he knows Sam is still hanging out with the girl.

The cop follows the path through the woods toward the Play-ground. A few yards from the Mill itself he spots Deanie Gauthier, messing with the padlock on the door. He freezes in the shadows of the trees.

That she uses the place as a refuge as well as a place to party in better weather he is well aware. He has taken the trouble to check it out, make sure it's reasonably safe, and also get a sense of the territory in case he ever has to come in and break up anything. So far there's been no serious trouble. Kids are going to get up to their shenanigans somewhere and he likes knowing just where. No one's being harmed; the Mill is abandoned property, technically owned by the town now because of delinquent taxes but of no in-terest to anybody at City Hall—just a pile of brick and stone on the Brook, picturesque as hell and utterly useless.

So now she's meeting Sam there. Woods smiles. Kids. Horny kids.

Not seeing him, in the camouflage of the trees, she tramps to-ward the Playground. She stuffs a shopping bag into the big waste barrel at the edge of the parking lot. She turns back and the po-liceman stands very still and she doesn't see him, as she takes an-other path, toward Depot Street.

Making his way back to the cruiser, the cop drives it to the Playground parking lot. When he heads for the Mill again, he has a flashlight hooked to his belt and a lockpick in his pocket. The padlock falls quickly into his hand and he lets himself into the Mill and closes the door behind him. First he pauses and sniffs the air, picking up nothing but old-abandoned-building smells. His flashlight beam shows him the tracked floor—lots of sneaker prints. Sweeping the light around the room, he is too low to pick up the hoop, high in the shadows on the wall. He follows his light to the watchman's cubby and chuckles. The mattress has been there awhile and her acidhead drawings on the wall, of course, but now there's a bedroll and a little space heater. And an old basketball tucked into a corner. Even more surprisingly, the flop is pungent with Chinese take-out. And ol' black magic of course, the effluvium of coupling. There's not even a trace scent of beer, pot or butts. Then the space heater registers again, the *electric* space heater, plugged into a wall outlet, and the bulb hanging overhead. Stepping out of the cubby, Woods lights up the fusebox and whistles in admiration. Swinging the flashlight toward the door, he picks out the switch. He crosses the room, flips it and finds himself in a crude homemade basketball court. Goddamn. The two of them come here and shoot hoops and screw. Sergeant Woods laughs until his eyes tear.

On his way back to the cruiser, the cop extracts the bag from the trash and finds it stuffed with Chinese take-out cartons. And a crumpled condom wrapper. No baggies with a litter of seeds and stems at the bottom, film canisters with herbal residue, empty Bud cans. Of course they could have hidden anything like that in the Mill or pitched it out a broken window or into the Millrace.

Slipping behind the wheel, he shakes his head and laughs again. Boy's got her working at her game, for Christ's sake. Probably Sam's idea of foreplay. The cop laughs until his eyes are wet and his stomach hurts.

Oh hell, nobody gives a crap about the Mill and they're not hurting it any. While they get their hormone fix, the girl isn't drinking, smoking reefer, and thieving. And that's about as good as it'll ever get for Deanie Gauthier. Sam could do better, but that girl, she can't. Least Sam's using protection. Praise Jesus. Kids this age, these things don't last. For the likes of Deanie Gauthier, she catches the guy's name, it's almost over. She'll want to be partying again and quit him if he's not up for it, or Sam will finally get enough so he can think straight about her and he'll realize she's bad news.

Flipping open his log, Woods makes a note that after seeing a couple of kids around the Mill, he has been in to check it out. It appears the kids have been using the place for trysts but since they are both of age and there is no sign of illegal substances, the next time he sees one or both of them he will merely warn them off the property.

■ ■ ■

J.C.'s Sunbird is at the curb on Depot Street. The Mutant hesitates, immediately wary. She'd turn right around and go back to the Mill for a few more hours but her books are in her bedroom and she's got exams in three subjects next week. Shoving her hands into her coat pockets, she strides to the door, flings it open and enters the house with a regal arrogance that covers her nerves.

J.C. is at the kitchen table with Tony. She doesn't need to see the shit on the table to know they've been tooting awhile nor does she have to see, in the dimness, the condition of their eyes. She only has to hear the way they laugh at the sight of her.

"Sister D.!" J.C. exclaims. "Have a hit with us! Set you right up!"

His face is flushed and he's finding himself extremely witty.

Tony's amusement trails off as he leans over a line.

From the corner of her eye, she notes Judy on the couch in front of the tube. With the Jack Daniel's and a mug at one hand, and an ashtray in her lap. She doesn't need to look straight at her to know Judy's eyes are wet and glazed and the mask of her makeup is cracking like the face of an old doll left out in the elements at the town dump.

While Tony is snorkling, she slips away to her room, not daring to linger long enough to make an informed guess how much powder he and J.C. have done up. The most important thing is to get a shower. A little blow makes Tony horny; a lot makes him limp, paranoid and unpredictable.

She unlaces her high-tops first and kicks them off. Under the oversized sweatshirt, she unclasps her waist chain, steps out of the rig and drops it onto her cot. As she reaches for her boy's bathrobe on the hook on the back of the door, it moves away in faded red ripples like an ragged flag trying to find a updraft, as Tony jerks open the door. J.C. loiters behind him, like a royal consort on parade review, an expectant expression on his face.

She takes an instinctive backward step.

"Heard a story about you," Tony says genially. "Heard you partied with the whole fucking hoop team New Year's Eve."

She is backing away another step and saying no before he finishes speaking. Her knees are weakening and she can't think of anything else to say but no.

"Whole goddamn team," Tony goes on. "And Hot Shot. Here I try to look out for your best interests, I tell you to stay away from him and what do I hear? The overgrown retard's punching you around the school parking lot. How can I help thinking the stupid shit knows you better than he oughta. Well enough to get aggravated with you. I mean, I love you to death, darlin', and *I* get aggravated with you."

Knees backed against her cot, she struggles to control her shaking.

"I didn't do anything! It's a lie!"

When Tony reaches out, she flinches but his hand comes to rest lightly on her jaw and he smiles. "Show me."

Behind him, J.C. grins at her.

She wants to say no to him but she is dumb with the effort of being brave. For a long moment she meets his eyes and he meets hers and his mouth tightens. Slowly and shakily she smiles a crooked, prideful, courageous smile.

"Don't touch me," she whispers. "Don't you ever touch me again. I'll tell. Sam'll kill you."

Tony's fingers drop to her neck chain and close around it and he yanks her to her stocking feet and then off them. Her toes struggle frantically to make contact with the floor and the chain chokes her and she can't breathe. She doesn't see it coming, the pistoning arm, the fist that drives into the left side of her face at an angle as she flops and twists like a bass on a hook. There's a sudden stunning impact, a blinding explosion of pain from a force that rocks her head to the right and the sound of J.C. shouting as Tony flings her to the floor.

"Fuck!" Tony bellows. "My hand!"

In shock, she crawls, groping her way toward the cot. Red drops spatter the floor. She is half under it when he grabs her ankle and drags her back out. She kicks back, catching him in the kneecap, and he bellows again.

Using her cot as a handhold, she scrabbles to her feet. There is no thought in her head, just roaring terror and bone-deep pain. Her hand closes on the chains she has left on the cot. She swings out with all the force she has as she turns toward him, swaying between her and the door, the exit, the way out. The chains slice through the air and his face bursts in a spray of tissue and blood. She feels the impact up her arm and across her back and she staggers as he screams and J.C. screams and she screams too, ragged with the agony of moving her torn facial muscles.

She loses the chain at the end of its arc and it spins upward, over Tony's head, into the mirror. The air explodes with swirling flakes of glass, as if they were inside a snowglobe that some god has just given a good shake. Tucking herself into a crouch, she tries to protect herself. Tony judders through the doorway into J.C.'s arms and they dance a crazed drunken waltz toward the couch, where Judy sits, staring in dazed horror. Bloody flecks of spittle and blurred obscenities spray from the hole of Tony's mouth in the lurid mask of his face.

The Mutant wipes something from her mouth, stares at what looks like a mangled caterpillar and then, disinterested, flicks Tony's eyebrow away. On her knees, she searches frantically among the mirror shards to find her chains. Wrapping them around her knuckles, she climbs to her feet again and staggers toward the door, but J.C. is there first. She raises her chained fist but he surprises her. He shoves her out the door and down the steps and she stumbles into the snow. He pukes noisily down the steps behind her.

Hurtfully the cold maps the cuts on her hands and face. Wiping at the blood running into her eyes, she smears the warm fluid into streaks of warpaint. Shaking fingers hover over the left side of her face but she's afraid to touch it—it feels numb and slack. Loosening the edge of her headwrap, she pulls it down to cover the wound. The passage of the cloth moves the air against it and her throat screams, behind her swelling face, at the agony.

Somehow she is on her feet again, and tripping, and the snow, cold and icy as dead finger bones, grabs at her ankles, and claws at her through her socks. In blind panic and shock, she loses all sense of direction. She thrashes into the woods, moving instinctively downhill, toward the Mill Brook. It's harder and harder to move on her numbed feet, the cold is in her bones and her mind too, like a hallucinogen, some weird winter mushroom, slowing everything down. She begins to fall again, with a brittle lucidity, pivoting with heroic effort, turning her body on a cursed spindle toward the right, and she falls a long long time, through a shattered lens of frozen time. She doesn't have to get up again. Her right pupil blooms darkly and she sees the grain of the snow, transparent broken and fused crystals, glassy shards, billions of points of splintered light. A red star novas among them. They suck it pink.

■ ■ ■

To avoid going home, Sam spends several hours in solitary practice in the empty meeting house. He works to the echoing attenuated wolf howls and driven drumbeat of boombox cock-rock, sweating himself into the shakes.

The lights downstairs are dimmed when he finally lurches into the house. Standing at the sink, staring out past his own reflection into the darkness, he eats directly from a leftover casserole he finds in the refrigerator. Pearl appears in the doorway as he swallows the last of the milk right from the carton. She tucks her hands into the sleeves of her robe and watches without comment as he shoves the carton into the trash can with one hand and wipes milk from his upper lip with the other.

"Sorry I was a dink this morning," he apologizes.

She nods and suddenly moves closer, to touch his nose and mouth with her fingertips.

"Honey, what happened to you?"

"Accident. Just an accident."

She raises an eyebrow and pats his stomach. "Get enough supper?"

He burps expressively and they both laugh.

She reaches for the teakettle. "I'm making tea. You want some? There's cake on the table."

Grinning, Sam whacks off a huge chunk of the devil's food cake, his favorite, and she slips a plate under it for him. He finds some French vanilla ice cream and buries the cake in it, making Pearl laugh. He carries her tea tray upstairs for her.

Chewing on the nipple of a water bottle and shaking a ring of oversized plastic keys in spasmodic jerks, Indy sits, seemingly weighted by her thickly diapered bottom, on the bed next to Reuben, who is reading. She looks up at Sam at the same instant Reuben looks over the glasses on the end of his nose, and their faces crinkle with an identical delight.

And then Reuben frowns. "Ouch. You and Rick get into it again?"

Eyes downcast and red surging to his face, Sam tightens up, twitching for a way out.

"Sorry about this morning."

"We've survived worse," Reuben observes and with deliberate compassion does not pursue the question.

■ ■ ■

"Do you suppose he did have another go-round with Rick?" Reuben asks Pearl when the boy takes his leave, having asked with excessive consideration if it would disturb them for him to use the shower. "He's all sweaty, like he's been playing ball all day."

Sitting on the end of the bed diagonally to him, Pearl crosses her ankles and pens the baby between her legs. Dropping her keys, the baby crabs along Pearl's thigh. "In the kitchen he told me it was an accident."

Reuben folds his glasses and places them and his book on the nightstand.

"I wonder if he didn't try hanging his face off the rim? Went up to jam it and came down too close?"

Pearl touches her own mouth. "Ow. Be lucky not to lose some teeth."

"Or break his nose. He'd be embarrassed to admit it too."

Pearl hesitates. "Or maybe he *was* fighting again."

"He's always been a peacemaker, kind of kid who breaks up fights. But he's my son too. What he didn't inherit, he's learned from my example. When Bri beat Karen up, I was the one who taught Sam the proper response was beating the shit out of Bri. Taught him his fists were the answer, at least some of the time."

"Boys fight sometimes," Pearl points out. "With their friends, too. It doesn't necessarily mean anything. And Sam's always banging himself up on his own."

Reuben punches his pillow up. "Why aren't kids born with a suit of armor? They could moult, like armadillos."

Pearl laughs.

"Dunno. We break but we mend, baby. Yes we do," she coos to Indy.

27

■ ■ ■

Sun Still Slugabed Below the horizon, the world
dead as dogshit and shivering, Sam waits at the Corner. She's late
and it's frigging colder than the heart of the goddamn cosmos. To
improve the frigid hour, he parks and goes into the coffee shop,
which opens even earlier than the diner does, and buys a couple of
cocoas. Tips open the lid of his lunch bucket and props hers inside
to keep it from spilling and empties his and she's still late. People
waiting at the gym for him and she's—what? not doing her frigging hair, that's for sure. Shaving her head maybe. Must take some
time. Tesla on the radio, covering "Signs." A little gem of sixties
libertarianism. The singer demands to know what right a land-
owner has to post his property.

"Paying the frigging taxes and the mortgage on the woodlot you
just took a shit in gives me the right," Sam sneers at himself in the
rearview mirror. "So fuck you, you longhaired hippie faggot. Get
a fucking haircut. Get a fucking job."

But there's no one to laugh with him at his countryman's shuck.
And there's still no sign of Deanie.

Throwing the truck into park in the high school parking lot, he
grabs for his duffel with one hand and slams down the lid of his
lunch bucket with the other. An odd rubbery resistance registers

and the smell of cocoa instantly permeates the cab. Flipping up the lid, he sees the crushed cup, milky brown puddles on the waxed paper of his sandwiches, rivulets glazing the yellow of banana peel. Swearing, he claps the lid down again and shoves the pail into his duffel.

The girls' coach, arriving a few minutes before him, has opened the gym and practice is under way.

"Where's Gauthier?" Rick asks him on the court. "You finally back the truck over her?"

Sam ignores him but Rick's not the last to make inquiries. It's clear the shouting match in the parking lot on Friday afternoon is still a hot topic on the grapevine. With the abrasions on Sam's nose and the blue patch of bruise visible on his upper lip to add to it, conclusions aren't just leapt to, they're jumped, mugged and bushwhacked.

"What's the bald bitch look like?" Bither demands. "You give as good as you took?"

Having seen Sam with his face undamaged on Saturday, Mouth has no reason to assume any connection, but Sam reddens anyway, since after all, the conclusion is more or less correct.

Turning away from Mouth, Sam encounters Melanie Jandreau's uneasy glance and he goes stony, pissed off all over again about the parking lot fray. She chews her lower lip and wipes nervous hands on her sweatpants.

The girls' coach halts him at the door at the end of the session and draws him into a quiet corner out of traffic. "Do you know where Gauthier is?"

"She wasn't at the place I usually pick her up. I waited but she never showed."

"Gauthier's doing very well. Hate to see her sick again."

"Yeah." He shrugs and turns his shoulder and looks past her, in a hint at urgent deadlines, but she's unmovable.

"I was in the parking lot Friday night, Sam. Warming up my car. God knows I've had all I could do not to slap Gauthier myself on a couple of occasions but what was going on—it didn't look good or sound good. I don't know what's going on between you two but I can't look the other way if any kid in this school raises a hand to any other kid, I don't care who they are."

"I didn't hit her," Sam mutters. "I yelled at her, that's all."

"All right. If you even came close to belting her, Sam, it's time for you to back off. How'd you get your nose scratched?"

"Accident."

Blinking behind her glasses, she waves him along without any signal she's buying it as a satisfactory answer.

Going straight to the Office, he leans on the secretary to call the Mutant's home number before she gets put down on the list as absent without notice.

"No answer, Sam. Sorry. Maybe she'll turn up late."

"The last time she was sick," he points out, "nobody called. She might be home alone and too sick to reach the phone."

The secretary smiles sympathetically.

"Chill out. Nobody's going to kick her off the team today, Sam."

Between classes, he grabs Shas Grey in the corridor and asks her if she knows anything.

"You see more of her than I do, dub," she sniggers, and flits away down the hall.

In the weight room he progresses through his program but his mind is on Deanie's absence. He can see her in her tatty boy's bathrobe, barefoot and feverish. They don't take care of her, her mother and that dickhead. They put cigarettes out on her. It was the old women who got her medical care the last time.

He thinks about asking Chapin if he knows anything but it galls him to bring her up to the smiling shithead. Just the sight of the pusbag makes him want to kill him. But when he glances at Chapin, Chapin is watching him. Eyes darting, smile building and collapsing like a house of cards, the creep has an immediate attack of nerves and nearly drops the free weights.

■ ■ ■

At lunchtime, when Sam goes into the cafeteria, she's still not there. Mrs. Hobart gives him a resigned shrug.

Opening his lunch bucket, he stares at the contents. The cocoa has had time to work its way through the wrappings into the sandwiches and cookies, reducing a lot of his lunch to discolored muck.

Pete Fosse drops into the chair on the other side of Sam from Rick. "Hey, Slammer, how do you tell when a whore is full?"

On the far side of Rick, Sarah Kendall glances up sharply. There is preliminary snickering up and down the table.

"Her nose runs," Rick answers irritably. "Jesus, Petey, that's not only old, it's disgusting."

Amid the expected ribald outburst, Pete grins. "I just wondered if anyone ever noticed the Mutant's nose runs all the time."

Sarah makes an odd little noise as Pete laughs alone.

A shadow of distaste crosses Sam's features as he looks down into his lunch bucket but when he raises his head, his face is blank and puzzled.

"I don't guh-get it, Pete. It's not mechanically possible. I mean, women aren't hollow. And Gauthier's nose runs because she doesn't dress warmly enough for the weather." Sam frowns with mental effort. "And she's a smoker."

Pete looks up and down the table, checking his audience, which has fallen silent. Some watch closely, others devote themselves with sudden intensity to their lunches.

"Bullshit," he says suddenly. "You get it all right. The stupid act's worn real fucking thin, Sam."

Sam closes his lunch bucket deliberately and comes suddenly to his feet, rocking the table, sending sodas and milk cartons sliding from grabbing hands and setting off a chorus of alarm.

"Now that's funny, Pete. I was just going to say the same thing to you."

Fists clenching, Pete starts to rise. Todd Gramolini grabs his arm. Chairs scrape as Rick and several others prepare to leap into the fray but Sam doesn't wait to give any satisfaction to Fosse.

Leaving the cafeteria, he takes the stairs three at a time to the Office. The secretary glances up from eating her lunch at her desk and shakes her head no. Sam takes the stairs two at a time to grab his jacket from his locker. As he yanks the pushbar down on the exit, he realizes he is probably buying himself a suspension from school, more benchtime and team troubles. It makes him feel like he might puke but he keeps on going.

■ ■ ■

He makes himself keep to the speed limit. There are no cars in the driveway of the house on Depot Street and the house itself has an abandoned look. Someone's cookie toss is frozen on the front steps, looking more like plastic puke from a novelty shop than the real thing. He steps around it and hammers at the door but no one answers.

"Deanie!" he calls.

What if she's so sick—or hurt, what if she's hurt?—she can't get to the door?

He calls again. There is only silence and he steps back and kicks in the door. It lurches open into darkness, the only source of illumination the rhomboid of daylight centered with his own distorted shadow.

"Deanie!"

He listens but hears no breathing, labored or otherwise. Finding a lamp, he gropes the switch at the neck. The door to Deanie's bedroom stands half-open and the cot is made up and empty and sprinkled with bits of mirror glass. The front of her room is similarly peppered and there are also shards on the floor just outside her door. There are dark spots and splashes and smears on the linoleum and the door to the bedroom. As he drops on one knee to examine it, his stomach churns and a cold sweat breaks at his hairline and in his armpits. The blood is dried to maroon—hours and hours old.

"Son of a bitch," he mutters.

In a daze, he tacks from one locus to another, reading the signs. Someone did some bleeding on the couch, someone dripped blood to the front door. More splashes and spatters in her bedroom, where he notes her backpack, her gym bag on the floor. Her hightops flung in the corner. What's she wearing on her feet?

Panic wells in his throat and he spins around and bounds up the stairs to look in the other bedroom and she's not there either. He jerks open a closet door and stares at a few women's dresses, a couple of pairs of runover spiked heels on the floor. Stumbling down the stairs, he opens a door that leads to a back shed full of rancid garbage and boxes of empties and then another one that is also a closet—coats and boots. And he realizes how stupid he's being—she's not here, whatever they've done to her, she's *not here*.

If she's the one who did the bleeding, maybe she's in the hospital. Snatching up the phone in the kitchen, Sam punches in the numbers for the hospital. He lucks out. It is Sonny Lunt's sister who answers, a former Nodd's Ridge girl, and she knows him. Because he's Reuben's boy, and the answers are negative anyway, she answers his two questions promptly. Deanie Gauthier hasn't been admitted in the last twenty-four hours nor has she been treated as an outpatient in the ER. He hangs up before she can ask him why he wants to know.

Blinking in the sudden brilliance of outdoors, Sam scans the snow in the narrow yard, finds disturbing but ambiguous signs—a churned-up patch where maybe someone fell or maybe only some kid or dog rolled around, and here some very pale pinkness that might be more blood or maybe someone spilled a can of fruit punch, and then there is this depression, the right size and shape to be her foot in socks instead of her high-tops, outdoors in the goddamn snow with no shoes on and here's a handprint, hers, he's sure of it, the proportions that make her hands so beautiful, the snow reminding him of the color of her skin.

He curses.

Shoeless, she ran out into the snow and fell and she picked herself up and ran for the woods. There are no more distinguishable signs to his untrained eye but he goes a hundred yards into the woods. The strip of woods is thick with brush and undergrowth and tracked with paths tramped by kids headed for the Playground from all over this side of Greenspark. The uneven terrain falls in general toward the Mill Brook. If she ran from the house because she was afraid or hurt, instinct and habit would take her to the refuge of the Mill.

Bolting for the truck, he fishtails it onto Depot Street. In less than a minute, he abandons the truck on the verge of the other edge of the woods and plunges down the path toward the Mill.

The padlock is on the ground by the door. He leans into the door. A gentle shove creaks it open. Stepping through, Sam flicks the switch and the floods show him the hollow grubby vastness, the hoop that seems so pathetic in the harshness of the electric light. Again he listens, straining for the sound of breathing that will tell him she's at least alive. All he hears is the panicky hitch of his own breathing and the pigeon burble of the wind through a broken clerestory window. And then there is a tremulous sucking breath, mouthbreathing, a struggle for air through narrowed passages.

■ ■ ■

He traverses the space to the cubby, without being conscious of the passage or acquiring any memory of it. He's there and there she is, curled up fetally inside the shabby old orange sleeping bag on the mattress, the brocade headrag loosely scarving her bare head against the cold. With an inarticulate rattle in her throat, she moves inside the bag. They reach for each other simultaneously. She clutches spasmodically at the chains around his neck.

Training takes his fingers to the pulse in her throat and she's steady, her breathing's steady, her fingernails pale but not blue.

Space heater's on—assuming she was here all night, it and the sleeping bag probably saved her from hypothermia. She's clammy, pallid, she's lost blood, but as he gropes carefully, he finds no broken bones, no bleeding through the sleeping bag. Around her left fist and lower arm she has wrapped her waist chain rig as if for combat. She still wears the clothing she was wearing yesterday and she stinks of stale urine and old blood. The brocade covers half her face; the other side is smeared with dried blood, mucus, drool. Blood soaked into the brocade has raised the pattern in maple-leaf maroon and the stain is oddly beautiful.

Lifting the cloth away from her face to see what the source of the blood is, for a moment he cannot make sense of what he sees. Her flesh and her face chains have become one. It looks as if some terrible accident has opened her face right to the gums and her teeth are made of chains. The whole left side has lost its shape. It has no contour of cheekbone or jawline or temple and the eye is lost in swollen bluish flesh.

For an instant he thinks the bones underneath must be totally pulped and then he seizes on the idea it's edema, swelling from accumulated blood and fluid. This didn't happen today. She's been lying here since sometime after he went home—probably soon after, to judge by the color of bruising. Whatever happened in that house, she's a fucking mess. She crawled away like a wounded animal, to lie in her own piss and blood. She might have died of exposure out there in the woods if she hadn't gotten this far, and nobody fucking gave a shit, nobody cared.

He rolls her head as gently as he can against his chest and gathers her up.

She moans. " 'god."

"Not even close. I'm taking you to the hospital now, so just be quiet."

■ ■ ■

Though she's very light to carry, the bag is slippery and he's afraid of stumbling in the woods and causing her pain. By the time they reach the truck, he suspects he smells nearly as bad from nervous sweat as she does. He drives with a tense tenderness, her head resting against his shoulder. The ridges of her chained arm are palpable through the sleeping bag. With one hand, he tugs the arm free and unwinds the chains, reassuring her she doesn't need them now.

He touches the right corner of her mouth carefully. "What happened?"

Her breath hitches. On the exhalation, almost inaudibly she tells him. "Tony."

His fingers strangle the wheel and his teeth grind in his jaw as a murderous enmity engages the gears of his heart. At the sudden tightening of his muscles, she moans again. Taking a hand from the wheel, Sam caresses the right side of her face with his fingertips, finds wetness welling from her eye.

"What was it this time? You kite the whole fucking pack of butts?"

The bitter query releases a quiver that is almost a laugh.

"No," she whispers. The words are slow and effortful and thick with stiffened muscle. "You."

It is as incomprehensible as his first sight of the damage to her face and then his nerve ends begin to register it. He feels the blood drain from his face, the lurch of heart and cramp of gut, the sudden coldness as if his insides were shrinking away from his skin. And the hospital is in sight, for whatever good it will do.

■ ■ ■

In the cubicle into which they are shunted on arrival at the Emergency Room, the triage nurse wants her out of the sleeping bag. Deanie clings to him while he eases her out of it as if she would crawl inside him if she could only find the zipper. Trying to get her out of her clothes provokes her to near hysteria. The nurse puts out a johnnie and leaves it to Sam.

Sitting on the examination table, he continues to cradle her, holding both her hands. Now they are in the institutional embrace of the hospital, she has the shakes and can't stop weeping silently. He wipes at the right side of her face with a tissue, trying to clean it up a little. All the while he reassures her, the same short phrases that have little objective meaning beyond a kind of verbal caress.

"It's over, it'll never happen again," he promises, as the door opens to admit an unfamiliar middle-aged woman.

She is short and chunky and brisk. Her gaze sharpens as it passes over the scabs on his nose, her eyes go to Deanie's hands clutching his and then travel to the half of Deanie's face that is exposed.

"I'm Dr. Spellman. What do we have here?" the doctor asks, in a tone of conspicuous neutrality, lifting the linen brocade to look at the left side.

"Her face is too swollen for her to talk very well," Sam explains. He gives Deanie's name and his own.

"I see. We'll manage something. Would you leave us alone now?"

Deanie's nails dig into his hands as he eases her onto the table.

"I'll be right outside," he promises.

Closing the door behind him, he hears her ask Deanie what happened to her. Loitering by the door, he feels awkward and still in the way. From the examining room, the rhythm of the doctor's questioning voice spikes in frustration and Deanie sobs for him and he shoulders open the door and Deanie dives for him.

The doctor's cheeks are flushed.

"All right," Dr. Spellman demands. "You tell me what happened, mister."

Stiffening in his arms, Deanie speaks. She sounds as if she is trying to speak through a gag but she repeats herself and the meaning sinks in. " 's an accident."

He's too stunned to do anything but stare at her. Face and head exposed, she hardly looks human at all. Her face, what's left of it, is like a mask seated insecurely on the bones of the skull. Half of it is gruesomely ravaged, the face of the walking dead from a slasher flick. Yet her mouth moves, struggling against resistant fluid-filled tissue, against pain. All the desperate effort goes into telling a grotesque lie—she claims she went face first down the slide at the Playground, just goofing around, couldn't stop at the bottom and knocked herself insensible. Somehow she made it to the Mill but has no memory of it.

"It's a fucking lie," Sam says. Deanie's nails tear at his hands. "Shut up!" "Her mother's boyfriend did it"—frantically, she strikes at his chest with her closed fist: "No, don't tell!" "—he hit her." Sam continues with matching stubbornness. "His name is Tony Lord."

A little gleam comes into Spellman's eyes.

"Lord, did you say?" She smiles slyly. "What a coincidence. There's a fellow of that name in one of our beds. Lost an eyelid and some other bits last night. He also has a good many of the same kind of small lacerations as you, young lady. His story is he fell into a mirror while intoxicated. Did you fall into a mirror?"

Deanie doesn't answer.

The doctor is suddenly chillingly cheerful, as if she has finally gotten her rocking chair arranged with a good view of the guillotine and only needs to decide what color yarn she's going to work. She's also friendlier to Sam.

It comes to him she's been assuming he did the damage to Deanie, that he was the one Deanie was protecting, and feels himself going incandescently red in the face. For a moment he thinks he's going to vomit but he manages to steady himself.

"But let's take care of treating this first, okay? We'll deal with Mr. Lord later," the doctor goes on. "Any other damage besides your face?"

In a fainter, relieved tone, Deanie says no to her question.

"Let's get you out of these clothes."

Deanie whispers an unnecessary confession in Sam's ear. "I wet myself."

"We know." Sam grins. "Faster we get you out of it, the less you'll stink. Whew. Takes me back. I was a bedwetter myself."

Deanie's right eye widens.

Spellman brightens with interest. "Late-maturing bladder?"

Sam shakes his head. "Folks split up. I think I was telling them I was pissed off at them."

The doctor grins and Deanie tries to smile.

"Give me the shears. I'll cut her out," he volunteers.

Spellman watches as he scissors off the sweatshirt. Her blood might wash out of it, but she'll never want to wear it again. Still, he regrets having to do it. The chain of possession reaches from his brother, in peril far away in the Gulf, to his father and himself before it stops at Deanie. It has done its utilitarian job and then some.

"I've had EMT training," he says, to make conversation. "I do a Rescue shift, summers. Definitely qualified to slash up people's clothes."

The sweatshirt falls away, then the T-shirt underneath. Breasts aquiver and nipples rising in response to the change in temperature, Deanie snugs closer to him.

"Nice tits," he teases and she makes a noise that might be a giggle.

Spellman frowns.

"It's okay," he assures her earnestly. "Deanie and me have played doctor before."

Deanie shivers violently and Sam ties her into the johnnie before she lies back on the table and he cuts her out of her jeans and tights. When they're off, he shoves his head under the johnnie and makes a mouthfart on her navel. She kicks convulsively and her stomach shakes with silent laughter. He raises his head to find Dr. Spellman's face reddening and her mouth working with amusement.

"Thank you," the doctor says briskly, "I think."

28
∎ ∎ ∎

With a Brisk Eloquent Snap of her gloves as she peels them off, Spellman expresses the same anger and disgust that shows in the pursing of her mouth. "We need X rays. The edema confuses the issue. The chains have chewed up the epidermis. It's fortunate they had some slackness or your earlobe and nares would be torn through. After we take the films, I'd like to give you a general anesthetic and extract the chains and get this wound cleaned up. We'll keep you overnight and have a plastic surgeon check you in the morning."

As clearly as she has been able to say anything, Deanie says, "Can't pay."

"Worry about that later," the doctor says dismissively. "You have foreign matter embedded in your face and there's already signs of infection. Blood poisoning is a real threat, young lady."

"Not overnight," Deanie pleads. "Cuh-cost too much."

"She's not going back home," Sam says. "No way."

"Mr. Lord isn't very feisty at the moment," Spellman says. "If I have my way, he'll be handcuffed to his bed in short order."

Deanie claws her way up Sam to a sitting position. " 's just an accident!"

"Jesus," Sam mutters. "Deanie."

"You don't have to stay overnight, only a couple of hours to recover from the general anesthetic." The doctor pauses, struggling to soften her expression into something adequately reassuring to her patient. "I'm sorry. The law requires me to report suspected abuse."

"Deanie," Sam says, "you can stay with me and my folks but your best protection is putting that fucker in jail."

"Indeed," Spellman agrees. "Were you sexually assaulted, Miss Gauthier?"

"No," Deanie mutters into Sam's chest.

Spellman reaches for fresh gloves. "I'd like to do an internal exam."

"No!" Deanie insists.

The doctor appeals silently to Sam—can you get her to submit to this too? But Sam is in shock, first from Spellman's request and then from Deanie's answer. Having underestimated the degree, had he also missed the type of abuse? All his strength is on the outside, holding the battered creature who clings to him. Inside he reels through a storm of cutting edges, painful bright flashes flaying his own denial raw.

Spellman turns to notetaking and asks if Deanie is taking any medication.

"The Pill," Sam answers for her. "She smokes too. Cigarettes and weed."

"Quitting," Deanie objects.

Spellman raises an eyebrow. "You'd better. Nicotine contracts blood vessels and compromises healing. Your face is going to need all the help it can get, so keep it out of cigarette smoke. Other people's too. Same goes for marijuana, which you should also avoid because it can affect how well the Pill works, among other things. You got any other bad habits I should know about, young lady?"

"Just him," Deanie says, shrugging a thumb toward Sam, and actually raises a smile from Spellman.

■ ■ ■

Holding her hand through X ray, through prepping for the procedure, then waiting for her to come out of surgery, he has few tasks to distract him. One of them is calling the school.

"Sam Styles!" the secretary exclaims. "Where are you? You're in hot water, young man!"

Without answering her questions, he gets her to put him through to Laliberte.

"I'm at the hospital with Deanie Gauthier," he tells the principal.

"What happened?"

"She got hurt. She's going to be all right. She's in surgery. Things are kind of confused right now. DHS could be involved. There might be charges brought against her mother's boyfriend. I should know more tonight. I'll call you."

Laliberte reacts as Sam expects. "Oh my God. Did you suspect something like this when you left school today without permission? Why didn't you tell me, Sam?"

"I thought she might be sick again, the way she was before. I mean, I knew things were rough for her at home but I didn't understand what was going on. I didn't expect to find her beaten up."

"Well," Laliberte sighs, "what's done is done. We'll talk more later, when things are a little clearer. Better keep a tight lip, Sam, if there's going to be legal activity. You know our first interest is in protecting Deanie."

Locking the barn, Sam thinks, but locks his own lip instead. Got a beam in his own eye to extract before he goes after the splinter in Laliberte's. He knew—and so far as he knows Laliberte didn't—that Deanie was being abused. He found reasons not to do anything, just like Laliberte is busy finding reasons to cover the administration's collective ass after the fact.

Hunched in a plastic chair in the room where he's told to wait, down the hall from the surgical theater where Spellman is lifting the embedded chains from Deanie's face, he broods. If he conned the old lady at the front desk out of Lord's room number, he could find a window to break with whatever's left of the miserable fucker's face. The bad thoughts drive him to his feet. He can't breathe and he can hardly see. Tripping over his own feet, he stumbles down the corridor toward the Emergency Room and the parking lot outside, where he can get a dose of cold air and find some tires to kick.

At the desk, in conversation with a couple of staff, Sergeant Woods and the chief of police, Art Poloniak, observe his erratic progress.

"Speak of the devil." The Chief grins.

Woods finds nothing to be amused about. His dark eyes are full of concern. "How's Deanie?"

"Right now there's a doctor picking chain out of her face. How do you think she is?"

Sam's distracted freeform flow past Art Poloniak is arrested by the Chief's chubby but surprisingly quick hand. "Easy there, son. You don't need to take that tone with us. Where do you think you're going?"

"Nowhere. Out to the truck to get my Walkman and something to read while I wait."

"Come on down to the cafeteria," Poloniak says in a kindly way. "I'll buy you a cup of cocoa and you can tell us what you know about this mess. It'll kill some time for you."

Time. The word triggers a vague itch in Sam and his eyes go to the clock over the desk.

"I'm missing practice," he says stupidly.

"Nevermind," Sergeant Woods reassures him. "This is more important."

As he allows the pair of cops to lead him like a distracted toddler back down the corridor toward the cafeteria, Sam is in sudden withdrawal; his fingers twitch for the ball, his spine loosens and he wants to sink into the familiar aggressive half-crouch, his legs want to drive his body into the angles and leaps. He no longer wants to maim, mutilate and murder Tony Lord—the thought of further violence now sickens him—nor does he want to hide behind the wall of noise from his Walkman 'phones or to fall down the rabbit's hole of a book. He just wants the sweet rubbery ecstasy of the game to take him away from this endless corridor, the cops and their questions.

■ ■ ■

Smelling like unwashed armpit, the familiar cafeteria odor of overcooked food reminds Sam he has gone without lunch. All at once, he identifies a goodly portion of his queasiness, headache and emotional distress as sheer hunger. He orders two cheeseburgers and a double order of fries and a milkshake—better make it three and a triple on the fries—and a chef's salad to scrub his lights.

When he takes out money at the cash register, Sergeant Woods waves it off.

"Town's buying, right, Art?"

The Chief's twitching in the vicinity of the desserts but Sergeant Woods frowns at Poloniak's beltline and the Chief sighs and coughs up for Sam's grub.

"So tell us about it, Sam," the Sergeant urges as Sam forks up salad while he's waiting for the real food. "From the beginning."

Sam's immediately confused. "Beginning of what?"

The two cops look at each other.

"Today, let's start with today," Poloniak suggests.

Slowly, with much backing and filling, they sort it out.

■ ■ ■

Wolfing burger, Sam feels a drip onto his hand. He swallows hard and licks bloody juice from his fingers. From his mouth, his fingertips travel unconsciously in a diagonal from the left nares to earlobe and linger briefly at the corner of the jaw. He takes a deep breath. "Her face chuh-chuh-chains—" Sam registers Poloniak's undisguised amusement at his struggle and Woods's annoyance with the Chief. He spreads his hand over the side of his face. Emphasizing a word, any word, helps steady him. "Must a bin a gluh-glancing *blow*. Spellman said. Right on, would a broke her jaw."

Sergeant Woods clears his throat. "Our likely perp's hospitalized in worse condition than the victim and the victim's already told two conflicting stories."

"I hate these frigging domestic cases," Poloniak grouses.

"We want a confession from this bozo or the truth from Deanie," Woods continues.

Poloniak snorts. "Jesus. If she knows what the hell happened. She was probably as loaded as he was."

Noting Sam's fists clenching, Sergeant Woods drops a hand on his right forearm.

"If the mother was there, maybe she'll talk."

"If *shuh-she* knows what the hell happened," Sam mocks the Chief. "She was probably as luh-loaded as he was."

Poloniak's face reddens.

"Look here, bub—" he growls.

Woods intervenes.

"We'll be talking to her. He got himself to the hospital and never said word one about the girl being injured, let alone missing, so she went without care overnight in an abandoned building. If that's not negligence and endangerment of a minor, I don't know what is."

Poloniak agrees. "Time to have a look at that place."

"You come with us, Sam," Woods suggests, "tell us if it's the way you left it."

Sam has no desire to go back there and less to see Judy Gauthier but it's something to do while he is waiting for Deanie.

■ ■ ■

Being in the backseat of a police cruiser evokes a strong sense of guilt about every bad thing he has ever done. He hopes no one sees him as they drive through town.

"Sam." Sergeant Woods breaks in on his thoughts. "Have you ever seen any signs of prior abuse?"

The silence from the backseat draws the cop's eyes to the rear-view mirror.

"Somebody put a cigarette out on the back of her hand a few weeks ago. She said it was her mother. She was stealing Judy's butts."

"Did you believe her?" Poloniak asks.

Sam hesitates. "I wasn't sure anyone else would."

With his arm over the seatback, Poloniak cranes around to pursue it. "Do you know of anything else? She tell you anything else?"

"No. She's always bruised up. I thought it was from hoops. She's such a physical player."

Woods clears his throat. "You think there might have been sexual abuse as well?"

Sam meets Rick's father's glance in the rearview mirror. "All I know was she was scared of him and he didn't like her getting calls from boys. I always had to pick her up and let her off out of sight of the house."

Poloniak drums the back of the seat with his fingers. "This girl, she gets around, Sam. She parties a lot. You don't think maybe a guy who's practically her stepfather might be sort of frustrated with his girlfriend's daughter running around? He might try to exert some discipline?"

Sam's laugh is rusty. "Discipline? You should see her face. What's left of it."

"All right, Sam," Woods says soothingly, "nobody's excusing

the son of a bitch. We're just investigating. Trying to get a picture of what's been going on."

■ ■ ■

The house at the end of Depot Street is still empty, the door slightly ajar as Sam left it. While the cops pick their way around the debris inside, they make him stay in the backseat of the cruiser. The neighbors peek out of their houses and then they put their winter gear on and come out and stand around, staring at the cop car and at Sam, who sinks lower in the seat. Woods comes back to make the radio calls that put a serious investigation into motion. As Sergeant Woods takes him up the walk into the house, Sam hopes the neighbors are noticing he is not in cuffs.

Everything is just as he left it.

It hits him she'll need some clothes and her books and uniform, her high-tops and Walkman, from this house she should never have to go into again.

"She's going home with me. Be all right if I get clothes and things for her?"

"Better not disturb anything yet," Poloniak advises.

Woods peers into Deanie's bedroom. "Sam's already walked through the broken glass. We've taken the Polaroids of the bedroom, Chief. I think Sam can take her books and some clothes. I'll keep on eye on him while he does it."

Crunching glass with every step, Sam collects her backpack and duffel onto the cot with her high-tops. Rick's father stands in the door, tracking his every move. The drawers of the dumppicked dresser in the corner yield up the meager assortment of her ragbag wardrobe—so little of it. He recognizes all the pieces. It hits him how little she has. When he's stuffed it all into the duffel with her high-tops and her uniform and books and swept in a handful of tape cassettes and another handful of makeup, there's nothing much left besides some rolling papers and matches and candle stubs—her coat on a nail driven into the wall, her bathrobe on the back of the door. He takes them both.

This room of hers is nearly as horrible as the cubby in the Mill—worse, with those frigging creepy mirrors. Her belongings are as pathetic as a refugee's. It occurs to him now that she made a style of holes and rags because that was what she had—turned them in into a kind of sarcastic joke by flaunting them. That mirror mind of hers. Clothe herself in holes, scalp herself for a hairdo, ornament herself with tattoos, jewel herself with ugly slavechains.

As he withdraws from the room, he catches a glimpse of himself in a fragment of mirror still clinging to the wall. He feels a sudden jolting nausea.

"The cartoon," he says.

Sergeant Woods looks at him quizzically.

"The one she did on the wall at the Mill."

"I've seen it," the cop says. "Checking the place out."

Sam looks at him. Sergeant Woods returns a direct and candid gaze.

"Look again," Sam says. "Look again."

■ ■ ■

Depositing her things in the truck in the hospital parking lot, he glances toward the building. In the Emergency Room reception area, visible through plate glass, Poloniak is claiming a clear plastic bag with the clothes cut off Deanie in it. It hits Sam this really is a legal matter now. They're all going to be up to their asses in cops, lawyers and Department of Human Services social workers. Courtrooms and judges. Evoking all the emotional baggage of his own childhood, it makes him want to puke.

He turns back to the truck and reaches for his duffel to find his Walkman. Something clanks underneath the gym bag. He fishes out her waist and crotch chain rig. He holds it a moment, thinking. She had it wrapped around her hand and wrist like a weapon. The doctor said Tony Lord lost an eyelid and maybe the use of the eye—from flying glass? Did Deanie hit the mirror with the chain? Or use the chain directly?

Slowly, he tucks it into a jacket pocket. His chest feels tight and his eyes are dry and hot. Right this minute, Tony Lord is comfortably stoned on legal narcotics. Clenching and unclenching his fists, Sam leans against the truck, fighting the urge to prescribe a full dose of the chain in his pocket to good ol' Tony—feed the motherfucker the whole length of it, link by link, jam his throat full of it.

In the ER, he draws it out and hands it to Woods. "She had it wrapped around her fist."

Woods dangles the chain in front of Poloniak. "What do you think, Art?"

Poloniak jerks back his head. "Better hold on to it."

It goes into another plastic bag.

■ ■ ■

Assuming a gargoyle hunch in the plastic chair in the waiting room, Sam closes his eyes and seals out the world with the noise in his headphones. He feels his cells thickening, petrifying, on the ledge of waiting. Like a fallen archangel condemned to this plane of time, he curls his toes inside misshapen, threadbare high-tops, his oversized hands and fingers slack between the knobs of his knees protruding from the rips in his jeans. The Walkman 'phones make a robotic halo on his head as he perches meditatively on the edge of the chair with his ponytail splaying over his broad back.

Dr. Spellman taps his shoulder. Blinking, he knocks the 'phones from his ears and lurches to his feet.

"She's going to recovery now."

He reaches for the bindle of her shoes and clothing.

"What about her mother? Shown up yet?"

He shakes his head.

In the recovery room, Deanie is still unconscious, her face half-covered in surgical dressings, the other half still surprisingly dirty. But with the bandages on her face and around her head to hold the facial dressings in place, she is now recognizably a human being; she has become merely the victim of a nasty head injury. Hitting up a nurse for a face towel, Sam wets it down with cool water and gingerly does the best he can to clean the rest of her face.

■ ■ ■

Sergeant Woods closes his notebook as Dr. Spellman walks away.

Next to him, Poloniak scratches his head, which is broad and flat at the top, thatched in colorless hair worn a little long on top in inadequate compensation for its increasing thinness. He bears a resemblance to one of the amphibious short-snouted rodents—beaver, wolverine, water rat.

"You notice the kid's nose was scratched, upper lip bruised? You don't think he was in the middle of it? I'm not saying he busted the girl's face but maybe he did Lord's for him after Lord punched out the girl?"

Woods shakes his head. "Lord and the girl are all cut up. If Sam was in the middle of it, he should be too. I wouldn't be surprised if that chain is what did Lord's eye for him. Spellman did say she didn't think that was caused by flying glass."

Poloniak nods.

"Besides," Woods adds, "I saw the both of them late yesterday afternoon, Sam and Deanie—couldn't have been much before it happened—and he was headed for Greenspark and she didn't have a mark on her."

The Chief stares at him in surprise. "You did?"

"Logged it," Woods says. "Not their names, though. Look, Art, you know the kids use the Mill to party. We got an understanding, right? Better to know where they're partying than not? Well, the Gauthier girl uses the place as a flop too. That in itself suggests home sweet home isn't. Anyway, a while before Christmas, I rousted the two of them making out in the Playground lot. I've noticed him in the neighborhood a couple of times since and yesterday when I saw him in the vicinity again, I went down there to check it out. The girl was just leaving the Mill. I went in after her and there's no doubt about it, they've practically set up light housekeeping in there. I didn't see much harm in it, Art. Couple horny kids finding themselves a place to get it on. I didn't see any sign of dope or booze so I made the judgment call to look the other way."

Poloniak grins. "Just what I would a done. We don't want the kid benched on account of throwing his back out humping her in the cab of his truck, eh? I'm nervous about this. Aren't you, Woodsie?"

"God yes. His name on the blotter and we'll have a media circus."

"It's a DHS case. We can sit on it. I'll call Bill Laliberte and fill him in so he can keep the lid on at the school. He's got to know DHS'll be around anyway. We can trust the kid not to talk. He didn't even want to talk to us. The TV bozos get about three seconds of the kid stuttering and they'll decide he makes a lousy sound bite. It's a shame, you know?"

"Yeah. I feel bad for her."

Poloniak grimaces. "Yeah, yeah," he says impatiently. "She was tough enough to look at before. I guess he's so big he don't have to look at her face unless she sits on him. I mean the kid. Goodlooking boy like that and talented, goddamn he's good, and shit for brains otherwise." He sticks out an obscene fat tongue and waggles it. "Tongue-tied and numb as a hockey puck. What's he doing with this freakin' little pumpette when he could be screwing some nice cheerleader, shaves her armpits instead of her head?"

"Softhearted," Woods suggests. "Look, so far as we know now, he's peripheral to the case. Just a good Samaritan who brought the girl to the hospital."

Poloniak grunts. "Softheaded's what he is. Softheaded, softhearted, but mostly hard-on. Way I remember it, Woodsie, the Good Samaritan wasn't popping the victim." He notices Woods isn't laughing. "Lighten up," he says, with a broad wink. "I got money riding on that kid."

■ ■ ■

Hanging over his forearm, she gags into the shallow plastic dish. Sam wipes her mouth again.

"Hurts worse," she whispers.

"That's 'cause they're professionals," he assures her. "They know what they're doing. That's why you have to pay them so much—get it done right."

The nurse laughs.

Deanie tries to smile.

Dr. Spellman enters, with another of the little kidney-shaped dishes in one hand. Deanie's facial chains and the rings from her nose and ears are puddled in it. Tinged with blood, they are at once as gruesome and banal as pulled teeth.

"I have to turn these over to the police. You'll get them back eventually."

There's a typed sheet about cleaning the wound, dressings and bandages, and telephone numbers to call for questions and to make a follow-up appointment with Spellman. The doctor dispenses an assortment of medications: antibiotics and painkillers—enough samples to save the cost of prescriptions, Sam notes gratefully. She must have been listening when Deanie said she couldn't pay.

"No smoking," the doctor reiterates. "Wear a seatbelt."

"When can I play again?"

Deanie's muffled question startles Spellman.

"Basketball," Sam prompts. "Season runs another month, six weeks if the girls go to the finals."

"Oh." Spellman shakes her head. "I don't know. If there's a possibility of another blow to the wound in the next six weeks—" She purses her lips. "You should be able to go back to school in a few days but I think your season's over."

Deanie sucks in breath. "No!" she cries through the mask of bandage and swollen tissue.

Started by her vehemence, Spellman shakes her head.

"Really, young lady, I advise against it. I just closed a seven-inch wound in your face. I don't like the thought it was for nothing."

"Fuck my face!" Deanie blurts. " 's fucked anyway."

Spellman pales.

Sam tightens his arms around Deanie. "All right," he soothes, "all right."

She thrashes in the enclosure of Sam's arms, tearing the IV line from the back of her hand and sending the dish of vomitus spinning from the bed. Blood from the IV cut spatters on Sam's already stained shirt. But she is quickly too exhausted to maintain her hysteria.

In the truck he has started ahead of time to get it warmed up, the heat and whatever's left of the anesthetic in her system pull her rapidly down into semiconsciousness and she sleeps peacefully with her head on his thigh.

29

▪ ▪ ▪

"Home," he tells her in the driveway but Deanie is beyond response. Her head falls back against his shoulder and she is slack and boneless in his arms.

Glimpsing him through the window, Reuben opens the door. Sam carries her into the kitchen. From astride Reuben's shoulders, Indy chortles her delight at seeing Sam. Pearl looks up from stirring what smells like chicken soup. Her welcoming smile fades to concern.

"This is Deanie," Sam tells them, "she needs a place to stay."

Reuben hands Indy off to Pearl and follows Sam as he takes Deanie through the kitchen to the couch in the living room. Squatting next to her, Sam arranges cushions under her head. Reuben fetches blankets and watches anxiously as Sam tucks Deanie up. With a nod of his head, Sam indicates the kitchen and they all withdraw, leaving Deanie unconscious on the couch.

"Her mother's boyfriend busted her face," Sam informs them tersely.

Pearl sits down abruptly and Reuben moves closer to her, groping for her free hand. Indy's little face grows anxious at the tone of Sam's voice.

"Tell us about it, Sam," his father urges.

"The creep's in the hospital—I guess she fought back in spades—and the cops are looking for her mother. The DHS'll be involved. She needs a place to stay until she has a foster home."

Pearl converts her distress into practicality. "We'll make up the bed on the sunporch. Put a heater in there."

"She can have my room," Sam offers.

There is a pause for consideration.

"The baby crying might bother her," Reuben points out.

Sam hadn't thought of that. They're all used to it but she won't be. Everything's going to be strange for her.

■ ■ ■

Before he sits down to supper, he makes the call to the principal. Laliberte's had contact with the cops and in turn has informed both coaches of the situation with their two AWOL team members. The principal sighs heavily over the doctor's advice against Deanie playing again this season. There'll be a meeting in Laliberte's office first thing in the morning.

While they eat, Sam gives them a condensed version of the story he has now repeated three times—once to Dr. Spellman, twice to the cops. He omits his sexual involvement with Deanie, and the Mill, except as a place where he knew she sometimes took refuge. It's too complicated; he doesn't know how to explain it, nor does he know what may happen between Deanie and himself. She's been through so much shit, it might be months or years before she gets over it, if ever. He realizes abruptly she will have to stay in the house alone tomorrow and possibly another day or two while he is at school and his folks are working, and depending on how quickly she is able to return to school and the DHS moves to find her a foster home.

When he proposes staying home with her, his father points out gently that this is exam week. "With the physical shock she's experienced and the painkillers, she's liable to sleep all day anyway. Pearl and I can check on her every hour or so."

Pearl nods. "We're only a few minutes away, Sammy."

■ ■ ■

He moves her to the sunporch daybed off the living room, where a space heater has warmed up the glassed-in, heavily curtained porch to a sickroom temperature. The sunporch is bigger than Deanie's room in the house on Depot Street. Full of plants and wicker furniture and the mildewy smell of summer in storage, it offers privacy the living room couch does not. It has served as a guestroom on prior occasions when Pearl's stepfather visited. Norris has left behind an old man's ribbed cardigan, smelling faintly of cigars, draped on the back of a chair, and sentimentally, Pearl has not tidied it away.

Deanie comes around enough for him to spoonfeed her some chicken broth and afterward, she lies back like the baby after nursing—snake logy with mouse to digest, don't bother me no more. He gives her medication. When he offers her her pajamas, she barely moves her head in refusal. The painkillers knock her out again quickly.

When he goes up to his own room, it seems weirdly mundane to try to study. He doesn't use his headphones to create a fortress of noise for fear he might not hear if Deanie calls to him. The words blur and dance; he reads the same passages over and over again with no understanding, no memory of having read them before.

The phone rings and Pearl calls him to answer it. He goes down to the kitchen to take the call—there's lemon meringue pie, his favorite, to scavenge while he talks.

"Where'd you go to, Sambo?" Rick demands. "Ditchin' school is one thing but ditchin' practice again—Coach booted our asses all over the court like it was our fault."

"I left to check on Deanie. I was right to do it, too. That creep her mother shacks with broke her face. I took her to the hospital. Got to spend a couple hours telling your dad and Poloniak all about it."

"You're shittin' me!"

"Ask him. Doctor says she's done for the season. I guess I am too if Coach wants to bounce me."

Rick groans. "Jesus, man, I'm sorry about Gauthier, that's terrible, but goddamn, don't say things like that. I don't think I can take having to listen to Pete's bullshit the rest of the season, never mind having to play with him."

"Sorry to inconvenience you," Sam responds sarcastically and drops the receiver into the cradle.

■ ■ ■

His light is still on when he wakes where he has fallen asleep, face down among his books. For an instant he thinks it is Indy's cry that has broken his sleep and then he moves swiftly, shoving texts aside. He has reached the stairwell when Pearl sticks her head out of her bedroom door.

He waves her back. "I'll take care of it. She probably needs her dope."

On the daybed, Deanie moans and sobs in her sleep. He holds her, rocks her, and she comes around a little. The clock says she's not due for the painkillers for another half hour but he can't stand it and he gives her the pill anyway. Lying down next to her, he slips under the layered blankets and quilts. The warmth of his body calms her shivering and gradually she quiets and sleeps again. And so does he.

■ ■ ■

Overhead, the baby's crib creaks and shakes and a small voice shrieks cheerfully for mama-mama-mama. Sam opens an eye. The dark is threadbare, morning coming on. Narrow bed, narrow room, narrow girl against him. He holds her in the crook of his arm, bandaged head on his shoulder. She's still wearing the clothes he put on her at the hospital. He can feel the soft bulge of tit against his bare rib cage through her pajama top and he is suddenly intensely aware of having a piss hard-on. She exudes a smell of fever sweat and blood and urine and she's drooled in his armpit. Carefully, he shifts her and slips out from under the bedding.

His bare feet are noiseless on the stairs but as he reaches the landing, Pearl comes out of the nursery with India in her arms. She gives him a level look and a soft-mouthed smile.

"How's Deanie?"

"Rough night," Sam answers and moves past her.

In a few moments he has pulled on some clothes and gotten his books together. Gym bag in one hand, basketball under his arm, he raps at the bathroom door and his father mumbles permission to enter.

Thrusting his chin at the mirror, Reuben rinses his blade and cocks an eyebrow questioningly at Sam.

"Toothbrush," Sam explains.

Reuben steps back and Sam dips to open the cupboard under the basin and hook out an unopened tube of toothpaste with a free toothbrush attached to it. One of Pearl's quirks, reminding him of his father in its automatic bargain-seeking, is that she never actually buys a toothbrush but always finds the brand offering the freebie.

Downstairs again, Sam peeks in at Deanie. She stares at him with her right eye. The left one's closed with swelling. He squats next to her, pressing the new toothbrush into her thin hand on the pillow. "Ready to try the bathroom?"

She nods and holds on to his shirt while she swings her legs out and hauls herself to her feet. She sways and props herself against him, fighting the dizziness of anesthesia hangover. He walks her to the bathroom. "Want me to stay?"

"I can manage," she rasps and the little bit of crossness in it gives him a lift.

"Don't lock the door. I'll be right outside in case you feel faint."

He waits outside, listening anxiously to the intimate noise of her making water. She moans when she tries to brush her teeth. When she opens the door, she is using the frame to stay on her feet. She needs him to get her back to bed.

It feels odd, leaving the house—leaving Deanie behind, in his home, while he goes off to school. He knows Pearl and Reuben will check her regularly through the day but now that she's his responsibility, he doesn't quite trust anybody else to take it over for him. They don't know her; she doesn't know them.

■ ■ ■

"Hey, bud!" Rick calls across the parking lot.

Sam swings out of the cab and meets him on the walkway. He tosses Rick his keyring. "Later," he promises and lopes past Rick on his mission to the Office.

Laliberte, Liggott and the coaches are grouped grimly around the Office coffee machine, watching it cough and steam and dribble. Sam feels an immediate empathy for the machine and only hopes he's able to perform a little more efficiently. But by now he's got his lines down and the recitation's easier.

No one wants to take him to the woodshed over cutting classes and practice while on probation, though technically he should be suspended from school and booted off the team. Of course he's drawing on four years' credit but there's no doubt the administration's taking care of business too. They don't want an angry Sam pointing out in public why he broke the rules.

■ ■ ■

The practice slows and comes to a halt when Sam arrives. There are no secrets for long in a town this small except the ones everyone agrees to keep. It's apparent they know something—Rick for one and some of them have other sources—parents or sibs working at the hospital or Town Hall. Deb Michaud shuts down the sound system as the players drift toward Sam.

"We heard Gauthier's out for the season," she says.

Sam nods.

The confirmation raises a ragged chorus of dismay from the girls. Boys look at each other and then away in unease—except for Pete Fosse, who is theatrically bored.

"How bad is it?" Nat Linscott presses in a low voice. "We heard she got her face messed up."

Automatically, Sam's hand drifts over the left half of his face. "Chewed up from here to here." He stops, surprised by a sudden tightness in his throat, a dryness of his eyes.

Melissa Jandreau makes a face. "Oh gross."

Her sister Melanie's fingertips fly to the hollow of her throat, touching the delicate gold chain that carries her boyfriend's class ring.

Pete slaps the ball in his hand to the floor impatiently.

For a moment, Sam wants to stomp Fosse but as he stares at him, he becomes aware of the others, tensing. They have to play tonight, all of them, and they are all grappling with exams. Another go-round between Pete and himself will not help, nor will dwelling on the loss of Deanie Gauthier. He makes himself relax.

"Let's go," he says and the knotted atmosphere dissolves in the relief of activity.

■ ■ ■

Loitering artfully outside Sam's physics class, Rick falls in beside him. "How'd it go?"

Sam mimes gagging himself with a forefinger. "Be a frigging miracle if I passed it."

Rick groans. "More good fucking news. All we need is you washing out academically. What happened? This is funnybook fucking physics, isn't it? You were doing all right."

"Fell asleep over the review last night," Sam admits. "How you doing, slick?"

Rick turns up a casually triumphant thumb. "Hey, bud," he

chides, "you hung up on me, you dink. Like some junior high school twitch in a frigging snit."

Sam has to grin at the image.

"So I hit on my old man. You know he never talks about the job and I figured he'd just shut me down. Surprised the shit out of me when he decided to try to pump me for what I knew, which is fucking zip on account of you're as tight as Reverend Mother's brownie." Rick pivots and walks backward down the corridor in front of Sam. "He says the Mutant's staying with you and your folks for now—"

"Don't call her that," Sam blurts. "She's got a name."

Rick cocks an eyebrow.

"All right, all right. Excuse me. I'm a worthless human being and deserve to die a *fucking* horrible death involving electrodes on my fuzzies. Dad wouldn't tell me anything except what you told me. Wouldn't tell me if it was you stripped the shithead's face for him."

Reaching the top of the stairwell that drops to the corridor outside the cafeteria, Sam stops. "I wish. But I didn't. Deanie did it."

Rick grabs Sam's forearm. "Look, man, I really am sorry this shit happened to her."

Nodding, Sam stares down the stairwell, watching the traffic from the surrealistic vantage point of heads and shoulders, flowing down the steps with the rhythm of a falling Slinky. Clatter and chatter boil up from the foreshortened bodies. He plunges into it with a sensation of stepping off a cliff, and Rick follows.

■ ■ ■

At the lunch table Sam deflects conversation with an open textbook. Though he's read this material before and understood it, it's like somebody stirred it all up again, either inside his head or on the page. The more he stares at it, the less sense it makes and the more the conversation around him distracts. Exams are quickly exhausted as a topic and the coming games anticipated in detail but gradually reserve loosens, heads edge closer together and whispers of his own nicknames and Deanie's reach his warming ears. When he glances up, the faces of the girls are open as roses in their fullness; they are wide-eyed and excited, as if they were passing around the latest tabloid celebrity scandal. An outburst of prurient laughter from the guys around Fosse draws Sam's eye. Pete smiles fatuously at him and then leans toward Tim Kasten to make a further remark.

This shits, Sam concludes tiredly. He shovels the rest of his lunch and retreats to the library, where he falls asleep over the text.

■ ■ ■

At halftime, the girls have a comfortable margin on the Lady Bears from Breckenfield. Sam watches with his teammates from the upper bleachers. Chapin is several tiers below him, in the middle of a little entourage of druggie suckups—Grey, Lexie Michaud, Jimmy Bouchard—not a bunch of regular boosters. Chapin cocks back his rainbowed head at Sam and jumps his eyebrows as if he were raising a beer in his direction. Chapin must know about Deanie; the grapevine's been flashing it all day. But of all the people who have inquired after her, Chapin isn't one.

Spectators for the boys' game to follow begin to arrive, among them Rick's folks and Reuben, by himself. Distracted from his ruminations about the indifference of Deanie's so-called friends, Sam clambers across the bleachers.

"How's Deanie?"

"Zonked," his father says. "Probably the best thing for her, so relax. Pearl's home with her now."

Sergeant Woods climbs toward them. After asking about Deanie, he tells them her mother's finally been located, in New Hampshire, but in bad enough shape to be checked into the detox unit of the hospital in North Conway. When she's sobered up enough, the cops will try to find out what she knows, if anything. In the meantime, the Department of Human Services investigators have everything the cops do on the case, including the information that Deanie is with friends for the time being. DHS will make contact in the next day or so.

"They're shorthanded and not just investigators. Woman I talked to was very relieved the girl's with you folks because they're scratching for foster homes too in this county."

Sam's surprised by his own relief.

"Child's in no shape to be carted round anyway," Reuben observes curtly.

Woods chews on the barnside broad *a* and swallowed *r* of Reuben's pronunciation of *carted* a few seconds before he works it out, with a tickled grin.

At the end of the third quarter, with the Lady Bears down by twelve points, the boys leave the bleachers to change. The atmosphere is boisterous, anticipating a home-game knockoff of the Bears.

Lacing his 'tops on the bench next to Rick, Sam pays little attention to the horseplay around him.

"What brought out Chapin and that clusterfuck of burns?" he asks Rick.

Rick shrugs. "Wondered that myself. Somebody maybe told'm they could get high on the old boogers on the underside of the fucking bleachers or something."

Coach reins them in a little and they go out and do the job. For Sam, it's the only time he's able to forget about everything else.

In the locker room after the game, he gropes his T-shirt one-handed from his locker shelf. A scrap of paper floats from the shirt. The bit of paper seems to rise toward his hand as he reaches for it. It's a homemade stamp, a flimsy little rectangle of paper the size of his thumbnail, with all the substance of rice paper. The words on it are drawn in balloon style: *EAT ME*. When he looks up, everything is normal—the locker room smells and sounds and feels like a locker room and his teammates are doing exactly what they should be doing. No one is watching his reaction to the note. Casually, he makes his way to the toilets, goes into a stall and flushes the square.

■ ■ ■

A dumb animal misery glazes her eye as she looks out of it at him and there is a weary tension in the way she raises her head when he crouches next to her and touches the corner of her mouth in greeting. During the day she has gotten cleaned up. In her own threadbare flannel pajamas, she smells of body-warmed almond oil and the fever of drugged sleep.

"How you doing?"

"Sucky."

It's difficult for her to speak, with the swollen tissue stiffened up. The way she sounds makes Sam think of trying to hold a conversation with the dentist while numbed with novocaine and with various arcane dental devices hooked over a lip or stuffed between cheek and gums.

"We won. Girls and boys."

Smiling slightly, she relaxes against the pillows. "Good."

"Pearl and Dad take good care of you?"

"Smell the oil? She gave me a bath. Rubbed me all over with it. Changed the—" She touches her dressing.

"Had your dope for the night?"

She nods.

He tucks her up and kisses her forehead and she turns onto her good side with a long sigh.

■ ■ ■

His mind wobbles wearily around the rim of sleep but refuses to drop through. After a long time of waiting, he hears Indy stir. She begins to talk earnestly to herself and then to whimper. The swish of Pearl's robe and the pad of her bare feet hurry past his door.

He peeks into the nursery. Wide-eyed, Indy stares at him over Pearl's shoulder. Her fist is crammed into her mouth. A floorboard creaks under his foot, bringing Pearl spinning around to face him.

"Sammy!"

He rakes his hair back. "She okay?"

"It's just her teeth, sugar. Go back to bed."

Instead he goes to the head of the stairs to listen for Deanie and hears a low, troubled cough. He finds her sitting up on the daybed, rubbing her good eye, reaching for her pills. Taking the plastic pill vial from her, he undoes the recalcitrant cap.

"Brat wake you up?" she asks.

"No. She's teething; she can't help it."

"I'm cold." She lifts the edge of her quilts.

He slips in beside her and she tucks herself inside his arm, legs twined with his. He closes his eyes and visualizes the slow roll of the ball around the rim. This time, after several revolutions, it falls in softly.

30

∎ ∎ ∎

Ice Brocade Scales the windowglass under the rough weave of the curtains. On the exposed skin of Sam's face and neck there is a sensation of cold as if the frigid breath of an ice dragon is just beyond the glass.

He creeps away upstairs, through the threadbare dimness of predawn, to his own bed, where he stretches out because he can. The coolness of the sheets is unexpectedly pleasurable. It produces goosebumps and raised body hair. The chains around his neck feel like they are part of this same generalized reaction. Rolling onto his stomach, he masturbates slowly, no hands, stopping and starting, until he is in a kind of trance and coming is the dreamy jolt of a nocturnal emission. Very soon—while he is still drifting—he hears the bathroom door close firmly behind his father and he rolls over to turn off the clock-radio alarm before it can go off.

A quarter of an hour later, he crouches next to Deanie on the sunporch daybed. She lies on her side, knees tucked up, hugging herself for the extra warmth. The bruising that closed her left eye so it looked like an overripe black plum has a slit in it now, with a little bit of dark eye peeking out. Her right eyelid flutters and she licks her lips sleepily. A smile softens the exposed half of her face.

She has only the one pair of pajamas. From the clean laundry in the basket, he brings her Pearl's longjohns. In her boy's bathrobe and his socks for slippers, she may not be chic but at least she'll be warm.

She summons him into the bathroom after her shower but not to show him how she looks in the borrowed duds. Perched on a stool, she clutches the hem of his shirt while he unwraps the bandage from her head. Her scalp, untouched by the razor for several days, is downy with black hair, silky as Indy's.

Fixing her gaze on his face, Deanie's fingers scrabble for his hand and strangle his fingers. He grasps that his face at that moment is her looking glass. *Mirror, mirror, on the wall, how bad is it?* What he shows is how she will always see herself. He makes himself relax, giving her fingers a reassuring squeeze back.

Exposed, the wound is only the central feature of the map of discolored swelling that is the whole left side of her face. In muddy and streaked hues, her ear appears to have been shaped by childish thick fingers from a lump of varicolored clay. From eyebrow to jawline, her skin is the color of an August thunderhead. The healing edges of the wound melt into each other unevenly. It is livid as candlewax against the purple suffusion of old blood and fluid under the taut skin. It's no good lying about it because she's going to look in that mirror in a minute and see for herself. The doctor's instructions require no further bandage. She has to face the world barefaced.

"It's healing. It's better. There's still so much swelling, I can't tell how it's really going to look."

For a long moment after she turns to look in the glass, she is motionless. Her hands are slack in her lap. If she feels any impulse to touch the wound, she resists it.

He applies antibiotic ointment with the tip of a finger, as lightly as possible, and she manages to hold steady. Her right eye focuses on him and she rests the right side of her face against him.

"Gotta shave my head," she announces.

"You can't see out your left eye. You'll take an ear off."

"I'm a mess," she says with a shrug, "what difference could it make? Help me do it."

"If you're such a mess then you don't need to shave your head," he argues, but her mouth is already set.

First she wraps her head in a hot wet towel. When he squirts the shaving foam into his hands and lathers it over the moist warm furriness of her head, it triggers an unexpected nostalgia. He finds himself telling her about the toothpaste and shaving cream wars of his childhood. She hoots at the image of Reuben with toothpaste in his hair and Sam riding his back trying to smear it into his father's mouth. He has to reprimand her to stop giggling and stay still so he doesn't cut her.

Drawing his razor through white foam over the curve of her skull becomes another intimacy, the stroke of the razor another variety of caress. The scalp exposed before the straightedge is palely nude. A clean, fragile sculptural shape, the curve of bone, suture lines of the segments and beneath the opalescent skin, the pale iris veins—her head rests against his diaphragm as he shaves it, reminding him of other moments he has held it. At the hairline of her left temple, and also below her left ear, he exposes the dark invasion of scallops of bruise. It must hurt her but she does no more than close her eyes briefly. By the time he wipes the last curds of foam from her head, he is sweating heavily.

He catches a glimpse of himself in the mirror. Unshaven, dogtags and chains around his neck, in ragged sweats, he has a piratical air. Buccaneer Sam: yo ho ho. Hastily he lathers his face and scrapes it clean. Almost. The hard-used blade bites him several times. He blots his face with a warm washrag, uses the styptic pencil and makes a mental note to score some new blades after school.

■ ■ ■

Morning gym is intense and focused, all business. Everyone, he notes with a tinge of bitterness, seems to have forgotten that Deanie Gauthier ever existed. It's as if she died in some awkward way—suicide or maybe taken out by the cops while sniping station wagons from an interstate overpass. Without her, though, the girls are a lesser team—still basically sound on their fundamentals, a good depth of talent, but lacking the explosive drive she fuels when she is on the floor. She's a playmaker, an igniter. One of these days, they're going to regret her absence.

Through the day, Sam has opportunities to spend quality time with Pete Fosse, and then Fosse and Chapin simultaneously lifting weights. He deliberately seeks eye contact with each, trying to read their expressions, their body language, some signal as to which one of them left him the blotter square. But each shows him only a familiar blankness, intense with effort at their reps, in which there is no visible grudge, no anger, nor the slightest hint of triumph. Neither of them speaks to him but then they hardly ever do anyway.

■ ■ ■

It isn't until 'god comes looming in, looking concerned, that the Mutant realizes she has been waiting for him—wishing for him—to get home. The tightening knot under her wishbone dissolves and somehow the letting go causes a sudden leakage in her tear ducts that she blots hastily under the guise of untangling herself from the quilts.

He brings her into the kitchen, where their presence congests the normal routine. As 'god sets the table and his stepmother bustles, they bump into each other. They turn a few laughing dance steps to recover. Stepmom relates amusing tales of her day at the diner. 'god's old man arrives, picks up the baby and sits down at the table, next to her. Up close, it's even more striking how much father and son resemble each other. It's as if 'god had no mother at all. From gesture to walk to the sound of their voices, they are eerily alike, only their years dividing one man from the other.

The older man's eyes follow Stepmom with an intensity that makes the Mutant want to giggle; it is the first time she has seen someone literally unable to take his eyes off someone else. And Stepmom knows it—she looks at her husband like a cat over its shoulder, oiling its slinky way under someone's palm.

The kitchen conversation goes back and forth and 'god interprets for the Mutant—but it stops with her. It hurts to talk, of course, and she finds herself shying. They are strangers to her and their very warmth and openness are disconcerting. She isn't sure how she is supposed to respond. In fact, she is terrified of offending them. In the shape she's in, where else can she go? Who else will take her in? It is all she can do not to bolt for the safety of the sunporch. She shrinks into Sam's shadow.

"Maybe snow tonight, tomorrow morning," his father says. "How does a snow day sound to you, Sammy?"

"Like a trip to Hawaii." 'god grins.

The Mutant breathes in the reassuring soup smell that makes her realize how hungry she is. She distracts herself with her surroundings. The fixtures are old-fashioned, the paper on the wall shabby, but this dog-eared reality is more comfortable than the glossy magazine surface on the Chapin house.

The baby dancing on the man's thigh makes a sudden lunge at

her face. As the baby bats at it, 'god catches the brat's hand and the man hauls her back. He gives the baby a cracker. The brat crams it in her mouth, slimes it up and then takes it out and wipes it along his mouth.

"Da!" she declares.

"Da," the man agrees.

■ ■ ■

"We can eat any time now," Pearl says.

Reuben's grin fades. "The Gulf news today sounded bad. If nobody objects, I'd like to break the rule and eat in front of the tube to catch the news."

"No tube when we're eating." Sam explains the house rule to Deanie.

Pearl glances at the table Sam has set and then at Sam.

"I'll set up the trays," he volunteers.

A few minutes later, Sam bears a tray into the living room. She clings to him like a nervous shadow. In the living room, the only noise is the voice of the newscaster; the nightly news broadcast has been on the air for some time already. On the couch, his father has his arm around Pearl and the baby climbs back and forth between the two of them.

"The war started," Reuben says.

Eyes riveting on the tube, Sam sinks into the easy chair next to the couch. Deanie kneels before him, facing the tube. He draws her back, making his knees her backrest.

■ ■ ■

"Show me your room," Deanie whispers to him when they finish their soup.

The news is going to continue into special coverage. His father is rooted in front of it. Pearl has the baby to put to bed.

"After I do the dishes," Sam whispers back and then gets up to clean their trays.

With an anxious puppy air, she follows him to the kitchen.

"You can stay and watch the tube with Dad if you want," he tries to reassure her.

"Uh uh."

The way she scuttles after him, it's like she's afraid of his father. Probably everything about being here is extremely weird to her. Barely conscious when he carried her into the house, all she knows is sunporch, living room, bathroom, kitchen. She needs to get familiar with the place. A few days with them and she'll realize they don't any of them bite. Or put cigarettes out on each other.

"This is Pearl's house, really. Our old place is bigger." He hitches his head vaguely toward the window. "Up on the height of the Ridge. Big old farmhouse. Had a fire. We're just living here until it's fixed up again."

"Oh," she says. "You really own two houses? You must be pretty rich."

Bemused at the thought, Sam whips through the cleanup.

■ ■ ■

It's the first time he's ever brought a girl into his bedroom. He sniffs the air and is relieved not to pick up something like the vague and constant odor of piss that characterizes Indy's nursery. The room does smell more than a little of the locker room—sweat, sneakers, rubber, leather, oil of wintergreen. Parfum de jock. But Deanie is a jock herself. Maybe it'll make her feel at home. Her own little room, he remembers, had smelled of her, of course, and cigarette ash, candlewax, very faintly of dope—things burning.

This space is three times the size of the wretched little room under the stairs of the house on Depot Street. His bed is king-sized, spread with a handmade quilt. He has built it into a wall of shelving that accommodates his stereo system, his considerable music collection and even the handful of books he has read, like trophies. There is room for his bench and weights, for a scarred old oak rolltop desk and office chair, for a highboy dresser and a lowboy with a mirror. Braided rug on the oak floor, family pictures above his desk. The other walls are collaged with posters.

Sports icons take up most of one wall: Robert Parish, Kareem, Magic Johnson, Roger Clemens, Nolan Ryan, and his most valuable baseball cards, framed under glass. Three successively sized baseball bats dangle by their necks from a homemade rack, a shorthand graphic chart of his physical growth since Little League. His mitts and caps hang on a coatrack, along with a pair of cleats suspended by their tied laces.

The fourth wall is devoted to music. A handbill advertises a rock music concert at Wallkill which never happened—it was moved to Woodstock. Around it is a constellation of posters or copier blowups of album and CD covers. One depicts a trio of unprepossessing young men, self-labeled Puds, who composed a now defunct band called Big Black. Among others are an X-rayed skull from an album by Ministry, twin X-rayed fetuses from one by the Becketts, the stills from Godzilla flicks used as covers from two collections of Japanese pop, *Slitherama* and *Big Lizard Stomp.* There is one of an underground-band guitarist performing in a mask and Depends adult diapers.

A basketball stops the closet door from closing. Like a sculpture, a solitary ragged high-top rests on his desk. A stack of comic books spills from under the bed. On the closed door is taped the reproduction of the James Wyeth painting, *Pumpkinhead,* that she gave him. It strikes him he really is rich in comparison with her.

She kneels on his bed to reverently caress the matte black surfaces of his component system. "You got a lot of buckage tied up in this system."

"I save a lot of money, not smoking."

She flips him off. It hurts her to laugh aloud; she keeps it inside and it shakes her shoulders and brightens her visible eye.

"Your dad's worried about your brother, isn't he?" she asks.

"Sure."

"What do you think? Will they start up the draft again?"

"If it goes on long enough, I guess. Let's not talk about it."

He jacks a dub of assorted punk obscurities into the machine and sprawls on the bed next to her, plucking a text from his duffel on the floor. Watching her rummage through his music with the intensity of Indy grabbing at her toys tickles him. It's so normal. For a little while, it is almost as if all the bad shit hasn't come down on her.

"Amazing," she keeps muttering as she stacks up things she wants to hear. "The only thing," she concludes, "most of these yo-yos have in common is nobody but you listens to them."

"It's my special talent," he admits.

She snickers. "One of 'm anyway."

Presently she snugs into the crook of his arm to listen. It makes him feel good to have her there, warm and peaceful, next to him. Closing one text, he reaches for another and the vague awareness of her body intensifies. Her head is bent against him, right side pillowed on his chest, the upside of her face a soft-sculpture mask of misery, but she is tangibly female. He closes her in his left arm, supporting the swell of tit with his forearm. Under his lashes, he peeks. Through the thin material of the longjohns, the shadows of her areolae are visible. Rolling his wrist a little allows the tip of a finger to slip over the edge of one and it's so silky. Dozing, she does not respond but he does. Hastily he shifts her to a less accessible position and tries to concentrate on studying. He's a sick puppy, he chides himself, getting horny for her now.

He nudges her hip. "Hey."

She opens her good eye sleepily.

"You can't fall asleep here. Come on, I'll tuck you in downstairs."

Silently she complies.

After he turns out his own lights, sleep again evades him. From outside, a dim glow reflected from the porchlight leaks back through the ice frosting his windows. The peculiar muffle of snow descends on them like a Fortress of Solitude. When the sound of her distress comes from the tense darkness, he is relieved to go to her. Deanie never really wakes from her particular nightmare but he rocks and shushes and it quiets her.

■ ■ ■

The creaking of overhead floorboards breaks the crust of sleep well before dawn. Sam scoots upstairs and into his room and is sitting on the edge of the bed, yawning, when Reuben raps at his door.

"Looks like a snow day. Feel up to working?"

"For sure."

They have been working over an hour before the radio confirms school is out. All day Sam and his father and Jonesy free vehicles from ditches, ruts, and snowbanks, separate others from telephone poles and trees and other vehicles, jump batteries, and move snow hither and yon. Food is peeled out of waxed paper, consumed behind the wheel or in the garage, from one hand, while the other pushes a pen through some necessary paperwork or punches the cash register.

Through the day, Sam begins to feel like a human being again. He knows no more reliable way to get sane than to sweat hard and breathe the crystalline air of the Ridge all day. To plant his boots on the fractured bones of the Ridge and see the world from its astonishing vantage restores him to himself as nothing else besides hoops.

Thinking often of Deanie at home, he frets. At least she's healing well. Eating like she hasn't been fed in a month. When they call it quits, well after the supper hour, he is eager to see her.

Every light in the house appears to be burning on his arrival so it sits in a matrix of brilliance reflected from the glassy surface of the snow. They have visitors, as evidenced by a Greenspark police cruiser—Rick's dad—and Rick's Skylark in the driveway. Laughter and music are audible as soon as Sam drops from the cab of his truck. Crossing the yard, he touches the hood of the wrecker, still warm as fresh bread; his father has driven home.

Kitchen full—Pearl nursing Indy by the stove, his dad sitting down to his late supper, Sergeant Woods copping a cup of coffee and a plate that from the smell and the crumbs and flecks recently held gingerbread and whipped cream. Ginger and cinnamon and vanilla, oh my, evoke a gurgle from Sam's empty stomach. From the living room he hears the low timbre of Rick's laughter and Sarah Kendall's higher pitch.

Before Sam can finish stomping snow from his boots on the mat, Sergeant Woods rises.

"I'm just leaving," he announces. "Walk me out, Sam?"

For all the neighborly courtesy in his leave-taking, there is no real choice in the invitation. Reuben gives Sam a reassuring nod.

Putting the shed between them and the kitchen, Woods stops Sam on the porch. "Judy Gauthier says she can't remember what happened real well but she's sure Tony didn't hurt Deanie. Swears he never would do such a thing." Sergeant Woods chews his lip. "Tony admits he was loaded. He claims you were there, Sam." The cop's steadying hand falls on Sam's forearm. "Says he heard you belted her in the school parking lot Friday night and told you to stay away from her and you did his face for him. He says she tried to stop it and you hit her too."

Sam's thorax locks from his breastbone to the knot in his tongue.

"You should have told me about the business in the parking lot," says the cop, "but nevermind. I saw you leave, I saw Deanie after you left and she was okay. Lord told another story, bullshit about falling into a mirror, when he went into the hospital. He didn't bother to mention her being injured either at that time. Just now she gave me this bullshit she gave that doctor about an accident in the Playground. When I told her what Lord had said, she crawled into her shell and pulled the lid down on me. Maybe when she's had time to think about it, she'll come around. Has Deanie said anything more to you about what we talked about before? Lord and her?"

Dropping his gaze to his boots, Sam shakes his head.

"All right, then." The cop shuffles in the cold. "Lot of things could happen yet. The prosecutor doesn't like to spend money on anything less than a sure bet. The most important thing here is Deanie's safety. What do you think about a deal where we swap charges against Lord for Judy Gauthier voluntarily giving up Deanie to DHS custody?"

"Whatever," he mutters.

If Lord isn't charged, there are other ways to make sure the motherfucker never touches her again, and more certainly and permanently than the legal remedies.

Woods knuckles Sam's shoulder. "What you're not gonna do, my boy, is have anything to do with that pusbag. Don't you get the idea you can do to him what your old man did to that bastard who beat up your sister. It's not your job. You go after Lord, I'll throw your ass in jail, I don't care if it's the night of the state title. You get yourself in any kind of trouble at all, I'm coming down on you like an avalanche. We clear on this?"

Cheekbones hot at the ease with which the cop has read his vengeful thoughts, Sam nods tightly.

"I talked to Deanie by herself," Woods continues. "I haven't told your folks anything about this. I thought maybe you'd want to explain it to them."

Sam hears himself insisting to his father he never hit her, just yelled at her, and other people made it into something else. That would be the least of the explaining Woods was expecting him to do.

"I'm sorry about this," the cop says. "Try not to let it get to you too much. Go on with your life." Woods grins. "Don't let it get to your game."

He means it in the kindliest way, Sam tells himself, but inside, he wants to scream *What about Deanie's game? What about her life?*

31

 ■ ■ ■

The Way Girls Do, Sarah and Deanie sit on the couch, one foot under the other thigh, facing each other like they have to read each other's lips when they chatter. The everyday casualness of two teenage girls makes the condition of Deanie's face even more shocking.

Sprawled in an easy chair, wearing Reuben's headphones, Rick's jacked into Reuben's component system. Sam reaches for his hand and Rick simultaneously shakes with him and yanks off the 'phones.

Deanie tosses Sam a glittery knot like a metallic birdie. "Sarah made me a pair of earrings."

In his palm, it is a puddle of chain. He rolls it to his fingertips and shakes out an earring made of broken lengths of very fine chain, some of them with the odd bead or rice pearl attached, some with hooks and catches on them.

"You know how you wind up with all these busted chains you can't do anything with—" Sarah starts to elucidate and the expression on Sam's face stops her. "Of course you don't. Anyway, I did"—pointing at herself, she continues—"and I realized I could turn them into earrings. It was something to do."

They all look at her and each other and laugh. Blushing, she smiles and wags a hand at them dismissively.

Sam returns the earring to Deanie and she slips it through the hole in her right ear and turns her face to show it to him. The knot of fine chain ripples against the smooth grained ivory of her jaw and neck.

He has to clear his throat.

"Beautiful," he says.

She looks up at him with a shining eye. "I don't know if I can wear an earring on the other side anymore but—" She shrugs.

"Then you'll have a spare," Sarah quickly says.

Sam glances at Sarah's sneakered feet and then at Deanie's sockclad ones. They look to be the same size. Sarah's eyes meet his as if she is having the same thought.

Reuben appears in the doorway. He's wearing the question on his face: *Gonna eat tonight, boy?* If Reuben doesn't have to ask the question aloud, Sam doesn't even have to think about the answer.

■ ■ ■

Gingerbread and cream, Sam discovers, is as fine an appetizer as it is his favorite dessert. He is licking his fingers when Rick wanders in and helps himself. Sam heaps a plate with fried chicken and mashed potatoes and gravy, fills a salad plate with cole slaw and hooks a half gallon of milk from the fridge.

"Thanks for coming over," he says.

Rick shrugs. "No big deal. It was Sarah's idea, really. She's been messing around making jewelry since Christmas. Nobody's had a birthday yet she could unload any of it on."

Sam lowers his voice. "Ask her if she's got any spare high-tops, will you? Her feet look about the same size as Deanie's. Also Deanie needs clothes. Anything. You couldn't blow your nose twice on what she's got."

"I'll try to remember to bring my own snotrag, then. Sure, I'll ask." Throwing a glance over his shoulder toward the living room, Rick drop his head and voice as far as he can without outright whispering. "Somebody should take that shithead Lord's face off in strips, with a rusty razor."

"Later. Your old man just threatened to bust me first chance he gets. After the season's over, I'll take care of it."

Grinning, Rick rocks back in his chair. "Jeez, I'd love to watch."

Sam reaches for the milk carton. "In the meantime, somebody left me a hit of blotter in my locker."

Rick sits up and drops the front of his chair to the floor. "You're shitting me!"

"A stamp. After the game, it fell off my T-shirt, like somebody just tucked it in, passing by."

"Shee-it." Rick whistles softly. "Chapin was there."

"Could have been anybody."

"Somebody's playing dirty. You don't look out, you're liable to wind up prancing around stark naked with a hard-on in the middle of the game, bawling *If you're going to San Francisco, be sure and tie a daisy on your dick.*"

They both laugh softly.

"So I don't dare eat or drink or breathe too deeply at school?"

"No shit, you ought to just fucking lay waste—fuck up Fosse and Chapin both. Whoever planted the stamp on you, they both deserve a good fucking up anyway."

Sam shakes his head. "You're the guy threw a fist at me for trying to quit, so don't tell me you think it's worth the risk of getting canned right now. The one thing Laliberte isn't going to let me get away with is felonious assault. I'll just have to be paranoid for a while. I got the rest of my life after roundball season's over to settle scores. And I will, slick, I will."

"You gotta let those two pricks know they can't fuck with you and get away with it now!"

"No. I want Deanie safe from that creep and everything else back to normal," Sam says softly. "Don't you see, they win if they succeed in getting me to fuck up? Eyes on the prize. I want that gold ball for us, I want one for Deanie and the girls."

"Yeah, all right," Rick agrees with no enthusiasm. "All the same, you watch your back. And I'm watching your back too."

Across the table, they shake on it.

■ ■ ■

After Rick and Sarah leave, girl and cat curl together on the couch in a pale arabesque. Slowly stroking the cat's arching back seems to be as much effort as Deanie can manage, as if the visit had consumed all her meager store of energy.

It's a surprise when she says, "I'm going to school tomorrow."

Weak as she is, it strikes Sam as a terrible idea but then it occurs to him she'll be with him. He'll be able to keep an eye on her.

Then she tells him she has arranged an appointment to see Dr. Spellman after school. "I don't see why I can't play again as soon as my eye's completely open again. The wound's closed. It's not going to open up if I run or jump."

"What if you take a ball or an elbow in the face?"

She gives the cat a push and the cat takes the hint and jumps to the floor. Digging in between the cushions, Deanie extracts a rolled-up magazine and flops it open. It's a copy of *Sports Illustrated* and the page she shows him has a photograph of Detroit Piston Bill Laimbeer. Covering half of Laimbeer's face is a clear plastic mask.

"He's worn it almost the whole season."

Her right cheek pinks with excitement. She thinks she's found a way back to what she loves, the only place in the world she feels as good as anybody else. It's so little, stacked against what she's been through.

"It would be great if you could play again," he says.

Abruptly headachy, he tucks her in and heads for the bathroom to shower.

On his way to his room afterward, he knocks on Reuben and Pearl's door. His father sprawls on the bed in his clothes, eyes closed, baby asleep on his stomach. Pearl looks up from packing the diaper bag for the next day and gives him a warm smile. He hesitates, mutters goodnight and starts to withdraw. Reuben lifts a heavy eyelid and smacks his lips sleepily.

"Sammy."

"Judy Gauthier is covering for Lord. The cops are thinking about working a deal where Judy'd give up Deanie to DHS custody in exchange for no charges against Lord."

In the course of the recitation, Reuben gets the other eye open and manages a noncommittal, "Might be best."

Relieved to have avoided a full interview, Sam ducks out.

■ ■ ■

A choking cry breaks through his heavy sleep and brings him downstairs. Deanie sits on the edge of the daybed, shivering in sweat-soaked pajamas. He skins her out of the damp pajamas and into dry ones. The sheets are damp too. Bundling her into quilts on the couch, he changes the bed and then brings her back to it.

She's still trembling. He makes spoons with her. It's a comfort to him too to hold her close.

Hours later and at first only dimly, he becomes aware he is hard, cock nestled comfortably in the cleavage of her bottom. As his consciousness focuses, he grows harder. Her breasts rest on his right forearm. With a sigh, he makes himself lift his left hand, and gently dislodges her from his arm.

"Mmm?" she asks thickly.

"Go back to sleep," he mutters, swinging his legs out from under the quilts. He leans forward, pressing down. "I ought to go upstairs."

Her near hand scrabbling for his inadvertently touches his prick. Hastily he draws her hand away, flattening it on the pillow, weaving fingers with her. From under sleep-thickened eyelids, she peeks at him. He makes himself smile, brings her fingers to his mouth and kisses the tips and she closes her eyes again and turns her face to the unhurt right.

■ ■ ■

Morning rush is complicated by Deanie's preparations. When he comes down to shave, he realizes she has to use the shower so he takes his tackle to the kitchen sink and cuts himself twice in the small mirror propped on the window ledge, hurrying to finish before Pearl hits the kitchen.

Outside, the storm has left the ground treacherous. With no boots to wear and no treads left on her high-tops, Deanie has to accept his help just getting from the back porch to the truck and again when they arrive at the school. He carries all their gear in one hand, and wraps an arm around her waist to keep her upright. Skidding and slipping and swearing, she staggers against him but the cold and adrenaline bring a rose suffusion to her skin and a glisten to her eye. Any kind of normality is suddenly an adventure to her. They are laughing as he boosts her up the steps and through the doors.

The gym is already open and everyone else is waiting. The two of them go in happy—forgetful for the moment that anything has changed—and are met with a stunned silence at the damage to Deanie's face. There are gasps and downcast eyes and awkward efforts to be cool about it. Sam notes Fosse's reaction—a sardonic twitch of his mouth and an elbow into Todd Gramolini, who jerks away from Pete and glares at him. Todd's eyes return reluctantly to the Mutant, his face tightening, and then he too stares at the floor.

It's not as if they've never seen the toll the world takes sometimes. They have all gotten used to the sophomore with leukemia and the paraplegic junior in his wheelchair. They have become accustomed to Gauthier's old Mutant weirdness.

But this is different—this naked trauma that has distorted one side of her face. It would be one thing if it were merely the result of an accident but the knowledge that this was done to her with a man's fist is much more disturbing. Some of them played Romans to her gladiator in the parking lot, demanding she be beaten, much too close to the time when she really was. Stripped of chains, earrings and nose ring, she stands barefaced, all too fragile and female, in their midst. Her wound indicts them all and the shame and guilt are suffocating. There is an instant when the air is all unbreathable edges, a moment when they could as easily stone her as accept her.

Instinctively, Sam moves closer to the Mutant, ready to protect her.

"Gauthier," her coach exclaims from the door and Deanie spins to look past Sam and the moment passes.

Coach takes her by the elbow and draws her aside and the others go about their business. There is a sudden outbreak of blustering, almost hysterical joking, and none of it, conspicuously, concerns the Mutant.

After the coach lets her go, the Mutant takes a basketball from the rack and climbs onto the bleachers to watch them scrimmage. Sam immediately falls out of play and hustles her to the highest one to minimize the remote chance of her being struck by a loose ball, or being fallen on, say by a clumsy center tumbling ass over teakettle like an out-of-control missile.

When Sam looks her way again, she is resting her chin on her hands on the basketball. The wistful posture slackens the wind in his sails but then she lifts her head and sticks out her chin and cocks a mocking eyebrow at him.

■ ■ ■

In the weight room, no one talks of anything but the war. There is an undertone that wasn't there when they were all assuring each other it wasn't going to happen. The ones who say they wish they were there already, the others who say they'll go if called and the minority who insist they won't die for oil all speak with the same bravado, but what Sam hears most clearly is the first understanding it really is possible they could find themselves, one day too soon, in the desert. It really might be them doing the dying.

He lets the music on the boombox fill his head. He doesn't want to think about the war, where Frankie is. When they ask him if he will volunteer or what he will do if the draft is reinstituted, he shrugs and answers, "I dunno."

Whatever they have said in the spirit of macho, most of them feel the same way. Their open young faces are still those of boys, interchangeable with those in the Brady photographs of the soldiers who fought the Civil War thirteen decades ago. We dunno, Sam concludes. Frankie dunno, either. And he's right there in the desert shitstorm's weather system. Suddenly angry, Sam punches up the volume on the boombox.

■ ■ ■

Deanie has every excuse not to sit for any exams but she only has one scheduled for the day anyway and is sure she has it down cold. Still, the algebra exam is harder than she expects—maybe the painkillers are making her mentally sluggish—but she gets through it and that's one down. Afterward she is tired and beginning to hurt as her morning medication wears off. She is doled out her painkiller in the school nurse's office and allowed to lie down. 'god comes looking for her and makes her eat her lunch and sits with her until the dope kicks in and she gets sleepy.

When she comes to again, the nurse has left her desk on a coffee break. Deanie listens to the life of the school going on around her—a boy hoots down the corridor and is reprimanded in a genial way by a voice she recognizes as Paul Romney's, a trio of girls goes giggling by, someone a few doors away is giving an emphatic lecture. Doors open and close, a toilet flushes somewhere overhead, and the wet wool smell of cafeteria food creeps up the stairs and under the door.

She feels safe here in the bosom of the educational mill. If school is mostly bullshit and pettiness from the teachers and administration, if her fellow students frequently exhibit the social habits of sharks and hyenas, it's still a warm and busy place, a warren of hidey holes she knows better than anyone, even Mr. Moody the janitor. If it weren't such a long public trek, she would have long since swiped a key from old George and made herself a warmer ground than the one at the Mill.

Tugging the blanket up under her chin, she digs into the soporific warmth of her cocoon.

"Hey," J.C. says from the doorway.

Her heart bolts in the sudden cage of her chest.

He drops his books against the doorframe, seizes the lintel to chin himself and drops over the threshold into the room. Sticking his hands in his pockets, he tilts his head to study her, his eyes moist with concern.

"Oh shit, you're some fucked up," he observes.

Dry-mouthed, throat tight, she holds her breath. She dreads his touch but he keeps his hands to himself as he sinks to his haunches next to her.

"You know ol' Tony moved so fast I couldn't stop him, don't you, D.? I mean, I never thought he'd do something like that. No way. Anyway, you gave it back to him."

There is in J.C.'s voice a lilt of admiration meant to divert her from his cowardice, and worse—his fueling Tony with coke and gossip. Now he does touch her, his fingertips trailing along her forearm to her waist.

"Called Tony while he was in the hospital. He told me the cops didn't seem to know I was there. You haven't said anything about me, have you? I didn't really have anything to do with it. I don't see why I need to get involved. I mean, you're out of that shithole and into a better deal. I hear you're staying with Samson and his folks for a while, until the state finds you a foster home. That's a relief—really, I mean it. I knew the son of a bitch would go too far one day. But you fixed him." J.C. laughs.

"Leave me alone," she whispers.

He strokes her forearm. "You got Samson between you and Tony now. Smartest thing you ever did, D. You looked at ol' Samson and saw a guy whose lights all dim when he gets hard. A guy like that, somebody gets between him and his knothole, he takes it personal. I figure I was lucky not to be in that parking lot the other night. It coulda been my ass got kicked."

"All he did was yell at me," she says. "He'd never hit me."

J.C. smiles conspiratorially. "Right. And Tony Lord hasn't been balling you since you were eleven." He chuckles as if he is relating an amusing incident. His voice has not risen above a pleasant conversational level and his face is bright with wit and affection. His fingers close around her wrist and dig into it. "Just keep your tame gorilla on his leash, baby. And your mouth shut. You don't want the wrong shit turning up in his gym bag or yours. You don't want him freakin' out in the middle of the tournament. Things like that could happen, D."

She licks her lips. "Just leave him alone."

His eyes are moist with emotion. "I'm glad we're straight about that. I feel funny, D., I guess I always thought you and me, we'd be close forever. But everything dies, right?"

She stares at him. "Let go of me or I'm going to scream my head off."

J.C. drops her wrist hastily and springs to his feet.

"Chill out, baby."

"Get out of here, you chickenshit," she spits, her voice rising. "Now!"

Scooping up his books, he's gone. She huddles under the blanket and listens to the rapid squeak of his expensive high-tops propelling him down the corridor.

With no reason to trust the law to protect her from Tony's vengefulness, any more than it ever protected her from his abuse, she is only too aware of how much she needs 'god's muscle between her and Tony. She hates the way J.C. makes it seem calculating. It's survival. It's about as calculating as grabbing a life ring in heavy seas. J.C. Over the surface of the bandage, her fingers trace the line of her wound. Mouth trembling, she feels her eyes leaking.

■ ■ ■

The magazine flops open in Deanie's hand to the right page. Dr. Spellman peers at the photograph. She looks up and smiles. "You're very determined."

The girl smiles crookedly.

"This fellow, what's-his-face, he's a professional athlete. This is his living, his career. You're just sixteen, playing a high school sport." Before she finishes the observation, the doctor's tone slides into frustrated resignation. She sighs and asks Sam to wait outside.

He wanders back to the reception area and finds a corner to slump in. Helping Deanie fill out the form on the clipboard the receptionist handed them when they arrived was a jolt; this was going to cost more money. Again he printed his own name on the line for the financially responsible person.

"I'll pay you back," Deanie whispered as his pen twitched over the paper.

"It's all right. I got in a full day's work yesterday."

He doesn't add he's already signed his name to a cock-knocking hospital bill and paying it will keep him too poor to insure his bike for months. He watches the clock, anxious not only to escape a place where every minute seems to drag him further into debt but to get back to school—luckily they are playing the return game with Mount Grace at home—girls first.

The doctor crooks a finger at him.

In her small inner office she gestures toward a chair and drops into her own, behind her desk, to scrawl notes. "I'm going to contact the sports medicine team in North Conway to see if they can help us with a protective mask for Deanie. I don't want her on the court until she has one—and not before another week is up, anyway."

Sam paces the office. From the window, the Mill is visible. He rubs a circle of condensation from the glass to see it more clearly.

"Maybe you could persuade her to let me do a complete physical," Spellman says. "If she's going to take oral contraceptives, she must have the appropriate checks. And the two of you shouldn't be having unprotected intercourse."

Blushing furiously, he mutters, "We're not doing anything now."

"She might not want to for a long time. You'll have to be careful. She could be afraid of an inadvertent injury to her face. She may not be feeling very sexy. Maybe she'll want to be cuddled and comforted more than she'll want to have sex. It would be a good idea for both of you to get some counseling—her especially, but you too. Something like this usually takes time and professional help to get over."

"I don't know how I'm going to pay for any of this," Sam blurts. "She hasn't got the price of a pack of gum herself."

"Once she's in state care, she'll have Medicaid," the doctor tells him. "We'll work it out."

Leaving unasked the question of whether the state will pick up the bills that already exist, he follows her to the cubicle down the hall, where Deanie sits cross-legged on the examining table, reading the *Sports Illustrated*.

"All set, Deanie," the doctor tells her. "Call me tomorrow and I should know something about the mask."

Deanie grins crookedly and offers Sam a high five.

32

■ ■ ■

The Mutant Teeters on the catwalk under the roof of the gym in her imagination, the contest with Mount Grace wheeling beneath her. With very little effort she could be onto the walk from the top bleacher. She wipes sweating palms on her thighs. Excitement churns the pit of her stomach. She can't help flying herself mentally to the court and going through the motions with her team.

"You okay?" Sam asks. "I have to go change."

"Sure, sure," she responds, grumpy at being distracted from the game.

In the last quarter, 'god's old man arrives with Stepmom and the Brat in tow. To her surprise, they survey the bleachers as if they are looking for someone, wave at her, and then they come and sit down next to her, where they inquire how she feels and how the game is going. It makes her feel extremely weird, almost panicky.

The Greenspark girls pull steadily ahead. Then it's over, another W. The girls form a gauntlet for the boys to run, applauding them onto the floor before going to their locker room. When they emerge again near the end of the first quarter of the boys' game, they fill up the bleachers the boys emptied. Quietly Deanie slips down to join them. Coach grins at her and accepts a congratulatory high five but mostly her teammates ignore her. Fuck'm. Unknown to them, at this moment she is wearing a pair of Samgod's socks. She hugs her secrets to herself.

■ ■ ■

The boys appear to have recovered their purpose. All at once they are exuberant again, playing as if they were having fun.

On the way to the locker room at the end of the second quarter, Sam calls up to Deanie, asking her how she is doing. Okay, she signals, but she looks wiped out to him. Maybe he should have taken her home right after she saw Dr. Spellman. Some of the elation at being back on the court drains away. Being involved with someone, he reflects, is as complicating as he always feared it would be.

The atmosphere in the locker room is a happy, confident one, though Coach is sweating Rick's stamina. In practice Billy Rank has shown no signs of recovery from his slump and no one, Billy least of all, wants to have to depend on him. Tim Kasten's ankle is still bothering him. At least Fosse is taking care of business— not, Sam suspects, because of the asskicking Sam has given him, but because Pete could hardly miss Sam taking Joey Skouros to school during practice, under Coach's approving eye.

Despite a six-minute run by the Red Demons in the fourth quarter, Coach risks sending in Billy. Sam is out too, giving Pete more minutes. Next to him, Rick mutters and curses as Billy thrashes like a drowning victim and their comfortable edge shrinks. By the time Coach hooks Billy and Rick reenters the game, Rick is in a thoroughly ugly mood. In three minutes he picks up two fouls, going into the last quarter with a total of four—one more and he's out of the game. He gives the already miserable Billy an evil look; Coach catches it and chokes Rick's leash.

"Woods," Coach snarls at him, "take a Midol and cut the shit."

While Rick gropes for his focus, Sam tightens the defense, rejecting the first three Red Demon lobs. The frustrated Demons fail to notice Rick falling back past center court steadily until he is only a stride from the Greenspark goal. Sam makes the long pass to him. Rick goes up, reaching, as the ball arrives and directs it gently through the hoop. The belated Mount Grace defense skids into the paint with Todd Gramolini in their midst. He strips their small forward of the ball and hurtles it overhead, back out to Sam, loping across the center line. Sam leaps up to catch it, shoots it from midair and it drops, for three. For the rest of the quarter, the Big Machine runs smokingly hot and the Red Demons reel.

■ ■ ■

With bills to pay, Sam goes to work after the game, eating his supper on the job, and stays to close up with his father. The household is settled for the night when he and Reuben let themselves in—Deanie asleep on the sunporch, Indy asleep at her mother's breast upstairs. After the ritual of locking the house, they say goodnight to each other and go directly to bed. Tired as he is, Sam lies taut and sleepless for an hour and then slips downstairs and under the quilts with Deanie.

■ ■ ■

The Mutant wakes, shivering, before dawn. There is a thread of long blond hair on her pillow. She remembers him flinching away from her, disentangling his legs from hers, rolling hastily from the daybed. Dazed with sleep, she can't get her mouth to work, to make him understand she knows he can't help it; it happens to men in their sleep. It would happen to him if she weren't there. She doesn't mind, anymore than she would mind a puppy creeping into bed with them and tucking his snout in the nearest warm spot.

She focuses on the narrow strips of painted wood that form the ceiling of the sunporch. The downstairs rooms feel larger in their emptiness. The furniture stands like sleeping horses in a field, shadowy hulks separated by space and an altered state of consciousness. In the kitchen, the refrigerator hums faintly. Banked coals in the woodstove suddenly snap. She can smell the odor of their combustion. The world is full of forgotten smells since she quit smoking.

This particular room, the sunporch, smells distinctly of long-ago dead cigars, though no one in the present household smokes. There are bars in the bathroom, the kind people use to grope their way around when they're unsteady on their pins, so presumably some previous resident grew sick or feeble in this house.

Upstairs, bedsprings shift and the floorboards object to 'god's old man's weight as he gets out of bed. Stepmom speaks, a sleepy question, and is answered tersely but with audible affection before the man goes down the hall to the upstairs bathroom.

Stepmom's bare feet follow him and pass the door to the bathroom and into the baby's room. The Brat greets her mother with a slurry of meaningless syllables and rakes her plastic keyring noisily against the bars of her crib. Stepmom laughs softly and coos to her.

She slides out from under the quilts. The floorboards between the braided rugs are cold, even through the socks she wears, and the downstairs bathroom is even colder. She turns on the space heater.

Picking up the cake of Dove, she sniffs at it. It's still a little damp from last night. Her toothbrush leans against the lip of a jelly glass on the shelf above the basin. She tips it out and rinses the glass and uses some mouthwash. Looks into the mirror. Turns her face to look at the left side. The black and blue is mottled with yellow and maroon. The wound bisects the muddied colors like a shiny string. Though puffy and torn at the lobe, her ear is almost normal again, and her left eye is fully open, though heavily shadowed with bruise-coarsened skin so it looks desperately weary. Raising her hand, she covers the left side as much as she can. Her jaw works and she drops the hand and pivots away.

■ ■ ■

The pipes clank and the water clatters in the tin shower stall of the downstairs bathroom just as Sam reaches the bottom step. He raps urgently on the bathroom door but over the noisy shower, Deanie must not be able to hear him. Upstairs, his father is shaving. Not alone. Pearl is just out of the shower and is drying herself and the baby. The pisser is, Sam thinks resentfully, it's Saturday, a day Deanie could shower later. He grabs his jacket, unlocks the back door, steps through the shed and onto the porch and leans over the rail to piss into the bare branches of the lilac. Numbed, he can't get it started right away and he rocks from foot to foot, muttering curses.

Encountering his father as he comes back into the kitchen, he is still adjusting his fly. Reuben raises an eyebrow but refrains from observing that it's decidedly frigid for pissing out of doors. Sam shrugs and hangs up his jacket. He washes his hands at the sink and reaches for his razor on the windowsill over it.

He is rinsing it off when Deanie drifts into the kitchen, head already scarfed, high-tops gripped in one hand. She drops into a chair and hauls on her sneakers. He fills two mugs of coffee and sits down next to her.

"Can I go to work with you? I won't get in the way. Maybe I could pump gas for you?"

He looks at his father, who shrugs.

"I'm not going straight to work," Sam tells her reluctantly. "I'm going to the meeting house."

"For what?"

"Pickup game," Sam mutters.

Deanie brightens. "Yeah? Can I go?"

"You can't play," he points out.

"That's okay. I'll watch. Who's playing?"

"Some of the guys."

She grins. "Great."

She's at his elbow as he unlocks the side door at the meeting house. It feels a little like sneaking into the Mill together but he's embarrassed too, because she's about to see that the place where he practices on the weekends is a palace next to the improvisation of the Mill. She steps into the pale gold silence of the high-ceilinged hall and her eyes widen.

"My dad built this court years ago. Promoted the money from a summer resident. This guy likes to hack himself when he's around. Can't shoot straight but he's wicked fast. Sometime I'll show you his house on the lake. My dad's his caretaker. Anyway, anytime the hall isn't being used for something else, it's available. Just wear sneakers and bring a ball. Most Sundays, there's a regular pickup game. Dad usually makes that one. Pearl's started playing recently. She's somebody who can shoot straight."

"No shit?" Deanie spins the ball on her fingertips, twitches her hips at him, and then dribbles it down the court and hooks it in.

"Hey!" he objects. "You're benched, twink."

Passing the ball behind her, she flips him a digit and sticks her tongue out.

"Twink yourself, Godzilla!"

He lopes after her and tries to take it away from her. Giggling, she teases him with the ball but won't let him get a hand on it. He's tentative, intensely aware of her unprotected face, but she moves fearlessly. Suddenly he stops dead, raises his palms and backs to the sidelines.

"Oh come on!" she pleads.

Crossing his arms, he shakes his head no.

Her mouth turns down and she spins away and drives the ball down court with a furious rhythm. She shoots around for a while and then she trots back and stands in front of him. The ball pops up off the floor and she rolls it over the edge of her palm and holds it like a globe.

"Chickenshit," she taunts.

Sam extends his palm and she tips the ball into it. She slumps disconsolately next to the boombox. What is he supposed to do? She can't play.

The others come horsing in, pausing at the sight of Deanie, and shooting Sam looks that he ignores, and then shrugging her presence off.

■ ■ ■

Woven through the chatter and clatter of the diner, the speculation among his teammates continues about whether the draft will be revived and how each of them will answer it. Few of them have any deep interest in politics or could find Kuwait or Iraq on an unmarked map but that doesn't change the obvious: they are all prime cannon fodder. Sam sits there with his ears open, working his way once again through the arguments and thinking of Frankie. Deanie listens closely, once muttering "Bullshit" at some bit of macho posturing.

At the garage, he walks her through turning on the gas pumps and locking down the triggers on the nozzles and then the use of the cash register and making out credit slips. Soon she is ensconced at the desk with her textbooks to fill the down time and the volume on the radio cranked. She doesn't try to talk to him while he's working, earning her points not only with him but his father as well.

In the early afternoon they make the trip to North Conway to see about the mask. Once they are in the sports medicine clinic, the familiarity of the staff is a little embarrassing—Sam's doctor pops out of his office and wants to talk basketball and not incidentally weigh and measure him. Grown another half inch since the preseason but no more weight—typically running on high and burning calories by the short ton—not that he needs scales and tapes to know that the seemingly ceaseless alteration of his fabric continues.

Deanie hangs back, in her cautious, watchful mode. She is relieved by the matter-of-fact treatment of the staff. The origin of her injury might as well be just another athletic accident as far as these efficient enthusiasts are concerned. Though her still-swollen face is prodded and pressured in the course of examination and the making of the mask, the way they take it for granted she will do whatever she had to do to play again straightens her spine and lightens her mood.

The mask is clear rigid plastic, molded to her face. It does not fit flush to her face but sits upon a perforate footing of cushioning foam that allows for the passage of air over her skin. It is asymmetrical, curving close under her eye socket over the cheekbone, up against the side of her nose and cutting down past the left side of her mouth to the jawline and back to her ear. Held in place by the side of her nose and a piratically cocked y-shaped strap around her head, it is immediately painful. She is assured that when the swelling subsides, all she will feel is a sensation of light pressure.

Though she seems faded by the time they leave the clinic, she doesn't want to go home and rest. A little aspirin and she'll be fine, she insists. Back at work, she displays the mask for Reuben. He examines it critically and then gives it back to her with a laugh and a shake of his head. Delighted for her, he gives her a casual, spontaneous hug. Much to his surprise, she stiffens instantaneously and flails into a backward stumble out of his embrace. Face reddening with chagrin, Reuben tries to apologize to her. Like a headlight-stunned animal, she stays fixed in her panic, her mask clutched tightly to her chest.

Reuben in distress retreats to the far side of the garage. Still hangdog, he takes his leave shortly—headed for the farmhouse to punch up drywall.

■ ■ ■

Hearing the crunch of tires and the beat of an engine outside, Sam slides out from under a sedan in time to see the door slap behind Deanie. He crosses the garage to look out at her. Sonny Lunt is at the pumps, waving her off to wait on himself. She pivots and Sam opens the door for her.

"Where's your frigging coat? Are you out of your head?"

Ducking under his arm, she drops into the chair behind the desk.

"You want to get sick? You like the bench that much?"

She kicks back and thuds her high-tops on the desk. "Oh Christ! Don't start on me!"

He throws up his palms in disgusted resignation. Stiff-arming the kettle, he shoves it under the tap in the restroom to fill and thunks it, sloshing, down onto the stove. He punishes the fire with the poker and jams another chunk of wood into the firebox. By then he feels like a total asshole.

When he peeks at her, she is twirling the office chair childishly from side to side, her knees drawn up and her arms wrapped around them, her head tilted back so the throat is a long elegant line. He finds himself studying the shape of her bottom, the darker solid fabric that covers her crotch, and his groin is suddenly oppressively heavy. He tries to distract himself with the work at hand.

That's all there really is between them—rutting in the Mill. He knew when he did it that screwing her was the wrong thing to do but he just had to do it, didn't he? She had needed a friend, not another stiff dick. It would have been better all around if it hadn't happened. Now he can't take it back.

" 'This ain't no disco,' " he mutters, " 'this ain't no foolin' around.' "

The dry smell of hot tea steams under his nose and he looks up into her face. She holds out the mug of tea she has made him. "Want something to eat?"

He straightens up, accepts a donut from the bag.

"You okay?" he asks, wolfing it and dusting his fingers on his overalls.

"A little tired," she admits. "I'll be okay, though. This isn't exactly hard work, what you got me doing. I bet I could have worked for my old ladies today, no problem. I like the way this place smells. You get high from the fumes?"

Sam laughs.

"What are you doing?" she asks.

Telling her about it, several moments go by before he is aware his hand has fallen to her hip and they are leg to leg. He takes an awkward step back. "Gotta get this finished."

Crossing her arms over her chest, she goes back to the office with her head down, the bad side of her face cocked away from him.

■ ■ ■

His father returns to spell him for the dinner hour. Leaving her at the house—she's too whipped for even a feeble display of resistance—he goes back to the garage and stays late, and not just to get the hours. It's a relief to find her asleep when he finally gets home again. Though she takes fewer painkillers now, by evening, the discomfort's always worse so she takes the full dose.

He flops onto his bed and opens the notebook he uses for an account book. He works a few moments, figuring his debts and anticipating his wages. The hole is huge. One relief is it hasn't gotten deeper; the trip to the sports medicine clinic turned out to be a freebie. Whether it was Spellman doing them a good turn or not, he didn't know, but they were told it was the first opportunity the clinic had to use one of the masks and they would do it gratis as part of a study. Throwing down the pencil, he buries his face in his pillow, wondering if maybe it wouldn't be better to shitcan the baseball season and squeeze the hours for cash. His last high school baseball season—shit.

Hours later he wakes again and he doesn't know why, except he is on the alert for something. It is the absence of the sound for which he listens from the other side of sleep that makes him anxious. Rolling out of bed, he sneaks downstairs to check on Deanie.

The bathroom light is on; the door, open. She stands before the mirror in her longjohns. With her left hand, she tries covering the scar and then lets the hand fall as if it just weighed too much to continue to support.

"It's always gonna be there, isn't it?" she says. "Like a tattoo. Where everybody can see it."

He doesn't answer. She doesn't look at him. As swiftly as her knees slacken and her fingers close over the edge of the basin and she begins to rise from the balls of her bare feet, he moves, catching her by the hips and hauling her down out of her trajectory into the mirror. Though she struggles briefly, she's lost both momentum and surprise and there's no hope of overpowering him.

On the bathroom floor, he holds her tight. Shudders go through her in waves that make her body churn and twist. Still she stays dry-eyed. He rubs his fingertips over her mouth and she gasps and sucks at them, hard, and that's when she finally cries, silent tears sheeting to the edges of her face and down his neck as she clings to it, and into the hair on his chest.

The bedding still holds a little of her warmth when he tucks her into it. He wants to reassure her that the swelling is diminishing, the bruising growing gaudy as it heals—it won't always be as bad as it is. He wants to lie and tell her the scar will be unnoticeable, or easily covered with makeup. But a lie won't make it so, it will only make him a liar.

Exhausted, she falls asleep in his arms. Carefully, he shifts her off him and slides out from between the sheets. He lifts the top quilt and lies back down beside her with most of the bedding between them.

■ ■ ■

Bouncing unsteadily on her toes, arms reaching ecstatically, Indy seems to be practicing her free throws but she is only excited by the noise and chaos of the Sunday-morning pickup game. Deanie holds her firmly by the waist in the pen of her crossed legs while the baby does her toddler squat thrusts. But Deanie stays somber, clutching Indy with something like resignation. In her eyes, Sam sees the bad night, the nightmare reality in the mirror.

■ ■ ■

In the afternoon, they babysit while Reuben and Pearl go to the farmhouse to work. Now that Indy is walking—staggering from piller to post, occasionally working herself into a run with no brakes—there are baby gates in all the doors and at the top and bottom of the two stairwells. Indy wants to climb, so Sam folds the bottom gate of the back stairs and sits on a step within reach of her. He allows her to struggle up a few risers before returning her to the first step to begin again.

"You're getting a lot done on that essay for Romney," Deanie chides. "That's sadistic, letting her get a little ways and dragging her back down."

"She likes it."

Slipping, Indy bangs her mouth into the edge of a riser and wails. He picks her up and finds she has bitten her upper lip and it's swelling. Shushing her, he wraps a chunk of ice in a washrag and holds it to her lip. Almost immediately, she forgets the pain and starts to suck on the damp cloth. Lowering her into her playpen, he goes back to the table to go to work. Muckling onto the netting of the playpen, the baby clambers back to her feet.

"Da!" she yells at him.

When he looks up and grins, she bursts out in a tirade of gibberish that makes him laugh. Frustrated, she bangs her face into the netting and makes it hurt again. She bursts out screaming.

Deanie claps her hands over her ears. "Jesus!"

Scooping up her books, she boots it upstairs. His component system thumps on.

Sam shushes the baby. The baby's wet herself right through in the course of her tantrum. He offers her the rag with the ice in it and takes her upstairs to change her.

Deanie lies on her back on his bed, holding his basketball on her stomach with one hand, one arm over her eyes, Green on Red's "Rock'n'Roll Disease" playing. Her breasts quiver with the movement as she lifts the arm over her eyes to peek at him.

Though Sarah brought over a box of jeans and shirts and stuff—including a pair of high-tops—that she claimed to have culled from her overstuffed closet on orders from her mother so it would practically be a favor if Deanie took them off her hands, almost the only thing Deanie has put to use are the sneakers, which do fit her—better than her old ones, anyway. She helps herself to his socks and T-shirts as they come out of the dryer and it makes him feel funny—funny amused but funny in other ways too. It's some kind of comfort to her, he guesses, makes her feel closer to him, and maybe safer, so he hasn't said anything to her about it. He's trying to figure out a way to get money enough to buy her the kind of leather jacket with fringes the other girls are wearing.

He lowers Indy onto his bed. The baby beelines for the orange ball, slapping at it with the palms of her hands. Deanie lets it go and Indy embraces it, tasting it. Deanie laughs and the baby grins wetly at her. Sam takes the ball away from her and Indy stiffens, her little hands clutching after it, her body going rigid. He pushes her gently onto her back, peels off her leathersoled socks and tickles the bottoms of her feet. She chortles and pumps her legs maniacally. She twists herself onto her knees and scrabbles away. He catches her by the ankles and yanks her back. Immediately she's up again, trying to escape, totally into the new game. She squirms out of Sam's hands and dives onto Deanie, clutching at her clothes, climbing right up her. Alarmed for Deanie's face, Sam reaches for Indy and flips the baby onto her back like a turtle. Indy keeps on rolling over and he catches her again and flips her and she decides this game is even better. The baby begins to roll over and over for the fun of it, while they laugh at her. Sam stops her, finally, and rocks her in his arms to calm her.

Deanie flops back down again and crooks an arm under her head and her tits tent the T-shirt. She catches him looking.

He finds the wet rag and Indy takes it eagerly. When he puts her on her back, she stays there, tired out by her exertions. Kneading Indy's belly, he is intensely aware of Deanie's body within his reach. His old shirt against her bare skin. Indy's eyes roll up and she slackens, the rag still firmly clenched in her fist.

When he looks up, Deanie is watching him still. The fingers of one hand touch the tip of her breast in his shirt in invitation. Her hand takes his, moves it up under the shirt without resistance and he feels the beautiful thing, the smooth curve, and sucks in a panicky breath and snatches back his hand.

"Folks'll be back any minute," he says.

Her eyes darken and she rolls over on her stomach and hides her face in the pillow. He wants to comfort her, to explain all the reasons it's wrong to start again but he knows if he touches her a second time, he won't be able to stop.

"Fuck," she mutters, "I'd kill for a drag."

He makes himself get off the bed and make a business of taking an extra quilt from the closet to cover the sleeping baby.

"Want some cocoa?" he asks.

Mercifully, she nods and he goes downstairs to make it, and when he brings it back up, her eyes are closed and she's either asleep or faking it, so he covers her too and dims the light. King's birthday tomorrow, so they'll have the day off, and she can sleep all day if she wants.

33

∎ ∎ ∎

Taking that Face with Them, the Mutant sees in the shock in her coach's eyes the first morning back after the long weekend. So far, she's been on the injured list, no explanation, but as soon as she comes in range of even a smalltown rag's stringer's camera, there will be questions about what happened to Gauthier's face that nobody wants to answer. When Coach hinted she should maybe stay out of sight until her face is in better shape, she pointed out that the questions are inevitable, given she is going to be wearing a mask when she plays again. So Coach is tensed to bark something vague about an accident to the first question and then to develop difficulty hearing further questions.

'god likes the Mutant going to the game so he can keep an eye on her. He was cheesed at her for going back to work on the lunchline. Wait'll he finds out she's going back to work for the old women on Saturday too. He came backing and bumping his way into the serving area and *checked up on her* in front of everybody—wanting to know if she'd eaten her lunch and how she was feeling. She'd racked herself being glassily polite. And then had to be aware—she wouldn't look at them—of him sitting there with Nat Linscott two chairs away fluttering her fat eyelashes at him.

Unable to use her Walkman because her left ear is still too ten-der, the Mutant has to listen to her teammates around her. Linscott's in the seat in front of her on the bus so she gives it a good shove with her feet and gets a satisfying squeak out of Nat.

■ ■ ■

Head tilted, ears sealed with his headphones, Sam cuts out. He isn't worried about the upcoming matches.

After the rough night, he woke half an hour earlier than neces-sary. And then she was in the bathroom forever, scraping her head with his blade, so he couldn't shave, nevermind taking a leak. When he went out to start the trucks, his battery was dead and he had to frig around jumping it, cursing himself for not having plugged in the block heater. She left his blade looking like she shaved a tank tread with it. In the whole frigging house, there wasn't a blade fit to use. And when he finally got to sit down at the table, Indy promptly lobbed a gob of mashed banana onto his frigging game-day tie so it looked like he had blown his nose on it or maybe wiped a fistful of jizz on it.

In the truck he plugged in Duke Tomato to try to cheer himself up and she reached over and punched reject at the end of the first verse of "Tie Me Up." As the cassette jumped out, she didn't even try to catch it so he grabbed for it with fingers sticky from the pancake sandwich he was trying to eat one-handed as he drove, and probably ruined the tape. And then Deanie shoved his favorite seventies dub with T. Rex and Sweet and Queen and some other extremely fine shit on it into the slot at an angle and jammed it. He had to pull over and ease it out, and *she* was ripped at *him,* like it was his fault. And they were late getting to the gym—skin off his nose, not hers, since she was still benched. When he finally managed a shave in the locker room with a disposable he'd left in his locker, he cut the shit out of his face. In the corridors between classes, she looked right through him and walked away from him, as if she wasn't wearing one of his old shirts knotted and frayed over hers, and a pair of his socks too.

No surprise he's tired enough to check effortlessly into the Dream Motel.

■ ■ ■

Sitting on the bench next to Coach, the Mutant watches the warm-up. People gawk at her. Some of them make cruel remarks to each other behind their hands or in low voices. Nothing new in that. She holds her head a little straighter. Someone's shadow falls massively over her from behind. 'god's huge hands fold over her thin shoulders, squeeze her gently and then he's gone, up into the bleachers.

Time-out, quarter breaks, half—she crouches next to Coach in the heart of the clutch of girls, with a twin on either side of her, their hands on her shoulder and knee in unself-conscious solidarity. Unimpeded, even enhanced by their differences, energy—the will to win—flows among them and flowers in the bright, damp faces and eyes, the nervous flick of fingers through sweaty hair.

She leaps into the air a fraction of a second before the buzzer, her arms shooting up as if to dunk, and she comes down, pistons her elbows back, her fists closed, folding her body in a triumphant clench. Her eyes are closed tight in ecstasy when the camera flash goes off.

Slapping palms down the length of the parade line of the boys waiting at the locker room door, when she reaches 'god the Mutant dances like a raindrop hip-hopping down a windshield, rattles her fingertips off his as if speed-typing, and is gone, a whirlwind on the tips of her toes.

The instant of contact transmits her excitement to Sam and he goes out pumped and primed, the tensions between them blown away.

■ ■ ■

After the game, the mood on the boys' bus is one of raucous triumph.

"Smoked'm!" Bither crows.

"Bagged'm, tagged'm and shat on their heads, Sambo," Rick confides happily.

"Amen, Brother Slick. But I felt like a paranoid asshole, sharing your squeeze bottle."

Rick glances around at their teammates. "Yeah, well, they could try to fuck me up too."

Sam shakes his head. "It's over. Whichever one it was, made their point."

"Anybody fucks me up, Sambo, is gonna get severely fucked back."

It's being pumped from the game that's running Rick's mouth,

Sam knows, but he feels an empathetic surge of the don't-fuck-with-me's in his blood.

"All right!" he agrees.

High fives, to mark their mutual aggression pact.

■ ■ ■

On the road before theirs, the girls' bus arrives at the high school first and empties. Sam checks his truck from the boys' bus. Though she has a key and instructions to start it and keep herself warm should she arrive first, he sees no Deanie.

The planet under Sam's feet seems to take a sudden acceleration and his stomach climbs his spine. Grabbing his gear, he climbs over the backs of seats past startled teammates to get to the front of the bus. The doors can't wheeze open fast enough for him. He gives them a kick that produces a startled pneumatic squeal and an outraged "Hey!" from the bus driver. As the driver anxiously works the doors again and discovers, wonderingly, that the stickiness they have exhibited for weeks is suddenly gone, Sam bolts across the lot to yank open the passenger door of his truck.

The dark bundle on the floor is the very shadow of his fear. He stops breathing and reaches for her. Yelping, she raises her pale face from her arms. He sees in her startled eyes there is nothing wrong with her. Her whole body is shaking and he realizes she is cold.

Feeling foolish, he demands to know, "Why didn't you start the truck?"

"I did what you told me but it didn't work," she snaps back just as crossly. "I must a flooded it."

Silently he slips behind the wheel, turns the key she has left in the ignition and jollies the engine, which she has indeed flooded, to life.

"My fault," he mutters. "Should of made sure you knew how to start this thing. We'll practice it." A lightbulb goes on in his head. "Gonna teach you how to drive too."

That makes her sit up, amazed, not sure whether she has heard him right.

He plucks at his game tie and tears it off. "When I looked over here and I couldn't see you, I was scared shitless."

Her good eye goes wide, the one with the bad mouse leaking, and her mouth wavers. "I didn't mean to scare you. It was just warmer on the floor. You shouldn't be worried. Tony's in no shape to come after me right now."

He yanks up the parking brake. "There's a tire iron under my seat. In case you can't get to it, I'm putting a nail gun in the glove compartment so when you have to wait for me, you'll have some way to protect yourself."

Deanie stares at him.

"The fuckhead doesn't get any more whacks at you," Sam promises. "He comes within sight of you, I'm taking his fucking head off for him."

Still hugging herself against the cold, she protests, "It's not worth it."

His answer is unspoken: *Yes it is. Yes it is.* In the deep cold beneath his breastbone, a murderous bulbous urge nudges toward a blind and distant heat. It terrifies him and exalts him and makes his palms wet.

■ ■ ■

As he swings the truck from the parking lot to the looping driveway back to 302, Fosse cuts in front of him far too closely and at a speed that causes the Blazer to fishtail. Sam narrowly avoids rear-ending him. Though he knows rationally Pete's handling of the Blazer is just high-spirited horsing around triggered by the adrenaline rush of winning, he finds himself as furious as if it were a deliberate provocation.

Pete turns his head, craning at Sam through the Blazer's rear window. Bither and Tim Kasten are in the Blazer too and they also look back, their faces contorted by the rollercoaster excitement of the fishtail. Pete's eyes meet Sam's and Pete laughs. He straightens around to fix his eyes back on the road again but he raises his right hand, middle digit up, blindly and casually flipping Sam off. Pete's passengers are convulsed by the act; they writhe around clutching their guts, pounding the heels of their palms against their foreheads.

That's it. Sam gooses the accelerator. All at once the Blazer jerks and sags like a bad vaudevillian on a hook as the front bumper of Sam's truck climbs its rear bumper. Deanie yelps and flails and braces herself. Sam gives the truck another squirt and shoves the Blazer forward.

Alarmed angry blobs of faces waver in Pete's rear window now. Up and down the line of exiting vehicles, there is a chorus of horns. Deanie hoots with savage delight. Sam throws the truck into reverse and the guys inside the Blazer take another jolt. Shifting into drive again, he slams the truck's bumper back into the Blazer. Pete's vehicle jerks and shimmies and shudders a few more feet forward. There is a muffled shriek from Deanie as she bounces off the dashboard and tumbles to the floor.

The Blazer's door swings open, Pete jumps out and Sam shoves the Blazer harder. Pete dives back inside, the door flopping open and closed with the impact. The headlights of the other vehicles are flashing on and off and the horn chorus grows crazier and people are hanging out of their windows, like a bunch of fight fans in a blood frenzy. Sam backs up again. Pete flings open his door again but when he sees Sam's door jerk open and Sam moving, erupting from behind the wheel wearing his gunslinger's face, Pete has second thoughts. He tromps on the gas and skids ahead.

Sam settles behind the wheel again. The Blazer is scooting away from them, the rearview a forest of middle digits and snarls. Only then does he realize Deanie is still on the floor, with a hand clapped over the hurt side of her face. He lunges toward her.

"I'm okay," she chokes, as he pries her hand away from her face. "I just bumped it."

He can't see any further damage but she winces when he touches it.

"I'm sorry, I'm sorry," he keeps saying. The muscle in his jaw aches along with his throat.

The vehicles behind the truck begin to swing around it, blatting horns in passing. Headlights flare in the side mirror.

■ ■ ■

Deanie lies on her back on the daybed, bare head resting on her crooked arm. In the clean sweatpants he'll sleep in, Sam scooches beside the daybed and she rolls her head slightly to meet his eyes but not before he sees the puffiness over her cheekbone. Her pupils are big and wet with Percodan.

"The looks on those guys' faces—I almost wet myself." Her mouth curves in a smile that makes him smile back. "Next thing I know I'm landing on my face. It felt like getting punched again. I couldn't believe it hurt so much and all I could think was now I've done it, I won't be able to play. I should have had my seatbelt on. I was as mad at myself as I was at you."

"Maybe we should have gone to the hospital, got it checked?"

She shudders. "No way. It's okay. It didn't open up. By the time we got home the pain was already a lot less."

He knows who is most to blame. Going up to his own room, he sits on the edge of his bed and undoes the chains around his neck. He holds the puddle of chain contemplatively in his palm. Raising his eyes to the image of himself in the dresser mirror, he fills his mouth with the chains. The corners and angles of the tags bite into the roof of his mouth. The twists of metal chains scrub at the soft tissue of gum and tongue. He tastes not only the metal but his own sweat on it. Tipping back his head, he lets the chain slip slowly back toward his throat. Then he gags, leans over his knees and spits out the wet chains with their burden of cross and dogtag into his hands.

■ ■ ■

His mind refuses to give up the nightwatch on Deanie. But he hears nothing and spends the whole night in his own bed. He gets off to a better start, not even trying for the downstairs bathroom, just going straight out to water the lilac and then shaving at the kitchen sink. Truck coughs like a three-pack-a-day septuagenarian with emphysema but it starts.

■ ■ ■

Pete Fosse is waiting at the gym doors. "Hey Sambot, you're fixing my bumper you fucked up, right?"

"Wrong." Sam starts past him.

Pete grabs him by the forearm. "No, you're the one who's wrong. What do you think Wild Bill's gonna say about it? You just got off probation for kicking a ceiling down, dumbo."

Sam shakes off Pete's hand and deliberately studies the ring of keys in his other hand to find the one for the gym. One small blessing is Deanie has gone directly to an early makeup exam. This is not a moment he needs her underfoot or in anybody's face.

"Peteybird, you're the wrong guy to be trying blackmail."

Fosse's face reddens. "Fuck you, Styles."

Sam rolls the key in the lock and it clicks open. He glances at Pete. "I'll make you a deal," he says.

Glaring at him, Pete waits. Sam flops the ring of keys, splaying them over the palm of his hand.

"I'll tighten up your frigging bumper."

Pete blinks.

"In shop," Sam continues. "For ten bucks. As a favor."

A suspicious grin distorts Pete's mouth.

"And?"

"And nothing. Just don't fuck with me anymore. There's been enough shit going down. I'm willing to do you a favor and over-look what an asshole you are so I can finish the season with no more aggravation. This is no big deal. I need you as my backup and you need to be my backup if you want my job next year."

Pete wilts into sulkiness. "You're not invulnerable, Sambo."

Sam nods. "Neither are you, Peteybird."

■ ■ ■

Initially, the other players in the morning practice session are wary of the tension between Sam and Pete. Sam ignores Pete's attitude, electing to work him steadily into the ground. Eventually Pete runs out of the energy to maintain a sneer.

Taking a rest on the sidelines, Rick demands the skinny. "What's this shit Bilbo just told me about you and Pete playing bumper cars in the parking lot with Fosse?"

"You didn't miss anything," Sam says, "it was stupid. I got it straightened out with Pete before practice. I'm done playing these asshole you-shove-me-I-shove-you-back games."

"You think you got a choice, you're dumber than you look. Sometimes you fucking gotta fight, Slammer."

"Sometimes you fucking gotta grow up," Sam says. He smiles but Rick just shakes his head.

■ ■ ■

Rumor traces a distant seismic shimmy epicentered in the Office. A yearbook staffer passing through the Office on an errand reports Laliberte and the coaches in conference over the local weekly. By Wednesday noon, the day the paper publishes, stories having to do with the school are usually posted on the bulletin board outside the Office.

By end-of-classes this Wednesday the board sports the usual range of coverage. Some lines have been scissored from the one about the basketball games. To Sam, the empty slots in the news-print look just like the frames he puts down over what he's read-ing. They cover up all but short, one-line windows of text so the other words don't distract and confuse his eye—one of the learn-ing techniques Paul Romney taught him. In censoring the newspaper, the administration might as well have highlighted every copy and informed every kid in school they were going to be tested on the material.

While the girls have their afternoon practice—Deanie on the bench taking play-by-play advice from her coach—Sam slips out of the school long enough to pick up an unexpurgated copy of the weekly at the pharmacy.

Under the fold of the sports page there is a photograph of her. Black-and-white does not soften the damage to Deanie's face. If the stringer with the camera did not see it when taking the picture, someone had picked it up after developing the print. The censored lines of the article concern what the picture shows. Gauthier's facial injury is clearly more serious than the school has let on, the piece says, and raises immediate questions about when she will return to play, and whether she should in this season. Until school officials provide more complete information about the nature of the injury, the reporter asserts piously, the public can only speculate.

Obviously Deanie's coach has seen the article but she makes no move to interfere when Sam brings it to Deanie on the bench. He sits behind her while she scans it. She folds it, hands it back to him, returns her attention without a word to the drills her teammates are performing.

He climbs the bleachers to watch until it's time to change for his own practice. Rick and Todd Gramolini settle on either side of him and have a look at the paper.

The photograph makes Todd wince. "Aw, shit. Sam, I'm sorry about all the bullshit. I didn't know anything about the rat till it was done but I wouldn't have gone along with it. I've had enough of Pete's crap."

Sam offers his hand silently and Todd shakes it.

"Can we get through this season as a team?" he wants to know.

Sam shrugs. "That might be up to Pete."

"Break his fucking arm," Rick observes, "break his fucking leg. We don't need him. Skouros can do the job and he's not full of shit."

Todd laughs. "Jesus. I hear you say that and I'm laughing, Rick, but it ain't good, talk like that about a teammate."

"Pete's his own worst enemy," Sam counsels. "Maybe he'll break his own leg."

■ ■ ■

On the way home, he asks Deanie if she wants to stop and see the old ladies. She shakes her head. Her face will still be ugly enough to trip their pacemakers when she goes back to work for them on the coming Saturday, she assures him.

It tells him better than anything what she really feels about the photograph in the paper. It seems to him she no longer shaves her head as an act of rebellion but in abnegation, like a nun. Why else has she taken to covering it all the time? She ties the loose end of the headscarf to fall over the left side of her face. The strut seems to have gone out of her most of the time. She meets no one's eyes anymore and she moves like a ghost, weaving invisibility around her.

■ ■ ■

Next morning when he stares up at his own ceiling on waking and realizes again she has slept through and so has he, he thinks he should feel relieved. Her face is healing, the color fading and shrinking, the normal contours reappearing, despite his stupid antics. Give her time to heal inside too and she'll be herself again.

Then when she's gotten used to whatever comes next for her, the foster home—if it's no good he'll just take her out of it, that's all—then, they can start over and do it right. Be friends for a while and nothing else. Maybe after they've been friends awhile, they won't even want to do it with each other anymore. Lots of married people got bored with screwing each other, didn't they? It wasn't that big of a deal. Take into account he isn't too good at it and she doesn't even have orgasms, not any worth having anyway, and it's not like they'd be giving up seats in the Commissioner's Box at the fourth game of the World Series in a Red Sox sweep.

From his father's bedroom he hears the stentorian tones of a television newscast. The minute Reuben gets home now, he begins to cable-surf, running the clicker up and down the dial looking for the latest war news. Though they know Frankie is somewhere in the Gulf, the position of his vessel is classified. They have not heard from him since the war began. The talking heads on the tube claim casualties in six months of land war might run fifty, sixty thousand. The fuckup in Vietnam claimed, officially, about that number over more than ten years. American dead. The never-mentioned enemy loss was more than twenty times that number and no one wants to speculate on what the ratio of dead Iraqis to Allies will be. He shivers, wondering if Frankie will ever make it home and if he himself will be over there this time next year.

And who will look out for Deanie if he is?

■ ■ ■

Game day. Last game day on the bench. The Mutant blinks at the ceiling, rolls over to look down into her duffel, where her protective mask nestles on top of her books. She touches her scar, amazed again at the seemingly instant seaming of her tissue. The doctor drew the edges together and the cells sealed themselves, zipped together like that, in the first twenty-four hours. Going on ten days and the rest of it is obviously on the mend, so the delicate-minded don't jerk their eyes away at first sight.

In the bathroom, she checks in at the mirror. It's beginning to look the way it will for good. Her face aches sometimes but she doesn't need the painkillers anymore. She takes them to kill the nightmares. She'll be out of them soon.

She takes her disc of b.c. pills from the pocket she has sewed into the inside of her bathrobe. Looking at the loop of tiny pellets, like a chain of flavorless candy, she wonders why she's bothering.

34

■ ■ ■

" '*This Ain't No Disco!* This ain't no foolin' around!' " is the Mutant's cry from the middle of the pack in the corridor.

It is a group-grope heaven as the boys emerge from the Chamberlain locker rooms into wall-to-wall bodies. The girls squeal and jump up and down and throw themselves on guys and not just guys on the team but anyone quick enough to jam himself into the corridor after the double-eagle win against Chamberlain. The Greenspark boys are beginning to feel they are as unbeatable as the weekend sports pages will speculate. And the next time the girls take the floor, the Mutant will be back.

To Sam's eyes, she's back already. She's cast off her depression, that cloak of invisibility. Her eyes are feverish, her skin translucent and glowing, the fading bruises opalescent smears of color, the scar a pearly chain underlining the upsweep of her cheekbone, nose to ear. Her headscarf is low on her forehead, and she is beautiful—the narrow cameo oval of her face, the dark arch of eyebrows, the rich bitter chocolate of her eyes, her full mouth. He moves through the crowd toward her, elated, stunned and afraid.

■ ■ ■

After the bus ride home, she crows again in the truck. She flops back and props her feet on the dashboard.

The radio bellows and he clicks down the volume.

"Next game," she says. "I can't wait."

"Be great."

The look she concentrates on him makes him feel like dry pine straw under a lens, an intensification of light into a sudden dangerous warmth. "You were great tonight."

He breaks eye contact hastily, addressing himself to getting out of the parking lot. No matter how many times he's had girls look at him like that, it's still heady stuff that leaves him covering confusion about how he's supposed to deal with it.

She chatters on, comparing the two games, contrasting plays and players, dissecting and re-playing exhaustively, just the way they all did in the locker rooms, on the buses, and the way they will tomorrow at the lunch tables. He listens. He is good at listening, in compensation for being so bad at speaking. Unable to sit still, she twists on her knees like a little kid to talk and gesticulate. Then she picks up the basketball from the floor of the cab and hugs it.

She bounces into the house ahead of him and accepts high fives from Pearl and his father without apparent unease.

It isn't until Pearl takes the baby upstairs to bathe her that Reuben tells them the woman from DHS called at the garage earlier. "She says the medical report and the Greenspark cops' information that Deanie's mother failed to seek medical care for her or even determine how badly she was hurt gives the state grounds to take custody until an investigation is completed. DHS might have a foster home for Deanie in Lisbon Falls by the end of next week."

The color drains from Deanie's face.

Sam reaches for her hand under the table. "How will she get to school?"

Reuben sighs. "She'll be transferred to the high school there."

"No!"

Deanie's cry expresses Sam's own stunned disbelief but before he can say anything, she jerks her hand from his and rushes from the room. He starts to rise but the bathroom door slams and he sinks back into his chair.

"You see how she was when we came in?" Sam asks, keeping his voice low so it won't carry to Deanie in the bathroom. "She talked all the way home about being able to play again. They take her out of Greenspark, she's not gonna play basketball again this year."

Reuben shakes his head. "Might be best if she didn't, Sammy."

■ ■ ■

Sam waits on the daybed for Deanie to come out of the bathroom. From upstairs the tube in Reuben and Pearl's bedroom endlessly recycles the meager war news, in counterpoint to Indy's exuberant recombinations of the half-dozen meaningful syllables in which she now converses, complete with seemingly intelligent inflections. The earrings Sarah made for Deanie pool in a cut-glass dish on a water-stained deal table that has been cleared of plants to make a nightstand. A scatter of tape cassettes and a knot of bandannas lie next to the dish. He thinks of this room before she stayed in it: the fecund greenhouse smell of potted plants in a suntrap, the old cigar stink, dry wicker and chintz cushions.

Grasping the frame of the door, Deanie teeters on the threshold. Her eyes are pink and swollen.

"It isn't going to happen," he says, and the promise clarifies everything for him. "I'm not letting them move you anywhere."

She lets out her breath and he sees that she believes him.

"Hey," he says, "come on upstairs. I want to play you some stuff."

She floats behind him nervously and scampers past Pearl and Reuben's bedroom door even though it is closed. Flopping stomach down onto his bed, she is breathless with giggles.

Pulling his headphones down over her ears, he plugs in the Gear Daddies. Fast forwards the tape to "Boys Will Be Boys," which isn't ever going to get any air time because it tells its truth in the most accurate language. It makes him think of his sister and of Deanie too. Especially now, with DHS getting set to exile her to Lisbon Falls.

> She's fucked again,
> and she don't know why.

The lyrics make Deanie laugh with a brief and bitter merriment.

He doesn't know how he can honor his promise to keep her at Greenspark. If she goes somewhere else, Tony Lord can never reach her again. Better she should miss the rest of this season than remain at risk from that creep.

"That's great," she says, pushing the 'phones back and letting them fall around her neck.

"I know what to do."

That rivets her. She sits up and cocks her head like an attentive puppy.

"I'll sell the bike."

Her hands fly to her mouth.

And it all comes tumbling out without a stutter. Pay the medical bills and give her the rest and put her on a bus to his aunt in Oregon. Big city like Portland, there must be some good plastic surgeons. Aunt Ilene would find one. How much could it cost? What's left of the price of the bike should more than cover it. If she gets it done this summer, she should be able to play ball next year. Some high school in Portland would be lucking into a wicked hook shot. It isn't the same as staying here but she'd be safe from that shithead. And if she has to make big changes in her life, at least she won't be jerked around by some underfunded, understaffed state agency.

He'll be out of school in June, he reminds her. He could follow her out there. He might have a draft board on his ass but all that is beyond his control. Deal with it when it came down. If ever.

He spins a fantasy about what it will be like to live in Oregon, in Portland. Does she realize every week they could hear live music?—everyone plays Portland, sooner or later. He saw the laser Zep show there. She'd get off on it in a major way. Oregon's a lot like Maine—not so frigging cold—but also green and thinly populated, with ocean to one side and mountains to the other and people who don't care to live in each other's pockets. They wouldn't have to stay forever, just long enough to get her through high school.

"This is crazy," she keeps interjecting but she's into it, watching his mouth as if a shower of gold coins were falling out of it instead of this wild-ass fantasy. And when he tells her about the laser show he saw and imitates the heads in the audience, she laughs until she has to hold her stomach. She rolls over and buries her face in the pillows so her giggling won't carry down the hall to his folks.

He runs down and she rolls over on her back and looks up at him. She sit up and sniffs and wipes her eyes.

"Shit," she says. "I almost wish it would happen."

They have to look each other in the eye then.

"It's possible," he insists. "It's a fallback position.'

He sees she wants to believe it. He'll just have to make it happen for her.

"Come on," he says, "we gotta get you back downstairs."

The baby fussing and Pearl shushing her provides cover for Deanie to tiptoe to the stairs. Back in his room, he pops out the Gear Daddies and slots a mixed dub, a Duran Duran single in six different versions. Music for meditating on the day's game. They had smashed Chamberlain's zone so decisively, icebreaker through rotten ice, the other team had never recovered. The next one will be tougher. Have to be careful not to get overconfident, lose their edge. The season's going fast now. Everything's going fast. School. Everything.

■ ■ ■

Waking on his stomach as the tape whispers and then clicks over to the next side, he realizes he is still on top of the covers. The clock says 1:09. His headphones have shifted forward. He readjusts them as the power mix of "Violence of Summer" begins—the A side of the dub—and he wonders how many times the tape has looped through the machine.

Next to him, the bed shivers with someone else's weight. It's Deanie, kneeling on the edge, watching him. He laughs sleepily but he is intensely awake. On hands and knees, she crawls toward him, her eyes wide-bored to total blackness. She crouches next to him and he curves his hand around the back of her skull. Shaved that morning, it's as smooth and aerodynamic as the fenders on his bike. She lowers her face to his throat as if she were going for his jugular and he feels her tongue flicking along the chains around his neck.

Closes his eyes, the better to feel. She lifts her head and brings her good cheekbone next to his, as if they were dancing. Her body reverberates with silent laughter against his as she touches the left cushion of the headphones he is still wearing. Tracing her scar with the tip of his tongue from nose to ear and back again, it feels to him like a chain of silky pearls, irregular nodes knitted along a cool smooth string. He licks over her upper lip and to the corner of her mouth. She opens it and takes in his tongue.

She's been in his laundry again. His old T-shirt she's using for a nightshirt still smells like him. Inside the slack billow of the shirt, her tits curve into his hands and he shivers. She's got nothing else on.

She puts her hands inside his sweatpants and he closes his hand over hers on his cock. They pull his pants down together, and she folds over him and her mouth is wet and hot on his knob, and it feels like she's sucking the roots of the hair on his head.

He shudders all over and then she raises her head and all he can do is gasp and take the slippery darting of her tongue in his mouth. Her sex is in his hand, the silky pleat rolling over his palm. He slips in two fingers to churn the muscular channel. His thumb knuckles the heel of her sex and she jerks against him.

He slides his fingers out and his cock into her, tilts her into his hands and she arches to take him. Her hands find the small of his back, urging him deeper. Rocking gently with her, he wishes this could last forever. When he looks at her, she looks back with amazed, amused curiosity; what's happening here? Reaching up, he tips his headphones upside down, brings their faces cheekbone to cheekbone again, and widens the arc of the diadem so the right earpiece is available to her and the left to him. It makes them laugh to share the throb of the music, using it like an aural waterbed to reinforce their rhythm. He tilts her more, lifting her knees, pressing them back until she grasps the back of his neck as if she is falling and the contact of their genitals is complete, the movement is slight and intense. Her fingers clutch at the chains around his neck. Everything's hot and tight and ready to explode.

"Do it!" he chokes. "Do it!"

"Ohhh," she gasps, and then she hiccups. He can't help laughing and she laughs too. A few seconds later, he urges her again and she's happening with him.

It feels like falling, each cell rippling, whispering into its own exquisite tawny bloom, the sharp edges melting, dissolving, yielding into gravity, whickering through the golden fold of moment. Her body. The molten core spinning into lightness, a spark falling through space into themselves again, the fan closing. She stutters consonants to match, bursting out of her in a storm of shards.

■ ■ ■

Next to Pearl, Reuben rises to one elbow. "Baby again," he says. "I'll go."

Pearl's fingers close around his wrist. "No," she murmurs.

He pats her hip. "Go back to sleep. I heard the baby. I'll see to her."

Pearl opens one eye briefly. "Wasn't the baby," she mumbles.

Reuben scratches his head. "Sammy's having a bad dream?"

A slow smile curves Pearl's mouth. "No, dear," she sighs. "That was Deanie."

"Oh." Reuben tugs his right earlobe. "Sounded like it was on this floor to me."

Pearl rolls to her side and snuggles against him. "It was. From Sam's room."

Still logy with sleep, and distracted by his wife's hand on his thigh, Reuben can't quite absorb it. He wonders why Deanie and Sam have swapped rooms. "What's she doing there?"

"Coming, from the sound of it."

"What!" Reuben sits up and stares at her. "With Sammy?"

Pearl's soft laughter makes him feel like an idiot. "She's in his room. You want odds?"

He starts to swing his legs from the bed and Pearl catches him by the forearm.

"Get back into bed," she hisses. "This minute. You leave them the hell alone."

Reuben sinks back onto the bed. "Sammy?" he asks incredulously. "Deanie?"

He lies back down and stares at the ceiling.

"Jesus," he mutters. "She's such a freak. Are you sure?"

Pearl sits up. "Men," she says, bemused.

"She is," Reuben insists. "Sammy? He's really got that little bald girl in there with him and—?"

"And. He made her come."

Reuben smiles. "That's right."

For a moment they are both silent.

"And in the morning," Reuben mutters, "I'm gonna boot his ass all over the yard. Is he out of his mind?"

"Of course he is. Calm down and go to sleep. He's been downstairs with her nearly every night since he brought her here. This didn't start tonight and it can wait until tomorrow for you to take official notice."

He tugs her close and takes a deep breath. She closes her eyes.

■ ■ ■

Sam claps his hand over Deanie's mouth too late. They both freeze. Carefully, Sam dislodges his headphones and reaches up to kill the tape player. Reuben and Pearl have some brief conversation in their bedroom while he and Deanie look at each other. Silence descends and they let out their breaths and suddenly they are struggling to control an outbreak of the giggles. It takes them a while to settle down.

■ ■ ■

Reuben continues to stare at the ceiling. Girl's sixteen, that's something. But. Scalped and scarred and tattooed. Nevermind the hook shot, she's an acidhead and a potsmoker and cheap as dirt. He's heard enough about her, sitting in the bleachers and listening to people around him, to feel the same appalled heartbreak for her he feels for Karen. Like Karen, somebody got at her young and convinced her she deserved what was happening to her and now, whether she offers it reflexively, as submission or seduction, it's part of survival. Can't blame Sammy—not much. How's he supposed to cope with a girl who doesn't know any other way to go but too fast? Reuben closes his eyes. Sammy made Deanie come. Goddamn him, he'd better have taken precautions. All that child needs to make her wretched life complete is a big belly, courtesy of his horny kid.

Do as I say, not as I do—thinking of himself, knocking up Pearl on a drunken, careless night. A clear, sweet drunk it was and the carelessness a heartfelt abandon. He wasn't so impaired, nor indifferent either, as to forget there could be a baby in it. *Good enough,* he remembers thinking, to the extent he could think at that time. *Good enough.* Some love deserves its own expression in a new life. If you want to be pretty about it. More crudely, knocking her up is a time-honored way to get a woman's serious attention. Of her motivation he was ignorant and so remains—it may have been the same as his. They jumped off a cliff together, she as reckless as he, and it was a lovely freefall. He couldn't regret it or its complications anymore.

Sammy, his manchild, making that wench testify tonight, was unwanted by Laura. He had his way about it and it might very well have put paid to the marriage. This is just the useless speculation of the small hours. As much good to fret about it as worry about Frankie and the goddamn war, or about his lost daughter. He thinks of the baby girl in her crib down the hall and wonders if someday he'll be staring at the ceiling, advising himself not to stay awake over her. How do you do that? How do you not worry?

"Should have got the kid a dog when he wanted it," he says to the ceiling.

Beside him, a tremor of laughter goes through his wife's body.

■ ■ ■

Reuben scrapes mashed banana from Indy's chin back into her mouth. As Sam and Deanie descend the stairs—Deanie reluctantly—he spares them an irritated glance. Deanie freezes. Pearl looks up from filling lunch buckets and smiles encouragingly. Sam nudges Deanie toward the bathroom. She looks from father to son and back again before scampering away. Reuben wipes the baby's chin and rises from his chair. He reaches for his jacket and tosses Sam's to him. Without a word, they leave the kitchen.

In the yard, they start the vehicles. Sam listens to his truck's engine race before he idles down. His father opens the passenger door. The truck lists and then settles under Reuben's weight. Sam's long legs go slack as he slumps down behind the wheel. He makes himself meet his father's furious eyes.

"I want to ask you two questions," Reuben says.

"She's on the Pill," Sam counters swiftly.

Reuben rolls his eyes. "Isn't that grand? What's the answer to the second question?"

Sam shrugs.

"Jesus, Sammy." Reuben's voice gentles into weary puzzlement. "Are you out of your mind?"

Sam stares at the dashboard clock. "You don't understand what Deanie's been through—"

"That's exactly what I'm talking about," Reuben interrupts. "The child's a mess. She's vulnerable."

"Dad, if she gets shipped out to some foster home outside of this SAD, she won't be allowed to play basketball for at least a year."

Reuben shakes his head. "I missed something. What does that have to do with you jumping her bones?"

"Nothing. Can't you forget about that long enough to realize the most important thing is Deanie? All she's got is hoops. She'll go right down the toilet without it. Look, she's sixteen. Why can't she be emancipated, like Karen? Then she won't have to go into DHS custody and she can stay with us."

"Not us—with you. You want me to allow you to cohabit with a sixteen-year-old girl under my roof. You're working what you want around to what's good for her."

Sam shoves his hands into his armpits and turns his hot face away from his father. "If she goes, I go."

"Oh shit!" Reuben explodes in disgust.

"I'll quit school. Get a job and a place to live."

His father rakes his hair distractedly. "No, Sammy. That's a terrible idea."

"You don't want her here, we can live in the horsebarn, like you did, or camp out in the farmhouse until summer."

In the kitchen window, Pearl looks out at them. Breakfast is on the table by now but she makes no summoning gesture. Sam's stomach aches for the French toast he can all but smell across the yard.

"Sammy, you're too young to take on another person. Right now you're letting your dick think for you. You want her where you can fuck her." He pauses, studying the boy's face for signs that the deliberate crudity has had the kind of cold-water shock he sought. A misery of conflicting emotion works Sammy's features but what fixes them finally is an obdurate stubbornness. "You don't understand—you live here together and get it regular from each other awhile and you'll wind up marrying her—and you got a snowball's chance in hell of making it work!"

"I'm too young to get married," Sam says, "and anyway I never will—you get married, you just wind up divorced."

Reuben winces.

Ignoring him, Sam presses onward. "*You* don't understand. Deanie needs me and she needs me now. If I don't love her, she's going to think no one ever will—or can, on account of her face."

His father is silent long enough for Sam to finally look at him again.

"Oh Sammy," Reuben says, with enormous sadness.

The boy does love her, the mechanic sees, to think such a thing. Could be right about it too. If there's any one moment in that wretched little girl's life when uncritical love—maybe even passion—is necessary, it's probably now.

"It's my fault," Sam croaks suddenly. "I was with her that Sunday. He did it because of me, because she'd been with me. I'm going to sell the bike to get enough for her to have plastic surgery."

Twitching aside Sam's ponytail, Reuben cups the back of his son's neck. "Wrong," he says. "About whose fault it is, you're wrong. It's the man's who did it. Not yours. You'll make mistakes enough in your life without taking on guilt that's not yours. And don't sell your bike yet. It's crossed my mind a couple of times—maybe Lord or Deanie's mother has some insurance coverage that includes her. The other route is suing the bastard to recover damages."

On the way to the house, Reuben stops Sam again.

"I'll see about getting Deanie emancipated. I need to talk to Pearl about her staying before I go along with it. You two are going to do what you're going to do whatever happens, but I still don't think living together, here or anywhere, is a wise thing. It may still be possible to find another place for her to live where she has people looking out for her and she doesn't have to leave Greenspark and you can do what you feel you have to, taking care of her. You give some thought to that idea, Sammy."

Sam's relief at having this interview over is so huge, he would consent to nearly anything. Reuben has met him more than halfway. They'll work it out.

35

■ ■ ■

Nose Ring Glinting in her left nares, for the first time since she was hurt, eyes huge with mascara, Deanie waits by the door. She is already headragged and coated and holds his breakfast wrapped in waxed paper. Sam's stomach cramps as he falls violently in love with her again, or else, he decides, it's sheer hunger. He takes her arm, to steady her across the icy yard.

"What's going to happen?"

He waits until she closes her seatbelt before he lets a smile slide and explains about emancipation and how it means she could stay with them.

"Stay with you? Until when?"

"Till you're ready to go out on your own."

She closes her eyes. "Oh 'god."

"Or until you find someplace you like better."

"What about you and me?"

Sam finds her hand on the seat between them and squeezes it. "Oh, he's ripshit about it but he knows he can't stop us whether you live with us or not. He has to talk to Pearl, make sure she's copacetic, about you staying."

"It's none of their business," Deanie protests, "what we do."

Sam moves his hand back to the wheel. "It's their home too—

they pay the bills and he *is* my father. They've got every right to say what they like and don't like."

"They shacked up together before they got married—you told me they did."

"Sure. And they were adults when they did it, and they did get married. We can't get married. You're only sixteen. You got a lot of shit to work out."

Deanie fumbles in his cassette dump. "Yeah, and you're seventeen and stupid, that's another good reason."

"Eighteen in two months. You don't need to shit on me. I'm just saying it was different for them."

"Yeah, yeah. Whatever. I couldn't believe it when you came back into the house and neither one of you was bleeding. I thought we'd wind up spending the rest of the winter in the Mill."

Sam looks at her with interest kindling in his eyes. "If it comes to it—"

"Oh my 'god," she giggles, rolling her eyes.

■ ■ ■

"If I'd known they were already involved, I would have made arrangements for her to stay with someone else immediately," Reuben tells Pearl.

In the cab of his truck on the way to the diner, the baby squirms in her carseat between them.

"I'm supposed to be looking out for this child and my boy's climbing into bed with her," he continues. "Or she's climbing in with him. Whatever, they could both get hurt. And she's a mess to start."

Pearl sighs. "She's tougher than you think. You see a victim. I see a gutty kid who got herself out of an intolerable situation and into a safe place. Give her credit for picking Sammy. She couldn't have done better, could she? Give him credit for seeing past her self-defenses. Maybe they just need a little time to find their way."

Reuben looks at her. "Oh hell, the oatburner's out of the barn." He smiles. "From here on out, they're going to make their own decisions about what goes on between them. I just wish they weren't so damned young."

"There's something to be said for not knowing any better. Who'd do anything if they knew all the consequences?"

"It's a lovely question but it's irrelevant. We have to work with what we have," he points out.

"Sometimes we have more than we realize," she retorts.

"Indeed," he agrees. "Indeed. Sometimes we get more than we bargained for."

■ ■ ■

In the meeting hall before anyone else but she and Sam arrive, Deanie masks herself for the first time. Tight against her face, the mask feels stiff and impervious as an exoskeleton. She tugs at the straps. Even with the attention to ventilation, there is an immediate sensation of heat building up underneath it. And there is pressure, her facial bones reading the weight. Weirdly, the mask telegraphs back the topography of her face, the sweep and shape of her bones and the ridge of the scar.

Because the mask touches the lobe of her nostril, she has to remove her nose ring, which she replaces with a stud she made from an ornate old tackhead. She wraps her headrag tighter, over the straps, to make them a little more secure. It makes her whole skull feel heavy and tight. Blinking, she turns her head from side to side.

"This frigging thing cuts into my peripheral vision!"

Sam fans his fingers over her hipbones and presses back. "Open up. Head up. This is going to be fine. You'll get used to it." And if wishes were horses, he reflects to himself, the whole world would be knee-deep in horseshit.

She warms up slowly, doing stretches and slow laps. She is taking a ball through drills by herself and then with Sam when the guys begin to trickle in.

Rick goes right up to her and stares critically at her masked face.

"Awesome," he concludes.

She shoots her hip and struts a few steps and gets a laugh for the effort.

Still there is a certain tension. It breaks when she sits down to watch. Sam sneaks a glance at her; she has taken off her mask and holds it disconsolately in her hands.

Rick checks the clock and mutters something to Billy, who nods agreeably.

"Gauthier," Rick calls, "put on that hockey mask of yours and give me some competition."

The others stop moving and start grumbling.

"Come on, come on," Rick urges her impatiently as she fumbles with the mask. "We've only got twenty minutes before the Ladies' Auxiliary wants this place for a belly-dancing class."

Sam grins at her. "You staying for that?"

"I'm teaching it," Rick says.

Pete Fosse stalks off the court as Deanie stumbles onto it. Dupre follows. Several guys, Kasten and Bither among them, hesitate. Todd Gramolini holds his ground.

"Chickenshit," Rick yells at Fosse and Dupre. "She weighs about ninety-five pounds. Are you scared of her?"

The gibe evokes a sheepish look from Dupre. Pete gives Rick an *are-you-shitting-me?* smirk and a rigid middle finger.

But once they start again, it quickly becomes apparent they have a problem.

"Siddown," Rick tells Sam. "You're trying to protect Gauthier. It's driving her nuts and it's driving us nuts. Go on, get the fuck out of the way."

Sam looks to her for confirmation, gets a furious glare, and accepts his exile. Sitting on the floor with his back against the wall, he watches her struggle with the distraction of the mask, the way it forces her to change her habits to accommodate it. At first tentative, she becomes frustrated and then angry. She stalks off court and squats, trembling, to remove the mask.

"Good enough," Rick calls.

Todd takes a last lob at the hoop and a general exodus begins.

"This sucks," she says as he approaches her. "I suck."

"It'll get better," Sam tells her. "Wanna dunk?"

She makes a face at him.

He takes her by the hand and kneels, offering his thigh as a stepping stool.

"Come on," he urges.

With a giggle of surprise, she steps up, slings a leg around his neck and slips onto his shoulders. He grasps her knees and rises.

Those players still gathering their gear begin to laugh.

She holds out her hands and Rick flicks a ball toward her.

"No traveling," Rick calls.

Sam lets go of her knees and she drops the ball into his hand. Feeling like a camel with a rider on its hump, he dribbles it up the court. Just before the post, he pushes the ball down hard and lets it bounce straight up to her waiting hands. She rises on his shoulders, reaching for the rim, and as she stuffs the ball in, he ducks out from under her and she grasps the iron ring and dangles from it, shrieking deliriously. The others raise a cheer. Then she lets go and drops into his waiting hands.

■ ■ ■

Freddy Cape glances up from his paper as Reuben enters the Vallone Cafe on Main Street in Greenspark and rising, extends his hand. "Cowboy!" Freddy grins, reverting in an instant to the class clown of some two decades previous. "You come looking for me first thing in the morning, I flip on the meter. Fair warning, old man—if your wife booted you out again, I'm representing her."

Reuben laughs, tries a chair and when it wobbles, rejects it for a sturdier one. "I break my ass on one of these miserable chairs of Tommy's, you can sue him for me."

Tommy Vallone leans past him to fling a menu on the table. He slops iced water from a pitcher into a glass for Reuben.

"Up yours, you friggin' ape," he remarks amicably. "I hear you say you're representing his wife, Freddy? Take the sucker for everything he's worth."

"Nothing left to take," Reuben responds. "Freddy was my lawyer last time, remember? He let Laura have everything but my spare kidney."

While Freddy bows his head, Tommy applauds mockingly.

Reuben pats his stomach. "Just tea for me, Tommy."

Tommy rolls his eyes. "Jesus. I might's well go away to starve. I remember when you put away two, three breakfasts at a go."

"Twenty years ago, maybe. Don't burn it off like I used to," Reuben says.

Tommy slaps a toddy of hot water and a mug and teabag down in front of Reuben. He taps Freddy's paper, folded on the table. "Your boy had another cock-knocker of a night."

Reuben chokes on iced water and Tommy pounds his back.

"Wrong pipe," Tommy diagnoses. "You oughta be careful about that. I seen a fat old middle-aged fuck like you blow his pump right out one day, tryin' to cough up an ice cube."

Freddy Cape kicks back, laughing.

"Thanks, Tommy," Reuben says. "I'll keep it in mind."

Tommy pats his shoulder and moves away to wait on somebody else.

" 'Fat old middle-aged fuck,' " Reuben grouses. "Listen to him. He must go fifty pounds over what he weighed in high school. Bald as a baby's ass, too."

"You should have bought breakfast," Freddy advises.

"Right."

"I really hope you aren't looking for a divorce lawyer."

"No. I want to talk about an emancipation order."

Freddy cocks his head attentively. "Sammy? Don't tell me Laura's up to her old tricks."

"No. It's the Gauthier girl."

Reuben explains the situation.

"The immediate question," Freddy concludes, "is whether Judy Gauthier will go along with an emancipation. There's a lot going for the idea. The girl's nearly old enough to leave anyway. You wouldn't think Lord or Judy would be much interested in having her come home. No calls or contact since the incident, right?"

Reuben nods.

"Looks golden to me," Freddy says. "I'll be in touch to talk to her. If I were you, though, I wouldn't look for any insurance coverage on the girl's injuries. My guess is Judy's job doesn't offer insurance benefits and since Lord isn't married to Judy, Deanie isn't legally his dependent. And even if she wins a civil suit against him, I doubt Judy and Tony between them own anything besides their wheels and some returnable bottles. On that reassuring note— how's everything else?"

"Besides Sammy moving his skinhead girlfriend into his bedroom? Oh, I'm living on my wife." Reuben tugs an earlobe. "My hearing's wonky. Getting fitted for a hearing aid in my left ear next week. My oldest boy's in the Persian Gulf in the middle of a shooting war. Karen's—well, you know all about it, Freddy."

Freddy catches Tommy Vallone's gimlet eye and scribbles in the air, signaling for the check. "I'm sorry about Karen. If it would get her off the street, it might be worth supplying her the shit. You know the problem. There's never enough for an addict. You give'm a gram and it's gone and they want another one. You give her all she wants and she'll kill herself with it."

"Gonna kill herself with it anyway, the way she's going. Or she'll pick up the wrong guy, get strangled in a gravel pit by a maniac. Get AIDS. Sometimes I feel like she's already dead, you know?"

Rising from his chair, Freddy rests a hand on Reuben's shoulder. "Easy does it, cowboy."

On the sidewalk a few minutes later, the mechanic looks up and down Main Street. The brave parade of flags on the storefronts pop in the cutting wind of a brilliant day. His ears hurt. Used to be even on a cold winter Saturday, there'd be traffic, foot and wheel. Not anymore. Half the buildings boarded up, the flags a patriotic gesture that is almost cruelly ironic. The Mill Brook runs with raw sewage from the village and the town breathes the sickly stench of the paper mill at the Bend in South Greenspark where a branch of the Saco makes the southern border of the township. The smell of money, the old-timers always called it, but only the brimstone stink of that money seems to linger here.

Karen and Deanie, he thinks. Maybe Deanie Gauthier's my second chance. I better not fuck this one up.

■ ■ ■

In the Rodrigues sisters' upstairs bathroom, the Mutant swishes the johnny brush through the water in the toilet. The old women have fallen behind and there is a lot to do to put the house to rights. First they had to fuss over her and prevaricate about how well the wound is healing and how invisible the scar is going to be. At least they didn't pretend it wasn't there.

It was funny to see them blow their gauges over Bigger. Creaking old ostriches were dribbling in their snuggies. Maybe it is some kind of yearning after missed motherhood. Then again, Mrs. H. in the cafeteria had about a billion brats and she's the same way, another old puss who just adores boys and young men. There is this weird compulsion to stuff them full of food. Fatten them up like they were going to eat them some day, like the witch in Hansel and Gretel. Of course Miss Reggie and Miss Katherine seem to want to fatten her up too. The Mutant pinches her arm. Still too bony to make a meal, she decides.

She tries to summon up the picture of the nude descending the staircase, trying to recapture her old feelings about it. If she could see it today, maybe it would be different, richer, more resonant. A cigarette, a joint, would be such a relief. She had an orgasm, she came. She knows what that means now. She's warm, fed, in a safe place with people who are kind to her. She might even actually play hoops again. 'god loves her. He said so. Why does she want to scream?

■ ■ ■

In the late afternoon, Sam picks her up again and brings her home for supper. Entering the house with a new awkwardness, they are met by a surprisingly disinterested welcome. His father and stepmother seem more focused on each other than the errant lovers. Their flirtatiousness is positively embarrassing. Reuben rises when he finishes eating, kisses the baby and then his wife, twice, before he reaches reluctantly for his jacket.

"Got to go back to the garage and finish a couple jobs I promised. Be home early."

"I'll ride with you, Dad," Sam says, and stuffs a last chunk of sourdough into his mouth as he rises. Shrugging into his jacket, he stoops, ears burning, to kiss Deanie's upraised face. Watching him stumble over his own feet and grope for the doorknob, she smothers a giggle behind her hand. Reuben bends over Pearl again and takes a longer, promissory kiss, before he follows Sam out.

Pearl and Deanie look at each other and burst out laughing.

■ ■ ■

When the men return from work, Pearl has retired with the baby and Deanie is curled up on the couch, watching the late news.

"I'll lock up," Reuben volunteers, but his eyes fix on the screen and he sinks into his favorite chair and zaps to the late-evening war coverage.

Deanie takes Sam's hand and follows him up the stairs. Halfway up, they roll their eyes at each other and bite their lips.

Leaning against the bedroom door as he closes it, Sam whispers, "Jesus, I can't believe I just brought you upstairs with me."

Giggling, she throws her arms around his neck and he picks her up and plops her onto his bed.

■ ■ ■

At the end of Monday-morning practice, the girls' coach plants herself between the Mutant and the gym doors. "You work with Sam this weekend?"

The Mutant nods.

"Good. He made you open up, didn't he? I wish I could clap one of those masks on all of you. You notice the difference?"

"Yes'm," the Mutant admits. Sunday had been better. A lot. Recalling it evokes the wild swings between elation that he had been right and resentment that this huge improvement only cost her half her face.

"You're feeling okay? No facial pain?"

The interrogation is inevitable, she has to go through it to get to play, but it still makes her impatient.

Coach pauses, takes a quick look around to make sure no one else is in earshot. She squints and a flush mounts in her cheeks. "Anybody giving you grief? About your face or the mask, either one?"

"No'm," the Mutant lies, without any effort at making it sound as if she believes it herself.

"How are things otherwise? You okay, staying with Sam and his folks?"

It's as good a time as any. The Mutant explains to the coach about being emancipated in order to stay at Greenspark. Coach suffers a visible flutter of alarm at the thought of Gauthier being transferred.

"Take care of yourself, now," she instructs gruffly, and lets the Mutant go.

■ ■ ■

A ghostly scorch of cigarette smoke tinges the air in the girls' room. The Mutant wrinkles her nose appreciatively but the smoker is long gone—no chance to bum a butt. She unwraps her headscarf, threads it through the belt loops of her jeans and studies herself bareheaded, fascinated as always at how quick and relentless hair is. Already the stubble emphasizes the shape of her head. To wear her nose ring again makes her feel less naked but she is disappointed that it does not restore her strength. She still looks like the victim of something, and feels diminished and disarmed. Her full hardware, her bad armor, would give the scar a forbidding setting and make her feel fierce again.

Other girls come chattering into the lavatory as she leans into the mirror to thicken her eyeliner. Cady Flemming parks her bony ass at the next basin and starts whipping up her hair in the front. She plies a hairbrush with one hand and a can of hairspray with the other.

"I hear a mirror exploded when you looked at it," Cady says around a wad of gum. "Or did you get your face caught in Samson's zipper?"

One girl moans, "Oh shit," and several others snicker.

A sideways glance shows the Mutant three of her own teammates watching and listening avidly. More than Cady's provocation, she resents their gawking.

She purses her lips in a kiss-off. "Stick your face in the toilet bowl all day, Flem, you're bound to hear all the shit."

The other girls gasp horrified laughter.

Eyes narrowed in rage, Cady turns her head slowly to stare at the Mutant. Her hair looks like the glossy artificial helmet of floss on a Barbie whose little girl owner has worked it so hard that it clumps into the separate root plugs in the vinyl scalp. She looks sick, like someone being slowly poisoned by low-level radiation.

"I didn't think you could get any uglier," Cady snarls. "Samson should finish the job and put your face in a bandsaw."

"Oh shut up, Cady," Nat Linscott breaks in suddenly.

"Yeah," Sarah Kendall agrees. "You're looking like homemade shit yourself."

Deanie's lungs feel full of sharp edges. In the mirror's seamless surface, the scar stitches from her nose ring to her earlobe. Her fists clench.

Nat shoulders by Cady to put her arm around the Mutant's waist. "Nevermind her," Nat murmurs.

Sarah steps closer as if to help protect her from Cady.

The Mutant sticks out her chin and swipes at her eyes. She laughs.

Nat smiles encouragingly and Sarah fumbles a wad of tissue at the Mutant.

The other girls begin to go about their business, murmuring and giggling. Cady Flemming sniffs scornfully and slings her handbag over her shoulder to head for the door.

Shaking off Nat, the Mutant steps into Cady's path. "Flem," she says, "Bigger wears buttonflies. My mother's boyfriend pounded my chains into my face. So now you tell me—what's your excuse for the way you look? Why are you eating yourself up?"

Cornered, the cheerleader looks frantically from girl to girl, looking for a way out. She opens her mouth, gasping and choking. Clutching her stomach, she bends over the nearest basin and vomits violently.

"Get the nurse," the Mutant orders.

"Right," Sarah responds and goes flying out the door.

The Mutant hesitates, then steps up and puts a supporting arm around Cady's waist. On the other side, Nat takes the same position. Over the sick girl's heaving back, Nat Linscott and Deanie Gauthier meet each other's eyes.

36

■ ■ ■

Huge Flimsy Flakes Tumble silently from the darkness as the boys spill from their practice. From the cover on the ground it's been snowing awhile. The truck chokes and shivers as Sam coaxes it to ignition. Deanie's attention is on tape selection; she holds up a cassette so he can read the label and when he nods, inserts it into the player. Wendy O., trying to pass as Joan Jett.

"Belt up," Sam tells Deanie, tugging at his own.

The truck's wipers sweep over the windshield to the heavy beat from the speakers. In the arc of cleared vision, Pete Fosse reaches his Blazer across the parking lot and shoves a key into the door lock. A sudden movement catches Sam's eye: a man erupting from a listing Buick station wagon parked behind the Blazer, striding toward Pete. Deanie strains forward against her seatbelt. As the wipers throw loose snow across the glass, the man raises an object in his right hand. The wiper clears the glass again and Sam sees it is a baseball bat. And he recognizes the man, a familiar face at games, one of the more rabid local fans. Dale Michaud. Lexie's father.

"Jesus Christ," Sam whispers.

In the few seconds he fumbles with the catch of his seatbelt, between the sweeps of the wiper, Pete turns and lifts his arms in defense as he tries to back away. Michaud takes a vicious cross-cut at the level of Pete's head just as Pete loses his footing and goes sliding into the man's spread legs. The man goes down with him, rolls away and comes up again as Pete scrambles to his feet and Michaud swings the bat, aiming squarely between Pete's legs. Tucking and swiveling to protect himself, Pete takes the blow on his left knee.

Sam flings open his door and hurls himself out to race across the lot toward them. The way that bat took Pete's knee and his face drained and pleated and he went down again so fast and never made a sound, he's out on one strike.

Michaud is raising the bat again over Pete when Sam tackles him. The last time Sam sacked a guy was in a pickup game with some of the football team in October. Coach had seen it and shit the bed at the thought of Sam risking an injury, though it was the quarterback who didn't get up for fifteen minutes. Landing on this guy feels the same as hitting that kid—like falling off a roof.

Michaud is a big guy, built heavy and low to the ground like his Buick station wagon. He reeks of heavy-breathing boozy sweat. But weirdly, crawling away from Sam, the man is crying. Not the way Pete is. Pete sounds as if somebody is trying to smother him. But Michaud wipes tears from his eyes and sobs.

Deanie has come to a sliding stop within a few yards.

"Get back in the truck!" Sam shouts at her.

Rick Woods throws his arms around Deanie from behind and drags her back another few yards.

As Sam rolls into a crouch, the man sits up. He's still clutching his bat. Warily, Sam looks for a way to take it away from him. Michaud brandishes it at him with a laugh. Sam shows his palms to signal his pacific intentions. Michaud wipes his nose with the sleeve of his plaid wool jacket.

Sam catches a glimpse of Todd Gramolini sprinting back into the school—to a phone, Sam hopes. Other players have ventured from vehicles or the school but keep a cautious distance.

"Oh jee-zus, jeez," Pete whimpers.

Michaud hauls himself to his feet against the Blazer. "I'm done with this fuck," he says.

Sam shakes his head. "You better just sit down somewhere and wait for the cops, man."

The heavy man looks contemptuously down on Sam. "You're

all the same, you fucks. The ones didn't take a turn watched it or joked about it. None a you stopped it, didja? Just let him do it, let'm all do it. I oughta take this slugger to every single one of ya. Right where you horny bastards live."

He sways as if he is on the verge of fainting. Rising hastily, Sam reaches out to support Michaud but the man shakes off his hand.

"She ain't even fourteen yet," Michaud says.

Writhing on the ground, Pete clutches at Sam's ankle and blubbers. When Sam crouches again to reassure him that help is on the way, Michaud shoves Sam from behind. Pete screams as Sam is driven forward onto him. Sam hears what's left of Pete's knee grate and abruptly Pete's shriek stops as he faints dead away while Sam struggles to get off him. Michaud lopes away toward his wagon.

On his knees, Sam stares after him. Deanie shakes off Rick. Sam rises to clutch her as she hurtles into him. A second later, she slithers from Sam's grasp into a scooch next to Pete. One hand wipes snow and tears from Pete's face and she moans in her throat.

Michaud's wagon spins slush from its wheels and waddles across the lot. As the first police siren pulses from the west, from Greenspark village, the wagon fishtails out onto the main road and spins east.

Rick kneels opposite Deanie. "Oh Peteybird," he mutters. "Petey, you are fucked."

"Where's he going?" Sam asks. "The Michauds live in town."

"Chapins' is east of here," Deanie suggests. "Maybe he knows about J.C. too."

Rick shakes his head. "What a shitstorm."

With the assailant gone, people leave the safety of their vehicles and the school to try to help or just to rubberneck. Sam sends Bither to promote a blanket. Pete is already in shock and they should keep him from getting any colder before the ambulance arrives.

He grabs Deanie's hand and yanks her toward the truck.

"Where you goin', Sambo?" Rick calls.

"Chapins'."

"What the hell do you think you're gonna do?"

Sam gives him no answer.

As they spin out onto 302, a rolling burble of colored lights due west signals the imminent arrival of a town cruiser. Deanie flops in her seat like a ragdoll.

"Belt up," Sam orders again. "Do it! For once! Please!"

"Rick's right! What are you gonna do?" she demands. "You're not a frigging cop. Why don't you just let Lexie's old man pound J.C. into the ground? Nobody deserves it more."

In his peripheral vision, Sam catches Deanie's fingers going directly to her face.

"I hope he does kill J.C.," she blurts. She hides her face with her hands. From behind her trembling fingers, the rest spills out in breathless gasps. "I hope the least he does is put that bat . . . in J.C.'s mouth. . . . I hope he ruins the fucker's face the . . . way J.C. . . . helped ruin mine."

The lights of an oncoming eighteen-wheeler blind Sam and he realizes he has crossed the center line. The truck's airhorn blasts like a banshee. As he swings the truck back across the line, the big rig tears by. It feels like it's sucking his truck right back into it. The whole vehicle vibrates violently before they escape the eighteen-wheeler's slipstream.

In the lee of the big rig, Sam slows the truck. He thinks he might have to throw up. Deanie undoes her seatbelt and crawls on hands and knees across the cab to put her head on his thigh. He strokes her jawline and feels the shudder go through her. He wonders if Michaud has got a spare slugger, or if the berserker might lend him the one he used on Pete, let him take a few strokes on Chapin.

Michaud has parked his wagon on the Chapins' snow-covered lawn. As Sam curbs the truck, the man plants himself next to J.C.'s car in the driveway and brings up the bat. Deanie clutches Sam's jacket and he helps her sit up. The bat comes down on the yellow Sunbird's windshield and the glass crackles and webs. Taking a deep breath, Michaud lifts the ash again and drives it down and the sheet of glass collapses inward over the dashboard. Snow begins immediately to drift over the tesserae of glass.

The front door opens, briefly framing J.C. in the houselight. He is barefoot, in jeans and a T-shirt that says *Kiss Me Where It Stinks—Greenspark, Maine*.

"Hey!" he shouts. "That's my car! What are you doing? Are you crazy?"

Michaud turns slowly to face him, with the mirthless grin of a hungry shark.

J.C. wavers, jumps back and slams the door.

Pleased with the reaction, Michaud pops his eyebrows comically and addresses the car again. He bashes a deep dent in the hood and then applies the bat to the headlights.

"Nice stroke," Sam murmurs. Conversationally, he tells Deanie, "My old man took a Cadillac apart with his bare hands once. I always wished I could have seen it."

Deanie is rigid, fixed on what Michaud is doing. She doesn't seem to hear Sam.

"What the hell," Sam murmurs. "J.C. can always get a new car. Too bad the cops'll be here before Dale gets around to him."

Quietly he throws the truck into gear and backs into a neighbor's driveway, turns around and heads back to 302. Almost immediately, the sounds of demolition are overwelmed by another burst of police sirens. Sam picks a driveway in front of a darkened house where no one appears to be home, swings in and kills his own lights.

He tightens his hold on Deanie. "What do you mean, Chapin helped?"

"He was there. Getting loaded with Tony. When I walked in and he was there, I knew it was just to get Tony coked and make trouble for me. He wanted to make sure Tony suspected I had something going with you. Tony'd never be able to intimidate you. J.C. knew Tony would react by hurting me. He was right, wasn't he?"

"The fucker," he mutters.

"Tony was so loaded he was gonna make me take my clothes off right in front of J.C. and my mother, so he could see if I'd been fucking someone. Like I was a bitch in heat. I couldn't stand him touching me again. I didn't care if he killed me, I was sure you'd kill him then. He was gonna hurt me anyway sooner or later."

The lights of the police cruiser wash over them, the pulse of the siren throbs without meaning, and they barely notice the police cruiser sweeping past.

■ ■ ■

Regardless of the dead lights, Sergeant Woods knows the truck too well to miss it, nor can he mistake the couple entwined within. He wonders why they have stopped short of Chapin's, where Rick has told him they were headed. But there's no time to find out what they are up to. The dispatcher has confirmed that Michaud is at the Chapins' and it's imperative to bring Dale's rampage to a halt before somebody gets killed.

The dispatcher's first call caught Woods on the western border of Greenspark, giving Sonny Lunt a hard time about the condition of the tires on his rig. It meant the youngest and least experienced man on Greenspark's small force, Mickey Farrell, was first on the scene. Disconcerted to find Lonnie Woods's boy on the scene, Mickey hadn't known what to make of Rick telling him that Sam and Deanie, for some reason, had decided Michaud was headed to Chapin's. With a little more sense of the kids Sergeant Woods was more inclined to assume Sam and Deanie knew something useful, a guess backed up by the dispatcher reporting a call from the Chapins.

■ ■ ■

"It's the lawyer," Sam tells Deanie at the sight of Freddy Cape's BMW in the driveway. "He's okay. He went to high school with my dad."

She swipes at her eyes, smearing what's left of her eyeliner and mascara, most of it previously transferred to tissues in a clumsy attempt at cleanup. Her tear-swollen eyes are a dead giveaway to the reception committee of Reuben, Pearl and Freddy, ensconced in the kitchen. When Reuben introduces Freddy with the explanation he is there to interview her about the emancipation order, Deanie acknowledges the lawyer with a nod and then bolts in the direction of the bathroom. Sam slumps into a chair at the kitchen table and gives them an abbreviated version of Dale Michaud's assault on Pete Fosse.

"What set Dale off?" Reuben asks bluntly.

Sam shakes his head in a mute profession of ignorance.

Pearl's concern is more immediate. "It shook up Deanie?"

Sam nods affirmatively, allowing them jump to the conclusion the violence, disturbing for anyone, was that much more upsetting to someone recovering from a beating herself.

Studying his son's face, blanked to hide his emotions, Reuben concludes Sam is covering more than distress or concern for Deanie.

■ ■ ■

When Deanie emerges from the bathroom, the lawyer asks to speak to her alone. Sam twitches restlessly around his bedroom, shuffling through cassettes, fanning textbooks and notebooks in search of homework that needs doing. When he finds some, he can't concentrate. He claps on his headphones and cranks the sound to a brain-jamming level.

At last, Deanie lets herself into the room. She skins out of her clothes and into her longjohns without speaking. He reaches across the bed toward her and pulls her up against him but before he can start anything, she nudges his headphones off one ear.

"The lawyer's still here. He wants to see you before Sergeant Woods gets here."

Reluctantly, Sam swings his legs off the bed. He tucks her in and crouches by the bed to kiss her. "Rick's dad won't get you out of bed to ask you questions."

She looks frail, the skin under her eyes like a bruised petal. It's going to be a rough night for her. He wishes he could stay with her, at least hold her until she drifts off.

■ ■ ■

Freddy is sucking up coffee at the kitchen table, which is is-landed with papers from his bloated briefcase. Reuben pokes at the fire.

"Deanie's in bed," Sam says. "She's wiped out. Anything Sergeant Woods wants to know, I can tell him."

"I'd be happy to hang out a little while and sit in on the statement with you," Freddy offers.

Sam shrugs. "No need."

The lawyer begins to collect his paperwork. Headlights flare in the window over the sink and they hear the cruiser's engine. Sergeant Woods parks behind Sam's truck and crunches across the thin fall of new snow to the house.

Met with Reuben's immediate inquiry after Pete Fosse, Woods answers, "He'll live but I think he's all done playing hoops."

"And Dale Michaud?"

"In the hoosegow. The only thing he's said to me was he hasn't been inside a jail since he was a nineteen-year-old Marine in the brig over a drunken brawl. Otherwise, he won't tell us anything."

The cop's undisguised surprise at Freddy's presence makes the lawyer laugh.

Sinking into the rocker by the fire, Reuben gestures Woods to a chair at the table. "Freddy's here to see Deanie about an emancipation order, Lonnie."

The cop cocks his head.

"That's what she wants." Reuben rolls his palms resignedly.

"To stay here. The only place the state could find for her is Lisbon Falls. She'd have to transfer schools and lose the rest of her basketball season."

Woods gives Sam a quizzical glance. "I'd like to talk to her too."

"She's gone to bed," Sam says, startling them all with the anger tensing his words. "She's had enough for today."

"All right," the cop says in a soothing way.

Parking himself opposite Sam, Woods opens his notebook, and puts on a pair of reading glasses.

"Sure you don't want me to stay?" Freddy offers in a low voice.

Sam shakes his head no.

Reviewing his notes, Sergeant Woods seems hardly to notice when Reuben and Freddy excuse themselves. They can be heard in the living room, clicking on the tube and settling down in front of prime-time war coverage.

Cautiously, Sam outlines the events in the parking lot and at Chapin's. The cop has to coax what Dale Michaud said out of him.

"Do you know what he meant? Pete is in no condition to do any explaining."

Sam studies his thumbs. "Mr. Michaud seems to think Pete and some other guys took advantage of his daughter. Lexie."

Woods peeks over his glasses. "The younger one?" The cop twiddles his pen and phrases his next question carefully. "Is it true?"

"I wasn't there," Sam says.

Woods pounces. "You heard something about it? You know who was involved? Besides Pete, I mean. I assume."

"There was some gossip. You know the stuff that goes around school." Face grown hot, Sam feels the truth like a hairball in his stomach.

"So tell me who else is supposed to have been there," the cop coaxes. "If there were a lot of stories around then a lot of people will be able to give me names and so on. You won't be the only one."

"I wasn't there," Sam repeats. "I don't know what happened."

Woods believes Sam's assertion he wasn't there, wherever it was and whatever went on. But he's convinced Sam can give him names. "Would it help any if I told you there may not be any criminal act involved? It depends on the ages involved. Statutory rape—the state doesn't call it that anymore, it's unlawful sexual contact—occurs if the victim is under sixteen and the actor is over nineteen, or if the victim is under fourteen and the actor is at least three years older. So if Lexie Michaud is fourteen—"

"Her father said she isn't," Sam says.

"All right. If she's thirteen and her partner was sixteen or younger, it wasn't unlawful. Unless she was sufficiently impaired. Age doesn't matter if a victim is too impaired to give consent. Then it's outright sexual assault."

Sam tries desperately to sort out the information. He is badly shaken by the realization he has apparently been mistaken about what constitutes statutory rape or whatever it's called now. Unlawful sexual contact. Lexie was wrecked. So was Grey. He didn't give much thought to Grey before. She was so far gone when he saw her, he doesn't see how she could have given consent. But maybe earlier she was capable. Aside from his uncertainty about the legal gravity of the incident, everywhere Sam looks, it seems to him obvious this will all come back on the team eventually. His original anger at Pete and those other idiots flares up like acid indigestion.

"I had an idea you and Pete were on the outs with each other." Woods continues to poke and prod. "What was all that about?"

"Pete's a jerk," Sam mutters. "He's been a jerk since we were in junior high. It's nothing new."

Woods tacks in another direction. "What about Chapin? He's not one of Pete's buddies. What's his connection to Lexie? Was he part of whatever the rumors claim happened?"

"Chapin's a sleaze. He goes after really young girls, the screwed-up ones. They're so easy to impress with how bad he is, you know?"

Sam's bitter vehemence brings a glint to the cop's eyes. "Deanie got involved with him about the same age, didn't she?"

"I guess. I never heard any cops showed any interest in it, though. Nobody kneecapped anybody over it. She doesn't have anything to do with him anymore."

"I won't argue Deanie's gotten a raw deal right down the line, Sam. Any sign she's going to talk to me about Lord? Not tonight—I understand she's exhausted. I need to know if we can count on her going to court to testify against Lord."

Sam knows he should pass on to Woods what Deanie has told him but he has promised not to tell. Chapin will always be protected by his parents' money and position. And nothing the law can do bears any resemblance to what Chapin has coming. At the right time and the right place, he will put it as right as he can.

"Not yet."

"We'll give her some more time."

"All the time she needs," Sam comes back swiftly.

Woods nods. "Of course. Let's go back to what happened today. Chapin claims he can't imagine why Dale Michaud wanted to turn his car to scrap. I tried to talk to Lexie. Mrs. Michaud came to the door and told me her husband could rot in jail for all she cared, how did he think she was going to support the family while he was in the slammer, and no, I wasn't talking to either of her daughters, maybe that fool Dale didn't know no better but there are some things you keep in the family, and since he had gone off and left her to handle it, she would, and hold her head up too. Dale's lucky his wife's not going to be the judge who decides his case." Grinning at Sam, the policeman flops the cover of his notebook closed and folds his glasses. "I'll get to Lexie sooner or later, of course, and Pete when he comes around, and J.C., again. I was hoping to get a handle on it before I tackled these people."

"Pete won't play again this year," Sam observes quietly. "Maybe never. If Mr. Michaud was right, that's not exactly an eye for an eye but it's close."

Sergeant Woods rises from the table. "Vengeance is a natural human instinct, Sam, but generations of experience have assigned it to God and the Law. Which sounds pompous as hell and I know the system sucks but it's the best one we've ever been able to devise. Don't you be getting any ideas from Dale Michaud. Whether Deanie ever gives us enough to act on against Lord, you stay clear of him. Understand me?"

Sam slumps in his chair. "Yessir."

"Thanks for your help. If either you or Deanie wants to tell me anything, you know how to reach me."

■ ■ ■

Cop, lawyer and mechanic loiter next to the cruiser, reflexively stomping down the snow as they make their farewells in the cold quiet country dark. Behind the house, the apple trees in the orchard sough and rattle nakedly in a passing wind.

"Get what you need?" Reuben asks Lonnie.

"No. Didn't get what I wanted, either," Woods returns, and the three men share a brief laugh. The cop addresses Reuben bluntly. "You got any sense of what the hell is going on? All I got is a lot of questions nobody wants to answer. If Dale Michaud had it straight, Pete and Chapin had unlawful sexual contact with Lexie and maybe some other guys did too. Sam knows something, Reuben. His words were 'I wasn't there.' But he wouldn't tell me where, or when, or who was there, nevermind any of what might have gone down."

"What if other kids on the team are involved?" Woods blurts, regretting it instantly.

Freddy Cape winces.

Reuben drops a hand on Woods's shoulder. "If they are, Lonnie, it's too late to do anything but deal with whatever's going to happen."

The cop nods, shakes hands with Reuben and Freddy and ducks into his cruiser.

The lawyer and the mechanic watch his lights slither and hop down the drive.

"At least he didn't say it out loud that Sam is covering for somebody," Freddy says. "Think it's Rick?"

Reuben grimaces. Stuffing his hands in his jacket, he shakes his head. "Rick's no angel but I don't think he'd do something like that. Why should he? He's going steady with Sarah Kendall."

"I saw them at the movies once," Freddy admits. "Looked to me like she had him thoroughly pussydazed."

Reuben laughs. "Poor Rick."

"Poor Rick nothing," Freddy objects. "All these goddamn kids not only get more than I did at their age, they're getting more than I do now."

■ ■ ■

Lonnie Woods finds Rick on his bed with the phone at his ear and signals him to cut off the call. Another time, he would step back out into the hall and let the boy say goodnight to Sarah in privacy, but he's in uniform, on duty and not happy about having to extract information from his own kid. Lonnie takes Rick's desk chair and spins it around on one leg to straddle it. Rick cradles the receiver.

"Spill it," Woods demands. "Everything you know."

Rick groans. "I don't know shit, Dad."

The cop grins without humor. "Lemme get that on tape for the next time you're mouthing off."

Rick flops back and stares at the ceiling. "I don't know anything. I saw Dale Michaud smash Pete's knee. Sam tackled Michaud and probably kept him from bashing Pete's brains out. Michaud took off and Sam followed him. It was Gauthier's idea Michaud might be headed for Chapin's."

"Why? Did she say?"

"No. She didn't have to. Everybody knows Chapin's been balling Lexie."

"Michaud right about Pete too?"

"Well, I've seen Lexie crawl all over Pete at the Corner, but shit, that's her hobby, sitting in guys' laps. Class A cocktease, you really want to know. Pete and J.C. don't party together though."

"So Sam saved Pete from maybe getting killed? I had an idea you two don't have much use for Pete."

"We don't," Rick admits. "If you think Sambo's got no use for Pete—he loathes Chapin, on account of you-know-who."

"All right," Lonnie sighs, meaning just the opposite. Everything about this business is all wrong.

A few minutes later, he finds himself rummaging under the seat of the cruiser for a stale cigarette. Locating a half pack, he taps the bottom with more force than he intends and the contents rocket out, spilling onto the wet muddy floor of the cruiser. Frustrated, he crushes the empty pack in one fist.

37

■ ■ ■

The Bat Swings Him or so it feels, the tug of its savage passage pulling the muscles across his back with it. He hears the crunch of the kneecap under it. Hears the sounds of glass breaking, metal shearing, the whicker of chains slicing the air and the meaty explosion of fluid metal into flesh. With a sensation of reaching, stretching for the last handhold on a rockface, and not finding it, he falls into the sound of the fist impacting on Deanie's face, driving her chains into her cheek. He feels it, the shock of the blunt force of a man's fist driving at full strength, the chewing metal like teeth before it, destroying the silken texture of skin, biting into the thin mask of musculature wrapping facial bones as thin as porcelain. He feels the rupture of blood vessel, the crushing of tissues, the eruption of spittle and blood inside the mouth. The closing of the throat behind the scream.

He swings the bat from his shoulder into the oncoming ball and it connects with a crunch of bone as he sees how big it is, and just as it begins to break up, that it has a face: Tony Lord's— exploding, splattering, spraying, once and for all, before the irresistible drive of his bat. Not wood, he thinks, aluminum. He steps into the box again, and this time the ball has Chapin's face.

■ ■ ■

Deanie whispers sleepily, "What's wrong?"

Wiping his mouth with the back of his hand, he reaches for the glass of water on his nightstand.

"Bad dream."

He fans his fingers over the curve of her skull at rest in the crook of his elbow. The stubble is downy.

"Must be catching," she murmurs.

He finds her hand, wraps her fingers around his cock. She rolls over tight against him. He doesn't know why it helps, sweating together, making the sweet machine thrum, but it does. When he wakes again in the predawn, she is still in his arms, a faint smile curving her mouth.

■ ■ ■

"Pete's out for the season," Coach tells them shortly, as they gather for morning gym.

The news settles over them oppressively.

"We'll miss him on court. You guys are gonna have to work harder to make up for the loss. You know the drill. Organize somebody to buy him a card and pass it around for signatures. Styles, get these people started and see me in my office."

A few minutes later, Coach hunches at his desk, hands cupped around a paper cup of vending-machine coffee from the teachers' lounge.

"This is lousy," he says, leaving Sam unsure whether he means the brew or the loss of Fosse. There is a long, despairing coachly sigh. "The question is, is Skouros up to the job?"

"Yessir."

"I know Dale Michaud," Coach announces abruptly. "He lives around the corner. Couple times a week, we run into each other walking our dogs at night. Stand on the curb and shoot the shit while the dogs sniff each other." The coach's eyebrows flex and knot with piss-off. "Lemme tell you something, Sam, just between the two of us. If Pete had screwed my underage daughter, I'd a done more than kneecap him. I'd have taken that bat to his nuts. I tell you, I'm disgusted. I don't understand it neither. So far as I can see, this school is wall-to-wall twitches, ninety percent of 'em willing to put out. Don't tell me Pete Fosse couldn't have found one who's at least of age to haul his ashes for him."

"Yessir," Sam agrees.

Coach hammers the desk with both fists. The paper cup of coffee jumps violently and spills. He seems not to notice the liquid flooding over his desk.

"Goddamn it," he cries, "I will not have this kinda crap going on. Not on my team. You hear me! You tell the rest of those hard-ons too!"

Sam, fascinated, stares at the spreading puddle of coffee on the coach's desk. The sharp acrid odor assaults his nose. "Yessir."

Coach notices the coffee at last. "Oh shit," he says.

Sam clears his throat. "May I go back to the gym?"

Coach flops a dismissive hand. "Sure, sure. Is Gauthier really going to wear that mask to play?"

"Yessir."

He rolls his eyes. "Sweet baby Jesus."

Sam retreats, pondering how he's going to phrase Coach's instructions to the troops.

■ ■ ■

"Crazy fucker," Chapin explains, to the small circle of visibly attentive listeners in the weight room. Getting his version into circulation. He's noisy—noisier than usual, close to babbling, the edgy brittle hysteria in his laugh. J.C. can't keep his baby blues, with their pupils like BBs, from tracking Sam as he moves from machine to machine. When Sam encounters his gaze, J.C. tries to harden his expression, flash a little of his own particular brand of cool amused contempt, but an almost rabid terror shows through the inadequate mask.

His workout finished, Sam wipes his face and drifts toward the shower room. As he passes the equipment cage, he turns to look back and finds J.C. still watching him. Sam grasps the wire and rattles it against the diamond racks of baseball bats. A matching tremor goes through Chapin.

On the bench in the locker room, Sam tightens the laces of one high-top. Then something lets go and he is holding one end of the lace, and the other dangles from the eyelet. He rummages in his duffel for his spare pair of laces and sets it on the bench next to him, then bends to tie the other high-top. And something lets go again and he's holding another broken shoelace. This time he examines the ends. His stomach lurches. Most of the way through the lace, the break is smooth, and then the shoestring frays. It has been cut through almost completely. Closer study of the first broken lace reveals the same thing. While he showered, someone sliced through each shoelace far enough to ensure they would break at the first application of tension.

Sam doesn't have to read at grade level to get this message: the cuts could have been less drastic, so the ties didn't break right away but went on quietly fraying with the stress of every tightening and tying and of the flexing and pounding of his feet. The mental vision of pushing off to make a shot, and coming down on a suddenly unsupported foot and ankle, brings a line of cold sweat to his upper lip.

Reaching up, he unhooks the padlock dangling from his locker. He closes it and gives it a squeeze and it pops open. Way too easily. Now he can see the way the shackle no longer sockets properly into the body. It's been popped before, by Fosse to leave the rat and by whichever one of them left the square, and now by Chapin. He ought to have replaced it after the rat or installed a lock they couldn't break. Or beaten the shit out of both of them right on the spot. One thing for sure, this particular warning didn't come from Fosse.

Yanking out the old ties, he threads in the spares.

■ ■ ■

Duffel slung over his shoulder, one hand resting casually inside the fashionably open zip on the topside, Chapin loiters near the door, staring at notices on a bulletin board. At Sam's emergence, he breaks out a confident smile and then his eyes widen as Sam drops his duffel to surge suddenly across the corridor and bodyslam him against the board. As J.C. scrabbles, paper trapped between the corkboard and his thrashing torso crimps and tears and the plastic high hats of pushpins pinch and nip at him.

Sam gets a hand under J.C.'s chin and around his throat. "I've had enough of you, shithead."

J.C.'s hand trapped in the duffel squirms as if he is trying to work it free. And something rigid and hard pokes against Sam's stomach from inside the duffel.

"Leggo my throat," Chapin whispers, "or I'll blow you away, fucker."

Sam hesitates, then lifts his hand slowly and carefully.

Chapin digs the hard thing inside the duffel into the muscle of Sam's gut. "Just take one baby step back and then don't ya move a goddamn inch," Chapin murmurs. He clears his throat. "It's a three-fifty-seven, Sambot. Your shit'll be dripping off the ceiling."

Behind Sam, Tim Kasten stops in the doorway of the weight room and nearly trips on Sam's duffel. It takes only a quick glance to assess the situation and he pauses, uncertain about whether to proceed and risk getting caught in the confrontation between Sam and Chapin. Rick appears and starts to brush by Tim, who catches his elbow and holds him in place.

"And I thought you were just glad to see me," Sam says.

Chapin snickers. "Very fuckin' funny, asshole. Take a walk with me." He keeps his voice so low Sam has to bend to hear it; Chapin speaks directly into Sam's ear. "This is too public."

"Fuck it," Sam mutters. "Shoot me, shithead. Go ahead. Spend the next thirty years at Shawshank. You'll be a fat old man when you get out, with a doorknob in your asshole to keep it from falling out on you. I'll be dead but trust me, it'll be a slow thirty years for you."

Chapin's grin freezes. He digs the thing in the duffel deeper into Sam's stomach, drags it down a little until it slips into Sam's navel. Gives it another shove.

Sam is surprised at how tender his navel is; it hurts. Suregod, if it isn't the barrel of a gun biting his belly button, it's a goddamn good fake. Close up to Chapin, he can smell the stink of crazed fear coming off J.C. and he can feel the tremor in J.C.'s muscles—it doesn't matter whether it's terror or toot, the guy is wired with it and might do anything.

Chapin makes a heroic effort to appear sane and reasonable. "What the fuck, Slammer, this is self-defense. You threw me into the wall, remember? I'm just trying to get along. Just take a walk with me a little ways and we'll work it out."

Sam glances back at his duffel.

J.C. shakes his head no. "Come back for it."

Rick takes a step toward them and Sam thrusts his chin out in warning. Chapin smiles winningly at Rick. Full of questions, Rick's gaze travels back to Sam, who moves in response to a slight tug from Chapin. The bottleneck at the door of the weight room breaks and the others move in the direction of their next class. Rick, Kasten and Todd Gramolini fall in a few steps behind Chapin and Sam.

Chapin glances back at them but they hang in, not hiding their interest in whatever is going on between Chapin and Sam.

"Things are kinda crazy," Chapin tells Sam conversationally. "You were there last night at my house. Watched that crazy fucker wreck my car. You and D. I find out from the cops that crazy fucker went after Fosse first, all over that dim little cunt Lexie. I don't like how this shit is coming down at all. You two are fuckin' with me. I don't like being fucked with, man. Lay off me, or I'm gonna fuck back so hard somebody'll get dead."

Sam shoves into Chapin and knocks him off balance. Rick and the other two start forward but Chapin recovers quickly. He tightens up against Sam, the tip of the gun barrel digging angry and hard into him again.

"Stupid!" Chapin spits. "You wanna be on the receiving end of a bad accident or what?"

"Chickenshit," Sam needles. "You haven't got the balls to blow your own load. Why don't I just take that toy away from you and put it up your ass?"

Chapin's face is a sheen of sweat. All at once, the pressure of the thing in the duffel lets up. Chapin grins weakly. "Shit happens, Slammer. That's all I want you to remember. Shit happens."

"*To all.*" A glint comes into Sam's eyes and his voice rises into sonorous preachment, ringing down the corridor, arresting students and staff in their passage. "*Time and chance . . .* brother, that's right, shit *happeneth to all . . . All things come alike to all . . . one event unto all.*" Startled, Chapin jerks away from Sam, who now grasps his forearm with passionate intensity. "*That which is crooked cannot be made straight; and that which is lacking cannot be numbered,*" Sam informs him fiercely.

"Testify, brother Sam'l, testify!" Rick cries out, skidding to his knees with his hands upraised.

Laughter begins to break out up and down the corridor and others call out encouragement.

"Tell it like it is, brother!" "Amen!"

"Fucking asshole," Chapin mutters, shaking loose his arm and fading into traffic.

"*The wise man's eyes are in his head but the fool walketh in darkness,*" Sam bellows after him. As Rick and Todd and Tim Kasten close on him, Sam falters. "Shit happeneth to them all," he concludes in a tone of some wonderment.

"What the fuck was that about?" Rick demands.

Lowering his voice, Sam confides in his teammates. "That crazy fuck says he's carrying a three-fifty-seven in his duffel. I think he's booted to the moon, too."

The three other boys are incredulous.

"I'm not shittin' you," Sam insists. "He had something shoved into my gut that felt like a gun barrel and he was threatening to blow me away."

Rick shakes his head. "What an asshole."

"We ought to take that duffel away from him, find out if there really is a gun in it, before he hurts somebody with it," Sam says.

Kasten raises his palms and steps backward. "I'm late for my next class. I'm not messing with Chapin, guys, sorry. If he's got a shooter on him, somebody should call the cops."

"Me," Todd volunteers, already pivoting in the proper direction. "I'm going to the Office."

"I'm outta here," Kasten says and trots down the emptying corridor.

"In the meantime," Sam tells Rick, "I'm taking that gun away from Chapin."

Rick grabs Sam's arm. "Are you nuts? Let the cops disarm the asshole. If he really is freaked, you coming after him might make him totally psycho."

Sam lowers his head obstinately. "Maybe. And while we're being so careful, what if he takes it into his fucked-up head to go after Deanie? If he's got a gun, I'm taking it away from him now!"

Sam strides back to the weight room and recovers his duffel, then heads in the direction Chapin took.

Rick skitters after him. "Where you going?"

"Senior lockers."

"You really think he might leave it in his locker?"

"Not if he's really freaking but it's a place to start."

Doors are closing up and down the corridor. A teacher hesitates in the crack of one. "Gonna be late, boys," she warns.

"Yes ma'am," Rick agrees and quickens his pace.

"Go to class," Sam urges.

Rick gives him an exasperated glare. It's one thing to face off with Pete Fosse and another to be messing around with a fucked-up druggie in possession of a Dirty Harry Special. He'd really rather be in class—except for the fact his next period is fourth-year French and Chapin's taking it with him.

Another tardy senior hurries away from the lockers as they approach them. His footsteps fade down the corridor as Sam leaves his duffel in his own locker and drifts to Chapin's. Rick plays lookout while Sam pops the padlock with a quick squeeze. No duffel inside.

Sam closes the locker and shakes his head at Rick.

"Okay," Rick says. "Obviously he took it to class. Which happens to be my next class, too. If he looks weird, acts weird, I'll take Madame aside and tell her about it. You go to the Office and tell Wild Bill."

"I'm going with you as far as your class," Sam insists.

Rolling his eyes, Rick gives up.

A glance through the window in the door, however, reveals two gaps in attendance: Woods and Chapin.

"Where is the busy little crab-ridden asshole?" Rick mutters.

"Calming his nerves," Sam guesses.

He pivots suddenly and bolts back down the hall in the direction from which they came. Rick is a step behind him when Sam reaches the boys' room around the corner from the stairwell. Holding a finger to his lips, Sam carefully pushes open the door.

There is no one at the urinals or basins and all but one stall door hangs open. As they let the door close behind them soundlessly, there is a sharp inhalation from the closed stall. They look at each other. The duffel is visible in the gap between the floor and the stall door. So are Chapin's Reebok Pumps, and his crumpled jeans around his ankles.

Inside the stall, J.C. sighs, "Oh shit."

Again Sam raises his finger to his lip. Rick's eyes widen with curiosity: *what next?*

It happens as quickly as a practiced, flawless steal. Sam is next to Rick and then he dives across the room, sliding on his belly across the floor, long arms and outsized hands under the stall door and seizing on the duffel as the first startled gasp escapes J.C., yanking it out as Chapin screams in outrage. Sam rolls to one side, then onto his feet.

The stall door flies open and Chapin stumbles out, tripping on his jeans and shorts as he tries to haul them up and run at the same time.

"Son of a bitch!" he shrieks.

Rick holds the restroom door open as Sam bolts through it. Just before Chapin reaches it, Rick lets it go. It swings back and Chapin takes it full-tilt boogie with a satisfying thunk.

In the corridor, Sam has the duffel unzipped. He drops it and holds an enormous gun over his head in triumph. "Got it!" he crows.

"Freeze!" Lonnie Woods booms, skidding into firing position from around the corner and the stairwell.

Both hands grasping the gun high over his head, Sam goes rigid. He stops breathing and his heart jerks in his chest and flips into overdrive at the same instant that his bladder cramps.

"Shit!" Rick hugs the wall.

The boys' room door bursts open and Chapin, blood pouring from his nose, staggers out, jeans and shorts hobbling him by the ankles.

"Freeze!" the cop shouts again.

Chapin staggers toward Woods.

"Goddamn it," the cop screams at Chapin, "freeze!"

Arms outstretched, Chapin continues to stumble and lurch toward him, moving like a man struggling through deep, crusted snow. The cop takes an instinctive step backward and attempts to raise his gun above Chapin's head, either seeking an angle to use it as a bludgeon or just trying to get it out of Chapin's reach. Chapin trips over the strictures of his own clothing and pitches forward onto Woods, who tries to sidestep him. The two of them take a brief, grotesque dance turn together. Blood from Chapin's nose spatters Woods's face and blouson. Then the cop's heel slips over the edge of the top stair and the two of them are suddenly no longer dancing.

They are falling. Woods grabs the newel post and Chapin grabs him. The cop has no hands to spare—one still closed around his gun, the other clawing the post. Chapin flails like a drowning man and before Woods can let go of the gun and offer a hand, Chapin is past him. With a weird, hobbled motion, Chapin seems to be stepping down the stairs an inch above their surface as he descends. He wails thinly before his head bounces off a riser and he becomes a boneless scarecrow.

■ ■ ■

Faces peep out of doors up and down the corridor. Behind the doors is hubbub, students surging from their desks, teachers trying to restore order.

"You okay, Dad?"

The cop accepts Rick's helping hand to get to his feet. Breathing hard, he moves like he has wrenched some muscles.

"Yeah. Chapin isn't. Is he shot too?"

"No, Dad. He took the door in his nose."

"It's Chapin's gun," Sam tries to explain.

"Yeah, Dad," Rick choruses. "Sambo took it off Chapin."

Holstering his gun, Woods starts down the stairs.

"Sergeant Woods," Sam asks, "can I unfreeze now?"

Over his shoulder, the cop throws Sam a withering look. "No," he says. "You just stand there till I tell you otherwise," but the sarcasm in his voice countermands the order. Descending to Chapin on the next landing, the policeman calls "All clear" up the stairwell.

■ ■ ■

Through the window of the principal's office, Sam can see the two police cruisers and the ambulance doors closing on the stretcher. A state police sedan pulls up and Poloniak trots down the steps of the main entrance and talks to the Smokey. The ambulance lights pulse on and then its siren and it spurts down the drive.

"There was white powder spilled in the stall and he had a tube of it in his breast pocket. He declined to say what it was. Now let's have the straight shit from you," Sergeant Woods says. "For a change."

Sam relates the morning's events with his usual terseness but without stuttering more than once or twice.

"So Chapin apparently got it into his head Dale Michaud trashing his car over Lexie was something you incited. It hadn't occurred to me to look at it that way, Sammy, but did you put a bee in Dale's bonnet?"

The only response Sam can make is an incredulous laugh.

"I had to ask," Woods goes on. "Rushing in there, that was risky, Sam. Somebody could have gotten seriously hurt. Why didn't you wait for us?"

Sam leans forward intently. "Deanie could have gotten dead, that's why. Or somebody else."

"This is all about Deanie, basically. You and Chapin going around about you taking his girl away from him."

"She was never his. Not like that. He's shit-paranoid. He's afraid she's gonna shop him. The fuckhead was there when Lord busted her face. It was Chapin's shit Lord was fucked up on. He isn't just a user, you know. He deals. I don't mean laying off a little of this or that on some friends to pay for his share either."

The cop nods. "You're not telling me anything I don't know." He sighs. "If Deanie wants to shop him, we'll listen, but a first offense is likely to result in probation. That's if we get a conviction. A good defense only has to cast her as a spurned girlfriend and you as his rival. If Chapin were a little bigger, it might be worth the trouble, but—you understand? We bust him, somebody else picks up his business tomorrow. Anyway, he's got himself a busted skull and I don't know what else from that tumble down the stairs." Woods wants to be warmer. But he's convinced Sam is still holding back significant knowledge of what set off Dale Michaud. It makes him angry. "Sammy, I don't give a shit who you promised not to tell or who you're protecting about what but you think about this—if you have any knowledge of any felony and you don't cough it up, you're an accessory after the fact."

Sam bites his lower lip. Slowly he raises his arms and his large hands lock at the back of his neck in a gesture Lonnie Woods abruptly recognizes as what Sam often does when a ref calls a foul on him. *I'm guilty,* it says. *I surrender.*

But though the policeman waits a long anxious moment for the rest of the confession, that's the end of it. The arms come down, the hands hang slack between the kid's knees, poking out of his jeans, and Sam hangs his head, brooding.

38

■ ■ ■

Rumor Wires the Entire School as if they'd all been tooting up in that stall with Chapin. A hundred versions of what happened circulate, wilder and more extravagant legends in the time-honored tradition of turning the swatting of seven flies into the slaying of seven giants.

Just before lunch, Coach again commands Sam's presence. "You okay?"

"Yessir," Sam assures him.

He is frantic to catch up with Deanie. By now, the tall tales must be scaring her witless. He has sent a reassuring message by way of Rick but he wants to make sure she is okay himself.

"You should have let the cops handle it," Coach tells him.

How many more times will he have to listen to this piece of Monday-morning quarterbacking? Before he can get a mental list started, Coach breaks his concentration by shifting the subject to the day's game. Fosse is out and there is nothing to be done about it except work with the remaining talent.

Half the lunch period is gone before Sam succeeds in escaping the Coach.

Deanie is in the kitchen, elbow deep in the pots and pans. Brushing the heel of her hand over her forehead, she leaves a smear of tomato sauce. He licks the ball of his thumb and wipes it away.

"I heard all about it," she tells him.

"Whatever. One of these days, the asshole will get out of the hospital. You see him coming, you run the other way, okay?"

The smile she gives him is ironic. "Like you did?"

■ ■ ■

As if a berserk armed druggie were not excitement enough, this is the day of the home rematches with Ravenswood. And the Mutant is back. As the girls' team emerges from the locker room for the first game, the reaction begins. It ripples up from the Ravenswood fans, the students, faculty and townsfolk bestirred by the rivalry to make the trip to Greenspark. They poke each other, lean into each other, snigger, make comments.

Deanie ignores them, gathering her concentration for the game. Freshly shaven, her head is as bald as a baseball. The clear plastic mask throws a glassy reflective light. Under the transparent shell, the scar is like a long crack in porcelain. The straps that keep the mask in place divide her head and face into irregular geometric shapes and have the contrary effect of appearing to hold the broken pieces together.

She could be, Sam decides, a comic-book heroine, the victim of some technological accident that rends her forever from a normal human existence, and in exchange gifts her with some unlikely superpower.

With a delicacy that is unexpectedly moving, her fingers adjust the mask. She catches him watching and her eyes are brilliant with irony. He thinks hard at her, telling her she is devastating, transcendent, the newest thing under the sun. Killer eyes, smart mouth, primitive profile, she wears her exoskeleton with the insouciance of a model flaunting opulent, overdone jewelry. The fingers of one hand rest on the wing of a hipbone as she leans into the huddle to take her teammates' hands, and the tuft of hair in her armpit is visible.

"Heal me, Lord!" he hears an adolescent male voice call mockingly from the other side of the gymnasium. "I bin struck blind by ugly!"

On either side, Rick and Todd pull him back down as Sam starts to rise in the outburst of jeers and laughing but it is really the warning look the Mutant throws him that keeps him in his place.

"Asshole," he mutters at the humorist.

On the floor, one of the officials speaks to the Ravenswood coach, who turns to her assistant coach. The AC stops laughing, arranges her face in a frown, and climbs the bleachers to have brief but harsh words with a group of boys wearing Ravenswood jackets in the area where the witticism originated. When she gets backtalk, she is promptly reinforced by Vice-Principal Liggott. The group of hecklers begin to exit, smirking.

From the floor, the ref warns that abuse of players from the bleachers will result in forfeit of the game. For all the good it does. The Greenspark girls tear up Ravenswood, 70–49, and twenty-seven points are Deanie Gauthier's, in thirty-two minutes of play. She dances down the waiting parade line of boys, her faceguard tipped up onto her crown like a welder's mask. She is glowing with triumph. Radioactive. She looks, he realizes suddenly, just the way she does when she's just had an orgasm.

■ ■ ■

When he takes the floor with his own team, he is deep in himself, unperturbed by Ravenswood's decision to target him. His team has practiced for this eventuality. By the middle of the first quarter, they have broken the three-guard gang-up completely. Once Ravenswood discards the futile strategy and reverts to man-on-man, it is just a matter of the Big Machine patiently chewing them up.

As the margin widens, the atmosphere on the visitors' side of the gym becomes mean and fractious. The buzzer brings down a rain of spitballs, stale popcorn, and drink cups, some of them not entirely empty. Lining up to palm off after the game, Sam rolls an ankle on a spill of ice on the hardwood and only avoids falling on his ass by grabbing onto Joey Skouros and Billy Rank. The losers are sullen, hardly making palm contact at all, let alone eye contact. Passing close to the stands, Sam takes a lunger in the face from an enraged red-faced old man.

Stunned, he wipes at his cheekbone, and stares up at the man.

"Hey, Pops," he calls up, "eat shit and die!"

"I heard that!" the Ravenswood coach screeches. "I heard that!"

"You're shittin' me!" Sam exclaims. "That old goat loogeyed on me!"

Rick and Todd seize him, trying to propel him into the locker room.

"I'm making a complaint about this," the coach screams.

Middle fingers rigid, Sam offers him a brace of birds as Coach throws himself between his star and the foaming Ravenswood coach.

"You goddamn idiot!" Coach explodes.

"That old shit hawked a looie on me! Look at the crap on the floor! I almost wrecked an ankle on that ice!"

"Shut up!" Coach commands.

Glowering, Sam withdraws into the locker room.

Anticipating trouble over this game, Poloniak has two police cruisers at the high school. The cops find themselves quelling parking-lot fistfights. Some Greenspark fans decide to give the Ravenswood buses a good rocking by way of imparting a few manners and Greenspark's finest are compelled to cordon the buses to get the Ravenswood teams safely onto them.

In the locker room, Coach tears up one side of Sam and down the other, explaining his deficiencies to the entire team.

Sam fingers his left earlobe. Maybe he should get it pierced. Deanie would like that. You have to start with a stud, he knows, until the hole is healed. A little smooth nub of a stud, like the one she wears in her nose. It's smoother than skin. To his tongue, it feels a lot like the button of her sex, that she let him kiss and tickle again last night. He closes his fist on his upper thigh in concert with the tightening in his groin.

"Are you listening to me? Coach snarls.

"No sir," he admits.

Some of his teammates snigger.

"What are you listening to? The wind blow between your ears?"

"No sir," he repeats.

"No sir, no sir," Coach mocks. "Just what are you doing, besides taking up space?"

"Thinking," Sam confesses humbly.

His teammates' snickers grow louder.

"Thinking!" Coach roars. "Thinking! And what great thoughts were you thinking, Einstein?"

"About whether to pierce my ear, sir."

With a moan, Rick covers his face, Bither shrieks, and the others are convulsed.

Coach's face is as purple as Sam's is red.

"Sweet Baby Jesus!" he moans. "You don't need another hole in your head, Styles! Get outta here, all of you, before I go borrow a gun from Chapin and put a hole in this moron's skull!"

■ ■ ■

On the way to school, Deanie reads Sam the game coverage in the Portland morning paper. There is another picture of her, fully as startling in her mask as the one the local paper ran of her while she was benched. Noting the officials had to warn against displays of bad sportsmanship and harassment of players by fans, a sidebar focuses on Gauthier and reactions to her return to play. It quotes an anonymous Ravenswood parent: "Hey, a kid who needs to wear a protective mask shouldn't be playing. It's too risky. She gets hurt again, who gets sued? Some player on another team? Their parents?" And an equally anonymous Greenspark fan: "You ask me, it's embarrassing. A person wears the school colors, they represent the school, they shouldn't look like some kind of skinhead Nazi. Makes Greenspark look bad. I don't care how good she is, she's only one player. Same rules for her as anyone else." What rules is she violating? the reporter asks the fan. "The ones they should have. Girls should look like girls. They should have hair on their heads."

About the danger of reinjury, Gauthier herself is quoted: "They lost. That's their problem, not what I have to wear for protective gear. How many of their players use mouthguards, rec specs, tape bad ankles and knees, whatever?" Deanie looks up from the paper. "I also said jocks for the guys but they cut that."

"Of course," Sam agrees.

She rattles the paper and continues.

The column notes Greenspark's backup center, Peter Fosse, is out for the rest of the season with a serious injury—a knee badly damaged in a fall in an icy parking lot.

"The guy from the paper never asked me anything how I got hurt," Deanie interjects. "I had myself all ready to bullshit him about it and what he wanted was a comment on this Ravenswood yupster's bellyache. Anyway," she points out, "since I've been out, we haven't lost any games and the only one you guys lost was the one those jerks threw away. You don't need Pete to win. My team doesn't need me to win, either."

"We could *use* Pete. He's more experienced than Skouros. And the girls do *need* you, Deanie. You're their edge, the difference between maybe and a sure thing."

She nudges his leg gently with her sneaker. "You're just trying to get into my pants."

He blinks but can't stop the pink in his face and she laughs at him.

■ ■ ■

The needle feels like a hard pinch as Deanie pushes it through his earlobe and that's all there is to it. Her hand falls and he sees his ear in the handmirror, the darning needle transfixing the center of the lobe. No visible blood. The discomfort is less than being stung. The most notable physical reaction is the one in his crotch.

" 'You have put a hole in me, seenyoor,' " he tells her.

Then he nuzzles between her tits again while she shoves the needle out the other side and daubs the hole she has made with alcohol and that stings, ouch and goddamn, that really stings. It hurts a lot more than the needle. It's as good an excuse as any to get himself a good titty facewash, though, which gets them both snickering. After a while she makes him stop fooling around so she can finish up disinfecting his earlobe. Then she puts the stud in, one of her old ones. When he looks in the mirror, it looks like it's always been there, except his earlobe is a little red.

"Now me," she insists. "Do me."

He's been dreading this part of the deal. There on the kitchen table are the five studs she wants him to reinsert but first he has to open up the holes in her left ear with the other needles they have sterilized. With nothing to keep them open since she got hurt, the holes have closed almost completely. She could merely shove the studs into the partially closed holes but is repiercing instead to prevent infection.

He draws out prepping her, bathing her earlobe and the curving edge of the pinna with alcohol-soaked cotton balls. The tension in his stomach is no longer the least bit sexy; he is scared to death he's going to hurt her. One of the reasons he insisted on her piercing his ear first was so he would know just how bad it hurt. If it turned out to be bad enough, he would refuse to do it for her. Even now, the thought of doing it five times raises gooseflesh. At least he doesn't have to try to center the first hole in the lobe or place any of them. They're all there, like machine-sewn button-holes that just need to be opened.

She kneels in a kitchen chair, her forehead on his chest. It's a mechanical operation, he tells himself, and focuses tightly on the delicate petal of flesh he grasps between thumb and forefinger. Steady, steady, as he places the point of the needle into the pucker of the closed hole, and they both hold their breaths and there is a tiny resistance and he punches it quickly all the way and the first one's done. They breathe again, simultaneously.

He wipes his hands on his jeans and picks up the next needle.

That was the easy one. The lobe is a little pillow of tissue. Millions of people puncture their earlobes and decorate them with jewelry—have for thousands of years. No big deal. But the four holes are not through soft tissue but what she calls her pinna, the curling edge. And it's mostly gristle, that stiffens the external structure of the ear the better to collect sound by lifting it away from the skull.

"Maybe you should put another one in for me," he suggests.

She knows he is chickenshit about this. "I told you, you have to wait and see if you're going to be able to keep a hole in your ear at all."

He takes a deep breath and inserts the second needle and her fingers dig into his torso. He does the others as fast as he can, three, four, five, while she murmurs okay, okay, okay, and when the last one goes through she shudders. Her eyes are too bright but she isn't going to admit to an instant's pain, though Sam would like to be able to go to the bathroom and vomit. His hands are shaking as he cleans her violated ear of the tiny drops of blood the piercings have drawn. He watches while she inserts the studs herself.

"Maybe we'll both be healed enough to wear earrings for the states," she speculates.

Sam grimaces. Five regular-season games remain on the schedule and then they will be in the regional playoffs. Beyond that he'd rather not think, not until they have clinched their chance. There are a thousand tales of little David schools skinning into tournaments by a fraction of a point and punching out the top-seed Goliath in the quarterfinals. And for every one, a matching thousand of top-dog teams watching the title they were sure they already owned slip into the hands of a hungrier one.

If the queasiness he is feeling is not actually hunger, eating might still appease it. He gets up and opens the refrigerator door. Rubbing his stomach, he considers the options. He takes out the milk and half a chocolate-coconut-cream pie, his favorite, and puts it on the table.

Deanie is still studying her ear in the mirror.

"You gonna wear your face chains ever again?" he asks.

"Sure. I figure they'll cover up the scar."

He pours milk into glasses and takes out forks and napkins. He halves the remainder of the pie and places the plate between them. Deanie waits until he has forked into one wedge of the pie and then takes a bite of the same section.

"I don't want a whole piece," she says.

He does but manages not to say so.

"What do you think? About my face chains?"

He's a little surprised to be asked. "It's your face. I like your chains. They're kind of dangerous though."

She touches the scar, as she does many times a day. He reaches out and takes her hand from her face and closes his hand around it on the table and she smiles at him. "You miss my other chains?"

It's not teasing. She wants to know.

"No," he says, shaking his head. "I don't miss them. I always liked them though. I like the contrast between your skin and the metal."

She laughs as if that's her favorite thing about him.

"Do you want some new ones? I could make you some in metal shop," he asks.

"Would you?"

In the living room, the tube suddenly goes mute and Reuben wanders into the kitchen. He glances at the paraphernalia scattered among the dessert plates—rubbing alcohol, needles, cotton balls—and squints at Sam's ear, but then is distracted by the remaining wedge of pie. He rummages for a fork and picks up the pie plate from the table.

"When you gettin' a tattoo?" he asks.

Sam and Deanie laugh. Reuben laughs with them.

"Thought I'd shave my head first," Sam says.

Reuben nearly chokes. "Oh shit," he finally mutters. "Sammy, I promised myself in 1967 I'd never make an issue of how my kids wore their hair and I'm not going back on that." He dumps the pie plate into the sink. "I think I'll say goodnight."

As his father ducks up the back stairway, Sam begins to clear the table. Deanie discards the used cotton balls and picks up the alcohol and needles.

"Could you put the milk away?" he asks.

Her mouth tightens. "You took it out."

Sam reaches past her, picks up the carton and puts it back into the refrigerator.

"Thanks," he says.

"Yeah, and fuck you very much, too."

"Jesus, Deanie, come off it. It wouldn't hurt you to do more around here, you know. Be a little more considerate. We've only got the two bathrooms for the five of us and no time in the morning to screw around. I'm shaving at the kitchen sink every day, cutting myself all to hell trying to get out of Pearl's way. You waltz in and tie up the goddamn bathroom for hours. You could help with the dishes after supper once in a while, offer to run and sort a load of laundry, anything."

"I helped clean up after supper last Friday when you went to work with your dad—don't tell me I don't do anything," she counters. "Just once you could tell me I was doing okay."

When he tries to put his arms around her, she twists out of his embrace and hurries from the room. He follows her, apologizing to her, to the sunporch, where she throws herself face down on the daybed. Sitting down next to her, he rubs his fingertips up and down the hollow between the prominent cords at the base of her skull.

"You're beautiful," he tells her. "You're hell with a darning needle."

The noise she makes into the pillow sounds suspiciously like a giggle.

"Best hook in the state," he continues. "Possibly in the known universe."

Definitely a giggle this time.

"You come louder than anybody else in this house."

Her body jerks and she pounds the pillow with her fists and shrieks. Rolling over, she bats him with the pillow. He knocks the pillow aside and tackles her, catching her by the wrists and pinning her to the bed with his weight while she wriggles and squirms under him. She grabs his neck and begins to moan and groan as loudly as she can.

"Ooooh," she gasps, "you're so gooood, oh 'god, oh shit,

oooh!" and fakes a long orgasmic ululation that leaves him red-faced and begging her to stop.

"You're gonna pay for this," he whispers into her ear.

■ ■ ■

A constipated squint wrinkles Coach's face and then an expression of outrage creases his long features.

"What next? You gonna shave your head and stick a ring in your nose like that skinhead? Sit around study hall and tattoo swastikas on yourself with a ballpoint pen? I just get used to the goddamn long hair and you guys start in with something else even uglier. You're worse'n the girls now, earrings and all the time you spend on your hair, it's either long hair and perms or these razor jobs look like the barber was your worse enemy. It's all the girls' doing, that's what."

Listening to Coach piss and moan, Sam holds his elastic between his lips as he gathers his hair in one hand, removes the rubber band from his mouth and twists it around his ponytail.

Rick slams his locker door shut and tugs Sam's ponytail. "What's it gonna be?" he asks in a low voice, as Coach drifts away to rip into Bither over something. "The ring in the nose or the Nazi tattoo?"

Sam closes his locker. "A cock ring," he confesses in a murmur.

Rick's shout of laughter spins the Coach around.

"What's so goddamn funny, Woods?"

"Nothing, sir."

"Twenty laps." Coach fines him on the spot. "Styles, you're so goddamn amusing, you can keep Woods company."

Before they have finished their laps, Rick's question and Sam's answer are legend among the rest of the team.

■ ■ ■

Chapin is recuperating from a fractured skull and various lesser bone breaks. He's quits with Greenspark Academy. He'll finish out his high school education at Ravenswood, as a boarder, next year. Let bygones be bygones, his father argued—the kid has suffered enough for what was, after all, perfectly normal experimentation. We all smoked some pot in college, didn't we? And the school doesn't seriously want to deal with a lawsuit over who's responsible for his son's injuries, does it?

Fosse has had his knee replaced. He's in a lot of pain. He wants to go home. He wants to kill Dale Michaud.

"I'd like to kill the fucker," Pete tells Lonnie Woods, though his mother is sitting right there next to his bed and gasps when he says it while his father tries to shush him. Pete won't be muzzled. "I'm gonna kill the fucker!" he snarls.

Woods lets Pete calm down again before informing him that as soon as his wife bailed him out, Michaud and Lexie caught an interstate bus in Lewiston the next day. The bus was headed for New York City where they could and probably did take a bus to anywhere, and there's no bucks in the Greenspark budget to chase Dale Michaud past, say, Castle Rock.

"So it doesn't seem likely there's going to be any prosecution as long as Dale keeps his nose clean."

"What about Lexie?" Sam asks when Rick's dad informs him Dale Michaud has jumped bail. "Must be a real treat, being on the run with her old man."

The cop finds himself thinking of Lexie at odd moments because of it. What's it like for her? Is she knocked up? Is Dale shaming her, ranting at her for her misbehavior and what it's done to the family, watching her like a warder transporting a prisoner, cuffing her every time he thinks she's flirting with some pimply kid at the cash register in some 7-Eleven? How long will it be before she escapes him and becomes another one of the kids on the street?

39

■ ■ ■

The Windows Light Up with somebody's head-lights. Sam lifts himself to his elbows to see who it is.

"Freddy," he tells Deanie, slipping off his headphones. "I'll go down and get the door."

She sits for a moment on the bed after he closes the door behind him and then she takes off her Walkman 'phones. It's not cold in this room or it didn't seem that way with him right next to her but now she shivers. From a shelf in his closet, she helps herself to an old misshapen sweater and pulls it over her head. It comes to her knees and she has to double back the sleeves until the wrists are at her elbows. It looks like she is wearing ankle-warmers on her forearms. The neck sags unevenly below her collarbone. She shuffles into her sneakers.

The lawyer stands up when she comes into the kitchen, disconcerting her. She goes to Sam, backed up against the counter, and leans into him. Freddy asks after Reuben and Pearl and Sam tells him they have gone up to the farmhouse with the baby to do a little work.

"You want me to stay?" Sam asks her.

She digs her nails into his hands.

"I'd like him to stay," Freddy says, unholstering his papers. "I saw your mother, Deanie. Lord was also present. Once they heard what you wanted, Lord became extremely angry. Your mother appears to be pretty much under his influence. In the end he offered a deal. She'll consent to emancipation if you make no charges against her or Lord. If you do make a criminal complaint or bring in DHS, Lord stated the two of them will make a countercharge against Sam."

Deanie moans softly in protest.

"As a deal, it's bullshit. You can go ahead and seek emancipation and once it's done, you can still make a criminal complaint against Lord. Your mother too, if you want. They can't stop you. The state can prosecute criminally or you can seek civil damages. Or you can let DHS take custody of you and assign you to a foster home. You have to make the choice, Deanie. You want to talk about it with Sam?"

"No." Her voice is shaky. "Just get me emancipated. Nobody hit anybody. Tell him that. Okay?"

She pivots, hides her face in Sam's open shirt.

Freddy looks at Sam over her bent head and Sam nods his consent.

■ ■ ■

At Breckenfield on Friday night, the locals are primed for her. She reacts to the jeers and mocking with a straight-spined strut and a cocked eyebrow that puts the jerks down with sheer guts. And then she plays her heart out. Gradually the blowoffs on the Breckenfield side are silenced by her control of the boards. The Greenspark bleachers, responsive at first to the humiliation of the opposing team, come to their feet immediately behind Sam when she executes a bravado steal and leaves the Bears yelling blame at each other. She double-pumps her fists in response to the surge of support from the Greenspark side.

In both the girls' and boys' matches, Greenspark beats Breckenfield, as Kevin Bither explains solemnly, "real bad."

■ ■ ■

If the weekend could be reduced to an ideogram, it would be two parallel wavy lines, like a long giggle. Shivering awake at the edge of dawn and going out to practice together at the meeting house. Wolfing breakfast at the diner before Sam takes Deanie to meet Miss Reggie at the supermarket. The old women waving at him from their kitchen window as he idles in the driveway and she runs back out to him when he picks her up. For their supper, eaten at the garage, he gets Chinese take-out and they have lemon-coconut cake from the bakery for dessert, Deanie's treat. She hangs out with him until he closes up. Sunday morning at the meeting house again, shooting, doing drills. Studying, listening to music, sharing the sports page, all reassuring and mundane events, in the course of which they are surprised by the sudden awareness of each other. Then they become rambunctious, tickling and pinching each other through the house and wrestling over the couch.

Off the court, or outside of work, Sam whistles "Froggie Went A-courtin' " all weekend. Miss Mousie, Miss Mousie, he finds himself whispering to her as they thrash, foundering in the current that sweeps them once again toward the edge of something like a waterfall. It's all right, he assures himself, this is just like tourney fever. It'll pass.

Deanie's notebooks rash out in giddy bagel-shaped flowerchild graphics to record such ephemera as how many baskets she shot in weekend practice. Sometimes she breaks out in a cold sweat and feels like she's going to throw up and wonders if Pearl is sprinkling hash in the brownies or lacing the coffee with windowpane.

She still wakes in the night, sweat-soaked and choking for breath. What begins as comfort becomes a frantic struggle for an instant's oblivion in which she punishes Sam, biting him, tearing him up with her nails. Once as he turns his head on the pillow, he sees her hand unclenching, the long fingers trembling, releasing strands of his hair like threads of spun straw and realizes why his scalp is tingling.

■ ■ ■

As the regular season began, so it ends, meeting Castle Rock— only away at the Rock, after both girls and boys again have taken the Cork Cougars and Hamlin Pipers down to defeat.

At the Castle Rock town line, the Greenspark buses are greeted with a jingle:

> Gauthier is bad and bald,
> Sam the Slam is big and mean,
> but CASTLE Rock
> has got the tools
> to jam the Big Machine.

"Hey, I resent that," Rick complains, "they didn't mention me."

Before they reach Castle Rock High School, though, each and every starter on both the girls' and boys' teams has been derided by name in a roadside insult.

Who Woodsie is
we think we know,
watch us
hold his scoring low.

"Well, I'se scared, Sambo, I'se jest scared," Rick squeaks in Butterfly McQueen's falsetto. "I don't know nothin' 'bout no hoops."

"Good ol' Woodsie, dark and deep," Sam teases, "with blondes to d-d-dick before he sleeps."

The boys on the bus occupy themselves with the new game of answering the jingles. By the time they reach downtown Castle Rock—two blocks with a Reny's five-and-dime, a cafe, a bar, a mom-and-pop store doing a heavy trade in video rentals, a video game parlor, a tiny barbershop, a sewing goods shop, a Western Auto, a laundromat, a Sunoco, two banks, and five boarded-up storefronts, among them a real estate office with a tattered for-sale sign on the outside of the plate-glass window, itself full of curling, yellowed three-by-five cards describing other properties on the market—the Greenspark players are hanging out the windows, reciting their own doggerel boasts and threats to pedestrians and passing traffic all the way to the high school. In response, the girls' bus provides rude cheers and then picks up the hastily composed doggerel and joins the recital.

Between the girls' squads, the game is one-sided but the Rockettes refuse to lie down and call it quits. The Mutant's irritation builds with the opposing team's persistence. When she glances in his direction—how am I doing?—Sam gives her the high sign. She gets his message and relaxes. Her shift in mood affects the players on both teams. All at once the game is looser. When the Rockettes' center slips and falls on her ass in a post scramble, the Mutant gives her a hand up and pats her fanny and gets a grin from the other girl.

■ ■ ■

The boys' game that follows is one of the hardest-fought of the schedule. The weeks of play since the last encounter have seasoned the Rockets into a tougher team. Priest and Clutterbuck are the best they have ever been. Of the trio of sophomores who start with them, Gary Seeds has emerged as a quick-handed point, Mike Fairbrother has taken enthusiastically to big forward and Nick Young now plays his guard position with confidence.

Sam is double-teamed by Priest and Fairbrother. The latter is only a middling shooter, does a little better at the stripe, but he can run and pass and he does have timing. Lucas Priest, of course, is far too devoted a student of Sam Styles's moves. They succeed in frustrating him just enough to make it worthwhile for them. Tim Kasten helps out the Rock with an overthrown pass that results in a turnover and then commits a couple of thoughtless, useless fouls, and comes down with the jitters. With Castle Rock up six points at the half, Coach subs Skouros for Kasten.

Greenspark ties up the score during the third quarter and Sam takes a breather while Joey Skouros fills in for him. Alquist subs for Joey at forward and Billy Rank spells Rick Woods.

When Lucas Priest attempts to climb straight up Joey on his way to the bucket, he gets a surprise; Skouros sinks like a ladder in a Road Runner cartoon. It is a highly inelegant flop but well worth the expression on Lucas's face as he sprawls in the opposite direction. Alquist plucks the ball from midair and is gone with it while Lucas scrambles frantically to his feet. The roar of dismay from the Castle Rock fans seems literally to buffet Lucas. Setting his mouth grimly, he looks very much like a man fussing with the fine-tuning of a television set, determined to get the picture to sharpen up.

Rick goes back into the game. Receiving a pass from Gramolini, he tries for a jump shot and comes down on his ankle as the ball falls through the net. Rick staggers against Seeds. Gramolini pivots and catches both of them as they lose their footing, Seeds by the elbow, Rick by the armpit.

Keeping his grip on Rick, Todd lowers him carefully into a sitting position on the floor. Coach and the officials gather around and examine the injured ankle. In a moment the decision is taken and Rick's benched, with the AC taping ice onto his elevated ankle. Billy Rank comes in for him and half a minute later the buzzer sounds. In the brief break between the third and last quarter, Sam is reassured by Rick that it's just a minor sprain.

Sam begins the fourth quarter with a three-pointer. Todd follows with a rebound deuce. Rank strips Seeds and passes it to

Skouros, who pops it in. It is in this last quarter that Billy Rank really becomes part of the Big Machine. All at once he is working with them effortlessly, nervelessly. The pleasure of having Billy come into his own makes the game for Sam. During the fourth quarter Greenspark builds a fourteen-point lead while holding Castle Rock scoreless. Sam delivers the last dish to Billy, who gets the last shot, taking the Rock by twenty points.

■ ■ ■

The mood in which Sam and Deanie make the drive home from Greenspark is wanton. Deanie's tongue is in Sam's ear, mouth, on his throat and nipples, her hands inside his shirt, between his legs, squeezing fifteen miles of hard. He begs her to stop before they reach the house. It is impossible to disguise their excitement as they come into the house. Throughout the meal, sitting next to each other, they hold hands under the table. The hidden hands occasionally release each other to wander to someplace squeezable or strokable. They cannot look at each other except in hasty peeks.

At last, Reuben crumples his napkin and unbuckles Indy from her high chair. "I'm taking baby cleanup tonight. Sam, would you and Deanie clear the meal and do the dishes?"

Sam stretches his neck and tries not to look at Deanie as her fingers dig into his thigh under the table. "Sure," he mutters.

"Thanks," Pearl says.

She looks so done in, Sam jumps up to give her a hug before she can leave the kitchen.

In a few moments he and Deanie are alone in the kitchen. They work swiftly, keeping their eyes and hands busy with the chores. While Deanie wipes the table, Sam fills the woodbox, and then they are finished. Deanie dries her hands slowly as Sam comes up behind her and takes the towel from her. She takes a deep breath and peeks up at him. Hand in hand, they begin a dignified passage up the back stairs. Midway up, their steps hasten suddenly.

■ ■ ■

Pearl is suddenly and completely awake, wondering if she ever really was asleep. It isn't the baby. Indy snoozes deep in baby dreams. The house is as quiet as it should be at—checking the clock-radio—half-past twelve: old house creaks and groans and whispers, a sudden whirring from the furnace. Reuben is awake, she realizes, as awake as she is.

He shifts his pillows, pulls her closer.

"Can't sleep?" she asks.

"Just waiting for it to be half-past Deanie again," he says. "Damn kids have been at it all night."

Her body vibrates with laughter against his. It makes him very aware of the sweet smooth weight of tit, the hipbone under his hand. Her hair tickles his chin. Inhaling the familiar perfumes of her shampoo and her own natural scent beneath it, he turns as if on a spindle, like a sunflower to the sun.

With one thing and another, he doesn't happen to hear half-past Deanie going off.

■ ■ ■

Tony Lord is on sick leave from his job and looking for a permanent disability pension now that he's legally blind in one eye. Fired by the convenience store after her last binge, Judy is not working either. The Greenspark cops are called twice to Depot Street by neighbors. She comes to the door, once in a dirty tieless bathrobe gaping over nothing underneath and once in jeans and a shirt darkened with blood from her nose. Each time, her face looks like a heavyweight boxer's after a savage title fight. And she insists, drunkenly, the neighbors are all assholes, there is no problem—she fell against a doorknob.

The emancipation hearing is a formality. Judy fails to show but has signed the papers—Freddy Cape doesn't tell Deanie that Judy gave up her signature for a fifth of Jack Daniel's while Tony was sleeping off the previous night's load.

The judge casts an uneasy eye over the wretched child. He can't find any serious fault in the arrangements cobbled together to assure her shelter, education and guidance by this mechanic and his second wife—own their own businesses and a little property, cash-poor but nobody goes hungry. And no, he doesn't like there being a youth unrelated to this girl in the same household but she's so bizarre-looking, it might even counteract the predictable rush of adolescent hormones. Of course he knows the boy, has seen him play many times and been impressed with his athletic talents but has also heard it said he's only half-bright. Oh well, the mechanic and his wife look solid. It's probably the best that can be done, given the shortfall of foster homes.

The judge barely looks at Deanie, nor does she look at him. She keeps her eyes downcast throughout the hearing, answering the few questions in monosyllables. The glossy wood of the table they sit at reflects her face almost as clearly as a mirror. The studs in her nose and ear wink dots of light off the overheads. Her eyes are dark and smudgy, like something drawn by a child. The scar between her nose and ear could be a ripple in the grain of the wood.

■ ■ ■

This February at war, awaiting the clash of ground forces in the desert, doesn't feel any different than any other year. February is always a waiting month. Waiting for winter to be done with it. Waiting for the furnace to stop running *all* the goddamn time. Waiting to be able to go outside in the morning and have the motor turn over on the first go. Waiting to be able to breathe out of doors without it freezing the hairs inside the nose and shocking the lungs. Waiting for the planet, in its lumbering pas de deux, to tip this particular latitude into the sun's face—oh for some heat in the daylight, some heat on the face.

Talk keeps you in the store or the post office or just inside and out of the cold a little longer. It kills the time, burns a few of the calories from that jelly donut you shouldna had. Talk about the weather. And the war. And about high school basketball.

In the rural states, high school basketball breaks up the dead of winter. Even though the tournaments are televised now, when the local kids make the cut, the little towns still automatically empty out, everybody headed toward wherever the tourney's being held that year. There's always joking about the last person out of town turning off the lights and remarks about what an opportune time it would be to burglarize East Bugswat.

With the last regular-season games in the books, it's time to study the tapes of the other nine teams qualifying for tournament play. Every possible clash between the tournament-bound teams is war-gamed until the players are as familiar with the characteristics of each team as if they played them regularly. Single elimination means everything rides on each game; lose and the buses go home. Two of the four lowest-ranked teams will be eliminated in preliminaries. In the boys' division, the eighth-ranked survivor is scheduled to meet number-one-seed Greenspark in the prime-time night game on the first of March. Number four in the girls' division,

Greenspark will meet number five, Comfort, in the quarterfinals during the afternoon of the same day.

■ ■ ■

Squirt-gun wars break out, spreading rapidly from the jocks to the rest of the student body. Bither is busted in a shootout on the stairwell when the vice-principal walks into the line of fire. He gets off with a warning.

There is a sudden escalation to shaving foam and then to cheese spray. Someone fills the inside of Bither's jock with cheese spray—Mouth himself, Rick Woods insists, probably to have a snack handy.

No locker or gym bag is safe. Jocks are discovered filled with shaving foam, toothpaste, liquid heat and depilatories. The insides of high-tops, sweats and uniforms are coated with Vaseline, with K-Y, with peanut butter. Lockers are slimed with various substances. Sam finds the interior of his stuccoed with marshmallow fluff, the goo studded with crushed Cheez-Its. It doesn't actually taste too bad.

When a teacher picks up the can of Maxwell House in the teachers' lounge to start the first pot next morning, she finds herself holding the bottomless cylinder as coffee grounds cascade over the counter. The sugar bowl is heaped with alum, the cookie tin filled with dog biscuits. Every tampon dispenser in the girls' rooms dispenses its contents all at once like a slot-machine jackpot. The fountains suddenly spurt green water and in the boys' room, wash basins and urinals run blood-red. When Coach's weight depresses the toilet seat on the pot in the teachers' lavatory, it sets off a police siren. The effects on Coach's chronic constipation are known only by scatological rumor.

There is a special assembly in which Wild Bill, twinkling with patient amusement, perches on the edge of the auditorium stage. When he calls on the vice-principal to deliver a sterner caution, Liggott is unable to rise from his chair in the first row. The student body is dismissed while the vice-principal abandons his Super Glued trousers for a pair of sweats volunteered by an assistant coach. The principal concludes the assembly over the PA system with the edict that the next stunt will be punished by suspension. No sooner does he sign off than there is a shriek of static like nails on a chalkboard and then a long, fluting (prerecorded) fart erupts from the intercom, followed by the principal exclaiming "Shut that goddamn thing off!" into the open mike.

The next morning, the grounds are festooned with toilet paper and the door to the Office is Super Glued. Once entry is gained, it is discovered that all the filing cabinets and desk drawers have also been Super Glued. Disgusted, the principal gives a jerk to his top drawer, the front panel separates into his hand and dozens of condoms spill out of the drawer. When Laliberte opens the door of his private lavatory, the popcorn the room has been packed with collapses onto the flailing principal. Laliberte begins, at last, to look a little ragged.

■ ■ ■

In the dull let-down light of too early in the morning, the buses load for Bangor. The kids are relatively quiet—sleepy, some of them, and some of them spooked and nervous. Nobody's fantasies of playing and winning ever include the mundane boarding of the bus. It's like the beginning of a journey of a thousand miles, one you have dreamed about and longed for, when you realize you're going to have to do it one foot at a time, and much of it will consist of sitting in waiting rooms, and then sitting on a bus, a plane, a train—time passing with the miles, and you're not there yet.

The coaches tick off their players on their clipboards and look anxiously at their watches. They meet a diplomatic halfway between the buses.

"I'm short a player," one coach tells the other.

"Me too. Lemme guess which one you're missing."

The boys' coach nods gloomily and shrugs his collar up against the raw of the day. "Would be those two. He never used to be late for anything, I'll tell you."

The girls' coach nods toward the highway. "There they are."

Cheering and applause rise from the idling buses.

The coaches shake hands and wish each other luck, as they will again later on debarking and yet again before their games. They don't like each other—she resents his seniority, his power and the sex bias of his funding; he knows it, and comes besides of a generation that suspects all female coaches of being lesbians—but like most coaches and indeed athletes, they are fundamentally superstitious.

As Sam brakes the truck, to the bellowing of two basketball

teams from the opened windows of the buses, Deanie flips them all off, which only increases the volume of their welcome.

"I told you we were gonna miss'm if you didn't hurry up," he chides her, grabbing their gear from the floor of the cab.

Deanie takes his free hand and slides out of the cab. "Oh shut up. You took your time, dub."

He heaves her gym bag up into the bus to Melanie Jandreau, who has jumped up from her front seat next to her sister to catch it. Deanie starts to brush past him. He catches her wrist and holds her at the bottom of the steps.

"You wanted to come twice," he reminds her in a whisper.

Deanie sticks her tongue out at him.

Her teammates react with applause, shrieks and faked orgasms. From the other two buses, he is being urged to get his ass on board.

"Promise?" he teases, backing to his own bus. In turning away from her, he trips over his own feet and nearly falls under the wheels. His teammates greet him with lewd suggestions as to why he is so late—several of them pretty much right on the money— and Coach shouts them down. As the buses move, there is an immediate distraction to be had in hanging out the windows, encouraging the whooping and cheers of their fellow students, teachers, parents and miscellaneous fans who have come to see them off.

As the boys' bus slowly passes the girls', Sam jams himself out his window and reaches across the gap to Deanie, kneeling on her seat to reach out to him. Their fingertips touch lightly.

■ ■ ■

Breathless, the Mutant sinks back into her seat. Billie Figueroa throws herself down next to her and hurriedly informs her that *everybody*'s gym bag on all three buses has been searched for contraband—this year including not just alcohol, drugs and tobacco, but Super Glue, squirt guns, slimy or sticky substances, anything in an aerosol can, anything that looks like a tool or hardware, balloons—basically anything that isn't absolutely necessary to the trip. Rumor has it a vast supply of rubbers was also confiscated.

As Billie chatters, Deanie realizes there is something new about Billie. A stud gleams from the right side of her nose.

"Look at you!" she exclaims.

Billie turns her head proudly from side to side, showing it off. "Bitchin', huh?"

Nat Linscott pops up from the seat in front of them. "That ain't all."

Slowly, Nat raises her baseball cap and reveals she has cropped her red curls to a tight cap and razored swooshes right to red fuzz on the sides.

"My mother just about shit!" she crows. She clasps her hands to her chest and imitates her mother, in an alarmed falsetto, " 'Oh my Gawd! Natalie Marie, what have you done! What about the prom!' "

40

. . .

Through Winter-Weary Countryside the
bus growls and wheezes while its riders settle down to the long
two-lane blacktop passage. Rick wanders back to his seat and
finds Sam heavily asleep. The stud in Sam's ear has been replaced
with a filigreed gold ring, which Rick recalls having seen in
Gauthier's ear.

It's got to be the weirdest coupling in the school's history. Rick
still can't quite believe it but there's also something predictable in
it—like one of those TV preachers getting busted with a hooker.
All the same, he still wants to punch the idiot out; it makes him
furious to know that one of these days the Mutant is going to fuck
Sam over but good. And Sam's the kind of guy, something like that
would half-kill him.

Imitating Sam, he hangs his headphones over his ears and closes
his eyes, but he doesn't sleep. He elaborates a long-running fantasy
about the Jandreau twins—half as smart as Sarah between the two
of them but twice as many tits.

■ ■ ■

Sam yawns and squints at the Bangor town line marker. He
stretches, wrinking his nose at the inadvertent whiff of the sharp-

ness in his pits. A deep breath of the whole bus would fell a dumpster-dwelling wino with the nervous funk. The decibel level emitted by their assorted suitcase blasters is paralyzing to the uninitiated. To them, it's a legal upper, a blood-pressure raiser, a testosterone pumper.

The mood on arrival is distracted, everyone suddenly aware it's almost high noon in Dodge. Spectators are beginning to arrive. TV crews are setting up. Uniformed cops loiter near the auditorium doors. The band hustles to unpack instruments and stands and cheerleaders posture with mirrors, lipstick, hairspray. The Boosters' Club makes for the second tier of the stands on the side assigned to Greenspark to hang banners.

Sam keeps the boys together long enough to line them up to high-five the girls on the way to their lockers. He gets his first look at the stud in Figueroa's nose.

He drifts with the rest of his team up into the stands where the green and silver is draped, looking for good vantage. The seats are filling up with folks from Greenspark and its tributaries—gran'mas and gran'pas, moms and dads and sibs, fellow students, teachers, administrators, run-to-fat middle-aged ex-high school jocks, and more—more of the population present than the smaller communities raise most Town Meetings, or Greenspark ever gets out to vote, even in a presidential year.

On the other side of the auditorium, the banners are royal blue for Comfort but the faces, frames and accents of the arriving fans are indistinguishable. These are not the athletic, slim-bodied, fresh-faced yuppie college students who fill the bleachers in beer ad sporting events. These are folks who really do drink beer and eat potatoes and red meat, donuts, pies, and fried food, and have the figures to prove it. Past youth, they sport guts and double chins and substantial rear ends, about which they kid each other. They discuss Weight Watchers meetings as they munch nachos with hot cheese spray on them.

Letter-jacketed brothers and boyfriends and buddies of the Comfort girls climb over seats and eat hot dogs while checking out the cheerleaders from Greenspark. Another cluster of letter jackets (maroon with white trim) appears among them: Archangels from St. Gabriel's, less interested for the moment in eyeing girls than in scouting the Greenspark Indians.

Except for the color of their jackets, the guys from St. Gabriel's are nearly interchangeable with the Indians—they even have one black player. There are two big boys, brothers, one of them a sophomore, the other a senior, both heavyset and hairy, with deep dents in their chins and pale blue eyes. At noontime they have heavy shadows on their jaws, the kind of bristle that must give their girlfriends wicked beard burns. Bet they stink some when they sweat, Sam thinks. Another St. Gabe's player could be Bither's cousin, wiry, with rubbery lips that have a natural sneer in them, little short nose, feverish eyes that look like they could come up cherries any second. A lanky, freckle-spattered kid with protuberant knuckles reminds Sam of Scottie, the senior guard who graduated Greenspark the previous year. The powerful short boy with the bullet head and Roman nose, St. Gabe's point man, is the same Gallic type as Dupre, Greenspark's spare off guard. And that square-faced blond kid could be Tim Kasten's cousin.

Rick leans toward Sam. "Stand up," he says. "Take off your jacket. Stretch and yawn. Let's see some articulation. I wanna see those bozos wet their buttonflys."

Sam rolls his eyes and responds lazily, "Eat me."

Rick laughs. "You wish."

The two school bands begin trading off: Comfort stumbles awkwardly through "Little Old Lady from Pasadena" and Greenspark drums the crap out of "Gloria," during which Sam provides Rick with lewd interjections by Jimi Hendrix. Comfort comes back with a more confident version of "Tequila." When it's Greenspark's turn, the band wheezes, bumps and grinds its way through "Louie Louie," managing to achieve a sound as sleazy and wasted as the original Kingsmen recording. The boys' team is moved to join in, bellowing the legendary lyrics passed down by three decades of youths with one thing on their minds.

In the middle of the buffoonery, the distaff Indians emerge from the locker room to warm up. The Greenspark side of the auditorium jumps to its feet to greet them. The Comfort gallery counters with derision. Greenspark's boys bellow the scatological lyrics more loudly—Bither bounding onto a seat to pump his hips until a security guard waves him down.

Though minus her hardware, the Mutant is nevertheless a sight to stir the crowd. Her skull gleams with almost the same plastic quality as her mask. The hair on her unshaven leg is emphasized by the smoothness of the hairless one and the rose tattoo draws the eye to her knee. Once she discards her warm-up jacket, her sleeveless jersey reveals her tufted armpits and the tattoos on her arms.

The other starters—Michaud with a new hedgehog 'do, Nat with her razored swooshes, Figueroa with her nose stud, the Jandreau twins with their eyes made up with so much eyeliner it looks like warpaint, every Greenspark player exhibiting some visual warning sign—are almost as aggressive-looking as Gauthier.

While their band obliterates "Wipeout," a block of Comfort students mime gagging and retching but not in a critical review of the hashed musical performance. It's directed at the Mutant. Others indulge in catcalls at her.

She's oblivious, doing what Sam told to her to do. As the girls warm up, she is using her feet to learn something about the floor, looking for the sweet spots Sam recalls. Between tournaments and exhibitions, he's played this floor more than a dozen times, as often as he's used some of the courts at schools Greenspark meets regularly. She's only played it twice. While he's told her everything he can remember, he wants to be down there with her, telling her—showing her—what he knows about it.

She alley-oops a basket and glances up into the stands, looking for him. Imitating her, he double-pumps his fist. He gets a grin from her. It takes her a few seconds to realize he has given the signal to the bandleader for the latest prank. As the Greenspark band begins its next piece, there is puzzlement among the many, delighted laughter among the enlightened—Greenspark's players, the student body—as they recognize "The Bitch Is Back."

■ ■ ■

Running to small and blonde, the Comfort Condors don't look much like predators. They look cuddly. Their starting center is all of five-seven and she's the tallest. The point's barely five feet from her size-two Reeboks to the root of her French braid. She's like a china doll.

Todd pokes Sam in the ribs. "Number twelve, the point—I'm in lust," he says.

"What's new about that?" Rick wants to know.

Once the game is under way, though, the dolly falters in the face of the Mutant's offense. Greenspark gets on the board first and is up seven points before the Condors recover and get their undersized center past Nat to lay up their first two points. Little Number 12—Sam checks the book; her name is Heidi McCandless—settles down and goes to work. She is quick, determined and an excellent floor leader.

The Mutant harries her, harries them all half-crazy. Her eyes blaze depthlessly in the pale oval of her face, with its bizarre exoskeletal half-mask. Her perspiration suckers her uniform to her body and her skin gleams wet under the lights. She is electrical. The spark leaps between her and her teammates and they move with the darting flashing rapidity of a school of fish.

Nat Linscott seems to become taller and heavier as she blocks the Condor center. Everywhere the Condor guards move, there is a Jandreau twin, until it seems as if they have been cloned into a quartet. With her hair in its rigid halo, Deb Michaud is always somewhere relentlessly useful to the Mutant. Greenspark runs and runs and runs. The Condors pant like little birds, their economical little breasts fluttering rapidly. Tiring, they begin to be confusable. They look at each other, they look to McCandless, and find only reflections of their own glassy china doll eyes. Hypnotized, stunned, mind-fucked—they struggle to catch up and are still running, exhausted and zombie-eyed, when the final buzzer catches them thirteen points in arrears, 61–48.

The Greenspark Indian girls advance to the semifinals.

■ ■ ■

The light outside is going and the air comes into the lungs knife-sharp. Almost everybody else leaves the auditorium in search of a meal. Sam urges Deanie—headragged against the cold—onto the bus so she won't miss a celebratory outing with her teammates. He watches the departure—waving at her, at his folks, who are there for her now as much as himself, at the whole contingent of two basketball teams, band, cheerleaders and an assortment of coaches, school administrators, Laliberte and Liggott among them, and the other kids' parents. The kids are exuberant and noisy but under control. Liggott has all but Super Glued himself to Kevin Bither. The hammer's been down on Mouth since before the buses departed Greenspark.

Sam leaves his gym bag on one of the chairs that form the bench on the Greenspark side. A couple of guys wield push brooms across the floor—a fat man and a thin man, like a couple of comedians from jerky old silent pictures. They pause to watch him stepping over TV cables at the ends and stroll onto the boards. Fingers in jacket pockets, he quarters the floor, rocking on his toes at certain points, once stooping to pick up a popcorn kernel.

"Hey, Sam, how's it feel?" one of the sweepers asks as he draws near them.

The question breaks his concentration. He blinks and then nods affirmatively.

"Got a ball with you?" the other asks. "Go ahead. We won't tell anybody, you want to shoot some."

Surveying the cavernous room for signs of officials, he moves to his bag. Nobody around to become officious—all out chowing down, likely. Just the sweepers, the camera crews testing their vantages, some old farts lounging in the upper sections, a trio of idling cops watching a TV monitor where the local happy-news team is making weak jokes at each other. Ball gripped between his knees, he twists a rubber band around his hair.

The first kiss of the ball on the floor cracks the silence of waiting inside him. It's as if a second set of eyelids opens for him and he is awake to himself and the world around him for the first time in a very long while—what a strange illusion, as if the ball carried some hallucinatory potion absorbed through the skin! Up the court he moves with the ball, *bop she bop,* partnered to it as a polo player to his horse and mallet. It's like the dream, he suddenly remembers, and that's why it seems so hyperreal. How wonderful it would be if it really happened, the girls in their birthday suits, all for him. Amused with himself, he dances around the ball, dances it around him. Spinning, he lifts himself from the floor, gently taps rubber through nylon and lands weightlessly on his toes, sweet and light, in a smattering of applause from the handful of loiterers.

Sam is unaware of the old duffers in the bleachers, tongues stilled, now moved forward to the edges of their seat, or that the cops' attention has shifted from the monitor to the floor, or that cameras now track him. He is no more conscious of anything besides the permutations of ball, floor, net and himself than a dog with a Frisbee.

When he picks up his father in his peripheral vision, Reuben nods toward the clock. An hour and a quarter have slipped by. There are more people in the seats—came in to have a look-see and stayed—and now early arrivals staking places for the game.

"Come on," his father says, "I brought you some sesame noodles and some tea."

■ ■ ■

With Deanie in her gypsy headrag perched on the railing next to him, he eats a little of the take-out in an upper section of the bleachers. Indy is fussy with sore teeth and Pearl and Reuben have taken her to walk the concourses behind the stand, hoping to distract her from the discomfort in her gums. He gives Deanie most of his noodles and pulls her into his lap. They put their foreheads together. The fringe of her headrag tickles his eyelashes. And then it's time.

■ ■ ■

Time. Time. Time. The word reverberates in his mind. Time to go to the locker room, time to change, time to listen to Coach, time to line up, time to lope out and through the stupid hoop onto the floor, time to stretch, warm up, time to go into himself, find his focus and all very possibly for the last time. However it comes out, this is the last high school tournament he will ever play.

During the introductions on the floor, he shakes the hand of the older of the two brothers he observed in the bleachers. In uniform—Number 11, Scott Barry—looks bigger. His blue eyes are sharply intelligent and he has a hard, polite smile, the kind of perfect teeth that cost money and are invaluable for a man with sound bites in his future. Hairy forearms, hairy legs, hairy chest, tufts sprouting from the armholes of his jersey at the back— probably Barry is as hairy-assed as Dupre, the Indians' champion furbearer. In contrast to all that black wiry hair, the guy's white skin seems bloodless.

"Good luck," Sam says to Barry.

Barry grasps his hand with both hands in the extravagantly friendly shake of a televangelist about to lift a wallet and smiles graciously. "You'll need it, shitkicker."

Sam turns up the wattage of his own smile. "Eat me," he murmurs sweetly.

The grin vanishes from Barry's face and he spins away to trot back to his men.

"They're friendly," Sam advises Rick as they circle together.

Rick laughs. "Fuck'm. They'll like us even better then."

■ ■ ■

One thing Sam guessed right; Barry stinks. Everybody does, of course, with nerves and then with the physical effort, but this guy—oh my fuckness, Sam gasps, turning his face away from Number 11's pits, full in his face as Barry tries to block him. Feinting, Sam waits until Barry comes to ground again and then pumps it casually over his thick head of hair. He whips back his elbow as hard as he can into Sam's gut. As the ball drops through, Sam looks to the ref but the guy just sucks the whistle and stares at Sam's raised eyebrows. Nor does he seem to hear Coach's scream of outrage.

From the close study of game tapes, Greenspark knows that St. Gabriel's plays physically, fouling to the max. St. Gabe's coach regards a game in which four out of five of his starters are not in foul trouble in the last quarter as a halfhearted effort, it's said. Whether the rumors are true or not, it is clear St. Gabe's players regard fouling as an opportunity to inflict permanent injury on an opponent. They use their elbows, their knees, their toes, their fingers, their heads, every chance they get. They use the goddamn ball, shoving it into faces and guts. Sam himself subscribes to the belief if you are going to foul, by accident or design, you should make sure your opponent feels it—purely as a matter of creating respect—but he prefers finesse to thuggery.

Rick exits hobbling in the first quarter, his left ankle tromped by the younger of the Barry brothers. Though he returns in the second quarter to play the rest of the game—pissed off and nearly as nasty as the Archangels—his momentary absence sends a wobble through the offense. Rank is shy, not stupid. Having seen what happened to Rick, he's understandably nervous.

At the half, the good guys have the bandits down by seven points and Sam is still holding himself back, saving something for the stretch. Near the end of the third quarter, he succeeds in forcing Scott Barry to foul him twice within a minute, both times in scrambles at the post. The second time, Barry is so enraged, he jerks his knee into Sam's crotch, an act that even the whistle-suckers see. Sam curls up quietly on the floor and throws up on the official's black shoes, thinking sourly that the jokers who are always saying sometimes you gotta take one for the team ought to try it. Number 11 takes a technical foul and is ejected from the game. Sam repairs to the bench to contemplate the constancy of human frailty.

After Gramolini shoots the technical with his usual competence, play resumes with Skouros trying to replace Sam in the middle. Both teams seem to lose their control and the remainder of the third quarter is a clumsy mess all around. The Archangels close the score to a point.

Sam returns to the game as the fourth quarter begins. He still feels weak and the ache in his testicles flares with every movement. He falters and Rick takes his arm and demands to know if he is all right. He shakes him off and lopes into position.

Sam is at the post when the Archangels' centurion point drives past Billy and Todd. It's a crazy move, with the wall of Sam waiting for him and a ref ready to call a charging foul but he keeps on coming. Sam declines the seemingly inevitable collision. He slides to the side and the point man starts past him, his hands coming up with the ball to lay it up. On Sam's right the younger Barry leans into him. Sam goes up. Barry staggers forward. Just as air is visible between the point's fingers and the ball as he tries for the lay-up, Sam's hand collects the orange neatly and sends it back out on a long arc toward Rick, backpedaling toward the other end of the court.

The gears grind and shift as Rick's quick jump begins Greenspark's fourth-quarter drive. All at once the Archangels find themselves in a new game. They get rougher. It costs them in short order the younger Barry and two other starters. Looking their way from the huddle around Coach during the last time-out, Sam meets Scott Barry's furious stare, the icy blue eyes pitted darkly with the knowledge of defeat. Sam gives nothing back. Scott Barry's history.

Rick makes a shot from outside that earns them a last three and the final score is Greenspark, 75; St. Gabriel's, 62. As the boys pass each other to shake hands, Sam pauses to tug his crotch and then offers that particular hand to Scott Barry, along with a huge moronic grin.

"Good game!" he says, crushing Barry's hand as hard as he can.

Barry pales and attempts to withdraw his hand. Sam keeps right on pumping it.

"Fuck you," Barry mutters.

"Not a chance," Sam returns with a wink, "but I'm sure you'll find someone."

■ ■ ■

The joyful noise his teammates raise, the horseplay in the showers and the locker room are at once familiar and strange. It will never be just this way again. It isn't just his own high school career whispering past with the speed of tape whipping by a tapehead but the team itself is also in its terminal days.

Rick slaps his shoulders. "We did it! What do you think of that, Sambo!"

Sam tugs his shirt across his chest and gropes for a button. " 'Vanity,' " he says, with a smile, " 'all is vanity.' "

Rick shakes his head. "So? I don't give a shit. Why do you?"

"I'll never forget these theological discussions of ours," Sam assures Rick.

"Right," Rick answers. "Blow me."

Sam grins. "I've already got a date but I can fix you up with Scott Barry."

Rick blows him a mocking kiss.

Exiting the lockers, Sam climbs the stands to shake hands with his father and kiss Pearl and Indy, before he joins Deanie in the seats the kids from Greenspark have taken over to watch the next game. Kinsale beats South Portland by a free throw in the last ten seconds and by then it's going for eleven and they won't reach Greenspark until one, nevermind home.

■ ■ ■

The boys' game flickers from the monitor at the front of the bus. Sam's unauthorized workout prior to the game, caught by the idling television crews, is used as a lead-in. It provides an opportunity for the commentators to recap his high school career and speculate upon his and Greenspark's expected performance in the tournament. Since his freshman year, Sam has been one of a handful of state-wide stars. This year's acquisition of an earring— exchanged for a stud at game time—not only increases the visibility that size and talent and his ponytail give him but reassuringly confirms he is merely another teenage with the same need for tribal signals as any other. He could be anybody's kid—and is, of course.

Everyone groans when Barry knees him. Sam shrugs off the chorus of rude commentary that follows to concentrate on the game itself. Only when it is over, in the break while the tape of the girls' game is being loaded into the machine, does he allow himself to think ahead.

The Greenspark teams have passed the first round. There are still two more games between each team and a regional championship, and if they make it, a third to settle the state title. The boys have a week to prepare to meet the Kinsale Trojans. Deanie and the girls will meet St. Mary's Crusaders on Thursday. Until then, there'll be practice and more practice. The next one will be a waste for most of them if the party plans he's hearing come off.

The old longing to be part of it burbles up. He wonders briefly if he could take Deanie to a party and count on her resisting temptation. No, he decides, and he doesn't need to tempt himself either. Immediately he plunges into gloom. She's going to be ripped at him when he tells her they're going home to bed.

But she never asks about partying. She gets into the truck and cuddles up to him and goes to sleep without a word and doesn't even wake up when he carries her into the house.

41

∎ ∎ ∎

Big Yellow Piglets in a Double Row, the buses all park together outside the Bangor Civic Center. From her window, the Mutant spots Sam's truck across the parking lot, nosing for a slot. Ignoring the faces raised to stare at her as spectators plod their way past the bus toward the auditorium, she ties off her headrag decisively and scoots between the seats to find the dub that skittered away during the ride.

Once she had been afraid the kids at school would make sport of her and 'god. And they did and still do, though not perhaps with the same viciousness—people can get used to anything, as they have her face. It all feels false, another reflection in a mirror. The real Deanie is invisible, as if her body with its scars and tattoos and chains and plastic mask is a kind of hologram of herself. Sometimes it makes her feel safe. Sometimes it just makes her want to feel and see if she is still there or has finally disappeared entirely. She's not sure she wants to know what they might do to her if miraculously they suddenly saw.

The other girls troop toward the auditorium. The bus is empty, the driver outside talking to another driver. Shoving the cassette into her duffel, she stays crouched between the seats, gathering herself to face the stares, and beyond that, to center herself for the

game. The bus shifts and she feels 'god walking down the aisle—
deaf and blind she would know his presence by means she cannot
entirely enumerate, subliminal perceptions of the dimensions of
space he takes up, the way he blocks a draft and vibrates a floor
with his weight.

Stooping over her, he massages the back of her neck, the span
of his palm and fingers engulfing the narrow stalk, the protuberant bones like a tightwoven string of bulbs.

She arches her neck against his hand.

"Worried?" he asks.

Her eyes crinkle with amusement. "Not about this bunch of
pussies."

Her coach climbs the bus steps and squints up the aisle. "What
are you waiting on, Gauthier, a printed invitation?"

"Be right along, Coach," Sam answers for her.

He straightens up and looks down at her, hand extended to take
hers and help her up. Staring up at him, she touches him on impulse and he starts.

"Jesus, Deanie."

Grasping his hipbones, she drags herself up the length of his
legs until she is on her feet, her face in his sternum. She presses her
thigh between his knees.

"Easy," he murmurs. "Coach'll be back here with a switch,
looking for you. Come on, it's going to be all right."

■ ■ ■

The multiple drums of the Greenspark band advise misleadingly
that "The Lion Sleeps." St. Mary's Crusaders, in blue and silver,
mesmerized from the tip, are still wide-eyed and dazed as the female aborigines from Greenspark make martyrs of them. Greenspark Indians, a walkaway 60 to St. Mary's Crusaders' 41—crunch,
crunch, yum yum.

Sam breathes a sigh of relief.

■ ■ ■

Rocketing up for the tip, he feels he is the soul of reason. Ball
to Rick, Rick to basket. Up and in. Hello, Trojans. *Soul of reason,* he telepaths to the wide boy in his face, *On the roll of the
season.* No reaction. The boy isn't tuned in. Possibly it's his haircut. Shaved close to the crown, where the wide boy's had the
barber—sheepshearer—leave an uneven clump of dirty-blond that

looks like dead, frozen grass that someone's been sliding on at the tag end of February. Boonie-ramp.

The wide boy has a partner, a lean senior with a goatee and no-color eyes. Defending, they double-team Sam, making him work for it enough for him to enjoy outwitting them. On offense, it is the wide boy who is the real threat once he gets in close. The senior likes the outside and shoots threes with depressing regularity. The pair of them will have to be neutralized. Fortunately, the wide boy is slow; they can run him into the floor. Watching Todd swipe the ball from the senior with the goatee, Sam confirms a weakness he saw in the game tapes: Billy Goat Gruff has a balloon for an ego—big, hollow, too easily pricked. Gruff has to stop and beat himself up over the turnover as if there weren't another three quarters to decide this game. His anger will be his downfall.

One by one, Sam's starters flash him signals that confirm the original strategy and they begin to dismantle the Trojans. Sam guns steadily until a few minutes into the third, when the Trojans collapse. He comes out for a rest and Skouros does well enough to leave him in until the buzzer. Greenspark Indians, 85, Kinsale Trojans, 62.

On the way to the lockers Sam evades the media but they are waiting for his exit, wanting comment on the fact both Greenspark teams have now advanced to the regional finals tomorrow. Cooperation with the media is part of his job but this year the coaches have consented to his silence, and to Deanie's. It would be too easy for her to become a focus, with her mask and her scar and her outrageous bald head, and leave the rest of her team feeling ignored. He shakes his head and shoulders his way through them. Winning is statement enough. Let some other kids have some spotlight.

In the stands, he finds Deanie with the other girls. The rest of his team settles around them, filling the rows with the green of their letter jackets. They stay to watch Castle Rock narrowly defeat Fremont. Above them, the Castle Rock banners are disorienting, the wrong colors to be under, and they are aware of being surrounded by Castle Rock fans. Who are aware of them in their Greenspark letter jackets. It takes some effort on Sam's part to keep the inevitable ribbing back and forth good-natured.

■ ■ ■

Good copy: both Greenspark teams are one win away from the regional title and in the boys' division, the struggle will be with traditional rival Castle Rock. The defending state and regional champ Greenspark boys will smite the Rock, the sports commentators predict, but Bricker has the edge against the distaff Indians. While the girls in green and silver have Gauthier, Bricker has a noloss record, three six-footers and an awesome senior point guard named Merrilee Constantine. She is built like a fireplug, is cuter than an Olympic gymnast, and is supposed to be the best floor leader in the state.

Freezing the picture on Constantine's exultant face, Deanie gives her a Bronx cheer and clicks off the game tape of the Bricker win over Oxford Hills.

"Relax," Sam tells her, "you got something she ain't got."

Deanie takes his hands out from under her shirt. "Right. My own plastic faceguard and a busted face to wear it over. That's a big edge."

"I meant me."

"And I'm supposed to sneak you onto the floor? Who are you going to play this game as? Billie? You'll need a nose stud, a buzz cut and more mustache."

Sam picks up the clicker and zaps on the TV. He rewinds the tape a couple of frames and replays it, freezing it again on Constantine. Seizing Deanie by the shoulders, he holds her head between his flattened palms and directs her gaze at the screen.

"Pay attention now," he tells her. "Take a good look at this girl. I will tell you three things about her that will win your game for you."

"Right," Deanie says. "I'm all ears."

"No you aren't, thank the living Jesus." Sam rewinds the tape. "Watch. She's gonna pass the ball left, move up court, and take it back, then she's gonna feint passing it, drive inside, and pass it right then, to her big guard, Number 10. She pulls it five times in this game. By the fifth time, Oxford Hills is starting to doubt that fake pass but they never got on top of it. You break that pass the first time she tries it and it'll break her confidence."

"Promise?" Deanie teases.

"Yup. Anybody can be beaten if they lose their nerve. One reason you work hard to be the best is so the people you're up against see right away you are. You make'm believe they can't beat you, and they can't."

"Right on, Coach. What's the second tip?"

"She pronates her left ankle, the taped one, when she pivots. If you move on her just as she pivots, you can catch her off balance. Make her hold the ball low and you can take it away underneath while she's trying to get on top of that ankle."

"Nasty guy," Deanie says admiringly. "You don't have some way of figuring out when she's got PMS, do you? What's the third secret?"

Sam grins. "She's never had an orgasm in her life."

Deanie whacks him with a cushion but he gets his hands up in time.

■ ■ ■

The white flare of a television strobe paints the Mutant's mask and for an instant, it's as if the flesh were stripped to the bone of her face. There is a fluid darkness at the lower edge that makes Sam sick to his stomach. The illusion passes and he registers the bite of his own nails in his palms. She rolls her head and her coach, crouched over her, speaks to her. Deanie's fingers fumble toward the mask, trail along the edge. The crowd in the auditorium buzzes quietly, waiting to find out how bad it is.

Merrilee Constantine hovers near Deanie. She looks to be near tears.

"I'm going down there," Sam mutters.

"Fuck you are," Rick says, hand on Sam's forearm.

Sam is still trying to absorb what has happened. A couple of minutes into the second quarter, the Mutant dove under Constantine to steal the ball, carried it to the floor in a scramble with Constantine and one of those six-foot Bricker guards and took Constantine's elbow in the face. She was flat faster than the big soft tires on a Corvette.

She sits up slowly, with her coach supporting her, holding something to her nose. A bloody rag. It's her nose she's bumped, just her nose, Sam thinks. Not her face. The wound didn't open. The faceguard worked. She leaves the floor, to the customary hand given the injured, and slumps in a chair with an ice pack on her face. Her mask is up on her skull and her tunic is splattered with dark blotches. Constantine stares after her, wringing her hands.

The Mutant lifts the ice pack and her eyes find Sam. She grins and then disappears behind the ice again. The AC stoops over her to stuff her nose with cotton balls.

She has succeeded in frustrating Constantine repeatedly in her favored fake-out and trapping her into two turnovers before the Bricker star adjusted her balance. Since then, it's been a slugfest between the two girls' teams, point answered by point, brilliant play on both sides that has kept them trading the lead the whole game.

It's no surprise to see the Mutant yanking her mask down, going back into the game after the half. Sam groans. Watching is almost more than he can bear. He's close enough to make out her swollen nose, with cotton visible in the nostrils. Her eye sockets are beginning to look bruised. He wishes they would swell up and close entirely so she could be taken out of the game.

As the Mutant comes back into the game, Constantine reaches out, touches her forearm and asks if she's okay. She grins and laughs. Her teeth are bloody. Constantine blanches.

Every time Constantine makes a move, there's the Mutant, blood leaking occasionally from her nose, her eyes blazing from their darkening sockets. She has to keep her mouth open; her breath must stink from the blood. Constantine falters, feints, tries everything and just can't bring herself to be as aggressive as she needs to be. She shakes her head, calls time, tries to pull herself together, get some pump from her coach, and for a little while she gives the Mutant a run for her money.

Then Billie rips the ball away from Bricker's center at the post and makes a long pass down the court to Deanie, who has drifted far from center court to make this play. Constantine has followed her and races to get between her and the net. When Deanie reaches up and collects the long pass and pivots on her, Constantine stumbles back in panic and sprawls on her tailbone, legs akimbo, her face crumbling. The crowd gasps as the Mutant's shot sails to the net. Sam sees the dark droplets spraying Constantine's tunic before the Mutant settles on the balls of her feet, her hand flying to cover her nose, blood gouting through her fingers.

As the Mutant leaves the game again, Constantine wipes at the drops on her white jersey. She looks rockier than the Mutant, who is sitting there under ice, making wisecracks to the AC. When the third quarter ends, Constantine is going through the motions and the Jandreau girls are hot. They put Greenspark ahead by six points. The Bricker players struggle to answer them. The center makes two points and Constantine is fouled and misses both her free throws. As the Bricker star turns away, wiping her palms and looking depressed, the Mutant comes back into the game. The look on Constantine's face is so shocked and woeful, Sam feels sorry for the girl.

"Jesus, she's scary," Rick says of Deanie. "She comes back like Freddy Krueger. Fucking Freddy Krueger." He looks at Sam with a new admiration in his eyes.

In the final three minutes of the game, Deanie Gauthier propels her team from a three-point deficit to a five-point lead. Faking out Bricker's four-guard chase of the ball, Deanie passes it behind her to Melanie Jandreau, who bounces it to Billie Figueroa for a base-line jumper, four seconds before the buzzer. Constantine reclaims the ball and wings it the length of the court to bang the glass with the kiss of defeat. Greenspark's band plows into "We Are the Champions" like a jetliner into a foggy mountainside.

As the kids on the bench erupt onto the floor, followed by the crowd, Constantine stands briefly alone, fingers spread on her hip-bones, blinking back tears, blowing a strand of hair out of her eyes. Her center lopes up and throws her arms around her and she bursts into tears.

The Mutant is lifted, laughing, to her teammates' shoulder. Her nose is leaking again. She slides down into the maelstrom of people engaged in promiscuous hugging.

Sam watches from the emptying stands. He should be in the locker room with his teammates, changing up. This is her moment. He has to see it but he can't join in. His presence on the court would take attention away from her.

The Mutant emerges from the mob on the floor and makes her way to Merrilee Constantine and embraces her. A thousand camera flashes seem to explode simultaneously and again a few minutes later, as Deanie is necklaced with one of the nets. Of the many memorable images of this championship, it is difficult to judge which is most striking—that of the opposing point guards, both in tears, both laughing, embracing each other, or the one of the Greenspark girls and their plaque, in which Deanie's mask, pulled down, reflects melting diamonds of light through the crumpled net around her neck.

■ ■ ■

Glittering with sweat and tears, the girls raise exultant faces to the boys emerging onto the floor through the gauntlet they have formed. As Sam passes Deanie, they give each other high fives.

"Come on, people," she shouts and the others pick it up.

As the boys warm up, Sam listens to the music of the court: squeak of high-tops, thunk of the glass, rattle of the hoop, the rimshot whisper of the net, all riding the bop-she-bop beat of the ball. Each player is a unique source of percussion on the floor but also moves in relationship to the other players, as each team moves in relation to the other and the goals. He hears a tight performance building in the oiled precision of the sounds and it pleases him.

He picks his jersey away from his chest in a nervous gesture and blows air up his face. Time. It's time. A time. One of the ones *for* something. Keeping and casting away, and the putting away of childish things. It seems to him the passage of time is speeding up. He is leaving something behind. He is rushing toward something else.

The Rockets' forward, Seeds, steals the tip Sam knocks to Kevin Bither. Clutterbuck makes the first lay-up and the Castle Rock stands are immediately hysterical. Todd Gramolini takes the rebound to the Greenspark net. Seeds lopes alongside Sam, who offers his hand in congratulation.

Seeds wears Number 40. He grins and shows his braces. He is an ugly kid, loopy mouth, eyes too close together, nose like a potato, milk-blue skin that looks as if it might sunburn under a nightlight, but he also looks like a hell of a good shit. Quick, too. Come a long way during the season. He and Lucas Priest work well together.

All of the Rock's starters seem to be in a good mood. Nobody desperate, everybody confident, ready to take advantage of anything they can get from the Indians. They'll have to, to have a chance. Here they are, deciding a regional championship, and both teams are so loose, it seems like an exhibition.

Playing against each other during the regular season, they are familiar with each others' strengths and weaknesses. Greenspark is, on the whole, bigger, more experienced—the Big Machine, the state champs. It has Sam Styles. The Slammer, the Sambot. Mr. God-To-You. The biggest job is to get around Sam Styles. Given this is the coda to his high school career, they expect him to be pumped for veins in his teeth. He can't be neutralized—bigger and better teams have tried and failed—but if they can cripple the rest of the Greenspark team, they have a chance to keep up with Sam and with a little luck, that's the game. Only need one point to take it.

■ ■ ■

Gleeful moments into it, they all know they are playing a beautiful game, a remarkable game. Castle Rock is playing over its head. Greenspark meets the challenge with delighted bravado. The Rockets lose the lead immediately to Greenspark but remain unruffled. The Indians take the ball, letting Woods, Gramolini, Bither and Kasten work the pick and roll or the outside shot, while Lucas presses Sam steadily, keeping him occupied, giving him a workout. That's okay; when their positions are reversed and Lucas is trying to get to his own post, the Slammer's walling it off. His own count likely to be held to single digits, Lucas grins and shrugs and takes care of business. The Rock picks up its first three fouls just trying to get around Sam, forcing the Rockets outside. Seeds and the Rock's best three-shooter, Nick Young, summon up miracles to get the ball into the hoop.

Once Lucas tries to get by Sam at the post and loses his footing. He skids and falls against Sam, who helps him to his feet and pats his ass and the crowd applauds. At the line, Sam shoots, his hands following the arc of the ball as it drops through, and Lucas, grinning, repeats the breaking wave of the motion with his own hands, and raises an approving thumb to Sam. It is an amiable, sweet-tempered performance.

During the half, Sam sightlines Deanie in the stands, with the other girls, not far from his folks. She's got a couple of shiners and her nose looks puffy and sore but she is radiant.

Rick's ankle is bothering him. Mangling a pass into a turnover, he limps down court. He shakes his head at Sam. Coach flicks a wrist at Rank. Billy just about explodes off the bench, he is so eager to get into the game. It is quickly apparent that the Big Machine is still running without a hitch. Kasten, Sam notes, is working better with Rank than he does most of the time with Rick.

Eyeing the clock, Lucas begins to lean on Sam. He draws Fairbrother down to double-team Sam. Toward the end of the quarter, Lucas suddenly realizes that Sam is playing tarbaby with him. Not only is he diverting Lucas's attention as well as Fairbrother's, while the rest of the Indians pound away, driving up the lead, but for each of the two fouls he manages to draw Sam into, Priest is nabbed for one of his own in return.

Lucas glances at the clock. He spits out a disgusted country, "Oh shit!"

Still there is scrap in the Rockets. They come out in the fourth with a wild who-wants-to-live-forever gleam in their eyes and play the best they ever have. There is a method in their madness; Lucas Priest crowds Sam into his third foul and for an instant, as Lucas grins his redneck's crooked-tooth grin at him, Sam is royally pissed off at himself. It's stupid, this late in the game and with a twelve-point margin, but he doesn't want to foul out, not of this game. Lucas steps to the charity stripe and makes his shots with the same deliberately mocking following arc as Sam used earlier.

Todd takes the rebound, passes to Rank, who starts it toward Greenspark's paint. Sam and Lucas move in the same direction, together.

"Sammy, you got a lace untied," Lucas kids.

"Lucas, you're tripping on your dick," Sam answers.

"Temper, temper," Lucas teases.

Todd makes a nice jump from the key and Clutterbuck claims the rebound. Kasten moves to strip Clutterbuck, the ball goes loose, and in a second, the players are in a snarl. Sam is sandwiches by Lucas and the other guy guarding him, trying not to inadvertently foul again. In that kind of free-for-all, the refs have their choice of fouls; it is random bad luck who catches one. Or gets caught. Lucas gets caught, fouling not Sam but Kevin Bither in the melee.

Mouth's first line shot wobbles around the rim forever and falls off and Seeds moves for it. Sam bops the ball from underneath and Lucas surges for it as it sails free. He trips on Seeds and his momentum carries him into Sam. One flailing hand grabs Sam by the wrist and the heel of one palm drives into Sam's mouth.

Coach is on his feet, demanding a foul call as Sam staggers back a step. His hand goes to his mouth, comes away red from a split in his lower lip. Lucas extends his hands in a who me? gesture.

The official calls an intentional on Lucas, bringing the Castle Rock fans to their feet in outrage. Castle Rock's coach is already there, his AC trying to restrain him from lunging onto the floor.

For once that night, Lucas Priest loses his composure. His face closes up in misery and his mouth tightens in a grimace of pain. Head down, he turns slowly toward the bench. Sam lopes to catch up with him, and seizes his hand to shake, an act that probably prevents the Castle Rock stands from showering the floor with debris in protest.

Lucas accepts Sam's hand draggingly.

"You were great," Sam tells him.

"Oh fuck you," Lucas blurts, eyes welling.

Sam breaks into a grin before he realizes Lucas isn't kidding around.

"I'm sorry," he mutters but Lucas brushes past him without another word.

Lucas's bitterness feels like poison, like bad luck.

Sam seeks out some glimpse of Deanie in the crowd. They are all singing "Na Na Na Na, Hey Hey Goodbye" and she is singing it with them, jumping up and down, fists pumping over her head in a little victory dance. Then she cups her hands around her mouth and calls something else and he can't hear it over the riot of noise but he knows what it is: *This ain't no disco. This ain't no foolin' around.*

Rick comes back into the game for the final moments. "We got this dicked," he advises Sam with a happy grin.

Clutterbuck knocks in a three-pointer with four seconds to go, making the final score Greenspark, 88, Castle Rock, 75; but the game's been over, the regional title settled, since Lucas Priest fouled out.

The Indians are already on their feet and leap upward as one at the buzzer, then flow around Sam. Almost immediately, though, he shoulders his way through his teammates toward the Castle Rock bench, and this time Lucas Priest, whose face is red with the effort not to cry, takes Sam's hand like a drowning man. Sam grabs his neck and yanks Lucas against him, and the two boys embrace roughly, as in sudden grief. When they separate, Sam raises Lucas's hand with his, in a gesture of triumph, and Lucas laughs shakily, and shakes Sam's hand again.

"This was your game," Sam tells him. "We won but this was Castle Rock's game."

A little while later someone thrusts a microphone in Lucas Priest's face and asks him what Sam Styles said to him and he repeats it, word for word, with the amazed grin of a small child who has just been handed a five-dollar bill.

42

∎ ∎ ∎

Not Since Sonny Jesus Was in short pants has Port Rose competed for a state title. All of Port Rose is in the stands, finally—a relief to the Twin Cities' cops, who have had to cope with the confusion of a couple of thousand Roseporters who have never before encountered a middle turn lane.

In the upper tier of seats on the Greenspark side, Sam Styles climbs into the section the boys' team has staked out. None of them enter the seats by the normal bipedal act of walking; they clamber over the backs, hop on the seats, and splash bonelessly into their chosen roosts.

The floor below shines like a field of gold. Used for the past several seasons by the state university at Orono, its paint is sapphire blue. It bears the university athletic program's mascot, a cartoon bear cub's head.

With his earring, a scrub of Roger Clemens–style beard around his mouth, and wearing the Mutant's brocade headrag, Sam is sufficiently piratical to amuse himself and inspire his teammates—as soon as they saw how it looked on him, they all hit up girls for bandannas and scarves and to a man have ragtied their heads.

Port Rose's colors are maroon and white by the book, but they look like raspberry and cream to Sam, a thought that makes him hungry. The food groups represented at the food kiosk are steamed hot dogs, nachos with hot cheese, popcorn, potato chips and candy bars, coffee and cola. The smells drift up the stairway from the concourse below, eliciting a rumble in Sam's stomach, but he still craves raspberries and cream. Fortunately, there is distraction in the girls coming out for their warm-ups.

In the creamy-raspberry flesh, the Whalers are a little more substantial than on the grainy videotape supplied by a Greenspark alumnus living within satellite-dish range of Port Rose's district. One of the Port's starters is a six-footer—Stacey Gould, Number 6. A serious young woman is Stacey Gould, with cross-shaped studs in her ears, and a whole congregation of backwoods holyrollers praying for her success.

One of the guards, Tara Pope, is a five-ten junior who looks as if she must go one-eighty. She's got some belly on her, but also a lot of visible muscle in her legs and arms. Her stats and the game tapes make it clear the weight doesn't slow her down any—and that she doesn't hesitate to drop it on an opponent if she can. A sidebar in the paper reports she's saving for college by pulling lobster pots with her old man on the weekends.

Two of the Whalers' starting guards are first cousins, Kelly and Heather Alley, both seniors with letters in track and field hockey. They don't look much alike but their stats are comparable and impressive.

The fifth starter, Vonda Alley, is a distant cousin of Kelly and Heather—and in fact of Tara and Stacey, because everybody in Port Rose is everybody else's cousin to some degree. Vonda, playing forward, is one of those bird-boned girls who look like a strong wind would carry her away but who somehow wind up working backbreaking twenty-hour days, birthing five or six yowens, burying a couple of husbands and living to be ancient. At three this morning, Vonda Alley sat straight up in bed and screamed *Gauthier!*

In Greenspark's road colors, the girls look—to Sam's appreciative eye anyway—totally savage, relentlessly bad. High-tops make the Greenspark girls' legs look muscular and sturdy. They have scabs on their knees and shins from floorburns. Most of them have taped ankles or knees or both. These girls sweat, the damp darkening the armpits of their jerseys and spreading in deltas from the cleavages of their breasts and buttocks. When angry or hurt, their faces redden, their mouths get wobbly and their noses run. Then they pick themselves up and go back to work.

Strutting past the tight-lipped girls from Port Rose, the Mutant's dark gaze smokes the Whalers and sweeps over the stands, looking for him. She turns up her fists, pulls them back slightly, smiles slightly.

"They're dead," Rick hoots. He elbows Sam to make the point. "They're fucked. You see the look in Gauthier's eyes. She's taking down names. Be heads going through that hoop tonight."

On Sam's other side, Todd grunts. "Don't be so sure. I hear Nat's got bad cramps."

"Period cramps? How'd you hear that?" Rick demands.

Todd shrugs. "Got my sources."

"Right," Rick agrees. "Your ass."

■ ■ ■

On the floor the Mutant drapes an arm over Nat Linscott's shoulder. "How ya doin'?"

Nat rolls her eyes. "Yucky. The Motrin isn't helping much."

"Shit. You ever tried booberry for it?"

"Big help, Gauthier," Billie Figueroa objects. "What do you think, we're going to ask if anybody in the crowd's got a number on them and then Nat's gonna squat there and smoke it."

The Mutant grins. "If your mom had a kitty over your hair, Nat, I wonder what she'd drop if you did a little weed right here. Hey, you know what helps me with cramps? Getting off."

The other girls groan in unison.

"Sure," Nat says. "Lend me Sam. We'll duck under the bleachers for a quickie."

"Right, right," Melissa Jandreau puts in impatiently. "Maybe if you move around some, it'll let go, Natski."

Nat shrugs. "Got no choice."

■ ■ ■

Nose to chin with Stacey Gould, Nat looks a little transparent around the edges. Gould controls the tip but Heather Alley can't get a grip on it and Melanie Jandreau has it away from her as quick as a cat takes a bird. The ball flies from one M cross court to the other M, and thence to the Mutant. Vonda Alley waves her arms in front of the Mutant, who stops dead and rolls her eyes. Tara Pope teams with Vonda to box the Mutant on the line. As

Pope hovers, legs and arms akimbo to keep the Mutant trapped, Nat and Billie peel off to come in behind Pope and Vonda Alley. Pope sneaks a peek at them. When Gauthier sees the tiny shift in Pope's eyes, she sinks suddenly and squirts the ball through the distracted guard's knees to Billie. And Billie's gone, racing toward the Greenspark net, with Pope and Vonda Alley in pursuit. Gould is positioned to block her at the net, with Heather and Kelly facing off with the M & M's. The Mutant spurts down the outside past Billie, the ball flashes between the two girls, and she rockets up, for two points right from the line.

Rocked, the Whalers founder. Greenspark racks ten points—Melissa for four, Billie for four, Nat for two on the foul line after Kelly Alley grabs her wrist during a jumper—before Tara Pope gets Port Rose on the board with a three. Attempts to double-team Gauthier are quickly countered and she moves the ball with a demonic slipperiness to the other Indians. The Whalers blow their hair out of their eyes and take a time-out right after Gould finally makes her outside shot.

The game steadies down. Slowly, the Roseporters struggle out of the hole into which they have fallen, making a vital shot here and again, managing to block Greenspark there and again. At the end of the first quarter, the immediate numbers don't show the effort—23–19 in the Indians' favor.

■ ■ ■

Sam doesn't like Nat Linscott's pasty color. She's missed her last three tries and made a turnover on a backcourt violation. A few seconds later, Tara Pope charges into her and knocks her to the floor.

"Oh fuck," Todd groans, "you see that truck hit Nat? Oh shit, she'll never walk again."

"Hell of a tackle," Rick agrees. "We could use some weight like that on the football team. She's got an ass you could hide a missile launcher under."

"Or in," Kevin Bither says from the other side of Todd. "I got one right—"

Todd yanks Bither's headrag down over his eyes to shut him up.

Nat goes to the bench to recover and Deb Michaud comes in for her and a moment later the quarter ends.

Greenspark begins the half with a demoralizing run—twelve unanswered points. The girls from Port Rose go to a time-out. Vonda

Alley smears tears across her rose-petal cheeks. Hands dropping to her knees, she half-crouches at the edge of the circle around her coach. She cocks her head and blinks up at the ceiling.

As the Whalers trot back onto the floor, Vonda and the Mutant pass each other. Gauthier's hand falls on Vonda's bony little hip in a reassuring pat. Vonda stares after the Mutant as Gauthier backs away, and spins toward her teammates, clapping her hands and calling out to them.

Port Rose comes back, with some help from an off-balance pass between the M & M's. When Melissa loses it to Kelly Alley's quick hands, Melanie goes rigid with fury at her sister. Melissa bugs her eyes and thrusts out her lower lip, repulsing the blame. While the pair of them are fuming at each other, Kelly is waltzing to the Port Rose net. Gauthier shouts at Melanie, who is supposed to be on Kelly, as she and Deb move to try to fill the gap. In the time it takes the Jandreau twins to get themselves back into the game, Kelly gets the ball to her cousin and Heather shoots it from outside.

That three ignites Port Rose. Their three-shooters come alive, breaking the defense inside the paint simply by blooping in over it. When the third consecutive three goes in for the Whalers, the Mutant calls a time-out. Greenspark readjusts its defense to control the outside shooters. Blocked outside, the Whalers go inside.

The Whaler offense doesn't go unanswered. The Mutant, Billie Figueroa and Melissa Jandreau rack points steadily. Deb Michaud misses her first two tries for field goals. When she washes out at the foul line, she is visibly upset. Just before the end of the third, the Whalers break into the lead by two points.

Nat Linscott replaces Michaud. She and the Mutant begin to take control of the game. The struggle becomes intense and stays that way. Out of tiredness and desperation, people begin to make mistakes. Sometimes the others are quick enough to take advantage; other times, the fumble is fumbled, the advantage lost before it can be taken. Nat suddenly reels and staggers and bolts from the floor as her coach calls time. The assistant coach follows her. Before Deb goes in for her, the AC comes back to say Nat's being sick.

Michaud shows her stuff this time. For five minutes she is scary, she and the Mutant, and the whole tenor of play becomes tighter, as if every player had refocused. Nat reappears to sit, pale and sweating, on the bench. When Melissa Jandreau fouls out, Nat comes back in. In a moment, Greenspark spreads its lead to ten again and the Whalers know it is beyond catching up. Still, they have cut it again to six before the buzzer. The Greenspark Indians are the State Class A Schoolgirl Champions, 1991.

■ ■ ■

Immediately the PA system booms a reminder to the celebrants that another game is going to be played on this floor tonight but that doesn't keep the stands from emptying almost completely onto it. The only people who stay in their seats are folks from Derry, come early to watch the girls' game in which they have no stake.

Sam finds Deanie and lifts her out of the mob to give her hugs and kisses. He doesn't want to let go of her but it happens, they are holding each other by both hands and then one hand and then there's somebody between them and he's pushed away, and then Rick Woods is tugging at his shirttails, reminding him it's past time for them to be changing up.

■ ■ ■

He sees her again as the girls pass them on the way to the locker rooms, after the ceremonies are over. She sees him, too, but it's just for a fraction of a second, like she's in a jet climbing at two hundred miles an hour and he's on the ground, five thousand feet below. It's a very new, scary sensation, being shrunk into a miniature of himself, who has always been the giant. He passes her the borrowed headrag and she is caught in the slipstream of whooping, shrieking girls.

At the locker door, she pivots and calls back, " 'god, you're looking monstrous."

He grins shyly and touches his hair. Before they left the house in the morning, she plaited it into a triple spine of knobs that begins at the front and bumps down the back of his head to the base of his neck.

At the unveiling in the locker room, Rick's reaction is typical of his teammates. "Check out the Slammer's 'do! It's bad!"

" 'spose you'll be shaving yourself bald next," Coach glooms.

"Dreads," Sam teases him. "Going for dreadlocks next."

Rick is even more delighted. "Rasta! Rasta Sam!"

"Dreadlocks? What the hell is dreadlocks?" Coach is totally mystified.

■ ■ ■

Sam lopes onto the floor, the boards gone gold beneath his big and educated feet. Above him the roof of light, to either side the walls of people, the hoops beckoning in their eager stances, the raucous bands in his ears, he knows he is not dreaming—and yet, living out the dream of countless boys and girls, he is.

Because East is home this year, Greenspark wears green and silver and the Ferrymen wear home whites, trimmed with Derry's silver and orange. The Derry team is a tall one, with four starters six feet or over. Three starters are seniors. All of them were part of the previous season's team that nearly took the whole shebang. Clean-shaven to a man, they all have their hair shaved up the sides to a cropped tussock. They could be cadets at some quasi-military institution, being stamped into a uniform mold.

Top gunner for the Ferrymen is a senior, Phil Malenfant, five-ten, playing point. Malenfant's quick as spit on a hot stove. He wears power shorts under his uniform in the style currently fashionable in the NBA. Malenfant is nearly at the two-thousand-point mark in four years of high school play. At center is Shawn Godfrey, another senior, six-five, and not far behind Malenfant in his high school point count. Godfrey fixes lashless pale blue eyes on Sam to flash a laser challenge as the two shake hands during the introductions. The other guards are Mark Tozier, Steven Starbuck and Jesse Blood, a formidable trio of gunslingers.

Facing Godfrey for the tip, it hits Sam this kid is scared. Maybe it's the stakes, maybe it's him but it's there, in the trickle of sweat at the base of Godfrey's throat and the almost imperceptible tic in the jaw. Maybe there is an extra edge of sharpness in the kid's perspiration that his nose is reporting to him. Sam smiles at him. Godfrey twitches like an animal on the verge of bolting. Okay, Sam thinks. Play it the way you like.

They rise together fluidly with the rising ball.

■ ■ ■

From Sam's tip, the ball falls toward Rick but suddenly he's shoved aside by Malenfant. Malenfant drives hard for the bucket and the other four Ferrymen blitzkrieg into the Greenspark defense, intent on smashing it. Greenspark has rehearsed for this event. Recovering instantly, Rick moves with Malenfant, forcing his drive one way and then the other and slowing him down. By the time the Ferrymen's point is at the three-point line, the rest of the

Greenspark players have stuck themselves to his cohorts and Sam Styles is at low post. There is no daylight to be seen.

Malenfant hesitates, debating a try for a three, and suddenly goes for it, but Rick is right there in front of him and the instant the ball spurts from the point's hands, Rick is up and after it, deflecting it toward Todd Gramolini, as Todd peels away from Starbuck. He receives it, spins, and passes it overhead to Sam, already rising to drive it up. Sam keeps on going with the ball and taps it through from above, to the screams of the crowd. He doesn't touch the rim but descends, knees bent to absorb the shock, almost gently.

The ball drops with Sam; Godfrey snatches it and spins around to find Sam there, along with Tim Kasten. Godfrey goes underneath to Malenfant but Rick dives on the ball as it passes, squirts it to Tim, who lays it up. Trying to stop him, Godfrey buffets Kasten's right ear, and the first foul is called.

Over the crowd sounds, Sam can hear the Derry coach screaming at his players: *Look out for the ball! Don't foul! D, Play the D!* His own coach hunches forward in his chair, as if thrusting his head out over his knees would give him a markedly better view of the game.

Derry has spent as much time studying them and planning for this game as they have. So have other teams in the past. The Ferrymen have no new strategies, nothing Greenspark hasn't seen before, only different players to try to make them work more effectively. They are the toughest team physically the Indians have ever encountered. While Godfrey is smaller than Sam, he is nearly as powerfully built, and a grim desperation fires his aggression. Malenfant is quicker by a small margin than Rick. Neither Starbuck or Tozier or Blood is as lithe and gymnastic as Todd Gramolini but Starbuck is an almost perfect counter to Bither and Tozier is a match to Kasten, who has turned in the steadiest performances of his career during the Western Finals. Before the first quarter ends, it is clear this game is going to be the long mudwrestle Sam expected it would be, a hyperactive brawl driven by an almost slapstick surplus of energy.

He maintains an unnerving idiot smile for the guy in his face, the guy he is blocking, or any Ferryman who comes close enough. Relentlessly he urges the Ferryman to take it easy, offers a hand up when one flops to the floor or crawls out from under a scramble, pats a passing ass encouragingly. Rick picks it up and then Todd, and the Ferrymen get pissed at being faced with a crew who seem to think this whole deal is a big joke.

In the second quarter Greenspark holds the Ferrymen scoreless for six minutes, while edging up their own numbers with arduous effort by seven points. The Ferrymen come out for the second half with veins in their teeth. The fierceness of their attack, which evens the score and then gives them a four-point edge, costs them wickedly in fouls. Malenfant and Starbuck both take the bench carrying four fouls each. Godfrey and Blood continue to play with three, and Tozier has two. On the Greenspark side, Sam, Kasten, and Bither are carrying two each and Gramolini has another three. The Ferrymen who come in to replace the starters are good but not good enough, and the Indians tie up the game before the third quarter ends.

The fourth brings Starbuck and Malenfant back into the game. Gramolini fouls Starbuck again and Coach shrugs and leaves him in. Starbuck makes his free throws and then Malenfant lobs in a three-pointer and Greenspark has a five-point deficit. When Sam earns a third foul against Godfrey, the game is again tied.

Godfrey goes to the stripe and the opposing players line up at the blocks.

When the clock starts again, there will be five minutes left, Sam notes. In this game, in this final, in his career as a high school basketball player. Five minutes.

It is a simple game, and like the music that speaks so strongly to him, it has a nearly infinite variety of expression. It can encompass head-butting brute strength and leather-lunged stamina, breath-sucking executions that require both intelligence and razor-edged timing, moments of slapstick comedy and occasions of an elegance of movement that a Russian toe-dancer would envy. Best of all, anything can happen—and does.

Godfrey overthrows and the ball bounces off the backboard. Sam steps into the paint with a feeling of something like reverence. One big hand collects the pumpkin and he pivots to face the Greenspark goal, knowing already the plays that will consume five minutes. Woods is already backpedaling past half court. Sam slings the ball and Rick is already turning as he receives it, surging into overdrive down the middle, and Malenfant arrives in time to feel helpless. The ball drops through.

For another four and a half minutes the struggle continues. Sam rejects two attempts by Godfrey, Starbuck fouls out and Gramolini makes the free throws to bring Greenspark ahead. Malenfant shoots a three. Gramolini takes an elbow in the nose and is benched by the rule that forbids flowing blood on the court. A pumped-up Alquist replaces him. A moment later, under the post, Sam's attempt to answer is fouled by Godfrey. At the line, Sam swooshes in another two.

Thirty-seven seconds remain in the game. Malenfant takes possession and heads down court. Rick lunges for the ball and trips on his own feet, into a header skid that leaves him on the wrong side of center court. Malencourt corners trickily between Alquist and Kasten and is suddenly in the paint, going for a jumper. Starbuck is just as suddenly between Bither and Malencourt and Sam is too close to the post. Malencourt's shot is a tight high arc that kisses the glass and drops through.

Sam takes the rebound and slings it overhead toward Rick but to Rick's surprise, Tozier shoots out of the traffic headed his way and strips him. Spinning, Tozier drops a three through the rim. Sam claims the ball again and this time hurls the ball from one end of the court to the other. It strikes the backboard at the Greenspark end of the court and falls off the rim—no good—as the buzzer sounds, leaving the game tied.

The Ferrymen have earned themselves an OT. Three more minutes. Each team returns to its bench for instruction and then the clock resumes. The tip goes to Greenspark but Alquist can't keep it; Blood and Malenfant are on him like wolves on an isolated lamb. Now Derry has possession, they find the Greenspark Indians, defending fiercely man to man, sticking like Velcro, between them and the goal. Every bit of energy is being expended as Greenspark stalls the Derry offense outside the paint and frustrates its three shooters with equal ferocity. Malenfant takes a furious desperate shot that whangs off the rim and bounces into Kevin Bither's hands.

A stunned grin freezes Bither's face as he hugs the ball for dear life. The official's whistle awards Greenspark possession and Bither delivers the baby to Rick with huge relief. The dangerous trek down court begins, Derry sniping and grabbing and bushwhacking, throwing up a half-court trap, and then all five Ferrymen align along the stripe like a line of cavalry on the horizon. The line falls back into a zone defense. Rick and Bither and Kasten on the outside play pass around to choruses of *boring!* from the crowd.

At a minute three on the clock, Rick begins to drive down the middle, meets Malenfant, Tozier and Blood, feints left as if to Kasten, stops, feints left again and steps back. The three move with him but he pivots and moves the ball back out to Alquist, who bounces it under to Bither. Malenfant, Tozier and Blood follow the ball and Rick moves suddenly inside, waiting for it as Bither spins around to hand it to him. Rick tries for a quick jumper but Godfrey is there, throwing him off, and the ball falls away.

Sam, on the rise, hooks it cleanly from above the forest of outstretched hands. He comes down, scattering bodies around him. He hears the thud of contact, the panting, grunts and gasps. Hears sneaker squeak and boards protesting and the punctuation of the ball as he drives it down. Hears limbs flailing around him, hears someone sob, hears a heartbeat as he rockets up. He jams the ball and descends into the roar of the crowd.

Time-out, with seven seconds left.

Tozier returns the ball to Godfrey and Godfrey makes a frantic pass to Malenfant, waiting at the Derry three-point arc. Malenfant spins and shoots and the ball goes flying past the glass and off the court.

Was it ever in doubt? the media cowbirds ask Sam later. Of course the game was in doubt. Derry played *hard* but Greenspark won, 77–75. They are all gamers, those boys from Derry, and nobody had a bad night. Derry just didn't have a good enough night. Greenspark scored when need be, and Derry didn't, and that's the game. It always is. And then it's over.

■ ■ ■

In the sea of celebrants Sam lifts Deanie to his shoulders. Like a princess in a howdah, her naked skull gleaming in the lights like the gold ball, she rides there regal and happy a moment—and then suddenly climbs to her feet and sways there on the broad plinth of him as he hastily grabs her ankles to stabilize her. She clenches her fists in triumph before straightening her legs to slide down onto his shoulders. At Sam's side, Reuben holds out his arms for her. Totally trusting, she lets go; he catches her, bounces her gently, and sets her on her feet.

The microphones bristle in Sam's face.

"Is this the most exciting moment of your high school career?" a young woman with TV hair asks.

He is supposed to say yes but he is so high he just blurts the first thing that comes into his mind. "No," he grins. He pauses for mental accounting. "It was third."

While the woman is blinking in astonishment, he takes the opportunity to escape. For the next few days, his teammates will speculate endlessly as to what two events could possibly surpass this one.

Outside, when the ceremonies are over and they emerge from the locker room again, ready for the trek home, the air is so cold the lungs contract. The arc lights gleam on the desiccated snow of an embankment that falls from the racetrack next to the auditorium. The brush edging the fence at the top of the embankment is red-gold, the color of willows when they begin to hint of spring.

■ ■ ■

Under a roofless sky, Greenspark Academy at 2:30 A.M. glows with light and vibrates with noise. It needs only smoke boiling from its foundations to complete the illusion it is about to erupt like an enormous clumsy pod into outer space, there to scatter seed to alien corners. An hour later, the parking lot begins to empty, the brilliance of the lights to fade and the sound to diminish. At 3:45, only the arc lights cast a sickly tarnish. A single boombox spews a pelvic thrust anthem into the shortening shadow of the night. On the outdoor basketball courts, Greenspark's class A state championship teams are playing a little mixed five-on-five. Dunking is allowed and everyone hotdogs outrageously. A solitary cop, there to make sure the school suffers no vandalism, watches the kids instead. The cop wants to smoke a cigarette but he gave away his last five stale butts to Sonny Lunt when he locked the logger up in the drunk tank. Here he was prepared to close his eyes and pretend to be cooping, in case they had themselves a prank to play, and the kids just want to play hoops.

So intent is he on watching the kids on the court, he doesn't notice the commandos sneaking up on the signboard out front to add to the legend *STATE CLASS A/WESTERN REGIONAL BOYS & GIRLS BASKETBALL CHAMPIONS 1991* the lower-case postscript: *We've got ALL the Balls.*

43
∎ ∎ ∎

Soft as a Fat Dirty Snowflake, the neatly folded
newsprint floats from the plain envelope with a Greenspark post-
mark onto the supper table Tuesday night. Sam drops the envelope
onto the pile of mail next to his plate and opens the piece of news-
print. Cut from Monday's sports page, it is a picture of himself
with Deanie on his shoulders in the vortex of the mob on the floor.
Their foreheads have been perforated by small black circles made
by a ballpoint. He crumples it hastily before she can see it. Fortunately, she is spooning mashed banana into Indy, who is remark-
ably cooperative for a change.

He doesn't know what to do about it. Maybe it's nothing. But
he finds himself looking around, tensing at sudden movement at
the periphery of his vision, checking the rearview mirror in the
truck when they are commuting.

On Thursday he is called from class to the Office. Lonnie
Woods is there, hat in his hand, trouble darkening his eyes.
Laliberte is so solemn, Sam's stomach turns over with apprehen-
sion. Has he somehow done something illegal as well as ignorant?
Then Deanie comes bouncing in, saucy as ever and popping gum.

Laliberte sighs. "Gum," he mutters and points at the trash can.

One look at them and Deanie's grin fades into wariness. She pitches the wad of gum automatically.

Laliberte clears his throat. "Sergeant Woods has something to tell you, Deanie."

"It's your mother," Lonnie says and Sam moves to Deanie's side, for whatever good he can do.

■ ■ ■

The neighbors bundle up to stand in the streets and watch, even after the body bag is carted past the TV cameras to the meat wagon. The state police lab van is there for hours and hours, and the TV people come and go, doing sound bites about a possible homicide. In broad accents the neighbors confide to the cameras that no one ever imagined this could happen, or they had always known it would. The newscasters lengthen their faces and note the irony of the tragedy in this week of what should be celebration in the life of a high school basketball star, the dead woman's daughter.

Tony Lord has vanished. Fled the state, the police assume, issuing the usual bulletins. Lonnie Woods tells Sam—not Deanie—that the evidence indicates Lord slept for several hours in the same bed with Judy Gauthier while she expired, of his last beating, probably on Sunday night. Rising from the squalor of their bed, he then took a shower, dressed and packed and drove away, leaving the furnace running and the thermostat set at sixty-eight.

Deanie does not cry. She lies in Sam's arms on the couch while they watch the evening news together and when the body bag is removed from the house, she hides her face but that is all. Over the next few days, she withdraws from everyone except Sam, and half the time, he can't reach her either. When she does talk, as often as not, she is muttering she wants a cigarette, she wants to get high.

He's not surprised to catch her going through his desk one night. She doesn't bother to deny she is looking for money but flies into a rage. Her stealing, she asserts, is what he deserves for taking most of her earnings to pay her medical bills. She's got a right to get stoned if she wants. She's earned it, stayed straight all the way through basketball season and now it's over and if he doesn't like it, he can go fuck himself. All the while she rages, she struts around, flinging off her clothes until she is barefoot and topless. The pain the words code falls on him like the needleprick of sleet.

In the lamplight that is the color of candlelight, she jerks herself around on the edge of hysteria, her small girlish tits quivering, ribs showing again because she hasn't been eating since her mother's death. More than ever, she gives off the frantic terror of a creature trapped. He opens his arms, holds out his hands and she throws herself at him.

She is on top of him, focused and sweating, and he smiles at her, trusting this is going to help, this is going to make a difference. Her face contorts suddenly, her scar grows livid, and she fists her hand and punches him in the mouth. Tears springing to his eyes, he reacts slowly. She sinks her fingers into his hair and yanks it violently.

Swearing, he grabs her wrists and twists until she lets go. Her eyes blank and she snaps at his face with her teeth. He throws her off him, onto her back, and his fist is closed, poised over her face without conscious thought. But he sees her, eyes clenched shut, mouth gone shapeless, cowering in the too familiar cringe, waiting for him to hit her. As he freezes, a drop of blood from his split lip falls on her face, on her cheekbone, and dribbles down the length of her scar.

He draws back his fist and uses the back of his hand to wipe his mouth, fingers quivering with too suddenly slackened tension. He gropes his way to the edge of the bed and sits at the edge.

"I can't do this," he tells her. "You need some kind of help I can't give you."

When he looks back at her, she is face down in the pillows. Her back heaves painfully as if she were trying to breathe water.

He finds an old T-shirt, sweatpants and socks and dresses her. Finds pants for himself and leaves the room to fetch her a glass of water and aspirin and then feeds it to her, as he once gave her painkillers. She's quiet by then, burnt out and limp. He is awake a long time after she goes to sleep. In her sleep, she hiccups and snuffles and draws long shaky breaths, just like Indy does after her tantrums.

His helplessness is like a wall he can't see around. In the morning, he tells her he's going to sleep on the daybed for a while. There is a stiff silence and then she insists she should be the one who sleeps there. It's not worth arguing about, so long as she understands he's not kicking her out, not out of his bedroom or his life, but when he tells her that, she crumples slowly into tears again.

It's pathetic how quickly she agrees to talk to Dr. Spellman about seeing someone, some kind of therapist. He says he'll go too, if she wants; they can work out the shit together. Anything to make her feel better.

■ ■ ■

No doubt with the ulterior motive of distracting Sam from Deanie's depression, Reuben asks him to tune up the Eldorado and take it for a spring wake-up run. Dutifully, when the job is done, on the first Sunday in April Sam and Deanie take the sedan into Greenspark.

The amazing thing is it seems to work. Just being in the Caddie, with its big mill purring under the long sleek hood, is relaxing. Deanie cranks a home dub up to maximum volume, parks her sneakers on the dash and settles back to let the music of Grunge Machine wash over her and out the open windows into the slipstream.

"Let's go to the school," Deanie suggests.

The tower of the Mill over the trees catches Sam's eyes.

"There's the Playground," he says.

Snuggled up to him in the front seat, Deanie draws her scarf from around her throat and ties it around her head against the cold. Her fingertips flutter to the new chains that underline her scar. Sarah has given her a new earring that dangles from her right earlobe—two miniature gold basketballs on a silver chain. She wears a sweater of Sam's that falls under her denim jacket to below her bottom; he wears his leather jacket open to the damp cold.

The big car glides down the incline of the access road to the Playground with the smoothness and power of a big jet landing. The ground is almost bare, with tattered patches of dreary old snow here and there, and the surface is slick where children's boots have beat it into a loose slurry on top of the underlying freeze.

With an avuncular courtesy, Sam opens the car door for Deanie and helps her out. He tucks her hand between his arm and torso and they walk slowly away from the sedan.

Then he seizes Deanie by the armpits, whirls her around until she is dizzy. They stagger happily to the turrets and crenelations of the fortress-playground. It occurs to him the best times together are when they pretend they are still children. Except for sex—and now he thinks on it, the best of that was a kind of play. He misses it, he's horny, but by unspoken agreement they have been careful not to start anything. They still sleep together but only sleep.

The two meetings they have had with the therapist have been miserable exercises in which he has had to listen to Deanie tear herself apart. At least afterward she seems more peaceful. His own confusion and helplessness are greater than ever. Often he finds himself thinking it's just never going to work and it might be better to hang it up. When she's strong enough to be on her own, of course, he amends, and refuses to consider the possibility she never will be.

He boosts her to the top of a playhouse ell so she is sitting at the height of his shoulders and squeezes her knee. With a laugh, Deanie bends to slide her fingers under his hair, clasps her hands at the back of his neck and kisses him. It's a sweet kiss, a little warmer than the quick peck they give each other at bedtime. She looks at him and does it again, not sisterly at all, and he's so relieved. Tentatively, they neck a little, and Sam slips his hands under the sweater to cup her breasts and she shivers. He pushes her back a little and kisses the crotch of her jeans, his lips cooled by her new rigging of chains. As she lies back on the roof with a sigh, the chains catch a flicker of rose-colored light from the taillights of a vehicle on the overpass overhead.

"It's cold out here," Sam says, "let's go to the Mill."

Sitting up, she cocks her head at him.

"Unless you don't want to," he amends.

"No," she says and it takes him a few seconds to understand she means the opposite. "Have to go back sometime."

The padlock's on the ground, rusting. Here too, there is evidence of passage, the patch of damp ground in front of the door churned up.

"Winos," she says. "Oh well, I suppose it's better than them freezing to death."

Inside the Mill is the familiar sink of cold, and the stench of things gone sour. Sam flicks the switch and the floods come on, shedding a sad light on the cavernous vault of the room. The hoop draws its gallows loop upon the ragged brick wall.

Deanie wrinkles her nose at the smell of the place. Raw human waste, somewhere around.

He grasps her by the elbows as she steps in front of him and holds her back. "Let me go first. There's any bums camping out here, I don't want them scaring the piss out of you."

While he goes to look into the watchman's cubby, she scuffs her feet on the floor.

"Shoulda brought a ball," she says.

"Your old one's still here if nobody took it."

But she goes back to her loose stone by the door and he hears the suck of the lid coming off the tin candle box.

Their flop's been used for sure. There is a strew of garbage—a broken beer bottle, empty canned heat tins, butts. There's a dirty blanket crumpled on the mattress. The heater's still there—probably kept whoever's camped here from pneumonia, if not death. The ball is gone.

Sam backs out as Deanie catches up with him. "Ball's gone. Nobody in there but somebody's definitely been around. Probably out boozing now."

They look at each other, reading the same thought in each other's faces. It's not their place anymore, just a hole in the wall that some bum is flopping in. If either of them had any urge for nostalgic lovemaking, it's dead now.

Sam takes her hand. "Come on, I want to look around."

Lighting candle stubs from the button box, they wander the empty spaces again, the rooms where something went on, some process, now obsolete and forgotten, that once consumed the hours and days and years of the workers and rendered up something of value to someone. Perhaps because they walk in the wavering, liquid candlelight, it's creepier than Sam remembers, with small sounds at the edge of hearing, as if ghosts are stirring. Rats, no doubt, vermin, pigeons living their verminous lives, and the structure itself that even in its long death continues to breathe like the brain-dead. The smell of the burning candles makes a peculiar, churchy incense that he thinks he will never forget for the rest of his life.

Toe to heel, they pace the length of the old power train and again Sam is entranced with the massive dinosaur bones of the ancient machine. From underneath, the draft from the Millrace carries more than chill; there is a chortle of running water under the thinning ice, and with it a sharp, metallic odor, as if the water were rusty.

At the foot of the tower, they find several steps collapsed with rot less than halfway to the first landing. It occurs to Sam the chance to view the town from the vantage of the tower may have passed irrevocably. All at once, he wants to restore the Mill and for a moment the fantasies flower gorgeously in his head.

Back in the main hall they pinch out their candleflames. By the floodlights the naked hoop looks so melancholy, he feels an idiot again for trying to make something here for her. The more he stares at it, the stupider it seems. Against the brick wall, it looks like something in a prison yard. When he looks back for her, she's gone.

He spins all around, panic turning the air to broken glass in his lungs. Then the ropes whisper and she giggles from above him. He spots her halfway up to the beams.

"Oh shit," he sighs.

She skinnies up the rope with a monkey agility that makes him tired. On the beam she toes along it a ways, sinks to her haunches and takes a baggie from her sleeve. She waggles it at him. "Come on up and have a toke, you tight-assed goon."

Sam closes his eyes for a long moment. The rustlings overhead inform him she is spreading a paper, spilling the shit onto it, rolling it up.

"Where'd you get that shit?" he asks.

From that tin box, maybe, or some other hole in the wall. She doesn't answer, not that it matters.

"I don't like this," he calls up to her. "It's a step backward. It isn't going to change anything, Deanie."

"Right. Not a frigging thing. So haul ass up here, 'god, and let's see if this shit still has some life to it."

She's gonna kill him, he glooms. If he goes up there, he's a dead man. He finds the end of the line and tugs at it. It's hung here another winter. Christ knows how much more rotten it may be. Probably got just enough climb in it for a bald witch to scoot up it and now it's ready to snap at the next two hundred forty pounds of mouthbreather. He squints up at her; she sucks on the doob and jumps her eyebrows in a Groucho moue at him. The smoke drifts down to him and prickles the inside of his nose. He wraps the line around his throat, cocks his head to one side, bugs his eyes and lets his tongue hang out and she laughs as if he had her in a headlock and was tickling her.

Unwinding it, he thrusts himself up onto it, feels it take his weight, and proceeds, making himself go cautiously when he wants to do it as fast as he can. At least this time there's light and he can see where he's putting his feet when he gains the beam. In a world of pigeon shit.

There is a shadow below and a whump. He raises his distracted gaze to see she has taken her sweater off.

"There," she says, "you're already high and you haven't even desecrated your holy lungs."

"Come on, Deanie. They're great tits. Now I want to go back down. I hate this. I'm not ready to die.'

"Poor baby," she mocks. "Okay. I just wanted to see that look on your face again."

He's trying not to look down, and ludicrously, not at her tits either, as if he's never seen them before.

"What look?"

"The one where you're scared I'm going to fall."

"It's still on my face, isn't it? Only now I'm scared I'm going to fall."

Hugging herself, she shivers. "All right. You go down first."

"Promises, promises," he mocks and she laughs. "No, you slide by me, gimme a good feel and get the hell down so I'm not pissing myself for fear you won't make it. Then I'll get me down."

Giggling, she squirms by him as instructed, and he laughs with her at the touch of her body. She is such a witch! With the jay in her mouth, she slithers down the rope and shakes it at him and then shakes herself, like a stripper giving the crowd what it wants.

He sticks two fingers in his mouth and makes a wolf whistle and applauds.

From the shadowed hole that is the doorway of the cubby, the man emerges so suddenly he seems unreal, like a lurching shadow himself. From Sam's vantage, he is foreshortened, the crown of a head, the tip of a nose, a chin, broad shoulders, the tops of workmen's shoes. Yet Tony Lord is instantly recognizable as he lunges for Deanie.

"*Motherfucker!*" Sam shouts.

Deanie grabs onto the rope convulsively, trying to rise again, but the man's arms are around her waist, dragging her back down. He is wheezing, squealing a kind of gibberish at her, a secret language made up completely of violent obscenities. Clinging with one hand to the line, Deanie bats at him with the other, claws at him, bucks with her whole body against his embrace.

The thirty feet between them and Sam is impassable. It is as if

Sam is on the other side of the universe. He cannot reach them either by descending the rope to which she clings or by jumping.

Deanie connects with Lord's bad eye and he squeals more loudly, and she makes a little progress up the rope before he seizes her knees and drags her back down again. His hands claw runners of flesh from her midriff and she screams.

Screaming with her, Sam steps off the beam.

■ ■ ■

Sergeant Woods glimpses the long black sleekness of the Eldorado from the overpass and shakes his head. The dashboard clock says past ten. Maybe he's a suspicious old poop and they're just larking on the Playground. The teenagers like the Playground as much as the little kids do. But he finds himself turning down the access road and pulling up behind the Eldorado with a burp and a blip.

"Shit," he mutters. "Better not be beer or smoke in that car."

Damn kids. Surely Sam and Deanie didn't need to be diddling in a parking lot, they must be getting all they want at home and if he was Reuben Styles he wouldn't be putting up with that bullshit.

And he flips his light into the sedan's backseat and it's empty.

■ ■ ■

Falling through thirty feet does not take very long but there is a fraction of a second of freefall into gravity's maw, or so it feels to Sam, almost the last thing he feels in the long heart-stopping launch from the beam to the hoop, and he almost misses—it has to be more than fingertips, and it is, the rough scaled metal of the hoop, curling under his fingers, taking the skin off his hands. His weight drops like a dead man's through the trap, the joints of his arms taking it just that next fraction of a second before the hoop tears free of the backboard as it separates from the exploding crumbling bricks, which dislodge neighbors of a hundred years and brings down a section of the wall. Even as he grasps the hoop, he twists his body out of its plummet and away, dislocating both shoulders in an exquisite burst that makes the last seven feet a fiery blur. Hoop, backboard and bricks descend behind him and over him, and over Deanie and Tony Lord, tangled together at the rope. The bricks explode on impact, filling the air with a rain of sharp-edged stones around him. The jolt of impact goes through Sam from the soles of his feet, which feel as if they are crumbling stone. It drives the long bones of his legs up into his hip sockets, telegraphing up his spine to the base of his skull and into the roots of his teeth and down through his shoulders and chest bones. He feels the articulation of all his bones in one instant. There is no breath to express the sensation, which is the most all-encompassing he has ever felt. It is like birth, a violent breathless expulsion into an unknown universe.

■ ■ ■

Though it is beyond Sam's knowing, he has given Deanie all the chance she needs. In the moment of distraction when Sam plummets from overhead, Tony's grip loosens enough for her to squirm a little higher up the rope. When everything comes down, hoop, backboard, bricks and Sam, Tony lets go, flinching, trying to get out of the way and she brings her knees up sharply into his balls. She hears the breath huff out of him. And then they are in the midst of the maelstrom of brick. Instinct brings her hands to her face as she drops to the floor with Tony limp on top of her. Before the brickstorm ends, she is crawling out from under him, skittering beyond his reach. Only then does she turn to look. The bloody heap that is Tony stirs, one hand groping for purchase among the debris. She stoops and snatches up a brick that has somehow survived nearly intact. She takes a hesitant step back to Tony's side. He stares up at her, his blood-streaked face contorting, and he raises his hands to protect it. She drops the brick onto his crotch. His body jumps and he gurgles strangely.

■ ■ ■

Sergeant Woods shouts and throws open the door but it's all over.

Deanie looks up at him impassively and wipes her running nose on her wrist. Naked from the waist up, bloody and torn, she is, bald head and hardware, perfectly natural in the total destruction. What looks like a basketball hoop lies on the floor, amid a lot of broken brick and a broken backboard. She crouches next to Sam but she isn't touching him. Her hands are tucked between her legs, as if she is cold. Sam is folded neatly on his right side, as if all his joints had suddenly turned to water. He's bloody—there's a lot of blood all over—but the cop can't tell at first glance what the sources are. It takes a second for Woods to register the other man, a slack mound amid the debris, and then he recognizes Tony Lord.

" 'god's not dead," Deanie explains to Lonnie Woods as if to make a careful theological argument.

"That's right, baby," he reassures her, groping for a pulse in Sam's throat.

"He's just very tired," she continues. "He's had a tough day. He flew all the way from up there"—pointing upward—"and probably he broke something, huh?"

She's stoned, the cop realizes, or in shock—but oh yes, there's a vague pot smell in the air. Both, then.

She fingers the earring in the lobe of Sam's ear. " 'This ain't no disco,' " she says and lets out a long quivering breath.

She sees it clearly, as she saw it happening. Tony was like fire on her, climbing up her body as she tried to climb the rope. And 'god jumped, she saw it, from above the white brilliance of the flood-lights, caught the hoop and turned as on a spindle, and the world fragmented, he tore it down with him, or it followed him, in tongues of tawny gold and red, from a maw of light. She saw the hoop bounce and roll like a toy, and then fall to its side, amid the rain of pain, the gnashing of bricks. She saw the blind red caul filling 'god's eyes, painting his face in streaks and checkers. She saw it and she sees it and she strokes it in her mind, no longer needing the photograph of the painting to know what she has seen.

Epilogue

■ ■ ■

October Flutters Maroon and Bronze, blood-red and gold leaf against a painter's blue sky outside the windows of the high school classroom. There are no students around; it is a parent-teacher conference day and the place is unnaturally quiet. A thin young woman sifts through the folders on her desk waiting for some parent to funnel in from the empty corridors. It's a warm afternoon and she has a window cracked to let in the tang of fall, her favorite season. The rumble of a motorcycle engine seeps in and is forgotten in the knock at the door that turns out to be the mother of a student, a harried, conscientious fortyish woman. Of course her kid is a good student. As a rule, the parents that show up for the conferences are the ones that don't need to.

Mrs. Mom is just taking her leave when there is a hesitant rap at the door and a young giant with a cane lurches into the room.

"Miss Carpenter?" he inquires.

She's still in shock, feeling the crick form in her neck as she stares at him. If he isn't seven feet tall, he's within striking distance. He wears a biker's leather jacket and torn jeans. He sweeps back his hair with one hand and an earring glints from one lobe. His blond mane is tightly braided in narrow rows up one side of his head and fountains in dozens of whiplike tight braids over the crown and other side. He wears a goatee of fine gold around his mouth and small circular dark glasses with gold rims. He props himself on an elaborately carved cane.

"I'm Sam Styles," he says, offering his hand. "I'm here for Deanie Gauthier."

Of course. Gauthier. Scarred and tattooed and with her stubble of hair elaborately patterned in razored swirls. No matter what the assigned subject, her essays always come back to basketball and religion. The kid writes about God—always spelling it god with a small *g*—as if she were going steady with Him. Gauthier's god is a very down-to-earth kind of deity. One of her essays, the teacher recalls, was about playing one-on-one with god, Who evidently dunks like nobody's business. The teacher has heard about the boyfriend; the other kids talk about him picking up Gauthier after school. They seem to be impressed with him but until now, she had no idea why.

"She keeping up?" he asks with an air of concern identical to the broad-beamed mom who has just left.

"Well, yes, she's doing very well," the young woman says.

"Good. Don't worry about Deanie getting her work done," he assures her. "We study together. I'm in school too. At the university." He seems surprised about that. "I have to study a lot," he confesses. "But I don't mind. I kind of like it, actually. History, that's what I like. I'm taking a course about the Industrial Revolution."

"How interesting," the teacher says and to her own surprise, means it. Kids are always surprising her. That's the biggest reason she's still teaching.

"If I make up my deficiencies," the boy explains, "I could be a walk-on."

"A walk-on?"

"On the basketball team. The coach promised me a tryout. Conditionally." He recites the information as if maybe he tells it to himself several times a day. "I have to get healthy. I'm in physical rehab." He touches one hip. "I'm so pinned together, I set off metal detectors." Grinning hugely. "I'm looking to play again next season. Coach'd have kitties if he knew I was out on my bike. Weather got to me, you know?" He fumbles a card from his jacket pocket. "You know anybody needs a car fixed, this is my number. I make housecalls. Deanie does housecleaning."

When he lurches away again, the young teacher wanders to the lounge for coffee and relates the story to a colleague. The other woman chuckles.

"Oh, those two. He's in some kind of remedial program for jocks at the university. I've heard there's very little chance he'll ever actually play and not much more he'll be able to complete a degree. Gauthier transferred up here to be with him."

"Oh. Well, they certainly are—flamboyant."

"You weren't here last year," the other one reminds herself, "I forgot. Well, anyway, he was a big high school star and so was she." The woman shudders. "She came out of an abusive home. Stepfather killed her mother. There was quite a dustup at the time about the fact she was living with her boyfriend and she was just a sophomore. I wasn't surprised. I used to run into it fairly often when I taught on the coast. These girls move in with their boyfriends just to get out of the house. Just kids. Could I see that card? My daughter's Datsun's been out of commission for a week and she's driving my car and I've got to do something!"

"What happens to them?" the young woman asks.

The older teacher shrugs. "Sometimes they grow up together quite successfully," she says. "You never can tell."

Afterword

■ ■ ■

If I may beg just a few more minutes of your time, I'd like to make amends to the championship basketball teams whose titles I borrowed in telling this particular yarn. Not fictional Greenspark Academy but the Old Town High School Indians won the 1991 Class A Schoolboy Basketball Championship of the State of Maine. In the years preceding, titles I attributed to the Greenspark Indians were actually won by Lawrence in 1990, and Morse in both 1989 and '88. The real Class A Schoolgirl Basketball Champion of the State of Maine in 1991 was Lawrence. The players on Greenspark's teams are entirely fictional and not based on any real present or past Maine basketball players or any real or present basketball players anywhere. However, none of the Greenspark players' athletic feats are unique to fiction.

Castle Rock and Derry, of course, were first mapped fictionally by another novelist who was kind enough to allow me to add to their histories. For those of you who are familiar with Castle Rock, the basketball season related in this particular yarn occurs in the spring before Mr. Leland Gaunt opened his curio shop in the Rock.

June 1, 1991, Bangor, Maine